MW00831489

UNBOUND

UNBOUND

Tales by Masters of Fantasy

EDITED BY

Shawn Speakman

GRIM OAK PRESS
SEATTLE

UNBOUND
Copyright © 2015 by Shawn Speakman.
All rights reserved.

"Madwalls" by Rachel Caine. © 2015 by Rachel Caine.
"Stories Are Gods" by Peter Orullian. © 2014 by Peter Orullian.
"River and Echo" by John Marco. © 2015 by John Marco.
"A Dichotomy of Paradigms" by Mary Robinette Kowal. © 2015 by Mary Robinette Kowal.
"Son of Crimea" by Jason M. Hough. © 2015 by Jason M. Hough.
"An Unfortunate Influx of Filipians" by Terry Brooks. © 2015 by Terry Brooks.
"The Way into Oblivion" by Harry Connolly. © 2015 by Harry Connolly.
"Uncharming" by Delilah S. Dawson. © 2014 by D.S. Dawson.
"A Good Name" by Mark Lawrence. © 2014 by Mark Lawrence.
"All in a Night's Work" by David Anthony Durham. © 2015 by David Anthony Durham.
"Seven Tongues" by Tim Marquitz. © 2015 by Tim Marquitz.
"Fiber" by Seanan McGuire. © 2015 by Seanan McGuire.
"The Hall of the Diamond Queen" by Anthony Ryan. © 2015 by Anthony Ryan.
"The Farmboy Prince" by Brian Staveley. © 2015 by Brian Staveley.
"Heart's Desire" by Kat Richardson. © 2014 by Kat Richardson.
"The Game" by Michael J. Sullivan. © 2015 by Michael J. Sullivan.
"The Ethical Heresy" by Sam Sykes. © 2015 by Sam Sykes.
"Small Kindnesses" by Joe Abercrombie. © 2015 by Joe Abercrombie.
"The Rat" by Mazarkis Williams. © 2015 by Mazarkis Williams.
"The Siege of Tilpur" by Brian McClellan. © 2015 by Brian McClellan.
"Mr. Island" by Kristen Britain. © 2015 by Kristen Britain.
"Jury Duty" by Jim Butcher. © 2015 by Jim Butcher.
"The Dead's Revenant" by Shawn Speakman. © 2014 by Shawn Speakman.
All rights reserved.

Dust jacket artwork by Todd Lockwood.
Interior artwork by Stacie Pitt.
Book design and composition by Rachelle Longé McGhee.

Signed, Limited Edition ISBN 978-1-944145-00-2
Trade Hardcover Edition ISBN 978-0-9847136-9-1
eBook ISBN 978-1-944145-01-9

First Edition, December 2015
2 4 6 8 9 7 5 3 1

Grim Oak Press
PO Box 45173
Seattle, WA 98145
www.grimoakpress.com

For those who enter the realms of imagination

And who find it hard to leave

"I propose to speak about fairy-stories, though
I am aware that this is a rash adventure."

—J.R.R. Tolkien

———————————

"I'm staying here to read: life's too short."

—Carlos Ruiz Zafón

CONTENTS

INTRODUCTION:
A GEEK TRYING TO DO GOOD

When I published *Unfettered*, I had one goal in mind: end the outrageous medical debt that had accumulated from treating my Hodgkin's lymphoma.

I did not do this alone. Two dozen of my friends came to my aid, donating short stories and artwork to produce *Unfettered*, a genre anthology featuring short stories by some of the finest writers working today. It sold unbelievably well and helped introduce many readers to new authors they otherwise would not have tried.

Once all the bills were settled and I was healthy again, I had a serious question to answer, though.

Should I continue Grim Oak Press?

The answer did not come to me immediately. I started the press to take care of my medical debt. We succeeded with that. Originally, I had no desire to continue it afterward. Owning a publishing house is hard work—quite possibly the hardest job in the entire industry—and I didn't want to see that work overshadow my own writing goals.

But upon reflection, I decided not using the platform that *Unfettered* created would be irresponsible. As Patrick Rothfuss is fond of saying, it is imperative—if nothing else—to make the world a better place than when we entered it. I fully believe that. And with Grim Oak Press, I think I can do that very thing.

Unbound is the beginning of an answer to my question. It is another unique anthology similar in scope to *Unfettered*. It features talented authors doing what they do best, and every one of them exceeded my expectations. And just like the first anthology, *Unbound* has no theme; the contributors were allowed to submit any genre tale they desired.

The result? An amazing collection. *Unbound* is sure to keep you reading when you open it right from the first, the stories as diverse as they are extraordinary. Jim Butcher sends Harry Dresden to jury duty. Rachel Caine creates mad walls in the Citadel. Terry Brooks revisits Landover, where Ben Holiday must deal with the worst threat ever—G'home Gnomes! Mary Robinette Kowal visits the stars with a reluctant painter. Mark Lawrence returns to his Broken Empire setting to reveal a Brother's name. And so many more stories. I enjoyed every tale in *Unbound*. I think you will too.

I published *The Dark Thorn* to learn how to publish *Unfettered*. *Unbound* in turn will give me the leverage and resources to publish *Unfettered II*, with all proceeds of that anthology going to alleviate medical debt for authors and artists who find themselves in the same situation I was in. This is the way I can pay forward the aid I received; this is the way I can do my part to begin making the world a better place.

I hope you enjoy *Unbound*. I hope you review it and share it with your friends and family.

It is the beginning of something far greater than myself.

Happy reading!

Shawn Speakman
Publisher, Grim Oak Press
October 2015

CONTENTS

INTRODUCTION:
A GEEK TRYING TO DO GOOD

When I published *Unfettered*, I had one goal in mind: end the outrageous medical debt that had accumulated from treating my Hodgkin's lymphoma.

I did not do this alone. Two dozen of my friends came to my aid, donating short stories and artwork to produce *Unfettered*, a genre anthology featuring short stories by some of the finest writers working today. It sold unbelievably well and helped introduce many readers to new authors they otherwise would not have tried.

Once all the bills were settled and I was healthy again, I had a serious question to answer, though.

Should I continue Grim Oak Press?

The answer did not come to me immediately. I started the press to take care of my medical debt. We succeeded with that. Originally, I had no desire to continue it afterward. Owning a publishing house is hard work—quite possibly the hardest job in the entire industry—and I didn't want to see that work overshadow my own writing goals.

But upon reflection, I decided not using the platform that *Unfettered* created would be irresponsible. As Patrick Rothfuss is fond of saying, it is imperative—if nothing else—to make the world a better place than when we entered it. I fully believe that. And with Grim Oak Press, I think I can do that very thing.

Unbound is the beginning of an answer to my question. It is another unique anthology similar in scope to *Unfettered*. It features talented authors doing what they do best, and every one of them exceeded my expectations. And just like the first anthology, *Unbound* has no theme; the contributors were allowed to submit any genre tale they desired.

The result? An amazing collection. *Unbound* is sure to keep you reading when you open it right from the first, the stories as diverse as they are extraordinary. Jim Butcher sends Harry Dresden to jury duty. Rachel Caine creates mad walls in the Citadel. Terry Brooks revisits Landover, where Ben Holiday must deal with the worst threat ever—G'home Gnomes! Mary Robinette Kowal visits the stars with a reluctant painter. Mark Lawrence returns to his Broken Empire setting to reveal a Brother's name. And so many more stories. I enjoyed every tale in *Unbound*. I think you will too.

I published *The Dark Thorn* to learn how to publish *Unfettered*. *Unbound* in turn will give me the leverage and resources to publish *Unfettered II*, with all proceeds of that anthology going to alleviate medical debt for authors and artists who find themselves in the same situation I was in. This is the way I can pay forward the aid I received; this is the way I can do my part to begin making the world a better place.

I hope you enjoy *Unbound*. I hope you review it and share it with your friends and family.

It is the beginning of something far greater than myself.

Happy reading!

Shawn Speakman
Publisher, Grim Oak Press
October 2015

UNBOUND

RACHEL CAINE

"Madwalls" was sparked by a photo that made the rounds on the Internet . . . of an abandoned house in China that was covered all over inside with handwriting on every surface. Without knowing anything else, I began to ponder why someone would write, and it collided with genies in my head and a somewhat Lovecraftian idea about the end of the world. So . . . welcome to the Citadel. Leave your electronics and your preconceptions at the door . . .

MADWALLS

Rachel Caine

On her sixteenth birthday, Samarjit Cole was taken to the Citadel to meet the captive. She wasn't expected to start her turn of duty yet, but it was necessary, her father said, to see it for herself, and to know what she would be facing when she did take up the role of Watcher.

"Did you read everything?" he asked her in the car on the way there. She pulled her long black hair back behind her ears and made a sound that could have gone either way. She'd read it. Twice. She just didn't like being questioned. "Because, I can't stress this enough, he'll play with your mind. You have to be prepared. You have to know the rules backwards and forwards. It's important, Sammy."

She sighed. "I know."

"What are you doing?"

She didn't look up from her tablet. "Explaining to my friends why I'm being dragged off for the whole weekend."

"Sammy—"

"I'm not telling them the truth, Dad. God. I'm not *stupid*." She sounded sullen and bitter, but she didn't feel that way. It was just a cover, because Sammy Cole was scared. Scared to the point that her fingertips were cold and clumsy when she tried to type out messages, and she finally gave it up and clicked off.

Being offline felt like being naked. Alone. She turned her head out toward the world, away from her father, because she knew he might figure out how she felt. "Where are we?"

He glanced over at her. Her father was a large man, imposing even in regular clothes, but today he wore a full dark-blue *chola* instead of his usual casual clothes, and a *dastar* turban to match, which was really not his usual style. The *chola* was reserved for special occasions. His long beard reached to the lower part of the steering wheel, and it was still mostly dark, with a few gray streaks in it. As always, Samarjit felt a conflicted surge inside when she looked at him; she loved her father, knew him for a good and kind and upright man, but she also wished . . . wished he wasn't so *practicing*. Her mother, Marta, was German and hardly ever thought about her Protestant church upbringing. It was her dad's calm, quiet, everyday faith that had driven them apart, or at least that was how Marta told it.

Sammy's father didn't say much about it at all. He said nothing but kind words about her mom, and although she knew he wished his daughter would embrace the Sikh faith and wear the *bana*, she couldn't see herself doing it. She respected him for following his own principles, though. In these times, when it seemed like having skin anything but the color of bleached porcelain prequalified you as terrorist, being a practicing Sikh was even harder than before.

"We're almost there," he told her. She turned the radio on but it hissed static all the way through the signal search, and she switched it off in frustration. Her dad had made her leave her headphones, which sucked, but he said it was important to listen. What she was listening *to*, other than him, she had no idea. "You'll leave your tablet in the car, along with your phone. No electronics of any kind inside the Citadel. Don't forget that."

"You've told me a million times. I know."

He reached out a hand and put it palm up on the velour seat between them. "I'm proud of you, Sammy. You know that, don't you?"

"I know," she said, and as the car rounded a vast, tight corner of the road, the trees broke apart on the stone of the mountain, and she found herself gripping his hand in sudden, electric fear.

The Citadel.

Surrounded by a no-man's-land of three separate fences, with nothing growing between them, the building was an enormous, lightless block rising far higher than she'd ever expected. It was real. *Real.* And suddenly, the weight of what she was expected to do hit her in ways that she had never expected. She clutched her tablet in her right hand, still holding onto her dad with the other, and had a wild impulse to take a photo of this place and send it to her friends. She knew she couldn't do that. Couldn't tell them where she was going, or why.

Because the world out there, down the mountain . . . the world couldn't know.

Chatar Singh stopped at the first of the gates and typed in a long string of code numbers at a keypad. The process repeated, with different numbers, at the next gate. The third required a retinal scan as well as a new code. "Once you begin, you'll receive your personal entrance codes when your duty period starts," he told Sammy. "You'll be expected to memorize them. They change every month, and you can't cheat and put them in your phone."

"Okay." Her voice was small now as the last gate cranked open. There were armed guards patrolling this last fence, in plain black uniforms with no insignia on them. No flag emblems. Her dad parked the Nissan in the lot off to the left; there were about thirty cars and trucks, all civilian models. "How long has this place been here?"

"Not long. Less than fifty years. But the Citadel . . ." He hesitated for a few seconds, then shrugged. "It isn't a place, exactly. More of an entrance to the place. You'll see."

She didn't want to let go of her dad's hand, but she knew she had to. He'd expect her to be courageous. He always had. "Before we go in there, I have to ask you something," she said. "You're not going to like it. But I—need to know."

"All right."

"Did you and Mom ever really love each other?"

It surprised him, and he stopped unbuckling his seat belt to turn to stare at her. "Of course! Your mother and I were very much in love. Our marriage was as it should have been: one spirit, two bodies. Why would you think . . . ?" He caught himself and shook his head. "Because of our divorce. Why wouldn't you?"

"Well, it is kind of a clue something went wrong. What? Because she won't tell me. Was it me?" She'd always believed that, in some vague, undefined way.

"No. Of course not." He was silent for a few seconds, and she saw the discomfort in the set of his mouth, the way he focused away from her. "She saw something that shook her faith. Made her doubt—everything. And she retreated. I couldn't hold her. I still love your mother, but we have to be separate now. It's better for her that way."

"Was it because of this place? Did she come here with you?"

"Once." He cleared his throat, as if it had suddenly started to pain him. "Did she tell you that?"

"No, I just sort of figured it out. It's why you told me not to tell her. Right? She wouldn't want me to come here. She wouldn't let you bring me if she knew."

"Yes. That's true. Your mother wants to protect you."

"And what do you want?"

He didn't answer. He let go of her and unfastened his restraint and was out of the car before she could draw breath to ask anything else.

There wasn't much choice. She couldn't cower in here like a child. Sammy popped the door and got out, remembering to lay her phone and tablet on the car seat at the last minute. *No electronics.* It felt weird.

Her father, standing, topped her by almost a foot, and she was not a small young woman; she liked sports, and exercise, and she had long legs built for running. Today, she wore jeans and a simple bright-blue top; she hadn't intended the color to match her dad's *chola,* but it almost did. She didn't wear the scarf anymore, though she had for a while. She'd gotten too much hassle for it in school, and since she wasn't a fully practicing Sikh anymore, it didn't seem worth it.

She knew he was disappointed by that and didn't know quite how to explain to him how sorry she was. But at the same time, not sorry either. She loved the religion, but being caught as a child between two faiths was . . . hard.

Her father's *chola*, the wide-skirted blue coat, should have looked like a costume, but it didn't on him. He wore it with the same casual ease as any other military uniform, which was what it was: a warrior's garb, complete to the ceremonial dagger, the *kirpan*, which wasn't really used as a weapon anymore. More of a tool for blessing, though she knew her father kept his *kirpan* sharpened, and he was allowed, by the faith, to use it in defense of himself or others.

Especially here.

"Our family only serves once a year," he told her. "You would begin next year, if you decide you have the calling. If you don't, I will continue until another of our relatives fills in. It's no disgrace, Sammy. I don't want you to believe that you have to do this . . . but at the same time, I can't deny you the opportunity to find out. That's where your mother and I have a difference of opinion. She wants to protect you. I want you to discover for yourself where your destiny lies."

There were guards on the doors—outer door, inner door, then next to a four-inch-thick transparent barrier that was the last checkpoint inside the big hall carved out of raw granite. Sammy studied the man and woman closely. The woman was of Chinese descent and had a lithe, whipcord look to her; the man was pure heartland American blend, with dirty blond hair and serious dark eyes. Both younger than her dad, but not by much.

"This is your daughter, Chatar?" the Chinese woman asked. She had a California accent and gave Sammy a warm smile as she input a code on her pad. Her partner, on the other side, mirrored her with a different set of numbers. "Listen, you'll be fine. Your dad says you're a very smart kid. Don't let the prisoner spook you, and do what he tells you. I'll be waiting right here when you come out."

"How is he today?" Her father asked her.

"About like usual." The woman shrugged. "Moods. You know."

"And where do we look for him today?"

The blond man consulted some kind of handheld device. *Oh, sure, he gets to have his phone. Thanks, Dad.* She felt an almost physical ache, being deprived of her stuff. Not that she was *constantly* on it, but being cut off completely felt so helpless.

"Third floor," the soldier said. "West corridor. He'll be needing supplies, like always." This man wasn't as friendly, that was glaringly obvious, and Sammy thought he was being rude to her, maybe prejudiced, but then when he finally looked past her father at her she realized that wasn't it at all. The man was worried. "Chatar, are you sure you want to do this? She's pretty young for this."

"She's the age I was when I first met him," her dad said. "And strong. She'll be fine."

The man shook his head but said nothing more.

Sammy jumped when a warning tone sounded, an amber light flashed, and the thick clear barrier slid back on both sides. Her father pushed her through and followed close behind, and she realized why when the barrier crashed back closed behind them with frightening speed. "There's no safety release," he told her. "If you get caught between the two sides, it will crush you. So don't get caught."

"Thanks, Dad, I wasn't feeling at all freaked out yet."

He laughed a little and put his arm around her. "You are doing fine, Samarjit. Just remember: you are here to serve. It's found that he is more . . . stable, when he has regular and changing visitation. Someone else will be here this afternoon, after we leave. Two visitors a day, seven hundred thirty visitors a year. We do not leave him alone for more than half a day, ever."

She knew that. She'd read the manual, every word, and she still couldn't quite understand *why*. Why her family had been chosen to be part of the visitor program. They weren't the only ones, of course; there were thousands of families rotating this task, and the book didn't say how it had started, but it had something to do with their ancestors, way back in time. The book was unclear about a lot of things, probably deliberately. More of a how-to manual, and not so much a backstory.

The hallway felt different beyond the barrier. The floors were still pure rough black stone, and so were the walls and ceiling, but there was a sense of . . . claustrophobia here. Ancient weight. And although she could see, she couldn't exactly say *how* she saw; there were no lights visible, just . . . illumination, without source. It felt very alien. Even the air smelled odd—fresh, but dead in a way, as if it had never circulated out in the world.

At the end of the black hallway was a large open room stacked with endless shelves and boxes of chalk. Just chalk. White, blue, sets of assorted colors. Her father grabbed three boxes and handed her one. It held assorted colors. Sammy looked down at the cover of it and almost laughed, because it was standard, everyday sidewalk chalk, the same kind kids used to play outside on the cement to draw skipping squares, bright suns, and crooked little houses.

"Really?" she asked him. He said nothing.

Next to the room were black stairs, three steep flights of them, and once they'd arrived on the correct floor, he held out a hand to stop her. "Stay still," he said. "Listen."

"Listen to *what?*"

He didn't answer. He'd closed his eyes, and his breath came slow and steady, and she finally, unwillingly, shut her eyes and listened, too. She heard nothing. An eerie, scary amount of *nothing*. She was used to noise, even at night . . . if it wasn't crickets chirping outside, it was the low hum of electronics inside that never quite went away.

Here it was utter, heavy nothing.

The sound of her breathing and pulse became louder. She'd never really paid attention to them before . . . and once those noises became familiar, she finally heard something else.

Her head turned toward it, and she opened her eyes. Her dad was looking the same way.

"You hear him. Very good," he told her. "He's moved. He does that. It's as if he knows we've asked where to find him. He does enjoy his games."

They turned left.

The halls were not featureless here. Well, they *were*; still the same black stone blocks as out in the hallway inside the barrier. But they were covered with a dizzying array of marks. Letters, words, symbols, figures, none of it seemed to have any continuity to it. One part of a wall held elegantly written out words in letters so tiny that Sammy's eyes burned trying to understand what she was seeing—thousands of words, crowded incredibly close together. Eventually, she realized it was in Italian. Two feet along, math equations sprawled in uneven lines in pink and green, and took up twenty feet of space. The other side of the wall had what looked like cave paintings—primitive, lean figures and running animals and spears. Those were in yellow chalk.

Seeing it, she finally understood what she was listening to in the distance: the faint hiss of chalk on stone.

They walked steadily down long hallways, every inch of the walls filled with *something*. A chalked epic poem she recognized from English class. A confusion of musical notation. More math, but this using symbols she didn't even recognize or understand. Chalk drawings of infinite complexity.

"It's all his?" she asked her father as they walked. It seemed impossible. Terrifying, in a way. "He did all of this? How long has he been here?"

"In the Citadel?" Her father shrugged. "For as long as I can remember. But the Citadel is not always where we entered. He's *here*. Just not always *there*."

That didn't make sense. None of this made *sense*.

The hissing of chalk was louder here, and her father slowed and pulled her closer. "Sammy. I talk, you don't. If he tries to speak to you, don't answer. Understand?"

"I understand." She didn't, but she would try.

He kissed her on the forehead and embraced her, and she realized that *he* was scared . . . not for himself. For her. "I love you," he said. "And I know you are brave. Now come."

It hit her how much she'd missed him, suddenly, and it was because of the scent of clean sandalwood and lemon and faint, masculine sweat. It unlocked so many memories of being a little girl, carried in strong arms, of playing in the sun, of love and joy. She melted into his arms and found herself on the verge of tears, suddenly, but then she remembered that she wasn't a little girl, and this wasn't a reunion.

She pulled back and made herself strong again.

"Remember," he said, "he isn't what he seems to be. Ever. You can't trust what you see."

She'd asked her father many times about the captive, but he had never answered her. The book he'd had her read hadn't cast much light on the mystery, either, and as they turned the corner, she knew why. After one long, unblinking stare, Sammy averted her gaze from the man kneeling in front of the wall. Her heart lurched, then pounded in a frenzied rhythm, and she felt hot, as if she'd stood in the full glare of the sun for too long. It wasn't that he glowed; he was just a man, on his knees in the corner, painstakingly chalking tiny words on a wall. A *young* man, beautiful, with skin the color of old bronze, and hair of silky black, cut loose around his face. He hadn't turned to face her.

She wasn't sure she could bear it if he did.

Her father had stopped with one hand on his *kirpan*. When she looked at him, she saw that he was staring at a spot in the middle distance, not focusing on the captive at all. It helped, when she tried it. She could see the outlines of the man, but not the detail. He could have been anyone.

That didn't slow her heartbeat, or calm her irrational terror.

"*Salve*, honored sir," her father said, in a quiet, calm voice. "How are you today?"

"I am well, Chatar," the man said. "And who is this lovely creature you bring today?" He had not turned, nor stopped his delicate, constant writing, even though the chalk was worn down to a thin sliver held tight in his fingers. He wore a loose white robe and his feet were bare.

He had called her lovely.

"I present my daughter Samarjit. We call her Sammy, for short."

"Samarjit," the man repeated, and in his mouth, it was glorious music. "It means *one who wins the war*. Did you know that, Sammy?" Except for how he said her name, he had no accent at all, to her ears, which meant he had an American accent like a newscaster's, from somewhere in the Midwest like Kansas or Iowa or Indiana. "When I was last in the world, it was still a name only for boys. I see that situation has improved."

She started to answer, because he was speaking to her, to *her*, but her father's touch on her arm reminded her better. She kept silent, and her dad said, "My daughter is true to her name. You may count on that."

"You haven't called me by *my* name, Chatar. Are you afraid to have her hear it?"

"She must decide your name for herself, as you know. What she sees is not what I see. What she hears is not what I hear. That is your gift."

"More of a curse, to be fair." The chalk snapped suddenly and fell from his fingers, and he scrabbled desperately around him for the pieces. His fingers trembled, and she saw his whole body convulse when the tiny fragments powdered in his grip. He reached out for a box next to him, and found it empty. "No. No. *No.*"

"Allow me," Chatar Singh said. He stepped forward and crouched a few feet from the man, opened the box of chalk he held, and extended one. It was white chalk, the same color as what had broken. He placed the box down in easy reach of the captive, and then the second box, filled with blue. "We are here to be of service."

The man sobbed and snatched the fresh chalk from her father's hand, and began scribbling frantically, as if he had time to make up. After a few seconds, he breathed easier, and the rhythm slowed to a more deliberate speed. "Thank you," he said. "You are a wise man. Have you explained me to your daughter yet?"

"Only you can explain what you are."

The man laughed. It sounded weird and hollow, and she thought that it might have been angry, too. "Of course, Chatar Singh. Now that she's here, I know why you love her more than anything in this world. It explains why you named me as you did."

Her father said nothing to that. He stood up and backed away, still staring into the unfocused distance, and made a formal bow. He turned and walked back to Samarjit, and whispered, "Take him your chalk. Do not get close."

She didn't want to do this anymore. She felt sick and light-headed now, and it was hard to breathe. But she couldn't let her father see her fear, could she? He expected more of her, and she had never wanted to disappoint him. Not the way her mother had.

She walked forward and crouched down, in exactly the same spot her father had chosen. She took the top off the box and slid that offering over next to the other two her father had delivered.

12

Her hand was still extended when the captive turned fast as the hiss of a whip, and his fingers wrapped around her wrist. The contact burned like a bracelet of heated metal, and she cried out and tried to jerk backward, but it made no difference. No difference at all. She was not strong enough to break free.

No one could be that strong.

"Samarjit." He sounded different, so close, so soft. Her name still sounded like a prayer on his lips. "Are you afraid of death?"

She looked at him, directly into his face, into the endless black fall of his eyes, the madness of his smile. The feelings that swept over her were indescribable . . . longing, need, anguish, horror, hunger, rage, so many, so fast, so intense that she felt burned black by them.

And then she saw him. *Truly* saw him. Not the pretty, pretty face or the flawless skin or silken hair. Not the disguise he wore to save those who came here.

She saw the whole world dying in blood and horror and pain and fear and fire, dying and being reborn, over and over. His lips were close to her ear now, close enough that his cool breath puffed against her hair. "I am not mad. The world is mad. It must be made sane." He smelled of burning and blood.

Her father was shouting her name, and she saw from the corner of her eye that he was lunging forward with his *kirpan* out and ready to strike. It took only a single, sharp glance from the captive to freeze him in place, with his *kirpan* half raised. She could see the panic in his eyes, the struggle to be free and come to her.

The captive held tight to Sammy's right wrist, and she could no more have broken that hold than ripped away her own arm. The screaming inside her faded to a whisper—not gone, no, never gone now, but she could keep it quiet.

"What are you?" she whispered then. It sounded rational, calm, controlled. It was not. *She* was not.

"Name me and we will both know," he said.

"I can't!" She stared past him, at the frozen-in-place form of her father, who was breathing in short, agonized gasps. There were tears running from his eyes down his cheeks, wetting his beard. "Please let

13

my father go," she said. "Please."

"If I let him go now, I will have to kill him. Is that what you want?"

"No!"

"Then he must stay there until you name me," the captive said. He was still writing with his left hand. He had never stopped, she realized, even as he held on to her. "What am I?"

"You're—you're a demon!"

"So speaks the Christian in you. What if I told you that this is *my* hell? And you are *my* demons?"

"I'm not!"

"Sweet Samarjit, you are exactly that to me. Demon. Master. Slaver. *Monster.*" He smiled wider this time, and she caught her breath at the sharpness of his teeth. "All these things, you are. And so you must name me."

"Or?"

"There is no *or*. Name me and I let you go."

"What does my father call you?"

"That's his name. It isn't yours. If you want to live, *name me!*" His face twisted into something no longer beautiful, and she saw his hunger, saw how he wanted to destroy her, her father, the Citadel, the *world*. He was a wounded and angry creature, hobbled and helpless, and it hurt to see it.

"No," she said.

He snapped her wrist.

She screamed. It was a high, thin, shocked sound, more surprise than pain at first, but the pain came fast behind in electric waves that pulsed red behind her eyes. "Let go!"

"Name me!" he roared and twisted her arm. More bones shattered. She shrieked and cried and battered at him, and while he broke her apart, one bone at a time, his left hand continued that steady, rapid scrape of chalk on walls. "Name me and live!"

"*Kaam!* Your name is *Kaam!*"

Oddly, she didn't even feel him let go. She only knew that he had turned away to focus on his endless, steady writing, and for a moment she clutched her arm close to her chest, trembling, unable to bear to move it . . . and then she realized the pain was completely gone.

Her wrist was whole. Her bones were unbroken.

Her father grabbed her and pulled her up and away, and she realized that he'd been released, too. He pushed her toward the door and advanced on the captive, on Kaam, with his knife. She knew he would kill him. She could see the rage.

Kaam raised his free right hand without turning from the wall and his constant, rhythmic writing, and said, "Anger is not your sin, Chatar. Thank you for bringing her. Now tell her the truth."

He was writing her name now. Over and over and over, in flowing white letters on black stone. *Samarjit. Samarjit. Samarjit.* Like a silent chant, madness and chalk on stone.

Her father stopped. She could see his muscles twitching with the desire to act, to protect her, but he sheathed the *kirpan* and backed away. Then he grabbed her and hurried her out of the room, down the chalked hallways, down the stairs. She didn't care where she went now. Part of her would never leave that room.

He pulled her to a stop at the thick plastic barrier. Through it, she could see the two soldiers standing guard, and the area beyond that was the world and not the Citadel. They were in the Citadel. That was the antechamber, worlds away. She understood now that what was out there was not . . . this.

This, here, was real.

The barrier, however thick, however secure, was not strong enough to hold in Kaam. All this high-tech security was a lie told by children to master their terror. A candle against a hurricane.

Her father was breathing so hard that she feared for him. His face beneath his beard looked stark and pale.

"God forgive me," he said. "God forgive me for bringing you to him."

"He didn't hurt me." He had, but it was gone now. What was broken was healed, except for the hidden things, secret things, which would never again be whole.

"It doesn't matter. Samarjit, your name is *on his wall.*"

"He said you'd tell me the truth. Please. Tell me—" She reached out to him, but he backed away. And on some horrible level, she understood why. She felt numb now, and the sound of chalk scraping on stone continued relentlessly in her ears.

She felt a shudder go through the stone beneath her feet, an awful, unsteady pulse, and grabbed for the stone of the wall beside her. "What is *that*?"

"It's him." Her father strode to the keypad and entered his code; he hesitated before he hit the last button and looked at her with unfathomably sad eyes. "You wanted to know what I called him," he said. "You named him one of the five evils in our religion. *Kaam*, for lust. For me, he was *Moh*." *Moh* was attachment. All Sikhs sought to keep their passions in balance—lust, greed, pride, anger. Even attachments like love. She had always been her father's biggest struggle, because his love for her had been too great, too out of balance. "He makes us destroy ourselves, Sammy. It's the only power he has. We have to go. *Now*."

He put the last number in, and the plastic gates slid open.

Her father plunged through.

Sammy didn't follow.

Chatar Singh realized at the last second and turned; the full blue skirts of his chola flared as he spun around toward her, but the gates were already crashing shut between them. Soundproofed, she realized. She couldn't hear his scream. Couldn't hear the shouts of the guards as they restrained him from the keypad.

She wished she could have explained it to him. She only knew that somehow, she had no choice.

He makes you destroy yourself, her father had said, and maybe that was true. But she also understood something else, something deeper than that. *We are his demons. This is his hell.*

She had to try to free the captive.

THE WORLD SHUDDERED again, and when she blinked, there wasn't a gate anymore. Where the gate had been was a black rock wall. The boxes of chalk were still in the room, and despite all the lurching and falling, not a single one had shifted on the shelves.

Something fundamental had shifted.

She could hear Kaam still writing, three floors up, the constant raw hiss of chalk on stone. She wondered if it was her name being written, over and over, like an incantation. It terrified her to think that it might be . . . and, she had to admit it, it thrilled her.

Sammy took the stairs two at a time, up two floors, then the third at a slower pace. Her ears led her straight to him. He'd moved again, into a pristinely clean room, and was just starting a new wall. He was lying flat on the stone floor, writing backward from right to left, and as he finished the first line, he moved up just enough to allow the letters space and began the next.

"You didn't leave with him," he said. "Sammy, that is not wise. How do you know I won't kill you?"

"Maybe you will," she said. "But I'm your demon, right? You're not mine. And as long as I stay away from you, you can't stop writing long enough to kill me. Can you?"

He tapped his right hand gently on the floor as he continued to move chalk over stone, and a bone exploded in her own hand and blew shards bloodily out from the skin, as if she'd been shot with an invisible bullet from the inside out. She screamed and clutched the hand to her chest, and blood flooded out over her shirt, sticky and hot. She almost fell.

He tapped again, and it was all gone. All fine. Her hand worked, the bones intact, skin unbroken.

She was still splashed with fresh blood.

"And now we understand each other," Kaam said. "But it's too late now, Samarjit. Too late to run from what you are."

She was shaking so hard that she sank down to a graceless sitting position, staring at him. At the movement of the chalk, drawing out words and phrases, lines and paragraphs. "What do you think I am?"

"Something new," he said. "Something extraordinary."

"Why am I extraordinary?" she asked him and settled into a crouch some feet away. He didn't turn his head.

"You stayed," he said.

"That's not really an answer."

"Oh, I have to answer to you now?"

"Yes," she said, "or I won't bring you chalk."

There was the slightest hesitation in his writing, a stutter, hardly even noticeable. "That's a stupid threat to make, Samarjit."

"It's Sammy, thanks, and I know. Answer me or no more chalk."

"You are extraordinary because I cannot answer that question."

"God, you do go in circles," she said, and laughed. She couldn't think why, because she knew she should be frightened out of her mind, desperately afraid. She had been, when she'd first seen him, but now that he had a name, *Kaam*, she was fascinated. She'd named him after a sin because that was what he made her think about. Sins. Sins of the body. Graceful, longed-for sins. "All right. These things you're writing. How do you know them?"

"How does anyone know anything, Sammy?" If she'd hoped that hearing her nickname instead of her full, formal one would sound less intimate on his lips, she was wrong. If anything, it was *more* intimate . . . as if she'd allowed him to see parts of her that were only properly meant for someone else. "I am remembering. Before it's all lost."

She wanted to ask him more about that, but she had bigger problems. "Are you what the Christians would call . . . the devil?"

He laughed. It was a pure, funny sound, contagious and joyous, and she found herself smiling when it was over. Tears glittered cool in her eyes. "No, sweet Sammy, I am not the devil. I am not God. I am not *anything*. That is the point. I am nothing, but this, this is everything. The act of chalk on stone. Words on the skin of the world."

"I don't understand."

"I didn't think you would. I am just answering your question."

She sat in silence for a while, watching him. He used up a stick of chalk to a nubbin, and before that crumbled into dust, he fetched another from the box with his right hand and passed it to his left to keep writing without pause. Smooth. Seamless.

Beautiful, really.

"You're going to have to let me go soon," she told him. "I'm human. I'm going to need food. Water. Bathrooms. Things like that."

"You'll find them downstairs," he said. "They're there when you need them. I don't have many visitors who want to stay, but when I do, I look after them."

She left and explored. He was right. There was a clean steel kitchen downstairs with a vast pantry stocked with food . . . and a microwave, which was good, because she was a terrible cook. The bathroom was the same black stone, sinks and shower and tub and toilet, but it was all beautiful. The towels were thick black cotton. In the bedroom she found next to it, there was a bed on a platform of black rock, with crisp white sheets. A mirror and dresser. A closet full of clothes in her size.

I am not the devil. I am not God. If he wasn't either of those things, she didn't understand him at all.

Days passed, or she thought they did; no watch, no phone, no clocks. Her father must have been driven mad with terror for her, but she didn't feel afraid. She had plenty to read, if she wanted; the walls were densely covered for ten floors with written works—entire books. Some were sacred, many more profane. Science fiction was next to Middle English texts she could barely read. Dry technical papers next to lush romances. The eighth floor was covered floor to ceiling with a mathematical proof that she finally figured out was part of a calculation of pi.

But most of the time, she found herself sitting in the room with him, kneeling close, passing him chalks. *We are here to serve*, her father had told her. Thousands of families took turns when the Citadel was in a place where the way was open, but for now, she thought, he only wanted to be with her. Only her. And she felt the heat between their bodies, the steady rising tide of desire.

His eyes were black—black irises, black pupils—and he never locked gazes with her again. His skin had a burnished, perfect look to it, as if it wasn't really made of human cells at all, but when their fingers brushed as she passed him chalk, he felt warm and real. She found she longed to trail a finger down that perfect skin. To see what he would do in return.

"Don't you ever rest?" she asked him, as he finished a piece of chalk and she handed him another. "Don't you *have* to rest?"

"There are many things I don't need. Food. Water. Sleep."

"You need someone to bring you chalk."

He smiled. It was too wide, too strange, and she felt a little pulse of disquiet. There were times when Kaam seemed perfectly sane, and she liked those quiet moments, but then there were times like this, when there was a wild, snapping energy inside him that frightened her. "I could make chalk appear," he said. "The ritual was meant to keep visitors coming here. I need visitors, Sammy. If I am left alone . . ."

"You closed the exits. To keep me with you."

"Yes. Do you want to leave me?" It was a quiet question, but there was a kind of resignation in it, too, as if he knew she would leave him soon.

She didn't know that. When she was here, next to him, her whole body burned, tingled, soared. When he brushed his fingers on hers it took her breath away and brought tears to her eyes. Kaam made her feel more alive than she had ever known it was possible to be.

"I don't want to leave," she said, and then forced herself to laugh a little. "Although you *have* to put in an internet connection and a computer, or I'll go crazy eventually. And my—" Her voice died, because for the first time in a while, she thought of her parents. Of her father, saying her name as the Citadel lurched and went away. Of her mother, who hadn't known she was coming here. Were they together, united in fear and grief for their daughter? Or was her mother screaming in rage at her father for taking her here, to *him*? The prospect made her feel sick.

"I could tell you that your parents are fine, but that would be a lie." His voice changed, grew tight and strained. His hand began to shake, though the shapes still formed perfectly under the moving chalk. He had abandoned the musical notation he'd been writing and instead shifted to letters. Her name, over and over. "I have taken their daughter away. They can never be fine again."

"Kaam—"

"Everything fades. Everything falls. Everyone goes away." As Kaam spoke it, he wrote it. Then again, in French. In German. "Go away."

She did. She wandered the halls, feeling ever colder away from the warmth of his presence. She thought about her mother and father, searching; she thought of her friends, who must have been terrified by now. Maybe they all thought she was dead. Maybe they were dead—for all she knew, years could have passed. Decades. She had no sense of time. *I should be terrified*, she realized.

But somehow, she wasn't.

On the tenth floor, written in the farthest corner, she found a letter written in Kaam's tiniest script, in English. It was a letter from him to her, Samarjit, and it poured out his hope, his fear, his longing to possess her in breathtaking ways.

He'd filled the tenth floor long, long ago. Before she was born, perhaps.

She reached out and touched her fingers to the chalk, closed her eyes, and said, "I feel it too."

He was there when she opened her eyes, writing frantically in the tiny spaces left between lines. *Samarjit. Samarjit. Samarjit.* Over and over and over, in letters she recognized and then alphabets she only vaguely knew. He wrote it in Punjabi, the language of the Sikh scriptures. In Chinese characters. In Cyrillic. In marks that no longer had meaning to modern eyes.

She put her arms around him from behind, and he stopped writing. The silence in her mind, which had been a constant hiss of chalk on stone, was deafening.

The one who wins the war. That was what her name meant.

And as he turned, she saw eternity in his eyes. It was not dark. It was bright and vast and full of terrors. *I am the one who writes*, Kaam said, and she heard it through her skin, through her soul. *And while I write on the skin of the world, that which would consume it, pauses.*

Kaam had stopped writing, because of *her*. Her father had told her: *The captive does not destroy. He makes you destroy yourself.*

You had to want to lose yourself in him.

She saw her skin begin to change, felt her mortal desires bleed away. Felt eternity reflected in her eyes.

Kaam kissed her, a soft and gentle kiss of longing, love, desire, sadness, and then he was free, a mist in the air, a whisper in her mind. She saw it clearly then, all the things her father hadn't told her: of the wise men gathered together in a long-fallen kingdom, knowing the end of days was upon them. Of binding a spirit, a *jinn*, a *si'lat*, to their service to hold it at bay, because they were weak and afraid to sacrifice themselves in the struggle.

They had kept him here in prison all this time, while their descendants kept watch. While they *served*. Knowing the end of the world, the end of everything and everyone, was on the shoulders of one poor, half-mad creature bound to their service.

Samarjit Cole was one of their blood, and one of their blood had finally freed him.

There was only one thing to do. One thing to keep the darkness at bay.

She knelt down, picked up the chalk, and began to write stories on the skin of the world.

I am the one who wins the war.

However long the war would last.

She felt him before she saw him, the metallic warmth of his presence, the whisper of his breath, and felt his arms around her. Her breath lurched in her throat as he pressed a warm kiss to the back of her neck.

Kaam would not abandon her. He was free to do as he chose.

And he chose to stay.

He knelt beside her, picked up a piece of chalk, and began to write with her.

PETER ORULLIAN

Why did I write "Stories Are Gods" for *Unbound*? That's easy. I mean, who *wouldn't* want to write a tale about an albino with brittle-bone disease? But of course, as with most things, there's more to it than that.

In my series, The Vault of Heaven, there's a place of science. A place where the people work to understand scientific law. It's called Aubade Grove. And Lour Nail—an albino philosopher with a rare bone disease—lives there. He's a character from book three of The Vault of Heaven. He's cantankerous. He's argumentative. And I wanted to write about him. About Aubade Grove.

But I also wanted to explore an idea—or at least frame it, since it's part of my ongoing world: the power of story. Does a story have a measurable relationship to the thing it describes? Do intangibles, or our belief, our . . . experience, of those intangibles affect mechanical systems—the world around us.

The original title of this tale was "A Story Proof." I still like the title. And I share it because it's how I began tackling the theme of *Unbound*. Since what we believe or don't believe about a story . . . what we're willing to defend or let go because of a story . . . says everything about who we are.

Also, I find Lour funny as hell.

STORIES ARE GODS

Peter Orullian

I eased to my knees beside her chair, breathless.

"Anna," I managed, huffing from my shambling jog to her convalescent room. I looked up at my love, anxious to hear her speak a word. Any word.

She looked down at me. "Lour?" I could see lucidity in her face—she'd used my name, knew who I was. But the real question remained in her eyes.

I glanced at the hand-mirror in her lap, its handle squeezed beneath her whitened knuckles. "Eight years," I said. "You don't remember?"

She raised the mirror, her expression like that of a disoriented child. The face reflected there was her own. Just older. Eight years of catatonia staring back.

"I was inside the Bourne," she said, quieter, her voice fragile. "I was taken by a trader. A highwayman. Sold." She looked at me, her brow rising, as though she hoped I could help her decipher the rest.

I put a hand over her fingers and gently pressed the mirror back to her lap. How much did I tell her? I didn't know it all, myself. But damn me if I didn't know what *I* had done. Things I'd thought about every day the past eight years as I'd sat in this very room hoping her distant, empty eyes would focus on me again—like they did now—and we could start over.

It wasn't the time to share any of that. Not right now. Maybe not ever. "How do you feel?" I asked. A safe question.

A feint smile rose at one corner of her mouth, looking more bitter than mirthful. "Muddled," she said.

"You're back in Aubade Grove, Anna." I glanced around the clean but rather bare room. "And this is a hospice, of sorts. They've been taking care of you."

"There's so much . . . missing." She struggled to find words, memories, her brow pinching. After a long moment, her eyes relaxed, no longer seeming to reflect inward, and her smile sweetened as she looked at me. "I remember you, though. My Lour Nail. And what did it cost you to have me looked after like this?"

I returned her warm smile. "I'm a philosopher by trade. A catatonic mind presents a unique challenge."

"I'll wager you've squandered countless hours telling me bad jokes, trying to pry me from my catalepsy." She swallowed, resting her voice a moment. Then shook her head in mild reproof. "That can't have helped the Grove's only albino win any arguments on the theater floors."

"Ah, but this is Aubade Grove, my dear. I convinced the college Savants that there was science to be had in observing and treating your condition."

She gave a small laugh. "Nonsense. The Grove colleges study the sky. The mind and body they leave to others. "

I shrugged and left her question unanswered. Wasn't important, anyway. The only thing that mattered was that Anna had returned from a long journey inside her mind. Deafened gods had I missed her. I would never have thought one could hold the hand of the woman he loves and feel so far from her. Know she was far from you. In mind. I'd had eight years of that.

"All hells, what are we rambling on about, you're back, my girl." I paused, happier than I'd been in . . . well, in eight years. "You're back."

"I'm back," she repeated, and inclined her head, so that our foreheads could touch. The way we used to.

Anna had been the *only* woman who'd ever touched me. Albinism has that effect. Or maybe it was my slight frame. A woman has a right to feel safe with her man. My bones seemed to break easy, besides. Physick men and blackcoats called it brittle-bone disease. I called it the nuisance that was my body.

"Why in every last hell did you ever marry me?"

It was a question I'd asked myself a lot over these years she'd held that thousand-league look in her eyes.

She pulled back, like you do when you want someone to hear *and* see your reply. "Why, because you're objectionable, of course." There was a wicked grin on her face now—a subtle thing, but there to be seen if you knew how to look. It wasn't a tease. In fact, that grin did more to punctuate what she said than refute it.

"Objectionable?" I said, a bit playful. I think I needed her to explain.

"You make me laugh," she clarified.

In truth, most of the time, I did so more by accident than design.

"It's all the popular positions I take in the discourse theaters, isn't it?" I laughed out loud, and very much liked the sound of it in her little convalescent room.

She shook her head, clarifying again. "It's the look on the faces of the opposing panelists that I like best."

Good hell did I love this woman.

I was a slight albino philosopher with unpopular opinions about most things. If there was ever proof of the abandoning gods, it was that *any* woman could love me. Let alone Anna, who many thought would be the next Savant of the College of Cosmology.

I smiled, more content than I had a right to be, and inclined to kiss her . . .

. . . when her eyes grew distant. Her cheeks slackened. And her thousand-league stare returned.

Just that fast, she was gone again.

Eight years.

After eight years I'd gotten eight minutes. If that. And now what?

Damn me.

I tried to rouse her. For hours I tried. Bad jokes. Unpopular philo-sophical arguments. Physical contact. Nothing worked. Eventually, the hospice workers gently ushered me out of her small room and onto the cobbled street.

It was dark hour. Maybe later. I didn't care. I stood there in the dark and chill, hating. Hating my bad luck. Hating the abandoning gods. Hating the Bourne and every last creature sent there by those gods during the Placing. The gods-damned creatures had bought Anna from a highwayman and made use of her somehow. Until I'd found a way to get her back—

"Pleasant evening, don't you think?"

I turned, un-startled, toward the owner of the deep, clear voice. A man stood against the wall of the hospice, his well-worn coat buttoned to the top. He looked like every field hand I'd ever seen. He didn't speak again for a long while, pulling a time or two on a tobacco stem, the end flaring in the dark.

Then he stood up and came close so that I could see his expression. Or rather the lack of expression. Empty, by those silent gods. His face was just plain empty. In philosophical terms, I'd say diffident. Lacking animus.

But that was my nerves trying to gain control of my fear, which had begun to gallop along irrationally. The Grove didn't have real enemies. Debates, sure. Spirited disagreements. But never hate. Never . . . apathy.

"Did you enjoy those few moments of clarity with your wife?" he asked.

A chill shivered through me.

I stared, unmoving.

"You're welcome," the man added.

My dying gods. Velle. Had to be. The Velle knew how to render the Will, cause things to move, change . . . stir. And they lived inside the Bourne, where Anna had been taken . . .

"You plan to take her back," I surmised, trying to sound defiant.

"Do you honestly think a single woman is that important to us?" The man took a long pull on his tobacco stem, savoring the smoke as it rolled from his lips and nose in slow streams.

"She must be," I replied. "Why else make a trip to Aubade Grove to give her a moment's clarity."

The man turned and began to stroll, clearly expecting me to join him. I didn't follow. Several strides down the small street he stopped. Never looked back. Waiting.

After several long moments of indecision, my skin began to prickle. A chill. But not of cold. Not temperature cold. This chill moved inside me. I shuddered as it touched my bones, as it caressed memories I'd successfully forgotten—about being an albino child, about how I'd rescued Anna. I felt like a cello string being played on a bitter midwinter morning, moments from snapping and ending that deep, dry note.

I dropped to my knees, staring up at the back of the Velle, who hadn't moved, save his head, which cocked back as if to some expectant pleasure.

That's when I felt the chill deepen. And in my mind images flared. Dark hovels rank with the sweat of childbirth labor. Long brackish ponds walked in by stooped figures harvesting mud-roots. Fields of short graves.

I agonized with the brutal suggestion of the images. My body and soul resonated in the night with the Velle, as if we'd become connected somehow. And just as my own dark secrets began to surface, the note ended. I crumpled to the stones, exhausted, defiled in a way one feels who's been caged and put on display as a *low one*. Something to be gawked at. Ridiculed. I knew those feelings. Oh, I knew them.

When enough of my strength returned, I stood and limped to the Velle's side. If I hadn't broken or cracked a bone in my left leg it sure felt like I had. But I shuffled alongside him as he started to stroll.

The man turned his indifferent eyes on me. "What do your stories say about the races in the Bourne?"

His question needed no answer. We both knew what the stories said. Whatever lived in the Bourne had been herded there, placed by gods who'd abandoned us all. And those races were kept in the Bourne by a barrier of some kind. A veil, the stories said. Raised by the gods to keep these *Quiet* races at bay. Keep them from coming into the Eastlands to test men. Test them with war. With death. With suffering.

He was merely reminding me of all this before coming to his purpose.

"There's an argument about to begin in your College of Philosophy," he said. "Not a Succession of Arguments," he clarified. "This won't involve your colleges of astronomy or mathematics or physics. Or even cosmology."

I looked up at the five great towers of the Grove, their observation domes looming hundreds of strides above. They formed an immense pentacle at the center of the city. Each college had its own tower. Libraries and research halls and discourse theaters connected the towers in a broad pentagon that held walking gardens at its center.

"The annual position forum, you mean." I hadn't planned to attend. Usually a waste of damn time.

"Aubade Grove's College of Philosophy has recently taken a charter from the League of Civility." The Velle turned down a narrow alley. "A few members is all. More of an experiment than anything else, at this point."

"I don't give a spit for the League," I said, grateful for an angry thought to combat the chill still rolling through me. "But the few who've signed on with them are influential with the college, that's a truth."

"They're responsible for this year's philosophical position. They plan to submit that the stories about the Bourne are misunderstood. They'll call to question the existence of the Veil that imprisons the Quiet. They'll argue to rationalize all of this as an unfortunate mythology. Put it away. Ignore it in the same way rational men ignore all irrational things."

Favoring my broken leg as I was, my boot caught on an ill-fitted stone and I fell. "Good gods-damn!" I was pretty sure I'd just broken my wrist trying to stop my fall.

The Velle paused, staring in the direction of the Grove towers. They ascended the night, carving dark pillars from the star-filled sky.

As I watched him, I began to have an idea about why he'd come to me. Of all the philosophers in the Grove—hell, maybe of all *people* in the Grove—I was one who held Bourne stories to be true. Anna had been taken there. And I'd once tried to go there myself.

"What do you want?" I asked.

"Simple." The Velle turned and stared down at me. "You will argue against them. You will be sure the *existing* philosophical position about the Bourne remains in place."

I forgot myself for a moment, and asked, "Why do you give a tinker's damn what a bunch of high-minded philosophers thinks about the Bourne and all its beasts."

A sharp pain erupted behind my eyes and nose. My eyes began to water. My nose bled. Then abruptly the stabbing sensation was gone. The Velle's brief touch.

When I'd caught my breath, I reframed my question. "I would have thought you'd prefer we pay you no mind. Attentive men prepare better. You know, in times of rumor and threat and war."

The Velle shook his head, and tossed his tobacco stem away. "We're not concerned with your little armies. Or your Sheason, who render the Will as we do." He paused a long moment, as if deciding whether killing me might prove a better course. After all, he was asking the Grove's frail albino to make his argument for him. I was awfully damn good on the theater floor—no false modesty there—but that didn't always matter in the ways it should.

"What we care about is the Veil," he continued. "We want to understand it, scientifically."

"That's not been a focus—"

"I know," he replied. "But you'll get to it eventually. And the concerted effort of the Grove colleges in understanding how it works is something we care very much about."

"Because in understanding it, you might be able to bring it down, that it?" The logic wasn't hard to follow. "Why in every last hell would I want to help you, then?"

He looked past me, back the way we'd come. "Because we'll find a way to bring it down, eventually. Because you might want to be considered a friend when we do. And because I can return Anna to you. Permanently."

End the catatonia he meant. My silent prayer for so long.

"There are risks, of course," he added. "Her mind has found a sanctuary. You'd be taking that away from her if I make her fully *awake*." His resonant voice came low, deep, almost from the stones beneath me.

I stared at him. *To get Anna back* . . . And I had no love for the League. Still, could anything he wanted of me be the right thing?

"And consider . . . it's the argument you'd have wanted to make anyway. You, of all people." He cocked his head—the first human thing I'd seen him do, other than smoke a stem—and asked an odd question. "Why 'Lour Nail'?"

It was a nickname. One I'd had since my youth. So long . . . that I didn't answer to anything else. I took out my compass, placed it in the palm of my hand, and held it toward him. The Velle bent down, reading the needle.

"It's out of true by a few degrees south," he said matter-of-factly. Then he nodded. "'Lour,' the alternate for 'lower.' And 'nail,' the astronomer's name for a compass needle. Clever. You have this effect on all compasses." It wasn't a question. He nodded again. "I felt it in you. Something in your blood. In your flesh. Heavier. Perhaps related to your white disease."

"Albinism, thank you." It wasn't humor or anger. Just rote.

That's when I saw the *most* human thing I'd seen from the Velle. An almost smile. In my experience, it takes practice to almost smile. It was a bitter thing. More mocking than amusement.

"Oh, that is poetry," he said.

I shook my head.

"You're wife. She walked into the Bourne with a slaver, didn't she?" The Velle's expression had already returned to indifference. "And you came to play the rescuer, but you couldn't cross the Veil. Something about you . . . Lour Nail, kept you out. Not that a frail albino could have done much inside the Bourne. Still, at least you tried. And still, poetic."

"I think you mean ironic," I said. "And I got her out, didn't I?"

The Velle pushed a wave of thought at me. It passed through my flesh, finding again those secrets I'd tried to hide. He caressed them a second time, making them ache and itch and burn. I clutched at my chest until he let go this resonant note. I felt something different that time, though. He could play this string long enough and loud enough that I'd drop for good. It was like poison already inside me. He had only to make it grow, make it the all of me.

And he was right. I'd have argued against this new position, anyway. Fool *new-thought* philosophers. It didn't seem to matter to them if their thinking was sound or not. Just putting forward challenges to *existing* thought was sufficient in and of itself these days. Wiseacres looking to make names for themselves. Damn fools.

"You don't need me," I finally said. "Why don't you go around to all the right sophists and clench up *their* hearts? I'm sure you can get them to agree with you."

He drew a deep breath, as one who appreciates a good question. "Your people have a different strength in masses. Or think they do. Makes them foolish. Makes them think they can win at things. They band together for a cause, even if they *can't* win. Besides," and he began to stroll away, "I told you, there's some poetry in having you do it, given what you are, and the wife I know you adore."

"What if I say no?"

He stopped at the end of the alley, his eyes cast up at the Grove towers. "Just remember that I'm not asking you to do something you wouldn't have done anyway." He paused. "And remember Anna. There are worse things than catatonia. She'd tell you so, herself . . . if she could."

THE COLLEGE OF Philosophy discourse theater hummed with excitement. And not just from Grove philosophers. Members of *all* the Grove colleges were there. As were members of philosophy schools as distant as Naltus Rey. The annual philosophical position that would be published from this conference would stir debate in them all.

I sat in the first row of the circular theater, because I knew I'd be taking the floor at some point. I didn't want to have to move too far. My wrist and leg were broken, bandaged tight, and the rest of me was sore as all hells from my little encounter with the Velle.

Hadn't seen the bastard again, which made me happy enough. But I didn't get the impression he was far away, either. Come to that, the discourse theater had several dozen rows. Big place. Lit with low-burning lamps. Good for thinking. But different than most of the other college theaters, which were brightly lit for demonstration. With his blank expression, the Velle could be sitting right here in the theater and it'd be hard to pick him out.

So, I didn't try. Would have given me the shakes to find him here, anyway.

All the same, I'd brought a friend. Martin. A trouper-turned-astronomy-shop-proprietor. Long story, that. But Martin liked coming to the theaters. For him, there was precious little difference between a rhea-fol play and these debates. Today, though, I'd asked his company because he had a calming, encouraging way about him. Maybe because he had a story for everything. Maybe because he had an uncanny knack for the stars.

My job was simple today: issue a challenge. The debate to confirm, refine, or refute the Grove's philosophical suppositions would happen later. Today, they would merely be stated. And either there'd be consensus, in which case, the panelists putting forward new thought would commit it to paper, or someone would call it to question, and a time for arguments would be set.

In some ways, this was very much like the Succession of Arguments the Grove used to establish new laws of celestial mechanics. The difference was that with Succession, one college put forth its hypothesis and defended it in successive debates with each college—so long as they continued to win.

But with the declaration of a new philosophical position, it was just Grove philosophers hashing it out amongst themselves.

Savant Leon Bellerex, who led the College of Philosophy, stood up from his seat—reserved in the first row. The hum of excitement quieted almost immediately. The doors were shut.

Two things I liked about Savant Bellerex. He wore the same robe as the rest of us. No gilding or color trim to draw attention to himself. Which isn't to say you wouldn't pick *him* out in a crowd. He had a presence about him. Gave you the feeling he'd read every book *you'd* ever read, and understood it twice as well.

The other thing I liked about him was that he didn't force the college into his own views. In fact, he let others lead the thrust of new thought, serving more to weigh and shape it. That, and he made sure any objections didn't go unheard.

He said, simply, "Let us begin. This year, Darius will be our lead panelist. He's young, but no less wise for that."

Laughter rolled around the theater, setting a nice tone for the conference. I smiled. We *all* did. No doubt that had been deliberate on Bellerex's part. Because what would follow was . . . well hell, some would call it heresy. Not philosophers. Heresy's not a word we use. But it would upset folks. That's for damn sure.

"The show begins," Martin whispered beside me.

Darius stood. All eighteen years of him. I almost laughed again. I don't think the young man had even a passing acquaintance with a razor, and here he was, strutting from the panel table to the center of the discourse theater. His shoes tapped a light rhythm on the boards. Other college theaters had marble floors, stones of different kinds. Ours was old oak. Felt thoughtful.

He came halfway to where I sat. That's when I saw it. The boy had to be this close for me *to* see it—in addition to all the rest, my eyes were bad. But there it was. Woven in dark thread against the black cloth of his robe—just below the College of Philosophy insignia—was the emblem of the League of Civility.

It wasn't unheard of for a Grove man to bear two allegiances, so long as the first belonged to his Grove college. But it was rare. And in some ways it was a louder statement.

I'd told the Velle I didn't "give a spit" for the League. That was true enough. But seeing their insignia woven to the robe of a man presenting new thought on the theater floor . . . troubled me. I couldn't say why. I didn't know much about the League. They apparently had a lot to say about reform. And if they moved beyond a probationary period in the Grove, they'd have the right to carry steel, as they did elsewhere. They'd have some policing duties, besides. Philosophers carrying blades seemed like a bad idea to me.

"Friends," Darius called out.

I smiled again. He was new to this, not realizing the acoustics of the theater were engineered deliberately so that a normal speaking voice may be used.

"It's a year of change," he began. "Even for men and women like us, change can be difficult. It forces us to reexamine what we believe. And what *we* know—maybe better than most—is that we are, in fact, little more than our collection of beliefs."

There was general assent to this sentiment.

I took a long breath to brace myself. Probably the thing I hated most about my own college was the pontification. I had an idea that it grew out of insecurity, since of the five Grove colleges we performed the least of the hard sciences. So, of course, we had to *sound* the wisest. Stupid.

"But that's what we're here to do: reexamine," Darius went on. "And today, it's one of the oldest stories that we will challenge. A belief that underlies faith-systems. A belief used to justify the wars of the First and Second Promise. A belief . . . without which we may well have to conceive new curse words."

A rumble of laughter.

Martin's laugh was cautious. He was a story man.

"My friends," Darius pushed on, "I speak of an ages-old notion of enemies held captive in the lands we call the Bourne. I speak of a Veil that many believe holds them there. I speak of a fable that gods placed them in these remote corners of our world because they were . . . undesirable."

All hells, this is going to get messy.

Muttering rose. General alarm at this new stance. Incredulousness. Some awe at the boldness of it. And underneath all that, a profound silence. Some few kept quiet, listening to a dangerous change being spoken with a civil tongue from the theater floor.

"Let's take a closer look at these suppositions." Darius began to pace, walking the ring and meeting the eyes of as many as he could. "If there are peoples in these far countries—and I think we can all agree that's true—why do we assume they're hostile toward us? Because a creation story tells us so?"

"Maybe because when they've come into the east, they've come in war." It was Mical, seated not far behind the panel table. His question was clearly a plant. He'd just done a bad job of sounding like he had a convicted opinion. Damn ninny.

"Nations of the east fight among themselves on the *right* side of this restraining Veil," Darius countered. "So, if these Quiet *are*, in fact, hostile, it's not divinely inspired hatred or vengeance. At least, no more so than our own petty wars."

A middle-aged woman seated halfway up the theater opposite me stood. She patiently waited for Darius's attention.

"Meghan, you've something to offer?" Darius kept an even tone. Meghan was well-regarded. It wouldn't do to antagonize her.

"Whether their hostility toward us is divinely inspired or not, I fail to see why we would challenge the idea of a Veil that keeps them from bringing war on us more often." She waited for an answer.

Darius raised a hand to cup his chin. A thoughtful gesture I would bet three thin plugs he'd rehearsed.

"Our feeling," Darius began, speaking as for the entire College of Philosophy, "is that we have no right to hold them there—"

"But we're not *doing* anything," Meghan countered. "If it exists, it's been placed there by someone else—"

"The gods, you mean," Darius jabbed back, while smiling.

"Does it matter?" Meghan softly challenged.

"Meghan's got salt," Martin commented under his breath.

Darius began to pace again, his eyes trained on his steps as one considering before speaking. "It does," he finally announced. "Because we lead with thought. What we espouse informs the opinions of kings and councils. It's irresponsible of us to ignore stories that are so clearly inhumane."

Meghan was preparing to counter, when I caught her eye. I made it clear to her that I had things of my own to say. No need for her to get too dirty too soon. I was made for dirty. She nodded almost imperceptibly in my direction and sat.

"And maybe there's just one thing more," Darius added, casting his gaze up and around the theater. "Have we ever considered that if this Veil is real, that perhaps the reason the citizens of the Bourne are angry and resentful, is precisely because they've been made prisoners there? I know I wouldn't like it."

Darius came around and sat again at the panel table. His colleagues, in turn, each stood and offered variants of the same thinking. It was classic philosophical argument: establish your thesis in the mouths of multiple advocates—made it seem to hold more weight. Another waste of good time.

A few more rose to voice concerns. But there were ready answers. And at the end of three hours, the room seemed to mull in general agreement.

Darius stood, looking grateful. I'd swear that was an affectation too. "If there's no direct challenge," he said, "we'll move to author these new positions and publish them as the Aubade Grove College of Philosophy's annual position."

"You're on," Martin said, gently elbowing me.

I was stiff from sitting so long. My bones hated it. So getting up was something of a chore. And though the Velle could chill me through, kill me with a thought, I still didn't like being pushed to do a thing. Before standing, I had to satisfy myself that I'd have made this argument anyway. But that was a short trip. Because I knew better about the Bourne. I knew it because of Anna.

There *was* still the Velle's belief that by keeping the stories about the Bourne unchanged the Grove would eventually decide to study the Veil. Learn how it works. And if it did, the Quiet might make use of that information to cross into the East. In force. So, maybe I should just keep my seat, let the League change the old stories, so the Grove would never have interest in studying the Veil. But, I figured, if I made my argument, won, and the Grove did someday discover how the Veil works, such knowledge could be equally used to strengthen it. And we'd have the knowledge first.

Also . . . there was Anna.

I got to my feet and stepped onto the theater floor. There were mutters.

"You're wrong," I said, because I just didn't have time or patience for stupid preamble.

As was customary, I let the theater empty before taking my leave. The purpose was to give any who wanted to throw in with me the chance let me know. None did. I knew I could count on Meghan if it came to that. So it didn't bother me that she walked on by. And Martin would help where needed, though he wasn't a member of any of the Grove colleges.

I stood alone on the theater floor for several long moments. There's a loud silence in that place when all the bluster's gone. I used it to think about Anna. I'd be a liar if I didn't acknowledge that a large part of making this argument was for her.

I let myself imagine one of our evening walks. We'd go beyond the Grove walls. Fewer whispers about a woman and an albino that way. Because even in a place of forward thought like Aubade Grove, people's observations often felt like judgment. Anna would amble slowly, so that I didn't have to work too hard—I had precious little endurance as it was. And we'd each take a side of some debate, often the side we least agreed with.

That's how I won her heart. We'd watch the stars on those evening strolls, and I'd do the one thing I did well. Argue. I didn't weave syllogisms. I didn't frame trick questions. I just had a knack for knowing why my opponent wanted to prove a thing, and then held that up for others to scrutinize.

Most of my colleagues thought me an ass. I assumed a healthy portion of that to be professional jealousy.

With Anna, though, it made her laugh. She wasn't mean-spirited. I think she just hated the sophistry as much as I did.

And now I had a chance to wake her from her catatonia. From eight years of her thousand-league stare.

I took a last look around, then made my way out. The hallway encircling the theater was dark. I navigated by memory. Ten strides on, something hit my head, knocking me to the ground.

Then boots rained down on me. My belly. My chest. My back. My ass. More than a few in my neck and face. One took me in the tender parts.

Pray they don't break any bones.

It seemed to go on forever. I could feel my skin bruising beneath my robe, feel the beat of my heart in several dozen places over my body.

Then silence returned, silence and labored breathing.

A moment later came boot-heels on the stone floor. Not hurried. Not someone rushing to help a stranger who's being mobbed.

Then a lamp flared to light in the darkness, and Darius stood there, staring down at me. The shapes of my attackers faded back. I'd never be able to identify them.

Darius shook his head. Might have been sympathy for the attack. Might have been reproof. Then he hunkered down, setting the lamp to the side so we could see each other clearly.

"Did you fall?" he asked with mock concern.

"I did," I said, spitting out blood, "I fell under the boots of your hirelings. Or is it just my good fortune you happened along and that my attackers didn't scurry away at your approach."

Darius's expression tightened. He'd missed that one. He waved at his cronies to leave.

Up close, I got a good look at the League insignia—four hands forming a squarish circle, each hand clasping the wrist of the other. Something brotherly about that, which made the attack another irony. I was used to ironies, though.

"You should be careful," Darius advised. "I understand in addition to your albinism, you're a bit frail in the bones."

"A nice attempt at discouragement." I smiled, being sure he saw my bloodied teeth. "And something you'd likely planned before tonight's performance."

"Performance?" His tone made clear that he knew what I meant, so I left it there.

"Is this the way the League does its work?" I pointed at the insignia on his robe. "Intimidation?"

"In actuality, we aren't members of the League. Not officially. Not yet."

"I see. Then it was my own philosophy colleagues who beat the pine-tar out of me. Is that what you want me telling Savant Bellerex? That you plan to win your argument through physical coercion?" I smiled my bloody smile again. Damn pup needed to learn how these games were played.

"I think witnesses will attest to the fact that you fell." Darius looked around at the shadowy figures retreating beyond the lamplight. "You're known for falling. Weak limbs and all."

"Are you really that afraid of a debate on this?" I shook my head. "Your deeper reasoning must be flawed—"

"Let me be plain." Darius hunched forward. "Change is coming. Change in the way we view things. It'll take time, but it'll come. The only real question is does the College of Philosophy adopt these views, embrace them. *Own* them. Or, do we serve those whose interests will set that agenda."

"The League," I surmised.

Darius kept a long silence. "I happen to agree with the League in its views on the Bourne. It's why I wear this." He pulled at the League emblem on his robe. "But what if . . . I'll make you a deal, Lour. If I win our argument, I'll kill the Grove chapter of the League."

"Why would you do that?" I didn't bother to hide my skepticism.

"Because if the College of Philosophy publishes this new thinking, it'll show the League that we're aligned with their credo." He nodded. "They won't feel any need to exercise oversight, to *influence* our opinions on topics that matter to them."

"If you win, huh?" I chuffed a laugh, spattering blood on his face. "You mean if I deliberately lose."

Darius said nothing, staring.

"You really are afraid of the albino philosopher with bad bones, aren't you," I mocked.

"You know what I think?" Darius spoke in a conspiratorial whisper. "I think you should leave the Grove."

"I make you that uncomfortable, do I?" I smiled. "Is it my skill at debate or my white skin that does it?"

He finally took his lamp in hand, and stood. "You're in an interesting position, aren't you, Lour? A philosophical position. You get to decide how to act based what you feel is the greater good. I'll be honest, I envy you."

He laughed and walked away. Other boots scuffed across the stone floors, retreating in the dark.

I shook my head and immediately regretted it. My body screamed with every movement.

When did philosophy get so dangerous? Damn me.

I COULD HAVE taken the pulley lift to the cosmology tower observation dome. I was the only Grove resident I knew that had been granted the privilege. Savant Scalinou—sixty-year-old leader of the College of Cosmology—didn't even take the lift. But I climbed the 998 steps anyway. Made my way with the cane I was now using. Took me an hour. Seemed right, especially since Scalinou had asked to see me. Though I *always* took the stairs, on account of our friendship. On account of respect.

Still, every step was a moment of hell. My whole body seemed a bruise. And I'd wrapped several parts of my arms and legs where Darius and his mob had put some hurt into my bones. I had at least two more breaks, sure enough.

I paused at the top of the stairs, winded. "We couldn't have met in your chambers? It had to be in the middle of the night in the middle of the sky?"

Scalinou stood beside his great skyglass, peering through the eyepiece. He laughed, his voice resonating through the long brass tube. Truth was, I loved this place. The slow, patient, thoughtful way of it. Anna and I had come here often to visit with Scalinou. Up here among the stars.

When I had my wind back, I limped with my cane over to the desk he kept beside his sky tools. "You heard, then?"

"You think you can win?" Scalinou said, still staring into his skyglass.

It was the wrong question. And that's why I'd been eager to keep this appointment. "Tell me what you know about the League?"

Scalinou finally sat back from his perch, wearing a pinched brow. "You look like the last hell. What happened to you?"

"I was born albino. And smart." I hunched my shoulders, which hurt not a little. "Bad combination."

Scalinou made a noise of agreement in this throat. Then, he motioned me closer, and nodded toward the eyepiece of his great sky-glass. An invitation. I leaned in and looked through the lens. I might hail from the College of Philosophy, but like any member of any Grove college, I had fundamental astronomy training. I was looking at an open stretch of sky where Pliny Soray—one of our planets—made her orbit.

And it looked a bit odd.

As I stood back, Scalinou was making a notation in his ledger. When he'd finished, he didn't comment on Soray, instead he answered my question.

"The League wants change. They want us to be more self-reliant. They want us spending less time looking to others for answers." He arched his back, stretching from his endless hunch over his instruments.

"When you say 'others,' you mean the gods, don't you?" This little argument was getting big fast.

"Maybe," he said. "It's a practical credo. Not bad for that. But the League does more than preach its unique philosophy. It's organized into what they call jurshahs, comprised of four factions: history, commerce, politics, and justice and defense."

"Sounds like government," I observed, already hating the League more.

Scalinou had a faraway look in his eyes. "When they formed political and militant branches . . . that's when things really changed. They've established garrisons in many cities. They sit on ruling councils. In many places they enforce the law—oftentimes, the very laws they've lobbied to establish."

"Sounds lovely." I sat in an open chair across from Scalinou—my legs were aching.

Scalinou gave a sour smile in the starlight. "It's hard to argue against ideas of self-reliance, of education, of ending slums and porridge lines. Trouble is," he took a deep breath, "once they gain a foothold somewhere on the basis of these ideas, they go further."

Recent news ran through my head. "They've passed laws in Recityv legalizing the killing of Sheason who employ their use of the Will . . . even when it's to help others."

He nodded. "I was the only Savant that voted against a League chapter in Aubade Grove. I don't blame the others. As I say, the League's core ideas are good ones. But," he looked down at his star ledger, "if we move past the trial period. If we install them as a part of what we do, as a means for keeping law . . . they'll go further."

"Like beating up albino philosophers?"

"I mean you and me," Scalinou replied, eyeing my several bruises. "Think about the Grove's five sciences. Astronomy, physics, and mathematics—those have practical value. But philosophy? Cosmology? We'll be seen as *im*practical."

I listened to the silence that fell between us for several moments before answering. "Because we don't add demonstrable value."

"Because we're predicated on opinion, judgment, ideology, belief," he added. "Funny that."

I laughed, seeing the immediate connection. "We're too much like the League itself, needing others to take stock in our ideas."

Scalinou looked up toward an open pane of glass in the observation dome. "It's not even about us, though. Think what will happen if they succeed in publishing this new philosophical position. If it comes from Aubade Grove of all places."

I sat, considering for the first time the repercussions. Our stories. The ones that had given us strength each time the Quiet had come into the east. They'd be challenged. Abandoned maybe. Our stories. The ones that led to ethics like giving kindness for kindness, mercy to balance justice. They'd be replaced with the League's brand of ethics.

"Damn me," I said, shaking my head at the futility.

"What?" Scalinou asked, as he poured us each a short glass of pomace brandy.

"You've given me another good reason to try and win my little argument . . ."

"But?" my old friend prompted, knowing me well enough to know there was more.

"But Darius told me that he'd abandon the League chapter in

Aubade Grove if *he* won." I took my drink and quaffed the whole thing.

"Was this before or after he beat the last hell out of you?" Scalinou showed his wry grin.

"Oh I know. Little jackbird has no intention of keeping that promise." I poured myself another glass and took a short pull. "Why did you want to see me, anyway?"

Scalinou pointed up toward the open pane—the same one his skyglass was pointed at. "Pliny Soray might be teaching us something."

I followed my old friend's gaze. "Can you dispense with the cosmologer's analogies? My head hurts."

He chuckled warm and low. "Some change is beyond us. Like a planet that may be out of true. We can observe, record, speculate as to possible outcomes. But some change," he looked down at me, "some change is *directed*. And the one thing I know you're good at, Lour, is getting at why someone wants what they want. Why does the League want this change? Maybe if you find the answer to that, you'll know how to win your little argument."

And that was the right question: Why did the league want this change?

"My argument's feeling not so little anymore," I said, finishing my brandy.

"No," Scalinou agreed, "quite possibly the most important philosophical debate in Grove history. And I can tell you this, even *this* argument pales in comparison to having the League here permanently *directing* philosophical thought."

I didn't bother to tell him about the Velle or Anna.

Scalinou rolled his shoulders, stretching. "How will you begin?"

"It's an argument about stories," I said, thinking out loud. "About what can be learned or believed because of them. So I guess I'm headed to the annals."

EACH GROVE COLLEGE had its own annals—extensive records and libraries. After talking to Scalinou, I wasn't sure winning my argument was the *right* thing for the greater good. Perhaps stories about the Bourne and the Quiet and the Veil could change. Should change. Perhaps losing them would cause no real harm. But something tugged at me every time I considered it. Maybe it was the idea that the League wanted to take some of our stories away. Reduce them to impotent fact.

And then there was Anna.

I could give her back her life. She deserved that. I did, too, by damn.

Regardless, I meant to do a little reading. An ideological stance in this debate would lose. I needed practical story-proof. For that, I decided to search first the annals in the College of Physics. And it had been Scalinou's planet, Pliny Soray, that had given me the idea. So it was only fair I drag the old cosmologer along. We probably looked a pair, two hunched old Grove-men puttering around the less frequented corners of the physics annals. We'd been at it for six days.

"Don't you think you'd have better luck with source documents on the old stories in your own college annals?" Scalinou asked. It was a protest against the many books we'd had to browse—physics researchers were copious publishers, and their annals were legion.

I paused, standing up to take a break from the endless reading that we did right there in the aisles. "You familiar with the hypothesis of Continuity?"

Scalinou looked up from the book in his hands. "You mean the existence of erymol, the omnipresent element? In and around everything, binding them all? The one that has failed twice in the Succession of Arguments? That Continuity?"

I ignored the sarcasm. We were both tired and irritable. "Your planet seems to be moving off her course. While down here, fundamental changes—like those proposed by the College of Philosophy—are cropping up."

"You think they're related?" Scalinou said with heavy skepticism.

"I don't know. But the concept of very different things bound together by something common got me thinking." I tested my legs, which had gone numb from sitting, and carefully started to limp-pace with the help of my cane.

"Ah, hells, you're looking for the 'science of belief,'" Scalinou tossed his book aside, a sure sign of his anger—he never tossed books.

"More like the science of stories," I corrected, and continued to pace, my legs tingling as they came fully awake. "I need to find anything we have that attempts to quantify or explain how a story affects mechanical systems—real things and how they behave. Gravity. Acoustics. If I can show that a story has a measurable relationship to the thing it describes, it would change our thinking on whether or not to rewrite the old stories, wouldn't it. The Bourne. The Veil."

Scalinou stood, shook his own legs, then pushed past me.

"Where you heading?" I asked.

"Physicists don't catalog anything not canonized." He waved me to follow. "We're in the wrong damn place."

He led us through two more floors of books, mumbling all the way. We paused at the top of another set of stairs, holding up lamps in the darkness—these levels weren't kept lit. The smell of dust was thick, and we'd stirred a veritable storm of motes as we started into a clutter of randomly stacked volumes.

After several moments, a sheering sound came muted through the blackness. We shared a look, and started toward it. Slowly, another light in the dark appeared, growing brighter as we approached.

The sheering sound stopped.

I gave Scalinou another look. He hunched his shoulders. On we went. After navigating two more aisles of piled books, we saw it. There on the floor, a lamp. Beside it, a book. And next to the book, pages cleanly shorn from the binding.

I pushed past my friend and got down close, putting aside my cane. I read the preceding page to what had been torn out. "They're removing anything that refers to the Bourne or the Quiet or the Veil."

I picked up a shorn page. It was from a book entitled, *The Science of Absences: A Physicist's Model for Pain and Loss.* I read a bit:

> *We should acknowledge that the pain resulting from a loved one's death is quite possibly more than internal anguish. Mechanical systems may well be affected.*

"Look at this." I held the page up to Scalinou, feeling close to understanding *why* the College of Philosophy—and the League—was pushing this new philosophical position.

Hurried footfalls. A dark shape emerged from the shadows, a cudgel in hand. The figure struck Scalinou. My friend crumpled in a heap.

The figure lunged at me, cudgel raised. I threw my lamp at my attacker and scrambled up the aisle, clawing my way to my feet. I grabbed a book lying atop another pile and turned, holding it up like a shield.

The cudgel struck my finger. Hurt like every last hell. Broke, no doubt. *Damn!*

I threw the book at the man. He batted it away as I grabbed another.

I couldn't tell who he was. His face below the eyes had been wrapped with a black scarf.

"You can't just rewrite history by removing a few pages," I yelled, trying to buy some time. "Or change physical law."

"You really don't understand, do you?" the man said.

I'd had enough of this, by all my dead gods. "And I don't think *you* have any idea who'd like to see your new philosophical position fail, or you might take a different view." I pictured the Velle and shook my head.

"There's nothing you can do to win," he said. "We're just *cleansing* the annals of deviant thought."

"I see," I replied, still backing away. "And do you realize you've just assaulted the Savant of Cosmology? I dare say you've put your whole supposition at risk on that alone."

The man chuckled, and rushed. I got a good hit on him with a voluminous book entitled, *Governing Dynamics*. But then he was on me. The cudgel came down again and again. I lost count before he got me good in the head, and I started to slide to oblivion.

Damn me but philosophy is getting dangerous.

I SPENT THE next few days with Anna, sleeping on the floor in her room. Seemed a safe place to be while I tried to heal up a bit. And after all the shenanigans lately, the slow way of things with someone who does little more than stare . . . well, it suited me fine. Beyond all that, I believed I'd found the only way I could win my argument with Darius.

So, I was waiting. Waiting for the Velle to come 'round.

On the evening of the third day, he stepped into the little room. I felt him before I saw him. Not frost or cold. Not heat. Not darkness. Not even anger. It was a subtle thing, because I was in Anna's room. But I felt like I might never be happy again.

The Velle had closed the door, and stood looking at me for many long moments. "You're running out of time."

"I can't win with rhetoric," I said. "You must have known that before you asked me to do this thing. And it seems the League has removed any documented Grove thinking on the topics of the Bourne. So, I don't have any precedents to cite."

The Velle said nothing. Waiting.

"But I think I know how I can win." I looked over at Anna.

The Velle followed my gaze. "You want me to waken her. So you can have her speak in the discourse theater."

I nodded. "Those that remember who she was before this," I looked at her vacant eyes, "they know she doesn't lie."

"They'll claim her illness is playing her false." The Velle looked back at me. "And I told you, waking her from her condition . . . there are risks."

I asked myself if Anna would want to live forever with her thousand-league stare. If she'd find some pain acceptable if she could be *awake* again.

I hoped I was right.

"Let me worry about Anna and the discourse theater," I said.

"Tomorrow," the Velle replied. "Just before the argument begins. Near the northwest door to the theater."

Then he left, his face as indifferent as it had ever been.

I turned and knelt before Anna, taking her hands in my own. Her eyes shifted in my direction. That was *something*, anyway. But she still held her distant gaze, as though she saw something far away, or a long time ago.

"What did they do to you up there, my love? What happened?"

Eight years.

Silent gods, I missed her.

THE PHILOSOPHY DISCOURSE theater hummed with expectation. Hundreds had already taken their seats, waiting. In the twilight shadows of an inner courtyard, Anna and I sat on a granite bench beneath a stand of aspen trees. I held her hands—always a comfort to me.

The hour had nearly arrived. Much longer and I'd be late to make my argument.

Then that feeling came again. Long unhappiness. The heavy-flesh feeling when you lose empathy.

The Velle came to stand in front of us. He gave me a steady look, as if weighing me. Then he turned to Anna. After watching her for a while, he reached up and took hold of an aspen limb. His chin dropped, his gaze focused. He raised a hand just a little.

And Anna began to stir.

Then shudder.

Then she bent forward, sobbing, as the Velle lowered his hand. The aspen limb had darkened, dried and split, as if it had lain beneath a scorching sun a dozen years.

The Velle regarded Anna and me a while more. Then he nodded—he'd kept his part, he expected me to keep mine—and walked away.

I held Anna until she sat up again, her eyes alive as if seeing the world for the first time. But her brow remained troubled. She turned toward me.

"Lour?"

I still had her hands in my own. "You remember now what was missing."

Fresh tears came. She nodded.

"I hate to ask it of you, my love, but here, tonight," I nodded toward the discourse theater, "I have an argument to make. An argument to keep a society of men from erasing stories, or at least removing their meaning."

"What stories, Lour?" Anna asked, her expression plaintive.

I hesitated. Maybe I'd gone too far with this. Asked too much. "Stories about the Quiet, Anna. And the Veil that keeps them captive in the Bourne."

She began shaking her head.

"To most of the Grove, these are storybook rhymes." I gave her a glimpse of what I was up against. "The annual position forum wants to refashion it all into mythology. No Veil, they'll say. No Bourne. No Quiet. Or, if there are races there, they aren't ill-formed of the gods and set against man. They're simply . . . misunderstood."

A small bit of ire crept into her face. I liked seeing it. "What do you need from me?" she asked.

Gods-damn I loved this woman. "I need you to tell *your* story. About being taken. Sold."

Her face grew sad, heavy. "And what happened to me there too. That's really what you're asking."

I wanted to tell her everything. About the League. About Darius. Even that she was *awake* because of a deal I'd struck with the Velle.

I said none of that. Instead I leaned in, touching my forehead to hers. Our gesture. She took a deep breath, and gave a painful smile.

She would do it. But I also understood that it would cost her. And I felt like a bastard for asking. But we both knew I didn't have a choice. Not if I was to win.

I'd known it before this, but it was clear again: Anna was the braver of us. By many stars.

I helped her to her feet and together we went into the discourse theater, each of us walking as though we were just learning how. Anna from eight years of sitting. Me with broken bones and cane.

The murmuring settled to silence. Part of that, no doubt, had to do with those who knew Anna seeing her up and alert. Darius and his elite selection of panelists sat across from us. He wore a look of slight surprise. And amusement, if I was any judge. That was a mistake of youth: Raising the ire of a brittle old albino. Young arguers have a life ahead to consider. They don't know it, but they feel a bit immortal. They don't consider death. But I'd lived with that certainty my whole life. Frail thin, I was. Not just white, but bones like winter kindling. And something strange in my body, besides—that thing that turned a compass needle south. I knew I had nothing to lose, was the thing. And Darius there, with his smug look, had no idea I would play my last card and coin.

I settled Anna in a chair and limped into the circle with my cane.

I caught the eyes of Martin, seated behind Darius's table in the second row. He gave me a wink—a stage encouragement, he'd explained to me once.

Darius stood. "The Aubade Grove College of Philosophy has put forward its forum position for this year. We've delayed publishing because of your challenge, Lour. Please tell me we haven't wasted a week's time for nothing."

His smile annoyed me. It was the kind that needed to be slapped. "Oh, you've *already* deemed it a waste, because you don't think you and you're little cronies there can be beaten." I looked over at Savant Bellerex. "And I'll guess you've spent the week lapping the Savant's hand like a currying mutt. To earn his favor. Young folks like yourselves tend to have more confidence when they inveigle. You understand what that word means, pup?"

Darius's smile didn't falter. "As irascible as ever, eh, Lour? Comedy is a good argument tactic. But maybe we can move on to your actual philosophical evidence?"

"I'd love that," I said. "Unfortunately, as it happens, someone wearing a League-emblazoned cloak is rummaging through the annals at night ripping out the very pages I'd need to show you."

I gave Darius a broad grin.

"I'm surprised," I followed, "that you overlooked that bit of logic."

"What bit of logic," Darius countered, "your lack of understanding that the College of Philosophy does work to collate uncataloged thought into uniform volumes for further study?"

Good recovery. "That what you call it? Well, then, how shall I argue when these night workers clonk me on the head to keep me from getting my hands on their shorn pages."

Darius laughed. "Are you sure, Lour, that you didn't fall? I know you're prone to it."

The theater laughed with him. But I gave Savant Bellerex a dark look. It would be enough to put a crimp in Darius's bid for a formal League charter in the Grove. For a while, anyway. Darius saw Bellerex's expression, and knew it. Made him right mad, too, though he covered that with his politic grin well enough.

I decided to press the point. "You know, pup, maybe you're right.

Maybe I fell under this little Leagueman's cudgel. So let's put that aside. Perhaps if you could just produce a volume of this uncataloged work, we could end this whole hootenanny."

Darius faltered. He opened his mouth to speak, and stuttered a bit, before shutting his lips.

That's when I knew. That's when I got to the *why* of this philosophical position being advanced by the League. It wasn't about the gods. Or even *stories* about the gods.

It was stories, themselves.

Because for the beggar and whore, for the poor and careworn, for any who hadn't two thin plugs to rub together, there was only one escape from the porridge lines and slums and worries. Only one thing they didn't have to pay for. A story.

Religionists wanted tithes, obedience.

Governments wanted taxes, loyalty.

Reformers wanted donations, conformity.

These were the "others" Scalinou had talked about. The "others" that made us less self-reliant. The "others" that came between the League and their ambitions.

But there was one above all these. Above religion and government and reform.

Stories.

Stories brought relief, comfort. Hope. They cost nothing. And expected nothing in return.

Stories are *gods.* I shook my head at the realization. *And the League knows it. They know that a powerful story will do more to ease a man's burdens than all the credos or philosophical positions the League can write. And they want to control our stories.*

Horse's asses.

"Certainly," Darius finally recovered, "just as soon as these volumes are ready, we'll share them broadly."

Sure you will.

"Now," he cleared his throat, "as to your evidence? What charade . . . I'm sorry, what argument will you make for us today?"

I took a long breath. There'd be consequences for what I was about to say. Shame, too. But I'd already lived with that a while. And I didn't suppose anyone in the theater could prick my conscience worse than I did myself.

"My wife," I motioned to Anna, "has been to the Bourne."

A chorus of whispers rose.

I saw Martin sit forward, like a man anticipating a story he might not want to hear.

"Really?" Darius asked. His incredulity silenced the theater.

"Yes, really," I said flatly. "Let's start with some ugly facts that even the College of Philosophy and your League of Civility can't deny. There's a human-trade across the Eastlands. People are being snatched. Enslavement, obviously. But to what end? Have we seen a rise in produce or shipped goods or any other measurable consequence of forced labor?"

"Wonderful question," Darius retorted. "We should investigate—"

"You do that," I said sharply. "And while you do, I'll just tell you the answer is no. Ugly as slavery is, it always, always results in economic boon."

"You're an economist now?" Darius countered.

Laughter around the theater.

"Hardly. Just old enough to care about more than what's between my legs."

The laughter this time came from the older of the crowd.

"And what does this have to do with the Bourne?" Darius came around to the side of his table, leaning against it, casual as you please.

"Oh, just this." I shuffled forward some. "These people being snatched? They're being taken into this Bourne you find so mythical."

Darius leveled his eyes on me and sauntered close. "Then tell us, Lour. If your wife was snatched, how was she taken through this Veil you'd have us believe holds the Quiet there . . . And how did you get her back?"

It was a damned good question. I had to give him that.

I took a long moment to look around the theater. The silent expectation grew heavy. Then I looked back at Anna, who watched attentively. She knew none of what I was about to say.

"When Anna went missing, I left the Grove. Many of you remember that." I nodded to a few who weren't entirely repulsed by me. "I was searching for her, of course. Any husband would have done the same. After three years, I'd found she was hardly the only one abducted. People were being taken. Lots of them. This slave trade was real.

"So, I sought out a trader willing to take me with him when he went to sell stock to Quiet hands. Inside the Bourne."

Darius furrowed his brow with exaggeration. "So, you're saying you've been there yourself?"

I shook my head. "I couldn't pass through the Veil. Walking through a canyon in the Pall Mountains, I just suddenly couldn't move forward."

"But your trader friend could?" Darius asked, with a hint of mocking.

"Ayuh," I replied, ignoring his condescending smile. "I'm sure it's something to do with whatever makes a compass read askew in my hand."

"And yet here is your wife," Darius persisted. "However did you accomplish this nasty business with the beasts of the Bourne, then? And really, how much longer do you think we should suffer this ridiculous distraction?"

That's when I did slap the insolent young horse's ass. People gasped. It was like listening to one of the Rhea-fol plays. The comedic ones, where exaggerated reactions by the crowd are part of the fun.

It actually made me laugh. Darius wasn't laughing though. And I knew I was on my last pardon.

I spared another look at Anna, and told the rest. "I had no idea why the races of the Bourne were buying humans. But I reasoned that if the only currency they cared about was human life, I'd simply *buy* my wife back from them."

The silence that came was heavy. Serious.

I nodded to the cumulative disgust. "I found a prison in Sever Ens. Paid the guards there to hand over three women being held in the pit indefinitely for murder. Paid that same trader I'd found to take them into the Bourne and barter them for my wife."

"You're something of a trader yourself, it would seem," Darius said, his slapped face forgotten.

"I'm not proud of it, if that's what you're hinting at." I stared defiantly at him. "But I'd do it again."

Darius's eyes were alive with thought. When his face finally relaxed, he'd found his way forward. "Though we study the motivations that underlie a person's criminal behavior, the College doesn't condone crime . . . of any kind." He leveled his stare on me. "And under no circumstance do we place the value of one life above another. It's contrary to every philosophical position the Grove holds. I can't imagine the pain of losing your wife, but what you did is unforgiveable."

"By whom?" I asked, wanting badly to slap him again. "You? The College? The Grove? Or these gods it seems you'd like us to put away?"

He opened his mouth to retort. I didn't give him a damn second.

"Because I don't need the forgiveness of a bastard pup who struts the discourse theater like he's nothing left to learn. And I don't need it from a College that has treated me like a walking sickness because I don't have the blush of health in my skin. And if this Grove of science is going to judge me, then it might as well start burning incense and saying prayers like the religionists it pits itself against. And I'd really love to know if you think I need the forgiveness of the silent gods."

I stopped, glaring at Darius. He was caught, and he knew it. He didn't want to admit of gods, or any of the rest of it. That was for damn sure.

The young debater stood his ground, though. And after several long moments, his wry smile touched light at his lips. Just enough that only I could see it.

"Very well, Lour," he said as a parent shushing a headstrong child, "let's suppose, for now, that all this is true. It doesn't argue for the existence of Quiet races bent on our destruction. It suggests only some phenomenon in the Pall Mountains. And slavery. Strange and maybe disconcerting things. But not stories to guide our science, or even our beliefs. Wouldn't you agree?"

I shook my head. Damn but this pup was good.

And that's when I turned to Anna. Understanding, she stood and came to my side, stepping slowly.

She shared a long look with Darius, then me. There was sadness in her eyes, and trembling. But she started to speak anyway.

"What Lour says is true." Anna swallowed loud enough that I heard it. "I was taken by a highwayman. I went up on the blocks and was sold. A pack of traders took me and several other women north over the Pall Mountains. Maybe two weeks' travel beyond it. I was placed in a pen. There were stalls for us. Flat bread each day. Muddy water."

Darius held up a finger. The bastard was interrupting. "And you're telling us you were held by Quiet creatures?"

"Bar'dyn," she said, no argument or anger in her voice. "Three strides tall. Skin like elm bark—hard, cracked, but pliable. And others. Smoother skin. Just as big. Wide, thick races. Powerful."

"A land of giants," Darius put in.

"Slight races, too" Anna added, "but just as . . . driven."

"Driven to what?" Darius asked, making a show of impatience.

Anna took my hand. The way she did on those rare occasions when she needed what strength I had for her.

"I was bred."

The anger in my mind almost put me down. My chest heaved, ached, for my dear one.

For maybe the first time, Darius had no response. I'd like to think it was a matter of decorum, as opposed to the calculated understanding that challenging such an admission would undermine his chances of winning the debate.

I caught a look at Martin's face, grateful for the sympathy I saw there.

After a painful silence, Anna went on. "It wasn't torture. Or amusement." Her brow creased. "They're trying to *accomplish* something. They're trying to *make* something." For all her strength, she began silently to weep. "Few of the children lived. Those that did were taken. The ones that I can remember, anyway. Sometime during those years, my mind left me. It's like I was living backward." She turned her eyes on me, and spoke in a broken voice. "Until the other night, when I awoke here, in the Grove, in a convalescent room. With Lour."

Then she shut down. She shook her head. A bitter look like shame— but not exactly that—took hold of her face. And she stumbled from the theater on weak legs. Her story done.

No one spoke.

I'm not sure how long it had been before Savant Bellerex stood and came onto the discourse theater floor. In a soft voice, "Those portions of this year's forum position that have to do with the Bourne and those that live there . . . will be removed."

Darius had an argument in his eyes, but he kept his silence until only he and I stood on the theater floor. It was an odd kind of company we kept. For my part, I didn't trust myself to move. Darius had stayed to say something.

"You win, Lour," he conceded, a note of humility in his voice. "I still don't think you had a story proof. But one thing I can promise you: the League will now come. I'll see to it. Formally. Fully. And with time, the position we argued today will be adopted and published."

"But not *this* year," I mocked.

He ignored me. "You won't see it, though. Because you'll be gone."

I'd anticipated this. Still, I hated to hear it. And it annoyed me, besides. "Gone, huh?"

"Legally, you could be sent to a nice pit for what you did," he said, conversationally. "But I'll spare you that. Just gather your things and leave the Grove."

"Because I make you uncomfortable," I said with a sour smile. "Me all white and fragile. Strange eyes and slow feet. I'm not a portrait of vigorous thought, am I? And I stick in your craw, hell the whole college's craw, for that. Albino with bad bones."

"By tomorrow," he replied, and strode away, boot heels clacking.

I'd thought I was alone. When I took a last look around, I saw a figure in the shadows of the top row of seats. He stared at me a good long while. Then got up, and disappeared through a door behind him. But even at that distance, even not truly seeing who it was, I felt him. The indifference. The Velle.

The creature out of the Bourne thought I'd done him a favor. I wasn't so sure.

He'd been right, of course. I'd have made this argument, anyway. But something was sticking in my own craw. How had he gotten through the Veil? If the stories were true, something was happening. Changing.

When I thought I could walk, I strolled with my cane through

Aubade Grove on my way to find Anna. I took in the five great towers and their observation domes hundreds of strides above me. I walked the great circumference of the inner pentacle and all the college theaters and annals and halls. I would miss this place. I would miss the pursuit of knowledge and thought and understanding of the sky.

Oh, I'd keep at it myself, wherever I went. But I'd be alone. That much I knew, even before I reached Anna.

"Don't let them do it, Lour," she said in her convalescent room. "Fight them."

I took her hands. "I have. And I won. But this fight I can't win."

"I'll come," she said, moving as if to pack, then realizing she had no idea what belongings she might have.

"You need the attendance of the blackcoats," I said. "For a while anyway. You're weak."

"And still stronger than you," she quipped, her eyes heavy.

"And still stronger than me," I repeated, hoping it was true.

She wrapped me in her embrace then. The one that was very tight, but not so tight that a brittle-boned man need worry. We touched foreheads. We stayed that way a long time.

"Thank you," she finally offered. "For getting me out. I hadn't remembered until tonight. And Lour . . ."

"You're remembering more," I deduced.

She found no words about it. I didn't ask her to try.

I promised to steal back into the city each moon cycle to visit. I told her she'd get stronger each day. I told her we'd find a way to be together again. They were the right lies to tell. Except for me coming to visit. That wasn't a lie. That I'd do.

I SETTLED NORTH of Aubade Grove a piece. Set to raising corn. My dad had raised corn. I'd been in my new home the better part of a month when the note came. Martin brought it himself. He stood by me while I read it.

Anna hadn't suffered the memories well. They'd gotten the better of her. She'd realized she'd never outlast those memories. And she'd found a way to escape. She'd had another moment of clarity—different this time, from when the Velle first touched her.

"I'm so sorry, Lour," Martin said. "She was a strong woman."

I gave him a puzzled look, even as my heart broke.

"For my stars, a woman who goes through what she did, then chooses to end her life to escape the memory of it . . . Damn brave. Oh, I wish she were still with us. But don't you go feeling anything but proud of that gal."

I cried. That's the only way to say it. I cried. She should never have loved me. She'd have been a college savant somewhere, if she hadn't stayed in the Grove because I was so frail.

Damn my bones. My sensitive skin. My humped walk.

You make me laugh, she'd always said.

And I *had* survived several run-ins while putting together my argument for the forum, hadn't I. I remember thinking philosophy was getting dangerous.

A dangerous philosophy.

That's gods-damned right. And that's exactly what I'd give them.

I showed Martin a thin look.

"I like what you're thinking," he said, smiling. "Whatever it is."

"Meaning you'd like to help?" I replied, folding the note and pocketing it.

"What you got in mind?" said Martin.

I looked up over my young crop of corn at a clear sky of stars above. "Did you know Pliny Soray appears to be *off*?" I pointed up at the wandering star.

"That I did." Martin stroked his thin white beard. "There's a sharp woman out of the College of Mathematics—Nanjesho Alanes is her name. She might be taking a run at another Succession of Arguments on Continuity. She knows about Pliny Soray. She's a friend of Scalinou's."

There was a connection in it all, somewhere. I could feel it. Almost like a compass needle turning south in my hand.

"League's coming," I said, still watching Soray. "Not today or tomorrow. But soon. And they hate the ideas about the Bourne and all it stands for."

"Ayeah?" Martin said, coaxing.

Darius had been right. I hadn't really proved my argument. I'd won. But that wasn't good enough. Not by a damn jot.

"I have a proof in mind," said I. "One that'll make them angry as every last hell."

"I'll get you some sky gear—instruments, notation, skyglass," Martin said, his voice as gleeful as when he replayed the pageants he used to perform.

"Dear abandoning gods, here we come," I raised a loud whoop that echoed out over my cornfield, the way my dad used to. "A story proof."

"Which story?" Martin asked, wearing a conspiratorial grin.

"Not *a* story." I shook my head. "A proof *of* story."

"To make Anna's account of the Bourne true to skeptics," Martin surmised.

This time I nodded. "That, and the stories every pale, weak slob holds close. The ones that give him grit when the world couldn't give a tinker's damn."

"That include philosopher slobs?" Martin put a warm hand gently on my shoulder.

I'll miss you, Anna. Dear silent gods, I will.

I was eager to begin. But not that night. That evening I stood with Martin for a long while, regarding the stars.

It's a good feeling knowing someone is no longer in pain. And it's a good feeling being on the front end of doing something you believe is important. And maybe irreverent.

Anna would have laughed at that.

JOHN MARCO

I don't remember when I saw my first automaton. I just remember being fascinated by them. It must have been on TV, or maybe at a carnival. Maybe it was one of those gypsies that tell your fortune from behind glass. Later, when I got my first computer, I hand-typed the program for ELIZA into its tiny memory, hoping the way that kids hope to create something that could talk back to me and be a friend. I read the science fiction magazines of the time, surprised every now and then to see a robot advertised in their back pages. Of course, I didn't have the money for one, and thinking back on it, I'm sure they wouldn't have satisfied me. They looked like little garbage cans. I wanted something as real as it was artificial.

I have this theory that every speculative fiction writer needs to write both a robot story and a dragon story someday. "River and Echo" is my attempt at the former. I could never get my computer to talk to me the way I wanted. Maybe that's why I became a storyteller.

I want to thank Shawn Speakman for letting me be part of this anthology. Imagination is perhaps the most "unbound" thing of all.

RIVER AND ECHO

John Marco

They say the plague started with a nosebleed.

The story goes that one day a tailor named Deon sneezed when a cat came into his shop. Afterward, he couldn't stop sneezing, his handkerchief turning red with blood. His wife washed the handkerchief and she started bleeding too, and then all the shopkeepers near the gate bled, first from their noses and then from their eyes. And they bled from their mouths, of course, because the coughing put holes in their lungs.

River's mother had died that way, but he wasn't sure about the story. For one thing his mother loved cats and never sneezed around them. They'd even had a cat of their own when he was little—which he wasn't anymore because he was nine years old now. River's father got the nosebleed too, but his eyes never bled, not even when pieces of his stomach showed up in his vomit. His parents had both died quickly, and that was good so they could go to the "better place" River's mother always talked about. All the city suffered like that before they died, but they all died fast. Even the humatons died.

All but River and Echo.

The thing that killed them didn't have a name. River called it "the plague" because he'd heard his father call it that, and his father was a professor. Still, no matter how smart they were, nobody had been able to save themselves or figure out what killed them.

Whatever the plague was, it had come from the enemy outside the city's walls. They had put the plague into the city and then come to watch it die. And every night there were more of them, hovering just at the edge of invasion, their campfires twinkling like distant stars. There were so many campfires now River couldn't count them. Even with winter approaching, they came. But they never came closer, and that irked River because he wanted to see them for real, and not just in the book Echo showed him.

At noontime the big clock in Concourse Square chimed. It seemed louder now with all the people gone. River had told Echo they could stop at noon and take a break from their work. The day was damp and the cold made his fingers ache where he'd clipped down his gloves. He dragged the humaton he'd found in the baker's shop onto the pile, then scratched another line into the cobblestones with his chalk. Each line meant a dead humaton for their army, and this latest made twenty-one. River stepped back and looked at the humatons and nodded. Twenty-one would look good on the wall. With weapons and helmets, twenty-one would look frightening. He was proud of his idea to set up his army atop the wall. With their metal bodies, they wouldn't collapse or rot the way people did. They didn't stink the way people did, either. To River, the humatons looked pretty much the same, except for the blue light of their eyes, which of course flicked off the moment they died.

"Echo!" River called out. "Where are you?"

The clockworks in his head meant Echo was never late unless he wanted to be. River looked around the empty square, expecting Echo to peek out from one of the stalls. Mostly everything was just as the shopkeepers had left it, when they went to the wild camp. Luckily, that was far from Concourse Square.

"Echo? Come on, I'm hungry!"

Finally he came, his big feet clanking on the stones. River turned quickly toward him, surprised to see Echo carrying two humatons over his shoulders. One had long, beautiful hair that almost swept the ground. The half of Echo's face molded to look human flushed with color, the closest a humaton could come to smiling. The other half whirred and clicked to make the illusion happen.

"I found these two in the furrier's workshop," Echo pronounced. The voice came from a rectangular slit where a mouth would be if he were human. It sounded alive, pretty much, but a little like talking into a bucket. Echo strode on toward the collection of humatons they'd gathered.

"He had *two?*" asked River.

"He was a furrier," Echo reminded him. "There are some beautiful pelts in his shop. I saw unskinned sable there just where he left them. We'll go back later to see. Let me show you this one with the hair."

Echo loved beautiful things. Shiny things. Beads of glass. He still collected them even though the city was dead. Gently he placed the two humatons near the one River had found. Almost all of the humatons they'd found were male; most of the female versions were built as girls, and too small to be frightening. The furrier's female was remarkable looking. Like all the humatons, her head was half human and half machine, all covered in luxurious hair. River knelt down next to her and ran his fingers through the blond strands. It felt completely human, like his mother's hair.

"That's twenty-three," said Echo. He didn't need River's chalk marks to count them. He could count anything just by looking at it. River was still playing with the female humaton's hair. Echo noticed this and said, "We can cover the hair with a helmet. Or cut it off."

"Oh, no way. Don't cut it." River looked at the humatons they'd gathered. Once, they'd been alive, like Echo. "I don't want to change any of them. I want to leave 'em like they are. That's what they would have wanted."

"If we want to scare the enemy, we'll have to change them. Weapons and helmets at least."

"Weapons and helmets, yeah, but that's it."

"Whatever you want, River. I can start bringing them to the wall now."

"I'm hungry. Let's take a break."

"All right. Take a break. I'll work."

"Leave it for now. Sit with me."

Echo hesitated. "This is what you wanted to do today."

"I know. We'll do it. But we'll break first, okay? We can set up the army later."

"Later we have your lessons."

River groaned, because there were always lessons. Echo had been built to give lessons. History, mathematics, philosophy—Echo knew them all. It was impossible to stump him, though River sometimes tried.

"We can skip the lessons," said River. "Just for today. You can do that for me, can't you?"

"Your mother and father would want them to continue."

River let the female's golden hair fall like sand through his fingers. "Why didn't my father build you with hair?"

"Professor Nous started losing his hair when he was twenty-one." Echo made a thumping sound, his version of laughter. "I'm you in the future, remember."

"Oh." River fell on his backside. He hated the thought of going bald like his father, but it didn't really matter now. There were no girls to impress or marry. No apprenticeships or professions. No reason to take a bath. All he had to do was defend the city. But setting up the humatons was a big job. They were heavy, and hoisting them up to stand guard atop the wall would be tough even for Echo. And first he had to dress them . . .

"Let's eat."

FOR THE FIRST month after the plague, finding food was easy. To River, the city was the whole world, and he had never been beyond its walls. According to Echo, the king's last census had put the population of the city at about twenty thousand—too many bodies to bury, of course, though most had gone to the wild camp to die. Those who had remained had died in their homes, mostly, sealing themselves away so only the rats and insects could find them. Despite the stink, River was glad the city had fed so many people. They had left behind stores and farms to explore for food, and he knew that if he kept on looking, he would always discover a new jar of pickled fruit or some cured ham to keep him alive.

Concourse Square, where they'd stacked the humatons, still had plenty of unspoiled things to eat. Besides the furrier and the baker's shop, there was a butcher who had persevered chicken meat in fat, jamming it into jars the size of human heads. The baker's stale biscuits softened nicely in the fat, and River smeared it on fearlessly. He and Echo rolled two barrels out of the brewer's shop, sitting atop them while River ate and drank a glass of the brewer's ale. When his parents were alive, he had snuck sips of ale from his father's mug. Now that they were gone only Echo could stop him, and Echo never did.

A black metal gate, twenty-feet high and forged into the city's wall, led into the square. In all his life River could not recall a time when the gate was closed, but it was now—closed and locked and wrapped with chains. The gate had been shut the same day the king ordered the flags hung upside down.

Like wild fire, they all said. That's how quickly the plague had spread. River had never seen wild fire, but he supposed it was pretty damn fast.

"Wild fire," he said between sips of ale. "Damn fast."

He was cursing a lot. His parents wouldn't have liked that. He felt bad for a moment then said it again.

"Damn fast."

Echo didn't answer. His blue eyes stared at the distant hills where the enemy waited. They were too far away to see in the daylight, but they weren't hiding. Every night, more and more of their campfires came, glowing around the city like a necklace.

"We should get to work," grunted River. He stuffed a biscuit into his mouth, saying as he chewed, "Just let me finish up."

Echo nodded only a little. His silence flustered River.

"Are you afraid?"

"No, I'm not afraid," replied Echo. "I was made out of you. If you're not afraid then I'm not afraid."

River chewed, swallowed, and took another big bite. Humatons could lie just as easily as people.

"You know," said River after a moment, "If we were going to die, we'd be dead already. Don't you think that's true?"

"Yes," agreed Echo.

"But we're not dead. I check my nose every night. You don't see me but I do. I look up there and I don't see any blood. Nothing. And I never sneeze. Never."

"That's very good."

"What I'm saying is that we're here for a reason. Whatever the plague is, it can't touch us. That's got to be the way God wants it, right?"

"God?"

"Yeah. God. Or whatever. He wants us here to take care of things, to make sure the enemy doesn't get through. That's why we didn't die."

"I like that story," said Echo. "But what about everybody else? Why are they dead?"

River shrugged. "God don't need them, I guess."

"But he needs us—a nine-year-old boy and a machine? Why not a hummingbird and a pencil?"

"You're not a machine."

"The story has to make sense," said Echo. "Explain it to me. Why did God choose us?"

River shrugged. "I don't know. He's God."

Echo approximated a sigh. "This conversation is a circle. It has no end. Therefore, no purpose." He slipped down from his barrel. "Keep eating if you want. I'm going to work."

DRESSING THE DEAD humatons was harder than River expected. They had already stripped the coats and hats from the fallen soldiers they'd found throughout the city, piling them in a stable at the far side of the square to keep them safe from the weather, but the trek between the stable and their undressed army tired River quickly. There were weapons to haul as well, mostly long-guns and swords, and these River carried two at a time, balancing them in his armpits while he carried the clothes.

Most of the humatons, like Echo, wore trousers and shirts and vests—the usual stuff for an upper-class citizen. The few females in their lot wore skirts, and River undressed them with a powerful curiosity, wondering if they—like the males—had been created sexless. To his disappointment they were, just as Echo had told him. Still, it felt odd to River to be taking their clothes off. It almost felt like he was hurting them, so he told each one that they were being dressed to defend the city, like heroes, and that he was sorry they were dead and couldn't dress themselves anymore.

One by one, River and Echo hoisted the humatons onto the battlements and watchtowers, sometimes using ropes to lift their heavy bodies and then positioning them to look fierce. The big clock in the square chimed as the hours past. The sun slipped away. Finally, they lifted the humaton with the beautiful hair up onto a catwalk near the gate. She looked very much like a soldier in her gray coat and trousers, but the sweeping blond hair remained a problem. River watched as Echo placed the silver helmet on her head.

"That's peculiar looking," said River. "She looks like a girl."

"I told you we need to cut it. It's too much to stuff under her helmet."

River took a step back. "From far away will they even see it?"

"Maybe they come closer at night when we're sleeping. If the wind blows her hair they'll see it."

"Yeah. They have eyes like eagles." River remembered that from the book. Eyes like eagles and scales like snakes—those were what he remembered most. "Does it matter? Who says a girl can't be a soldier?"

Echo's blue eyes flashed with frustration. "This was your idea. We should cut it."

But River couldn't. "Leave it." He put the long-gun he had chosen for her in her metal hands, closing the fingers around it. "I like her the way she is."

They stayed on the catwalk for an hour more, watching the hills turn black around them. As always, the campfires of the enemy winked into view, just a few at first, then many, many others. Some were closer now too. By the time the big clock struck eight, the hills were ablaze with them.

"I can smell the smoke," said River. His breath froze as it hit the air.

"What does it smell like?" asked Echo.

"Like wood. What else?"

"The book says they burn animals."

River breathed deeply through his nose. "No. Definitely wood." He put his hand on the shoulder of the blond humaton. "You think they can see us?"

"Yes. They always see us."

Echo's confidence made River grin. Every night for weeks they had climbed atop the wall to let the enemy see them. Just so they would know they hadn't won yet.

"Do you think they'll attack soon?" asked River.

Echo turned his head left and right, his gesture for no. He said, "I think our army will scare them."

"Ha!" crowed River. He leaned out over the wall. "You hear that? We have an army!"

The quiet hills gave no reply. A smattering of snowflakes fell from the sky.

"We should go home now," said Echo. "It's time for lessons."

IT TOOK NEARLY an hour for River and Echo to walk back home. The streets were dark and deserted, and despite his dexterity Echo was not at all speedy. River had long ago given up searching for plague survivors. A few times, weeks ago now, he had seen the shambling figures of survivors limping blindly through the streets, but they had all died quickly, and all River and Echo could do was try to answer their questions and comfort them. Now, they saw only dead folks in the streets, those who were too weak or too stubborn to go to the wild camp the way the king had ordered.

The Nous house—River's house—was in a good, green part of the city, with lots of trees to climb. River's parents had been given the house as part of his father's salary. It was near the royal university where his father taught and in close view of Castle Hill, though River had never once visited the castle despite his many pleas to do so. The castle sat dark and deserted now, its upside-down flag still flapping in the wind.

River looked longingly at Castle Hill while Echo opened the door to their house. The king and all his family had gone to the wild camp, just like River's parents. They had tried to stop the plague from spreading, but that seemed like a dumb idea now.

Like wild fire, thought River.

He helped Echo make a fire in the hearth, then sat down in his father's big, comfortable chair. The wooden shelves sagged with books, and a smiling portrait of River's mother hung over the mantel. Her name was Ellin but his father called her "honey," just like the color of her hair. On the table next to the big chair sat the pipe his father smoked every night after coming home from the college. The room stank of sweet tobacco. River picked up the pipe and stuck it between his teeth, watching as Echo looked over the many books.

"I don't know which to choose," said Echo finally. "I'm done with all these."

"Good," replied River. "Let's go to sleep."

"No." Echo ran his metal fingertips over the spines of the books. "Your lessons have to continue."

"So? Teach me something else."

"I've taught you everything here already." Echo's blue eyes dimmed. "Professor Nous always brought me new books."

The human side of Echo's face drooped in a way River had never seen before. The metal side of his face whirred and clicked.

"Your lessons," said Echo blankly.

River tossed the pipe onto the table and sat up. "Hey, you can just start from the beginning again. I never remember anything you teach me anyway."

But Echo's face didn't change. "We are the people now, River. We are all that's left."

"See, that's not right," said River. "We're not all that's left. There's all these books."

"We have to live for the people."

"Nope. We have to live for *us*, Echo. All the stuff the people did— that's all in the books."

"So we have to protect the books."

River saw his argument being lost. He took up the pipe again and put it defiantly in his mouth. "I need a match," he said, just the way his father used to say it.

Without a question, Echo took one of the long matches used to light kindling out of a brass container. He stuck it in the hearth, lit it, then handed it to River. River did as he'd seen his father do a thousand times—holding the flame to the remnants of the old tobacco until it smoldered and sucking in little puffs of air. Instantly his lungs burned.

"Oh!" he coughed. Water streamed from his reddening eyes. He kept the pipe in his teeth anyway. "All this stuff you're teaching me, Echo? That's all memories. I got memories." He choked a little. "Lots of them. So you gotta let me live. Okay?"

He kept the pipe in his mouth until he couldn't stand it anymore, then put it back on the table and caught his breath. He felt nauseous suddenly and collapsed backward into the chair. Echo had turned away and was looking through the endless books.

"What are you doing?" River asked him.

Echo held up a metal finger to quiet him, continuing to search, then hitting on the book he wanted. "This one." He flushed to show a smile. "Remember?"

The book made River sit up in the chair; he'd looked at it many times since the plague hit. Echo sat down on the arm of the chair. His fingers had been specifically built for turning pages and he leafed through them easily, his face lighting up when he came to their favorite illustration.

The thing was vaguely manlike, ten feet tall on two tree-trunk legs. Its arms were scaly, its body armored in brassy metal, and a pig-faced helmet capped the invisible head. In one hand it held a club, in the other a thick, straight sword. River stared at the picture. He still couldn't understand how a race that appeared so slow-witted had made something as deadly as the plague. Or why, with all their brutish size, they still hadn't attacked.

River sat back and thought a while. When Echo started reading one of the book's stories, River stopped him.

"No, don't read it," he said softly. He knew the stories all by heart. He looked at Echo, who seemed perplexed, and said, "You think they're scared of us, maybe? Because we're still alive, I mean? Because they don't want to get catch the plague they made?"

"I think that makes good sense," agreed Echo. "I think so, yes."

"That's got to be it. They're so big—they could attack us if they wanted. They're waiting for us to die." The thought made River laugh. "But we're *not* gonna die! I'm just a kid. I'm not gonna die."

"Your grandfather died when he was sixty-seven years old," Echo pointed out. "The Professor would have lived that long at least. So, you will too. Probably."

"Sixty-seven! That's forever." River leaned back comfortably in his father's chair. "We don't need an army. The enemy in the hills—they just got to see that we're still alive. That's all we got to do every day— make sure they see us."

"Very good!" said Echo. "Nothing else?"

"Well, no. There's lots of stuff. Like tomorrow? We're going to the castle."

THE SNOW HAD fallen through the night, turning the city a pure, clean white. By the time River dressed himself and stepped outside with Echo, only flurries strayed from the sky. River looked at Castle Hill, half a mile away—no problem in his coat and heavy boots. Echo had dressed himself too, wearing a pair of leather shoes that ran up his metal calves, protecting his feet yet allowing him to balance. He wore a cape as well, a ruby-red garment of velvet he had found in a tailor shop after the plague. He had described the cape as irresistible and was excited at the chance to wear it. As they trudged through the newly fallen snow, Echo looked up at the sky. He put out his hand to catch a snowflake, then brought it up against his mouth slit.

"What are you doing?" River asked.

"I've seen people catch snowflakes on their tongue. I don't have a tongue." Echo turned to look at River. "What do they taste like?"

"I don't know. Like water I guess."

"You should have done this by now," said Echo. "Do it and tell me."

Echo rarely gave orders. River stuck out his tongue and waited for a snowflake to find it. When one did not, Echo goaded, "Go after them."

So River did, laughing and not caring how stupid he looked as he dashed about with his tongue outstretched, first catching one stray flake, then another. "They taste like nothing!" he shouted. "Just cold. But kind of good . . ."

All the way to Castle Hill, River chased the snowflakes. And when they finally reached the hill and found the ornate gates of the castle open and buried in snow, he pulled in his tongue and closed his mouth at the majesty of the place. His father had been lucky. The king had called upon the professor many times, and River wondered what the castle was *really* like, before it was so quiet. The castle grounds were completely barren, with carts and tools left behind, and a few human-sized lumps in the snow. River and Echo walked through the unguarded gates and shuffled toward the looming entrance, a black mouth of a thing that should have been grand but now felt haunted.

"I have a toy guardsman at home," said River as he walked through the archway. His voice echoed beneath the stone. "Remember?"

"The one in blue and gold," said Echo. "With the silver long-gun. I remember."

The courtyard should have been filled with blue and gold guardsman, but instead there was no one to stop them. Soon they were in the entry hall, a frozen tunnel hung with paintings and tapestries, the floor stained by rain and snow. Echo chirped with excitement at the artwork, swiveling his metal head to see it all.

"There's so much!" he exclaimed. "Where should we start?"

"I want to see the throne room! My father told me it's all made of gold . . ."

River dashed forward, leaving Echo to clank on behind him. The lamps on the wall had all burned out, but the light from the stained glass windows was enough. River followed the big hall forward, spotting the enormous doors of the throne room. A roaring lion's head was carved into each of the open doors. Beyond them, River caught just a glimpse of something sparkling . . .

"God!" He stopped at once, putting his hands over his mouth and nose. He knew the smell at once. Echo shuffled up behind him.

"What is it?" asked Echo.

"If you could smell you'd know." River pointed into the throne room. "There's dead people in there."

So far most of the dead they'd encountered had been out of doors, where the cold had let their bodies decay slowly and the wind could steal the worst of the stench.

"You want to go inside?" Echo asked.

River grimaced. "I thought they all went to the wild camp. My mother and father said that's what the king wanted."

Echo walked up to the doors, through them, and into the throne room. He looked straight ahead, his blue eyes glowing in the dim light. "Oh."

"What?" asked River. He brought the tail of his coat up to cover his face. The stench was the worst he'd ever smelled, but he couldn't help himself—he followed after Echo into the throne room.

And there he stopped and stared at the throne, and saw the king upon it, slumped and dead, with his eyes rotted out and jaw open wide, the crown crooked on his fleshless skull, and the weird look of anguish on his bony face . . . and River puked his breakfast onto the golden tiles.

"Oh my God!" he gasped, gagging and retching and wiping his face with his sleeve. "Why'd he stay?"

Echo had no trouble at all looking at the corpse. "Because he was king." Slowly he walked toward the throne, across the blood-crusted floor, and when he reached the dead king he plucked the crown off his head. With his prized velvet cape he wiped it clean—clean until it gleamed—then headed back to River. River, who had fallen to his knees in sickness, waved him away.

"Put that back!" he cried. "You can't steal that!"

Echo rarely disobeyed River's orders, but this time he ignored them completely. He stood over River and placed the polished crown upon his head.

"You're the king now," he said.

River touched the crown. He looked at Echo as if his friend were mad. "I'm a boy. Just a kid. You know that . . . don't you Echo?"

"A king doesn't kneel," said Echo. "Get up."

DURING HIS FIRST week as king, River wore the crown wherever he went. He knew that as long as he stayed alive, the city and its knowledge was safe. Each night he and Echo went to the gate and looked at the campfires surrounding the city. They watched the numbers grow, fascinated by the way they inched ever closer. But River had no fear, for he knew the plague was in the city, the only weapon he needed to keep the enemy away.

And so he and Echo explored the city and lit bonfires and slept in strange beds. River ate whatever he wanted, cursed when he hurt himself, laughed inappropriately, and rode hogs like they were horses. Echo gloried in the library and its many, many books, studied the paintings in the castle and the royal museum, wore the baubles that nobody wanted, and made maps of the stars. Together they sang in the opera house and banged the instruments to make music. They slept late every morning, watched the enemy at night, and wondered.

But they never, ever went to the wild camp.

A week passed, and then two more, and soon the winter was fully upon them. River chased the snowflakes when they came, just as Echo had taught him. He did everything he could to forget his mother and father, but sometimes at night they visited him in dreams. The cold came like a tiger, stifling the stench of the dead completely, and because he was so haunted by his dreams, River finally set out for the wild camp.

Just as they were told, the camp was far in the corner of the city, a two-day walk for a humaton. River did not know what he expected to see there, but when he saw the barbed wire he could go no further. Beyond it, hills of bodies sat snow-capped. Dead soldiers guarded the iron gate, slumped and frozen. River knew then—in a way he'd never really understood—that his parents were gone.

Together, he and Echo treaded home.

They went to the gate every night and made sure the enemy saw them. River stopped wearing the crown. He didn't like being king.

They slept late every morning, read books and set bonfires, and waited for the spring.

RIVER AWOKE TO the sound of melting snow. In the room with the big chair where he slept, Echo had opened the window. Echo's face glowed as he tried to sniff the air.

"Do you hear that?" he asked. He leaned forward the way he always did when listening. "A bird!"

River was groggy but excited. He rolled out of the chair and went to the window, shielding his eyes from the stabbing sunlight. "I hear it," he said. "The sun . . ." He took a deep breath. "So warm."

"Spring," pronounced Echo.

"It's too early for spring."

"Nature makes its own calendar."

"That's not true and it makes no sense."

Echo's face flushed and whirred. "I want to go to the castle greenhouse and see if the lily bulbs are sprouting. Get your shoes on."

"I'm hungry."

"Later. Hurry."

There was no hurry at all, but River did as Echo asked, slipping into his shoes and his coat and stepping out into the warm day. The snow that had piled up outside their door was turning to slush, and the avenue that led to Castle Hill dripped and glistened. Over the winter they had cleaned up all the bodies they could find, burning them in their bonfires, and so the way was clear and empty now. They walked through the castle and its once-inspiring halls, no longer noticing the great artwork, and went straight for the greenhouse where Echo had spent much of his time. Someone had planted a row of lily bulbs, and Echo had tended them like a mother hen, protecting them from dangers that didn't exist and talking to them about the spring. River let Echo take the lead, hanging back among the pots of dead plants and loving the way the sun looked through the glass panes. He watched Echo clang toward the bulbs, bending over to inspect them. There was a long pause.

"Well?" asked River.

Echo stared at the dirt. The fleshlike side of his face turned the color of joy. "Oh." He had never sounded more human. "River, come see."

River went and examined the soil. It took a moment, then he noticed the tiny shoots of green sprouting from the dirt. "Wow." He looked closer. "You did it, Echo."

Echo beamed. River smiled at him—then saw something strange. A tiny stream of fluid dripped from Echo's nose.

"What's wrong, River?"

River stared but couldn't find his voice. He looked closer. He knew the drip was spirit oil, but it looked like blood.

"Your nose . . ."

Echo put his hand to his nose and wiped at it with his metal finger. His blue eyes flashed with realization, but somehow he remained perfectly calm. "River," he said. "You'll have to look after the lilies for me."

THE PLAGUE DIDN'T work the same on humatons as it did on people. The nosebleeds they got were really just leaks, and by the third day Echo was leaking everywhere. The spirit oil that kept him alive seeped out of every joint in his metal body. River tightened each one with bandages to try and keep the oil inside, but no matter what he did, more and more of the precious liquid dripped away. By the fourth day Echo could no longer walk, and by the fifth he couldn't see. He sat in the big chair, letting River tend to him and listening to the growing choirs of birds outside the window. Unlike the way humans died, the plague caused Echo no pain at all. River read to Echo to pass the time, stopped going to the gate, and only ventured outside at night to briefly watch the campfires.

On the sixth night of Echo's illness, River knew the end was near. Echo could no longer move his arms or legs; he could barely swivel his head. They had spent the day talking about little things, and River had yet to ask the question that truly frightened him.

"Will I get sick?"

The night was particularly quiet, and Echo's blue eyes still glowed softly.

"No," said Echo. "Don't worry about that."

River sat at the base of the chair, like he'd done so many times when his father sat in it. The pipe still rested on the table, unused since that first time River smoked it. The hearth was cold.

"Echo, are you lying to me? You do lie sometimes."

Echo was completely still. "I protect you," he said.

"So, is that the same as lying sometimes?"

"Parents love their children very much. Professor Nous wanted me to look after you. I hope I've taught you enough."

"You've taught me everything," said River. "But I'm afraid."

"You won't get sick, River."

River didn't know if Echo was telling the truth. "Tell me about the day you were born. I like that story."

Echo liked the story too. "I was born like all humatons are born," he said. "I was made in the mechaworks and brought to life by a piece of your fingernail and a tiny drop of blood . . ."

River listened, entranced. Echo had always been a very good story-teller.

Two DAYS AFTER Echo died, River dragged him on a cart to the gate at Concourse Square. He had dressed his friend in his beloved velvet cape and decorated his arms with bracelets Echo had collected over the years. Once again he rigged up the ropes and hoisted Echo onto the catwalk, standing him up beside the humaton with the blond hair. He didn't bother giving Echo a weapon. The enemy hadn't come, and River knew they never would while he was alive. It had been nearly a week since he had come to the gate, and River stood on the catwalk waiting for the sun to go down and the campfires to arrive.

"I'm here!" he shouted to the hills. "It's just me but I'm not gonna die! Not ever, 'cause I'm the king!"

He tried to sound defiant but felt empty inside. Not weak. Not sick. Just empty. He watched the sun die behind the hills and the shadows creep across the city. Straight in front of him, a single campfire came to life in the distance.

"Still there," River muttered.

He waited for the other fires to join the first. The minutes passed and the clock in the concourse chimed, but no other fires appeared.

Instead the single fire grew and grew, like one of the bonfires he'd lit with Echo, soon glowing so brightly it was hard to look upon. The strangeness of it perplexed River. He thought it might be a threat, but nothing about it was frightening. In fact it was beautiful, like a beacon, and he was glad he'd brought Echo to see it.

"What are they doing?" he asked as if Echo could hear him.

He wondered if they knew he was alone on the wall, and that the humatons around him were all just metal containers now, like cans or buckets.

"They've been watching us so long . . ."

River squinted at the fire.

"Waiting for me to die . . ."

They were always watching—everything he did.

"Or . . . watching me live?"

Suddenly he wished he'd paid more attention to Echo's lessons. People communicated with fire; he remembered that, at least. He remembered a story about a queen who died, and how her body had been laid on a pyre and set aflame, and how the people watched the flames and cried because they missed her. River put his hand over his heart and wondered if it was broken.

He moved in close to Echo's cold body and put his arm around his dead friend's shoulder. He smelled the pipe smoke on Echo's velvet cape. He remembered the day when the plague came, and how afraid he was, and how his mother and father were frantic, and how the city was full of screams. And how Echo, peaceful and composed, had taken the book with the monsters in it off the shelf and explained it all to him . . .

Like it was just another story.

MARY ROBINETTE KOWAL

I was an art major in college. It shaped the way I approach a lot of my fiction, but I keep coming back to one central question: what is the difference between an artist and a technician? See, I could render. I was really, really good at rendering and my technique was spot on. But my drawings were static and lifeless. It was workman-like, in fact. On the other hand, I had friends who had unique voices. I was endlessly frustrated by being able to *recognize* good art, but not being able to produce anything beyond the technically correct. Even knowing it was about "voice" didn't help me figure out a path to levelling up.

When I went into puppetry, I did so in part because I had a unique voice there. In that art form, I stopped being a technician and was an artist.

So this story is very much me still exploring that question. Because much like being able to recognize good art, I can still spot an artist but don't have any better understanding of how a person becomes one.

A DICHOTOMY OF PARADIGMS

Mary Robinette Kowal

Ducking through the hatch of the interstellar frigate *Triumphant Beast Descending*, Patrick stepped into the captain's quarters. She stood by a console mounted on the wall, with her hands on her hips in the sort of unthinking grace that made him itch to start painting.

Not that he was going to be able to do that yet. They were waiting in the flight path for the *Creative Fire*, which was carrying an original Picacio that was worth more money than God. Captain Dauntless had on the same snug space compression suit that most of her crew wore, ready for boarding when their target ship dropped out of its tesseract field.

"I was thinking about adding something to my suit, so you could distinguish me from the others." She turned and held up a bandolier made of heavy braided leather. It had a sequence of small guns clipped to it, which looked like throwbacks to derringers but were really single-shot blasters. The power supply was too small to get off more than one shot before needing to recharge.

He considered for a moment, trying to imagine what the boarding process would actually be like. Smoke? It would be nice to have that sort of atmosphere for her portrait. "How were you thinking of wearing it?"

She draped it over her shoulder like it was some beauty queen's sash. "Well?"

He pretended to consider, but really, anything his client wanted would be fine by him. In this case, fortunately, the bandolier *would* be a good addition. Even though the suit helmets were clear, it would help draw the eye to her. "I think that would be an excellent choice."

"Good." Then she spun back to the console. "Now tell me what you think of this." And she began to read from the screen.

"Patrick Windlass's latest portrait, done in his 'in the moment' style betrays all the symptoms of a hack. The hasty brush strokes, which could give the painting vitality in the hands of another, here are nothing more than gimmickry."

Goddammit. This is why he avoided the reviews. *A hack?* Gimmickry? When you could matter-print anything, the price on unique objects and experiences meant that artists were finally paid what they were worth. And Patrick's particular skill was painting fast and under any circumstances.

He pasted a smile on his face. "One learns not to be wounded by those who don't understand one's art."

"Yeah, well, at the moment, I'm wondering why I'm hiring you if it's going to get a bad review. Convince me it's worth keeping you."

Well . . . shit. Usually having to pay a deposit was enough, but no . . . he had to go and accept a commission from the infamous Captain Dauntless. "Of course, though I am surprised you lend any credence to someone else's taste. You wanted a portrait with your pirates attacking a ship to cement your status as a terror of space." As if having a painting would make anyone believe her name were really "Dauntless." She'd probably been born a Maude.

"Yeah. Vid will do that."

"Vid will show the facts, but not the emotion. You need an artist for that. *You* sought me for reasons that have not changed because of this petty reviewer. No one else has my ability to paint while in motion, under any circumstances, and capture a composite of the experience."

"Which this lady is saying is a gimmick."

He kept the smile steady, though his teeth ground together before he spoke. "Other artists are merely jealous of what my skill allows me to do and of the clients who seek my work. I have painted General Dahl while on the battlefield in the mountains on New Pluto. I was trusted to paint the final dance of Maria Amazonia before her retirement from zero-g ballet. The President of Uusi Suomi hired me to create his official portrait, which I did while he toured the Frozen Catacombs of Death. A gimmick? No. That is skill." Pure, unfettered skill, thank you very much. And if it happened to be harnessed to meet current market needs for "unique" art then there was no shame in that. None. He was *not* a hack.

"That all sounds fancy enough but—"

A klaxon went off, saving him from answering her doubt. Captain Dauntless ran past him as if he didn't even exist. She sprinted toward the bridge trailing a string of curses behind her.

"What is it?" He started after her.

Another crew member answered him as she ran past toward the shuttle bay. "The *Creative Fire* is early."

Patrick skidded to a halt and spun back toward his cabin. He was going to need his easel.

THERE WAS AN appalling lack of smoke on the ship they boarded. The interior curving corridors had little to distinguish them from any other ship, except for the bodies strewn on the floor. A pair of burly guards flanked him as they moved through the cramped corridors of the ship that the pirates had attacked. Their sole job was to give him room to work.

Patrick stepped over the bleeding corpse of a spacer and tried not to see it. He swallowed against the nausea. Inside his helmet, his breath hissed in his ears, stinking of the curry he'd had for lunch. This was like being a war journalist. Right? You couldn't let the dead affect you.

Right . . . except in a war everyone had signed up to be there. These people had been minding their own business and— He wrestled his mind to a halt before he lost his lunch. He had a job to do, even if he was "a hack."

His Stedi-Easel 5000 balanced in front of Patrick as he followed the captain. Without it, he would never have been able to paint on the fly like this. It was strapped around his waist and used a set of gyroscopes to maintain the canvas at a perfect level relationship to his body. He wore it at a slight angle, so he could see past to his subject, but even so his vision was limited.

Patrick shoved his fan brush back into the holster on his utility belt and whipped out the #8 sable. Sliding it through the seal on the vacu-palette, he loaded Mars black on the brush and tried to capture the line of the captain's shoulder as she leveled a blaster at one of the passengers. God. Why did she have to keep looking back and smiling at him? This was not at all the "in the moment" painting that he was known for. Usually he'd build the painting from the entire experience, working out the composition and the pose as he went in a compilation of moments. Dauntless kept practically posing. Like the way she pulled the passenger toward her—

He knew that passenger.

Patrick fumbled the brush and laid a hard streak of black down the page. Captain Dauntless was holding his mentor. He hadn't seen Lila Kirkland since he left the art academy back in '47. He shook his head and holstered the #8. It didn't matter.

The subject of the painting was Captain Dauntless, and right now, he had a line of paint down the canvas. He snatched a rag from his utility belt and smudged the wet paint into smoke. There wasn't actually smoke in the corridor, but there should be. Goddammit, this was a space battle. With pirates! There should be smoke.

Or was that the hack talking? The artist who just had a series of gimmicks. He bit his lip and pushed the paint into swirls of light and shadow.

"Patrick?" The easel must have been what caught her attention, because right now Lila Kirkland was staring at him instead of the gun pointing at her chest.

He cleared his throat and had the Pavlovian response of sweat and a cracked voice. "Ma'am?"

Captain Dauntless frowned and shook the older woman. "Hey— no chatter or I end you."

"No—" Patrick bit off the rest of his reply as she glared at him. What was he *doing*? He'd just seen Dauntless kill half a dozen people because they were in the wrong place, and he was trying to make her angry? But . . . but this was Lila Kirkland. He *knew* her. She'd trained him. He swallowed. "It's better with a victim—a *living* victim—in the painting. It shows you dominating and represents man's essential inhumanity to man, which is so endemic of our modern era." God—that sort of pseudo art babble had always made Professor Kirkland furious in his Academy days, but clients ate it up. "Also, the essential contrast between your youth and her age better represents the vitality of conquest against a stagnant society."

Professor Kirkland's pained eye roll could have been scripted. His fingers itched. His description had been a ploy to keep Dauntless from killing the older woman, but by God . . . that *would* be a good painting. He reached for the #8 and said something he thought he'd never say. "Just hold that pose, okay?"

Captain Dauntless sneered, but she held the pose.

Of course, that also meant she was still holding a gun on Professor Kirkland. Patrick worked with the speed that allowed him to do this—to paint on site—while in the far corridors other crew members finished rounding up stragglers. As he slid his brush over the canvas to create the smooth dome of Captain Dauntless's helmet, he cleared his throat again. "You know . . . that's Lila Kirkland."

"Who?" Captain Dauntless raised an eyebrow, and he switched to working on her face to catch the expression.

"The artist. Painted *Sunday in the Martian Canals with Bradbury*." It was *only* one of the most pivotal pieces of post-post-retro modern art and kicked off an entire punch card punk movement. Dauntless just looked at him as blankly as if he'd started chewing cud. He mentally kicked himself. *Remember who the client is and speak her language.* "It sold for over two million solar."

That got Dauntless to give a low whistle, which fogged the inside of her faceplate for a moment. He moved from painting her face to catching the line of Professor Kirkland's jaw on the canvas.

"If she gave a good review . . . more people would see your portrait."

Patrick stared at the painting, willing Dauntless to care about publicity. That had to be why she hired him, right? Why she had that stupid name? It had to be enough to let her keep Professor Kirkland alive.

"You think she would?"

"Maybe." He stared at the canvas and knew the answer would be "no." He was a hack and always had been. "She taught me everything I know."

"So . . . it would be a favor to you to let her live?"

He lifted the brush from the canvas. "Yes."

"Then you can talk about giving me the painting for a better price." She bared her teeth and raised the blaster higher.

"Absolutely."

"*If* it gets a good review."

He swallowed and stared at Lila Kirkland, begging her to lie about art, just once in her life. "I'll do my best to make sure it does."

The first thing he did was paint over the smoke. And then he started to paint in earnest.

THE FIGHTING HAD quieted to the point that they clearly had control of the ship. Captain Dauntless continued to hold the pose—something he'd never asked a client to do before—while crew members came to her with reports. Her arm with the blaster sagged with fatigue, the point drifting from Professor Kirkland's chest to her midriff. It would be just as deadly either way.

Patrick lifted his brush from the canvas and slid the viewing lens over his face. You couldn't back away from a Stedi-Easel, because it was strapped to you, but the lens gave him the illusion of stepping back to view the painting at a distance.

On the canvas, Captain Dauntless stood with her shoulders back and the bandolier draped over her compression suit. Behind her, the long corridor of the ship vanished in a curve. Splashes of red and black showed where bodies had been, but no smoke masked the crisp lines, so everything seemed to be anchored around her. Leaning against one wall, as the only element of softness in the painting, was a captive. Dauntless held the woman by one arm, while the victim's other hand pressed flat against the wall, almost in supplication. The woman stared out of the picture, as if she were the subject instead of the captain. She seemed to be pleading with the viewer.

Patrick tapped his brush against the edge of the canvas. It wasn't who he'd been hired to paint, but . . . it was the right painting. He should wipe it and make Dauntless the focus again. But it was *right*. It was probably the best thing he'd painted in years, and God, that was a depressing thought.

"Are you finished yet?"

He slid the viewing lens out of the way, hesitated for a moment, and signed the painting. "Yes."

Slipping the release on the Stedi-Easel, he pivoted the canvas to face Captain Dauntless but he watched Professor Kirkland.

"My boobs should be bigger."

Patrick snapped his gaze back to Captain Dauntless. "Pardon?"

"The bandolier. It's making me look flat."

"Oh." He made a show of thinking about his client's input. They *always* had some. "I can adjust that but . . . I wanted to demonstrate your power and not let the viewers' perception of your femininity get in the way of your abilities and mastery of space. By catering to the expectations of body images, we risk presenting the idea that a woman must use her appearance for domination, but that has not been what I've witnessed in the time spent with you. No, madam. Your strength is within."

Professor Kirkland coughed.

Patrick hurried on. "But if you would like, I can definitely adjust the bandolier to make your other assets more . . . present."

"Maybe . . ." She turned to Professor Kirkland and jerked her chin at the painting. "What do you think? Going to give it a good review?"

"May I?" Professor Kirkland pulled her hand from the wall and gestured to the painting. Despite her apparent calm, a slight tremor shook her hand. When she painted, her hands had always been so steady, so confident.

"Sure. But don't try anything. I've got crew crawling the ship." Dauntless released the older woman and kept the blaster trained on her.

"Of course." The professor straightened, stretching her shoulders in a gesture he remembered from art school. The critique was coming.

The bodyguards assigned to cover Patrick shifted their weight as if evaluating the aging artist for possible threats. There was no way they could be prepared for her raking wit during a critique. No hired gun could protect him from *that*.

He was twenty years old again. Sweat slid down his neck and he blessed the suit for containing his sudden stink of fear. Professor Kirkland crossed her arms, raising one hand so that it lay alongside her neck, and she considered the painting.

For a brief moment, her gaze flashed up to Patrick's face and she winked. "Well . . . I must say that Patrick's statements about the dominance of your position are quite correct. I find that he's invoking a dichotomy of heterogeneous paradigms that hearken back to Yert and Mingle, while, of course, speaking to the heart of the question of what it is to be human. Also . . . your boobs are glorious." She raised her hand from her neck and waved it in a line down the painting. "See the clever thing he's done with the bandolier? It appears to caress your bosom and suggests a line leading to the crotch as though to warn viewers that you are not to be trifled with. This, madam, is a defining painting."

Captain Dauntless frowned and looked at the painting as if she'd understood any of the absolute tripe that had come out of Professor Kirkland's mouth. "So . . . that's a good review?"

"As good as I can give." She smiled brightly. "And I promise to post about the painting in glorious detail."

Patrick had no doubt that she would. He could deal with the humiliation, if Dauntless let her live.

Dauntless nodded and turned to the nearest bodyguard. "All right. Load her into an escape pod and hold the rest of the crew for ransom. Or space them. You know the drill."

Sagging with relief, Patrick turned the painting back to face him. He pulled the fixative sheet in place to protect it on the way back to the good ship, *Triumphant Beast Descending*.

Lila Kirkland leaned forward as he did. She whispered, "It's really not bad. And your brushwork is lovely."

He stared after his old professor as the bodyguard hauled her down the corridor. His brushwork was lovely . . . He studied the painting and grinned. It really wasn't bad.

JASON M. HOUGH

Enter my time machine for a moment, will you? Way back in 1985, when I was but a freshly minted teenager, my friend and I spent our summer writing a novel. For reasons I can't quite remember now, we decided to write a murder mystery set in nineteenth-century British-occupied India. The main character of our story was a dashing young soldier named John Crimson.

When I was invited to be part of *Unbound*, I knew immediately I wanted to revisit this setting and character, because I'd been thinking about that time period a lot while writing my futuristic spy thriller, *Zero World*. In that novel, some references are made to the dawn of sound criminal forensics, and how that moment in history is something of a turning point for a civilization. To explore that in detail, while also being able to return to a story that's been kicking around in my head since childhood, was an irresistible call.

I hope you enjoy reading it!

SON OF CRIMEA

Jason M. Hough

On Old Kent Road, still six miles from London, the horses grew nervous. Their rhythmic trot became a stutter, their silence a chorus of fearful neighs.

A bend in the lane, with a hill falling away to one side and a wall of trees crowding the other, hid the source of this fear from John Crimson's view. But the horses sensed something. Smelled it in the cool air.

Bandits, he naturally concluded, and thudded the ceiling of the carriage for the driver's attention.

"Sir?"

"Stop here," he said. His boots slapped in the muddy lane a few seconds later. He had no weapon, not while off-duty, but the driver did. Crimson held his hand out and, unspoken command understood, the man handed over a wooden baton without complaint. They had chatted amicably on the ride out to Canterbury, Crimson quizzing the old man about the state of the highway and the old man asking all manner of question about the more storied cases recently spilled from Scotland Yard.

"What is it?" the driver asked, voice low now. He'd been half asleep, from the dazed look on his face.

"I'm going to find out. Be ready to move, would you?"

"'Course, sir."

Crimson hefted the truncheon in his left hand and started toward the bend in the lane, keeping to the wooded side of the ancient road. Above, a sky of bulbous gray drifted lazily north on a chill wind. Crows watched silently from the high branches. Behind, the horses tapped about with their hooves and let out shuddering breaths. Crimson eyed the driver, willing silence as well as an order to calm the beasts. The old man fetched carrots from a basket on the bench beside him and tossed them into the mud between the two steeds. Their heads dipped in unison, lips practically reaching out for the treats, the cause of their worry temporarily forgotten.

Satisfied, Crimson turned back toward the bend. He walked forward at a casual pace, eyes scanning the trees on his left and, across the narrow road, the lip of the hillside. Farms stretched out below, but the immediate bank was not visible from here. A great place for an ambush, Crimson thought. Place a watcher in the trees, have the rest of the crew lay prone on the hillside, ready to swarm up and surround any passersby. Were it he, he would have a log or some other obstacle blocking the lane at the apex of the bend, forcing carriages to slow and stop.

No obstacle lay at the midpoint of the curve, however. What he saw instead was much more surprising and did nothing to calm his nerves.

A lone woman stood there, peach-colored dress muddy at the fringe. She held a shade umbrella in one gloved hand and a spyglass in the other, the device trained on the farm below. A brown leather satchel rested in the thin grass beside her, stuffed to overflowing. She looked, Crimson thought, like a provocative painting. *Lone Woman on Road, 1835*, a museum placard might say.

Golden hair curled about her shoulders, and she stood tall. Sturdy. Proud, or perhaps confident.

Crimson cleared his throat.

The sound did not startle her. She simply lowered her spyglass and turned, one eyebrow arched. "Hello," she said simply, yet it was enough to know she was a foreigner. Dutch perhaps, or Swedish.

"I," Crimson began, then paused. She unsettled him just as she had the horses. Yet there seemed to be no danger about her. Surely she was no lure in a brigand band. She was simply out of place. An oddity. "What are you doing out here alone, Miss . . . ?"

"Penar," she said. "Malena Penar."

Twenty feet still separated them, but she held out a gloved hand regardless, resting the spyglass atop her luggage between the two leather handles.

Crimson cast a glance across the tree line, saw nothing. He crossed to her side of the lane and leaned out, far enough to scan the surrounding slope. No bandits lay in wait. Just a carpet of long green grass marred here and there by jutting white stone.

"Inspector Jonathan Crimson of Scotland Yard," he said with deliberate volume, and took her offered hand.

She grinned. "I feel as if a child rescued after falling in an abandoned well."

A strange thing to say. Crimson had no reply. He tipped an imaginary hat, earning another smile.

"Crim-son," she said, sounding it out. "A criminal's son on the police force? How interesting."

He'd seen that apprehensive look his entire life. At least she hadn't made a remark about the color, as most were quick to do. "Son of Crimea, actually. And you haven't answered my question. What are you doing out here?"

"I'd hoped to glimpse a ghost," she said.

SHE RODE BESIDE him, her bag secured on the roof next to his own. Against the clatter of hooves and the sprawling countryside, her story came out. Traveling not alone but with her brother. Wealthy siblings from Scandinavia, in England to scout possible investments on behalf of the family confectionary business. Dairy farms, she explained. While visiting the nearby village in Kent she'd heard a peculiar story. A nine-year-old girl had apparently fallen into a well just across the field from that bend in the road, a decade ago. Local legend had it that her ghost could sometimes be seen to crawl from the stone circle and drift through the high grass, just before twilight.

"Rubbish," Crimson muttered.

Malena's ill-tempered brother had apparently said as much. When she'd demanded they stop and watch for the apparition, he'd flown into a fit of rage and decided to deposit his sister at the side of the road rather than indulge her superstitions. He'd taken their carriage on to London, leaving her to fend for herself. "How lucky you came along."

"Indeed," Crimson said, swallowing his own prejudices against those who believed in things like ghosts. "If you like I can search the archives, see if this incident with the girl even happened."

"That won't be necessary. I just thought it curious and wanted to see for myself, you know?"

"I do." Yet Crimson's thoughts had turned to her brother. Whether Malena wished it or not, he felt a powerful urge to find the bastard and instill some manners into him via his nose. It was one thing to disagree on matters supernatural, it was another to leave a woman alone on a country road.

"And you?" she asked. "You are one of these, what is the word, 'coppers'?"

"A police inspector, yes. Under Superintendent Goddard."

"Are you out here working on a case?"

"Attending a wedding in Canterbury, actually. Or was. On the way back when we found you."

"Your own wedding?" The barest hint of a smile played at the corner of her mouth. Something wicked about it.

"A friend's, alas." He smiled and she returned it warmly.

HE FOUND HER well educated and very bright. Also vaguely cruel, yet her lack of British modesty somehow transformed this into an endearing quality. She found his occupation mildly disgusting, yet this seemed to only increase her curiosity about the finer details of the work. The last five miles to London went by altogether too quickly.

A dinner followed tea the next evening, and then again the evening after that. She had only two more weeks in London and wanted to see a show, so he offered to take her.

Of her brother there was no mention.

On the fourth day after meeting Malena Penar, Crimson found himself talking like a lovestruck schoolboy about her to Henry Goddard. His superintendent listened thoughtfully, though, and invited him to bring her along to their already planned dinner that evening. "I'll bring Annette," Goddard added, "so the lady does not feel intimidated, and you and I are less inclined to talk shop."

"OYSTERS AND PORTER, nothing fancy," Crimson explained to Malena in the lobby of her hotel. "Pub fare. Sort of a tradition. I hope that is all right?"

She said it was and he led her through the damp and crowded streets of London at twilight, her arm entwined around his. She'd dressed somewhat somberly, though her mood did not reflect this in the slightest. Dark gray coat and dress, white blouse, and a silken black scarf around her neck, pinned in place with a circle of worn gold. A Roman coin, perhaps.

A puddle in the lane, no larger than Crimson's shoe, nevertheless caused Malena to insist they walk around rather than simply step over it. "Old superstition," she said. Then, at his dubious expression, added, "From my country. A spirit, it is said, will have no reflection."

Despite the attraction he had toward her, this reminder of her belief in such nonsense, however casual, made something in the back of his mind twitch. A little voice, easily muzzled, telling him to walk away now, that she wasn't right for him.

He kept beside her all the same.

Their path winded for a quarter-mile until, on Fleet Street, he led her through the aging front door of The Rainbow, where Mr. and Mrs. Goddard already waited at a table for four overlooking the street outside.

In a pool of candlelight beside a rain-streaked window they ate oysters, drank good ale, and talked nothing but shop. The presence of the visibly pregnant Mrs. Goddard did nothing to stem Malena's curiosity about the sordid underbelly of London.

"It's quite easy," she said, "to picture the two of you gentlemen kicking in the door of some burglar or pedophile and hauling them off to jail."

"Do we look so rough around the edges?" Goddard asked.

"Oh, absolutely," Malena replied. Again that hint of wickedness. Crimson felt a ripple of electricity course through him at the way she held herself. Undaunted. This was not a woman to keep at home and have dote upon you. This was a woman to travel the world with. To slog through jungles or across the savannah. He could picture her with a musket on her hip as easily as in her unmentionables. Crimson took a long pull from his porter.

"Of course those days are all but over," Goddard was saying. "John and I rely on intuition, on years of working these streets, to find the villainous. We kick in doors, as you so delightfully put it, because we simply know in our gut that the perpetrator is within."

"And yet you say this will change? To what?"

"Something more . . . methodical," Goddard said.

Crimson smirked. This was a discussion they held almost daily in Goddard's office. The coming intrusion of science into a job that thrived on finesse and gut feel.

"That sounds dull," Malena observed.

"It's quite fascinating actually." Goddard rested his forearms on the table and leaned in, dropping his voice to something conspiratorial. "You see, the scope of what we're dealing with here only grows. Too big for men like us to keep in our heads."

"Speak for yourself," Crimson said, and tipped his mug back to disguise his smile.

Malena laughed, but her attention never wavered from the superintendent. "Are you going to start talking figures and equations?"

Goddard's face scrunched up. "Not exactly, though you're close to the mark." Sensing the impending loss of his audience, Crimson's superior quickly went on. "I'm going to talk about India."

Malena cocked her head, confused.

"Oh not this, Henry," Annette said, face sour, one hand across her bulging torso. "I'll be sick."

"India?" Malena prompted.

"India," Goddard said, a twinkle in his eyes despite his wife's displeasure.

Annette looked to Crimson for help. He shrugged, and she let her gaze fall to her plate, annoyed.

"You see," Goddard said to Malena, "what we're dealing with here in London is nothing compared to a certain W.H. Sleeman."

"I don't know the name," Malena said.

"You will. Everyone will, I believe."

"Why? Who is he?"

"Major Sleeman," Crimson interjected, "is administrator of a small province within the colony."

". . . A province with more crime than London?"

"*Vastly* more," Goddard said. "And not just crime, my dear, but murder. Murder on an unimaginable scale. A sprawling cult of stranglers known as the Thugs. Their crimes are so numerous and broad that Sleeman, out of sheer necessity mind you, has invented entirely new investigative techniques just to get a handle on it. He's written me, detailing the situation. Remarkable work, and by God I think he's going to crack them. The horrors he faces, Malena! Mass graves. Strangled and mutilated bodies by the hundred—"

"Henry, please," Annette said, face gone green.

Goddard went on, patting his wife's hand absently as he spoke. "He'll be knighted for his efforts, believe me. 'The man who brought down the Thugs and ushered in the era of modern investigative techniques.'"

"Superintendent Goddard is going to visit Sleeman in a few weeks," Crimson added, desperate to reinsert himself into the conversation. "See it all firsthand. He studies the region daily on a globe in his den."

This was the wrong thing to say. Annette went wide-eyed at the remark and hissed something at her husband.

"Not now, dear," Goddard said to her through the side of his mouth.

"Our child will be born while you're halfway around the world?

Just so you can see piles of strangled corpses?"

"Later."

"Will you even make it back before the baby's first birthday?"

"Later!" Goddard snapped.

But Annette would not be quieted, and soon the couple made their excuses and left Crimson alone with the Scandinavian heiress. This change of circumstances was not unwelcome, but to Crimson's disappointment Malena spent the next hour distracted and sullen, as if she'd been the one to argue with Annette Goddard. Or perhaps Crimson's accidental disclosure of Goddard's plans had left her unimpressed. Whatever the case, she'd gone cold. Withdrawn.

The bill came and Crimson paid. Malena sat and waited, patiently, fingers fidgeting with the coin at her neck. The scarf . . . Crimson stared at it. It had been black, he could have sworn. And yet she wore a blue scarf now. A trick of the light? "Did you change scarves?" he asked.

Malena glanced at him, perplexed. Suddenly annoyed. "Pardon me?"

He gestured to it. "I could have sworn it was black."

She shook her head, the matter settled. "Please take me back to the hotel, John."

A POUNDING ON the door of Crimson's flat woke him, well before sunrise. He opened it, bleary-eyed, to the breathless sweat-soaked figure of a policeman. "Super needs you," the boy said. "There's been a break-in."

"Where?"

"He's at home."

"I mean the break-in."

"At his home," the man repeated.

"Christ," Crimson said. "Anyone hurt?"

"Don't know sir. He asked for you."

Crimson dressed in a hurry and rushed to Goddard's, a dozen blocks away in an upscale neighborhood. Out of habit Crimson went to the back of the house, which crowded up against a narrow alley and, beyond, a richly foliaged park laced with footpaths. The sun had yet to rise, and back here the city was nearly pitch black. An officer waited in the alley, lantern in hand, and ushered Crimson inside without a word.

Silence draped the house, until floorboards creaking under Crimson's feet announced him. Goddard stood in the main hallway, leaning against a wall with his hands clasped in front of him. He stared into the open door of a room, candlelight spilling out to paint him in dancing shades of yellow. Crimson came to stand next to him, saying nothing. His superior wore a stony expression, face lined in deep concentration.

The room was the study. Shelves of books lined the walls. A globe on a pedestal stood in one corner. Dominating the space was Goddard's oak desk, a gigantic slab of lacquered wood mounted on four massive legs. Crimson had been here many times before and always marveled internally at the cleanliness of the place. The order. An absolute contrast to the chaos of Goddard's office at Scotland Yard. He'd explained once that this place was the one room he could go to and not be distracted by the piles of work, or the chores of running one's household. An oasis of order.

The room was a disheveled mess.

Papers strewn everywhere. Books pulled off the shelves, laying face down and spine open on the carpeted floor. A safe embedded in the sidewall stood wide open, contents splayed out on the ground around it. And, opposite the globe on the back wall, a single narrow window was cracked a few inches ajar. Cold air spilled in. The window creaked in the breeze, swinging in then out, as if breathing.

Crimson ignored a sudden chill. He took a step forward. "What was stolen?"

He stopped abruptly, Goddard's hand suddenly pressing against his chest to hold him at the precipice.

"Let's do this carefully," the man said. "Methodical. As Sleeman would."

Crimson found himself nodding. "Yeah, all right."

"Tell me what you see."

John Crimson took in the room again. He shrugged; the answer seemed obvious. "Someone was looking for something. In a hurry. Money or jewels from the safe will be gone, I suspect."

To his surprise, Goddard shook his head. "We're meant to think so."

"Sir?"

His boss gestured expansively. "All this," he said, "should have made a hell of a noise. But I heard nothing until a breeze made that window clack against the frame, waking me."

"I . . ." Crimson said, and swallowed. "I don't understand."

"This is staged, John."

"There was no break-in?"

"Oh, there was a break-in all right." He seemed about to say more, then fell silent.

"Still a bit confused here, sir."

Goddard sighed, but not, Crimson thought, from annoyance. The man was trying to convince himself, as if trying to work out a magician's trick at a West End show. "The burglar, or burglars, came in through the window. They were after something specific. The safe, perhaps, I'm not sure yet. Then, once in possession of their prize, they proceeded to quietly and methodically create this mess."

Crimson studied the room again, still confused. He was about to ask how Goddard could know they made the mess after the robbery, but then he saw it. "No footprints," he said.

"Very good, John."

"They came in through the window. A flower garden out there, if I'm not mistaken."

"You are not mistaken."

"Their boots or shoes would have been damp at the very least, muddy more than likely. Yet the papers on the floor are unblemished."

"Not even rumpled."

Crimson pictured a thief walking backward toward the window, scattering papers in their wake. "We may find muddy footprints on the carpet then."

"Indeed. In fact you can see some, in a gap just there," Goddard said, pointing.

Something still didn't add up. "Why go to that trouble, though? Why not take the boots off at the sill and make the whole thing clean?"

"It is a mystery, isn't it? I suspect," the superintendent said, "all will become clear when we know what was taken, and that is no small task.

There's so much detritus here I'm half convinced the thieves brought some papers with them just to add to the mess."

"Only you will know what is missing, of course, but I'll help in any way I can. There may be more clues we have yet to spot."

Goddard grasped Crimson's shoulder. "Now you're thinking like Major Sleeman. Let's get to it then."

HOURS LATER, AT 7 a.m., Annette brought them eggs with thick-sliced toast coated in butter, plus a carafe of steaming Arabica coffee. They ate in the hall, at Goddard's insistence, so as to not contaminate the room. Fed and caffeinated—it was by far the best coffee Crimson had ever tasted—they returned to the laborious task, with Crimson surveying every inch of the room for possible clues while Goddard attempted to catalog the spilled papers and other debris from his mental recollection of the contents prior to the invasion.

There were indeed the hints of muddy footprints on the rug below the scattered papers. Crimson also found a single black thread dangling from the window's protruding hasp. Silk, he thought. An unusual textile in London, but it made sense if one wished to move about with stealth. He wrapped it in a paper envelope, wondering what Goddard would do with such a clue. Take it to the cloth vendors and the fine clothiers, perhaps? Look for a match in color and thread quality, then scour the billings for a possible suspect. Rather thin. Likely a waste of time. Crimson stuffed the paper in his pocket.

The clock struck nine when Henry Goddard, kneeling on the floor beside stacks of papers, rocked back on his heels and ran a hand over his tired face. "I don't understand."

"What is it? What's missing?"

"That's just it. Nothing."

"What?"

"It's all here, John."

Crimson cast a glance about the room, deflated. "Whoever it was sought something specific and did not find it, then."

Goddard reluctantly agreed. Neither of them commented on the implication: trespassing was a much less serious crime than theft, no matter the stature of the victim. He sent Crimson away then, saying he would stay home a few days to sooth the nerves of his pregnant wife, asking Crimson to manage affairs at the Yard as best he could.

Two days passed with Crimson drifting through his duties, his mind equally distracted by the crime scene within Goddard's home and the lack of contact with the lovely Malena. She'd vanished from his life as abruptly as she'd entered it. Inquires at her hotel were rebuffed on grounds of client privacy. Upon presenting his Scotland Yard warrant book, the clerk admitted no one by the name Malena Penar was on their current guest list, nor, upon Crimson insisting they check, even on their list of clients from the last few weeks.

"What about the name Penar?" he asked, thinking of her brother, how he'd left her on Old Kent Road, and what else a man like that might be capable of. Intuition made a vein on his temple begin to twitch.

"Nothing, inspector. Look for yourself."

"I think I will," Crimson said, and for the next hour he pored through each entry. He found nothing either, though one name made him trip up twice during his search. A current resident by the name Mona Pendisio. M. P. Crimson flipped the book around and tapped it. "I'd like entry to this room, please."

The manager came with him, along with a porter holding a ring of keys. No one answered at the knock, so Crimson stepped aside and let the door be unlocked. The two men waited in the hall as he entered with truncheon in hand.

An empty room. Bed unmade. Closet wide open, devoid of clothing. Drawers left pulled open.

And, unmistakably, her scent. It lingered in the air, as if she'd just left.

The manager came in a step.

"Remain in the hall," Crimson barked. "This may be a crime scene."

The man backed out, aghast, hands raised in apology. Crimson kicked the door shut in his face. He turned back to the room, stepping farther inside as a hundred thoughts fought for the full attention of his mind. Why stay under a false name? Or had the name he'd known been the false one? Had she left in haste? Fled from her brother? Perhaps he'd taken her. Perhaps he'd packed her belongings while she waited, bound and gagged, in a carriage in the alley below.

Crimson recognized this last as pure fantasy on his part. The overactive imagination of a man who'd seen more horror in his twenty-five years than most would see in a lifetime. Yet he also knew what people were capable of.

He closed his eyes, drew in a deep breath through his nose and let it out through the mouth. Theoretically this cleared the mind, gave one the ability to see things as they were. Henry Goddard said so, anyway. Crimson felt daft, but when he opened his eyes he found the technique had worked.

The room was not, in fact, empty. When he'd kicked the door closed, something had moved. A length of cloth, black and shiny, hanging from a peg on the inside. Malena's silk scarf. The accessory had been black when he first saw it, then she'd changed it for a blue one but claimed to have done no such thing. Here, now, hanging in space against the white-painted door, it seemed to announce itself like a bold challenge.

And suddenly John Crimson felt a weight. A physical burden, wrapped in a piece of paper and stuffed into his pocket. A knot of dread twisted in his stomach as he removed the yellow square and unfolded it carefully. Inside, the single strand of blue silk waited like a serpent. Blue! It had been black when he'd taken it from Goddard's window. His throat went dry as he picked up the thread. He lifted it, and lifted his eyes at the same time, to the cloth hanging from the door. The black scarf, now blue.

Transformed, somehow. Impossibly. Supernaturally.

Crimson shook his head. He felt like the butt of a joke. Some prank being pulled on the school yard. This was no innocent jest, though. A home had been robbed. Malena had used him to get to Goddard. She'd . . . she must have sought something. Heard something during that dinner. But what? And why leave this bizarre, almost magical, clue?

Of one thing he felt sure. This was a challenge, somehow. A test. He vowed, then and there, to pass it.

Blue cloth in hand, he fled the room and raced to Goddard's home.

CRIMSON FOUND HIS superior much as he had two days prior: standing in the hallway, staring into the invaded study.

Only this time the superintendent's face brightened at the sight of his inspector. "I've cracked it, John," he said.

"I . . . you have?" he asked, the scarf temporarily forgotten.

"Something *was* stolen. A single piece of paper, no wonder I'd missed it."

"What piece of paper?"

Henry Goddard looked at him. "Sleeman's letter, of all things. I don't understand why. It contained only the logistics of my visit. Still . . . what's wrong, John?"

Crimson had turned to look at the room, as if it might now divulge some explanation. It did not, not exactly. But tidied now, everything back where it had been before the robbery, Crimson noticed something that had slipped attention before. "The globe, sir," he said.

"What about it?"

"Did you move it while cleaning in here? Bump into it, perhaps?"

"No. Why?"

He and Goddard walked together to the ornate sphere.

The world had been angled so that India would be front and center in the magnifying glass, a single red pin pressed into the surface to mark Sleeman's base of operations in Jubbulpore. Crimson had noted this marker months ago, even discussed it with Goddard. It served both as a reminder of the coming visit to that place, and a talisman through which Goddard hoped to channel some of Sleeman's investigative ideas.

But the globed had been turned.

"What on earth?" Goddard whispered.

The Black Sea, not India, now loomed beneath the circular lens. The word CRIMEA sat in the very center, bold and blindingly obvious.

"Son of Crimea," John Crimson whispered.

Then he showed Goddard the scarf, and the thread from the window hasp.

PART TWO

Months of agonizing travel followed.

Crimson spent most of it alone in his meager cabin, dividing his time between attempts to unravel the mystery of the color-shifting scarf and studying everything he could find about Major William Sleeman. The scarf proved stubborn, remaining blue since leaving the abandoned hotel room. As for Sleeman, the man proved a prolific writer, leaving no shortage of material to pore over on the journey. Yet for all he learned about colonial politics and the murderous Thugee Cult, he could not imagine why Malena Penar—or whatever her name really was—had done any of this. The whole endeavor defied logic, and so he'd quickly given up trying to comprehend it. The answers waited in the jungles of central India, it seemed. He hoped so, anyway.

Between the frayed nerves of Goddard's wife and the impending birth of their child, plus the pin in the globe that seemed aimed for John Crimson himself, it had not taken more than an hour for the two policemen to agree that it should be Crimson, not Goddard, who would board an East India Company steamship bound for Alexandria. They had learned, later on the same day that the modified globe had been discovered, that a Mona Pendisio had booked passage to India the day after the robbery. She'd taken a sail ship on the slower course around the Cape of Good Hope. Crimson, it was decided, would steam for Egypt, ride hard overland to the Suez, then sail on to Bombay. With any luck he'd present himself at Sleeman's home several weeks before the woman had even set foot on the subcontinent. Then he would wait for her, and confront her.

"She may never arrive at all," Goddard had said, "but learning her motives is not the primary purpose of this journey. You are my representative to Sleeman. Learn all you can from him. Write down everything, because this time next year you'll be training our whole department in his techniques. Understood?"

What ate away at Crimson's confidence was the fact that this seemed to be exactly what Malena wanted. The scarf, the pin, Sleeman's stolen letter. These clues had been deliberate. She wanted him to follow, of that he felt absolutely sure. And she'd given him the chance to arrive ahead of her. Had their meeting on Old Kent Road been planned as well? He thought very probably so.

It was the why of it that gnawed at his gut, churning with each mile of sea and land he left behind him until finally, after almost six months, the sprawling skyline of Bombay appeared on the horizon.

HE SPENT ONLY one night in the teeming, sweltering city. Hundreds of miles of overland travel still awaited him, and yet his only safe option— to embed himself in an army regiment bound for Sleeman's province— would not work. No suitable dispatch would happen for another four weeks, and Crimson's intuition told him time was of the essence.

A rail line made close approach to Jubbulpore, leaving a manageable fifty miles of foot travel. However, Crimson quickly learned the trains were not running due to a tunnel collapse three days prior, so that path was moot.

That left two alternatives. The first was to travel with a merchant caravan. A logical choice, as common sense said there was safety in numbers. Yet Crimson had learned much from reading Sleeman's letters over the last few months, and the Major devoted a significant amount of his words to the methods employed by the Thugee. It seemed they preyed upon this very notion of safety in numbers. They posed as merchants, trickling in to caravans in the days leading up to a departure, then traveling alongside them for days or weeks. They made friends, they dined with their traveling companions, shared stories and supplies. Then, somewhere out in the vast rural plains or forests or jungle, the Thugee would strike. They were not brigands who waited at blind curves in the road. No, the cunning bastards earned the trust of their victims. They traveled alongside, then struck in unison when least expected. Through some complex and silent system of hand signals, the Thugs would spread among the other merchants, slip rolled-up scarves around their necks, press one foot against the lower back, pull, and twist. A coin knotted into the center of the scarf would press against the windpipe, resulting in suffocation. The hair on Crimson's neck pricked up every time Sleeman mentioned this sinister technique.

The bodies were looted, then grotesquely-yet-expertly mutilated so the limbs could be folded in such a way that a full bleed-out would occur within hours. Buried in shallow graves, yet drained of fluids, the bodies would rot into the earth without notice. Because of the crude infrastructure of the country, it would be weeks or even months before anyone even realized their traveling merchant relative had failed to return. Before Sleeman these disappearances were attributed to the supernatural, or simply the deliberate removal of oneself from an unwanted marriage or overbearing family. Disturbed and disgusted by the Thug's techniques, Crimson couldn't help but admire the cleverness of the system. They were rarely caught, at least before Sleeman took his interest in their activities. Indeed, as far as Crimson could tell the Thugs were essentially tolerated by the larger population. To be killed by them was to have been duped by their methods and their deities, and thus the fate deserved.

Thus John Crimson could not travel with merchants, though part of him almost wanted to just to confront these killers firsthand. It seemed almost a test of investigative skill to see if he could spot them before they struck. The problem, however, was that he would be hopelessly outnumbered. He could see himself standing in a jungle clearing, pointing and shouting "Aha! I knew you were Thug!" even as fifty or sixty of them surrounded him, the rest of the caravan dead or dying. These were people who made murder and robbery a way of life, starting as young as eight years old. Fine inspector of the Yard or not, he'd be no match for them.

So he rode, alone, eschewing even a guide. The police warrant book he carried had no pull whatsoever with the colonial force, so he purchased a horse for a considerable sum from a regimental stablemaster with an understanding of reimbursement if Crimson returned the animal in good condition at the conclusion of his "ill-advised adventure." Again common sense seemed to run against reality. Everyone he spoke with while provisioning himself seemed to think traveling alone in India was suicide. He should wait, travel in a large group, surely!

He couldn't blame them. To cling to the common wisdom, no matter the evidence right in front of one's nose, was an affliction as old as love.

Each night he made camp well off the roads, which were little more than well-beaten game trails in truth. His skittish horse, bearing the unoriginal name Bucephalus, neighed at anything that came within twenty yards. He ran well enough during the long, blisteringly hot days, but at night the animal seemed to sleep with an eye open and that suited Crimson just fine. From the very first night he slept like the dead.

Fifty miles outside Bombay the foot traffic all but vanished. When Crimson did come upon other travelers he stormed past them at a gallop, eyeing each of them as a potential Thug, though he knew this was likely incorrect in every instance. Most ignored him anyway, uninterested in the goings-on of the British.

For a week straight he pushed the horse across a landscape of shocking variety and beauty. Endless dusty plains and dense jungles. Villages and their denizens alive with a riot of color and sound. Ancient temples half-consumed by vegetation. Forgotten monuments to uncountable Gods. He rode past all without so much as stopping to eat, and by the end he found that, more than anything, he craved human contact. Relief washed over him as the white spires of Hindoo temples finally poked out about the dense trees, and the town of Jubbulpore came into view.

THE TOWN WAS no more than dirt roads woven through a scattering of low buildings, some in the native style and some clearly built since the East India Company arrived.

He visited the garrison house first, intent to stable Bucephalus and continue on foot. But the ranking officer took pity on the dusty ruffled man before him and offered to send a runner up to Sleeman's estate on the north edge of town. Crimson was afforded a hot bath, a hot meal, and a sideroom in which to make himself presentable.

Word quickly came back that Sleeman and his wife, Amélie, had gone out on one of their "expeditions" and may not return for several days. As the town had no proper hotel, Crimson was offered a soldier's bunk in the garrison house or, if he preferred, a place to pitch his tent in the vast drilling yard behind. Beyond that the only option seemed to be staying at one of the temples, an idea Crimson disliked because it seemed somehow blasphemous. He decided not to decide, asking instead where Sleeman had gone. He would meet the man today even if it meant hiking until dusk.

But neither the officer nor the runner had any inkling of where their superior was. The runner offered to go back and ask at the house, but Crimson shook his head. "I'll go myself, if that's all right. Tell me the way."

On the dusty main road through town, he tried to imagine himself living here, among such poverty and ragged wilderness. He became so lost in thought he almost missed the beggar who had spoken to him. The words trickled into his head as if come from a dream. "She fell in the well."

Crimson spun, walked a pace back. The man looked at least seventy years old, limbs like bones covered in old, untreated leather. His face was a pinched landscape of wrinkles all surrounding a toothless smile. "What did you say?"

The man just grinned and held out his bowl.

"Repeat yourself," Crimson rasped. "Who fell in a well?"

The beggar only nodded, his bowl bobbing up and down in unison with his head. He mumbled something in the local tongue.

Crimson, annoyed, moved on, feeling once again on the ignorant end of a cruel joke.

A native met him at the outer gate to Sleeman's estate. The home, a vision of dignity and taste surrounded by squalor, stood back a good hundred feet from the ivy-covered wall. The servant, immaculately dressed and impossibly thin, spoke perfect, accented English.

"What is this expedition the Major is on?" Crimson asked, after making introductions that elicited no reaction.

The dark face scrunched up. "No place of mine to say, sir. You may wait inside if you wish, though I know not if they will return on this day."

Crimson tried another tack. "I'm here on behalf of Henry Goddard, whom I believe the Major was expecting. Goddard could not make the—"

The small man interrupted him. "Oh! I see! We were not expecting another so soon."

"Another?"

"The Major is so sorry for your loss. He will want to speak with you immediately."

"Explain yourself, man. What are you talking about?"

"I speak of the woman, of course. The one who vanished."

OVER CHAI IN the parlor, and with infinite patience, Crimson drew the story out.

On the surface it all had the air of truth. Nearly six months ago a woman had arrived in Jubbulpore, going by the name Pendisio. She had a letter of introduction, supposedly penned by Goddard himself, stating she was his apprentice and requesting that she be allowed to "shadow" Sleeman for as much time as needed to learn the details of his investigative techniques. After two months she had concluded her work and left with a caravan bound for Bombay. The caravan, Major Sleeman learned weeks later, had never reached its destination.

When prompted the manservant provided Crimson with a perfect description of Malena.

He sat back in the deeply cushioned couch, too stunned to speak. He'd traveled the fastest possible route, only days after she'd fled London. It had taken almost six months. And yet Malena had been here, by all evidence, just days after leaving England on a boat that most likely was yet to even reach the subcontinent.

"She must have a twin," Crimson muttered. No other explanation made sense. Even so, why do this? And how could the pair have coordinated any of this over such a distance? Even a simple letter could not arrive any faster than he had.

"Sir? A twin?"

"I need to find Sleeman, and I need to find him right now."

The thin man nodded, and gave directions.

In a jungle clearing less than two miles away Crimson found them. How strange, in that verdant place of color and beaming sunlight and clouds of insects, to find a proper English couple studying the mud.

Sleeman matched Crimson's imagined portrait almost exactly. Tall and proudly upright. A bald pate, with brown hair above the ears that flowed down to frame his cheeks in long, fashionable sideburns. He wore his military uniform, immaculate save for muddied boots. At present he stood with one foot atop a fallen log, pointing at a dark cavity in the wood.

The woman with him was Sleeman's wife Amélie, whom Crimson knew to be the daughter of a French Count who had fled that nation after Napoleon's coup. Even from this distance her beauty was obvious. She crouched, boots as soiled as her husband's, and rooted around in the notch on the tree trunk with a gloved hand. The two were talking quietly. Equals, Crimson could plainly see. He stepped into the clearing and spoke. "Major Sleeman?"

The pair came instantly alert, Sleeman's right hand moving to the hilt of a small sword worn at his belt. Amélie stood and moved a step to be at her husband's side, not behind him. Her eyes brimmed not with suspicion but curiosity. Crimson liked her already.

"Announce yourself, young man," Sleeman said.

"I am Police Inspector John Crimson of Scotland Yard."

Sleeman gestured to the dense foliage surrounding them. "A bit far from your jurisdiction, isn't it?"

"I believe we're looking for the same person," Crimson said. "And I fear some scheme, which I cannot yet explain, has been hatched against you."

He expected shock, or even outrage. What he saw instead was something like fascination. The prospect of a riddle about to be solved.

Seated on a blanket beneath a cathedral-like tree, the Sleemans told him what they knew.

Mona Pendisio had indeed arrived almost six months earlier. Though Sleeman had been surprised at her appearance, he had been in contact with Goddard for almost a year and so he did not question this. She had, after all, a hand-written letter from the man as means of introduction. "I have many letters from Goddard. The writing is a perfect match, I assure you."

"I believe it. Please, go on," Crimson said.

There wasn't much else to say. She'd truly shadowed Sleeman for two months. Observing his investigations, even sitting in on interrogations. She'd been so silent Sleeman had all but forgotten she was there. "A fine woman in polite conversation, but when it came to the work she was nothing more than a fly on the wall. She took her notes without comment, never offered her opinion on anything she saw here, and left with little fanfare."

A month later, when a garrison officer arrived from Bombay with supplies, it became apparent that Mona had not arrived in the city. The Sleemans had been investigating the disappearance ever since, suspecting another Thugee attack as this was the method by which the cult operated.

"And what have you learned?" Crimson asked.

"Not much, I'm afraid," Sleeman admitted.

Crimson glanced around the clearing in the forest. "This will sound strange, but is it possible she fell into a well?"

Sleeman considered this for a moment, then shrugged. "Possible, I suppose. There are enough around. But that does not explain the rest of her caravan."

Crimson nodded. "What brings you out here, then? It's far from the road, or any trail I've seen."

Amélie answered. Despite being raised outside her mother country, she still spoke with a thick French accent. "A villager found footprints in the soil," she gestured where the fallen tree bisected the space, "there. Long washed away, unfortunately."

"Footprints don't seem so odd," Crimson observed.

She shook her head. "This villager helps in our gardens. He thought the prints mine, for he'd seen them before in our flower bed many times. These prints were made by my own boots, which I'd given to Mona as a gift."

Major Sleeman nodded, contemplative. "She was certainly ill-equipped for this place. An odd choice for Goddard to send. Quite dull, really."

"Goddard didn't send her," Crimson said flatly. Then he told them all he knew, deciding to leave nothing out despite the strangeness of the story. The Sleemans hung on every word, exchanging the occasional baffled glance. "And so Goddard sent me in his place via the fastest possible route. I should have beaten her here by weeks, but she arrived months ago."

"So she has a twin," Amélie said.

"My thought exactly."

Sleeman grimaced. "This is a lot to consider, and the day grows short. Come back to the house with us and we'll ponder this over supper."

"If you don't mind," Crimson said, "I'd like to look around a bit."

"It's not safe after dark."

"Because of the Thugs?"

Sleeman gestured to the forest. "They do not work that way. They'll befriend you in town or on the road and offer to travel with you, then strike when you least expect."

Like Malena, Crimson thought.

"No," Sleeman said, "it is the wildlife you need to fear."

"I'll be all right," Crimson replied. "You found only the footprints here?"

"We never saw them ourselves, but the gardener said they were in a line parallel to this fallen tree. None before, none beyond. I don't understand how that's possible, but I have no reason to doubt the man. Still, embellishment driven by superstition is part of their culture, so who can be sure?"

With that they said their farewells, gathered their gear, and walked back toward town.

John Crimson stood in the now silent glade and just observed. It was possible, he thought, that someone had tried to cover footprints here, but missed Malena's due to a shadow cast by the log. After so many months it would be impossible to prove that, however.

What if, instead, the footprints had been left deliberately? Another hidden message, perhaps even directly to him, like the globe turned to Crimea. He studied the log for several minutes, keenly aware that the Major and his wife had been doing the same thing when he'd found them. The renowned investigator had a similar intuition, and that gave Crimson a touch of hope. Yet he found nothing.

The log pointed south toward town and north toward ever-denser jungle. Crimson then noticed something he should have seen instantly. Where had the log come from? There was no stump from which it had been cut. No broken branch above. It had been placed here, and based on the moss growing atop it, the length of wood had been here for some time. This in and of itself was not remarkable, but when combined with the footprints . . .

Crimson began to walk north, in a line parallel to the tree. At the edge of the clearing he stopped and studied the thick foliage. Sweat soaked his clothes now. Insects made the air around him buzz. He rubbed his eyes, willing more light to spill in as the sun crept lower in the sky. Weak golden beams lanced through a thousand tiny gaps in the canopy.

Nothing out of place. Crimson frowned, growing frustrated. He pushed into the undergrowth and began to walk, as best he could, in a line congruous to the direction the log seemed to point.

Half a mile later he'd all but decided to give up when something ahead caught his eye. A patch of gray amid the greens. Instinctively he slowed to a silent creep, pushing leaves and branches aside, ignoring the sting on his hands from some plant that irritated the skin. The gray began to take the shape of a small pile of rocks.

Not a pile, he realized, but a wall. Man-made, of that he had no doubt. Ancient, from the mold and the black grime between the stones.

He circled it and realized it was not a wall, but a well. A very old abandoned well.

Satisfied he was alone, Crimson swallowed hard and approached the circular structure. Holding his breath and feeling so much the fool for his sudden fear, he peered over the rim.

She fell into a well, the beggar had said.

Despite that, Crimson expected darkness, or perhaps stagnant water. Only a dark corner of his mind expected the curled body of a woman, dead six months.

What he saw instead was a stone floor, just six or seven feet below the ground. Despite the surroundings there were no leaves or even dirt marring the surface. No sign of water, either. It looked as if recently swept by a broom. A chill ran up John Crimson's spine and as it spread across his scalp he heard a voice. Not a real voice, but one remembered. Malena's, when he'd first spoken to her on Old Kent Road.

I feel as if a child rescued after falling in an abandoned well. She'd said that. The word "abandoned" such an odd extra detail. At the time he'd found it a bit strange, but mostly endearing. A woman struggling with a learned language, still a bit off.

And now here, in the middle of a jungle in India, he'd been guided to an abandoned well by footprints she'd left. What sort of well only descended six feet and held no water?

On a whim he reached into his bag for the blue scarf. The length of cloth he pulled from its depths was blue no longer, though. Nor had it shifted to black. The fabric was an impossibly brilliant crimson red.

Teeth gritted against a sudden, rising anger, John Crimson sat on the edge of the well and then pushed himself down to the floor.

His feet found only air, though, and then he was falling into absolute darkness.

JOHN CRIMSON WOKE to a blinding white light. He lay on a thin mattress that felt like gelatin covered in silk. Tight bindings made of something like porcelain held his wrists, ankles, and torso to the surface.

Malena stood nearby. She had slicked her hair back and wore an outfit like nothing Crimson had seen before. Pale blue in color, it looked almost like a second skin, so tight around her body. She had her arms folded across her chest, and a look of simple curiosity on her face. Wound around one fist was the scarf, and every time she moved her hand a new coloration rippled across its surface. Red, blue, green, yellow, black, white, then clear as glass.

"Where . . . where am I?" Crimson managed.

Malena's mouth tightened into a thin line. "We have much to learn from each other, John Crimson. But first I must give you a new life. Sleep now."

Something tickled the back of his neck, followed by a sharp sting of pain. The world melted into nothingness.

THAT VERY EVENING she broadcast her findings on the system-wide channel, plus a narrow-beam lanced out to the waiting skip drone at the Conduit's entrance.

We are discovered, or nearly so. A riddle carefully laid out has led an Earthling directly to me, rather than earning a claim of witchcraft or something similar as has happened so many times before.

Due to this, and other information I have recently gathered (see attached), I am forced to conclude that Earth has reached the divergent moment. It is my estimation that within several decades Earth's forensic sciences will be sufficient to detect us with no possibility for continued attribution to the supernatural.

Therefore I am ordering a full evacuation from the Zero World, effective immediately (with the exception of the Linguistics Operatives, who may remain for no more than six days in order to ensure final implantation of the guided lexicon, or as much as is possible at any rate).

We will observe from orbit until such time as even that is impossible (my estimate: fifty years local standard), at which time only myself and a core team will remain in system for continued intellectual harvest, to continue the search for our missing Wardens, and of course to protect the Conduit itself.

Thank you for your cooperation. A harvest conclave will begin in sixty-two months, Prime standard. I look forward to seeing you all there.

Monivar Pendo Tonaris
Warden
World 0

In the days and weeks that followed, they left. Silent vessels, inky blotches against the night sky, rising up toward the stars by the dozens.

TERRY BROOKS

This story came about the way most do—with a call asking for a contribution to a planned short story collection. Mostly, I turn these down. I hate writing short stories. Too constricted. Too many demands. They take forever. But this was Shawn—my Web Druid and friend. He was the one asking, and I did owe him a story for reasons too complicated to go into here. It suffices to say that once upon a time I had promised him something new and ended up giving him something used. So when he asked again, I couldn't very well refuse. And this time I had to write something original.

Turns out both of us were thinking it should be a Shannara tale. But I was burnt out on that series and not inclined at present to write another word, short or long. An alternative was needed. I hadn't written anything in the Magic Kingdom world for a while, and I thought I might try that. I decided to center the story on the G'home Gnomes—something light and fanciful, distancing myself from the big, dark epic fantasies of Shannara.

Fine and dandy, but what was the story? Easy enough to come up with something centered on the endlessly bad decisions or foolish behaviors of Filip and Sot and their sorry friends, but a real threat was needed too.

And then it occurred to me that there had never been anything written about where the G'home Gnomes come from. Nothing about their women and children. Nothing about how they procreate. If these inept creatures were so bad at everything else, wouldn't they be equally bad at birthing and raising offspring?

Wouldn't catastrophe be only one bad choice away?

And maybe a dragon?

AN UNFORTUNATE
INFLUX OF FILIPIANS

Terry Brooks

On that late spring morning it wasn't the weather that ended up ruining Ben Holiday's day, although the air was gray and coolish and uncomfortably slimy. It wasn't his teenage daughter Mistaya either, who of late had proved typically troublesome in that teenage sort of way. She was back in school in the Old World, having talked her way into being reinstated after being booted out the year before for behavior unbecoming a student of Carrington Women's Preparatory. Nor was it the larger world of Landover, which it sometimes seemed was bent on intruding on Ben Holiday's peace of mind for the express purpose of disrupting it. It wasn't even Questor Thews making an ill-advised attempt at summoning yet another peculiar form of magic that was well beyond his somewhat limited abilities.

No, on this morning, it was a simple visit.

"High Lord?" a tinny voice called out from the other side of his closed bedroom door.

His eyes opened, and he lifted his head from the pillow. He had been awake earlier, up before the sun. But after deciding he had few demands on his time that day, he had chosen to stay in bed. So seldom did he get such an opportunity these days. As King of Landover, he ruled over an entire world of very strange creatures. As such, much of what he did involved protecting them, frequently from each other or, rather sadly, him from them, and when momentarily freed from this effort he tried to keep the wheels and cogs of his makeshift government chugging away.

So, a day of just lounging in bed would have been a gloriously pleasant indulgence! Joy, happy happy joy! There he was, drowsing, undisturbed and without a care in the world—which maybe should have been a warning—when the voice called out a second time: "High Lord?"

The voice sounded familiar. And not in a good way. No, instead it nudged to life rather aggressively a recognizable clutch of dark memories that had been buried, if never quite eradicated, by the passing of the days.

"Is he in there?" a second voice whispered, similar in tone but just different enough to be distinguishable.

"He must be. He sleeps in there, doesn't he?"

"He might have gone out."

"Where would he go?"

"Anywhere he chooses. He is High Lord."

Ah, Ben thought in dismay. The light dawned. "Go away!" he shouted at the door. "Far away!"

Gasps sounded. Breath exhaled in a mix of distress and awe. A jumbled muttering of indistinguishable words ensued. A shuffling of feet preceded the sound of bodies crowding up against the door in an effort to get closer.

"Great High Lord!" cried one voice.

"Mighty High Lord!" cried the other.

Filip and Sot. If not his worst nightmare, then something close.

He squeezed his eyes tightly closed in disbelief. How had they gotten in here? Weren't there supposed to be guards protecting him from intruders? Wasn't he safe even in his own bed?

"Go away!" he repeated.

Filip and Sot. Troublesome even for G'Home Gnomes, a variety of Landoverian Gnomes that were otherwise mostly innocuous. Most Gnomes—the good kind—nested in the northern stretches of Landover, up around the Melchor Mountains. Where they behaved themselves. Where they didn't eat their neighbors' pets. Where they didn't steal everything that wasn't nailed down. Where they didn't start fires in people's living rooms just to see what would happen. All of which the G'Home Gnomes did without a second thought. This was a tribe so reviled by everyone that they had been told so often to "Go Home, Gnomes!" that the name had stuck. Unfortunately, no one, themselves included, could remember by now where that home was or how to get the G'Home Gnomes to go back there.

Ben had tried everything. The complaints had piled up and he had been left with no choice. He had consigned them wholesale to portions of his kingdom north, south, east, and west, at different times but with similar results. He had placed them in compounds in an effort to curtail their wandering ways. He had confined them behind chain-link fencing and, when that failed, barbed wire. He had assigned guards. He had cajoled and threatened and finally given up. You could only do so much; you could only give a problem a certain amount of your time and energy before you were forced to pronounce it a hopeless endeavor.

Filip and Sot were the worst of a bad bunch, the extent of his annoyance enhanced by the fact that they inexplicably worshipped him.

"Great High Lord!" they called out through the door, chanting together. "Mighty High Lord!"

On and on and on.

He gritted his teeth. His thoughts were best left unvoiced, so he kept them that way. Instead, he climbed out of bed to meet his fate, already pretty much knowing what it was. Not in the specific, of course, but generally. Each appearance by these two always prefaced a disaster; only the nature of it varied.

He yanked open the door furiously. Two wizened, somewhat monkey-like faces looked up at him in adoration from three feet down. Eyes wide and adoring, beaming smiles revealing sharpened teeth, they bowed low.

"Great High Lord."

"Mighty High Lord."

"Stop saying that!" he snapped, causing them to flinch. "How did you get in here, anyway?"

"Oh, it was easy, High Lord," Filip explained. "We just climbed the wall."

"You climbed the . . . Wait. That wall is a hundred feet high!"

"They wouldn't let us in through the gates, High Lord. They sent us away. They would not tell you we were here. So we climbed. It's very easy for Gnomes to climb walls."

Note to self, Ben thought. *Find a way to make castle walls too slippery to climb.* "What about the guards? Didn't they see you?"

The Gnomes looked at each other in confusion. "It was very dark. No one could see us."

Ben stared. "You climbed the wall *last night?*"

"It was necessary, High Lord!" Filip said.

Sot nodded eagerly. "We have a problem, High Lord. We need you to solve it."

"We couldn't wait for morning," Filip added.

"Not out *there*," Sot declared, gesturing vaguely. "So we climbed the wall and waited outside your door."

Ben pictured this and was appalled. But only for a second because it was so typically them it didn't bear dwelling on.

"We have a problem," Sot repeated.

"We do," Filip agreed.

"Of course you do." Ben made a dismissive gesture. "When have you not had a problem? But you have to go through the gates and the front door and ask to see me! You do not get to see me by climbing walls and sneaking around to find my bedroom door and waiting for morning to barge in uninvited! And waking me up! I was sleeping!"

Both Gnomes nodded sagely. "We slept a little too," Filip announced, missing the point entirely. "Can we tell you about our problem now?"

Ben gave up. "Sure. Why not? Come right on in. No need to stand on ceremony. Mi casa es su casa. Feel free to make yourselves at home."

He stomped back into his bedroom and threw himself down on the bed. The Gnomes took this as an invitation and jumped up beside him.

Ben was too worn down to do anything about it. He did have enough presence of mind to wonder where Willow was. She had been there last night, hadn't she? Usually that meant she was there in the morning. But for some reason she wasn't today. Probably heard the Gnomes outside the door and was smart enough to get out while the getting was good. Still, it was strange he hadn't heard her go.

"We have a new pet," Filip began, and right away Ben held up his hand.

"Tell me you didn't eat it."

"No, no, it's *my* pet."

"When has that ever stopped you?"

"It is a special pet," Filip announced.

"A special pet," Sot echoed.

"I found it," Filip added.

"Sort of," Sot said.

They looked at him, waiting.

"So what's the problem?" Ben asked cautiously.

"My pet was stolen," Filip announced, a frown adding further displacement to his wizened features.

"Sort of," Sot repeated.

There was a nuance to these last two words that Ben didn't miss. "Stolen or not?" he pressed, none too gently. Time was wasting.

Filip was looking daggers at Sot. "It was my pet!" he snapped.

"You both found it," Sot replied.

"It was mine!"

"It was his too!"

"Wait a minute," Ben interrupted. "Someone else was with you when you found it?"

Filip made a freshly reworked expression of disgust by clearing his throat loudly. "Shoopdiesel."

Another G'Home Gnome that was always making unfortunate decisions and wreaking havoc as a result. Mistaya had encountered this one after her discharge from Carrington. But it was Ben, still in Landover, who was now stuck with him. Still, unlike Filip and Sot, Shoopdiesel never spoke. As far as Ben was concerned, it was his sole virtue.

Ben rubbed his eyes wearily, wishing he were back asleep. "So you and Shoopdiesel found this pet together?"

"He is my pet!" Filip declared vehemently. "I want him back!"

It was at this point that the bedroom door opened and Willow walked in. His wife took in the sight of her husband sitting in bed with a pair of G'Home Gnomes and raised an eyebrow.

"This isn't what it seems," Ben said quickly.

Willow, ever calm and steady, nodded. "Is it about the pet?"

Ben stared. Well, who knew?

ONCE THE GUARDS had been summoned and the G'Home Gnomes had been carted off to await Ben's call to bring them back (would he actually do something that foolish?), Willow sat him down to explain what she knew about this pet business. It was hard for Ben to ever avoid being distracted by his wife when they had these sorts of conversations. She was an exotic creature and he was desperately in love with her, so his distraction was understandable. Born to a woodland nymph so wild she refused afterward to remain behind to raise her daughter, and a river sprite that had spent his life trying to persuade her to come back, Willow had told Ben on their first meeting that in accordance with arcane fairy lore he was meant for her. She subsequently provided further evidence of her exotic nature when she demonstrated quite abruptly that she could change into the tree for which she was named, explaining that the transformation was a part of her genetic makeup. In order for her to survive, she was required periodically to take root in the soil of her birth world, something that seemed very odd even in Landover.

All this had a tendency to stay with you, married or not, children or not, King of Landover or not, and it did so with Ben. His fascination with his wife was further enhanced by the fact that she was beautiful and smart and altogether too headstrong. Where Willow was concerned, you never wanted to take anything for granted or assume she would do what you expected.

So in the matter of the mysterious pet, he was not caught off guard entirely when she surprised him once more.

"The pet belongs to Shoopdiesel, and I gave it back to him," she said. "He had it on a leash, it had his name on its collar, and he took it back from Filip when Filip stole it from him."

"Wait, wait." Ben held up both hands. "How did you get involved with all this in the first place? The last thing I remember was you sleeping next to me in bed."

She gave her emerald hair a shake. "Caeris woke me early to tell me there was a Gnome with a strange animal at the gate asking to see me. She thought I should speak with him right away. She wasn't wrong about this. I found him in a very distraught state."

Caeris. Her new handmaiden from her home in the Lake Country recently arrived to provide her with a companion and helpmate. Ben had approved. "She just came into our bedroom and woke you in the middle of the night?"

Willow shrugged. "She has my permission to do so, when she judges it important and does not in any significant way disturb us. I trust her."

Ben hesitated. There was nowhere reasonable to go with this. "So you spoke to Shoopdiesel? But how did you do that. He doesn't talk."

"He signs. His own Gnomish language, which I can understand. He doesn't need words with me."

"But you should have woken me. I would have gone with you."

She smiled and ran her fingers though his hair. Silken strands of moss (she was various attractive shades of green all over) trailed across his skin, tickling him. "What sense would that make? Do you really need yet another problem to add to those you already have?"

He had to admit he did not. Even though now, it appeared, he had one anyway. "Filip seems to think the pet belongs to him. Are you sure about Shoopdiesel?"

She shook back her long green hair and leaned down to give him a meaningful kiss, making it last long enough that he was soon kissing her back.

"Does any of this really matter just now," she whispered, pressing up against him.

He was pretty sure it didn't.

When he went down a bit later to announce his decision regarding the fate of the mysterious pet, he was feeling considerably better about things. He noticed as he was giving his verdict to Filip that Sot was nodding along agreeably, even while Filip was shaking his head in disgust. That pretty much confirmed what Willow had told him and he already suspected—the pet was indeed not Filip's. He emphasized that this was the end of the matter and he fervently hoped never to hear another word about it.

Then he sent them packing.

It was only later in the day that he thought to ask Willow what sort of pet the Gnomes were fighting over.

"I don't know," she admitted. "Some sort of lizard, I think. I've never seen anything like it before."

"Didn't they tell you what it was?"

"I'm not sure they knew."

For reasons he could not explain, this was vaguely troubling.

An entire week passed without further involvement with the three G'Home Gnomes. During that time, Ben tended to the business of the Kingdom and gave little thought to the mysterious pet. Willow left for a visit with her father in the Lake Country, where she also planned a surreptitious rendezvous with her feral mother. Court Wizard Questor Thews announced the beginning of yet another attempt to change Court Scribe Abernathy back into a human (he was currently a dog). Bunion, the Kobold scout and Ben's personal bodyguard, caught a bog wump prowling outside the castle grounds and dispatched it. A delegation of Lords of the Greensward appeared to negotiate for higher rates on the farm crops their serfs grew in the rich black earth of the midlands, and a second delegation, this one from the River Master, came knocking to complain about the Greensward's ecologically damaging farming methods.

Things were back to normal.

Until day eight, when the G'Home Gnomes reappeared, all three at once, and none of them were looking very happy. They managed not to climb the walls to Ben's bedroom, but simply showed up at the gates during business hours and were allowed into the throne room to present their latest request, demand, complaint, announcement, or whatever it turned out to be this time. On this occasion, it was a little of each.

"Great High Lord," Filip declared, bowing low.

"Mighty High Lord," Sot added, bowing even lower.

Shoopdiesel, as usual, said nothing.

Ben was sitting on his throne, something he did not much care for save when he wished to impart a certain impression, which he very much felt was necessary with these three. *I am King; you are not. I am not to be trifled with; you are not to waste my time.* He sat tall and straight and tried hard to look stern. He just hoped that his demeanor would suggest to them that they would get on with it and depart as quickly as possible.

As if.

There was a momentary pause in the proceedings as Sot prepared to speak, and then suddenly Shoopdiesel threw himself on Filip and began beating him. Filip, who already looked like he might have gone a few rounds, fought back valiantly but sustained a number of fresh bruises and cuts before Sot could pull Shoopdiesel off.

Once separated, all three stood panting hard and looking at the floor.

"I thought you were friends," Ben said finally, still a little dazed by the sudden display of violence.

"Hah!" snapped Filip.

Shoopdiesel stomped his foot.

Sot stepped forward. "Filip ate Shoopdiesel's pet."

At that moment Willow walked into the room, heard Sot's pronouncement, shook her head in dismay and, having clearly decided this was nothing she wanted to become involved in, turned around and walked out. Ben wished he could do the same.

"Why did you do that, Filip?" he asked the offender.

Filip pouted and refused to speak. Ben looked at Sot.

"He was angry, High Lord. He thought the pet was his and should have been given to him. So he ate it." A small hesitation. "He wasn't thinking clearly."

Nothing new there. None of these three was given to clear thinking. It might well seem as if they weren't given to thinking at all, but only to acting impulsively. "All right," he said after further thought, "what do you want me to do about it?"

None of them said anything, but after another few moments Shoopdiesel began gesturing wildly while making honking noises that could have indicated almost anything. He sounded vaguely bird-like, but the honking was long and loud and really annoying.

"All right!" Ben shouted. "Someone just tell me what you think I can do about this!"

"Shoop wants another pet," Sot answered. "Of the same kind. We want you to help us find one."

"How am I supposed to do that?"

"You are High Lord Ben Holiday. You can do anything."

Ben rolled his eyes. "Not in this case. What I can do is send you back to where you came from and tell you this matter is over and done with! Find yourselves another pet! Or better yet, don't find another pet!"

As if in response to this pronouncement, Filip began to choke and hack in the way of a cat with a hairball. Sot started pounding him on the back to help him clear his throat, and then Shoopdiesel joined in, beating on him for the most part, it appeared, for the sheer pleasure of doing so, intent on getting back at him for eating his pet.

Soon, all of them were beating on one another.

Ben jumped up, fighting down his anger and frustration, and called for the guards to haul them out. But before that could happen, Filip began to retch violently, down on his hands and knees, head lowered, drool running from his mouth. The hacking was bad enough that even his two companions stepped away, their wizened faces crinkling in distaste. Even the approaching guards hesitated, pulling back uncertainly.

Then Filip began to vomit, throwing up chunks of raw meat, one after another—a couple, a few, half a dozen, a dozen, more. He kept doing this long enough that it soon became clear that whatever was afflicting him was completely out of control.

Willow ran back into the room, rushing toward the hapless Gnome. But just then he stopped retching and sat up again, a dazed look on his face. As he did so, the chunks of meat scattered about the throne room floor began to move.

Willow turned around and departed once more.

The little meat bundles were growing legs and starting to walk around. Ben wasted no time on waiting to see what else was going to happen.

"Send for Questor Thews!" he demanded. "Now!"

Shoopdiesel and Sot hauled the unfortunate Filip back to his feet, and the three of them stood watching the meat bundles lurch back and forth.

"Babies!" Sot declared exuberantly. He clapped Filip on the back. "You're a father!"

Ben could hardly believe what he was hearing. Filip—a father? "He's not a father! You don't give birth to babies by throwing up! Males don't give birth at all!" He hesitated, examining this claim. "Wait a minute. G'Home Gnomes don't, do they?"

But no one was paying any attention to him, least of all the newborns, who were gaining speed and confidence the more they staggered about, bumping into each other and the curious Gnomes, their blunted features slowly taking on definition. They were four-legged chunks with a tail and a head, their faces scrunched up and wrinkled, all of them looking not unlike smaller, uglier versions of the G'Home Gnomes.

OMG, Ben thought. *Maybe they do!*

All of the Gnomes, even Shoopdiesel, were looking decidedly pleased by the unexpected appearance of the regurgitated meat lumps, thumping each other on the back and talking excitedly about raising children and the joys of fatherhood, ignoring what to Ben seemed a clear indication that they were losing touch with reality.

Finally, he shouted anew, "How can they be your children! They're pieces of undigested pet!"

The Gnomes ignored him completely, chatting and laughing among themselves, now engaged in nudging the little creatures about with the toes of their boots. The baby meat lumps seemed to like this, scrambling away and then racing back, frolicking about the throne room like puppies. At one point the commander of his guards caught his eye and silently beseeched him for directions. But he had no directions to give, and he simply motioned the guards away. Throwing out new parents and their newborn children, no matter how odd the species and the circumstances, seemed heartless.

At least the Gnomes weren't fighting anymore.

Finally, Questor appeared, his multicolored robes and bright sashes flashing brightly, his white hair and beard looking windblown. The moment he saw the babies, he threw up his hands and rushed over, dropping to his knees to join the G'Home Gnomes in playing with the little creatures. Ben wanted to rush over and drag him away but settled for exercising patience instead. When it appeared that patience wasn't going to be enough, he shouted at Questor to get over there and tell him what he was dealing with.

"You're my Court Wizard, for cat's sake! What are these things?"

Questor smiled benignly. "I have no idea. But they are rather cute, aren't they?"

Having witnessed the manner of their birth, Ben was not inclined to agree. But that wasn't the point. Cute or not, it troubled him that no one knew what they were. So he filled in Questor on the backstory and asked if any of what he said raised red flags or unearthed buried skeletons.

"Not a one," the other admitted. "But perhaps the squabble over pets is ended. There are enough there for everyone to take a handful. So they can all go home and stop bothering you, High Lord."

A fine idea. All for it.

"Clear everyone out," Ben ordered the guards, knowing a favorable opportunity when he saw one. "Parents and puppies outside, and then point one and all in any direction but this one! See that they have an escort for the first mile."

He took time to congratulate the G'Home Gnomes and clap them on their backs while surreptitiously herding them towards the doors leading out.

"But mighty High Lord!" Filip exclaimed at one point, turning back. "I want the chocolate one, and Shoopdiesel wants him too! Make him give it to me!"

Ben patted him on the head and leaned down. "If you fail to settle this between yourselves, I will take the pets away from you and keep them for myself! I will not let you keep even one of them, no matter how much you beg and plead! Are you hearing me?"

Filip started to say something and then thought better of it. Instead, he nodded, tight-lipped and red-faced, and raced away, catching up to the others and trying to snatch the chocolate one from the guards, practically knocking down Shoopdiesel in the process. The pushing, shoving, and arguing continued as they continued along the hall and disappeared from view.

"I hope that's the end of this business," Ben muttered to himself, thoroughly sick of having to deal with it.

Questor Thews came up beside him, stroking his white beard and nodding in satisfaction. "I think we can safely say that the matter is settled, High Lord. We should not have to hear anything more about the Gnomes or those little creatures, whatever they are."

Ben Holiday nodded. He was inclined to agree.

They were both wrong.

ANOTHER WEEK PASSED. A week of relative peace and quiet. A week without a fresh appearance by Filip, Sot, Shoopdiesel, or any of their new family. Word filtered back that by agreement Shoopdiesel had gotten to keep the chocolate baby pet while Filip had been allowed to name the whole pet family. Not surprisingly, he decided to name them after himself. He called them Filipians.

So for seven days the G'Home Gnomes and the Filipians hovered on the fringes of Ben's thoughts, but no word of further disturbances regarding any of them intruded on his personal or professional life.

On day eight, things changed.

Ben was finishing up with a delegation of farmers from the Greensward who had come to lodge a complaint about unfair treatment at the hands of the Lords of the Greensward—a tricky proposition due to the fact that Landover still tolerated feudal laws in that part of the Kingdom—when Questor Thews appeared at the rear of the assemblage making frantic gestures to catch Ben's attention. Excusing himself momentarily, Ben brought Questor forward.

The Court Wizard leaned close, keeping his voice low. "There is a problem, High Lord, that requires your immediately attention."

"Tell me this doesn't have anything to do with the G'Home Gnomes."

Questor pursed his lips. "If I did so, I would be lying."

Ben sighed. "All right. What is it?"

"The baby Filipians? They grew up. In the process, they seem to have found a way to multiply." He glanced over his shoulder at the farmers, all of whom were leaning forward, trying to hear what he was saying. "There are rather a lot of them."

"Multiply," Ben repeated, an unpleasant picture entering his mind as he did so. "Sort of like before, perhaps?"

"Exactly like before."

Ben felt like screaming. "You're telling me Filip began eating his own children?"

Questor pursed his lips so hard they disappeared into his beard along with his mouth. "Not only Filip, but Shoopdiesel and Sot as well. Apparently they thought this was a good way to cut down on the population. And, of course, they were hungry. The babies, I am told, did not protest. They seemed rather eager to be eaten. Perhaps so they could multiply. Perhaps they knew what would happen. Perhaps this is an example of the circle of life. I don't know. But now we have an entire forest full of Filipian babies, all of them running around without supervision, waiting for the inevitable, I imagine."

Inevitable, indeed. Ben felt like "inevitable" was the exact word when it came to G'Home Gnomes. "What do you suggest?"

Questor's brows knitted like kissing caterpillars. "Round them up and dispose of them in some way."

"Destroy them? We can't do that!"

"Really? Then let me provide you with fresh incentive. The babies have taken to eating crops out of fields and vegetables out of gardens. Like locusts. They seem insatiable. If we don't do something, we will have a riot on our hands. These farmers you are speaking to? Once they find out what is happening to their livelihood, they will be back with pitchforks and torches. I don't think you should wait on that."

Ben closed his eyes in dismay. Questor was right, of course. But there was something inherently wrong with what he was suggesting too. Still, they had to put a stop to this whole business before it got totally out of hand.

So he sent Questor off to make preparations and went back to his discussion with the Greensward farmers, hurrying them along with their litany of complaints and promising to do what he could to help improve their situation. It took some time to convince them he would be able to do anything, but in the end they agreed to wait and see.

By midday, he was riding out with Questor Thews and a small band of soldiers, headed for Longthorn Woods, where the G'Home Gnomes and the Filipians were currently ensconced. It was a warmer, sunnier day than when Filip and Sot had appeared in his bedroom and this whole business had begun. Ben took some measure of satisfaction in this pleasant change of weather, ready to find reassurance and comfort anywhere he could. He had thought about bringing Willow with them, but in the end had decided there was nothing she could do to help and she might be better off not knowing what was intended.

Bunion led the way, scurrying ahead eagerly, traveling much faster than any of the rest of the company, making sure the way was cleared of obstacles and potential dangers. The Kobold was so swift that when he reappeared it always seemed he came out of nowhere. It was so this morning, as they neared their destination and Bunion flashed into view with a Filipian baby clutched in his teeth.

Ben did not assume the worst, although those who did not know Kobolds might. Kobolds did not eat baby animals. They looked fierce and could be ferocious; but they were selective eaters. Mostly, they flashed their teeth when angry or threatened, which that was enough to ward off enemies or others intending to cause them harm. A show of one's potential fate is sometimes enough to discourage the making of a bad decision.

Bunion dropped the little creature on the ground where it began scurrying around playfully, trying to climb onto the Kobold, possibly to get back into its mouth. Who knew? Bunion said something to Questor (Ben had not yet mastered the Kobold tongue sufficiently either to carry on or even understand a conversation) and went still.

Questor gave Ben a look. "He says there are hundreds more waiting up ahead, running about like little rodents. In point of fact, there might even be thousands. He saw no sign of the Gnomes."

"Probably off looking for some other form of trouble to get into." Ben made a face. "Why do we have so few men with us? Don't we need something closer to an entire army to get these Filipians under control?"

Questor shook his head. "More men would just get in the way. Besides, trying to round up these little creatures by hand would take days. There are far too many of them. Magic will do the job more quickly and efficiently. I have something in mind."

Right away, Ben was worried. But he could tell by the way his Court Wizard spoke and the set of his jaw as he did so that there would be no arguing him out of it. There was nothing to do but hope that whatever Questor Thews had planned, it would work out better than it usually did.

His concerns were magnified when they reached Longtooth and saw how many Filipians the over-hungry G'Home Gnome breeders had produced. They were everywhere, running about through the trees, climbing over logs, grassy hummocks, deadwood, and themselves. They had not yet blanketed the ground, but they were getting frighteningly close. It appeared as if the entire forest was carpeted with romping Filipians.

Ben climbed down off his horse and stood looking at what must have been thousands of small bodies. How many Filipian pets had the G'Home Gnomes managed to eat to reproduce like this?

The answer was provided moments later by the reappearance of Bunion, who had disappeared back into the woods and now re-emerged dragging a decidedly miserable Filip behind him. Filip wriggled and moaned, but it was probably more from overeating than mistreatment.

Bunion tossed him down at Ben Holiday's feet, and the unfortunate Gnome cried out in a plaintive voice, "Mighty High Lord! I don't feel so good."

"No wonder," Ben said. "You appear to have eaten hundreds of your offspring."

Filip nodded sadly. "They just taste so good. I can't seem to stop."

"So now you have created hundreds more. All because you can't control your appetite. Do you intend to eat yourself to death? Because right now, I would not be troubled by that."

Shoopdiesel and Sot staggered out of the trees, equally fattened by Filipian pets. Neither spoke, both moaning as they clutched their distended bellies.

Ben was beyond disgusted. No one had ever told him he would have problems of this sort. It was bad enough having to deal with the witch Nightshade and the dragon Strabo and the Lords of the Greensward and the once-fairy of the Lake Country and all the rest of Landover's odd denizens without having to be plagued by G'Home Gnomes and Filipians too.

"Questor," he said quietly. "Will you please use whatever magic you've prepared and put an end to all this."

"No, great High Lord!" Filip exclaimed.

"No, mighty High Lord," Sot pleaded.

No, Shoopdiesel indicated wordlessly, using unmistakable gestures in place of words.

But Questor was already voicing the required spell. The air darkened to twilight and thickened with heavy mist; the temperature dropped precipitously and the sky filled with black clouds and lightning that streaked from horizon to horizon in jagged bolts. It was an impressive display, made all the more so by the fact that it was Questor Thews who was making it all happen. Ben found himself stepping back in trepidation, worried about where it was all going to lead.

"ARRRAZZZ MANTLE BOT!" shouted the wizard.

A whirlwind swept into the woods, scattering leaves and twigs and debris everywhere. Ben had to shield his eyes against its force, but he was able to discern large numbers of squirming, thrashing bodies flying through the air, picked up and swept away on the back of the wind. One might have thought the world was coming to an end and the souls of the departed were being lifted Heavenward—save for the fact that the things flying about were clearly Filipians.

The maelstrom of bodies and debris continued whirling as both king and attendants ducked frantically and in some cases fell to the ground, covering their heads in dismay, none of them even a little reassured by the fact that it was Questor Thews exercising the magic in play. But finally the wind died away, the skies cleared and things went back to the way they had been before.

Except for one thing.

Thousands of Filipians lay piled in mountainous heaps, all limp and unmoving, all immobile and seemingly lifeless.

"You've killed them!" Ben gasped, snatching at Questor's robes.

"What?" The Court Wizard stared at him. "Killed them? No, no, High Lord! What do you think I am? A barbarian?"

Ben didn't care to answer that question and simply stared at the piles of Filipians. "Well, this is all well and good, but what are you going to do with them once they wake up again?"

Questor rubbed his hands gleefully, a troubling eagerness reflected in his sudden smile. "Just you watch."

A second bout of magic-wielding ensued with Questor gesturing and chanting. Only this time the air stayed calm and the sky stayed clear and there was no thunder and lightning. Instead, rainbows appeared at every quadrant of the horizon, huge and brilliant arcs spanning the color spectrum and suggesting sugarplums and candy canes and the like. Slowly the heaps of Filipians began to encapsulate themselves in vast cocoons that took on the appearance of giant wasps nests, a comparison Ben found unavoidable and decidedly unpleasant.

Questor finished and gave Ben a knowing look. "Patience, High Lord," he said with a wink.

Ben waited. He had little choice. Long minutes passed and nothing happened. He began to grow uneasy, especially when he saw Questor frown in a way that suggested he was starting to become uneasy too.

More minutes passed. Endless minutes.

"Uh, Questor," Ben said quietly.

Then abruptly the mounds of encapsulated Filipians began to quiver and shake, a clear indication that something was about to happen. Everyone, Questor included, took a cautionary step backward and more than a few blades and spear points were directed toward the mounds. Bunion, who was standing next to Ben, hissed loudly, showing all of his considerable teeth as he did so. There was no mistaking his feelings on the matter.

"Questor," Ben said again, a little more urgently this time.

Yet when the mounds split apart, neither demons nor monsters emerged, but thousands upon thousands of butterflies in a colorful swarm of radiant wings. Fluttering in random flight paths, they were clustered in such droves as to turn the air about Ben and company into a dazzling kaleidoscope.

All too quickly, the patterns fragmented and then in seconds the butterflies disappeared into the nearby woods and were gone.

"There you are, High Lord," Questor declared, clearly taking great delight in the shock and awe reflected on Ben's face. "Problem solved. No one hurt, no one killed, and the world made a slightly better place."

Ben had to agree. It certainly appeared that way.

But, then, where Questor was concerned, appearances were often deceiving.

TORSHAK THE TERRIBLE was prowling the woods just north of Sterling Silver, searching for food or gold or trouble, all of which gave him great pleasure. Torshak was a Troll from the Jorgen Swamp, not all that far from the Fire Springs where Strabo the dragon made his home. He liked to brag that once upon a time there had been an encounter between the two, and it had not gone well for him. Although, if you considered the fate of so many others, apparently he had accomplished the impossible—he had escaped with his life.

But not, however, without souvenirs for his trouble, he was always quick to say, pointing out the ridged scars from claws and teeth and rippled flesh from burns that layered his mighty forearms and hands. He had been ill-used by the dragon, and one day he would make the beast pay. Didn't matter that it was his fault—which it was, he admitted—for trespassing on forbidden ground and then attempting to remove healing stones from the fire ponds in which the dragon bathed. He had been attacked and forced to defend himself against a much larger aggressor, which was patently unfair.

Which was not, as it happened, even slightly true. He had received his burns as a result of his own carelessness in building a campfire while drinking and not because of a direct encounter with Strabo. But that was how he liked to tell it—that he faced down the dragon, fought him to a standstill, and escaped with his life. It made a much better story, really.

So he blamed the dragon for what had happened and still, to this very day, swore vengeance far and wide. At every opportunity he would say to anyone who would listen, "One day, there will be an accounting. No one trifles with Torshak the Terrible and gets away with it! No such fool escapes my wrath!"

Which was when he began calling himself Torshak the Terrible and not Torshak Pudwuddle, which was his real name. You can understand why he might decide to do this.

Torshak liked to reinvent his own history. It made sense he would do so with his name.

On this morning, perhaps two weeks after the demise of the Filipians, he was feeling particularly wrathful. His head hurt terribly from the after-effects of consuming copious amounts of alcohol the previous night at a tavern in the village of Stink Whistle. That, and the blows struck him by the tavern owner when Torshak revealed he could not afford to settle his bill.

So, hungry and hurting and hugely disgruntled, he was looking for something to make himself feel better. Hence the search for food, gold, or trouble. Not very imaginative, but well within his manly comfort zone.

What he found, however, was something else entirely.

The first creature landed right in front of him, an insect more than twelve feet tall with a colorful wingspan larger still, claws each the size of Torshak's hands and mandibles that looked exceedingly sharp. It shrieked and rumbled when it saw him, making an unpleasantly eager sound. Torshak had no idea what this creature was and didn't think it necessary to find out. He began to back away, sensing that this was going to end badly for him if he stuck around.

But he only got as far as the wall behind him. Wheeling in dismay, he discovered another of these terrible creatures, this one no less terrifying than the first. He backed away in a different direction, seriously worried now. He was rapidly running out of space.

Then a third creature appeared, this one larger and more formidable in appearance than the previous two, descending from the sky and blocking his way once more. Now he was hemmed in on three sides with no room left to maneuver. He did some quick thinking—well, quick for him, anyway—trying to discover a way out of his dilemma. It occurred to him that if he were nimble and quick, he could duck under their wings or between their legs and flee to safety. But he possessed neither of these attributes, and in his present state—still hung over and aching from the blows he had received from the tavern owner—he was having trouble moving at all.

So he took the only course of action open to him. He drew himself up, faced them squarely, and roared, "I am Torshak the Terrible!"

Turned out the creatures didn't care.

They ate him anyway.

Then they began to follow his tracks back toward the unfortunate village he had come from.

IT WAS LATE the following day, and Ben was sitting with Willow out on the balcony of their living quarters watching a spectacular orange and purple sunset when Abernathy appeared. Talking dogs were not unheard of within the Kingdom of Landover, but you never wanted to make mention of it to the King's Scribe. Abernathy viewed himself as a victim of an incredibly careless and unfeeling Questor Thews who, once upon a time, had changed him from a man into a dog. He had used magic to do this, but magic ill-conceived and ill-applied, even given the urgency of the moment and the circumstances that required that this happen. Bad enough that he had done this much damage, but then Questor had found himself unable to change Abernathy back again. Although he had repeatedly tried, to date he had failed to make any real progress.

Well, except for once, but that's another story for another time, for which you can be thankful.

Abernathy still thought of himself as a man rather than a dog and struggled mightily to convince others to do the same. After all, he had his human hands and brain and voice, even if the rest of him was a Soft-Coated Wheaten Terrier, and those were the parts that counted. His vocabulary, in point of fact, far exceeded that of others at Sterling Silver and gave him a decided advantage in any conversation.

Not that he required much of an advantage on this occasion.

"High Lord, it appears we have a problem with the village of Stink Whistle," he announced. "A rather serious one."

Starting with the name, Ben thought. He had never heard of Stink Whistle and would have been perfectly happy if things had stayed that way. The one thing he knew he would never do was ask how the village got such an unfortunate name in the first place.

"What sort of problem?" he said, trying to sound interested.

"People are being eaten by large insects."

"Have they tried bug spray?"

"These are not normal insects. They are gigantic, carnivorous creatures. Literally, villagers are being snatched up and consumed."

Willow frowned. "What species are we talking about? I don't seem to remember insects like that anywhere in Landover."

"Precisely," Abernathy said.

Ben nodded slowly. "So, what you're saying is?"

"These insects are the direct result of ill-considered and ill-conceived magic," his scribe declared. "That's what I'm saying."

"Magic conjured by whom?"

"Questor Thews, once again practicing magic without a license to the detriment and regret of all." A pause. "I've warned you about this before, have I not?"

"Repeatedly." Ben exchanged a look with Willow. "I don't seem to remember him saying anything about creating giant insects, however. Are you sure he's to blame for this?"

Abernathy drew himself up, a sneer tugging at his dog lips. "Quite sure. Our overconfident and marginally skilled Court Wizard botched his attempt at transforming Filipians into butterflies, it seems. Some of those butterflies have become monsters with wingspans of twenty or maybe thirty feet and prefer humans to plants as food. Stink Whistle is bearing the brunt of this failure."

He looked so self-satisfied that Ben could hardly stand it. "Perhaps we should feel a little compassion for our friend?" he suggested.

"Compassion?"

"Yes, you know. Sympathy. Empathy for his unsuccessful, though well-meaning, attempts to do the right thing? I'm sure you will agree that none of this was intentional."

"I'll agree to nothing of the sort." Abernathy actually growled. "As for empathy, when he finds a way to turn me back into a man again, then I will extend him compassion and whatever else he requires. But not before!"

He barked at the conclusion of these last three words, something he almost never did. Ben sighed. "So how, exactly, do we know these creatures are Filipians? Or were Filipians, anyway?"

"After eating a villager or two, they regurgitated pieces of them. A characteristic that might remind you of another species?"

"So we now have more babies?"

"No. Now we have body parts. The kind that simply lay on the ground, waiting for someone to dispose of them. Rather a lot of them at this point since the creatures have eaten five villagers and seem eager to continue eating as long as there is anyone in Stink Whistle for them to devour. The residents of the village have barricaded themselves in their homes, which for the most part are constructed of stone and therefore safe enough. For the moment, the beasts can't get at them."

Which might not be true for very long, Ben knew.

He got to his feet. "Assemble a company of soldiers. We better go see what we can do."

For the first time, Abernathy hesitated. "Perhaps it might be better to wait until morning? Haste does not benefit those who rush to . . ."

Ben shook his head, cutting him short.

"Right now."

So off they went, a small army of the High Lord's finest soldiers along with Bunion, Questor, Abernathy, and Ben himself. Willow had given momentary thought to coming but she had done this so many times before that she decided it would be better for everyone if she remained behind. Having a woman along on a rescue mission always seemed to upset everyone, possibly because men always worried they would end up having to save the woman when it usually ended up being the other way around. Which was how she knew life mostly worked, even if men didn't want to admit it.

They rode horses north toward what had become known of late within the confines of Sterling Silver as the Filipian Woods, just beyond which, Ben knew from consulting with Questor, they would find Stink Whistle and the marauding insects. They covered ground quickly, moving at a fast pace, anxious to get as far along as possible before sunset. They didn't accomplish much, of course, because the sun had already been setting when Abernathy brought news of the need for a rescue. So they ended up riding most of the way in the dark, although two of Landover's moons were out that night and provided sufficient light to allow for safe passage.

It was well after midnight when the company finally arrived at the outskirts of Stink Whistle. Although Ben was expecting to hear sounds of mayhem and destruction, he heard nothing but the steady clop of their horses' hooves. No shrieks or screams; no grunts or roars. Only silence. When they rode down the main road leading into town, they saw no one. Apparently, they had arrived too late. It appeared the hunt for food was over, the beasts sated and the villagers devoured.

Ben spurred his mount forward, fearing the worst. The rest of the company followed, weapons drawn. They proceeded cautiously, peering into shadows between buildings and encroaching groves of trees, watching for movement. There were glimmers of light in windows, but shutters everywhere were tightly closed. They came upon the remains of a horse and something that might once have been a man, but nothing like the carnage they had anticipated. There were no body parts scattered along the roadway. No villagers fled through the streets and alleyways, seeking shelter from their hunters.

More gratifying still, there were no signs of new baby Filipians.

Huh, Ben thought as they reached the center of the village and came to a halt.

They were sitting atop their horses, looking around in puzzlement, when a nearby door creaked open and an old man stuck his head out. "They're gone!" he snapped.

Ben walked his horse closer. "Which way?"

"How would I know that? I've been hiding in my house for two days! Are you the rescue party we've been waiting for?"

"I suppose so," Ben said.

"Took your sweet time getting here, didn't you? Get after those things before they decide to come back! You got to figure out which way they've gone first. They fly, you know, so they could be anywhere!"

Ben looked at Questor, who shrugged. "Where is everyone?" he asked the old man.

"They're hiding in their houses, you dang fool! You think they want to get eaten like Jens Whippet or that Forney kid? Who are you anyway?"

Ben didn't think he wanted to answer that question, so he smiled bravely and said, "You can come out now. The monsters are gone."

"Says you!" snapped the old man and slammed the door.

Ben shook his head. "Questor, Questor, Questor."

"I am terribly sorry about all this, High Lord," the other replied quickly. "But how was I to know those Filipians could continue to change into other things once I magicked them."

"It would have been a good idea if you experimented on one of them."

"Magic is unpredictable, High Lord. Never forget that."

As if this were a possibility where Questor was concerned. Ben searched the empty, darkened skies. "Do you happen to have any magic that might let us track these things? Anything that would tell us where they've gone? We have to find them before they attack anyone else."

Questor looked at him indignantly. "Of course, I do," he said.

THEY RODE ALL night, making their way to the northeast of the kingdom, crossing into the southern reaches of the Greensward. Although they searched for signs of the winged creatures, they saw nothing, and no one they came upon had see anything either. By the time they had reached the Eastern Wastelands and still not experienced even the smallest sighting of their quarry, it was beginning to feel to Ben as if they were looking for a needle in a haystack.

It didn't help matters that Abernathy and Questor were bickering nonstop. It got bad enough that Ben thought about sending them both home. Except he needed Questor (well, maybe) to help him search out the creatures they were hunting. And sending Abernathy back would require he also send an escort to protect him. That would embarrass his Court Scribe immensely. Better to weather the bickering, even if it was driving him crazy.

When they were nearing the Fire Springs, he called a halt. Going further would mean entering Strabo's domain, and that was never a wise idea if you didn't have an invitation. Not that the dragon offered many, but you had to at least ask. So he sent Bunion ahead to inquire of the dragon if he had seen the winged creatures. It didn't pay to take anything for granted where Strabo was concerned. He tolerated Ben as Landover's King, but that attitude could change at any moment given his mercurial nature. Strabo was nothing if not unpredictable, and Ben had experienced the consequences of this more than once in the past.

With the arrival of dawn, Bunion returned. Always a difficult creature to read, let alone understand, he was particularly inscrutable this morning, his wizened face scrunched up with what appeared to be laughter, his rough language so punctuated by odd mutterings that even Questor couldn't manage to understand him clearly.

"It appears he found Strabo," the wizard said. "But I can't quite make out the result. He seems to be laughing about something."

Not very helpful, Ben thought, resigned to maybe trying to talk to Strabo himself, a not very compelling prospect. He thought about sending Questor, but the dragon had less regard for Landover's Court Wizard than he did for Landover's King. He seemed to feel a kinship for Bunion however, although Ben could not imagine why that would be.

The problem resolved itself while the soldiers were still waking, after being allowed to sleep for several hours, when a dark shadow fell over the entire company and Strabo sailed slowly out of the heavily misted horizon east. Everyone backed away immediately, save Ben. He was King, after all. He couldn't very well show fear even when he was experiencing it. So, instead, he stepped forward to meet his fate.

Strabo landed, and the ground shook. The dragon surpassed huge in the way a mountain overshadows a flatlands. He was a massive beast, all black scales and horny protrusions, great wings carefully folding back against his armored body. He loomed over Ben as if he intended to crush him. Intimidation being a large part of his persona, he crowded Ben's personal space and forced him to look skyward just to meet his baleful gaze.

"Holiday," he hissed, his breath hot and raw enough to melt iron. "I had hoped never to see you again. How unpleasant it is to find out I was wrong."

Ben straightened. "Just once I wish you would start a conversation with me that doesn't include an insult."

The dragon laughed, great jaws parting, revealing a hint of the fire that burned deep in his throat. "And what fun would that be? Tell me, does your neck hurt from having to look up at me? Do you regret that you are so small and puny? Others in your situation do, usually just before I eat them."

"I'm sure. Can we skip the threats and just talk?"

"Conversing with you is so boring. You have such trouble holding up your end of the conversation." His emerald eyes scanned the rest of the company. "Is that Questor Thews? Is he still Court Wizard? How pathetic! You really ought to find someone competent. Isn't he the whole reason you're here?"

Ben was caught off guard. "You know why we're here?"

"Let's just say I have my suspicions. I must say I keep wondering when you are going to get around to governing your kingdom in a reasonable fashion. Thus far, the concept of governing seems to have eluded you. You appear to believe that once you were named High Lord you were no longer required to do anything but sit on your throne.

Chaos reigns, your retinue of handlers wring their hands and engage in pointless efforts to do something, and no one seems to understand that it's your fault."

"Exactly what is it you think I should be doing that I am not?" Ben demanded, now thoroughly put out. "Who are you to sit in judgment of me? Who causes more trouble in this kingdom than you?"

"That is entirely beside the point. I cause trouble because that is what dragons do. This is not supposed to be the case with High Lords of Landover. High Lords are supposed to govern ably and keep things in balance. This is where you have failed, time and again. I cannot help but feel we would all be better off without you. Maybe it's time for a new King."

"Oh, fine!" Ben snapped. "You want to overthrow the present regime and bring in someone more able. Hasn't that been tried before? Hasn't it repeatedly failed? Miserably? You can wail about me all you want, but I am still better than the twenty-seven or so other Kings you had who all fled for their lives in the first week of their rule." He paused, calming himself as best he could with a forty-ton dragon looming over him. "What is it you are trying to say? What is your specific complaint?"

"*Specific* complaint? I have no *specific* complaint. I am in *general* dissatisfied with your efforts at ruling." The dragon sniffed. "But enough of that. I just wanted to voice my displeasure while I had your attention. Tell me what you're doing here, and we can all get on with our lives."

Strabo flexed his back muscles, and all of his considerable spikes stood on end. He yawned to emphasize his boredom and smacked his dragon lips lazily. "You know, I do like your queen though, the pretty sylph, so much better than you. Dragons are like that. Gracious and sentimental where ladies are concerned. We have a soft spot for such lovely creatures, especially when they are of the once-fairy. Such exquisite creatures." His nostrils flared. "Why am I wasting my time telling you all this? Why am I doing all the talking? Speak up, will you? I don't have all day. What are you doing here?"

Ben took a deep breath. "Apparently, you already know the answer to that. Three winged creatures of considerable size are rampaging through the countryside, killing people and destroying property. I want to put an end to it. Have you seen them?"

152

"Of course, I've seen them. They were trespassing on my property, trying to steal cattle from my personal feed lot—cattle I had spent considerable time rounding up."

"Stealing, you mean," Ben interrupted.

"Semantics," Strabo countered.

"So where are they?"

Strabo regarded him with an expression that somehow managed to convey scorn and disgust. "Why should I waste my time telling you? What do you think you can do about it?"

Ben shook his head in disbelief. "Oh, I don't know. Rid Landover of them, perhaps?"

"Really? Do you think you're up to it—you and this ragtag band of inept minions? Because I don't."

Ben gave up. "Just tell me where you saw them."

Strabo released a rush of smoky breath that engulfed Ben and left him feeling slightly singed and deeply violated.

"Look, Holiday. These are not the sorts of creatures that listen to reason. You will need to put an end to them. Termination with prejudice. I would have eaten them and let them burn to crisps in my stomach, but as even you realize by now, no one in his right mind eats Kringe."

"Wait a minute." Ben held up one hand. "You know what these things are?"

Strabo paused. "Don't you?"

"No. Why would I?"

"You are King of Landover, aren't you? Read up on the history and cultural development of your domain and its inhabitants, why don't you? Certainly Questor Thews must know what Kringe are."

"I've never heard of them either!" Questor declared from somewhere in the deep background.

Strabo spat out several gouts of fire that sent everyone but Ben scurrying for safer ground. "I forget how very young and ill-informed you all are compared to me," Strabo sneered. "Kringe are a form of changeling. Very dangerous because they make themselves look harmless so you will take them in. Nasty little beasts. Sneaky mean. They've been around for a very long time, although most died out a while back. I should know.

I assisted in hastening their departure. But they are a persistent species. Sort of like humans. That's what you've been mucking around with, the two of you. I suppose I shouldn't be surprised at your stupidity."

"They started out as pets!" Ben snapped. "They didn't look dangerous."

"I'm sure they didn't. But perhaps you've heard? Appearances can be deceiving?" Strabo shook his head as he looked past Ben at Questor. "You tried using magic on them, didn't you? But you don't get rid of them that way. That's not how it's done. Kringe are exceptionally hard to kill. As you have discovered, even if you should eat it, it will come back to life. Not that I can imagine anyone doing such a loathsome thing. Even the dog." He nodded toward Abernathy. "But I hear it's been tried by others."

Ben decided not to pursue this line of thought. "So how *do* you . . . rid yourself of them?"

Strabo leaned close, lantern eyes glowing. "Brute force, Holiday. Like unpleasant bugs, you stamp on them. You squish them flat."

Ben swallowed. "With your foot?"

"What do you think?"

"I think my feet are sort of small for squishing something that big."

Strabo straightened, giving Ben space to breathe again. "You might want to give that some consideration. Better to know your limitations, Holiday. Better to recognize them before you find out the hard way how big they are. Unlike your feet."

"Just point me in the right direction," Ben snapped. "I'll find a way to deal with the Kringe."

"Oh, you will, will you? How do you plan to accomplish this? Will you grow your feet bigger? Or make the Kringe smaller? Maybe you can just keep stomping on them over and over until they are flattened? That should only take a week or two, if you are persistent. And if they agree to remain still and not simply eat you."

Ben held his ground. "Well, what do you suggest?"

"I suggest you turn around and go home until you find a better way of dealing with things. This task is beyond you."

There was a long pause as Ben and the dragon eyed each other. Ben felt his chances for accomplishing anything slipping away. Strabo was right about him. It was difficult to accept, but when you came right down to it his reign as King of Landover had been largely ineffective. He should be better at what he did. He should be able to accomplish more. He was the ruler of an entire kingdom and responsible for its inhabitants and their welfare. Yet so much of what happened seemed to simply overwhelm him, to defy his best efforts and end up requiring others to provide solutions.

Now a talking dragon, no less, was taunting him with his failures. It was humiliating.

When he had left his old world behind after the death of his wife and daughter and abandoned the practice of law in the wake of his discouragement over its inadequacies and failings, he had thought coming to Landover to become King could provide him with a fresh start and a chance to accomplish something important. Never mind that he knew rationally Landover could not possibly exist and his chances of becoming King were next to zero. Never mind that he found on his arrival that nothing was as he had thought it would be and virtually everything occupying this strange world seemed to be set against him. What had mattered was that he believed in his heart of hearts it might be possible to start anew. Here was the chance he had been hoping for. This new life was what he had come searching for.

When it turned out his faith might be rewarded, he had been both flustered and excited by its prospects. But by now, almost twenty years into his reign, his expectations and hopes had taken a beating. He was weary of the struggle, and more and more frequently he wondered if he had accomplished anything at all. That he was married to Willow and was the father of Mistaya were things he could point to with pride. But they were not things he could point to when claiming he had achieved anything. It didn't seem enough to be able to say he had set out to be King and now he was. It didn't seem adequate that he had made the transition from lawyer in one world to King in another without being able to identify what exactly he had accomplished by doing so. It didn't feel sufficient that he had spent the better part of his twenty-year rule putting out fires.

Kings, he thought, were supposed to rule. But how much ruling had he actually done?

He wasn't a ruler. Not really. He was mostly a manager.

How could he take any pride in that?

Yet Kings really *were* managers when you came right down to it, weren't they? Kings didn't rule their kingdoms, no matter what they might tell themselves; they managed them. Just like leaders of countries everywhere, even back in his old world. All those leaders of nations seeking to make great changes and leave deep footprints? Mostly what they did was manage things as best they could while try-ing not to muck up the status quo. Those who ruled in any other way did so by domination and brute force. He could never be like that. He wasn't built for it. Maybe that was what Strabo expected of him but it wasn't what he was prepared to give.

Besides, he knew he was better off as a manager than he would ever be as a ruler. It suited him perfectly and gave him something he could feel confident about. It provided him with goals he could reasonably expect to attain.

And just like that, he had an idea.

"In spite of what you think," he said suddenly, breaking the silence, "I take my position as King of Landover seriously. I know my responsi-bilities, and I know what I must do to exercise them. But I know that I have my limitations too. Obviously, this is one such time. Stamping out giant insects is not an integral part of my skill set. So I have a better idea. You do it for me. For me, as your King, and for Landover, as your country, and for yourself so you may receive Landover's Gold Medal for Exceptional Service."

Strabo glared at him. "What are you talking about? Aside from the fact that I have no intention of helping you, there is no such award."

"As a matter of fact, there is. It was conceived of and designed by Landover's Queen Willow. The award was her idea. New, yes. No one has yet proved worthy enough to receive it. But you could be the first.

I have reason to think I can persuade her to award it to you. I will certainly recommend it, since I have no reason to want to have any further dealings with the Kringe. If she agrees, she will bestow it on you personally."

"I don't have any need of medals or awards or . . . that sort." He paused, thinking. "Of what is this metal is it made, Holiday? Gold, perhaps?"

Ben nodded. "Featuring a fist-sized emerald set within the center of a graven image of your face, since you would be its first recipient. Also, there is something to be said about being the center of attention at an awards ceremony featuring a Queen as lovely and kind and good as our own. Don't you think?"

Landover's histories recorded that dragons, even ones as large and ferocious and uncompromising as Strabo, had a soft spot for beautiful women and precious metals. Hopefully, offering both together would prove irresistible.

Strabo had gone silent, looking off into the distance. Ben waited, holding his breath. "Hmmm," the dragon mused. "An attractive offer, I admit. The pretty sylph giving me an award. It does seem appropriate, even for so paltry a task as this one." He paused. "But, I wonder. Could it be designated as more of a Lifetime Achievement award?"

"Done!" Ben said at once. *Yes!* "Congratulations. Recipient of the first Gold Medal for Exceptional Service to Landover! This is a proud moment for all of us."

The dragon drew himself up and nodded. "I suppose it is, isn't it?"

Ben smiled. "Now all you have to do is rid us of those flying insects, and an awards ceremony can be scheduled."

Strabo spread his wings wide. "Wait right here."

Lifting his great horned head, he breathed out a stream of fire that momentarily swept the sky and rained ash and smoke all over Ben. Then he spread his wings, and with an earth-shaking roar lifted off. Wind from his passing flattened grasses, scrub, and living creatures alike before he disappeared into the blue of the midday sky and was gone.

After awhile, from not too far off, there came the sounds of stamping. The earth shook and the air was filled with further roaring, and then there was silence.

Seconds later Questor appeared at Ben's elbow, his wizened face pinched with distaste. "Well, that was unnecessarily showy," he declared.

Ben nodded and turned away. Unsurprisingly, he was in a much better mood.

SEVERAL DAYS LATER, he received another unannounced visit from the G'Home Gnomes. Filip, Sot, and Shoopdiesel appeared on his castle doorstep in the company of a fourth gnome. This latest addition to the little band was another of those he had previously encountered and survived, an ingratiating fellow called Poggwydd. This time he didn't wait for the gnomes to be brought in, but went down himself to greet them at the gates. He ushered them inside and took them the kitchen, sat them down and had them fed. While they ate, he sat with them and waited patiently to learn what had brought them here this time.

Finally, when Poggwydd finished his meal, he cleared his throat loudly and rose to his feet. The other three immediately rose with him, heads lowered. Only Poggwydd spoke.

"On behalf of my companions, I want to assure you, High Lord, they are very sorry for all the trouble they have caused. They regret they were so foolish and unthinking in their behavior regarding the . . ."

He paused and leaned close to Filip. "Yes, the Filipians. All of them wish to apologize for their actions. They have promised not to try to find any more of these . . . creatures. And further promised never to try to bring one home again. All they ask is that you forgive them and tell them you are still their friend."

He stopped talking. All of them waited on him, the three with downcast looks occasionally glancing up to reveal expressions that would have been downright heartbreaking on most creatures but merely looked muddle-headed on them. But Ben had seen those looks before at other times and after similar promises, so he knew they were as genuine as G'Home Gnomes could make them. It was just too bad they couldn't ever seem to follow through.

Manage, not rule. He said the words to himself and smiled.

He faced the Gnomes squarely. "I do forgive you," he said to them aloud. "And I am still your friend."

Curiously enough, he meant it.

HARRY CONNOLLY

When I started working on The Great Way, I planned to write a big, sprawling epic just like the books I love to read. Unfortunately, the story I'd intended to tell in a single volume expanded so much that it became a trilogy of more than 370,000 words, even after I'd pared it down to only two point-of-view characters. There just wasn't room for subplots that set the scene or deepened the stakes.

But when Shawn invited me to take part in this anthology, I realized I had a chance to feature a few of those forgotten characters; their tales would not have to go untold. So I resurrected one of those subplots and wrote it so it could stand alone for readers unfamiliar with the larger work.

The story below takes place concurrent with the events described in *The Way into Chaos*, the first book of The Great Way.

THE WAY INTO OBLIVION

Harry Connolly

In Holvos lands, every patch of blue sky was a kindness. The end-less rainfalls made the canals overtop themselves monthly, it seemed. Where farmers in other parts of the continent struggled to find enough fresh water, here they dug drainage canals and prayed for an early end to spring floods. Song knew they could use a bountiful year, if the news from the north was accurate.

Despite the fact that a rare clear sky granted even rarer visibility, Alinder deployed the scouts far ahead of the troops, checking in three times a day. So far there had been nothing unusual, but they were only three days' walk out of Rivershelf, and war had broken out.

At least, that was the rumor. Peradain had fallen, quite suddenly, and the conquered peoples of the Peradaini empire, Holvos included, were without a master for the first time in generations. Rumor also had it that King Ellifer and his wife had been assassinated by soldiers wearing dyed furs, and that the prince—old enough now to take the throne himself—had fled in terror.

She glanced at the Red Salt River on their right. The ridge road had been built to give troops a commanding view of the waters, allowing

Alinder to see clearly that there was no one on the far bank. The fin of a river shark glided upstream and the okshim beside her, always skittish creatures, jolted forward, rattling the cartload of supplies they pulled. Alinder hurried ahead of them; when the beasts became nervous, they sometimes kicked.

It was peaceful here. The salt grass, the rice paddies on the western side of the road, the river rippling in the breeze. Her homelands were beautiful and now they belonged to her again.

Song knew Alinder herself did not much care what happened within the imperial capital. The Little Spinner never slowed; everything that began also ended. The thought made her smile. Peradain was less than a month's travel by road, but she had never loved her master just because his whip hand was near.

One of the scouts came running back along the ridge road to make her report to the captain. Alinder gestured to her children: *Come along.* The captain would not think to include them, but they were Tyr Holvos's heirs and they needed to learn.

Shoaw and Shawa did not run, but they did not dawdle, either. The three of them took up places beside the captain before the scout arrived. A slight twist in the corner of the captain's mouth betrayed his annoyance but he could not order them away. Alinder was elder sister and counsel to the tyr, and her fourteen-year-old son was the tyr's eldest male heir.

With a sudden thrill, she realized that, if Peradain had truly fallen, there was nothing to stop them from throwing out the whole business of kings, tyrants, and tyrs, and return to the traditional rule by family council. The tyr system, imposed on them for the convenience of the throne in Peradain, was no longer necessary. Goose bumps ran down Alinder's back as she imagined herself seated beside the tyr her brother as his equal. Finally.

"It is as we feared," the scout said. Alinder was startled by how young and scrawny she looked. She still had pimples on her cheeks. Not much for fighting, probably, but a capable spy.

"What numbers for our enemy?" the captain asked.

"None," the spy said. "The enemy has come, broken the gates, and withdrawn again. They have left okshim carts and supplies in the courtyard."

"And the troops within?"

"Many dead, captain. More are missing."

"Could Ronnet have engaged this enemy without sending an alarm to the divisions in the south? He knew his duty."

The scout had no answer and the captain didn't seem to expect one.

"We must withdraw," Alinder said. "Not all of us," she added quickly, before the captain could voice his objection, "but if the enemy has come so far, the tyr's heirs should return to the walls of Rivershelf."

Shoaw shook his head. "I won't. I'll accompany the troops to the outpost, so I can help care for the wounded." He turned to the captain. "We'll need the cart and okshim, won't we? To carry the wounded back home?"

"He's right," Shawa added. "If the enemy has withdrawn, we should help. I want to help."

Alinder silenced her with a scowl. "If the enemy that overthrew Peradain has struck against us, we—"

"It cannot be the same enemy," the captain said. "Even if they had come by river on the day Peradain fell, they could not be so far south after three days' journey." Of course, this is what Alinder had told herself before she agreed to accompany the troops to the station. Now that they were close, she began to doubt her certitude. The captain looked over her head at the troops behind them. "At worst, this is the work of Veliender bandits. We continue." Clearly, the tyr's family was welcome to join them or return south alone.

"Mother, it will be fine," Shawa insisted. "The scout said the enemy has withdrawn. Are we not safer with all these troops around us than alone on the road? At the first sign of danger, Shoaw and I will flee. We're faster than any northern soldier."

She wasn't faster than an arrow, but before Alinder could say it, Shoaw's bodyguard cleared his throat. "We'll watch over them." He nodded to his partner. "We swear it."

Shoaw was already at the fore of the column of troops; his sister ran after him. The bodyguards hurried to catch up.

"They're good soldiers," Elz said. Alinder was startled to hear his voice. Her own bodyguard was with her always, of course, but she rarely noticed him anymore.

She followed the troops northward, wondering if the tyr her brother—her little brother, even though he was almost into his fourth decade—had also realized they could return to the old ways of their people.

WHATEVER ALINDER HAD expected to see when they reached the fortified outpost, this was not it. The wooden gates were not broken, they were splintered. And the dead before the walls . . .

Not just bodies. Body parts. These soldiers had been torn apart.

The captain surveyed the carnage. "All ours," he said.

For a moment, Alinder thought he was claiming the victims' possessions for himself, but then she could see it, too. Every tunic, shield, and fallen banner bore the Holvos black and green. Either the enemy had carried away their dead, or the attack had been a one-sided slaughter.

"And here!" a soldier cried, much too loudly. Alinder and the captain turned toward the river and looked behind them. A wooden walkway led down the slope to a small pier. Two high-backed little canoes were tied off there. In the grass were the mutilated bodies of Holvos scouts.

"This was no battle," she said.

The captain said, "Take your children south."

A soldier gasped, and they turned toward the outpost. There, strolling through the gateway like a well-fed mountain bear at its leisure, came a creature like nothing Alinder had ever seen before.

It was huge, and it went on all fours, with its hindquarters low on crouching legs. Its shoulders and head resembled a bear's, but its torso was broad and flat, and all four of its legs ended in hands. Strangest of all, the fur that covered it was the same delicate pale color as the purple nightshade Alinder's grandmother had grown in her garden.

It turned away then, looking north. Alinder noted that its head came halfway up the wall. This thing was half-again as tall as the captain; they were all like children beside it.

"One moment, Captain." Alinder said as he was about to shout an order. She slid the sword from Elz's scabbard and ran behind the okshim. With all her might, she stabbed the tip deep into the haunch of the beast on the left.

It did not kick immediately—an okshim had flat, horned feet, which could have torn her leg off—but it did let out a high-pitched cry that gave Alinder goose bumps. She scrambled back, and the beast's kick missed her.

The cry of pain and fear startled the other okshim into motion, driving it forward. Both beasts went together—okshim always pressed flank against flank, if they could—jolting the cart so severely that a cask rolled off the back.

The captain waved the spears back, and they cleared a path. The huge creature that had emerged through the broken gateway turned toward them, alerted by the okshim's cry.

Alinder turned toward her two children. Their bodyguards stood behind them—*behind them*—gaping in surprise.

"To Rivershelf. Now."

As soon as the words were out of her mouth, a tremendous roar sounded from behind her. The guards began dragging Shawa and Shoaw down the road. Elz took back his weapon.

Alinder spun toward the sound of that terrible roar. Fire and Fury, it was like nothing she'd ever heard before. A grass lion might roar this way, if it were burning with rage and hunger.

The okshim balked, their forward flight from Elz's blade halted by the sudden threat from the front. The captain had already withdrawn his spears, putting the animals in the vanguard, and though the okshim lowered their great curved horns, they did not charge.

At that moment, a second creature leaped onto the wall from inside the station. Then a third. A fourth followed the first though the shattered gateway. All stared at the assembled soldiers like starving men before an unguarded feast.

With his spear, the captain jabbed at the wounded okshim again. It mewled and jolted forward. Both beasts, encumbered by their cart, charged toward the gigantic creatures.

The captain had understood her plan. Let these creatures feast on injured prey, while the troops—and the tyr's family—withdrew. Alinder's skin crawled when she looked at them. There was something supernatural to them, she was sure of it. One of those Fire-taken Peradaini scholars must have gone hollow and, in their madness, created these *things*. Song knew it wouldn't be the first time.

The first of the creatures grunted as the okshim charged, but barely glanced at them. Its gaze, and the gaze of its fellows, remained fixed on the humans. The limping okshim and their cart rumbled by them unmolested. The animals continued north, fleeing up the road.

The first of the great creatures—Alinder thought they needed a name but she could think of nothing to call them except nightshade-bears, and her grandmother wouldn't approve—stepped toward them, moving almost tentatively, as though worried it might spook its prey.

"Sprint line!" the captain called, and Alinder moved to the edge of the road so the spears could form up. These were a contingent from Fifth Rivershelf, and the tyr her brother had outfitted them with steel helms and the latest long spears. They drilled all through the day, shouting and sprinting in full armor through the streets and courtyards of the city.

And it showed. They came together effortlessly, five wide and eight deep, then ran toward their enemy with shields high and close, their points steadily aligned.

It did them no good. One of the enemy grabbed a corpse by the ankle and flung it, gore spraying from a crushed skull, into the line. The body knocked spears down like a stone from a catapult, and then the thing was among them, swatting aside spear points and slamming soldiers into the ranks behind.

Other creatures leaped down into the marshy borders of the road, coming up on the soldiers' flanks even before the captain could call for a defensive redeployment. Spears found their mark—many of them—shedding the monster's awful gray blood and eliciting roars of pain, but none of the wounds seemed to be mortal, no matter where they struck.

A cold shiver ran through Alinder. These soldiers were going to die. The entire column could not have killed two of these creatures, let alone four.

She glanced back along the road. Shoaw and Shawa were making good time, but the outpost had been built on a high point of the ridge road. They would be visible for miles.

The okshim had been no distraction at all, and Fifth Rivershelf would not be enough of one. Not to save her children.

"We must withdraw," Elz commanded, seizing her elbow. "We should have—"

"No!" Alinder yanked her arm free. "The tyr's heirs need time. Nothing else matters."

He looked into her eyes, his expression going blank with surprise. She intended to die here, for her children. It occurred to her that he might abandon her.

"I will guard you," he said, his expression going flat, "as best I can."

They turned just as the last half-dozen spears lost their will to fight. As their fellows lay broken and moaning around them, the last rank threw down their shields and spears and fled toward Alinder, and Rivershelf beyond.

It did them no good. One of the creatures pounced on them, slamming them to the ground, then lowered its head and bit.

"They aren't killing them," Elz said. It was true. Most of the spears were grievously injured but still conscious. The creatures moved among the fallen soldiers, biting each as though tasting them.

"Perhaps they have already eaten their lunch," Alinder said.

Glancing back at the road behind them, she saw her children and their guards. Fire and Fury, couldn't they run any faster than that?

One of the creatures raised its head and looked at her.

"It's time."

Alinder knew they could do little against the creatures themselves—every wound Fifth Rivershelf inflicted had already healed—but maybe she could move them off this high vantage point before they saw her children.

She ran down the wooden walkway toward the pier. He followed, backing up with his shield high and his spear point low.

"Hoh-wa!" Alinder shouted. "Follow us! Come down among the tall grasses!"

Elz immediately began to shout similar remarks, although of course the creatures couldn't understand. Alinder took hold of his sword belt, steering him along the walkway so he wouldn't step off and fall into the mud.

It took a moment before a grunt appeared at the top of the walkway—perhaps they wanted to taste every spear before they went after new prey—but when they did, they seemed hesitant. Two more appeared together, staring hungrily at Alinder and her guard, then warily at the river.

The fourth creature bounded partway down the hill, then scrambled for the wooden planks when it slipped in the mud. Alinder and Elz reached the thick salt grass at the bank of the river. Great Way, they were big.

Were they afraid of water? It seemed so. Every sane person knew to fear what lurked in the deeps, but—

Alinder's thought was cut short when the nearest creature leaped—splintering the planks beneath its tremendous weight—and struck Elz with its massive claw.

The bodyguard took the blow with a grunt and flew back into Alinder, colliding very hard with the left side of her body. She spun as she fell from the pier onto the nearest canoe, its hard wooden edges digging painfully into her ribs. The cold, briny water of the Red Salt River splashed into her eyes and mouth.

Elz hit the canoe, too, rolling it sideways and crushing it beneath their combined weight. Alinder thought she could hear, under the cracking wood, bones breaking. Great Way, she hoped they weren't hers.

The current pulled her from the riverbank. Fighting to the surface, she clutched at the shattered bow of the canoe. Her ribs hurt, but she didn't think anything was broken.

Elz lay still in the water, face down. Alinder had gotten him killed. She felt a twinge of regret, but she would have sacrificed ten thousand just like him for her children.

The creatures had retreated up the slope toward the road. The one that had leaped at her was frantically scraping wet mud from its strange, long-toed hind foot.

As she floated downstream, they followed her, running along the bank to grunt and roar their frustration. Fire and Fury, they were beautiful and terrible.

Alinder was all too aware that she was leading them toward River-shelf and her children. She kicked toward the sucking mud and thick grasses at the bank, hoping to slow her progress and lure the things to come after her again. Was the river shark nearby? Perhaps it would strike one of the creatures if she could lure them into the shallows.

It didn't work. The creatures would not approach the water, and soon they were distracted by something on the road to the south.

Alinder knew what they'd seen. It would have been a comfort to lie to herself, to hope that an old paddy farmer had wandered into the road, or a pack of Redmudd raiders were nearby, or *something*.

The beasts raced southward, and she floated along after them, clinging to the broken bow of that canoe. She knew what she would find.

Her son was first, lying on the slope beside the ridge road. She didn't need a second glance to see that he was dead; no living body could be so twisted and so still.

She saw Shawa moments later, kneeling at the edge of the road. Her left shoulder was bloody, but she did not seem badly hurt. Beside her were the two bodyguards. Both were injured; neither was dead.

Shoaw's bodyguard saw Alinder in the water. The man had the decency to look ashamed, but not to fall upon his sword.

The creatures were also there, of course. They stood over the injured as though guarding a meal. Alinder knew the creatures had faced scores of well-trained soldiers and that every injury had closed without so much as a suture. Still, Elz's "good soldiers" ought to die in the effort, if only for form's sake.

Alinder kicked toward the muddy riverbank. If those guards ought to die in the effort of saving her child, so should she. She didn't even have a weapon, but she knew the emptiness inside her was going to turn into grief and rage soon, and she would rather be dead than endure it.

Besides, a distraction might give Shawa a chance to leap into the river—

Her daughter—so frail-looking—noticed her, then shook her head. *Stay away.*

That look froze Alinder. Was Shawa telling her not to throw her life away, or that an attempted rescue would only make things worse for her? Alinder did not care a tin speck for the former, but the latter? It seemed that there was something here she did not understand, and if she blundered and made things worse for her little girl . . .

Hesitation made the choice for her; the current carried her slowly away. The creatures roared at her but didn't leave their victims unguarded. In fact, they prodded Shawa and the guards northward, toward the outpost—

Alinder thought this was the time she would weep, but tears wouldn't come. Her little daughter, so slender and fragile, had accepted death. Her son, the rangy, serious, restless boy that she'd once believed would become tyr over these lands, lay twisted in the mud like a heap of laundry.

Fire had taken her son from The Great Way. She could have tried to comfort herself with a trite saying about the Little Spinner and how she never slows. She could have cursed Fire for the death it had brought, or called to Fury for aid. She could have prayed to Monument for the strength to endure. She could have begged Song to remember, as Song always did.

In the end, she did nothing. She was nothing. *The world conspires to take everything from us in the end.* She had been reduced to a lump of meat floating toward the ocean. Something there would devour her and it would mean nothing. Her son was dead. Her daughter would soon be dead. Alinder had, by mischance, saved her own life and failed her children.

THE RED SALT River picked up speed as the land gently sloped downward toward the sea. Night fell shortly after Shawa receded from sight, and Alinder clung to her broken piece of canoe through the long hours, dozing sometimes, staring up into the starless darkness when she woke. Dawn brought a chilly gray light. There would be no patches of blue sky today.

Rivershelf appeared suddenly, when Alinder passed around a bend and the ridge road no longer blocked her view. The pink granite walls stood an astonishing four stories high, almost as tall as the walls of Peradain itself. It was the Holvos's loyalty during the last rebellion that had earned them such an engineering marvel: King Ellifer had sent his own team of building scholars to cast the spells that created it.

Alinder thought it was an ugly thing, but there was no denying its power.

Once, she'd thought her son would stand atop those walls. Once, she'd thought they would be his.

She did nothing to catch the attention of the fisherfolk preparing to spike giant eels at the shallow river's end—she wouldn't even look at them—but they pulled her from the water anyway. They recognized her immediately, and she was so cold and weary she had to be carried in a blanket.

The guards atop the walls said the tyr her brother was near the ocean gate, so the fisherfolk carried her along the plankways that surrounded the city wall on the east and south. Here, the scholar-made pink granite walls came right to the stony edge of the bay.

Then they passed the southeastern corner of the city.

Alinder had been to the southern edge of Rivershelf, of course, but never outside the wall. The waters of the Red Salt swirled and eddied here, flowing through the rocks, over the cliffs, and into the perilous ocean below. She looked at the bay stones, seeing the blood-red salt encrusted on those rocks.

Her father had told her the cliff was slowly crumbling. The waves below and the water running overtop had the continent in a slow retreat. One day, he'd said, the foundations of the southern wall would collapse, and it would topple fifty feet into the ocean below, leaving the entire city exposed. Then the great beasts of the sea would be able to reach up with their long tentacles and pluck the Holvos people from the streets.

Alinder could picture it in her mind: the colossal noise of tumbling stone, the screams, the futile prayers for Fire to pass them by. The deaths. So many deaths.

She shut her eyes. Her son had been killed. Her daughter had been stolen. The Holvos heirs . . .

The images returned. The screams. The falling granite. The shocked faces of the citizens, all of whom thought there would be at least another decade of life and happiness, another year, another hour.

Alinder knew her thoughts were a slender shield against her private grief. Soon, the tears would flow. To stop them, all she had to do was roll out of this blanket into the swirling waters below. She would be swept over the cliff, and die from the impact at the bottom or be swallowed alive like a grain of rice by one of the great beasts.

But she didn't. Her daughter was injured but still alive. A single square couldn't best those four creatures, but Rivershelf had long held more than a single square. Even if her daughter couldn't be saved, she might be avenged.

The ocean gate was barely larger than a door; no carts or wagons needed access to a cliff top that faced the open sea, nor could they travel the plankways. Fisherfolk called to the guards as they approached. Explanations were made, messengers sent, blankets laid across her. Something stank like an open chamber pot. So much activity, but Alinder shut her eyes against the city. She imagined the voices around her screaming, the footfalls fleeing in terror.

The tyr her brother would be coming soon, and so would Eslind, the wife of her younger brother Ilinder. When they arrived, she would have to explain what had happened. The truth would become undeniable. There was no return to her old life—she knew it—but to speak her losses aloud would be like declaring allegiance to grief.

Alinder opened her eyes at the sound of Eslind's voice. She had arrived first, her baby boy in her arms. The new heir, now that Ilinder and Shoaw were both dead. There was no ambition in her expression. Of course not. Only concern.

Behind her was a great curving wall of timber the like of which Alinder had never seen before, and that could have no use at all.

Finally, Alinder began to cry.

Not long after, her face still wet with tears, she stood before the Holvos court and the great stone chair.

The tyr her brother did not believe her.

Not that he thought Shoaw was still alive, or that the spears had not fallen, or the outpost remained intact. He didn't believe in the creatures she described.

"Describe them to me again," he urged.

She did, listless but still grateful for the distraction. A time was coming where she would have no distractions left. She did not think she could endure it.

Alinder described it all again, how the creatures' wounds had seemed to heal quickly, how they threw soldiers like crockery, how they killed like a grass lion in a chicken coop.

A thump of wood on stone echoed through the Holvos great hall. Alinder had been asked to tell her story in front of the court. Linder himself sat in the stone chair—not a throne, never a throne, not while they were ruled from Peradain—while his general, his spy catcher, his tax collector, and other influential figures stood at the periphery, whispering at everything she said. The only familiar faces missing were the Peradaini secretary and the bureaucrats he used to keep Linder in line.

The thump had come from the butt of a general's spear, struck against the ground. "My spears are not chickens to be plucked!"

Alinder sighed. "You're right. They were brave soldiers, and well trained, too. But it was four against your forty, and these creatures struck down your spears the way you would slap aside a child with a sharpened stick."

The general didn't like that, and neither did the tyr her brother. "Are you sure," Linder said quietly, "that they couldn't be men in disguise?"

"I have been closer to them than I am to you now."

"Of course. I should not have asked again. Allie, I loved Shoaw. He was a smart, courageous boy, and what happened to him will be avenged. As for Shawa—"

"We must search for her," Alinder said. "Not with forty spears, but four hundred. A large force might frighten the beasts into retreat."

"I will see to her return," the general said, "personally."

"No," Linder said. "Not yet."

Alinder gaped at him. "Not yet? NOT YET?" Her voice shook. "Shawa was alive when I last saw her. She may be alive still—"

"Yes," the tyr her brother interrupted. "And I love her as if she were my own child. We are Holvos, are we not? What people in all of Kal-Maddum values family as we do? However! We have to look after the city, the lands around us, and the people living on them as well. I learned long ago to take the measure of an enemy before engaging them. We need to send out scouts."

"Scouts!" Alinder remembered the pimply girl who had made her report to the captain. "Lin, scouts will not free my daughter. My only child. Any delay might see her *torn apart*." The last two words were ragged in her throat.

The tyr her brother was maddeningly calm. "Allie, we have been waiting *years* for Ellifer to pass from The Way. That he was Fire-taken during his Festival is . . ." He waved his hand as though brushing aside a housefly. "Lar is not the man to rule an empire. He has already abandoned Peradain and the Palace of Song and Morning. I don't have to tell you what that means.

"We are ready. We have been ready for eight years, waiting for the Throne of Skulls to pass to that scholar-prince. We have become wealthy, have armed our troops with steel, and have drilled them incessantly. I would match a Holvos square against any in Kal-Maddum. Peradain is ours for the taking, and . . . Allie, would you risk all that we have worked for to rush into battle against an unknown enemy?"

Alinder looked down at her hands. They were shaking. "Lin, I would send every Holvos spear and bow after her. I would press knives and hammers into the hands of every citizen able to hold one and march them upon the road. For my daughter, I would empty the city—"

"My tyr!"

A messenger boy dressed in the colors of a city guard stood in the doorway. All turned toward him; the boys would not interrupt unless there was an emergency.

The messenger bowed low. Irritated, Linder called. "Speak."

"My tyr, there are strange beasts at the walls."

From the guard post above the northern gates, Alinder, the tyr her brother, and his council stared at the long slope between Rivershelf and the marshes. The creatures moved among the yellow grasses, their fur standing out like spatters of dye on white linen. Now, he believed.

"What of those?" Linder asked, pointing to smaller, dark blue creatures.

Alinder shrugged. "There were no small ones at the ridge road outpost." Linder frowned and stared at them as though he might discover their secrets from the safety of his wall walk.

Silence. The world suddenly seemed utterly unreal. Was this really Alinder's life, to be standing here, exhausted and poisoned by grief?

"Fire pass us by," one of the sentries muttered. Alinder followed his gaze.

At first, she couldn't see what had alarmed the archer. The brightly colored creatures were withdrawing down the long stony slope into the marshes.

Unlike most of the large cities on Kal-Maddum, Rivershelf did not permit shacks and slums to cluster against the outer wall. Even the skin tents of migrant herders, usually so commonplace this time of year, were missing.

There. Human beings trudged up the slope from behind a clump of trees. Some were old, some young, some male, some female . . . They weren't rushing for the safety of the gate and the city walls. They shuffled like condemned prisoners.

One of the little children raised her head and Alinder felt a sudden spasm of recognition. Shawa.

Alinder cried out. She looked so tiny from up here, and the bloody stain at the shoulder of her tunic so large.

The girl, with all the others around her, moved listlessly into a stony clearing, then dropped to the ground like puppets with cut strings. They did not move again, nor did they appear to want to.

Linder stared out at them, his jaw set. Silence had fallen over the guard post, as everyone waited for the tyr to make a decision.

"General, although this is not my heir, it appears we must send troops after all."

The general nodded. "My tyr, we have a contingent of spears stationed at the north gate, two hundred strong. Let me take them out personally. I'll escort the injured inside the walls and kill a few of those beasts. Then we'll mount their heads on pikes, to discourage the rest."

"Only two hundred?" Alinder asked. "You—"

"Leave some spears to guard the gate," Linder interrupted. "If the beasts do not flee at the sight of you, bring back more than one color, to discourage them all." The general nodded to them both, then left.

The tyr her brother turned on her. "Alinder, you may be the older sister, but I am tyr. *Tyr.* I set the taxes. I make the laws. I command the troops. You stand at my shoulder because tradition makes you an advisor, but you will not come between me and my military again."

"Tradition." Alinder said. "Such a sour word when you say it. What did you mean when you said 'although this is not my heir'? Would you have marched out immediately to rescue my son?"

"Of course! I told you that family is important, but I have a people to care for. Shoaw was going to be tyr someday. King."

"Those are the ways of Peradain, Lin. *Peradain.* You talk as though Ellifer's ghost stands at your shoulder. The Holvos once ruled as a family, through a family council. Are you still planning to lay power on the male children of our line, as though Peradaini steel still commands it, or will you return to the tradition of our people?"

The tyr her brother—little Linder, who had put little muddy handprints on the hem of her dress before he could speak a word—looked at her with a cold, stony expression. The skin on her back prickled and she had no idea why. It's not as if her own brother would order her execution . . .

Linder snapped his fingers. The messenger boy who had interrupted the council stepped forward. "Get to the eastern gate. Tell the commander to open the sluices and fill the moat. Quickly. I want water flowing before the general returns from his errand."

The boy sprinted off. Linder was still angry but he said nothing. Whatever he'd intended to say or do to her, it would wait.

"They're just lying there," one of the archers said.

"Why don't they proceed to the gate?" the tyr her brother demanded, as though she possessed some hidden expertise she had not yet shared.

Alinder was wondering the same thing. Still, her brother made the question sound like an accusation. "Perhaps they're exhausted," she snapped. Alinder was exhausted herself. "All have clearly lost a lot of blood."

The tyr her brother couldn't argue with that. Soon, they heard the sound of the drawbridge lowering, then boots marching along the road. The square came into view, ten spears wide and ten spears deep, points spread in a fan. The general had only taken half the contingent.

The ambush, when it came, was sudden. A great flower-colored beast charged out of the tall grasses, matted stalks still clinging to its fur, and rushed the square. The general barely had time to shout a command before it leaped above the row of spears and landed inside the formation.

Later, Alinder would remember thinking there was a strange beauty to the battle. The square did not break right away, but the spears within rippled like water, flowing away from the creature and then suddenly rushing toward it again. It bellowed in agony as steel slid into its body, but all heads had turned toward it and none were ready for six other creatures that charged out of the grasses.

Two were the smaller, darker beasts. Their fur was deep blue like the most expensive dyes from the east, and she could see protective ridges along their backs and shoulders. Had she thought them small? In fact, they were only smaller beside their purple cousins; each was at least as long as a human being, with a deeper chest and more powerful leg muscles.

Creatures ducked under the spear points. They went over. They swatted soldiers to the ground like stalks of salt grass. Archers stood on the walls, arrows nocked and ready to offer support, but they had no clear shot to take.

There were screams, too. Many came from the meadow below, when soldiers were pinned to the ground and bitten, but some came from the guards around her.

In the end, it appeared that only six were killed. The others were grievously injured, and while the dead were devoured in broad daylight, the others were bitten—once—then herded toward Shawa and her listless gathering.

Linder held his fists against his chest. He had spent a fortune on steel weapons and constant drilling to create an army that could win him the whole of Kal-Maddum, and it was not enough.

When he spoke to her, his eyes were wide with rage and spittle flew from his lips.

"Did you urge her to this?"

Alinder had no idea what he meant. "Urge?"

"Shawa. Your daughter. Did you tell her to linger before my walls like bait, to draw out our spears? To undermine me? Surely you don't expect me to believe those *animals* set a trap for us."

The terrible empty space in Alinder's belly turned over. Was her brother accusing her of treason, of murdering her own son to take his worthless stone chair? She stared at him, waiting for him to realize he was speaking madness.

Instead, the tyr her brother addressed the guards beside her. "Take her to the iron tower. She is to have no visitors without my leave."

The iron tower was not made of iron. It was quarried black stone, but with black iron bars in place of a banded oak door. Alinder was locked in a cell on the top floor.

She wept until exhaustion took her, then wept again when she woke. Food was brought at sunrise and sunset, but no one spoke to her, and she did not care.

There was one exception: Three days after her imprisonment, a soldier appeared at her barred door. He explained that her daughter, Shawa, was no more.

Alinder had expected this news, but she was not prepared to hear what had happened. The soldier claimed that she had transformed into one of the creatures—he called them "grunts" after the sounds they made. In fact, all of the humans who had been bitten were transforming into the smaller, dark-blue creatures.

Alinder did not respond. He withdrew.

For the first time in days, Alinder stood and went to the balcony.

The iron tower was built atop a hill near the southern wall, and it was tall enough to look over the walls to the sea. What's more, the balcony itself had no bars; any prisoner who felt they had endured enough were free to pitch themselves onto the stony courtyard below.

Shawa was alive—transformed but alive. Alinder stared over the wall, beyond the cliffs, to the gently rolling sea beyond. Something was floating just beneath the waves—something gelid and repulsive, like a corpse as wide and long as Rivershelf itself. Then a section split like a tearing seam, formed a mouth, and lunged upward at a sea bird.

Alinder watched it float westward along the cliffs until the sun set. This world was full of terrible things, and her daughter had become one of them.

The days passed. Alinder sat on her cot or stared out to sea. Sometimes she heard screams of terror or wails of grief. As the days wore on, redeployments along the walls became more frantic, and so many funeral banners were raised that they obscured her view of the city.

She saw no more creatures break above the waves but she knew they were out there. When she felt especially lonely, she went to the northern side of the tower, which had no windows at all, and laid her cheek upon the chill stone. Her daughter was out there somewhere, ready to pluck Alinder and all her people out of the air like sea birds.

Just as the ocean held its terrors, the land had her Shawa.

FINALLY, AFTER THE moon had waxed, then waned, then began to wax again, Eslind appeared in the darkness on the other side of the barred door.

"It's time to go."

She slid the key into the lock, then swung the door open. Alinder did not get up.

"Allie," Eslind said, as though trying to wake her. "Allie, we must go. The city will soon fall, and I've convinced Linder that we cannot leave you behind."

"Linder?" she croaked. There was a bowl of broth on the floor. Alinder drank from it to sooth her throat.

"Allie," Eslind said, kneeling before her. Her baby—the heir—lay in a sling at her breast. So beautiful. "Do you remember the day we buried Ilinder? You swore that we would always be sisters. Now, Linder is taking me and the baby out of the city, in secret, and I insisted that he bring you, too. Will you come?"

Alinder stood. Eslind smiled and hurried to the stairs. "Quickly! The archers are upon the walls, but they have nearly run out of arrows. The moat has been blocked and the walls nearly sundered. Quickly!"

Two hulking guards awaited them, shields on their backs and swords on their hips. They held clay oil lamps with stubby linen wicks. There was a hint of sunrise in the east, but only the lamplight let them scurry through the dark alleys.

They did not turn northward, as Alinder hoped. She wanted to top the walls to look for her child. Instead, they turned south toward the ocean.

Pounding echoed through the city. The streets were full of wailing. The destruction Alinder had imagined that terrible day was here, but it had come from a direction that no one expected.

Eslind and the guards led her through the little ocean gate, then out onto the cliffs themselves. Alinder stopped at the edge. "What are we doing? Going to the sea?"

The heir began to fuss, and Eslind became impatient. "There isn't time! There isn't—Monument sustain me. Allie, some of the fisherfolk have been dumping sewage into a cove, a space where the waters are calm. That caused a bloom of red. No one is sure what the red stuff is, but the great beasts of the sea avoid it like poison. Look below."

She pointed to the foot of the cliff. A long wooden boat was moored there, in the shelter of a rock spur. "Linder has collected barrels of the red stuff, and of dried sewage, too. He's going to sail along the cliffs with the barrels submerged beside the hull. That should protect us until we reach the beaches of Espileth. There's no love between Holvos and the Simblins, but surely the steel weapons in our hull will buy us sanctuary."

Alinder looked around. There were great booms built along the top of the cliff, and a sturdy wooden ladder running down the rock face. She remembered the long, curving wall of timber she'd seen on the morning she was fished from the bay and the terrible stench of human waste. How long had the tyr her brother been planning this retreat?

Then she glanced to the east and saw, perched upon a rock, one of the blue-furred creatures. She suddenly felt as though she couldn't breathe. The thing stared at her, and she stared back.

Was that her? Was that Shawa? The plankways between that stone and the ocean gate had been destroyed, but Alinder felt herself drawn to it like an iron pin to a lodestone.

"Don't worry," Eslind said, "they can't come closer. The beasts don't swim."

Alinder looked down the long ladder. "My brother is down there?"

"Yes, now we must hurry. The gates will break before full daylight."

Alinder extended her hands toward the oil lamps the guards held. "Give those to me, and help the heir and his mother!" The creature— the grunt—was behind her. She could feel it watching.

The men gave her the lamps, then one climbed onto the ladder. The second helped Eslind down, then went after her.

Alinder leaned out over the cliff. The lamps were heavy with oil, but she did not need strength to throw them. Only drop them.

The burning wicks fluttered as they fell, but they were still alight when they struck. One fell into an open hold, spraying flame inside. The other broke through the top of a barrel, and the contents lit up like a flare. Within moments, the entire bow of the ship was aflame. Burning men leaped into the sea. A second barrel ignited with a sound like thunder, and the ship began to list.

The guard at the top of the ladder stared down into the flames, but Eslind, her helpless babe held close, stared up at Alinder, her eyes wide with shock.

The world conspires to take everything from us in the end. But Alinder still had one thing left. One chance to stop being prey and start being predator.

She went back through the ocean gate, toward the wailing of terror and despair. Toward her daughter.

DELILAH S. DAWSON

Sometimes I like my villains more than my heroes. In this case, Monsieur Charmant and Coco play a part in my third Blud book, *Wicked After Midnight*, but I felt like the reader was missing out on so many delicious details. Why did the magician have a metal orangutan, and why was that metal orangutan . . . downright depressed? What evil deeds went down in his strange shop? It was all too easy to descend into the darkness with Monsieur Charmant and watch him become obsessed with the only woman in Paris who didn't fear him, the only one who could tell him no. The inspiration behind *Wicked After Midnight* was basically vampire Moulin Rouge, so it was even more fun to push my villain into the decadent, glittering world of Toulouse Lautrec's cabarets, where everything is designed to entice and delight . . . even as poison lurks under the surface. If you like the story, I hope you'll consider checking out the entire Steampunk Fantasy Blud series, which starts with *Wicked as They Come* and includes three books, four e-novellas, and several short stories.

UNCHARMING

Delilah S. Dawson

The magician wasn't in his shop when his next sweet obsession slipped through the front door. She ducked into the darkness as they all did: shyly, clutching a wrapped package as tenderly as a sick babe, and perfuming the air with her terror and bewilderment.

It always took them that way—losing their magic. And Monsieur Charmant thrived on it.

From his underground laboratory, the magician twisted his mustache and shivered in anticipation as the girl pushed the door open with one hand and a shudder. The sound of her slippers on the boards nearly sent him over the edge as he removed his lab coat and shrugged into his natty red-and-white striped jacket. He could imagine her there, seeing the dark bowels of the alchemist's shop for the first time. She'd be beautiful, off-balance, fresh from the surgeon and still wearing the tracks of her silvery tears.

First she would see the heads of carousel horses crowding by the door, their lips pulled back in fury, showing fangs. She'd gasp and stumble back, knocking into the chair where unfortunate humans sat to trade their blood—or worse things—for coin. Oh, how fast she would gulp and lurch away when she saw the collection of antique surgical instruments hanging on the wall, rusty with long-dried fluids, reminding her of what she'd just lost. Perhaps next, she would seek the safety of his bookshelves only to find grimoires made of daimon skin and jars of dead floating things blinking back at her. Or perhaps she had woken the hound that waited behind the counter, grinning, tongue out, to growl at just the right time.

He was an artist of torture, this magician. He'd built his lair as lovingly as a conductor conjures an orchestra for just this purpose: to drink the fear and hopelessness of each new girl who entered his shop to bargain her past against her future.

A low growl went up, and a feminine shout signaled the perfect moment for the magician's entrance. After adjusting his bowler and straightening his bow tie in the mirror, he took the stone steps up, throwing open the door in the floor with a wave of his arm. As his head crested the boards, he found the girl just where she was supposed to be, backed into a corner and held captive by the monster hound. But instead of cowering and crying, as they so often did, she had stolen an umbrella from the stand and was fencing the ravenous dog-beast as if she thought she had a chance of besting it.

Foolish girl.

Beautiful foolish girl.

Oddly intriguing, damnably delicious, beautiful, foolish, foolish, foolish girl.

"*Arretez*," he barked at the dog, and it froze. "*Dormez.*" It fell over, already snoring, the floorboards shaking beneath its massive shoulder.

But the girl didn't toss down her umbrella. She pointed it at him and twitched her hips like a great cat preparing to pounce, the wrapped package flopping over one arm.

"Charmant," she spat like a curse.

His name was heaven on her trembling lips. She hated him. But she feared him more. And he drank it in like wine, his perfectly curled mustache twitching as he bowed deeply.

"Charmed, I'm sure. Welcome to my shop, mademoiselle. *Je suis a vous.*"

Turning his back on her, Monsieur Charmant strolled behind his counter and held out a hand invitingly. The scale waited, tared to deny the girl what little riches she might know from here on out. Usually, at this point, the girl minced forward and handed over her bundle gently, dashing away tears as the paper was unwrapped.

But this girl—she threw it at him. The package hit Charmant in the face with the weight of a halibut and slapped wetly to the glass counter, opening a tiny starburst crack where the bulk of it landed. That was the moment the daimon magician's heart cracked, too.

He would have this girl. He would possess her. And more than just the amputated limb that fell from the brown paper as he pulled the twine bow loose.

"Ugh." She drew away, disgusted by what had, until a few hours ago, been her tail.

Charmant looked up at her. At the part of her that still lived, that still blushed a delicate lavender. Every daimon was born one color but could change, like a chameleon, as it suited them or as emotions took them. She wore violet like a cloak of dusk. And he would see her disrobed.

Her tail, on the other hand . . .

"They all turn that color, when they're removed. Dead white. Just a chunk of meat." But his fingers caressed it from the still-bloody base all the way to the delicate stinger as if it was the finest ivory. His own, still-attached tail curled in desire, held slightly behind him where she couldn't see.

"Weigh it and pay me for my meat, then."

His lips turned up at the corners under his mustache. "So anxious to leave me, *mignon*? I am a powerful man. I know things." One eyebrow quirked. "I have friends."

She took a deep breath and straightened, wincing only slightly at what must have been considerable pain. Oh, how he longed to see the line of stitches. Would it be neat or crooked? Was the wound puckered the color of wisteria, still dotted with a bright red line? He licked his lips at the thought, lifted her tail onto his waiting scale, and leaned heavy fingers on the metal edge.

"Don't cheat me, alchemist. I know what you are. I know what you know. I know what you consider *friends*."

"Oh, but you really don't."

Her gaze challenged him, and he took his thumb off the scale and stepped back, both hands in the air.

"Seven kilograms. That's sixteen hundred francs, payable—"

"No!" She rushed past him, her floor-length gray skirts snapping. The brush of her sleeve against his guaranteed she'd get her way. At least at first. He could wait a little longer to cheat this girl.

The scale read eighteen pounds, and the girl's skin burned over a fierce magenta as she pointed. "Eighteen pounds, you monster. You'll take your pound of flesh, but you'll pay me for every drop of blood I've shed." Charmant nodded and stretched out both hands to rewrap the tail, but the girl smacked his fingers with the umbrella she still held and muttered, "Don't touch me, any part of me. I'll have enough of that tonight at the cabaret."

"Eighteen hundred francs, then. In silver."

"No. In trade."

She was lavender again, the perfect foil to the acidic chartreuse of his own skin. His last girl had been the green of spring grass. And this new girl wanted trade. How utterly delicious.

"What do you wish in trade, Mademoiselle . . . ?"

She took a deep breath and pointed with a shaking finger. "My name doesn't matter. And I want that."

The necklace in the glass case wasn't the flashiest of pieces, but the gold was real and the opal was cursed. It was worth twice what her tail was, even once he'd processed it into the many expensive components that, had she known of them, would've turned the girl's stomach and sent her running from his shop, from Darkside, from Paris altogether.

She had taste. But, yes, the opal was cursed. He held a hand to his heart, pained.

"You drive a hard bargain, mademoiselle."

"Madame."

She held out her hand, and he wanted to kiss every blister, run his tongue over the cracked skin between her fingers. He did the math in his head. A *madame* with hard-used hands, willing to amputate her tail and enter the cabarets? She was desperate, possibly a widow, at the very least destitute. Yes, he would give her what she wanted. Or what she thought she wanted.

Her fingers flicked open and closed. "The necklace. Now, *s'il vous plait.*"

Charmant kept his face neutral, his eyes flat as he used a scrap of velvet to withdraw the opal from the enchanted cabinet that protected him from the more troublesome effects of his trinkets. The lovely thing about alchemic magic was that one could truly kill with kindness, if one knew the right sort of spell. Without touching the stone or the chain, he arrayed the necklace on his counter in an enticing curl. She snatched it up as if he might change his mind and fastened the gold links around her swanlike throat, tucking it down the neck of her gown where it would nestle like a newborn snake against the crushable little bones.

"You know, madame—"

"My task is accomplished. *Au revoir.*"

He tipped his hat. "*A bientot,* madame."

She spun and marched to the door, her balance still off as she pushed through and disappeared. It would be at least a week before she'd learn to sway her hips properly without a waving tail. Another week still until she'd healed well enough to learn the dances of the cabarets, including the ones she would dance on her back.

In three weeks, he swore he would come for her.

He FOUND HER in the fourth-best cabaret. His costume was flawless, from the black silk topper to the perfectly tied cravat to the fashionable indigo of his skin. It was hard for him to hold on to such a dark color, but a few grains of the right powder helped. She was lavender, of course. Settling into a different skin color was all but impossible when a daimon was in pain. She'd be lucky to accomplish periwinkle until she had healed, much less show any grace performing the steps of dances that had not yet become rote. Good. He liked her that color, like a morning flower waiting to be tenderly defiled by a hummingbird.

It was intermission, and he ordered a drink and settled at the bar. The girls mingled with their patrons to the tune of a brass gramophone, their voices musical and cloying. He saw through it, but he saw through everything.

"You look lonely, monsieur." The girl looked up at him through long, red feathers glued inelegantly to her plucked eyelashes.

"Then you're not looking hard enough," he answered, spinning away from her and taking his drink along on the hunt.

He stalked his prey across the waxed floor, edging past tuxedos and sidling past wide skirts engineered to lift quickly without the trouble of petticoats. He saw no one but her. He heard no voice but hers, her laugh still strangled with the pain of a creature cornered. He sipped the steaming liquor in his glass but tasted only her blood, a delicacy he'd kept for himself when divvying up the meat and magic of her tail. He could smell her now, so close.

"Coco, bebe, I must tell you a secret," a young man said as he leaned in toward the delicate petal of her ear.

Charmant muttered a few choice words under his breath and flicked his fingers towards the fellow's hat, which flew across the room on a breeze no one else felt. When the fellow turned away to fetch his costly topper, Charmant took his place.

"Mademoiselle Coco, I don't believe we've met," he said, a genuine smile stretching his lips, which felt naked without his trademark curling mustache. But she would've remembered that, and he was banking on her forgetting, even if it took a dash of powder from the right packet in his pocket.

"Ah, but you already know my name, monsieur." She looked down, a clumsy coquette who hadn't yet found her feet in flirting. The thing he called his heart jerked in his chest.

"Please call me Thierry.

She tipped her head. "Thierry, then. You look familiar. Have we met?"

Fear flashed behind feathery lashes. Did she recall the hunger in his eyes as he watched her in the shop, or did she seek to hide her other life, her old life, the one that had hardened her hands and heart? As much as he loved her fear, he hated her doubt.

"This is my first time in the Moulin Bleu, *cherie*. But I find that I like what I see. Perhaps you would indulge me with a private audience later?"

It was a bold move, but they were both bold, in their own ways. She raised one eyebrow and straightened her spine as she had in his store.

"I do not give private audiences, monsieur. If you'll excuse me? Intermission is nearly done."

Chin up, shoulders down, she sashayed to the curtain. He sipped his drink and watched her over the steaming rim as she slipped behind the velvet.

Intermission was not over. And neither was his game.

MONSIEUR CHARMANT COULD not sleep, could not dream. His laboratory called to him.

She called to him.

There had to be a spell somewhere that would work, a powder or distillation that would draw her out and bind her to him. It was odd, how he didn't want to steal her and force her; he wanted to lure her and possess her forever. Rolling out of bed, he slipped into his robe and through the hidden door to his cutting table. The bristles were thick on his lip and chin, dark black against the acid yellow. Each night, he took out his brush and cup and soap, daubing his face with thick cream and shaving it away with a sharp razor. Each morning, the damn thing grew back, stubborn as Charmant himself, stubborn as his acid yellow skin. Each night, after shaving, he closed his eyes and forced his skin to shiver over indigo, placing a grain on his tongue to hold the color long enough to pursue the violet girl who obsessed him.

His Coco.

Most dancing girls chose new names, extravagant nicknames that they hoped to see on posters one day, hanging in the streets and lauded in the newspapers and magazines. But Coco? Where could a Coco go in the cabarets? No one would whistle through two fingers for La Coco.

Not if she kept flubbing every dance scene, snarling through every comedy act, insulting every suitor.

Not if she kept turning down *him*.

He was drawn to her every night, but she sidestepped him and avoided his questions and laughed away his concerns for her calloused hands and sleepless eyes. She gave away nothing, and her dancing did not improve a bit, and he liked her the better for it.

Monsieur Charmant was unaccustomed to being denied what he wanted most. And it was driving him mad. How else could he coax the damnable creature? Her fire was what called to him. But her fire was also what drove her away. Up to his elbows in grimoires, he couldn't find quite the right thing. It wasn't love he wanted. It wasn't compliance. It was utter possession that still left her eyes fiery, her chin high, her wound unhealed for his pleasure. And that's when it occurred to him. He knew someone who might be able to help.

He was almost out the door when he remembered he was still barefoot, in his nightshirt.

What was she doing to him, his Coco?

WITH HIS HAT brim pulled low and his skin a threatening shade of red, he stared out the window at hill after hill of boring moor grass, willing the train to hurry faster toward the dreadful creature he sought. The witch had settled in London, although few knew it. He had his ways of discovery. And she owed him for a tricky bit of magic ten years gone.

A day's worth of the fastest travel available felt like ten years. He would miss the show at the Moulin Bleu tonight, but if he found answers, it would be worth it. Not only would Coco be his forever, but if the trick proved successful and repeatable, there's no telling what he could earn in trade. Money had been important to him once. Now it was power and possession, the tang of owing that hit the air every time a client gave more than they really had. His hunger for fear, for terror, was what had originally led him down the dark path of alchemy. But it wasn't about sustenance anymore. He was a connoisseur, and he had wicked needs.

By the time he disembarked outside the tall walls of London, he was hungry enough for fear that he walked too close to old women, glaring at them with yellow eyes. Each tiny gasp was a drop in the ocean of his desire, and he longed for more. Whistling a few discordant notes, he called a host of feral rats upon the company and struggled not to laugh as the frantic humans ran in all the wrong directions, screaming. Sated, he walked right past the guards at the gates in the chaos.

Ducking under an outcrop in the cliffs below the towering city, he squinted, hunting for the right stone. A drop of blood rubbed on the dirty gray rock was all it took to open a crack into the catacombs so similar to those under Paris and yet so different without the beautiful mosaics and intricate configurations of bone. So plain, these Londoners. He slipped in like a maggot into the eye of an ossified corpse.

The witch's secret was the same as his own: the best place to craft magic is deep underground. She had no shop topside, but he'd heard she kept a grand studio of magic and herbs deep under the heart of Londontown, where the bones of mighty kings and queens slept and withered. She was here, somewhere; he could feel it thrumming in his blood like a moth battering against a lantern. The witch had needs, too. And since he had brought her choice gifts, he knew they could palaver.

Monsieur Charmant was surely the most dapper creature to grace the catacombs in decades, at least while alive. He passed some moldering carcasses long gnawed to the bone and stripped of everything magical. Poor London. With so few daimons, most of the magic was held in the hands of the fiends, and all of it was stolen. A charmer could buy powders and charms, tinctures and wands, a word here or there. But a daimon's tail was the root of magic itself. That's why the girls had to lose them before they joined the cabarets, of course; no client would wish to pay for the time of a woman with any power.

Although he'd never been in these particular tunnels before, Charmant carried a compass that led him, step by step, toward the witch's lair. His leather-soled shoes tapped the rock with jittery impatience, and whenever something dripped on his dashing red-and-white striped suit, a whisk of his fingers and a few murmured words sent it from his shoulder to the floor with a rude splat. He liked it underground well enough, but he preferred his stone-walled lairs to be clean and have a little style besides.

"Who's that tip-tapping on my bridge?"

The voice came from everywhere and nowhere and held a hint of a smirk. She wanted to play, did she? *Bon.* He could play.

"It is a stranger, lady. And I have in my possession the one thing you can't possess."

Her cackle echoed eerily. "That so? How *charming.*"

A light blinked on like the goddess of fireflies, leading the way. He followed, grinning.

"So my reputation precedes me. You know that I'm serious, then, Erzabet."

The light grew, and a twisted shadow fell over his lizard-skin shoes.

"I know you wouldn't walk into my lair to lie to me, Charmant. You know what I can do."

"And I know what you cannot do as well."

She sighed in disgust. "Come in and have a cuppa then, you smarmy bastard."

Charmant smothered his mad snicker as he stepped into her lair, not so unlike his own. She had no door, and she had predator skulls instead of carousel horses, but it was the same jumble of meaningful talismans, amusing diversions, and serious ingredients for the most powerful spells. The witch sat close to a glowing hole in the floor where a smokeless orange fire smoldered. Her shoulders were humped like a vulture, her face wrinkled and sagging with age. But her eyes were sharp behind the smoke curling from her pipe, and it didn't escape him that the raven perched on her chair could pop out his eyes as easily as a child shooting marbles.

Her head tilted like an ugly rock eroding. "If you think you can make this mug beautiful, Charmant, I can't wait to hear how. I've tried every spell, every cream, every snake oil. I'll be trapped this way for at least two hundred miserable years, and I can only hope to take down as many smug, pretty people as I can." She took a long draw on her pipe and held it, waiting.

"Madame, has it escaped your purview that you are, in fact, an idiot?"

The witch spluttered smoke, but a snap of Charmant's fingertips sealed her lips.

"You keep trying to make yourself beautiful, but that's impossible. You can, however, make yourself younger." He snapped again, and her mouth opened with a cough, billowing white smoke.

"Years ain't free, last I checked, daimon."

"Then steal them." Charmant pulled a small bag from his jacket pocket and dangled it just out of the crone's reach, minimal as it was. "I'll give you a year of my own to prove my solution."

"Name your price."

He licked green lips, twirled his mustache. "I wish to take possession of a soul."

The witch's head fell forward, showing gray hair marching down her back. Her cackle built from a burble to a mad cawing, and she threw back her head, showing old, ivory teeth in between shining white fangs.

"So you wish to trade impossibilities. I accept."

She held out her hand, and he stretched out his, and acid yellow met dead white over the cherry-red fire.

"But there's a catch," the witch said, eyes dancing. Charmant squeezed her age-spotted hand with skin gone red with fury, and she squeezed back with bones of iron.

Too late. The deal was done.

THE EXCHANGE HAPPENED quickly, each magician anxious to steal away to savor their new toy in solitude. Charmant shook the black dragon scales from his bag and bound them to the witch's right hand with whispered, slurry words. They sank into her withered skin, invisible.

"Grasp my hand and focus on my life force, on drawing it away like a handful of water. I promised you one year. Take a single moment more, and you'll suffer for it." He held out his bare hand, and his tail rose up over his shoulder, the barbed end aiming for where the witch's heart ought to be.

Erzabet's corpse-lips curled up as she reached for him. He braced himself for the jolt of panic he knew was coming. After focusing for a moment, he felt it—one year and one day, gone.

As his tail reared back to strike, the witch cackled and stumbled out of reach. "It was a leap year, Charmant. And damned if it didn't taste fine." Withered fingers traced the cracks around her eyes. "A few more handshakes, and you won't even recognize me."

The magician swallowed down his growl and held his other palm out flat, wiggling his fingers.

"You mentioned a catch."

He would have bet any amount that the witch's smile couldn't have been wider, but now it stretched wider still.

"You can possess a soul, but once it's out of the body, it can't be put back. Flesh rejects its wrongness."

"What the hell sort of bloody good does that do me? I'm not making a terrarium!" His skin shivered over with tiger stripes, his regrown mustache uncurling.

"Not my problem. You said only that you wished to possess a soul. You didn't say anything about what you wanted done with it. And you'll possess it. There's just not much you can do with a soul, sadly."

Charmant threw his hat into her fire and watched it burn, cursing the clever words he'd practiced in his head on his way down to the cavern. He should've known better and gone for detail instead of beautiful, succinct phrasing. Witches had no appreciation of poetry. But perhaps something could be salvaged.

"I can't possess it while the creature in question lives?"

"The creature will live, but soulless, a lump of breathing meat. You'll enjoy that, I'm sure. The soul's not yours until you yank it out. But it will belong to you, know you, be unable to raise a hand against you."

"And it can't be placed into another body?"

"Sadly, no. Flesh will reject a foreign soul."

Charmant's head shot up. "Flesh will reject it. But other materials won't?"

Erzabet's rheumy eyes twinkled. "Maybe. Maybe not."

The daimon's fingers wiggled again. "Then hand over the charm and free me to pursue this puzzle, witch."

She hobbled to a shelf hacked into the cave wall, rummaged in a dainty box, and returned with a spool of invisible thread. Dropping it into his hand, she gestured to a tiny knot winking in the firelight. "Get her to swallow that. Feed the thread to her. When it goes no further, reel it back. The glowing bit of fuzz that pops out will be her soul."

Charmant's eyes slid sideways. "How do you know it's a she?"

Erzabet laughed and waved him away. "Because everyone knows a man's soul is worthless."

BACK IN HIS own underground lair, Charmant lovingly folded his striped jacket and draped it over a chair. With a grim smile, he removed his cufflinks and rolled up his sleeves. His lab coat slid over his shoulders, perfectly tailored and charmed to never show the years of layered stains painted by blood, oil, and ink. Glancing in the mirror, he grinned at the dapper murderer he almost always found there. His mustache was flawless, and soon his spell would be, too.

He'd already dragged in another table, the pitted wood pre-fit with shackles. In the corner waited a stack of abandoned, run-down, or stolen clockworks, smooth faces and long limbs and rusted hooves jumbled together. Carousel horse legs, a dancing bear, a comical orangutan, a robot butler, a cluster of curves pulled from a burned-down bordello: they formed a tangle of steel, brass, and copper. But Charmant didn't see a mess. He saw a potpourri of possibilities. A few uncharred automaton dancers were mixed in, and he had already selected the base from which he would build his masterpiece.

Plucking a gas-powered saw from the perfectly arranged table of instruments and opening a fresh jar of silver solder, he flipped down his goggles and set the blade to a slender metal neck. The fluid that spilled out was close enough to blood to make him smile.

IT TOOK NEARLY a week of sleepless slaving to construct a vessel worthy of his Coco. With complete freedom over form, he fed his deepest desires into polished metal. Her legs tapered daintily, her hips swelled like a violin, her neck was more swanlike than a normal spine could allow. She was better than anatomically correct in every way. The face took the longest, as he had only sketches of his beloved and a poster stolen from the cabaret's wall to go on. He made her lips just a little poutier and curved up, her eyes wider and her eyelashes longer and hard as springs. With stroke after stroke, his sandpaper smoothed the metal and solder down to the softness of a girl's cheek, and soon the once disparate parts were unified with the perfect coat of lavender. The lust he felt while painting her nipples a rosy pink on mountains of shaded purple spoke plainly of satisfaction at a job well done. The automaton was, in a word, flawless.

Dressing her was a joy. Years of trade had amassed a collection of dresses and fripperies that would've made any real girl envious. With his usual impeccable taste, Charmant selected a celadon green gown, daringly low cut and trimmed with gold. Once slipped over the metal girl's head and over her still but pliant arms, it required loving tailoring with needle and thread. He giggled as he took in the waist, amused that his perfect woman required no corset and would never grow fat or old. The powerful limbs would never raise against him, never turn him away. A clever bit of spellcasting, that.

Finally, finally he stood back to take in her full form. All she lacked was hair, and he would stop by the wiggist later to fetch the most beautiful curls money and treachery could buy. He took off his lab coat, unrolled his sleeves, slipped on his jacket, and checked the mirror. The man he found there burned with an unnatural fever, his skin unconsciously matching the celadon gown and his mustache drooping and overlong. Whipping off his goggles and straightening his cravat, he twitched away his concerns and slid a hand under the automaton's back, his other hand under her neck. Lifting her for the first time, he shuddered. The daimon magician of Darkside Paris had held dragon eggs, unicorn horns, and once, a beating human heart. But until this moment, he had never known true awe. Clutching her to his chest and giggling madly, he danced a waltz, just a few turns around the cavern.

It would be even better when she fought against him as much as the spell would allow, tiny hands pushing him away but unable to bruise.

As if she could escape.

After planting a chaste kiss on her firm, red lips, he tucked the automaton into an armoire he'd fitted with hooks and manacles, just so. Closing the door on her stupid, beautiful face, he shivered to himself and made his final preparations. Tonight, his Coco would belong to him.

Forever.

"Do I KNOW you, monsieur le duc?" Coco's smile was more of a smirk, her legs crossing and uncrossing in irritation as he slid the champagne flute across the table.

"This is my first time at the cabaret, *ma chere*. And I find myself mesmerized."

He stroked his full beard contemplatively and glanced around the room as if hunting for a better toy. The courtesan's eyes shot to the duke's crest on his ring and the diamond pin in his cravat.

"You seem bored, my lord."

The man's dark eyes flicked to her, his blond eyebrows shooting up. "And you seem to be rejecting the finest vintage of champagne Paris can offer."

The girl looked taken aback but quickly recovered, swigging down the champagne as if her life depended on it. Glancing back, the man noticed the cabaret's Madame glaring daggers at poor Coco as she slopped the champagne down her front. He allowed himself a small smile. Couldn't let a human duke go, could they? Especially when he'd already paid.

Coco spluttered and giggled. "It's delicious, monsieur."

His hand cupped hers around the flute. "Then have some more. I have another bottle in my apartments, if you'd care to join me."

Coco's eyes shot over his shoulder as she obediently drank.

"It would seem I have no choice, monsieur. I'd be glad to accompany you."

He rose and smoothed his tailcoat. Tipping his tall hat and gathering his cane and the champagne bottle, he held out his arm to her.

"Please join me, then, mademoiselle. For I so very much wish to know you better."

SHE STRUTTED OUT of the cabaret, slunk out the door, and hopped into the waiting hansom as if being chased. Once he'd climbed in beside her, she wedged herself into the corner and glared at him.

"I don't like doing this," she all but spat. "This is not a life I chose. So use me if you must, but know that I'll hate you for it." His fingers twitched against the velvet, and she sneered and added, "But you'll pay me first."

In answer, he held out the champagne flute, again full.

"I've already paid your mistress. But after a few sips, my dear, you might not mind as much."

She grasped the crystal as if it were a viper. "I will always mind."

"I admire your ferocity."

"Overpowering me, I suppose, will make it all the sweeter for you."

He smiled, lips just a bit green beneath the peach-colored powder.

"Perhaps it will. They do say hunger is the best sauce."

SHE KEPT UP her hissing cat act right up until the coach stopped at the yawning mouth of a dark alley.

"These . . . are not fashionable apartments, then, my duke?"

"Surely you didn't expect to be entertained at the palace, *ma cherie*?"

He disembarked and reached a hand for her, and she stepped onto the slick cobbles. Before her fear could still her limbs, he dragged her down the alley and toward the arching gates of Darkside.

"Monsieur, I don't think—"

"Good. Don't think. Just follow."

His hand clamped painfully down on her arm as he propelled her into the twisting streets of his domain. She tried to break away from him once, but he caught her around her neck and waist and carried her with more strength than his slight body should have possessed. "I beg you to struggle, darling. But cry out and it will be your last."

She bucked against him, and he drank in the delicious beauty of a terrified mind and body fighting for dignity and safety. But her fine lips remained pinned, and he couldn't help himself. He brushed his nose down the trail of her neck, drinking in her fear with eyes rolled back in ecstasy. And this was simply the *amuse-bouche.*

The familiar black door opened at a whispered word, and she fought for real as she understood, finally, where he was taking her. The high whimper escaped past closed lips as she faced the shoppe's carousel horses, the bloodletter's chair, the jars of glaring eyeballs. This was where he'd first seen her and known he had to possess her, and this was where she had given up the last part of herself she'd owned in exchange for the locket shimmering on her neck. Thanks to the curse, it had been worse than nothing to her. And now she knew she'd gained nothing.

When he scooped her up to carry her down the stairs, she struggled and writhed, but she was no match for his arms, his lust, his magic. Her duke tossed her onto the scarred wooden table and clasped manacles around her slender wrists. And that's when she let out her first scream.

"You monster!"

Charmant turned to his mirror, digging too-sharp nails into his cheeks. The peach peeled away to reveal acid-yellow skin lit with desire. The beard fell to the ground with one good tug, and he tossed the blond wig into the fire, where it stank of wet wool and burned meat.

"It's just like the fairy tales, then, my love. You be my beauty, and I will gladly be your beast." He twirled the tips of his mustache in the mirror and turned back to her, love shining in his eyes like a wrecked train's headlights sinking deep into a loch.

"I am not yours," Coco spat.

"Oh, but you will be."

Charmant snaked fingers into his waistcoat pocket and pulled out a spool. When he gave it an experimental tug, Coco's shoulders jerked up, a look of terror and disgust twisting her fine features.

"What . . . what is that? What is in my throat?"

"Merely a bit of fishing line, my love. A consequence of fine champagne. Relax as I reel in my prize."

The thread was invisible between his fingertips as he rewound it around the cylinder. Coco's body convulsed as if she might vomit but couldn't find her own throat. Ragged retching started deep within her, and her eyes rolled back to show all whites broken with angry red veins. With one final, happy pull, Charmant tugged past the last bastion of resistance, and Coco's body bowed up from the table with a high, gargling scream.

The tiny bit of glowing fuzz that floated on the end of the invisible string resembled a firefly's light, and Charmant caught it deftly between thumb and middle finger. Coco's body flattened onto the table, mouth open and eyes blank. With his other hand, Charmant stroked the pale lilac wrist, checking for the pulse. Warm, alive. But mindless. So sweet.

Holding the soul-light carefully, the magician used every lens on his complicated artificer's goggles. Even at the highest magnification, he could discern no body, no form, no composition, which confirmed several things he had always assumed about what composed a soul: namely, that it was a useless bit of fluff.

He'd kept the armoire closed to avoid frightening Coco, although, in hindsight, it didn't really matter. Now he unclasped the door and threw it open to reveal the beautiful automaton waiting within.

But . . .

There was something wrong. His construct: she had fallen apart completely.

One of her arms had sloughed off. Her face had running holes for eyes, the rust eating farther and farther into softly painted cheeks. Stains the color of old blood seeped through her celadon dress, and the wig had fallen to the ground in an acid-etched heap of fur.

Every muscle in Charmant's body clenched—except those two fingers that held Coco's soul.

It had to be the solder. That brand new jar he'd opened, just for her. Every place he'd melted silver powder into the metal, every seam—they were all broken. Where had he bought it? Who had dared to sell bad solder to the most powerful alchemist in Paris?

He would find out later. And end them.

But for now, he held a soul. And its glow was weakening.

He tried shoving it back into Coco's fine mouth, but the blasted thing stubbornly floated back out, just as the witch had gleefully promised. Next, he tried to tuck it into a jar, and then a wooden box, and then a clay pot. But outside of his own fingers, the thing could not be contained and gently floated about as if gravity was merely an amusing idea. Charmant's goat eyes dashed around the room, frantic for some way to capture the soul until he could craft another flawless, timeless body that he alone could control.

And then he remembered the automaton's heart. It was iron and hand-hammered and didn't include solder. Perhaps it, alone, had survived. And iron was prized for its immunity to magic.

With one hand, he ripped open the celadon dress. A tug on the chest plate split the torso in half, the once-perfect breasts falling apart and clattering on the ground. There, in the center of the complicated mechanisms within, sat a perfect iron heart untouched by the foul, rusting acid. But it was useless without a body to move, and the damnable witch had said the thing wouldn't last long without a body to inhabit. With a growl, he ripped out the heart and tossed it on the table, where the wires dangled from it like tree roots wrenched out in a storm.

Charmant dug through the pile of automaton parts he'd so recently plundered to build his masterpiece and found nothing but useless chunks. Half a face, a leg, a belled metal skirt filled with cogs. Nothing was complete enough to hold the heart. Nothing had the wires, the capability of connecting with the soul as he'd dreamed.

Except . . . no.

Not that one.

It was finely crafted but inelegantly shaped. It was . . . hideous.

An abomination.

The soul-light was dimmer now, almost spluttering.

He hadn't much time.

He had even less choice.

With a feral growl and a savage yank, he ripped the body from the pile, scattering bolts across his once-spotless laboratory. A few hooks, undone, revealed a flawless chest cavity and a smaller, more primitive mechanical heart still connected to sensitive wires.

The soul-light fizzed like a candle flame about to sputter out. With a fingernail, he unscrewed the cover on the iron heart and slammed the soul-fuzz inside, flipping the door back until it clicked.

For the first minute, he held a hand over the top, praying to the bloodier gods that the damned thing would stick. It was all he'd ever wanted, and he'd held it in his hand. And now he just wanted to be rid of it. The way it stuck to him, clung to him like her harsh words—the thing needed to be captured and kept contained.

His hand trembled as he revealed the cold iron underneath. The soul-light stayed put, did not try to float out. First came a tiny click. Then the tiniest bloom of warmth. Then a glow that shone through the tiny seams. And then the heart was beating, the cogs turning, the fingers twitching experimentally.

And Charmant breathed again and went to enjoy a cabaret girl's soft, pliant, senseless flesh while waiting for Coco's soul to ignite the body of the metal orangutan.

The alchemist was, after all, a practical creature.

He could never have the Coco that obsessed him.

But now he had both her body and a new servant, one who had no choice but to serve him until her metal rusted away, until the long, clever fingers shattered to dust. The metal golem was bound to him with the darkest magic, unable to lift a hand to harm her master. As he climbed off the table and cleaned himself with a handkerchief, he couldn't help smiling, twirling his mustache.

Yes. Perhaps this wasn't the possession that he'd intended, but it was a possession nonetheless.

THE NEXT MORNING, Charmant woke covered in blood. Coco's body lay beside him in his bed, her arms tied to the post as they'd been when he'd drifted into beautiful dreams. But her skin was dead, cold white splashed with red. The daimon dancing girl's throat was slit in a wide, gaping, mocking smile.

Across the room crouched a metal orangutan holding his razor with long, dextrous fingers.

MARK LAWRENCE

One tip when writing a two-hundred-word introduction is to burn off at least twenty-four of those words in a tip about writing introductions. Eventually, though, you will be forced to tackle the topic in hand, which is: why this story, why here? Before that I should note that my introduction is a mild spoiler regarding the subject of this story, and so the purist may wish to skip what follows for now.

Why this story, why here? Actually, at Shawn's invitation I submitted a completely different story and "A Good Name" was destined for the *Unfettered II* anthology. But *Unfettered II* had to be pushed back, and I needed the rights to this tale back in my hands on a shorter timescale so that it could be bundled with my other "brother tales" later in 2016. So here it is. And that also covers the choice of subject—I've been writing backstories for the outlaw comrades (or brothers) of Jorg Ancrath, the main character in my Broken Empire trilogy. And this is one such!

A GOOD NAME

Mark Lawrence

The scars of his name still stung about his neck and shoulders. The sun beat upon him as it had always beaten, as it would continue to beat until the day came at last for the tribe to put his bones in the caves beside those of his ancestors.

THE YOUNG MAN held his name tight, unwilling even to move his lips around the shape of it. He had won both manhood and a name in the heat and dust of the ghost plain. Long Toe had led him out a name-less child. He found his own way back, bleeding from the wounds of a thousand thorn pricks. Long Toe had patterned him with the spine of a casca bush. In time the scars would darken and the black-on-brown pattern would let the world know him for a man of the Haccu tribe.

"Firestone, fetch me water." Broken Bowl rose from his bower as Firestone approached the village, dusty from his long trek.

Broken Bowl watched his cattle from the comfort of his shaded hammock most days. Men would come to buy, leaning on the twisted fence spars, chewing betel until their mouths ran bloody, spitting the juice into the dust. Half a day spent in haggling and they would leave with a cow, two cows, three cows, and Broken Bowl would return to his hammock with more cowrie shells for his wives to braid into his hair.

"I'm a man now. Find a boy to bring you water." Firestone had known Broken Bowl would test him. Many of the new men still fetched and carried for him as they had when they were boys. Broken Bowl might only have worn his scars five years but he had wealth and he could wrestle a cow to the ground unaided when the time came to bleed one. Besides, his father led the warriors to battle.

"Don't make me beat you, little man." Broken Bowl slid from his hammock, and stood, tall, thick with muscle, honour scars reaching in bands from both shoulders nearly to the elbow.

"I'm not making you." Firestone had carried Broken Bowl's water and his "little man" for years. He was neither little now, nor ready to carry another gourd from the well. On the ghost plain Long Toe had tested him, broken him nearly, left him dry long enough to see the spirits hiding in the dust, hurt him bad enough to take the sting from pain.

Broken Bowl rolled his head on his thick neck and stretched his arms out to the side, yawning. "End this foolishness, Firestone. The young men bring me water. When you have fought alongside the warriors, when you have Hesha blood on your spear, or a braid of Snake-Stick hair on your wrist, the young men will carry for you too."

"You're still a young man, Broken Bowl. I remember when you came back with your scars." Firestone's heart beat hard beneath the bone of his breast. His mouth grew dry and the words had to be pushed from it—like ebru forced cover before the hunters. He knew he should bow his head and fetch the water, but his scars stung and his true name trembled behind his lips.

Broken Bowl stamped in the dust, not just ritual anger—the real emotion burned in his bloodshot eyes. Two men of Kosha village turned from the cattle pens to watch. Small children emerged from the shade of the closest huts, larger ones hurrying after. A whistle rang out somewhere back past the long hall.

"Do you remember why they call you Firestone?" Broken Bowl asked. He sucked in a breath and calmed himself.

Firestone said nothing. He knew that Broken Bowl would tell the story again for the gathering crowd.

"Your brother found you bawling your eyes out, clutching a stone from the fire to your chest." Broken Bowl rubbed his fists against his eyes, mocking those tears. "Your father had to take the stone from you and he cursed as it burned him."

Firestone felt the eyes of the children on his chest. The scars there had a melted quality to them. One of the Kosha men laughed, a lean fellow with a bone plate through his nose.

"Your name is a lesson, Firestone. About when to put something down and walk away." Broken Bowl cracked his knuckles. "Put this down. Walk away."

Firestone carried no weapon, he had a spear in his father's hut, warped, its point fire-hardened wood. Broken Bowl had a bronze curas at his hip on the leather strap that held his loincloth. The larger man made no move to draw it though. He would beat Firestone bloody but do no murder. Not today. Even now Firestone could fetch the water and escape with nothing more than a slap or two.

"Harrac." Firestone whispered his true name, curling his lips around the sound. Every prick of that casca spine lanced again through his skin as he spoke his name—all of them at once—a thousand stabs, a liquid pain. He threw himself forward, the lion's snarl bursting from him.

Perhaps he was faster than he had thought—and he had thought himself fast. Perhaps Broken Bowl hadn't taken him seriously, or had expected threats and stamping. Either way, when Harrac leapt, Broken Bowl reached for him too slow, fumbled his grapple, and the top of Harrac's forehead smashed into Broken Bowl's cheek and nose.

They went down together. Broken Bowl hammering into the dust, Harrac on top, pounding the edge of his hand into Broken Bowl's face. Broken Bowl threw him off—the man's strength amazed Harrac but didn't daunt him. In two heartbeats he was back on his foe. Broken Bowl managed to turn onto his side but Harrac threw his weight upon the man's back as he tried to rise. Harrac drove his elbow into the back of Broken Bowl's neck, brought his knee up into his ribs, pressed his face into the ground with his other hand. A red fury seized him and he didn't stop pounding his foe until the men of the village pulled him off.

Harrac sat on the ground, sweat cutting paths through the dust caking his limbs. The crowd about him, an indivisible many, their words just noise beneath the rush of his breathing and the din of his heart. From the corner of his eye he saw five men carry Broken Bowl toward the huts. Later his father came, and Broken Bowl's father, and Carry Iron in his headman's cloak of feathers, and Long Toe, Ten Legs, Spiller . . . all the elders.

"I am a man," Harrac said when he stood before them, with the village watching on. "I have a name. I have a man's strength."

"Then why do you not use it as a man?" His own father, three of Harrac's grown brothers at his shoulders.

"I would not carry water for him," Harrac said.

"Maybe nobody will have to carry water for my son again." Red Sky made the sign of sorrow, his hand descending on a wavered path. "There is no disputing your right to fight him. But you fought as though he were our enemy, not a brother."

"I . . ." Harrac drew in a long breath. "There is only fighting or not fighting. Fight or do not. He didn't ask me to dance."

A muted ripple of laughter through the children, but the men exchanged glances. Red Sky turned to look at Harrac's father. Carry Iron looked too, the blackwood club in his hand.

"You must go to Ibowen, Firestone. Tell the king what you have done. He will send you back to us, or he won't."

It made no sense. Why would Harrac's own father try to steal his victory? Were they jealous? Just three days a man and already he had humbled Broken Bowl. Harrac felt the red tide of anger rising in him again. He set his jaw and looked Carry Iron in the eye. "I will go to the king."

He turned and started walking, knowing they all watched him, knowing the stories and talk around the fires tonight would be his.

Pride and anger bubbled in him, a bitter taste in his mouth. He spat his own blood as he walked, red as betel juice.

A mile on, Harrac stopped by the marula trees, anger, pride, bitterness, gone, as if it had leaked from him, colouring his footprints. He crouched in the shade wondering what madness took him, sore in every limb. He carried no food, no water, he didn't even know the way to Ibowen. West, past the River Ugwye. Not the best of directions. Lion country too. No place for a man alone.

He sat for the longest time, staring at his hands, the same hands that had beaten Broken Bowl. He remembered the looks shot his way as the men had carried Broken Bowl toward the huts. A mix of disgust and horror, as if he were a rabid dog rather than a warrior. Harrac's eyes prickled with tears, though he couldn't say who they might be for.

Three days he'd carried his name before disgracing it. One day recovering, two days walking, and just minutes beneath the eyes of his village. Long Toe had said there were deeper secrets to a man's name but that the elders did not teach them, only pointed the way across the years—they were learned, or not, as a man carried his name beneath the sun. Long Toe said the secrets lay in the Haccu songs and stories, and in the way men lived, set in full view. Harrac wondered what the king-of-many-tribes would say. If he was sent away he would never know the full truth signified by his true name, earned in pain and suffering.

RAGGED TAIL, THE eldest of Harrac's three younger brothers, came to him as the sky shaded red in the west. He bought a hard slab of bread-cake, a grass bag of lebo nuts, and a gourd of water.

"Broken Bowl has woken." Ragged Tail watched his brother with wide eyes as if he were a wild creature off the yellow grass, seen for the first time. "He has broken ribs but Long Toe thinks he will recover."

"Ribs?" Harrac didn't even remember hitting him in the side. He drank from the heavy gourd. "You fetched me water, 'Tail."

"You're my brother." He didn't sound entirely sure.

Harrac put his hand on 'Tail's shoulder. "Fetch water whoever asks you. Make all men your brother." He took the gourd, the bag, and the bread-cake, then started to walk.

"You're not coming back?" 'Tail called after him.

"I'm a man now. I can't just say sorry. I have to do what Carry Iron told me to do."

Ibowen lay farther from Harrac's village than he had ever imagined, and the city itself lay farther beyond his imagination still. First he discovered a road—a trail beaten into the ground by the passage of many feet, marked with stones, rutted with wheels. Then came the houses. It seemed that a thousand villages had gathered together. It started as clusters of huts made from mud and straw, though taller than those of the Haccu, but before long the buildings became mud-brick, hard-angled, longer than the long hall, taller than a man holding his spear above him. Harrac walked through a wholly alien landscape, without grass, without views to the distance, hardly a tree, everything edges and windows, noise, strangers, multitudes, none of them interested in his arrival. They spoke strange languages here, or familiar ones with strange voices.

At length, following the directions of a man who recognised his Haccu scars, Harrac came to the high mud walls of the king's palace. He circled, tracking around the perimeter, passing dozens of houses that put Carry Iron's hut to shame. The palace gates stood taller than an elephant, thick timbers bound with an extravagance of iron, gates that would stand against a hundred men.

A multitude camped around the entrance, naked children, men in loincloths, priests with bird-skull necklaces and the ia-lines painted red across their arms and chests, warriors with spears and so many honour scars they almost lacked the skin for more.

Two warriors stood by the gates, splendid in leopard skins, ostrich feathers in their woven hair, iron-tipped spears, curved iron swords at their hips. Strangest of all though, the man standing in conversation with one of the pair, his back to Harrac as he worked his way through the seated crowds.

Where the man wasn't covered in folds of white linen, he had the palest skin Harrac had ever seen, white as fish meat on his hands, an angry red on his forearms. And his hair—a white mass of it beneath a broad-brimmed hat of woven grass.

Harrac came closer still and realised how huge the man was. Head and shoulders above the guardsmen, but both of those were as tall as any man Harrac knew, and this man stood thick with muscle, far broader across the shoulders than Broken Bowl, a white giant.

The man turned as Harrac approached.

"A boy fresh in off the grassland." The white man grinned down at Harrac, his teeth showing amid the thickest beard, cut close to his chin. He watched for a reply, then narrowed his pale blue eyes. "Did I say it wrong? You look Haccu to me."

"I am Haccu."

"What's your name, boy?"

Harrac found himself on the point of speaking his true name to a stranger. "Firestone. I'm a man of the tribe." He turned to the closest of the plumed guards. "My headman sent me to speak with the king."

The guardsman nodded, unsmiling, toward the crowd. "Wait."

Harrac looked back. The people seemed settled in for a stay of days or more, food supplies heaped beside them, shelters erected to provide shade. "For how long?"

The guardsman stared ahead as if no longer seeing anyone before him. Harrac felt his name scars sting, his pride pricking him even in this strange place of walls and iron. He stood, immobile, held between the angry heat in his blood and the cold fact of his station. Older and more important men than him sat waiting by the roadside—the doors belonged to the king-of-many-tribes. And still he couldn't walk away.

"Ha! The boy doesn't like to wait." The huge foreigner grinned still more broadly. "And who does? Especially in this damned heat!" He reached out to slap Harrac's shoulder.

Harrac caught the white man's wrist. He felt ridges of scar tissue beneath his fingers. "I am a man."

"Of course you are. Firestone wasn't it?" The man looked surprised, though with his face half covered in beard it was hard to tell. "I'm Snaga ver Olaafson. May I have my arm back?"

Harrac released Snaga's wrist and the big man made a show of rubbing it. The scars there were ugly—nothing ritual about them—matched on the other wrist.

"Snaga?" Harrac asked. "Why do they call you that?"

"It's my name." Again the grin, infectious. Harrac found an unwilling echo of it on his lips.

"Your true name?"

Snaga nodded. "We don't view it the same where I come from. A man wears his name. None of this hiding it."

"You are from the north. Across the sea. The lands of Christ, where men are pale." Harrac felt pleased he had listened to the wisdom of the elders at circle and remembered enough of it to keep him from seeming ignorant before this stranger.

"Ha!" Snaga nodded to the side and led off into the shadow of the wall, raising a hand toward the two guards. "I'm from the utter north. Across two seas. My home is a place of snow and icy winds and our gods are many just as yours. The men of Christendom call us Vikings, axemen, and they fear us."

"Snow?"

Snaga sat cross-legged and patted the ground for Harrac to join him. "You have to learn to trust me before I tell you about snow. I wouldn't want you to call me a liar."

Harrac crouched, wary, eyes on the straight iron sword now laid across Snaga's lap. "You don't have an axe." All Broken Bowl's cattle and cowrie shells might buy him an iron sword, but not one so long or heavy as this.

"I left my axe with my son." Snaga's smile became thin. "A good lad. Big. He'd be about your age, Firestone. When I sailed from home—oh, it was autumn some . . . four years ago now. Odin take it. Four years . . . ?"

Harrac didn't know "autumn" or "Odin"—they didn't sound like Haccu words—but he knew about listening.

"Anyway, when I sailed I consulted a vo— . . . a witch, and she told me if I sailed in that season I wouldn't return to the shores of the Uulisk. So I left my axe, Hel, with my son. My father wielded that axe, and his father. I didn't want it to be gone from our people."

"Why did you sail then?" Harrac had never seen a sea, or even a lake, but he knew the Nola pond that came in the rainy season and it seemed no great leap of imagination to picture it many times as wide with men crossing the waters on wooden rafts. "If the witch said—"

"A man can't live by prophecy. I had a duty to my clan mates. How many of them might not have come home if I stayed in my hut? How would my son have valued me or my axe then?" Again the smile. "Besides. I might go back yet!"

"What happened?"

"Sailed too far, into warm seas, lost too many men, got taken captive, taken south, sold as a slave, taken farther south."

Harrac's eyes returned to the scars on Snaga's wrists. The Snake-Stick tribes dealt in slaves with the moors beyond the north mountains. Took men captive too sometimes. Only the ghost plain stood between the Haccu and the Snake-Sticks with their ropes and markets where men were sold like cattle.

"Did you escape?"

"Your king bought me for his guard. The Laccoa." He nodded back at the wall.

Harrac knew a dozen stories about the Laccoa. If there were a more dangerous band than the king-of-many-tribes' elite, the elders of the Haccu had no knowledge of them.

"The Laccoa has slave-warriors?" Harrac knew they had men from many tribes and even lands beyond the king's domain, but he hadn't heard of any enslaved to fight.

"Not any more." Snaga patted the sword across his knees. "I won my freedom after our first battle. Salash from the deep Sahar had taken a desert town. We took it back."

"The Salash—"

"There's a better question you should be asking." Snaga cut across him.

Harrac sat back on his haunches. He looked across at the waiting crowd. Old men playing mancala with wooden boards and shiny pebbles. Tribal warriors hunched under their spears, chewing betel, merchants seated on cushions beside their mounded wares.

"Why is a warrior of the Laccoa sitting to talk with me?"

Snaga nodded. "Because you have fire in you." He gave Harrac a narrow look. "Why did you come here?"

"I beat a man. My father sent me to tell the king." Harrac felt more guilty saying it out loud before a stranger than he had before the people of his village.

"Was he an enemy? This man?"

"The son of the leader of our warriors. A warrior of repute and a rich man."

"What was it that made you attack him?" Snaga asked.

"He told me to fetch him water."

"What really made you attack him?"

"He told me—"

"No." Snaga slapped Harrac across the face, a heavy, casual blow, so unexpected that even Harrac's speed couldn't help him.

Harrac surged up, toward the Northman, but Snaga planted a hand on his scarred chest and pushed him back without apparent effort. "Why?"

"Because he was there. Because he was big." Harrac's face burned with the blow.

"Now you know why I'm sitting with you, Firestone." Snaga stood, brushing the dust from his robes. "Because I saw the killer in you."

Harrac stood too, willing himself not to rub his cheek. "I'm sorry for what I did. I hope Broken Bowl gets better. I don't want to be a killer."

Snaga shrugged. "Perhaps you're not. I was the same at your age, too ready to put my fist into someone's face for looking at me wrong. Full of fire and anger, without reason or anything to aim it at. Young men show the world a fierce face, and behind it? Confusion. Lost angry boys not know their place in the world yet. That's just how some of us grow—most grow through it, some die, some are stuck with it. Those are the true killers, blood to bone.

"Killers who fight against what they are make better soldiers than those who don't. Marry a killer's instinct to a conscience and you may not get a happy man, but you get a useful one." He started walking back toward the gates. "Come on. We'll see if you've got enough in your arms to match what's in your head and heart."

"But—" Harrac hurried to catch up. Snaga waved at the guards to open the gates. "I need to speak with the king. Then go home."

"Better to serve first—speak later. Our king is not a kind man." Snaga led on through the gates. "His justice tends toward . . . harsh. Go to him once you've wet your spear in his service though, and you'll get a more reasonable judgment. Oomaran appreciates warriors."

Harrac stopped, with the gates closing behind him, narrowing away the world he knew, the path home. "I'm not a killer . . ."

Snaga came back, put his hand to Harrac's shoulder to steer him. "My life didn't end the day they put chains upon me. I endured. So will you. Perhaps we'll both go home in the end."

Harrac looked up at the giant. "Why don't you? Go, I mean. You're free."

"Free and a thousand miles from the coast. Lacking money or the skills to travel these wilds. But most of all? I'm a Northman." He held out his arm and pulled back the sleeve of his robes. Harrac wasn't sure if he was more shocked by the skin, white as the linen itself, or the sheer amount of muscle heaped upon the bone. "It's dangerous for a Haccu to travel out beyond the tribes he knows. Even in the lands that pay tribute to the king-of-many-tribes there are villages where you would be speared or find an arrow in your back. For me—ten times as hard." He patted the sword at his hip. "Not so good against arrows, and Afrique is a land of hunters." Snaga looked back toward the gates. "If I'm ever getting out of here it will be in a war party, a small army—a band of brothers, men bound to each other. No man's an island. Not even the ones that think they are. Especially not them."

HARRAC PROVED HIMSELF strong and fast, balanced in hand and eye. A year proved him hard enough of mind and spirit, ready to endure, ready to bleed. A second year proved him ready to kill.

Snaga sat with him that night, backs against a baobab tree, away from the low fire set to draw in any remaining enemy. They had found the tribeless raiders at noon, a large band of men outcast from many nations. Camped without care, secure in their numbers. They called themselves sand-wolves. Jackals would be closer. Most carried hide shields, machete, spears. A group of ten Laccoa broke among them, having crawled through the scrub beneath grass mats. Snaga led them, laying about with his heavy sword in a red carnage before running for the casca bushes that hid the rest of the Laccoa.

Harrac had waited among the bushes with his bow and his spear and his sword, a curved blade—only the Northman carried straight iron. He had crouched among his brothers, sweating. Each time the casca thorns pricked him it seemed that he heard his name spoken—Long Toe calling it as he had the first and only time it fell upon Harrac's ears. More thorn pricks, and other voices spoke his name—his father, Broken Bowl, his brothers, a chorus, all of them calling him home, calling him any place but there among the thorn bushes with the sand-wolves racing toward him howling for blood.

He loosed two arrows and brought at least one man down. Another died upon his spear, set into the ground, a longer thorn amid the casca spines. In the clash and chaos of blades Harrac had kept his head, the red heat running in his veins, all thoughts of running burned away. There had been a joy in it. Aloor of the Nuccabi had fought beside him, fat and strong, a clever warrior without mercy. Three Stars of the Haccu had fought on his other side, tall, serious, turning to grey, a master of the sword. Three Stars had fallen, taken by a wild swing of a machete. Harrac's blade had all but severed the head of the man who killed him.

Now, sitting with Snaga against the baobab he felt sick. The visions wouldn't leave him—flesh laid open to the bone, men screaming, limbs parted from bodies, more blood that he had imagined possible.

"You learned a lesson here today, Firestone." Snaga kept his eyes on the night. He spoke low, amid the whirr and chirp of the darkness. "It's a lesson that will burn you, but if you hold it close even so, it will make you the man you were meant to be. That's the first lesson—choosing what to hold on to, even if it scars, or marks, or changes, or ends you. We may not understand why we choose one thing to take close over another, but it is important that we do, and keep them tight. That faith makes us one with the gods."

Only the night spoke, the endless, ageless voice of the dark.

"Do you hear me, Firestone?"

"Harrac."

"What?"

"My name is Harrac."

"Thank you," Snaga said.

THREE YEARS PROVED Harrac ready to sacrifice.

"You should have gone to the king last year. You're a blooded Laccoa. Oomaran would have sent you home with cattle, or at the least paid you a handsome fee to stay." Snaga scanned the bush land around them. Dust trails rose in several places.

"I wanted to see you go home," Harrac said. The Snake-Stick would find them soon. The bush offered many places to hide but the surviving Laccoa left a trail any skilled hunter could follow, and they didn't have time to disguise it further.

"I was tracking raiders," Snaga said, glancing back at Harrac. "Not going home."

Harrac watched the Viking and said nothing. As leader of the fifth Laccoa division, Snaga had the right to make such decisions, but tracking Snake-Stick raiders for ten days had taken them far beyond prudence, out past the furthest reaches of the king-of-many-tribes' influence. Out to lands where even the Laccoa must tread lightly. The Snake-Stick raiders had led them into Ugand territory and set up an ambush with their allies.

Snaga grinned. "I always said the only way home for me was with a band of brothers around me." He looked around at the Laccoa, their ranks thinned but the core of their strength remaining. "We made it farther than I expected. Another week and I could have shown you the sea!"

"I would liked to have seen it," Harrac said. "The gods were not with us though."

Snaga pointed to the east. "You have the command, Firestone. Take the men and head back. If you reach the grey scrub you'll stand a good chance. When the Snake-Sticks come, disperse and make separately to the great rocks we saw after the river."

"It's a good plan." Harrac sat back in the creoat bush and ran his whetstone along the length of his blade another time. "Why are you telling me to lead?"

"I'm going back along our trail to make an ambush of my own. You know what I can do if I get in among them."

Harrac didn't argue. He knew where that led. He gathered the men and told them the plan while Snaga crouched a way off, scanning the bush. Nine of the Laccoa would not leave without arguing. Harrac sent them to Snaga and the big man held each by the shoulder, speaking softly to them, extracting a promise. They returned one by one. Hard men, killers, eyes red.

Harrac led the band away.

SNAGA FOUND HIS spot a few hundred yards back along their trail. The Snake-Sticks were close now, some still letting their dust rise to spook the Laccoa, others moving with more skill, almost unseen save for the occasional alarm cries of a kessot or the flutter of minta birds taking flight.

Snaga rolled under the skeletal branches of a thellot bush, letting the dust cake him, drawing about him armfuls of the ancient seedpod cases that lie in drifts beneath the thellot. Thus disguised he lay in wait.

The hunting party came by presently, confident in their numbers though stepping carefully so as to raise the dust only to waist height. Three slender, long-haired Snake-Sticks led an Ugand war party, squat men with long, thin spears and heavy clubs of knotwood. Three dozen in all perhaps.

Snaga rose silently and ran into the midst of them while a Snake-Stick tracker paused to study the confusion in the trail. The Viking loosed his roar only at the last moment when the majority had turned their heads, if not their spears, his way.

His heavy sword sheared through the neck of the first man he reached, ploughing on to slice the next from collarbone to hip. The thrust of his foot broke a man's knee. He drove his pommel into an Ugand's face, then spun, arm stretched, scything his blade through every man within his arc. The dust rose about him, battlefield smoke, the dark shapes of men closing on every side. Red slaughter followed.

SNAGA LAY ON the ground, head raised, resting on the leg of a dead Ugand. The Ugand dead sprawled on all sides, the dust spattered with their blood, reaching out in dark arcs in all directions, too much even for the thirsty ground to swallow. Close on forty men butchered, tumbled in untidy heaps, broken-limbed, red gore spread wide.

Three spears pierced the Viking: gut, thigh, chest. Harrac knew at least two of them were fatal wounds. His own leg had given out, perhaps broken, his eye closed by an Ugand club.

"You came back. I told you not to." The blood around the spear in Snaga's chest bubbled as he spoke.

"Just ten of us. Aloor is leading the rest back as you ordered."

"How many . . . now . . ."

"Just me and you, I think. Some of the Ugand ran away."

"They'll bring the other parties quick enough."

Harrac nodded and pulled himself closer to the Viking, wondering if the other men of the Viking tribe were as deadly. He would guess that Snaga had felled twenty of the enemy by his own hand. Even with the spears in him he had fought on, snapping off the hafts—falling only when there were no foes left to stand against him.

"I—" Snaga coughed crimson. "I'll tell you a Haccu secret."

Harrac grinned. He hoped the Ugand would kill him quickly. "You don't know any Haccu secrets, old man."

"Harrac." Snaga had never spoken his name before. He paused as if forgetting where he was. "My other son is called Snorri. You would like him." Snaga set a hand to Harrac's shoulder. "You Haccu with your secret names." He coughed again. "But the old Haccu, the wise ones, know this truth." His voice faded and Harrac leaned in to hear, wincing at the pain in his ribs. "Your secret names are gifts, to share with those you honour or love—but it's your use-names, the ones young boys are so eager to shed, that say the most about you. The names you wear in full view, simple, ordinary, shared with friend and foe alike. That's where the truth lies. The stories behind them are the stories of where you came from . . . where you're going."

Harrac saw the shapes of men moving through the bush on several sides now. He reached for his sword, dulled by use, the point snapped off, lost in some Ugand's corpse. "I won't let them take me."

"Find something worth holding to." Snaga didn't seem to hear him, his eyes fixed on the sky, sharing the same faded blue. His fingers gripped Harrac's shoulder with surprising strength. "Tell my boy . . . tell Snorri . . ." And the hand fell away.

The Ugand broke cover, screaming, and as Harrac struggled to stand a heavy net fell about him from behind. He tripped and fell, roaring. The first of the screaming Ugand reached him, spear raised to skewer him. Snaga's sword carved the leg from under the man. A second Ugand drove his spear through Snaga's neck, but the Snake-Stick who had netted Harrac stepped over his prey to guard it.

Harrac lay without motion, eyes on Snaga, now pierced by still more spears as if the Ugand couldn't believe so big a man truly dead. The Snake-Sticks would sell him north, a prize Laccoa, a fighting slave for some sultan's army or the blood-pits of a merchant prince. Snaga had said his life didn't end when they put chains upon him—Harrac too would endure. The net tightened about him and he said nothing.

Snaga had found him at the gates, a boy-turned-man, angry, with blood on his hands, and he had held to him. Perhaps to replace his own lost son, but there was no shame in that. Snaga had spoken of Harrac, offering guidance, but so often he truly spoke of himself, his own struggles, his own choices. He had been right though. Firestone was the name that said most about its owner and Harrac had worn it without shame before those he loved. Both of them, Snaga and Harrac, were men who looked for something to commit to—something to guard— and once sworn to their cause, both would die for it.

Harrac grunted as they lifted him in the net, the Snake-Sticks carrying him, hanging from a pole between four men, the Ugand whooping around, raising dust, thick as their anger. He watched until the bodies of friend and foe became lost. He travelled unseeing now, cocooned in the net, hemmed in by bodies. Perhaps it was like this to travel the oceans, swaying and bouncing with the waves. He had no knowing what lay ahead of him. Things as far beyond his imagination as Ibowen had been when he first walked from his village. Maybe there would even be snow. All he knew was that he would carry his name with him: Firestone. He had asked Snaga how it would sound in the tongue of the north.

"Kashta, my friend. That's how we would say it. Kashta. It's good name. Hold it close."

DAVID ANTHONY DURHAM

The idea for the world of this story came to me on a sweltering midsummer day. I'd just mowed the lawn and retreated inside for a tall glass of ice water. I was home alone, so I settled down on the couch to rest and try to cool down. On the coffee table I noticed a book. It was an encyclopedia of Egyptian gods that my son had borrowed from our Egyptologist neighbor. I picked it up and, absently at first, flipped through it. I'm glad I did.

There were things about that particular book on that particular day that sparked my imagination: shape-shifting gods in a vast variety of forms and with personality traits ripe and ready for comedic fiction, time-traveling magicians, hieroglyphs that suddenly seemed the perfect vehicles for magic, and that divine sun raining down on everything. Perhaps influenced by knowing the book had been intended for my son, I imagined all of these things from a lighter, more playful perspective than I might otherwise have, and I came up with a solarpunk take on ancient Egypt. It's rather unlike anything I've written before: aimed at young readers, humorous, action-packed, and fast-paced.

This story is my first published offering in this world—an offshoot of a longer piece I'm contemplating. As it's new territory for me, I jumped at the chance to submit it for *Unbound*. I hoped Shawn would be willing to experiment with me. Fortunately, he was.

ALL IN A NIGHT'S WORK

David Anthony Durham

The night had been uneventful, peaceful even, tranquil and quiet. A real easy-going pleasure.

I should've known that was a bad sign.

There was a reason I was relaxed. Khufu—the prince I was assigned to protect since I'd turned twelve and become what's called "the Prince's Shadow"—was away on a secret trip to Heliopolis. While he was gone, I got to pretend to be him. I pretty much just went through the routine of things Khufu normally did when he was home. It didn't fool anyone in the palace, but we liked to keep the routine up so that the prince's enemies didn't know he was out of the protection of the city.

My real name is Ash, usually just a humble bodyguard. But tonight . . . I was playing the prince!

That's why I was laying against the cool sheets, bowl of figs and sweet cakes next to me. A few low torches lit the sumptuous room. I'd had a hot bath, a massage, been sprinkled with flower petals, and wished good night by servants a few hours ago. Honestly, it felt sort of like being off-duty, having a little holiday.

That's were I was wrong. I nearly ended up dead because of it.

I'd drifted off and been sleeping for a while when Meres, one of the palace servants, tiptoed in. Waking, I watched him through slitted eyes, pretending to be asleep. Meres is a nice old guy. I figured he was carrying through with his nightly chores. Come to check the room was safe, verify that I was sleeping, and all that. He'd done all that earlier in the evening, but he was getting up there in years. Could be he just couldn't tell the difference between me and the prince—or notice that it was closer to sunrise than bedtime.

When he walked over and stood beside the bed, I figured I should say something. I didn't get the chance to.

Through the cracks of my almost closed eyes, I watched Meres grin strangely. He rubbed his hands together in devilish enthusiasm, and then he changed shape. The old man vanished. Instead, he became a cross between a crocodile and a sea squid. He had twelve tentacles instead of arms, with barbs at the ends of them. His long snout was lined with a jagged bristle of teeth. With that, I knew exactly what he was. Not a kindly old caregiver. He was one of the bau. He was the spirit of a dead demon that has been enslaved by an evil magician. They can be sent out on missions. Stuff like trying to kill a prince while he was sleeping. They're horrible monsters, but they shape-shift into other forms. They only drop their guise right before they kill.

Opening his jaws, the bau blew a breath of fetid vapor down toward me, and then he lunged.

As the bau's jaws descended, I kicked with all the strength I had. My foot smashed into his lower jaw, slamming it shut. I grabbed it with both hands and held it closed. That's the thing about crocodile jaws. They put all the muscle into bone-crushing bite power, but they're pretty easy to hold shut. I'd had experience with this, you see.

The bau's eyes bulged with surprise.

I planted both feet on his chest and thrust him upward, flipping him over. As he flew over me, I let go and scrambled away. The bau crashed down loudly, smashing a couch to bits. For a moment, he was all flailing tentacles and roaring anger.

I hope the noise would attract the palace guards. I snatched the spear I kept hidden under the bed. It's one of my favorite weapons. I considered hurling it at him, but as he lumbered forward I got the feeling he might be able to knock it away with one of those tentacles. Then I'd be weaponless. Better to hang on to it. I stepped toward him. Using the spear like a staff, I went to work.

Despite the bulk of his upper body, this bau had spindly legs. I swung low, trying to take them out. The demon jumped. Pretty nimble, really. I swung high, but one of his tentacles batted the spear away. I tried jabbing at his chest. Bad move. He grabbed the shaft and nearly yanked it out of my grasp. I only got it back by using it to pull myself forward and swing up on. I planted a roundhouse kick across his jaw. He loosened his grip. I hit the ground running away from him and pulled the spear along with me.

I needed to rethink. Clearly, getting in close with the spear wasn't working. Throwing it was risky, but the barbs on the bau's tentacles looked nastier the more I watched him slash them around. No, better to keep my distance and nail the beast.

When I had a clear shot at him, I planted my feet and hurled the spear with everything I had. The spear sailed toward him, iron point glistening and the shaft behind it driving forward. It should have pierced through his chest and pinned him to the wall.

It didn't.

He twisted to one side. The spear slipped by a hair's breadth from his body. Even his tentacles managed to curve out of the way. The spear slammed into the wall and stuck solid. The shaft swayed with the force of the impact.

The bau's face wasn't exactly the easiest to read, but I had a feeling he was looking pleased with himself. He came at me. I did the only reasonable thing. I ran for the exit. The bau beat me to it. I skimmed away and kept moving. I tried to dislodge the spear from the wall. No dice. It wouldn't budge. I had a quiver of throwing knives in my own room, but the bau wouldn't let me escape the prince's quarters. Instead, we kept up a deadly game of chase. To slow him down, I chucked anything I could at him. Chairs, bowls, vases, cushions, those silky soft sheets:

whatever I could get my hands on. Between the bau's bellows and the crash of things breaking, we really made a racket.

Where were the palace guards? They should've been here by now.

"A little help would be appreciated, guys!" I called.

If they weren't going to show up to help me out, I was going to have to pull off something unconventional, something that would catch the demon by surprise. It took me a while to come up with my bright idea. I only figured it out after about the fifth time I'd jumped over or slid under the spear jutting out of the wall. Just because it was stuck didn't mean it couldn't still be used as a weapon.

The next time I ran passed it, with the bau hot on my heels, I grabbed the butt of the spear shaft. Using my momentum, I pulled it to one side, feeling the tension build. I held it for a second, until the demon was heading right at me, and then I . . .

I'd like to say that I released the shaft and watched it swing around and hit the bau right in the gut. That was my plan. It didn't go that way. Before I could let go, the tension on the shaft yanked me off my feet and sent me hurtling into the bau's midsection. I thudded into him, knocking him back.

I struggled to my feet, winded. The bau didn't let me catch my breath. He rose too, rubbing his tummy and looking offended. I turned to run again, but I noticed something. Using the spear like a catapult must have loosened it. It lay on the floor, freed from the wall. I snatched it up, set the shaft against the base of the wall, and turned, aiming the point behind me. The bau didn't see the spear until it was too late. The force of his own body drove the point into his chest. His face—which was so close to mine I could've planted a kiss on his scaled snout—registered the pain of the injury for a moment. Then it changed. It lost the fury of the fight. It grew soft with relief. His body lost its flesh and blood substance and he faded into vapor.

With that, I sent him back to the spirit world.

I STOOD PANTING, glad to be alive. In the eerie silence of the room, I wondered again where the guards were? I mean, seriously, there was no way they could've slept through that! I'd give them an earful when I found them.

Then I had a horrible thought.

I dashed out of the room, down the passageway to the guard post. What I saw confirmed the worst. The two guards hadn't been sleeping. Not unless you mean the sleep that never ends. They were dead, cut to shreds by the bau's barbed tentacles. Gruesome. They probably never knew what hit them. One minute old Meres was chatting with them. The next they were getting sliced and diced and gnawed on.

Meres was going to be horrified when he found out what happened. Chances were he was fast asleep in his room, with no actual role in this. He'd hate it that his form had been used to deceive the guards to their death. And almost to my death, for that matter.

Anger surged up in me. Two people dead, and for what? A foul attack on the prince, obviously. Whoever sent that bau hadn't even done their homework well enough to know the prince wasn't in the palace! Whoever enslaved the creature wasn't the brightest. A clever magician would've dispatched the bau on his mission and then hightailed it out of there. If this guy wasn't clever he was probably still nearby, hoping to verify that the bau had succeeded.

And if he's nearby, I thought. *I can catch him!*

I still had the spear in hand, but I figured it wouldn't hurt to get a bit better armed. In my room, I strapped on my knife belt. Three razor-sharp blades, each of them perfectly balanced for throwing. I'd sent a few demons back to the underworld with these.

Next, I flipped open the locked box on my desk. The stylus lay there, a slim sliver of writing tool. It was a beauty, a present from Lord Thoth, the god of scribes and magical knowledge. He gave it to me when I began my magical training. It wasn't just any old stylus. It was a magician's primary instrument. Instead of writing words on papyrus, it wrote magical hieroglyphs. I called them "glyphs" for short. Write the correct glyph in just the right way, and almost anything was possible.

The only problem with the stylus was that it didn't work at night. That's why I didn't have one at hand to turn the bau into a chicken or something. Egyptian magic isn't like the stuff practiced outside of the

Nile Valley. For us, magic is gift given to us each day, when Lord Ra—the falcon-headed god—joined with the sun. It's kinda complicated. But the basic idea is that when the god and sun merge, the light they shone down on Egypt had magic in it. It's how we powered our sun barges and skiffs. It's what energized our excavation tools and supply transports. And it's what gave our spells life.

At night, of course, magic didn't work. Good thing sunrise wasn't far away.

I slipped the stylus under my belt and took off. My plan was a reasonable one. I'd alert the palace security force about the bau and the dead guards, and have them sound the alarms. If the magician was in the city, we'd nab him. Good plan, right?

Well, it never happened.

THE MOMENT I ran out of the prince's compound I saw him. It would've been hard not to.

The magician was mounted on an enormous, horrible winged creature. It was all beak, two big choppers that were so massive it barely seemed his body should be able to fly with it. Its glowing orange eyes turned and simmered on me. Its taloned feet gripped the peak of the glowing obelisk it perched on. No doubt about it: it was a winged spirit, a flying demon that powerful magicians could bend to their will.

The magician himself—it was obvious he was the wicked magician at this point—started when he saw me. He wasn't expecting to see me alive. His stern features hardened even more. He cursed under his breath, and then barked a command. The bird's wings flared out, pitch black, blocking out the lightening morning sky. The creature leaped. It slammed its wings down, creating a great rush of air that almost knocked me off my feet. The mount and rider carved away, rising with each wingbeat.

"No!" I cried. He was getting away! I didn't stand a chance of hitting him with a knife, and the stylus was still powerless. I ran to the edge of the balcony, wishing I had wings. My eyes followed the shape of the creature as it grew smaller. It was so frustrating!

I had just about given up hope when I heard a sound behind me. Spinning, I saw a messenger beetle. He was short, just up to my waist, with a hard green shell that protected his wings. He walked upright on two legs, but he had the full insect allotment of six. He looked to be off on some early morning business.

"You there, beetle!" I snapped. "Can you fly?"

The insect turned. Realizing who I was, he bowed an honorable greeting. "Yes, I've just recently received second class flier status. I would be first class, but—"

"Good," I interrupted. Rude, I know, but there were time issues to consider. "Fly me."

"Fly you?" He looked perplexed. "I carry messages, not . . . boys."

"You do now. I command you with my authority as the Prince Khufu's Shadow. Take me in pursuit of that magician." I pointed.

The beetle stood a moment taking in the view of the winged creature flying into the night sky. "You're joking," he finally said.

"I wish I was."

"You've picked the wrong beetle." He wiggled one of his antennas. It had a noticeable crook in it. "I've got a faulty antenna. Lord Set snapped it once, and it never healed properly. Means I have a hard time flying straight."

Watching the winged creature grow smaller, I said, "I'm sure you'll do your best." I tossed my spear aside. There'd be no way to hold onto it with what I had in mind. I snatched the beetle up, flipped him over, and grabbed him by his lower legs. Once I had a good grip, I swung him into the air and leaped off the balcony.

"B-B-BUT," THE BEETLE cried, "my antenna!"

His shell cracked open and his wings whirred to life. We dropped terrifyingly toward the terrace below us, but at the last minute the beetle got enough control to pull us out of the fall. He flew forward. I held on, dangling beneath him, legs whipping about.

"Follow that bird!" I shouted.

"I'll try!" was his answer.

Considering how he looped and twisted, rose and dove and veered from one side to the other, I found that hard to believe. I admit that I was an awkward load for a beetle to carry, but this was ridiculous! I could barely tell that we were heading in the right direction. We certainly weren't gaining on the magician and his mount. I was starting to think I had picked the wrong beetle after all.

"Fly straight!" I yelled.

"I told you I can't! Busted tenny."

Fortunately, the little guy had strong wings. He kept us aloft. The grounds of the palace scrolled by beneath us. Soon we were over the city itself, and then further into the farmland that stretched off to the south. I was on my own now, no guards to call on for help.

At least the sun would be up soon. The lightening sky to the east proved it. If I'd been thinking straight, it would've occurred to me that the only problem with my being able to use my stylus was that the magician would be able to use his too. That should've worried me, but you can't think of everything when you're dangling a hundred feet in the air, holding on to the scrawny legs of a faulty beetle.

"They've landed at the temple to Anubis!" the beetle said.

I craned my head around to see. I caught a glimpse of the magician dismounting from the demon bird in front of the massive temple. That's all I saw, though, before the beetle veered again. "How hard is it to fly straight?" I yelled, my anger rising.

The beetle said, "Ah . . ."

He wasn't answering me. I thrashed, trying to get a better view of whatever he was seeing. "What?"

"Uh oh . . ."

"What?"

"Oh, no . . ."

I didn't have to wait for his answer. He swung around, giving me a perfect view. The magician was nowhere to be seen. He must've gone into the temple. The demon bird, however, had risen back into the air.

"He's heading straight for us!" the beetle said.

Exactly. The creature's enormous wings made short work of the distance. He flew toward us at incredible speed.

"What should I do?" the beetle asked.

"Make evasive maneuvers."

The beetle's voice rose to panic pitch. "Make what?!"

"Fly weird!" I said. "That shouldn't be hard for you."

He did. He flew plenty weird. He darted side to side. He zigged. He zagged. He rose up and down. He carved loops. All of this was *before* the demon even reached us.

When it did, it just got crazier. The demon swooped in. Its massive beak snapped at us. It lunged and twisted, eyes fixed on us with murderous intent. The beetle flew so chaotically that he nearly pulled my arms from my sockets. I flailed about, legs going this way and that, barely able to hold on.

All of this happened in midair. From my perspective, the world below shifted and heaved as we moved. I tried not to think about that. What I needed to do, I knew, was sink one of my throwing knives into the beast. With all the motion, it wasn't going to be easy. My timing had to be perfect.

We corkscrewed between the demon's massive head and the flare of its wing. If I'd believed it was intentional, I'd have praised the beetle for his skills. Only, he was screaming like a maniac as he did it, so I doubted it was planned. We stalled out for a moment above the demon. I saw my chance.

I let go with one hand and, swinging one-armed, I yanked a dagger from its sheath. Quick as I could, I aimed at the demon's head as it turned to snap at us. I threw.

Would've been a good shot, except that the beetle zinged to the left at just the wrong time. My knife missed the demon. It flew end over end out of sight, falling to the earth.

"I had a clear shot!" I screamed.

The beetle babbled in response. He spoke so fast that he pounded words together in a way that made no sense at all. He kept at his crazy flying, and I grabbed my second knife.

The next time I got a shot I was upside down. The beetle was doing one of his somersaults. We were underneath the demon. As the beetle flipped to avoid him, I swung around. My feet touched the great bird's belly. I ran along it a few steps. I should've kicked him, but I was focused on using my knife. I aimed at the beast and threw.

Would've worked, except that my running feet got in the way. I kicked the knife before it sunk home. The blade careened away. I grabbed for it, but the beetle, in his wisdom, twisted around the demon and rose at a furious rate. Looking down at the demon as it beat its wings to rise with us, I considered my options.

I only had one knife left. I wasn't going to hit the fiend like this. The beetle was clearly exhausted. The way the demon was roaring up toward us, both the beetle and I were going to be demon food. If I was going to have any chance of hitting him, I had to be able to really aim at him. I knew what I had to do.

"Beetle," I said, "if you can, catch me before I splatter."

With that, I let go of his leg. I plummeted downward, toward the demon bird.

THE FORCE OF the wind tore at me. It roared in my ears. But at least I was dropping in a direct line. I locked my legs beneath me and fell straight toward it, making my body as lean as possible. I tore my final knife free. I cocked my arm back, waiting for the perfect moment.

The demon bird couldn't have been happier. He pumped his wings even more furiously. His eyes bulged with anticipation of the treat that was about to drop into his gullet. The bird cranked open its enormous beak, so wide I could see right down his throat. That was the moment I wanted.

I hurled the knife downward, using every muscle in my body to zing it fast and true. It disappeared into the demon's throat. A direct hit. A few seconds later, I did the same thing.

It's not easy to describe the sensation that followed. For a moment, I slid down the slick tube of the bird's throat. I heard its beak snap shut with a crash, and for the briefest moment, I landed in the sopping, gooky blackness of its stomach. I can say with certainty that I know exactly what it feels like to get swallowed by a giant flying demon. It wasn't the first time something had swallowed me. The giant serpent Apep had me in his cavernous tummy for a while that time I had to save . . .

But that's a different story. I really should stay on topic.

So, I was swallowed by the beast, but only for a moment. My knife had done its work. It struck home to the creature's heart. As it died, the demon burst into a cloud of green smoke and then vanished. I was free. And in midair.

This time, I'll admit I didn't fall in a terribly graceful manner. I screamed bloody murder and slashed at the air with my arms and legs, as if I could somehow swim in the sky. I couldn't. The world rushed up toward me. I picked out the exact spot I was going to get pulped, just a bit of barren ground, not a remarkable spot at all. I closed my eyes and awaited the impact.

There certainly was an impact, but it wasn't between me and the ground. Something slammed into my back with so much force it knocked the wind out of me. Six thin arms clamped around my chest. The beetle! He'd caught me! If I'd had the breath to, I would've shouted for joy. Instead, I just panted.

The beetle still flew in his chaotic style, but I didn't mind anymore. We were safe for the moment.

He skimmed over the palm trees and brought us in for a landing on the wide, smooth stones in front of the temple. My feet touched down, running. We gradually came to a stop. The beetle released me. I dropped to my knees, and then to all fours. The beetle flopped down on his back, arms limp, gasping for breath. For a time, neither of us did anything else.

I took stock of the situation. One bau down. One demon bird out of the picture. I was two for two so far. Only the magician himself remained, and I knew where he was. He was obviously the type of scoundrel that liked for others to do his dirty work. Even if he knew more magic than me—which I assumed he did—my combat magic would give him a run for his money. That was my specialty. I figured my chances were at least fifty-fifty. I could work with that. I'm the optimistic type.

When I had my breath back, I stood. The sun had just begun to emerge out of the eastern horizon. "Lord Ra," I said, thankful for the magic his rising brought with it. I slipped my stylus from my belt and held it up to catch the first rays of the sun. I felt the life ignite in it.

I helped the beetle up with my free hand. "All right," I said, "you got me here. You caught me. Saved my life. Thanks for all that. Do me one last favor. If I don't make it out alive, take word of my death back to the palace."

"Great," he said, with more sarcasm than I thought insects were capable of. "I love delivering happy news to royalty. You're not seriously considering going in there, are you?"

"I have to go after him and finish this up properly. The last thing I want is for him to get away. He'd only plot another, more deadly, attack. I don't really have any choice."

"It's your funeral," the beetle said. He sat down, looking dejected. He began caressing his bent antenna.

I started for the temple but hesitated a moment. The little guy was pretty down. "Hey, beetle," I asked, "what's your name?"

"Babbel, messenger beetle, second class," he recited. "It would be first class, except for . . ." He exhaled. "You know already. The tenny. Can't fly straight, as you experienced."

"No, you flew wonderfully. Wouldn't have had it any other way. Your evasive maneuvers were . . ." What was the right word? ". . . special. If things work out, I'll put in a good word for you. Maybe get you bumped up to first class."

He looked up, hopeful. "Really?"

Starting for the temple entrance, I called back, "It's a promise, Babbel." I meant it too. I keep my promises. Of course, if I didn't come out alive I wouldn't be able to, but that was just one of those unavoidably troublesome details.

I jogged between the massive, imposing statues of Anubis, the jackal-headed god, and into the dim interior of the temple. I drew an illumination glyph with glowing lines of crackling energy. They hung in the air in front of me. It didn't glow as brightly as I wished because the thick stone walls sheltered it from sunlight. Still, there was enough for the spell to work. I circled the glyph in a cartouche and then slashed it into life. A candle-like flame sprung from the tip of my stylus. It would have to do.

Like all temples dedicated to gods of the underworld, this one was pretty grim. Lots of shadowy corridors, black stone pillars. Not an actual person in sight, but everywhere I turned, statues of Anubis and his servants lurked as if waiting to pounce. Long, pointy ears, canine snouts, glimmering white teeth, and large red eyes. It all made me a bit jittery. I kept moving, holding the stylus high as I did.

I wondered why the magician had come here. Anubis was an underworld god, but that didn't mean he was evil or anything. He was pretty well respected, really. Chances are the magician didn't have anything to do with Anubis. Maybe he'd just fled for the first structure he saw out here, hoping to lose me in the maze of dark corridors. I wasn't going to let that happen.

I explored the main level of the temple carefully, looking behind every statue, down each spooky hallway. Nothing. I kept checking the main entrance as well, to make sure he didn't sneak out and run for it. I would've spotted him if he tried. No, after my thorough search, I concluded there was only one place left for him to be hiding in. The sacred vault.

Pretty poor hiding spot, I thought.

If there was one thing I knew about sacred vaults it's that there was only one way in or out. One stone door opened on to a ramp leading down into it. Once I had him cornered there, he'd have to deal with me. Even better, he wouldn't be able to use magic in there. It was too far away from the sun, too deep in the temple, embedded in solid rock. I wouldn't be able to use magic either, but that wasn't a problem. I could take out one old magician with my bare hands.

I slipped my stylus back under my belt and descended the ramp into the dank, dim chamber.

A VOICE SPOKE out of the dimness. It sounded sinister, condescending. And disturbingly calm.

"I'm disappointed," the voice said. "I had expected you to be bigger.

241

It appears you are hard to kill. Judging by the scrawny look of you, I can't figure out why."

The magician stood in the center of the room. He circled the altar to Anubis, the centerpiece of the vault. A faint illumination from above highlighted him. I couldn't quite tell where it came from, but it wasn't magic. It looked like sunlight. Faint as it was, it wouldn't be enough to a power stylus.

The way the light fell down on him exaggerated his features, his sunken cheeks and heavy brow. No one would call him handsome. He looked the part of an evil magician, though. The dark cloak that draped his shoulders was classic. He said, "How underwhelming. You're just like any other boy."

"Says who?" I asked.

"Oh, my name isn't important. Not to you, at least."

"Embarrassed to give your name? I would be too if I was a magician that summoned demons to do his dirty work. You'll notice I've defeated both of them. I barely broke a sweat while doing it." I felt smug and didn't mind showing it. "You'll be the easiest yet. It's just you and me now. No magic for either of us."

"True enough," the man said. He glanced up. "Down here, there is but this faint glimmer from the world above. Beneath it, we are equally powerless. This is not going to give you the advantage that you think it is, I'm afraid. You really are a rash little boy."

A rash little . . . The nerve of this guy!

I moved closer. "I would've expected a powerful magician to be smarter than you are. Next time you make an attempt on the prince's life, make sure that he's actually in the city. Your target was never in danger. I'm not the prince! I'm his Shadow."

There, that should put a wet blanket on his attitude. When he realized that I had the fighting skills to wipe the tiles with him, he'd probably beg for mercy. That wasn't quite what happened.

He grinned and looked more confident than ever. "That's where you are mistaken, boy. I wasn't trying to kill the prince. He's worth more to me alive in any event."

A sense of dread got hold of my toes and began creeping up my body. This guy really should be looking more worried. I defeated his bau. I made a pincushion of the winged spirit. I'd tracked him down with ease. Why didn't he seem a bit more concerned?

As I circled the altar table, he did the same. He kept the stone surface between us. "You still don't get it, do you?" he asked. "It was you I was after all along."

"Me?"

"Yes, yes. You. Ash. The Shadow of the Prince. Khufu's protector and close friend. You, young man, are a nuisance, one that I intend to remove. Once I have, the prince will be easily manipulated for my purposes. And I will have stopped you from achieving your destiny."

I must've looked as confounded by that as I felt.

"This is better than I thought!" the magician said. He was having a grand time. "You really don't know how important you are. You don't even know *who* you are! Even better, you're going to die without knowing."

In a way, he was right about some of that. I knew *what* I was—the Shadow of the Prince. That's pretty much the thing that defined my life. It's what I'd trained for up until my twelfth birthday. At that point, I was summoned to the palace. I went through a rigorous testing— along with other kids that had been trained as I had. We even had to fight demons. By the end of a week of trials, I was the only one to make it through. Because of it, I became the prince's bodyguard. More than that, I became his friend.

So that was what I was. And proud of it! What I didn't know was who I would've been if I hadn't been a Shadow. I was taken from my parents at birth to begin my candidacy. I never knew them. By tradition, I never would. Only my role as Shadow mattered now. I sometimes wished I knew about my parents, and about where I'd come from, whether or not I had any brothers or sisters. All that stuff. But most of the time my job was enough. I didn't know what the magician was up to, but I wasn't going to let him play mind tricks on me.

Our circling around the table had put me in the position the magician had been in when I entered. He, on the other hand, now had the exit ramp to his back. I didn't like that. He might be trying to confuse me, waiting for the right moment to bolt out of here. I jumped up onto the table. No need to circle it when I could go over it.

"You can ramble all you want," I said. "I'm not falling for it. You tried to kill Prince Khufu but got me instead. Don't think you can talk your way out of it."

He cackled. Literally, he threw back his head and cackled. He began backing toward the exit. He was trying to hide it, but he was definitely moving that way. I balled my hands into fists, jumped down, and moved toward him. Enough talk. It was time for action.

"Ravenous One!" he called. "I have need of you!"

That stopped me in my tracks. "What did you just say?"

"You thought I lured you here to fight me?" the magician asked, still inching backward. "No, that would be beneath me. There is someone else who is keen to rip you to pieces. You know her. She goes by many names."

I realized, to my horror, that something was descending the ramp toward us. Judging by the heavy crunch of its footfalls, it was something big.

"You can call her the Devourer of the Dead," the magician continued.

The foulest reek I'd ever smelled wafted down into the chamber. It stank of dead things. Rotten things. Evil things.

"She is sometimes called the Eater of Hearts."

A shape lumbered into view behind the magician. It towered over him.

"She'll even answer to She Who Is Great of Death." He moved to one side, to allow the creature to step past him. The evil thing came into view, its eyes and teeth and claws all glimmering. "Surely, you know by now to whom I refer."

I did. "Ammut . . ." As I whispered the demon's name, I realized just how big a fool I'd been.

THE MAGICIAN BACKED away, saying, "I will leave you to it, Ammut. Enjoy." He turned and disappeared up the ramp. A moment later, I heard the stone door grind shut. And that was it. I was trapped.

With Ammut.

The problem with Ammut was that she combined the strengths of the three deadliest creatures in Egypt. The demon had the head and jaws of a Nile crocodile. Her midsection was that of a lion, including the savage claws. And her lower portion . . . well, she's got the rump of a hippopotamus. Her victims could be swallowed whole, ripped to shreds, or sat upon. Simply put, there were no good options with Ammut.

As she strode toward me, several things occurred to me all at once. I was alone, without magic to call on and weaponless. In fighting the bau I'd lost my spear. With the demon bird I'd given up my daggers. Trapped as I was in a subterranean room, my stylus was useless. Maybe the magician had done his homework after all. He had managed to deprive me of all of my weapons.

Ammut came at me with her hippo legs stomping, her lion arms spread wide, her jaws open and slathering. She was all stampeding rage. The old girl was faster than she looked. Not as quick as me, though.

I faked to the right, just enough to get her to turn that way. Then I dove low and to the left. I grasped one of her ankles as her foot crashed down. The idea was to trip her. Didn't work. Ammut just walked forward a few more steps, me hugging her chubby leg, getting yanked up and down. When she realized where I was, she lashed at me with a paw bristling with long claws. I released her leg and rolled behind her. That got me away from the claws, but it put me in the line of fire of her rump. I scrabbled away just as her heavy bottom crashed down on the stones.

Before she could rise, I ran up her back. I reached over her head and got a grip on both her eyelids. She bellowed and thrashed about. Hauling myself up to the crown of her alligator head, I let go with one hand long enough to plant a stiff-handed chop right between her eyes. Then I grabbed both lids again and hauled back with all my weight. I let go when I couldn't hold down anymore. Her eyelids slapped back against her eyes. She howled with pain and fury.

I landed on my feet, feeling pretty impressed with that little move. The feeling didn't last long. Ammut was on me in no time, just angrier than before. Going toe to toe with her, I punched and kicked, ducked and dived. She slashed at me. She tried to stomp me. Her neck shot forward at unexpected moments. Her jaws slammed shut so near me I felt the heat of her breath. Her spittle sprayed my face.

It wasn't an even contest and we both knew it. I landed blows every now and then, but they hardly fazed her. Punching Ammut in the gut was like driving your fist into a furry stone wall. I did no real damage. She, on the other hand, did. Hitting her hurt me; my knuckles grew swollen and bloody. Once, when I didn't dodge fast enough, she slashed her claws down my leg. She even stepped on my toe. That left me limping and off-balance. It was only a matter of time before her claws sunk into me and held. Then it would all be over. So I did what I'd done in similar circumstances in the past.

I ran. I darted and dodged. I slipped between Anubis statues and slid under the altar table. I even dashed up the ramp once to check the door, just in case I could budge it. No chance. Maybe if I had time to work at it slowly, but I couldn't open it in a rush, that's for sure. Before long, I'd crisscrossed the entire chamber, touching each of the four corners of it. Ammut lumbered behind me the entire time. Truth was, I was going to get tired before she did. We both knew it.

When I leaped up onto the table, it wasn't so much that I had a plan in mind. It was more just that I hadn't been there for a while, so I figured why not? As Ammut shoved a statue of Anubis out of the way, sending it crashing into jagged pieces, I scanned the room. I couldn't see any place that I hadn't been already. Nothing I could use as a weapon. I looked up into the narrow opening that let that faint light in. It was just a long chute that stretched upward. I couldn't say how far up it went, but it ended in a pinprick of light. Daylight. It drew me like a moth to a flame.

Ammut barreled toward me. I bent my knees and jumped straight up.

FOR AN AWFUL moment, I dangled from the narrow rim that ran along the inside edge of the chute. That was as high up as I could leap. Ammut appeared beneath my feet. She climbed up onto the table, rose, and reached for me. I planted one of my feet on the tip of her snout and pushed off. It gave me enough upward motion to jam my body into the chute. I had to press my back against one side and my feet against the other. By putting force against both sides, I managed to stay crammed between them, just out of Ammut's reach.

She was a bit too close for comfort, though. As the demon raged beneath me, I worked my way toward that pinpoint of light. It offered hope. Maybe it was a way out.

It was hard going. I had to inch my feet up one by one, and then press back with my arms to scoot my body a little higher. Then I had to do it all again and again. The chute stayed uniformly narrow all the way up. The stone was so smooth there was nothing to hold on to, no ledges to get purchase on. Keeping up the pressure on the walls was a constant strain. By the time I reached the top, I didn't have much left in me. What I did have left nearly drained out of me when I saw what the light was.

The chute narrowed in the last few feet. The opening was a small triangle, just wide enough to fit a hand through. There was no way I could squeeze my whole body through it. I could see the morning sky clearly, bright blue and beautiful. So close, and yet I was still trapped, and growing weaker every second. I wasn't getting out of here this way, but maybe if I could reach into the light . . .

Leg muscles quivering and burning with the exertion, I held myself in place. With one hand, I felt for the stylus. I got ahold of it and stretched it up toward the small triangle of light. Sweat stung my eyes. My grip on the stone slipped a little. I extended the stylus as far as I could, but it wasn't enough. The sunlight was still out of reach.

One foot slipped. Gasping, I got it back in place. But I couldn't hold on any longer. My legs felt like molten iron. There was only one thing I could do.

With the last of my strength, pushing off with my legs and with the arm that had a grip on the wall, I lunged upward. I thrust the stylus point up into the sun. For the briefest moment, the tip of it flared as it absorbed Ra's energy. And then I fell.

I had never drawn a spell in mid-plummet before. Bit of an advanced technique, one I hadn't received training in. I wasn't even sure if it would work. Still, I wrote a fast, simple glyph. It wasn't fancy. Nothing elaborate. I slashed it into life as the walls of the chimney opened, dropping me back into the chamber. I saw Ammut, waiting with open jaws and grasping claws, a look of rapture in her reptilian eyes.

That was the last thing I saw before I smashed down on her, riding atop my spell. It appeared beneath me at the last moment. A stone. That's what I drew the glyph for. It must've been quite a surprise for Ammut. Instead of devouring me, she got crushed between a falling stone and the stone table on which she stood. The force would've turned a person to pulp. With a demon it wasn't quite as visceral as that.

Riding on top of the stone, the impact knocked the breath out of me. I lay stunned for a moment, and then slowly climbed to my feet. Every inch of me was achy and sore, scratched and bruised. I coughed. The air around me swirled with an unpleasant green vapor. That was all that remained of Ammut. The moment the stone killed her, her demon essence disappeared from here and appeared back in the underworld caverns that had spawned her. So it went. Ammut couldn't really die. She could only be defeated for the day. Chances were we'd meet again.

Limping, I climbed the ramp back toward the exit. I didn't want to hang around down there any longer than I had to. It took a while to get the stone door open, heavy as it was, but eventually I managed it. I slipped through and stumbled out of the dark interior of the temple. The light of day shone wonderfully warm on my face as I emerged into it. The fresh air was sweeter than any I'd ever tasted. I sat down, enjoying it.

Babbel flew toward me, weaving and chaotic as usual. He landed in a tumble, got up, and dusted himself off. He sat down and took in the view beside me. "So," he said, "you lived."

"Can you believe it?"

"No, not really."

"All in a night's work," I said.

After a minute, Babbel added, "I'm glad you're pleased with yourself, but . . ." The beetle hesitated.

"But what?"

"Well, *you* lived, but so did the magician. He got away."

Babbel seemed to have a way of seeing the dark side of everything. He was kind of a downer.

He was also right. The unnamed magician was still out there. When he found out I was alive, he wasn't going to be happy. I'd been wrong to be so cocky. Clearly he had planned every stage of the trap he led me into. He'd only miscalculated in one aspect; he'd expected me to be larger than I was. If I had been, I wouldn't have been able to fit up the chute. I'd be demon food. No, the guy deserved respect—the kind reserved only for your worst enemies. As with Ammut, I knew I hadn't heard the last from the magician. For today, though, I'd done as much as I could.

"Hey," I asked, "how about a lift back to the palace?"

Exhaling, Babbel climbed to his feet. "Sure, but don't make any jokes about my flying, all right?"

"Deal," I said.

TIM MARQUITZ

"Seven Tongues" is a story in the Tales of a Prodigy world, featuring the eunuch assassin Gryl. I'd originally imagined I'd write a Demon Squad story, my primary urban fantasy series, when I was offered a slot in *Unbound*. However, it struck me a few days later that I could add to the Tales of a Prodigy world I was building and include Gryl instead, the character having debuted in *Neverland's Library* and who was featured in *Blackguards*. With *Unbound* I was being given the opportunity to weave Gryl's story across three different anthologies before I'd even begun to write his debut book. That appealed to me, my being able to give a kind of prelife to the gritty, soft-hearted assassin in an episodic style that perfectly complements the nature of *An Empire of Tears*, the Gryl novel I've finally gotten around to writing.

SEVEN TONGUES

Tim Marquitz

The clouds gnawed at the moon, devouring it in slow, steady bites. It wasn't until the last shimmers of light had been swallowed by roiling gray that Gryl crept toward the small caravan camped in the valley below. The coins wrapped tight in his purse weighed upon his conscience, a promise of blood unfulfilled, but dawn would see their burden lifted.

He'd tracked the caravan across the quiet plains of Andral for six days, drawing closer until he'd spied it crossing the southern border of the Ural Province, the land butting up against the foothills of the Jiorn Highlands. The air had grown colder the last few nights, each breath brisk in his lungs, pleasantly bracing after the trek across the warmer clime of Andral. Memories of the north sprang unbidden to his mind as he tasted the moisture on the breeze, felt its frost-borne kiss gentle upon his cheeks.

They were bittersweet, those recollections, for Gryl had first come to the Shytan Empire in the frigid clutches of winter, on a mission of war. He'd been little more than a slave then, a Prodigy whose entire existence served the cruel whims of his Avan Seer mistress. Still, he had earned his freedom in the snowy north, born again at the Avan defeat.

That freedom came with a price, however. Scarred from toe to pate, only his face unmarred by the sorceries embedded in his ruined flesh, he would forever be an outcast, his disfigurement a glaring reminder of an enemy who'd come to the shores of Shytan and left destruction in its wake.

Yet it offered opportunity as well.

Opportunities like the one that had brought him here in search of a slaver who preyed upon children just finding their feet, leaving them desiccated husks before their tenth year. Gryl's jaw tightened at the thought, his teeth clenched. He'd seen this man's *work*—if Althun Rathe could be called a man—on display in the pens at Amberton and the shanty towns beyond, eyes devoid of life, the dead in shuffling husks only playing at life. It might well be too late to save the poor wretches who'd come before, but a taste of steel would keep this particular wolf from the rest of the flock.

Gryl drifted toward the camp, his steps silent in the gloom, his only resistance the cloying spider webs chaotically weaved within the tall grass. He brushed them aside, his target just a few short yards ahead.

The caravan was little more than a dozen wagons turned into a loose circle, one lone coach parked conspicuously in the middle of the rest. All wore the signs of their miles, tattered and patched canvas pulled over warped frames, the material more brown than white. No insignia announced their trade to the world, but there was no mistaking the cages set upon a trio of the hardier wagons, tarps tied so tightly as to define the bars. Shades of rusty orange stained the cloth with checkerboard lines.

Twice the number of men were clustered about the wheels of the center wagon, wrapped in blankets and threadbare cloaks. Emberstones crackled in a small pit beside them, casting wisps of shadows, the light of the stones reaching no farther than the first of the sleeping men. Gryl listened to their muffled symphony of snores and shallow, steady breaths as he stepped over the hitch between the nearest wagons and moved into the circle. He'd heard tale of Rathe's confidence but to leave one's camp without sentries, even in the peaceful foothills of Jiorn, was foolishness tantamount to recklessness.

Gryl inched his way onto the wagon in the center, its rear flaps threaded with gold, the only marking setting it apart from the rest. The priest Delvin—Gryl's one true friend and confidant in Shytan—told him as much as he slid the coin across Gryl's palm, whispering of the slave traders who'd ridden through Caesins just a week before. He had said there was a Xenius among the captives, one of a rare breed of beings whose magic could be tapped to perform miracles, their magic gifted to another. If this rumor were true, Rathe deserved far more than Gryl intended, but death would have to do.

He worked at the ties with one hand, his dagger clasped in the other, and peeled the flap open just wide enough for him to slip inside. Darkness greeted him yet it held no secrets from his eyes. A smattering of sturdy chests filled the left side of the wagon. Heavy padlocks secured their iron clasps, no doubt protecting Rathe's sordid earnings. Above them, dangling from the ribs of the wagon, hung a variety of chain leashes, hooked collars swinging at their ends. They stunk of copper and shame, and Gryl pulled his gaze away before his anger got the best of him, letting his eyes settle on the lump of worthless flesh that lay on the floor beneath a stained down quilt.

A worn boot jutted from under the near end of the covers and a wild mop of dirty brown hair splayed out across the wagon's floor at the other. He could see the barest of fluctuations at the covers, even breaths sounding in the dark. *Rathe sleeps well for a bastard.* He didn't so much as twitch while Gryl considered his fate. He felt his purse growing lighter as his blade closed upon its target. Retribution had come. *Poison or clean steel?* He thought of the company of men outside and left his envenomed dagger in its sheath at his boot. Swiftness would be his friend here, the lingering torture of the poison a delay he could not afford. *Besides, dead was dead.*

He seized the quilt, pressing it downward to hold his target in place, and sunk his knife into the mop of unruly hair. The blade slid through bone and brain and struck the wooden floor of the wagon with the barest of *thumps.* Gryl let a smile play across his lips. He'd have to deal with the others soon enough if he wanted to free their captives, but he'd earned his coin with Rathe, however merciful he'd been. All that was left was to collect his proof. Gryl peeled back the cover, and he felt his face flush. His smile withered.

Instead of retribution revealed beneath the quilt, he found the body of a boy still years from manhood despite his fair size. Bile filled the back of Gryl's throat, and he swallowed it back. The boy spasmed in his death throes, foam spilling from his mouth, but he didn't make a sound. His eyes spoke volumes of his silence. Though they were open wide, they stared into the distance, but not with the coming of death. A haze soured the blue of them until the edges faded to gray, focus lost in the swirl. The boy had been drugged to keep him still. Gryl had murdered one of the poor souls he'd come to save.

The heat of shame threatened to overwhelm him, and sweat beaded his brow as another realization struck home. *Rathe had known he was coming.* He cursed under his breath and yanked his blade free as a sullen *twang* sounded outside.

Something ripped through the canvas cover of the wagon and punched him in the shoulder, slamming him into the collection of chests at his back. His head struck a corner and his eyes filled with swaying will-o'-the-wisps. The wagon shook with the impact but the frame held, allowing Gryl to regain his balance. He dropped to his knees and pulled a chest in front of him, wood scraping against wood, as his vision cleared. His head pounded despite the metal of his skull-cap. The shuffle of booted feet reached his ringing ears. The wagon was surrounded.

"Not what you were expecting now, was it, Assassin?" a voice rang out, roughened by a lifetime on the road, campfire and trail dust. "I'm thinking not." Grim laughter resounded.

Gryl said nothing, his fingers playing about the shaft of the cross-bow bolt embedded in his upper arm. The leather of his armor had slowed it just enough that the quarrel hadn't struck bone. *Lucky thing that.* He ripped it free of his shoulder without so much as a whimper—his mistress having long ago bled the well of his agony dry—and tossed the bolt away. His guilt, however, would not be so easily cast aside.

A moment later, another bolt flew through the canvas above, only to tear its way out through the back.

"Don't be shy," the voice went on. "I know you're in there. The spiders warned me you were coming." The man laughed.

Gryl glanced at his legs to see the shimmer of webs still clinging to him. He ran his hand across them and watched as they flickered, tiny, almost invisible sparks lighting up at his touch. He knew then why Rathe hadn't needed guards; he'd set a ward about the caravan and Gryl had traipsed right through it. *Who's the fool now?*

"Come on, Assassin. I didn't spend good coin to bring you here for you to hide away like some child behind his mother's skirts," he said, the smile obvious in his voice. "Isn't it funny what a priest will believe when it comes to his little pet mystics? A few choice whispers and here you are, though you have your tussle with Korbitt to thank for giving me the idea. Brilliant work there, I have to say."

Gryl let out a weary sigh at the slaver's admission and loosed his second sword. The trap was sprung, no point in pretending otherwise.

"To what purpose, Rathe?" he asked. "Is your preference to die with your eyes open, or do you simply enjoy instigating a challenge you can't win?"

The slaver chuckled. "You've mistaken me for prey. I've hunted your kind since your hooded masters loosed you among us." There was a rattle of chain, and Gryl reached out with his broadsword and sliced a narrow slit in the canvas so he could see his would-be killer as he spoke. "Mementos of six of your brethren adorn my throat, but seven seems a more agreeable number to me."

A wooden chest between him and another crossbow bolt, Gryl glanced out at Althun Rathe. He saw the slaver amidst his men, holding a thick silver necklace out before him. Slabs of shriveled and blackened meat dangled from it like giant, salted leeches. Gryl's eyes narrowed in his efforts to identify what the man held up. His breath caught in his lungs with recognition.

There on the chain, hooked as clearly as bait, were six withered tongues.

"Do you see them, Prodigy?" Rathe called out. "I'd offer up their names as proof, but I have to be honest. I never asked. You'll just have to take my word for who these silent lumps once belonged to."

Gryl stared at the dark-eyed slaver as he returned his grisly necklace to its place beneath his leathern breastplate. Clean-shaven, his long hair pulled back into a tail behind his head, the man looked nothing of the hunter he claimed to be, short and frail-looking, thin almost to the point of being emaciated. His face was smooth and without a hint of scars, an unlikely visage for one claiming to have murdered six of Gryl's kind. Though he had no sentimentality toward the other Prodigies beyond their mutual suffering at the hands of the Seers, Gryl knew each to be as efficient as himself in the arts of war. They would have left their mark on Rathe were his words true. Gryl most assuredly would.

"Then, by all means, come and collect another if you've the appetite."

"I've that and more, Avan scum." Rathe grinned, teeth gleaming in the night. "Draw him out," he said to his men, and Gryl felt a cold chill settle in the pit of his stomach.

A burst of light and the acrid scent of flaring pitch told him what was coming even before the canvas erupted into flames. The temperature soared in a heartbeat. Tendrils of fire reached for him through the blistering roof like raking claws, ash and cinders cavorting in some infernal dance. The air grew heavy, and black smoke nipped at his throat with every breath. Rathe had planned his ambush well, but the man had no sense of what Gryl had survived in order to gain his freedom. A little smoke and flame was nothing.

Gryl grabbed one of the chests—not surprised to notice it was empty—and hefted it above his head so that the burning canvas rested against its painted surface. He held his breath, hoping there would be no more bolts shot into the wagon, and waited for the chest to catch fire. The moment it did, he pulled back and hurled it with all of his might. It struck the wooden ribs of the wagon, weakened by the flames, and crashed through, tearing the canvas from the frame and taking the chest with it. It flew into the circle like a burning star fallen from the firmament.

The chest crashed among the men, flinging fire and splintered wood in every direction as they scattered, but Gryl wasted no time admiring his efforts. He turned and slipped through the wooden supports on the opposite side of the wagon and leaped into the night. Only when his boots struck the ground, his blades at the ready, did he take a breath. The cool air was a balm to his scorched throat, but Rathe's men offered him no respite. They were on him without hesitation.

Gryl expected no less.

The first ended his days with a sneer plastered across his lips, Gryl's sword speared through his eye and sunk deep into his skull before the man even registered it. His body swayed to music no one could hear after the blade was yanked loose, his body fooled into thinking it still lived. Gryl turned from the still-walking corpse and dodged a quarrel that whistled past his back. The crossbowman grunted and reached for another bolt on instinct rather than his steel. The move cost him his life. A vicious thrust found his groin before his fingers settled at his quiver. He opened his mouth to scream and Gryl filled it with his dagger, sliding it in until it struck spine, then twisting it sideways to rip it loose from the man's face. The slaver fell away to the sound of clashing steel, his companions having closed upon Gryl.

It did little good.

Raised to kill since birth to the exception of all other endeavors—his early castration assuring he would have no loves other than the blade—Gryl was a hurricane among the thatch huts that were Rathe's men. The scent of copper clung to the air as blood rained down in warm tempests, lifeless bodies toppling in a macabre ballet. Men screamed and died and more took their place until there were none left to do so. Gryl stood in the ruin after the last blow had fallen and let the crimson drip from his blades, the remnants of the slaver crew pattering to the grass, a pitiful epitaph to their efforts.

But he was not yet done. Rathe still lived.

Gryl circled the wagon, its fiery demise lighting a path through the carnage. Over the crackling hisses and pops of the fire, he heard the mutterings of Rathe's captives for the first time, their voices given wind with terror, drifting to him across the circle.

"Quite the display, Assassin."

The children went silent at hearing their master speak, their hopes dashed at the sound.

Gryl drew to a halt as Rathe stepped from the shadows. The slaver was not alone. Held before him was a young girl, no older than eight. The orchid of her wide eyes stood out against her pale and frightened face, her Xenius lineage on full display. Her pure white hair hung over the blade that rested on her collar bones, doing nothing to lessen its menace. Rathe stood behind her, one hand clasped at the scruff of her neck, offering up the grin of the victor.

"Is this the prize you've come to wrest from my hands, Prodigy?" He shook the girl as he would an errant puppy. "Seems hardly worth losing your life over."

Teeth bared, Gryl met Rathe's gaze over the girl's trembling shoulder. "And yet it's you who hides behind a child rather than cross steel," he said. "Perhaps you're not as certain of your skills as you boasted."

The slaver's grin widened, threatening to eclipse the fire. "Or perhaps I'm everything I claim and then some. Only one way for us to be certain."

Before Gryl could say another word, Rathe sunk his sword into the girl's neck, his smile never wavering. She went to scream but there was only the whisper of her life's blood spewing from her throat. Gryl's stomach knotted, nearly doubling him over in his disgust. The Xenius girl saw none of his discomfort. She squirmed, frantic to draw breath, clawing at her wound with reddening hands, but Rathe had no further use for her. He threw her behind him like discarded trash before stepping forward to meet Gryl.

"Now there's nothing to stay your hand."

The mercy Gryl had aspired to earlier fled the reins without a fight. Two children were dead this night, one by his own hand, and no amount of vengeance would return them to this realm. It would, however, bring grim satisfaction to see Rathe suffer something other than a quick death.

Rather than charge, Gryl knocked his skullcap from his head to reveal the patchwork of scars beneath. He slashed at the straps holding his leather vest and tore it away so his disfigured torso gleamed bare in the firelight. His blood warmed as he drew upon the sorceries etched into his skin. Worms of agonies past gathered sentience, his scars coming to life, slithering serpents beneath his puckered flesh. He glared at

Rathe, willing his magic to pluck the man's foul deeds from his soul, but no ghosts stirred the air between them. Only the void answered his call, emptiness bringing his spell to naught.

"You dare pit your powers against mine, but as you can see they are found wanting." Rathe laughed, the temperature dropping at its heels. He patted his breastplate. "Soon there will be seven tongues hanging over my heart." The slaver advanced like lightning on the cusp of a storm.

Gryl brought his weapons up but only barely managed to deflect the slaver's single sword with both of his blades. The blow sent him scrambling backward, boots digging into the grass to keep from toppling. Never had he faced someone so swift or powerful, not even the monstrous Thrak berserkers. Gryl's arms tingled from the blow, yet Rathe stood his ground, his smile eternal. The slaver had true power after all.

"After the display with my men, I thought you might be the one to provide me a true fight," the slaver said. "Appears my faith in you is misplaced."

As is mine, Gryl thought, shaking the sting from his limbs, but only death would still his determination. He darted forward tall, feinting high before dropping low to gut the slaver. Rathe followed him with casual ease, meeting Gryl's strike and twisting it aside with plenty of time to do the same to Gryl's dagger, its blade no closer to success than the first. And still a third movement drew a line of fire across his ribs, sending Gryl stumbling. He pressed against his wound with his forearm and gasped at the perplexing feeling of long-dead nerves firing anew. Gryl cursed. *At least I didn't scream.*

Rathe eased about with callous disregard, resetting his stance as though they'd only been sparring. His chest barely rose with each breath while Gryl's bellowed, the unfamiliar pain sapping his energy far too soon. The slaver seemed not to care.

One moment he stood tall, taunting, the next he was before Gryl, driving a fist into his cheek. There was a dull *pop* as bone gave way and Gryl's vision blurred on his left, his eye swimming in a shattered socket. This time he did cry out, but Rathe quieted him by driving his pommel into Gryl's gut. Sanguine spittle flew one direction and he flew another. The ground reached out to cradle him before he could react, but there was none of a mother's love in its touch. He felt a rib *snap* at her embrace. Misery made a home in his flesh as he scrambled back to his feet. Gryl tasted blood and humiliation on his tongue, and he wondered if it would be the last thing it would taste before Rathe clawed it from his mouth to hang morosely about the slaver's neck.

"It's a pity you're the last of your kind here in Shytan," Rathe said, drawing closer as though he strolled through a crowd of well-wishers, each reaching out a delaying hand as if they might be graced with his glory. "I might well have to plan a journey across the Demarcean Sea to your homeland to find more Prodigies to put to the test. I wonder how many are left since the Empress sent your people scurrying home."

It was a question Gryl had often asked since he'd exiled himself to these foreign shores, but even if he had the answer he would take it to the grave rather than offer Rathe any more satisfaction. *He's had more than enough already.*

The tang of copper filled Gryl's mouth, and he spit to clear it but the taste lingered, much like the taste of his impending defeat. Rathe lingered too, in no hurry to re-engage, happy to draw the moment out.

Gryl raged at the man's arrogance, but he was angrier at his own impotence. "I'm not dead yet."

Rathe only laughed. "Soon enough." He inched forward, a cat playing with a wounded mouse.

Gryl moved away from him, trapped in the circle of the wagons with nowhere to run, his eyes rooted on the slaver as he advanced. He needed a moment to think, a moment to plot, though he wondered what that might earn him. *Nothing so far.* He wound his way past the fire pit, veering away from the useless emberstones only to feel something scrape against his heel. Gryl went to step over it only to realize it was fingers clasping at his boot. His head snapped about so he could bring his good eye to bear, surprised at what he saw. The Xenius girl was still alive, if only barely.

Her blood stained the grass in an ever-widening pool around her. She swam in it, one purple eye staring up at Gryl, its color draining with every heartbeat. There was nothing he could do for her, though it set his chest to aching. He whispered a prayer to the Xenius goddess

Ailih on behalf of the child, for what his heathen voice was worth, and went to pull his foot away. The girl gurgled, blood bubbling from her throat, and tapped his heel with the tip of a bloody finger. She raised her hand one last time, finger pointing, and then it went limp, splashing dead into the pool.

"A shame she had to die," Rathe said, still closing at a glacial pace, "but she was weak. Hardly a shining example of her kind."

Gryl stumbled back, keeping the distance between them, but the blood splattered across his boot was a portend of things to come. He stopped then, his vision—blurred as it was—coming to rest on an image smeared in crimson across his heel. Gryl forced his eye to focus and felt his heart flutter with recognition at what it was. The child hadn't pawed at him for help. She'd drawn a symbol on the slick leather of his boot in her own blood. A symbol written in the ancient script of the Xenius; a symbol he knew.

A word filled Gryl's skull as he translated the scrawl, bringing the barest of hopes with it. He spun about to survey the wagons bunched behind him, their canvas covers pulled tight against the cages beneath. Gryl raced to the one the child had so desperately tried to point at and drew his sword across the ropes that held the tarp in place. He'd only cut the last when Rathe snatched him by the throat and slammed him to the ground.

More bones snapped as he hit, his weapons bouncing free of his hands, but only a blessed numbness washed over him in place of pain. He was moving beyond such mortal concerns, he knew, even the slaver's magic losing its hold over him. Rathe stood above, feral grin in place, his presence looming.

"Impressive heroics, Assassin, though I'm not certain what you hoped to attain by your efforts." He gestured to the wagon, all pitiful faces and rusty bars, the concealing cloth gone. "At least now you have an audience to your death." Rathe struck a thoughtful pose. "Now, should I take your tongue before or after I kill you? What say you?"

Gryl's head lolled as he fought gravity's efforts to drag it down. He ignored the slaver and looked to the prison wagon, sorting through the faces that stared at him with pitiful eyes. At last, he turned back to Rathe and snarled. A numb arm reached for the dagger at his boot, fingers barely seizing upon the pommel to draw it awkwardly from its sheath.

"I admire your conviction, Prodigy. You honor me by fighting to the last, but if you believe this tiny little blade can bring me low, you're more a fool than I could ever have imagined."

Gryl settled the hilt in his hand, barely able to feel its metal in his grasp. He coughed blood from his throat and let it dribble down his cheek. "It's not . . . not . . . for . . ." The words leaked out slowly, but Gryl forced a pained smile to his lips as he flung the knife. ". . . you."

The blade flew through the bars and thudded loudly into the leg of a child who'd been standing at the front of the cage. He shrieked and fell into the other children, their gathered mass keeping him from dropping all the way to the floor. His waxen face grew even paler as he howled, clawing at the knife.

"What have you done?" Rathe screamed, driving his sword downward to skewer Gryl. His eyes were wide, wild.

Gryl squirmed at the last moment, the blade piercing the meat of his side rather than his bowels. Still, it ran all the way through, grating into the ground beneath him, pinning him down. Instead of clawing at the sword, he reached out and clasped his arms and legs about Rathe, pulling the slaver into him, holding him tight. It was as if he clung to a giant, pleading not to be crushed beneath his weight.

"No," Rathe screamed, over and over as he thrashed, unable to break free, resolving at last to slamming his forehead into Gryl's face.

Gryl's nose shattered on the second blow, but he turned his head aside to see the boy he'd stabbed begin to spasm and writhe. Then he went still, slumping into his companions, purple eyes sliding shut. The pressure on Gryl seemed to lift.

Rathe postured up to smash his skull down once more, but Gryl turned into the blow, slipping around the slaver's jaw and sinking his teeth into the man's throat. Rathe howled as Gryl chewed, tearing at the rubbery flesh until it sprung a leak. His mouth flooded with blood and Gryl rolled his head away to spit it out, warmth splashing down over his swollen and ruined cheek.

Despite his injuries, he clung to Rathe until the slaver's life drained away, his furious resistance turning to shuddering trembles as the magic left his body, its source severed. Only when he felt the man slip loose of his coil did Gryl release his hold and push Rathe aside.

"Not dead . . . yet," he whispered, yanking the sword from his side with a hiss.

He could feel his every wound pulsing as he dragged himself across the wet grass to the wagon. Once there, he clasped at its wheel spokes until he could sit up, propped against its hard wood. The children shied away while he dug for a pouch stashed within the inner pockets of his pants. At last he found what he was looking for and pulled a tiny vial out, holding it up to the wagon.

"Give . . . him this," he said as clearly as he could, waving the vial before the children. "Take it. Pour . . . his mouth."

Time dragged on as he waited, his shoulder throbbing and nearing its limits. Then, just when he feared he could hold the vial within reach no longer, a small, cold hand snatched it from him. Gryl let his arm flop to the ground. He groaned as his head lolled to his chest. The children muttered and whispered above, their words incomprehensible to Gryl, consciousness slipping away with every ragged breath.

His one good eye looked again to the mark on his boot as his vision closed in, and it brought a smile to his lips, despite it all. He read it once more.

Brother, it said.

He sank to his elbow as the last of his strength fled his body. Above, he heard the Xenius boy gasp as the antidote took hold, and Gryl let out a grateful sigh. *He'll be all right.* Rathe had stolen the boy's magic, forcing a choice upon Gryl: kill the boy or let Rathe win. Neither sat well with him, but in the end there'd been no real choice. Gryl's only real regret was that he could do nothing for the girl Rathe had murdered, but at least her brother would live. That was something.

"Stay . . . put," he managed to say before the darkness came for him.

His final thought before he lost consciousness was that Rathe would have to settle for six tongues in whatever hell he found himself.

It was a fair number still, but far better than seven, Gryl thought.

SEANAN MCGUIRE

It is a truth universally acknowledged that when I am told to write anything I want, the odds are extremely high that I will write a Fighting Pumpkins story. This team of vaguely Halloween-themed cheerleaders has been one of my favorite subjects for years, mostly because they embody my personal philosophy of horror movies: that absolutely anything can be successfully scary if it is approached with absolute seriousness. The Fighting Pumpkins may be teenage girls in retina-searing uniforms, but they take themselves and the situations that they wind up in completely seriously. Which just makes things more ridiculous.

I'm also a huge fan of horror, and gross-out humor is a big part of the horror genre. I wanted to write a story that involved cheerleaders yelling about pooping basically constantly. The various members of the squad are recurring enough that at this point I know how they'll react in almost any situation, and the thought of putting them in this specific situation was just, well.

It was too funny to pass up.

FIBER

Seanan McGuire

The trouble began when Laurie discovered that Jamie Lee Curtis yogurt. You know, the stuff that's marketed at, like, middle-aged moms who want to reclaim their youth, or at least the ability to have regular bowel movements again. Anyway, Laurie *loves* Jamie Lee Curtis, for reasons that are a mystery to anyone whose taste in popular culture has matured past the early '90s. Also, Laurie is frequently too lazy to chew. So when Jamie Lee Curtis said "come, my children, and eat of my poop yogurt," Laurie was first in line.

Well, Laurie's mom was, on account of Laurie is also too lazy to go to the goddamn store. It's sort of a miracle that Laurie wasn't too lazy to go out for the cheerleading squad, except for the part where once you wear the orange and green uniform of a Fighting Pumpkin, you basically have a license to cut class. She became a cheerleader because it allowed her to be even lazier. Now that was dedication.

Anyway, we were driving back from an away game against the Devil's Spoke Scorpions—a bunch of lazy jerks whose cheer squad was *barely* deserving of the name, much less their pom-poms—with Jude behind the wheel, Marti in the front, and me, Laurie, and Colleen jammed into the back. The rest of the squad had gone on ahead in the football bus, choosing comfort and efficiency over the freedom of the road and being stacked like cordwood in Jude's backseat. Which, well. The bus was seeming like a better idea with every mile we drove, since Laurie was slurping down yogurt like it was about to be made illegal, while Colleen balanced her notebook on her knee and scribbled in her weird shorthand. We couldn't even really have a conversation, since Marti had all the windows down and the radio cranked all the way to "moving noise violation."

At the same time, I hadn't had this much fun in ages. Largely because I had been a zombie up until the homecoming game, when the weird girl we'd found in the woods had flung herself into the post-game bonfire, burning up and being forgotten by everyone who wasn't on the squad in the same instant. There had been no body, no bones; only straw, and the faint scent of singed pumpkin-flesh. And I had come back to life. My heart had started beating, the scars from my autopsy had scabbed over and started to heal, and I had found myself with a lot of explaining to do.

My parents were still sort of in shock, and viewed me as something between a miracle and a test. When I'd explained, very earnestly, that my return from the grave was connected to the cheerleading squad, they had opened their checkbooks, made a substantial donation to the school, and bought me a new uniform. Being alive was pretty cool. Even if Marti did need to learn how to turn the music down.

Then Laurie looked up from her yogurt—strawberry with extra fiber—worried her lower lip between her teeth for a moment, and said, "I need to go."

Colleen kept writing. Marti kept howling along to a Katy Perry song that had been pretty much incomprehensible *before* it became a duet with a tone-deaf cheerleader. I blanched, leaning away from her. The worst thing about coming back from the dead: bodily functions. It didn't matter what it was, if it came out of an orifice, I didn't want anything to do with it. Doubly so if the orifice it came out of wasn't my own.

Laurie scowled, guessing—rightly—that Jude hadn't heard her, and repeated, more loudly, "I have to *go*."

The car continued to hurtle down the road as fast as Jude's commitment to safe driving would allow. The howling of the wind mingled with the howling of pop music and cheerleader, creating an unholy trio that could only be pierced by something even worse.

"I said, *I HAVE TO GO!*" shouted Laurie. Colleen jumped, her pen drawing a thick black line across the center of the page she'd been scribbling on. Marti swore, loudly enough to be heard over the song. And Jude hit the brakes, slamming us all forward. I gasped, closing my eyes.

To become a zombie, you have to die. That's just Necromancy 101. And I, well, died in a car crash when my boyfriend-at-the time decided that he wasn't too drunk to drive. I couldn't put all the blame on him. I had been too drunk to stop him. End result: while I don't mind riding in cars, I don't like it when they swerve, or brake abruptly, or do anything else that feels like losing control.

"Dammit, Laurie, you scared the crap out of Heather," snapped Marti. I could hear her, which meant she had turned the radio off. That was a nice change.

"No one was listening to me," said Laurie sullenly. I opened my eyes. Laurie had her arms crossed and was sulking at Marti, who had twisted around in her seat to glare into the back. Jude had pulled off to the side and was also twisted around, although her expression was more concerned than accusatory. Her sleek black hair fell in perfect wings to either side of her face, held back with a pumpkin-shaped hair clip that would have seemed immature, if not for our school mascot. Being a Fighting Pumpkin meant never needing to apologize for shopping at Claire's.

"What do you need, Laurie?" asked Jude.

"Can we—" began Laurie.

Jude held up a hand, stopping her. "Please don't," she said.

We all had our little quirks, like me having been dead for a while, or Marti being allergic to gluten. In Laurie's case, "quirk" was another way of saying "people generally did what she asked them to do." She could turn a simple request into an order, just by phrasing it the right way. Jude had been working with her on finding ways to say things without making them an irresistible compulsion for the people around her.

(Laurie's parents were both perfectly nice, perfectly normal people who didn't seem to understand why anyone would want to do anything apart from what their daughter asked. But Colleen, who was the squad's record keeper and had access to all the Fighting Pumpkins handbooks, going back to the foundation of the high school, said that she was pretty sure Laurie's great-grandmother had been a river nymph of some sort. Some things can skip a generation or two. Like gills, or an irresistible voice.)

"But I need to *go*," whined Laurie. "I gotta go *bad*."

"Can't you just piss behind a bush like a normal person?" asked Marti. She sounded annoyed. That was pretty normal. Marti generally sounded annoyed by anything that wasn't all about Marti, which made her a perfect mean girl attack dog for the rest of us. Any time someone started to question why the Pumpkins did things a certain way, we'd just point Marti at them and run in the opposite direction. After she was done stripping the flesh from their bones with her tongue—metaphorically speaking, anyway; she wasn't a real flesh-stripper—they were generally way more willing to tolerate the rest of us being a little odd.

"No!" Laurie shot a horrified look at the back of Marti's head. "I don't need to go number one. I need to *go*."

Colleen looked up from her notes and said, in a surprisingly clinical tone, "She's been eating yogurt for the last hour. By now, her colon is probably ready to explode. She needs to—"

"I am begging you not to finish that sentence," said Jude. "We'll stop at the very next place we see so you can use the bathroom, all right, Laurie? Do you think you can hold it for just a couple of miles?"

"I can try," said Laurie. She sank deeper in her seat. "Just hurry, okay?"

"I'll hurry," said Jude, and hit the gas.

ONE CAR, FIVE cheerleaders, and a totally disregarded speed limit: these are the things that dreams are made of. Jude drove like a girl who desperately didn't want to have her upholstery cleaned, until an exit loomed up ahead of us, complete with a large, hand-painted sign advertising JACK'S COFFEE * GAS * HOMEMADE BEEF JERKY.

"I bet they have a bathroom," said Laurie, with strained enthusiasm.

"I bet they have a man in a hockey mask waiting to carve our faces off and wear them like pretty little masks," said Marti. "I don't want to stop here. This looks unhygienic."

"I gotta *go*," said Laurie.

"I don't know—" began Jude.

And that was when Laurie, sensing that the bathroom was about to slip out of her grasp, did the unforgivable. "Jude, can we please stop? This place seems nice."

"Sure, Laurie," said Jude, and swerved for the exit, ignoring the way Marti and Colleen were shouting for her to slow down. I didn't shout. It wouldn't do any good now that Jude was on a mission, and I had a better task to perform: glaring at Laurie like I was willing the flesh to melt right off of her bones.

To her extremely slight credit, Laurie grimaced apologetically and whispered, "I'm *sorry*, I know I'm not supposed to put the whammy on squad members, but I have to *go*."

"You didn't put the whammy on a squad member, you put it on the squad *leader*," I whispered back. "You're going to be lucky if you don't spend the rest of the season sitting on the bench as a punishment for treason."

"I wasn't aware that we were a totalitarian government," said Colleen, adjusting her glasses as Jude got the car back onto an even keel. "There's nothing in the bylaws about treason charges."

"Shut *up*, Colleen," snarled Marti.

Laurie crossed her legs, looked apologetic, and said nothing.

We were approaching the end of the exit, which looked exactly as promising as an area that played host to Jack's Coffee should. Heavy weeds choked the fields in every direction, broken only by the shapes of twisted, claw-like trees. None of the trees had leaves, naturally; that would have been too friendly, and too welcoming to travelers. It was like we were driving into a bad horror movie from the late 1970s, before anyone had discovered concepts like "production values."

Then we came around the bend, and things got worse.

Jack's Coffee, Gas, and Homemade Beef Jerky was a wooden shack with two antique pumps shoved into the cracked concrete out front. One of them was listing to the side at an alarming angle. The other had a sign on it that read "Out of Order." Completing the picture was a green porta-potty, shoved off to one side with a piece of cardboard declaring "Customers Only" taped to the front.

"Go be customers buy something I don't care what," wailed Laurie, launching herself out of the car as soon as it started to slow down. The door slammed shut behind her as Jude brought us to a full stop.

The sound was the trigger: Jude's hands tightened on the wheel, her shoulders going abruptly stiff, before she leaned forward, attention focused on the fleeing Laurie. "We've stopped," she said.

"Yes," said Colleen.

"I did not want to stop."

"True," said Marti.

Jude made an irritated noise. "She whammied me."

"Yes," I said, opening my door. "And then she whammied us all. Excuse me, but I need to be a customer and buy something."

Grumbling and muttering, the other three cheerleaders followed me as I climbed out of the car. We were an odd streak of color in the blasted landscape: we had changed out of our uniforms after the game, choosing comfort over remaining encased in cotton-poly blend, so we were all in jeans. But our sweatshirts and hair bows were in various permutations of the school colors, orange and green, the high school social structure equivalent of those deep-sea fish that look like rainbows and will poison the shit out of anything that tries to eat them. Even with most of the squad elsewhere, we moved like a pack, smooth and fluid and completely united.

The door was unlocked. That was good. It creaked like a prop from a Vincent Price movie. That was bad. Nothing creaked like that unless it had been abandoned for twenty years, or was being intentionally damaged by a local horror enthusiast.

The interior wasn't much better, although to be fair, it was precisely the sort of place that had been promised by the exterior. The floor was bare, splintery wood, and looked like it would give way under any but the most cautious of treads. There were shelves, which meant that the place could continue to claim to be a "convenience store," no matter how inconvenient it actually was, but those shelves were virtually bare, and the boxes and cans they *did* hold were all brands I didn't recognize. Judging by the hairstyles and clothing of the grinning kids on the cereal boxes, some of the groceries had been here since my parents were in high school, if not longer. Eating anything sold in this store would probably be a quick ticket to food poisoning.

"I am going to strangle Laurie with my bare hands," said Marti philosophically, as she looked around. "If anyone wants to dissuade me, feel free, but it's not going to work. She's going to die, and I'm not going to be sorry."

"At least prison jumpsuits are orange," said Colleen. She took a dainty step forward. The floor creaked, but held. "Maybe they have gum."

"Does it still count as gum after it's fossilized?" I asked.

"Can I help you girls?" The voice was calm, clear, and sounded like it belonged on the radio, maybe trying to sell us a new car or something. I jumped anyway, spinning around with Marti, Colleen, and Jude only half a beat behind me. (Coming back from the dead hadn't changed my reflexes back to human normal, and the horror movies lie about how quickly zombies react to the possibility of a good meal: at my best, I could pluck squirrels out of the trees. These days, I'm just a little quicker than the norm. Which is still uncannily fast, especially when compared to the people around me.)

The man in the doorway matched the voice. He had brown hair, brown eyes, and a chin that should have been immortalized in story, song, and the occasional soft-focus photo shoot. Only his clothes spoiled the effect, since I'd never seen a piece of prime beefcake wearing dirty brown zip-up mechanic's overalls before. They were at least three sizes too big, and still managed to look amazing. The thought that if he looked that good *in* them, he'd look even better *out* of them occurred briefly. I shoved it down. This was the time to buy expired sodas and rock-hard gum, not to indulge our carnal natures.

Besides, while I was willing to share most things with my squad, the idea of adding my love life—or lust life, as might have been more accurate—to the list just didn't sit well with me.

"Hi!" said Jude, falling immediately into her role as leader. She offered the stranger a winning smile. (Literally winning. That smile had put us over the top at cheer camp, twice. When it came to bringing home the gold, the power of Jude's orthodontist could not be ignored.) "Do you work here?"

"Oh my God what the fuck," muttered Marti, slapping her forehead with one hand. Louder, she said, "Jude. He's wearing the logo of this shit-shack on his left boy-boob. If he doesn't work here, he's a murder-hobo, and we need to leave."

"Please forgive my friend; she was raised by wolves, and she doesn't really understand how to interact with normal people," said Jude. She glared daggers at Marti before flashing another smile at the stranger. "I was just hoping you could sell us something. Our friend is using your bathroom, and she's really into following the letter of the law."

"Ah, the 'customers only' sign got another one," said the man. He looked amused by the whole situation. I wasn't sure whether that was a good thing or a bad thing. We were sort of a house of horrors once we got going—most people found us less "amusing" and more "terrifying give them whatever they want so they'll go away."

I'd say it was because we were a bunch of sometimes semi-supernatural weirdos who flung each other into the air for fun, but honestly, the semi-supernatural thing didn't seem to have anything to do with it. Every cheerleading squad had their own version of our repelling field, effective on high school students and high school graduates alike. Once you've known the terror of large groups of girls in short skirts and spirit bows, you can never truly be free of it.

Only this fellow didn't seem to be batting an eye, either out of fear or because he wanted some barely legal cheerleader action (also not uncommon, unfortunately). He was looking at the four of us with an expression of vague amusement, like we were the most adorable things that had ever darkened his doorstep. That made me nervous. No, more than nervous: that made me *wary*. Never trust anybody who can look at a group of teenage girls in short skirts and not react at all.

Those are almost always the people who are hiding something.

"We don't get much business around here," he said. "How'd you like some homemade beef jerky?"

"Was it made this decade?" asked Marti.

"Yes," said the man, looking amused. "It was even made this year. I'm Chuck, by the way."

"Jude," said our squad leader. She pointed at the rest of us as she listed, in turn, "Marti, Colleen, and Heather. Our fifth Fighting Pumpkin should be here shortly."

"If she didn't fall in," said Chuck, and laughed at his own joke before starting toward the counter. "Come on. I'll show you what we've got."

The beef jerky was kept up at the front counter in a variety of old apothecary jars. Anywhere else, they would have looked charmingly antique. Here, they fed right into the overall horror movie décor, making it seem even more likely that a man with a machete was going to spring out at us at any moment.

"Oh, look, teriyaki," said Colleen happily, and removed the lid from the first jar of jerky.

The smell hit me immediately, blunted by a heavy coating of teriyaki, but unmistakable all the same. I actually moaned, the sound rising involuntarily from the depths of my throat and causing all three of my teammates to whip around and stare at me. Jude, especially, went pale. She extended one hand like she was going to take my arm, only to pause and pull back, unsure of what she was supposed to do.

"Heather?" she said. "Are you . . . feeling all right?"

The man in the overalls raised his eyebrows. "Your friend sounds hungry. She a big fan of jerky?"

"Actually, she's a vegetarian," said Marti smoothly. She plucked the lid from Colleen's unresisting fingers and clamped it back down over the jar. The smell of teriyaki jerky stopped invading the store, although it lingered in my nostrils, dreadful and cloying, like smoke, or permanent marker.

Jude frowned, eyes still locked on my face. "Heather?"

I struggled to make my jaw unclench. My heart was hammering, and my lungs ached—I hadn't exhaled since the jar had been opened, freeing that terrible, wonderful scent. I tried to focus on my heartbeat. It meant that I was still alive. Living people had choices. They could choose whether to moan or not. They could choose whether they were going to stuff their faces with jerky or kick some terrifying gas station asshole in the balls. They were *alive*. But in the moment, I didn't feel like I had any choices at all. I couldn't move.

The door banged open behind me and footsteps pattered into the room, followed by Laurie demanding mulishly, "Aren't you guys done *yet*? The bathroom was *way* gross. I had to raid the glove compartment for wet wipes. By the way, we're out of wet wipes. Do they sell those here?"

"Just a second, Laurie," said Jude. Her eyes remained fixed on me. "Heather? Are you feeling all right? Do we need to step outside? Because we can step outside, if that's what needs to happen. We can always come back in and make our purchases after you've had a chance to take a few deep breaths and maybe sit down."

"Maybe she just needs to eat some jerky," said Chuck. "In my experience, most vegetarians are just people who haven't had enough beef jerky in their lives."

That was the last straw. My jaw finally obeyed my orders to unclench. As soon as I could move again, I grabbed the nearest arm, which belonged to Jude, and yanked it—along with its owner—farther from the jars of jerky. "*Human*," I hissed.

Jude, who hadn't risen to leader of the Fighting Pumpkins cheer squad by being slow on the uptake, gasped. Marti and Colleen looked at me blankly. And Laurie skipped over to the counter and reached for the nearest jar.

"This looks delicious!" she chirped. "Sorry about the, um, you-know from before. I just really had to *go*."

Marti's hand clamped down on Laurie's wrist before she could take the lid off the jar. "How about you *reverse* the you-know so that we can all leave, hmm?" she said. "I don't think Heather's feeling much like jerky right now."

Chuck, who had been looking increasingly confused by the ruckus we were making, frowned. "Now, hang on," he said. "We enforce a strict 'customers only' policy with our bathroom facilities."

"Oh, like what, you're going to shove it back up her ass?" snapped Marti. "How about we leave a dollar on the counter, and you call it all good?"

"Wait, why is my ass involved?" asked Laurie, sounding alarmed.

I found my voice again. "It's *human*," I said. "The jerky is made from people."

"Are you sure?" asked Jude.

"I know what human flesh smells like," I said, letting go of her arm. "I know what it tastes like, too. None of you need to know that. We need to leave. Laurie?"

"Um," she said, pulling away from the jerky jar. Marti released her wrist, enabling her retreat. "No one has to buy anything, let's just leave."

"Oh, no, sugar," said Chuck. His voice had dropped down into his chest, becoming dark and gravelly. I whirled, putting myself between him and the rest of the squad.

His overalls weren't too large anymore. If anything, they were too small, clinging to his body like they had been painted on, seams threatening to split with every move of his densely muscled arms. Hair covered his neck and hands, and ran up the sides of his face in some of the most impressive muttonchops I had ever seen a man grow in under a minute. His eyes had gone from charming brown to piss-yellow, cold and somehow rancid, like they were windows for a soul that had gone bad.

"No, no, no," he said, showing a mouthful of jagged teeth. "You agreed to the contract when you used the bathroom. Customers only. If you want to break it, you're going to pay."

"Oh, goodie," said Colleen faintly. "We found a wendigo. I always wondered if they were real."

Chuck snarled and lunged for her. Marti kicked him in the throat as Jude kicked him in the balls. I elbowed him in the side of the neck for good measure before I grabbed Jude again and hauled ass for the exit, trusting the others to follow. The wendigo, meanwhile, was in the process of folding in half and dropping to his knees, thus proving the old adage that you should never forget to wear a cup to a cheerleader fight. No matter what kind of junk you're packing in your pants, a good boot to the groin is going to put you down if you don't have protection.

The door hadn't latched all the way. I hit it shoulder-first, bursting onto the porch in a shower of splinters and deeply confused termites. All I needed to do was get Jude to the car. The others could look out for themselves, or I could double back for them once I was sure that our captain was safe; saving her meant saving the team, at least symbolically. It was less than twenty yards to safety—

Twenty yards, and three more wendigo, their mouths bristling with teeth and their chins slick with drool. I came skidding to a stop, aided by Jude, who grabbed the doorframe with the hand that wasn't clutching my shoulder. Her fingers dug in to both the wood and my flesh. We halted.

"What the *fuck*," demanded Marti from behind me. I glanced over my shoulder. Wendigo #1 was still crumpled in a heap on the floor. He was going to be pissed when he recovered. Marti, Colleen, and Laurie were all standing there, ready to run, which gave them a clear line of sight on the new wendigo. "Why are we in a horror movie? I just had my nails done!"

"Because we're always in a horror movie," said Jude. She squirmed out of my grasp, grabbed Laurie, and shoved her in front of us. "Tell them to back off," she ordered.

"Um," said Laurie. She looked terrified. That showed more of a brain than was normal for her. Clearing her throat, she cupped her hands around her mouth and called, "Hey, monsters! Don't eat us!"

The wendigo started laughing.

"I don't think it worked," said Laurie, dropping her hands. "Why didn't it work?"

"Maybe because they're mangy cannibalistic monsters, and not members of the Computer Club," said Marti.

"It's not cannibalism if they're not human," said Colleen.

"Should we really be standing here discussing this when we're about to be eaten?" asked Jude, just before the wendigo we had left inside the shop—good old Chuck—slammed into her from behind and sent her sprawling into me. I slammed into Laurie, and all three of us went down in a heap, with the wendigo on top of us.

He didn't stay there long. There was an enraged scream, and then he was fleeing from Marti, who was attempting to use his head as a kickball. Wendigo #1 fled to the dubious safety of wendigo #2 through #4, falling into place among his pack. He snarled. So did they. I picked myself up from the porch, grabbed Jude *and* Laurie this time, and fled back inside.

"Barricade the door!" I shouted.

"*Way* ahead of you," said Marti, shouldering me out of the way as she hauled a shelf from its place in the middle of the room to prop against the door—which no longer latched, thanks to our earlier exit. "Okay, Colleen, you're our genius. How the fuck do we get past these things?"

"I've never *seen* a wendigo before!" protested Colleen. "They're supposed to be mythological!"

"Like zombies, mind-control, and attractive high-waisted jeans, and yet here we are," said Marti. "Figure something out!"

Jude had picked herself up from the floor. Smoothing her hair with one hand, she asked, "What was that you said about the jerky before, Heather?"

"It's human," I said. My mouth flooded with spit. I swallowed it, trying to push back the memory of how *delicious* people had been, back when I was dead and they were my natural prey. "Teriyaki-flavored human, but still human."

"Wendigo are cannibals," said Marti again, shooting a glare at Colleen that dared her to argue the definition of "cannibalism." Instead, Colleen just looked thoughtful.

"So the jerky is probably other people who stopped here for gas or to use the bathroom," she said. "That gives me an idea."

"We'll try anything," said Jude.

"Just remember you said that," said Colleen.

CHEERLEADERS NATURALLY COME in two varieties: the ones who throw, and the ones who get thrown. We gussy our roles up with lots of extras, like "who stands on the bottom of the pyramid" and "who does the big tumbling passes," but at the end of the day, some of us had our feet on the ground so that the rest of us could get our heads as high into the clouds as possible. Jude and Marti were both bases. Colleen and Laurie were fliers. I was a switch—I could fill either role, as needed, although most of the time, I was too busy doing cartwheels for my teammates to fling me around.

Using me as a stabilizer, Marti and Jude knelt down and allowed Colleen and Laurie, respectively, to climb onto their backs, where the two lighter girls locked their knees around the ribcages of their bases. That left Colleen and Laurie with free hands, and the leverage they would need if they had to launch themselves into the air. Jude handed me her car keys. I handed Jude and Marti each a jar of jerky, which they passed up to Colleen and Laurie.

"This is a terrible plan," I said.

"Go, Pumpkins," said Jude, and kicked the door open.

The wendigo were still outside—true to Colleen's supposition, they had decided to wait us out rather than destroy their own shack. It was always nice to deal with responsibly minded monsters. Jude and Marti screamed as they ran. I dove for the space between them, hitting the ground on my hands and going into a tumbling pass that would have been illegal in competition; I was pushing myself high and hard, without pausing to breathe or give my spotters time to adjust for my position. It was the sort of stunt that breaks necks.

Like the neck of the wendigo I landed on halfway across the yard. There was a sickening crunch as he went down, and the smell of blood and piss filled the air. Hitting someone in the base of the skull with a hundred and forty pounds of fast-moving cheerleader will do that. Another of the wendigo howled, swiping at me and drawing four lines of burning pain down the back of my thigh. The smell of *my* blood— human enough to trigger that maddening hunger, even though it was my own—filled my mouth and nose, obscuring the stink of wendigo. The wendigo howled.

"*Now!*" shouted Jude.

On cue, Colleen and Laurie opened their jars of jerky and began pelting the wendigo. The wendigo howled and snapped, grabbing the jerky before it could hit the ground. Two wendigo went for the same piece of jerky. Then they went for each other. Colleen spiked her jerky jar, hard, off the remaining wendigo's head—and then I was too far ahead of the action to see what was happening any more.

Jude hadn't bothered to lock the car in her rush to get inside and buy things. Thank fuck for that. I wrenched the door open, jammed the keys into the ignition, and hit the gas, sending the car rocketing toward the fray. Jude dove out of the way, taking Colleen with her. Marti and Laurie were a few feet away, still throwing jerky to the wendigo.

"Get in get in get in!" I screeched. Jude threw Colleen onto the roof and dove in through the passenger side door. Marti didn't bother letting Laurie go; she just shoved her through the open window to the backseat and slung her legs in after her, leaving her own torso hanging over the edge. Reaching up, she grabbed Colleen's arm, stabilizing them both. I hit the gas again, and we were off, accelerating away from the shack and toward the freeway, with one cheerleader on the roof, one halfway out the window, and three wendigo in pursuit.

"*I hate all of you!*" I screamed.

Jude put on her seatbelt.

We hit the freeway at just under seventy miles per hour, weaving as I tried to keep the car under control without flinging anyone off into space. Colleen was whooping with glee. Marti was screaming incoherent curses, her meaning clear only from her tone. The wendigo were hot on our trail, which was somehow more terrifying than anything else about our situation. Shapeshifting cannibal monsters were one thing. Shapeshifting cannibal monsters that could run at seventy miles per hour were something entirely different.

A convoy of big rigs was making its lumbering way down the other side of the highway. I said a silent prayer to whatever god looks after cheerleaders and fools, and jerked the wheel hard to the side, sending us careening across three lanes and cutting off the lead truck in the convoy. Horns blared. Tires screeched. Colleen squealed.

Wendigo splashed. Everywhere. Three wendigo could generate a *lot* of splash. Colleen squealed again, but this time it was in disgust, not delight. "It's in my hair *it's in my hair!*" she wailed.

"Shut up," snarled Marti.

I kept pulling on the wheel, steering us onto the shoulder. I turned the hazard lights on, stopped the engine, and slumped backward in my seat, panting.

"Oh my God," said Jude.

"That sucked," said Marti, pulling herself in through the window and starting to pick bits of wendigo out of her hair. "Somebody get Colleen off the roof."

I got out of the car and helped Colleen down as Jude slid into the driver's seat. Colleen had been right in the path of the bursting wendigo: she was covered in gore, although she wasn't injured. I was the only one who'd actually been hurt. Marti broke out the first aid kit, and we did some roadside medical care while Colleen toweled herself off. Then it was back into the car and back on the road for home.

AN HOUR LATER, Laurie piped up from the back seat: "I need to *go*."

Everyone groaned.

Marti threw the rest of Laurie's yogurt out the window.

ANTHONY RYAN

This story grew out of a desire to explore a fantasy narrative from the antagonist's point of view—after all, Dark Lords and Ladies are people too, right? If you cut them, do they not bleed? Sometimes yes, oft times no, but that's beside the point. I've often wondered what was going through Sauron's head when the Men of the West were at his gates and his Nazgûl still hadn't managed to find the Ring Bearer—pondering the wisdom of taking up residence in a giant obsidian tower a few miles away from an active volcano, maybe? Also, as a short fiction novice I wanted to test the long-standing advice of constructing the story as the climax of a much longer narrative. Fortunately, in Sharrow-Met, a name and a character that had hung around my ever-crowded imagination for some time, I found the ideal vehicle for this tale, although it wasn't until the giant war eagles and talking velociraptors turned up that I felt ready to start writing. Enjoy.

THE HALL OF THE DIAMOND QUEEN

Anthony Ryan

She loved to watch them run. Victory's reward was the spectacle of flee-ing men, the raging panic and fear a tangible delight as the Raptorile and Tormented broke their ranks and the blackwings streaked down from above, talons flashing and beaks gaping wide. This had been a harder battle than most, the foe an army some forty thousand strong led by a veteran warrior king of typically noble aspect. She could see him now, standing atop a small hill, two-handed longsword raised high as his most loyal retainers clustered around him for the final stand. She felt a faint tick of recognition as her unnaturally keen sight found his face, lined with age but still handsome beneath the beard, and the eyes a pale shade of blue reminding her of the sea.

There is only the Voice. The Voice brings great rewards and dark glory. Those deaf to the Voice are Abominate.

The mantra came unbidden, an automatic response to the surge of memory, banishing the images with a brutal ease that always stirred her gratitude. *All memory is a lie*, the Voice had taught her long ago. *Beware its seduction, my Sharrow-met.* She soon knew the recognition for what it was, watching the king reorder his ranks below. She couldn't hear his words but didn't need to; "Fight!" would be his exhortation. "Fight on or all is lost!" *Another doomed hero. And there have been so many.*

She laid her gauntleted hand on Keera's neck, playing the steel fingers through the great bird's ebony feathers, whispering a soft command. The blackwing tilted in response, banking hard to circle the hill where the noble king made his stand, now ringed by at least a thousand men. Ever more were rushing to join him, fear waning and shame surging at the sight of his example. Kilted clansmen from the northern vales with their double-bladed axes, strongbow-wielding plainsmen from the south, barely armed crofters from the western shore, all rushing to stand with the great king against the surging horde.

Such courage, she mused, guiding Keera lower. *A shame, but one such as he will ever be deaf to the Voice.*

She had Keera ignore the outer ranks and swoop low over the king's house guards, steel-clad talons tearing through their armour like scythes through corn, blood rising in a sweet-tasting vapour that beaded her skin, hot and fresh. Keera rose from the hilltop with a warrior clutched in each claw, then cast them away, rent and torn, their blood like rain on the terrorised faces of their fellows. A few bows thrummed but the arrows flew wide as Keera's wings fanned the air into a gale. The king stood alone now, she saw, his guards forced back by the bird's fury.

She hissed a sigh of anticipation as Keera folded her wings, bird and rider plunging down in a black streak. She had intended to inflict a quick but spectacular death. Not, of course, out of mercy but as a demonstration to his men, the final blow to their teetering courage. The king, however, contrived to frustrate her, diving clear of Keera's snapping beak and delivering a swift backhand stroke with his sword. The bird screamed as the blade found her eye, dark blood gouting as she reeled away, wings spreading in panic, then settling into unnatural stillness at a touch from her rider's hand.

"The Voice is kind," Sharrow-met told the king as she dismounted from Keera's back. "And never shirks from offering friendship to a valiant foe." The offer was perfunctory and she knew the king could hear the amusement in her tone as she strode towards him, her hand going to the long, black-bladed scimitar strapped across her back.

"The Voice offers only death to the valiant," the king replied in a low voice, eyes grim with implacable resolve as he crouched in anticipation of combat. "And slavery to the cowardly . . . and the deluded."

There was an additional weight to this last word that gave her pause, a sense of resigned sorrow. Once again she scrutinised his face, the recognition swelling anew, summoning an image of a man and a woman standing in a garden, his eyes an echo of the ocean beyond. *Can't you see the trap in his words?* the man was saying, leaning close to the woman, a keen desperation evident in voice and manner. *You think he promises life? The histories are clear. All the Voice ever brings is death . . .*

There is only the Voice. The Voice brings great rewards and dark glory.

The vision shattered as the mantra took hold, calling forth her rage, the Dark Glory rising fast, singing in every muscle and nerve as she drew the scimitar. She attacked without preamble or restraint. On occasion she had let these encounters last, allowing her doomed opponent some measure of hope. It made the deathblow so much sweeter, the final realisation in their eyes a tasty treat to crown the moment as the scimitar's blade bit deep. But there would be no sweet moment here, she knew that. This was a day for the all-consuming fire of the Dark Glory, the most cherished gift bestowed by the Voice.

The king was skilled, still swift and strong despite his age, moving with the fierce grace of a born warrior as he parried and whirled, his longsword a flicker of shining steel. *A display worthy of a song*, Sharrow-met mused as she hacked his sword arm off at the elbow then brought the scimitar up and 'round in a scything slash that took away his legs. She stood back to watch him die, the blood draining to leave his noble aspect bleached and empty, but still he clung to life, and his eyes . . .

"Sharrow-met!" She turned to see Harazil descending to earth on the back of his blackwing, a bloodied axe clutched in his fist and a brace of freshly harvested heads dangling from his bird's harness. "Victory, Greatness." The Shar-gur captain pointed his axe at the field and she raised her gaze to witness the disintegration of the noble king's army. The Tormented had broken the ranks of those choosing to die with their king and now moved among the wounded, pale, silent figures going about their business with customary efficiency, killing the maimed and chaining those fit to join their ranks. Beyond them the Raptorile war-packs displayed no such restraint, surging through the fleeing mob, steel-barbed tails whipping like angry snakes as they leaped and bit and tore, pausing after every kill to voice their victory shrieks before bounding on.

Sharrow-met turned again to the king as he choked out a few words, too thick with blood and pain to be discerned but nevertheless spoken with a fierce conviction. She crouched at his side, leaning close with a raised eyebrow. The Dark Glory had faded now, leaving an odd sense of sorrow she had never quite accustomed herself to, and she found she had little appetite for the killing blow.

"I . . ." the king rasped, dimming eyes meeting her own. "I prayed . . . to the Twelve Gods . . . that I might never . . . see your face . . . again . . ."

Harazil's axe came down in a blur, neatly severing the king's neck as his lips moved to form a final, forever unknown word. "Abominate scum," the Shar-gur grunted, snatching up the head and brandishing it at her, back straight and eyes averted in careful respect. "My gift to you, Greatness."

Sharrow-met rose from her haunches, ignoring Harazil's gift and turning away. Her eyes tracked across the sights of slaughter and beyond, over fields of green and gold to the pale, jagged outline on the horizon. *Mara-vielle, City of a Thousand Spires.* The greatest prize yet won by the Servants of the Voice and the last free city on this continent.

"I beg the honour of leading the Vanguard, my queen," Harazil said, voice heavy with anticipation. Like all the Shar-gur his lust for her recognition was ingrained and insatiable. Should she command it he would slice open his own belly in a trice, an order she had been tempted to issue more than once. "I will secure the city's treasures . . ."

"Be quiet," she told him in a murmur, eyes still lingering on the distant spires. She could feel it again, the upsurge of recognition, though she fought to keep it muted. By rights she should surrender herself to the comforts of the mantra but the doomed king's eyes were bright in her mind and there was something enticing about this new sensation, something that made her endure the pain of unwanted visions. *He knew my face.*

"Muster your Tormented," she told Harazil, striding to Keera's side. "Make due assessment of the chosen. Await my word before commencing the cull of the unworthy."

She peered at the blackwing's ruined eye, running a soothing hand over the bird's neck as she took hold of the red-jewelled amulet about her neck. Holding it close to Keera's eye she chanted a soft invocation, calling forth the jewel's power, tendrils of red light snaking forth to lick at the wound, damaged flesh reforming and knitting together. Keera gave an appreciative squawk as the healing completed, the remade eye bright and new, possibly keener than it had ever been, though Sharrowmet knew it would always ache. The Voice's gifts carried a price; her own body was as smooth and free of scars as a new born babe, but there were times, usually at night when she sat through the sleepless hours, when the pain of long-healed wounds was enough to make her cry out, though she never did.

"Send word to the Raptorile to advance upon the city." She climbed onto Keera's back, the bird's wings thrumming as they caught the air and bore her queen aloft. "They will find me at the Hall of the Twelve Gods."

Silence. No screams, no flocks of people casting terrorised glances at the sky, no weeping mothers cradling infants, no old and sick hobbling in the wake of the young as they all fled towards imagined refuge. Just silent spires overlooking empty parks and streets. There were some signs of disorder, upturned carts, doors left open in haste, various detritus littering the broad avenues. But no people, and the people were the true spoils of any victory, for what was the Voice without ears to hear it?

She spent an hour scouring the city, swooping low and high, her marvellous Voice-gifted eyes alive to the slightest movement, but finding nothing. Eventually she guided Keera towards the four tallest spires rising from the centre of the city. Each had been constructed from different coloured marble—red, gold, white and black—and were linked by a series of bridges. They were deceptively fragile in appearance, narrow with fluted buttresses, like a web spun between the spires, but strong enough to have stood for centuries. Each tower rose from the corner of a rectangular structure, itself more than a hundred feet in height, its walls decorated from end to end in marble reliefs. There were three great panels to each wall, one for each of the twelve gods, their legends rendered with a level of skill and detail as yet unseen in all the cities she had taken.

So many years of labour and expense frittered on art, she mused as Keera fanned her wings to alight on a plaza adjacent to the structure's monolithic doors. *More energy expended on defence and they might have stood a chance.*

The doors were open and the space inside cavernous. Painted murals flowed over walls and ceiling like a tide of colour frozen in time. These, she knew, were the epics, the part-mythic tales of Maravielle's origin and rise to greatness; mighty heroes and learned scholars, self-sacrificing warriors and wise statesmen, and, naturally, kings of noble aspect. She found him towards the rear of the chamber, the mural painted high on a wall overlooking a raised dais where a vacant throne sat. The mural was more recent than the others, the paintwork more vivid though it depicted a man considerably younger than the warrior who now lay headless on a hill several miles away. He seemed troubled, his aspect one of sombre reflection as he stood regarding an empty ocean. Her eyes went to the inscription painted above the king's head: *Therumin, The Silver King.*

Therumin. So now she knew his name at least, as he had known her face. She turned, surveying the opposite wall and pausing at the sight of a patch of ruined plaster, a jarring interruption to the finely worked beauty on either side. Moving closer she saw it to have been the work of vandalism, and not recently. The fragments of surviving paint were dim flecks of colour amid ruined plaster yellowed with age. Whatever had been depicted here had been wiped away, expunged with considerable violence, though she noted the inscription was partially intact: ...*amond Que..n.*

The Diamond Queen. She knew this name, her spies had spoken of it. Some tragedy to have befallen the ruling family years ago. The tale had little bearing on her plans so she paid it scant mind, concentrating instead on the reports regarding Mara-vielle's copious wealth. *They are strong*, Harazil had cautioned but she just laughed. *We are stronger, and we have the Voice.*

A skitter of claws on stone drew her attention from the ruined mural. A Raptorile scout party had entered the hall, tails curling in alarm and forked tongues darting to taste the unfamiliar air as they crouched and squinted at the murals, exchanging puzzled profanity in their sibilant speech. They were greenbacks, hailing from the southern jungles and smaller than their red-backed desert cousins, but no less fierce and just as devoted to the acquisition of trinkets. Seeing her, their pack-chief issued a guttural, commanding snarl, and they all fell into an immediate servile posture, approaching in a crouch, claws outstretched to proffer their loot as was custom.

The pack-chief extended the clutch of pearl necklaces in her claws, seeking acknowledgement and forming the human words with uncanny precision, "By your leave, Sharrow-met." For all their apparent savagery, these were intelligent creatures, possessed of memory and senses far beyond human understanding, though their superstitious lust for shiny things made them ever her slaves. *When they die the treasure will buy them protection from eternal torment*, the Voice had told her. *For their prey awaits in the next world, hungry for vengeance.*

She was about to raise her hand and issue the customary response, "The Voice grants rich reward, sister," but paused at the sight of something amid their ranks, something in a tall silver frame. It caught the light with dazzling brightness before the angle changed slightly, revealing the sight of a tall woman in cobalt armour, the hilt of a scimitar jutting over her shoulder. This was a beautiful woman, Sharrow-met saw, perhaps a few years shy of thirty, pale of face with high cheekbones and a delicately curved chin, a face made porcelain in its flawlessness. Her hair was a silken jet cascade, tied back with a silver braid, and her eyes . . . *blue eyes, blue like the sea . . .*

"Get rid of that!" she grated, casting her hand at the mirror and turning away.

A rasping snarl, the multiple crack of whipping tails then the harsh clamour of shattering glass. When she turned back the mirror's unfortunate owner lay dead amid its shards, her plentiful blood sufficient to conceal more hated reflection. It had always been this way, as long she had served the Voice, which was as long as she could remember; she could never abide the sight of her own image.

"She was newly hatched, Sharrow-met," the pack-chief said, her words devoid of any inflection, as her kind could learn a human tongue with remarkable speed but never the emotions that coloured it. However, the floor-level crouch and rigid tail made her contrition clear. "I was remiss in not providing clear instruction."

Sharrow-met gave an irritated wave and moved to the empty throne, running her hands over its finely carved back. "You bring me your spoils but no captives," she told the pack-chief, sinking onto the throne and finding it more comfortable than expected.

"We found none, Sharrow-met," the pack-chief replied, still lowered in the servile crouch.

Could they have fled? she wondered. Had the battle been no more than a desperate ploy to delay her advance and buy time for the people to flee? She quickly dismissed the notion as absurd. *There is nowhere for them to flee to. Every kingdom, duchy, and city on this continent now belongs to the Voice.*

"Carry my word to your sisters," she told the pack-chief. "Search every inch of this city. Go deep, into the sewers, the catacombs. The war-packs are forbidden loot until this is done and I will execute one of my soldiers for every hour that sees no captives in my hands."

SHE DIDN'T SLEEP; such things were lost to those so steeped in the Voice. The Shar-gur still slept, albeit fitfully, and the Tormented required at least some rest in between their many labours, but not her. As night claimed the city she ascended alone through the hall's upper levels, finding only a succession of corridors and rooms, all furnished to varying degrees of finery and all empty. There were more mirrors of course; it was a continual point of puzzlement to her that the people she conquered were so addicted to their own image. She shattered

294

every glass she found, suffering the brief glimpse of the porcelain-faced woman before her armoured fist broke it apart.

She found what she assumed to be the king's rooms on the highest tier of the white marble spire, sparsely furnished with few comforts, though he had maintained an extensive library, all now destined for the fire, as the Voice had no tolerance for books. The adjoining chamber was more interesting, a suite of spacious apartments shrouded in cobwebs. Every surface was thick with dust, the drapes on the windows ragged with filth, the mouldings and cornices turned yellow with decades of neglect.

She judged this a woman's chamber, a woman of some importance given the finery of the dresses hanging in the cupboards and the contents of the jewellery box on her dresser, adorned with a large oval mirror thankfully so thickly webbed it betrayed only the most shadowy reflection. *Diamonds*, Sharrow-met saw, plucking a necklace from the box. *No rubies, no sapphires. Only diamonds.* Her gaze went to the bed; large, luxurious and, if not caked in dust, surely fit for a queen. *The rooms of the Diamond Queen, left untouched for many a year.*

The amulet around her neck gave off a sudden heat, issuing the faint thrum that told of the Voice's imminent blessing. Her heart began to pump faster in anticipation; it was only at these moments that this happened. Not in battle, not when exacting just punishment on the Abominate, only now when the Voice chose to bless her was she reminded that, for the many gifts that had changed her, she still retained a human heart.

I sense you are troubled, my Sharrow-met, it said, the amulet thrumming with every wondrous word, her flesh tingling as the sound washed through her. It was a more subtle reward than the Dark Glory, but no less appreciated.

"The city conceals its citizens somehow," she replied, a slight quaver to her voice. "I would have them hear you, know your rewards as I do."

There is sorcery at work here, I can feel it. A great spell, woven with skill, but still just an illusion, a glamour, to be shattered like the mirrors you hate so much.

"How? How do I shatter it?"

How is any illusion shattered? The trickster relies on the ignorance of his audience when dealing his cards. But those with eyes to see the trick are never fooled. Truth, my wonderful, terrible child. Shatter it with truth.

The amulet gave a sudden deeper thrum, and she convulsed as the pulse of pleasure cut through her, so pure and unrestrained it was almost an agony, leaving her crouched and gasping, gauntlets gripping the edge of the dresser tight enough to splinter the wood.

"I deserve no reward," she groaned, shuddering. "Not until the Abominate are secured."

This war is won by your hand, Sharrow-met. I reward as I see fit. Finish our business here quickly, for we have an ocean to cross and much work to do.

Then it was gone, the absence making her gasp once more, blinking away grateful tears as she raised her gaze, finding it momentarily captured by the gleam of the vanished queen's diamonds.

A flicker in the mirror, something moving behind the cobweb veil.

She came to her feet in a whirl, the scimitar scraping free of the scabbard. Nothing. Just dust and rotting luxury. But she had seen something in the glass, and her eyes never betrayed her.

A sound, no more than a breath, or a faint gust of wind, and her eyes snapped to a tiny plume of dust rising next to the door beyond the bed.

"Come out!" Sharrow-met commanded, striding forward. "Your king is fallen. This city belongs to the Voice. Come out and know his blessing!"

The door slammed aside, hinges broken by the power of her kick . . . and she froze at the sight that greeted her.

Mirrors . . . A hall of mirrors.

The hall was perhaps thirty feet long, narrow with a tiled chequerboard floor, and its walls were covered in mirrors. Like the other rooms the floor was thick with dust, but not the mirrors. Oval mirrors, square mirrors, tiny disc-like mirrors, all gleaming clean and bright as if just polished that morning. Sharrow-met's eyes darted around the hall, finding no one, and no other door. The rooms ended here in this hall of hateful glass. Fortunately the dark prevented clear reflection, but she knew if she took just one more step into the hall the image of the porcelain-faced woman would surround her, bouncing from one glass to the next, inescapable and implacable; she would never be able to shatter them all fast enough.

Another sound, another soft breath, the dust on the chequerboard floor rising to swirl briefly before drifting down with a soft hiss. Sharrow-met took a slow, deliberate backward step and turned around, her heart once again doubling its rhythm though there was no Voice to stir it.

She heard no other sound as she strode away, iron-shod boots drawing a dull echo from the dusty floor, but she felt it, as clear as if it had been shouted: an invitation from whatever waited in that hall. *Come in . . . come in and see . . .*

THE WIRY CAPTIVE writhed in her grasp, chains rattling as she lifted him off the floor, face reddening as her steel fingers tightened on his neck. "Captain Harazil tells me you were Mage-Ascendant to King Therumin," she said, angling her head to scrutinise his face, seeing little sign of wisdom, and less fear than she would have liked. "Your spells held back my Raptorile for a time, as I recall. Five hundred redbacks burned and blasted to ash. Their pack-chief would very much like to know how you taste. Shall I feed you to her?"

The mage grunted, mottled features bunching, a vestige of a snarl visible on his lips and defiance shining in his eyes. She relaxed her grip, pulling him close enough to smell the stench of unwashed flesh and dried blood. Harazil had plucked him from a pile of bodies on the battlefield, a senseless near dead wreck of a man, but somehow the spark of resistance still lingered.

"What glamouring web have you spun here?" she asked in a whisper. "By what means do you hide the Abominate from my eyes?"

She saw a frown flicker across his brow, genuine puzzlement in his gaze before his resolve returned and he stared back, unblinking and silent.

"Not your work then," she said, dropping him to the floor where he lay gasping. She put his age at somewhere near forty, if not a little younger. Most mages were far older, wizened mystics feeble in body but rich in knowledge, though never accruing enough to thwart her. "You have a name?" she asked him.

She expected him not to answer, maintain his silence regardless of consequence as was often the way with these dutiful types. So it came as a surprise when he coughed and rasped out a reply, "Dralgen."

"That is not a noble name," she observed, moving to sit on the throne, appreciating once more the feel of it, as if it had been made for her. She had called Harazil to the Hall of the Twelve Gods that morning, the Shar-gur arriving with his elite guard of Tormented and his prize captive. The Raptorile were still scouring the city, hunting through every dark place with tireless efficiency, finding only rats and abandoned pets. True to her word she had ordered the deaths of six Raptorile and six Tormented so far and had begun to toy with the idea of executing one of the Shar-gur as the ultimate example of their queen's will.

"You were born to the gutter, were you not?" she enquired of Dralgen, hoping to fire his temper. She had always found anger more effective than pain in stirring a reluctant tongue.

The mage, however, seemed to find no cause for resentment in the question, barely glancing up as he voiced his reply. "I was raised in an orphanage . . . the king's orphanage."

"Where, no doubt, his servants were quick to spot your talents. How powerful you must be to have risen so high."

She watched his muscles bunching under the besmirched skin, chains tightening. She could feel him searching for his power, reaching inside himself to summon the fuel his words would shape. "Don't waste your time," she told him. "You are bound by chains of iron, forged by my own fire and quenched in the blood of mages. As long as they touch your skin, your power is quelled, as I think you know."

She felt his power recede, seeing his muscles relax though his gaze retained an aggravating heat. "I know nothing of any glamour," he grated. "You had best kill me and have done, for I have nothing else to say to so pestilent a soul."

Harazil stepped forward, three-tongued whip raised high, halting as Sharrow-met raised a hand to wave him back. "So keen to earn a noble end," she said. "Fitting for one so steeped in failure. But sadly I am unable to oblige. Harazil, how many captives did we take yesterday?"

The Shar-gur's answer was immediate, "Six thousand two hundred and twenty, Greatness."

"How many for the cull?"

"Five thousand three hundred and eighteen."

She returned her gaze to the prostrate mage. "An unusually high number, but not untypical among my more stubborn enemies. Still, it leaves me near a thousand Tormented to swell my ranks." She beckoned one of Harazil's guards forward, a tall, powerful man, his head shaved down to a bone-white scalp. He was bare-chested save the iron chains criss-crossing the hard muscle of his bleached flesh. He strode to within a dozen feet of her—Tormented were allowed no closer to their queen—and dropped to both knees, head bowed.

"Tell this man your name," she commanded, keeping her eyes on Dralgen.

"I need no name," the Tormented replied in an automatic monotone. "I need only the Voice."

"Where were you born?" she continued.

"I need no past," came the toneless reply. "I need only the Voice."

"Are you in pain?"

"Pain is the gift of the Voice. Through pain I know the truth of his words and the wonder of his reward."

She smiled at Dralgen. "Wonderful, isn't he? The product of years of conditioning, a being of absolute servitude, freed from the burden of memory, pride, or identity. In time he may become formidable enough to warrant elevation to Shar-gur and become a great captain in service to the Voice. Are you not jealous?"

She expected more defiance but Dralgen wasn't looking at her. Instead his gaze was fixed on the kneeling Tormented, features drawn in a mix of fear and sympathy.

"I'll spare you his fate," she went on. "You and all the other captives. A merciful death for every soul, if you will . . ."

"You saw her," he said, turning to her, expression defiant once again, but also displaying a certain amused twist to his lips.

"What did you say?"

"You went to her rooms, didn't you? I can sense the taint of her touch. Did she speak to you?"

Sharrow-met stared at him in silence as his smile broadened further. "Why do you imagine those rooms are left untouched?" he asked. "Not even King Therumin could stand to take one step inside. *She* has been waiting a very long time for a visitor, and now she has you."

"And who is she?"

His smile transformed into a laugh, his mirth echoing about the cavernous hall. "A blessing who became a curse," he said, laughter subsiding as she loomed above him, scimitar in hand. She couldn't remember rising from the throne or drawing the blade, her heart once again thumping hard with no whisper from the Voice.

Who is this to stir my fury? she wondered, placing the tip of her scimitar under his chin, watching the humour transform into grim but unrepentant acceptance. *No more than another broken spell-weaver. And yet he makes me so very angry . . .*

"Take a look in one of her mirrors, great queen," Dralgen said as she raised the scimitar. "You'll find all the truth you need."

Truth . . . Shatter it with truth.

SHE RETURNED TO the upper levels after the confrontation with Dralgen, resisting the impulse to hack Harazil's head from his shoulders when he had the gall to question her decision to spare the mage.

"Greatness?" he said, eyes wide in his colourless face as she stepped back, sheathing the scimitar.

"Secure him close by," she repeated in a faint whisper, meeting the Shar-gur's eyes. It had been enough to see him stumbling to his knees babbling abject contrition, but still . . . *He questioned me.*

She sat in the Silver King's library, a scattering of books littering the floor. She had hunted through the shelves for a time, seeking some mention of the Diamond Queen, finding much in the way of history and legend but nothing useful. She could see the entrance to her rooms through the open door, the same sense of invitation rising every time she glanced towards it. *Come in . . . come in and see . . .*

For the first time in many a year she felt a chill. She was clad in only the black silks she wore beneath her armour, having discarded it on returning to the spire. Normally she had little regard for the vagaries of climate, it made scant difference amid the constant ache of her invisible-but-present scars, but tonight she felt it, an icy cut straight to the bone that made her rise and seek out the king's bedchamber. She dragged a blanket from his bed and draped it about her shoulders before returning to her vigil in the library, sitting in clenched immobility until the chill abated and a soothing warmth spread through her, allowing her mind to wander.

As ever the Black Vale was the first image conjured from her memory, the mountain holdfast where the Voice built his army and raised a girl to Greatness. Her earliest memory was of the day a Shar-gur had placed the amulet about her neck. She had no clear notion of how old she had been but guessed she couldn't have been more than eight, just a small girl standing atop one of the obsidian tors overlooking smithies and training grounds where the Tormented laboured. She remembered her eyes had been sore and her cheeks damp but had no notion why that could be. Nor did she yet know her name.

The Shar-gur had been named Zorakath, a mighty champion to one of the now vanished hill-tribes before he had heard the Voice a decade earlier, now risen to generalship over forty thousand Tormented. "Sharrow-met," he had called her. *Wraith-Queen in the ancient tongue.*

The Voice was her father, she understood this on some fundamental level, but Zorakath had been her teacher. She had been at his side when he led the first wave of Tormented against the eastern duchies, grown to adolescence by the time he overran the lake-lands, and gained womanhood the day she watched him die at the Battle of the Pass. The mages of the Westlands had reached a concordance by then, stirred into panicked unity by the inexorable advance of the Voice. Near a thousand had stood together at the Pass, their spells searing fire and ruin into the ranks of the Tormented. Zorakath took his blackwing in a vertical dive into the midst of the mages, wreaking havoc until their fires consumed him. Sharrow-met made ready to command Keera to follow the Shar-gur's example, but the amulet had thrummed, the subsequent command implacable and absolute. *Return to me. I have a task for you.*

And so he had sent her south, alone but for Keera and the chest of looted treasure. The memories shifted, accelerating into a blur. The duels she had fought with various pack-chiefs, spilling blood to earn the right to speak to their sisters. The vast tracks of jungle and desert, the breeding grounds where dull-eyed males tended the endless rows of eggs, and everywhere so many of these clever, wonderfully fierce creatures, willing to fight and die on promise of ever more trinkets. It took ten years, but when she returned it was at the head of an army, one no number of mages could halt.

Come in . . . come in and see . . .

The compulsion lurched anew and something moved beyond the half-open door to the Diamond Queen's chambers, a flickering shadow accompanied by the faint whisper of dust sliding over faded tiles.

Fear now, she thought. *First memory, then cold, now fear. But those who hear the Voice have no need of fear.*

She rose to her feet, letting the blanket fall away, striding forward to slam the doors aside, ignoring the chill of the floor on her bare feet as she made for the hall of mirrors. "I have seen a thousand miles of horrors!" she hissed aloud. "I have seen cities burn and rivers turn red with the blood of my enemies! What do you imagine you can show me?"

But still she paused at the entrance to the hall, her disgusting human heart thumping in her chest as her eyes played over the silent walls of glass. She realised she had left the amulet in the king's chamber with her armour, its absence a keen ache in her breast. *Truth*, she reminded herself. *The mage said there is truth here, and the Voice commands I seek it out.*

A sound behind her, the faintest sigh of an indrawn breath heralding another bone-cutting chill. She shuddered as the skin on her back prickled, knowing something had reached out to caress her flesh. More unheard but undeniable words, effortlessly pushed into her mind: *I knew you would be beautiful. Go in, now . . . Go and see . . .*

302

There was little light to see by, only the faintest gleam on the edges of the mirrors, and every glass seemed like a portal pregnant with the threat of sights unwanted.

There is only the Voice. The Voice brings great rewards and dark glory. Those who hear the Voice have no need of fear.

She repeated the mantra several times over, drew a breath, and stepped forward, the lingering goosebumps on the back of her neck a clear indication her unseen companion had followed her through the door. She paused at the first mirror, her eyes roaming over the gilt frame, steeling herself for the sight of the porcelain-faced young woman. Instead she saw nothing. The mirror held no reflection, just a rectangle of black glass in an ornate frame. She frowned and was about to turn away when the icy caress came again, a numbing touch to her shoulder, holding her in place.

Wait . . . It searches for you . . .

It took a moment before she saw it, a barely perceptible glow in the centre of the glass, growing slowly until it filled the entire mirror, an opaque swirling haze that soon coalesced into a recognisable figure. The girl was small and thin, pale of face and red of eye, her lips colourless and chapped. She wore a fine dress that seemed to jar with her sickly appearance; blue silk and sequins that matched her eyes. She stood gazing into the mirror, head cocked at a curious angle and a motley rag-doll dangling from her hand. Tentatively she reached out to touch the mirror, then drew back, small face bunching in a puzzled frown.

"Does she see me?" Sharrow-met asked in a whisper.

A shadow only, her companion replied. *A possibility . . . A twist in her future captured by the glass.*

Sharrow-met's gaze roved the girl's face, taking in the hollowness of her cheeks before lingering on her red-rimmed eyes. "She has a sickness."

From the day she was born. It happens sometimes. Those born with the power can be too fragile to contain it. But she never complained . . .

Abruptly the girl turned from the mirror, glancing over her shoulder at a slim beckoning figure, too shadowed to make out. The girl gave the glass a final bemused glance before clutching her doll to her breast and scampering off. The mirror misted over once more, then slowly faded to black.

"You knew her," Sharrow-met said, finding her skin suddenly beaded with sweat despite the chill at her back. "What was her name?" Her companion said nothing, though the cold air shifted, impelling her towards the next mirror.

This one was wider, the black glass misting, then forming into an impressive view of a garden on a summer's day. The same little girl played in the foreground, a little older now but somehow even weaker in appearance, a certain fatigue evident in her movements as she made her doll dance. Beyond her a man and a woman stood side by side, the woman talking with great animation whilst the man stood staring fixedly out at the glittering sea in the distance. The mirror conveyed no sound but Sharrow-met knew with absolute certainty the words spoken by the woman: *I sensed no lie in his promise . . .*

She remembered it all. The feel of the grass against her skin, the sun on her back, the scent of the orange blossoms, and the voices of her parents arguing a short way off. *Raggy*, she thought, sheened in sweat and limbs trembling. *The doll's name was Raggy.*

She saw the man round on the woman, a tall man of noble aspect, handsome as his wife was beautiful, made suddenly ugly by anger and fear. "Can't you see the trap in his words?" the man had demanded in a tone she hadn't heard before, causing her to look up from Raggy's caperings, as the little girl in the mirror looked up now. The man leaned close to the woman and Sharrow-met found herself mouthing his next words as he spoke them: "You think he promises life? The histories are clear. All the Voice ever brings is death . . ."

She whirled away from the mirror, eyes shut tight, gasping as the cold enveloped her, the chill cutting even deeper, making her cry out and sink to her knees. "There . . . there is o-only . . . the V-voice . . ." she stammered through misting breath. "The Voice . . . b-brings great . . . rewards and . . . and . . ."

This was where it found me, her companion's words invaded her mind with calm ease. *In this hall, this place of power and wisdom. For this was to be my legacy, the finest collection of enchanted glass in all the world. A blessing for those who came after me, twisted into a curse. For this was how the Voice found me. Lacking form or substance, it lives in the artefacts of power; the blessed blades of great warriors, these wondrous mirrors, the jewel you wear. It came to me and whispered of wonders, of impossible reward . . . I can save her, it said, and through the glass it sent a vision of what you would be, the warrior queen, so strong, so beautiful, so much more than the sickly girl who broke my heart with her every rasping cough. He sent his Shar-gur captain on a great bird to take you, and though I knew my husband would hate me for all the ages, I gave you to the Voice. He promised one day he would return you . . . and now he has.*

"The . . . the glamour," Sharrow-met gasped, the chill now gripping her like a vice. "You wove it!"

My husband shunned my company from the day I gave you away, forbade my presence at all councils and formal gatherings. I spent my remaining days in these rooms. I knew by then, you see. I knew what I had done . . . One day he would send you home with fire and slaughter. So for years I sought an answer in these mirrors, rarely sleeping or eating. I suppose I became mad after a time, and when my body finally died, I barely noticed, and my labour continued.

The icy fist closed ever tighter, squeezing the air from Sharrow-met's body, her back convulsing into a spasmodic arch, a shout of pain filling the hall.

Open your eyes, my daughter. The grip tightened further and Sharrow-met's shout became a scream. *Open your eyes and see!*

Her eyes flew open, stinging and streaming from the cold, and there before her stood a woman, or rather the mist of her own stolen breath formed into the shape of a woman. Sharrow-met choked, her empty lungs unable to give sound to the words she sought to speak: *What is my name?*

The face of the spectre shifted, becoming more solid, the features recognisable as those of the woman in the glass, her expression sorrowful but not unkind. Her lips moved to form a silent reply, the words conveyed to Sharrow-met by other means. *Mara, we named you for the city.* The spectre of the Diamond Queen smiled then raised her arms, every mirror in the hall suddenly filling with bright light, banishing shadow and invading Sharrow-met's eyes with a searing pain.

Now, my daughter, the Diamond Queen said as Sharrow-met tried vainly to scream once more. *Now it is time for you to see . . .*

SHE HAD THE mage brought to the top of the white marble spire in the morning, a pair of Tormented forcing him up the steps and onto the balcony where she waited. Sharrow-met noted his evident exhaustion, though his defiance remained undimmed. She turned her gaze to the city, eyes tracking over the Shar-gur gliding above on their blackwings to the Raptorile prowling the streets and parks below, crouched low as they hunted, blind to their prey.

She could see them now, clustering together in fear, crouching in doorways, some sitting in the parks, slumped and accepting of their fate, and all surely baffled to the point of near-madness as to why the monsters who had seized their city paid them no mind at all. The people were everywhere, revealed the instant she made her way from the Diamond Queen's chambers to the great hall below where they huddled in their hundreds, some crying out in terror as they realised she could see them, mothers clutching infants, the elderly staring with grim resolution. She had wandered the city for hours, clad only in her silks, heedless of the cold whilst the jewel about her neck throbbed constantly with the Voice's entreaties. *She lied, my Sharrow-met. You are mine. You have always been mine . . .*

"Remarkable," she said now, gesturing for the Tormented to bring Dralgen to her side and nodding at the streets below. "Don't you think?"

Dralgen said nothing, wariness and puzzlement dominating his sagging features.

"You can't see them, can you?" she asked, reaching out to touch a finger to his head. He stiffened momentarily in pain, then blinked like a man waking from a troubled sleep. On looking down at the city, his eyes grew wide and a soft gasp of amazement escaped him.

"Perhaps the most powerful spell ever woven," Sharrow-met said. "Thousands of souls hidden in plain sight by nothing more than the will of a long dead woman. My mother was surely the greatest of mages."

"Therumin spoke of her power," Dralgen breathed. "But this . . ."

"Did he tell you?" she asked. "Did his people know they faced destruction at the hands of his heir?"

He shook his head, gaze still fixed on the newly revealed populace below. "He was a greatly sorrowful man. His daughter stolen, his wife driven to madness and death in grief. Sometimes I wonder if he hungered for your coming."

I prayed . . . that I might never see your face again . . . "No," she murmured. "No he did not."

Her hand went to the jewel resting on her breastplate, now visibly thrumming as her steel fingers closed on it. *I made you,* the Voice said, and for the first time she heard something new in it, something beyond the serene certainty, something more than the unfettered affection it had always shown her; a faint, fearful whine, like a petulant child caught in a lie. *I was lonely, so I made you. Have I not shown you love, my Sharrow-met? Was not the Dark Glory everything I promised?*

"Yes," she replied, lifting the amulet's chain over her head and laying the jewel on the balustrade before her. "Everything and more."

It began to scream as she drew the scimitar, a shrill, desperate exhortation reaching out to the Shar-gur. *Sharrow-met is Abominate! Kill her! KILL HER! KI—*

The scimitar's pommel came down in a hammer blow, driven with all her unnatural strength, the Voice choking to silence as the red jewel shattered into a cloud of sparkling dust. She glanced up to see the Shar-gur had been quick to answer the Voice's call, six blackwings formed into an arrowhead aimed straight at the spire, Harazil in the lead, axe held high. She could feel his rising hate and wondered if it had always been there, hidden behind unfaltering loyalty all these years, festering away as he waited his chance.

She turned to Dralgen, reaching out to touch his chains, which fell away in an instant, leaving him gasping with the shock of release. She glanced at the two Tormented, both staring at her in abject bemusement. She blinked and the clasps holding their chains in place shattered. They both cried out in unison, falling to their knees, a great chorus of agony and wonder rising from the city as she turned back, her will reaching out to free every Tormented under her command.

"I'll bring the Shar-gur to you," she told Dralgen, leaping over the balcony. "Kill as many as you can."

She plummeted for twenty yards before Keera caught her. The Shar-gur may still belong to the Voice but Keera had always been hers. The great bird's talons snatched her from the air and Sharrow-met swung herself onto the harness on her back, immediately guiding the bird in a low sweeping pass over the plaza below. The Shar-gur had the advantage of height, and she needed speed to have any chance of executing this stratagem. Behind her the Shar-gur's blackwings screamed and air thundered as their riders forced them to greater efforts, Harazil's hate-filled challenge cutting through the din.

Sharrow-met guided Keera into a climb, sending them soaring high, ascending to the same height as the spire in a few beats. Keera folded her wings and they spun in the air, turning to face the pursuing Shar-gur, their formation tight as they rounded the spire and drew level with the balcony where Dralgen waited.

The mage's fire caught Harazil first, searing away his bird's left wing in a blaze of white flame and cinders, sending both rider and bird spiralling towards the plaza below. The torrent of flame swept through the other Shar-gur, killing two and wounding the others before it flickered and died, Sharrow-met seeing the mage's slim form slumping in exhaustion. She took Keera in a dive through what remained of the Shar-gur, scimitar flashing, the blackwing's steel-shod talons rending the flesh of her own kind. The frenzy of battle was different without the Dark Glory, no surging exultation or joyous thrill at the spatter of blood on her skin, just the grunts and jolts of savage contest. The Shar-gur were mighty indeed, stolen heroes from once great kingdoms, but they were not her, and although they died hard, still they died.

She decapitated the last of them as he fell from the back of his mortally wounded bird, head and body describing strangely identical bloody spirals as they tumbled towards the earth. Sharrow-met followed the corpse down and had Keera land outside the door to the great hall, near to where Harazil lay amid the smoking remains of his bird. She stepped down from Keera's back, wincing from the stinging cut on her cheek, certain to scar now there was no jewel to heal her. *Finally, a crack in the porcelain mask*, she thought, wondering why the notion made her laugh.

She noticed the city-folk gathering on the steps to the plaza, plainly fearful but edging ever closer. She knew they would kill her; once they realised she offered no more threat they would take bloody vengeance for their fallen men. She paused to play a hand through Keera's feathers, whispering a final command. The bird gave a brief squawk, perhaps in reluctance, but nevertheless spread her wings and ascended into the sky once more. Sharrow-met watched her rise to circle the spire before striking off on an eastward course, towards the Iron Peaks where her kind made their home.

Sharrow-met held up the scimitar's blade, dark with the blood of Shar-gur and blackwing alike, then tossed it away with a grimace of disgust before slumping down on the steps, weary and waiting for the peoples' judgement.

"Abominate!" She turned to see Harazil rising from the corpse of his blackwing, face half-burned and smoking, one arm charred to the bone, but the other whole and strong enough to raise his axe as he stumbled towards her. "You are deaf to the Voice!"

Sharrow-met's eyes went to where her scimitar lay and found her weariness so deep she had no desire to reach for it. So she simply sat and watched the maimed Shar-gur lurch towards her, spitting hate with every faltering step. "You were always unworthy! The Voice should have chosen me! I will make him an offering of your traitorous heart! I wi—"

The Raptorile fell on him in a blur of lashing tails and flashing teeth, a full war-pack of thirty redbacks, soon joined by more. Harazil was transformed into a flailing, dark shadow in the midst of their frenzy, killing many but never enough. Sharrow-met looked away as the shadow was shredded to nothing. She wondered at her own surprise, for the Raptorile, like Keera, had always been hers, she it was who led them to much meat and so many trinkets after all.

They formed a tight cordon around her as the city-folk drew closer, warning hisses and raised tail-spikes enough to force them back. She could see the tall, pale figures of former Tormented amongst them, some still plainly astonished at their liberation, others clutching weapons with enraged intent.

"Move back!" She turned to see Dralgen emerging from the temple doors. He waved his arms at the people, voice croaking with weariness but still loud enough to hold a note of command. "This is Princess Mara! Risen to save us. Move back!"

At her nod the Raptorile made way for the mage and he came to her side with a bow. "My queen."

She groaned and got to her feet, surveying the people crowding the steps, more thronging the streets beyond, their ranks swelled by the unchained Tormented. Their expressions varied: fear, joy, relief, but through it all a simmering and growing anger.

"Hardly," she told Dralgen. "I think, perhaps, these people are deserving of a new dynasty."

She turned to the Raptorile, gesturing for the most senior pack-chief to come forward. "Send word to gather your sisters," she said. "We leave this city by nightfall. They may keep their loot but take nothing else. None are to feed."

The pack-chief assumed the customary servile posture, but paused before bounding off, her tail describing the shape that indicated puzzlement. "Where now for the hunt, Sharrow-met?"

She glanced down at her scimitar and one of the redbacks quickly scooped it up and brought it to her, crouching low as she proffered the hilt. Sharrow-met returned the weapon to the scabbard on her back and turned to the east, where the sun rose high over distant mountains. "There are many shiny things," she said, "in a place called the Black Vale, far to the east. The treasure of a hundred kingdoms. Follow me there, and you can have it all."

The pack-chief bobbed lower but still hesitated. "And what reward awaits you there, sister?"

"Silence," she replied, feeling a smile spread across her lips. "I shall be content with silence."

BRIAN STAVELEY

There are almost as many Hidden Farmboy Princes as Mysterious Master Swordsmen in the annals of epic fantasy. Usually we see the story through the eyes of one of those princes. He comes to understand the truth about his past, eventually defeats his foes, claims his birthright, etcetera, etcetera. What does it look like, though, to live in the same town as one of these heroes, and not some idealized, Renaissance-faire town brimming with minstrels and mead, either, but some miserable medieval backwater afflicted by famine, banditry, disease? This was the question I set out to answer in this short story, and I'll admit I had a great time poking fun at a few other tropes as well: Why are the bad guys always so incompetent? Why are the princes in question so clueless? This isn't really a nice story, but then, not every tale is a fairy tale.

THE FARMBOY PRINCE

Brian Staveley

We weren't fucking stupid.

It was obvious even early on, even when we were just pimply kids, that Royal wasn't one of us. His skin was too smooth, for one thing; while we were busy popping zits and digging dirty fingernails into our blackheads, Royal's skin seemed to glow. Dirt just didn't stick to him the same way it did to us. Even when he'd been slopping hogs all day long, he didn't stink the way we did. He wouldn't wash his hair for half a year, and it still looked like silk. Mine? I had to hack it off with a kitchen knife each spring.

Did I mention his name was *Royal?*

If that weren't enough, there were the midnight visitors to consider. Two Streams is the sort of place that city-folk call a hamlet; I'd call it a shithole. A couple of streets, mostly mud mixed with piss. A slouching tavern, half burned-down when Twisted Nick got drunk and set the kitchen on fire. Pigs everywhere. It's not the sort of place with much to offer a well-dressed traveler on his high horse, but ever since Royal showed up—Sera's cousin's orphan from out west, they told us—we started seeing more of these strangers, men and women in silk and muslin worth more than our whole farm, coming and going long after the last lights had burned down.

They'd sit in the tavern trying not to grimace, holding one of Nick's filthy tankards as though he'd filled it up with some pox-victim's phlegm instead of ale, which, considering Nick's ale, was about right. They'd ask questions they had no reason to ask: *How's the harvest this year? You have any good farmers?* As if they gave any sort of a shit about the harvest or our farmers. Eventually, they'd make some sort of excuse to head out Sera's way, where they'd pretend to study the pigs without ever taking their eyes off Royal.

It was obvious. Even Brick-Leg Jack knew the kid was a prince—maybe a prince in hiding, but still a prince—and Brick-Leg Jack was too drunk to remember his own name half the time.

The only people who didn't seem to be in on the joke were the sinister sons-of-bitches in black cloaks who showed up from time to time. They'd hiss, and gnash their teeth, and skulk around for a few days, asking questions that were even more obvious than the questions from the rich bastards with the nice horses: "Have you sssseeen any orphanssss?" they'd ask. "Ssstrange orphanss?"

We knew who they were talking about. How could you *not*? There was only one strange orphan in town. We could have handed Royal's lily-scented ass over to them, but we didn't, mostly because it was more fun just to fuck with these guys.

"Sure," we'd say, pointing. "That little hog over there lost his mother just last week." It was worth it for the hisses of vexation. By god, those pale, pockmarked sons-of-bitches were dumb.

There was just one—a tall, gaunt hisser with fingers like claws—who seemed to understand we were pulling his leg. He went for his sword, which was a bad mistake. I don't know what kinds of towns he'd been lurking in earlier, but if you go for your sword in Two Streams, you'd better be ready to drop some motherfuckers. We were on him in a blink with bricks, sticks, fists—whatever came to hand, really. He left town half-dead, and we never saw him again. Looking back, maybe we should have let him have the little prince. Would have sidestepped what happened later, at least.

And then there was Royal himself. Despite about a thousand signs, he had no idea who he was. Seemed to think he was just a hog farmer like the rest of us, despite the fact he had the only teeth in town that were straight and white and all accounted for.

Funny thing was, he wasn't a bad farmer. Those of us who grew up in Two Streams hated getting up in the mid-winter cold, freezing our tits and dicks off slopping hogs that would try to take a chunk out of your leg more often than not. Royal didn't hate things; he didn't seem *able* to hate. Like I said, he was different than us; that poor bastard would have slopped a whole kingdom full of hogs and thanked you for the chance to do it. It was easy to take advantage of him, but he didn't care—would just look at you with those serious eyes and ask if there was any other way he could help.

At first we didn't trust his work ethic. Seemed too much like the set-up to a joke or a punch in the face. Every day, though, he was out there, in the gray rain or on the hottest day of summer, working his noble balls off. He never cheated. Never lied. We'd shave the dice so he lost every game, and he never complained. He was kind to everyone. A strange guy, but hard to hate, and for a long time it worked out fine.

Then, sometime around his sixteenth birthday, the strangers started coming more often, sometimes two or three riding through in a month. And there were rumors, too, little shards of news out of the east: *Discontent. Rebellion. War. The end of the usurpers. The true king to rise; the old flag to fly again.*

Well, we might have been born in the sticks, but we knew just what the fuck *that* meant. To be clear, we didn't give a pickled shit about who sat on the throne. The throne was hundreds of miles away. One royal family or another, we'd still have wood to split before winter. We'd still be slopping hogs, swilling Twisted Nick's shitty ale, feeling each other up in haylofts. We weren't against Royal's family and we weren't for it. People might say that what happened next happened because we were jealous, but it's not true. What happened next happened because we knew what it would mean for the old flag to fly again. We knew what it would take.

I tried to warn him.

"Royal," I said. "You gotta get outta here. Get south. Now. Before the weather turns."

He just smiled at me. "Why?"

I wanted to tell him, but how do you tell someone *that* dumb that he's a prince, that he's being groomed to be king?

"The speckled pox," I said instead. "It's coming this way."

His eyes widened, but he didn't flinch. Did I mention he was brave?

"Then we'll face it together," he replied, clapping his hand on my shoulder as though we were friends, as though he knew the first thing about me. "This is my home too."

"No," I said, shaking my head. "No, it's not."

He looked a little hurt. "I know I wasn't born here . . ."

"That's not it . . ."

"I know I wasn't born here," he said again, talking over me. He could be firm when he wanted. You could imagine him sitting on a throne, handing down edicts or orders or whatever. "But because of you, because of friends like you, I've made this my home."

The next day, a group of us, a group of his friends, got together. We told him we were looking for a lost hog down by the south swamp, and of course he wanted to help. Didn't matter that it was pissing down rain, that the ground was more mud than dirt—he was going to help us find that hog. Almost made you feel bad for him, but this was no time for feeling bad.

We waited until we were deep in the swamp, and then we did it. He was strong and fast, but he was trusting, and we'd been butchering ornery hogs all our lives. There was a quick orgy of knives, Royal clutching his chest, staring at us, perplexed, then sinking to his knees. It would have made a fine song, but the only instrument in town had been Peet's warped lute, and his wife had busted that over his head a year earlier. No songs for Royal, which was just as well, considering.

We heaved the carcass into the swamp. If he didn't sink, the animals would go to work on him, and the rest would rot before anyone came looking.

If someone was writing the history, I'm sure we'd be the villains, and I *did* feel a little bad. I think we all did. He was a good kid, after all, real kingly material. Here's the thing though—no one thinks about what happens when a great king returns to claim his throne. He doesn't just ask politely for the usurper to step aside—usurpers don't do that. That's the whole point of being a *usurper*. No, for a great king to claim his throne, there has to be a war, when there's a war, a bunch of poor bastards are going to die, and we had no illusions about who the poor bastards were.

We hated slopping those hogs, but slopping the hogs was better than catching a spear in the guts or an arrow in the eye. It was better than sleeping night after night in the mud while our feet rotted off. It was better than wandering over half a kingdom killing people or getting killed, raping farmers who lived in the wrong place, taking their shit or burning it down. You get a war going, and that's what happens—all to put a different pair of buttocks on the fucking throne. We weren't heroes, but at least we helped stop a war.

Life in Two Streams was shit, but it was life. Sometimes you have to make sacrifices; it's a tough break, but that goes double for princes.

KAT RICHARDSON

I wanted to write a story from the villain's perspective. But one of the problems with writing from the bad guy's point of view is that he or she then becomes the protagonist and, perforce, no longer the villain—it's their story after all. So the challenge I'd set for myself was to write the villain who knows that he or she is the villain and remains so until the end. I couldn't use someone else's character but I could use an archetype, and while I was thinking about archetypes, it occurred to me that the Evil Sorcerer Who Keeps His Heart in a Box has several things in common with the Damsel in the Tower. So I took those ideas and several other classic fairy-tale tropes and spun them together. Initially I called the story "Heart's Blood," and blood does play a part, but by the time I'd revised it, the story had shifted a bit—becoming a tale about hearts and love and the folly of thoughtless desire.

HEART'S DESIRE

Kat Richardson

I have no choice but to kill you, heart of my heart. It is all that is admirable in you—love, compassion, resolve—that seals your fate. Now I trudge up the tower stairs blinded by tears that burn with bitterest salt. I hear the golden eagle's wings beat the air as he lands on the parapet, the stone still chilly in the pine shadows thrown by the rising sun.

I cuff the water from my eyes, though the bird will not care that I weep. "Where is he?" I ask.

Many leagues, by morning's light,
No closer still by dark of night,
Across the river that mountain stream
Delights by glacial freshet.

"Bother you and your metrical poesy, bird." The eagle is too much like me—a killer who fancies himself a poetical soul. Perhaps you will find me as amusing to begin with, as vain and flowery as the bird. "Does he know of me? Does he come hither?"

The bird spreads his wings and bobs his head. *He prepares, Mover of Stones. His distance is yet great and I have had to seek many of my cousins to learn his flight.*

"On the far side of the river, beyond the mountains. . . ."

The eagle bobs his head again.

"I had not expected him to rise so far away," I say. "Is it not strange that this should be?" Oh, liar that I am, this comes as no surprise, but I enjoy the bird's discomfort at being asked a question any deeper than a dish of salt.

The eagle shuffles side to side and tilts his head. *Perhaps one of my cousins carried him in her gullet when first you cast your stone.*

I throw my hands up in frustration. "And perhaps the wind gave wings to pebbles and the gravel speaks to the river that passes over it— each just as likely since nature gave beauty to such a one as you."

The eagle ruffles his feathers in annoyance. *Why belabor me, Mover of Stones? It is no fault of mine if my answer does not please. I shall take my lovely self away if I offend you so.* Piqued, the bird extends his wings again and makes as if to vault into the sky.

"Oh, bird, bird, don't be so quick," I say. "I am intemperate this morning." No more so than ever, but the eagle is easily hoodwinked since of Power, Beauty, Brains he has only two. I take one of the scraps of rabbit flesh from my pocket and hold it aloft. "And I have brought you a tidbit."

He lets out a cry of delight and leaps into the air as I toss the meat upward. The morning light gleams from his golden feathers as he wheels and snatches the bait. You will find him as easy to dupe, I have no doubt.

The eagle lands again and tears the meat, devouring it. And I speak to my spell, which twines through him as he dines upon it. He feels it stir and change him, growing like the thicket that springs up around my tower, but he is too greedy to stop eating the enchanted flesh until it is too late. *Oh, wretched creature!* The bird screams and springs upward, talons extended. *You have poisoned me!*

I lunge and throw my arms around his neck as he expands. My weight pulls him back to the tower's roof and though he rakes me, rends me into pieces, I do not bleed.

The eagle shrieks and flutters, content that he should escape my grip if he cannot kill me, though that is, of course, as impossible as the other.

Now he is as large as a hunting hound.

And now as large as a horse.

I let go and lie on the roof as the torn shreds of my body draw together again.

The eagle flaps his wings, but he is too heavy, now, to fly. *I shall take your eyes, betrayer!*

I roll myself small beneath him and say, "But how shall I behold your loveliness if you blind me, Eagle? And you are lovely—more beautiful than the sunlight on water."

The eagle hops back and perches on the parapet as I rise again. He cocks his head to stare at me with eyes now as large as golden cauldrons. *You think me lovely now? But I am huge and cannot fly! What beauty is that?* He tilts his head in curiosity. *Water comes from your eyes. Is it pain that brings it—I hope so!*

"It is your beauty that brings tears to my eyes," I lie to him, for it is only regret. But he is much too foolish to question my flattery. "And I can restore your flight."

I throw the other piece of meat onto the farthest apron of the tower roof.

The eagle regards it with hunger, but he does not lunge for it yet, though I can see his constant appetite in his gaze. *What will you inflict upon me this time, Mover of Stones?*

Already he forgets his ire. "Only what I have promised," I say. "I will restore your flight and you will remain as mighty and beautiful as you are now. But there is a task. . . ."

The eagle lets out a small sharp cry. *As always!*

"You are bound to me by our mutual nature, no matter what you will," I remind him. "And do you not delight in proving your strength and cunning as I do . . . ?"

He eyes me and clacks his beak as if he imagines how delicious my innards shall one day be. I doubt he has the brain to realize that prey that cannot die is prey that can be tormented for eternity. Alas for us both when he does.

He shuffles foot to foot and spreads his wings, casting a shade over the tower. *What would you have me do?*

"Go to him. Lay a trap. Let him think you in his debt or power. In discharge of this debt, carry him safe across the river and the mountain, so that he will come here all the sooner. But tell him nothing of me."

But to fly so far . . . and carry one of your kind . . . !

"It will be as nothing to you—see how vast and powerful you are! Once you dine upon the meat, you can fly across the valley in a single beat of your wings."

The eagle considers it, turning his head side to side. Then he snatches up the bit of rabbit and gulps it down. My spell enfolds him, illuminates his form in light more golden than the rising spears of the sun.

He launches into the sky and beats high into the brightening blue. Oh, how glorious is this thing I have made for your doom! And the horror of it pains me until fresh tears well from my eyes and I clutch the stone edge of the tower so that I shall not fall to my knees. I am a wretch, and you bring me to this.

The bird returns, raising a wind as he cups the air to land on the parapet again, so pleased with himself that he stops to preen. *Soar! Oh, flight and feathers! I rule the sky!*

"And shall you undertake my task, Eagle?"

Yes! But. But, how shall I entrap him?

"He is a human and believes all animals are stupid," I say. "Leave one of your golden feathers in his path—even the smallest of them will be as long as his hand—just where the river is widest or where I have cast the mountain sheer and daunting in his way. When he picks it up, you have but to descend and attempt—unsuccessfully—to take the feather back. But fail carefully or all is lost. Once he believes he has the upper hand of you, tell him you will carry him toward his heart's desire in exchange for the feather. He will, of course, accept, and as this tower holds his heart's desire, you will carry him to the edge of the wood. No farther. For a goal too easily won is a prize without value."

Your kind is strange. I prefer the prey that comes easily.

I shrug. "Indeed, as what truly intelligent creature does not?"

He preens a bit more and there is barely room enough on the roof for us both.

"Fly, my friend. Find him."

The eagle leaps into the air and beats away. When his form is a distant shape against the mountains, I sink to my knees and weep.

I HAVE SHARED such dreams . . . dreams that draw you to me by the weakness of your nobility, visions of perfection and irresistible desire. Lies and truth bound up as we two are bound together in life and love and death. I have sent them each night since I knew what I must do. While you tarried, the tale spread, bringing others who batter themselves against my obstacles to drown, to fall, to die pierced by thorns and crushed by vines. Not one survives while my forest and my brambles drink their blood. Had you only heeded my sendings earlier, they would not have died.

I climb to the tower every night before I dream. The bat arrives first and then the owl as night thickens. The hedge below the tower grows denser by the day, winding between the trunks of the lofty evergreens as thick as marsh fog and more dangerous, but no news comes. . . . I begin wondering if the eagle has failed me, for he has not yet returned. Perhaps I should send the owl. . . .

But as the darkness draws in tonight, the bat flutters to the tower top and hangs himself on the bare limb I've left there for him, wedged into the crenellations of the parapet.

There is a breeze from the mountain that smells of carrion.

"Indeed, Master of the Evening Sky?" I ask.

Would I tell you something that was not true?

"You never have."

And never will. I have no need to lie, Swarmcaller.

"Everyone lies."

The bat chirps his laughter. *I shall bear that in mind when I converse with you.*

My grief for you has made me incautious, and I would regret my candor, but regret is something I shall have to learn to live without. And the bat, at least, has the virtue of humor—a trait I share with neither the eagle nor the owl, who possess it not at all.

"What does this wind tell you?" I ask.

A man draws near—flies leap from the trail of his leavings and they taste of his journey. The eagle accompanies him, so he has neither eaten the man, nor been killed by him—though that might be a battle worth seeing.

"What would you know of battles, Leatherwing? Your kind does not duel or fight."

My kind are wiser than to kill each other over a bit of land. But battles draw such delicious insects, spiced with tales! And your kind are amusing in their battle array—surging together and churning like a confluence of rivers. It's a good thing your kind have not learned to fly, for then we *should have to learn to fight! Would we not look proper fools flapping through the night bearing tiny swords?*

I chuckle at the thought. "Like a battalion of idiots."

The bat bares his tiny fangs in mock anger. *Do you call me an idiot? Perhaps you mistake me for an eagle. . . . I fear I've been insulted. Should I challenge you to a duel, Swarmcaller?*

I look at him askance, but smile as I say, "That would not be wise— as the challenged, I choose the weapon."

But pity me! Would you be so dishonorable as to choose one I cannot wield?

If I were an honorable creature, I would not, now, be plotting your death. A sudden pang squeezes my chest and I must shut my eyes against it, shedding a tear as large and hard as a pearl. "I will choose that which suits me," I reply.

I cast a spell into the air and send a buzzing cloud of gnats toward the trees below, rife with my own sorrows and stories.

The bat looks first to me, before he makes to fly away after the fast-moving flight of his supper. *Coward.*

Then he falls from his perch and swoops to follow the swarm away into the twilight.

I send away my only friend and draw you to your fate here, where you will be powerless against me. For yes, I am a coward, as much as I am a monster, but I am not a fool.

For two nights I see neither bat nor eagle and return to my chamber alone to cast my dreams. The forest of thorns has grown thick and full all around my tower and there is no path to me but by my art or through the air. I have made it difficult for you, knowing you as I do; like me, you crave challenge and have no time for that which is acquired without effort. So much comes easily to you now, that it was inevitable that you would seek me, though you do not know the price that you will pay in finding me. I am the prize that holds a hidden sting, death at the heart of love. I despise myself, but this will pass. . . .

Late in darkness the owl comes, swooping to the parapet on silent wings like a windblown flurry of snow.

She lays a shimmering crystal on the parapet and turns her head to regard me with a somber gaze.

I pick up the pretty rock and bow. "Well met, Queen of Night. What passes?" I ask and put the stone away in my pocket.

I have taken a mouse that crept into the forest from the shadow of the eagle this afternoon.

"What did it say before you devoured it?"

She hacks and spits its rendered carcass—only bones and fur and long tail—onto the parapet between us. *Ask it yourself. I do not cross-examine my dinner.*

I take up the pathetic bundle and sort it with my fingers, muttering memories to it, willing it to recall its shape and life. The remains rise and take their form, bones assembling into skeleton, fur wrapping about, until the dead mouse stands in my hand, squeaking. I listen closely to its tale, holding it near my ear, feeling the twitch of ghostly whiskers at my cheek.

Sharp beak by evening, where the bramble roots make a den beneath the hazel. As I cross a field of grass, the eagle—monstrous large—roosts above an oak waiting for daylight.

I consider what it's told me. "At the base of the hills where an oak stands beside a field that spreads to my woods. The owl caught you near the bramble and a hazel tree, only the distance a mouse could run from evening into night. . . . I think I know the place," I say.

The owl blinks at me. *Another day will see him to the edge of the thicket.*

"Yes. And then another to the tower, if he can pass the thorns." My breath stumbles in my chest and I look back to the mouse. "I will ask a favor of you, little one."

The remains squeak and tremble—even dead it is afraid of me. I part its tattered fur with my fingertips and take two of its tiny ribs. The creature's cries wring me with pity. "There, Mouse, it will soon be over and you will live again. Find the man and lead him to your ribs, which will rise up into a gate. When he is through, touch your bones and they will return to their proper place as you will return to life. Then scamper fast back to your home and be at peace."

But he is far. . . .

"Never mind it. I will bring him closer." I work my magic over the sad bundle of remaining bones and fur and the mouse stands again as if alive, though it is only an illusion for now.

I breathe into its mouth and ears and it looks up, speaking like a man, "My thanks, Mage."

"Do not be foolish with my gift, Mouse."

It trembles again. "Never!"

I place it on the parapet and watch it scamper away down the vine-grown walls of my tower.

The owl regards it hungrily, then turns her gaze back to me.

You place much faith in the rodent.

"It will do as I ask."

Why trust such a one? They are foolish and easily frightened. Why not ask the bear to drive the man to your hidden path?

I shake my head. "The bear could not resist his impulse to do the man harm. I would rather that he comes without violence."

Why?

"Now that he walks in my domain, every drop of his blood shed is as a drop of my own. The longer he takes to come to me, the greater the danger."

My plan proceeds and the ache within me builds with every step you take in my direction. I walk to the edge of the parapet and look over, but the view down is obscured by night and the constant stream of my tears.

You should find some other way . . .

"It is none of your concern, Owl," I snap. "There *is* no other way. I have studied and I have searched and if I would gain the greatest potential of my power, it must be thus."

But this pains you.

"Little worth doing comes without pain." There would be much more if not for my plan. I shall not abandon it, though it means your death and my own agony.

I pick up the tiny bones and hold them out to the owl. "Take these to the place where the hidden path lies at the edge of the wood and lay them on the ground there. Then summon the bat to me. And leave the mouse to its own devices."

The owl stares long at me, keeping her own counsel. Then she blinks and takes the bones in her beak, flying away with neither word nor sound.

You must not delay, nor wander far afield, for I cannot bear this much longer. The path is strewn with horrors—with the bodies of those who would have the prize that was not meant for them and met their end, instead. By your gentlest feelings I will compel you quicker to my side.

I draw my knife and weave my sending around your name, my illusion of perfection cast to dreaming night—for you would never come to me were my image otherwise. Then, I stab the blade into my chest and fall to the tower roof, blood drawn from those who've died before you spreading all around as I cry out into your dreams. I know you hear me, see me fall, and feel my pain as your own. I hear you in the darkness, startled from sleep and shouting your distress, compassion, love. . . . You will rescue me—you must. And soon, for my creatures and my plan ensure it.

But for me this pang, this bleeding, is nothing. You must come and you must die and that is the greater torment. I sob for you until I sleep, wrapped in blood and watched by cold stars until the bat comes.

His fluttering awakens me and he leaps to roost as I climb to my feet, streaked in blood.

Are you clumsy, Swarmcaller? I have never seen you fall before.

"I do not fall—I sleep."

I don't care for your pajamas. . . .

"At least I do not ask you to wear them. I have another task for you."

I guessed as much. What now?

"Only this," I say. "Take your kin and drive the man across the field and toward the hidden path. He will encounter a mouse in the morning who will show him the rest of the way. Be sure to leave the creature in peace and only harry the man faster toward the tower once night is falling. I'd have him here by tomorrow's sunset."

The bat snickers. *You grow impatient.*

"That should be warning enough for you, Leatherwing. Your charm may not be proof against my temper."

But will your temper be proof against my charm?

"We shall see. . . ."

By morning the eagle has stooped to my tower and I have restored him to his natural size—I need him no longer, and his appetite is as gargantuan as he is. I fear for my woods were he to continue in such a state.

He stands at the edge of the parapet and glances at the forest below. *He comes.*

"Well I know it, bird," I say. I feel you close.

And yet, you cry. Why does this not bring you joy? Or is it that you mourn my beauty now that I am diminished again?

"Bird, you are as beautiful as ever, so there is nothing to mourn."

But you are not as beautiful as I . . .

"Think you that I should be jealous? Who could be as lovely as you?" I ask. But my vanity is pricked and I call forth the semblance I wear in your dreams—tall and fair as dawn, kind-eyed and cherry-lipped.

Startled, the eagle cries out and bolts into the sky.

I feel your attention turn toward my tower and in the moment a thorn tears your sleeve, pricks your arm. . . . I gasp and feel the poison burn your flesh.

You must not die. You must not. Not yet. Not but by my hand. I cast a spell out to the thorn and take your wound to myself. Agony like wildfire rages through my body and brings me to my knees, but I must not cry out, since you will hear me and turn again, drawn to my aid. I could fly to you and end this, but that would not accomplish my goal, for the spell has a mind of its own and you must come to me of your own will, no matter the hardship, else my heart will be too weak and we both shall die.

I go below to my rooms in the tower to heal myself and prepare. I needn't stay above now that you are so close; I feel your presence as my own true north and know every step you take. I drink the draughts and cast the spells, cure my wounds, and lay the treasures of my love aside.

I know of your amazement in meeting the small ghost of a mouse. I feel the rush of wings as the bats drive you to the gate and through it to my path. Your fear and resolve wash through me as the gate vanishes and you must wind alone along the path to my tower. Your wonder ignites in my breast as you see the white stone walls rise before you at last.

I climb again to the tower's top, clad in my fair illusion, and walk awhile where you can see me before I descend again without acknowledging your presence. Elation leaps within you as it does in me and you rush to the wall that separates us.

I feel you press against the door, heart beating fast, flushed with yearning that warms me like a fire.

You break the lock with your sword and begin up the stairs. . . .

Round and round, rising up the interminable steps, your breath fast with excitement. I leave my chamber and return again to the roof, panting with you, rushing toward the light that you might see the sun one last time before you die.

You follow, drawn by the fleeting glimpse of my hem, my sleeve, my hair . . . always out of reach, tantalizing. Oh, how your heart beats, how it thrills, and I am entwined in love that binds like cutting wire.

Upon the roof of my tower I cast my circle wide and you ascend within it.

My back is turned, my illusion still intact. I feel your breath stop in your chest, feel your heart leap. You raise your hands to touch me, even from a distance drawn to me. My own breath comes short and wild.

You take a step, then two to bring us close. . . .

I slam the door and turn to you—my heart, my love, my life—as the sky begins to flare toward sunset. And in its changing light I am myself alone.

You stop short. Your confusion is like cold water.

"You are not she," you say.

I smile my bittersweet expression, for you are as beautiful and beloved as ever in my dreams and scrying. And you are here, drawn to your fate. "But I *am* she," I say, and let the face that you have loved take form across my own. I let it fall away to leave my own true face, dark where you are bright, a mirror of yourself. "And I am he. I am you, as you are me, heart of my heart."

You scowl and step back, filling us with your fear and horror. You draw your sword. "You are a sorcerer and mean me ill," you say.

My remorse and resolution twine in our fear and my tears flow again. I tremble with effort. "Not yet a sorcerer, but I do mean to kill you, my heart—for that is what you are and a sorcerer needs no heart."

You strike at me as I draw close—close enough to touch you. But your stroke is no more mortal than the raking of the eagle's claws—you cannot kill me, for I do not bleed.

But you do, and I stab my knife into your throat.

We fall together as your blood flows over me, covering my skin, filling my mouth, blinding me. I lay your body on the tower roof and kneel beside you.

My guilt compels me to speak—if I could only leap through time until this were over I should hold my tongue, but, though I try, I cannot. You are my weakness, even as I feel you dying. "Once we were one, my heart, but I put you from me—all my better feeling, my mortality, and frailty. I cast you as a stone, far away. But perhaps I should have held something back, for such was your goodness and humanity that you sprang up again as a being more perfect and more pure than I, yet tied to me. My own beating, living heart, eternally mine. You plague me with your emotions, your desires, your love. I do not want them. They are my weakness. So today, heart of my heart, I shall murder you and be plagued no more with mortality or feeling."

You say nothing—what can you say, indeed, with your throat slit from side to side?

I plunge the knife into your chest and cut to draw forth the tiny sliver of stone as black as jet that is all that remains of the once-large heart I threw away. The greater perfection around it has grown to be you and this hard cinder is the one cold, hard thing within you—the one thing that ties me to you, still.

My breath steadies and I grow colder as you die, all feeling flowing from me like the blood from your body.

I draw the shimmering crystal from my pocket—the stone the owl brought to me—to bathe it in our blood. This will serve as my heart now. The stone has turned black but for a single brilliant star.

I hear a rustle of wings and look up, the two stones in my hands.

The eagle, the owl, and the bat assemble on the parapet as the last red light of sunset touches it. They watch me with cold eyes as the bond between us dissolves. . . .

Your life snuffs out like a candle, and the kernel of my heart crumbles between my fingers. I—too late—know I have been a fool, reached for immortality and the chill of power unleavened by emotion, and all that remains in me now is horror, swiftly fading.

The creatures watch me without feeling—the feeling that I endowed them with by my fancy and the empathy by which I bound them, now as dead as you are. What I saw as weakness was the sinew and fiber that binds resilience to power into true strength, and what remains without it is as brittle as ice. I have deceived myself to my own doom and slaughtered you for nothing.

The crystal in my other hand goes black . . .

Now they come for me, heart of my heart.

MICHAEL J. SULLIVAN

I admit it, I'm a long-time gaming geek. When I started back in 1984, I played on a Compaq DeskPro outfitted with an 8 MHz 8086 CPU and an awesome monochrome display adapter. I said I was a geek, remember? During the golden age of computer gaming, otherwise known as the 1990s, each month brought quantum innovations, spurring a host of inventive game designs. For me, the pinnacle was reached with the invention of the MMORPG (massive multiplayer online role-playing game), and my wife and I became lost in the world of *EverQuest* from 1999 to 2001.

In the land of Norrath, we made many friends as we rose from a pair of pathetic magic users to guild legends, and I saw how the lines blurred between reality and the virtual world. People speak of how computer games are a waste of time. But a great many good things grew out of those days. One of them was a fertile seed of an idea that I pondered well over a decade ago . . . and still do. This story is the result.

THE GAME

Michael J. Sullivan

Jeri Blainey's blissful ignorance shattered before dawn on the morning of July 30th when the "Ride of the Valkyries" ringtone jolted her awake. She fumbled for the glowing iPhone, charging on the hotel room's nightstand.

"Yeah? What? Who is this?" she asked, pressing the smooth glass to her cheek.

"What the hell did you do, Blainey?"

Even groggy and disoriented she recognized Brandon Meriwether's voice. She sat up, wiped her eyes, and noted the clock's red LED digits shining 5:04 in the dark. She managed the math . . . two o'clock in the morning in Oregon.

Why the hell is he calling at this hour?

The convention wouldn't start for another five hours, her meeting with FiberNexSolutions wasn't until eleven, and her presentation was at two. Any last-minute changes could wait.

"Mr. Meriwether?"

"Blainey, if this is an advertising stunt, you should have cleared it through Dickerson. Are you doing this, or is it someone on your team? People think it's real. They're freaking out. I want you to shut it down. Now!"

"I'm sorry. I . . . I honestly don't have a clue what you're talking about."

"Don't give me that, Jeri. This is serious. Have you seen the news? This isn't the 1930s, and you're no Orson Welles. Publicity is all fine and good, but people can be pretty unforgiving about having their chains yanked so hard. And oh how they love to litigate! It's practically an American pastime. Amnesty International already has more than 68,000 signatures on a petition at the White House's page. I just dodged a call from there—the freaking *White House*, Jeri!"

"The *President* phoned—and you didn't pick up?" Her fingers groped across the top of the nightstand. Finding the lamp, she switched it on.

"No, not *him*, some staffer. I need answers first. If a petition gets 100,000 signatures in thirty days, the White House *has* to respond. Did you know that? I looked the damn thing up!"

"Mr. Meriwether, I honestly have no idea what you're talking about."

"Are *you* running Troth?"

Troth? The Realms of Rah *character? My god, is Brandon drunk?*

"Troth? No. I was sleeping until you woke me."

"Then who is? Ajit? Get him to stop. Shut the game down if you have to. But I want this nonsense to stop. Right now!"

"Mr. Meriwether, you're not making any sense. No one on my team is in the game. We've been working sixteen-hour days the last five weeks. Everyone is exhausted. Maybe you should back up a bit and explain."

A long silence followed. Jeri could hear him breathing—hard, heavy puffs.

Jeri stuffed a pillow behind her back and realized she needed to urinate.

"Troth is off the script," he said, his tone deadpan serious.

Maybe this is a dream?

A software bug in a massive multiplayer role-playing game wasn't cause for phone calls from the White House and petitions from Amnesty International.

"Troth?" she asked. "He's the NPC that starts the Spectral Robe quest."

"I guess."

Jeri drew hair away from her face. "What do you mean he's *off the script?*"

"Which word didn't you understand?"

"Are you saying Troth isn't giving out the quest anymore?"

Jeri couldn't fathom how this could be a problem. The game always had glitches. If Meriwether had called to say the game was completely error free, *that* would be noteworthy. She couldn't make any connection between the virtual world and the White House.

Unless terrorists are using the game as a meeting place to chat and plan. She'd heard of that happening, rumors at least. *But what does that have to do with Troth?*

"No, Jeri, he's not giving out the quest anymore," Meriwether said. "The last report spotted him in the Chimera Tavern in the Forest of Dim."

She almost laughed. Being president of DysanSoft, Meriwether wasn't a developer and didn't know anything about the way things worked.

"That's impossible. NPCs can't—"

"And he's been asking questions."

Her desire to laugh died. "What do you mean he's been *asking questions*? Asking who? Asking what?"

"Players. From the reports I've seen, he started by talking to other NPCs but gave that up because players have been more responsive."

This was tripping well past bizarre, and Jeri doubted if even her unbridled subconscious could dream up this concoction. "What *kind* of questions?"

"Jeri . . . he asked, '*Is this a game?*'"

"No way." Jeri switched on the phone's speaker and dropped the device on the bed. Then she powered up her portable Wi-Fi hub and grabbed her laptop.

"I saw a YouTube video. Looked pretty authentic. I need answers, Jeri. You understand me?"

"Already booting my rig. I'm on it, and I'll call you back." She hung up. As bizarre as the conversation had been, one point was cause for real concern, and she was certain Meriwether had no idea what that was.

WHILE JERI WAITED for her computer to boot, she found the television remote, and the flat panel came on. Jeri typed her logon name and password, then rushed to the bathroom while the machine finished loading.

"... that would kill Troth, wouldn't it?" a male voice from the television asked.

Troth! Holy shit! They're talking about Realms of Rah *on TV!*

"That's unclear," another man responded.

"I think we should repeat that a lot is unclear at this point. Dysan-Soft has yet to make any statements other than to say they are looking into the situation," said a third person, this time a woman.

Jeri didn't recognize the voices, but it didn't matter. Morning news shows were all the same: a bunch of men in suits and a blond woman in a skirt.

"It's probably just some form of guerrilla marketing. Some gimmick to get free advertising. Well, I guess it worked, but it could end up backfiring. If your brand scares people, it becomes toxic. The creepy Burger King commercials lost the fast food giant market share," added one of the men.

"Well I, for one, am plenty scared," the woman said. "I've never cared for video games and don't let my kids play them. They're dangerous—they really are. How many Columbines do we need before people start realizing this? Millions of kids are being desensitized to violence, losing what little social skills they might have, and becoming psychopathic shut-ins. Am I right? I mean if Congress would have passed some legislation to regulate gaming, we wouldn't be here. We have no idea what this *Troth guy* might start telling our kids. With all the hype, they're bound to listen to him. This could be the start of some online cult, a way to mind-control our children!"

"Well, if it is a person or a corporation that's doing the puppeteering, for whatever reason, that's one thing," one of the men interjected. "But let's go back to the idea that it might be real. *That* changes everything. In a way it's like discovering life on Mars, right?"

"I think it's dangerous and should be turned off, unplugged, or whatever the heck they need to do to protect our children." The woman again. Her voice grated.

There must be thousands of applicants for every opening on television. Why do they have to hire every reactionary, irritating moron with a teeth-drag-on-fork voice?

"But if it isn't a hoax—and again I want to repeat for our viewers that nothing has been confirmed—let's consider the possibilities. Artificial intelligence may have advanced to the point of achieving sentience, and Troth is—"

"What do you mean by *sentience?*" the woman asked.

Jeri cringed. *Are they paying her to act stupid?*

"I mean *I* know what it means," the woman said, and Jeri imagined she had gotten some rolled eyes from the others. "But I'm sure *someone* in our audience isn't familiar with the term. It's just not that common of a word, you know?"

"*Self-aware,*" someone else said. "Troth appears to be self-aware, the definition of intelligent life. That would mean he would have rights, including the right to exist. Turning off the server could be interpreted as murder." This voice wasn't as clear as the others, and Jeri guessed they had a specialist weighing in via satellite.

"Which brings us to the Amnesty International petition which now has over 325,000 signatures."

Jesus, how long has this been going on? I only went to bed six hours ago!

"Which is just ridiculous," the woman said. "I still think the person behind this is a pervert trying to lure our children away, or some cult leader. But even if Professor Hubert is right about this whole *awareness thing*, it doesn't change the facts. This Troth character is not alive. He's a bunch of electronic dots, or what do you call them? You know, pixies."

Several people laughed.

"Pixies?" Jeri said to the bathroom tile, which gleamed under the overhead light. "C'mon. "My grandmother is seventy, and even she knows computers aren't made of fairies."

"Pixels," someone corrected.

"Whatever. As I said, I'm no expert on video games. I thought I established that." Her tone was defensive. "But this Troth doesn't even have a body, so how can he be alive?"

Any doubt that the woman was more than a talking head vanished. No journalist would tarnish her own industry this way, just as no priest would admit the Bible was on his to-read stack right under *Fifty Shades of Grey*.

"An amoeba is alive; a germ is alive, and they don't have bodies— not like we do, at least."

"But this Troth thing can't exist outside of a computer."

"And people can't exist outside Earth's atmosphere, either."

"Of course they can!" the woman nearly shouted. "They're called astronauts."

"Astronauts aren't existing outside the atmosphere, they bring it with them, contained in ships and suits. Troth could do the same thing. Just put a laptop running *Realms of Rah* on a spaceship."

"But that's not the same. Troth can't build a spaceship and pilot it."

Jeri flushed the toilet and rushed back to the bed without taking the time to wash her hands. She checked the bars on her portable hot spot, logged into the DysanSoft network, and started downloading the most current version of the game. Once the progress bar was snailing along, she grabbed her iPhone. Normally a dedicated text-based life form, Jeri shied away from calls, but she made an exception this time. Muting the television, she held down the iPhone's power button.

After the musical chime, she said, "Siri, call Ajit."

The iPhone's virtual assistant echoed back, "Calling Ajit." The irony was impossible to miss.

Two-fifteen in Portland and Ajit picked up on the first ring. "'Bout time, Jeri."

"Talk to me."

"We've got nothing back here. Customer Service woke me about four hours ago because of a flood of support tickets. Forty-five minutes later Twitter exploded. I got the team together within an hour."

"So it's not you or anyone else messing around?"

"Nope. We're all in the conference room, and this kind of interactivity can't be programmed. The conversations are fluid and responsive."

"How many servers are we talking about?"

"Just Angoth. Troth is well behaved in staging and he hasn't done anything freaky on the other servers."

"Sounds like a hack then. Danny maybe?"

Jeri felt the list of possibilities dwindling fast. Despite what she'd told Meriwether, she suspected it *was* someone from her team—someone retaliating for so many long hours leading up to this weekend's GDC East. She expected the guilty to step forward and apologize profusely. Then she'd take care of smoothing things over with the brass and write a carefully worded press release. The possibility that a hack might originate outside DysanSoft was a bigger concern.

"Danny wouldn't do it," Ajit replied.

"He might."

"He was pissed about being fired, but he wouldn't. I don't even think he could. Jeri, Troth isn't in even in Eridia any more. He's in *another* zone. Hell, I wouldn't know how to do that. Do you?"

And there it was. The elephant that had been in her room since Meriwether's call now waved hello with his trunk.

"Jeri . . . Jeri? You still there?"

"Yeah, I'm here. Just checking my download. Almost done. So what's going on now? What's the current status?"

Jeri tabbed out of the download window and brought up Chrome. Doing a search on Troth returned 323,000 results. "Is this a game?" was in the title of the top seven.

"It's late, but it didn't take long for people to swarm to the Forest of Dim," Ajit said. "We were afraid of a crash with so many players in a single zone. Game play was laggy as hell. So we kicked everyone off the server and disabled logins. Only Zach is in there now."

One more possibility down. The thought of a hacker was a thread she had been holding onto, but now even that tendril to reality snapped. *Or has it? Anyone who could figure out how to puppet a non-player character across zone boundaries might be bright enough to have their own hidden access. Right?*

"Can Zach still interact with him after kicking everyone off? Is Troth now on what appears to be a programmed script?"

"Nope, no change. Zach and Troth have been having quite the conversation."

"Tell her about the parents." Steve's voice came from the background.

"What's that?" Jeri asked.

"Well, of course, we wanted to see things firsthand, so Zach hailed Troth. Sure enough, instead of giving the cloak quest he says, 'Hi, my name's Troth. Nice to meet you.'"

"At least he's friendly."

"Oh, he's that all right. Then Zach says, 'I'm in search of the Spectral Cloak.' You know, to see if that would jar anything. Guess what Troth does?"

"He doesn't give the quest, I take it."

"He asks Zach if he remembered what his parents looked like."

"You're shitting me!"

"No! But that's not all. The two of them have been having a conversation for hours—*hours*—about families and memories. I gotta tell you Jeri, I'm no Turing judge, but if I were, I'd say Troth passed with flying colors."

"What does Steve say? He's the AI egghead."

"Steve has been feeding Zach prompts, and he concurs."

"You're telling me a guy with a PhD from MIT can't tell if Troth is real or code?"

"No, not at all. I'm saying he *can* tell, and he's convinced Troth *is* alive."

"Alive?"

"Sentient."

Ask me if I know what sentient means and I'll fire your ass right now. She actually paused to see if Ajit would.

He didn't. Instead, he lowered his voice and said, "Things are kinda freaky back here, Jeri. I've asked security not to let anyone out of the building, and you wouldn't believe the number of news trucks in the parking lot. Pinkerton has called in extra officers. And Samuel is roaming the halls proclaiming the Good News of Troth like John the Baptist."

"Our Sam? Samuel Mendelburg, the atheist and professional skeptic formerly of Staten Island? That Sam?"

"A total convert now. He actually called it a *miracle*. I shit you not."

Samuel famously refused to accept that the country of France existed, because he'd never personally been there. When Julie from the quality assurance team explained she'd had a layover in Paris the previous summer, he replied, "That doesn't prove anything. All you know is that you sat inside an airport for a few hours. They all pretty much look the same. You could have been anywhere."

Jeri sighed. "Let me guess. You guys have been glued to the television and Internet sites, haven't you?"

Ajit sounded defensive. "Well, yeah, a bit, of course, but I wouldn't say *glued*."

"I think you're getting wrapped up in all the hysteria that's out there. Maybe you should try doing something more constructive. Of course Troth can pass the Turing test—because a *real person* is puppeteering him. I want you to go through all the files on the server and compare them to the files in the staging area. My guess, you're going to find something that's been changed, or shouldn't be there in the first place."

"Jeri, we aren't complete morons. We did that already. The code is *exactly* the same. And before you ask, all the firewalls are in place, and there are no connections except for Zach's, and he's logged in through a hardline. I'm telling you there is no one running Troth, and the mirror system has him doing exactly what he's supposed to."

"Well, there has to be something. Maybe there's a trigger that sets Troth into some subroutine and he just *seems* self-aware. My money is still on Danny."

"If Danny added this sub before he left, then firing him was the stupidest thing you've ever done, because Danny has to be a genius. I mean he'd make Einstein look like Homer Simpson, seriously. But I don't think our systems even have the computing power needed to do what Troth is. It'd take something like IBM's Watson, and even that falls short of what I've been watching these last few hours."

"Do you have any idea how crazy you're sounding? Or just how serious this is outside our company? Meriwether is dodging calls from the White House, for Christ's sake. He wants this dealt with—*now*! Why don't you just shut down, reformat the disks, reload the last code from before Danny left, and I'm sure everything will be fine."

"I can't," Ajit said.

"Of course you can."

"Okay, let me rephrase: I won't."

"Ajit, did you put your kids up for adoption recently? Because I could swear you still need a paycheck, right?"

"You won't fire me. You need me."

"Excellent point. I'll just tell Steve to do it. I can afford to lose him."

"He won't do it either. I doubt you'll find any of us who will. Listen, I'm telling you, no one could code Troth to do the things he's doing. And since the system is secure, no one can be running him. I think we have to accept that when you've eliminated the impossible, whatever remains, however improbable, must be the truth."

Jeri sighed again. "Ajit, I've read Arthur Conan Doyle too. But do you know what Edison said? 'When you have exhausted all possibilities, remember this—you haven't.'"

"But Jeri, what . . . what if this *is* real? What if Troth is—I mean he could be the very first man-made, sentient artificial intelligence. A new life form. You coded Troth, Jeri, so in some sense, you could be considered his God."

"Project Lead is fine by me, thank you. I'm sure being God has its perks, but I don't think the insurance plan includes dental."

"And Project Lead doesn't grant you unlimited power. Can you reload the server from Indianapolis?" Ajit asked.

"You know I can't."

"Then you are reliant on us, and I'm serious about no one here being willing to jeopardize Troth's existence by resetting the server. But you haven't seen what we have. Before you make any decisions do me this favor—see for yourself. Look, I've already opened a password-protected port for you to log in with. Go, talk to Troth, and afterward, if you still think it's Danny burning the Golden Gate behind him, then fine."

"You'll reload the previous version, then?"

"No—I'll resign. I'm not a Nazi."

Jeri opened her mouth to admonish him for making such an insensitive joke. She wanted to let him know this was serious. Before she could, Jeri realized Ajit wasn't joking. His tone was dead flat. He meant it.

"You're serious?" she asked.

"Absolutely."

Jeri looked at the clock on the nightstand: 5:25. "I'll humor you until four o'clock your time, that's it. What's the password?"

"I_am_the_lord_your_god."

"Cute."

JERI SAT AT the little desk in the corner of her hotel room wearing pajamas that consisted of sweatpants and an oversized T-shirt that read: *Come for the breasts. Stay for the brains.* The only noise was the gurgle of the little in-room coffee maker drooling into a paper cup and the rhythmic pattering of her avatar's feet racing through a dense forest of ancient trees while on *auto run*.

The clock read 5:45 when her avatar reached the Chimera Tavern, built in a lonely section of forest cleared of trees, where stumps had been lazily left behind. The stumps were a telltale sign that the Tavern had, at least originally, been a player-built establishment. NPCs were programmed to clear stumps and fill in holes. The rickety one-story public house with quad dormers looked like a cross between a dive bar and the log cabin on a syrup label. The roof had a dusting of snow, as did the ground and the pine trees around it. *Realms of Rah* ran on half-scale time—for every one day in the real world, two passed in-game—so the two worlds were rarely in sync with each other. While it might be the heat of summer on earth, winter was coming in the Forest of Dim.

Jeri's avatar paused on the porch.

Inside the hotel room, the coffee maker had stopped gurgling. Jeri crossed the room to add cream and sugar to the pale-gray dishwater that bore as much resemblance to coffee as the movie *I, Robot* did to Asimov's book. Feeling chilled, she adjusted the room's thermostat. Outside, a faint dawn competed with the parking lot's floodlights for the right to illuminate the world.

She sent a text to Ajit, asking him to tell Zach to log out. She didn't want to talk to her lead programmer or Zach for that matter. When Ajit texted "Done," she sat back down at the computer, sipped from the coffee cup in one hand and entered the tavern by right-clicking on the door with the other.

The sound of the door creaking played through her tinny laptop speakers as a room lit by the warm glow of a fireplace and three candle-filled chandeliers was revealed. Two NPCs sat at a table in the middle of the room, playing checkers. The one on the left was Dashion the Huntsman, a gimpy one-time hunter who gave out a series of low-level quests: gathering wood for the fire, killing an elusive but nonaggressive stag, and then a more challenging quest to eliminate an aggressive bear. Upon finishing those, a final quest for Dashion's bow was granted, sending the player deep in the forest to a cave filled with spiders. When the gamer went there, he or she could find broken remnants of the weapon. Returning them to Dashion, he'd fixed the bow's broken string and give the player a "+10 to hit" weapon, explaining that he was too old to use the bow anymore.

Across from Dashion was Edgar Sawtail, whose only purpose was to play checkers with Dashion. Neither NPC ever left the tavern. They didn't even get up to stretch or eat. These were two of the lobotomized inhabitants who had caused some of the most talented game developers in the industry to leave DysanSoft.

Realms of Rah, presently in its fourth year and fifth expansion, was unlike its predecessors, such as the once popular *EverQuest*, *World of Warcraft*, *Control Point*, and *Elan Online*. *RoR* reached for the Holy Grail of MMORPGs—a living world. Seven years of development had resulted in the creation of an autonomous simulated ecosystem. Chaos-based weather patterns eroded landscapes, while winds dispersed seeds from mature plants. The seeds could sprout if they landed on good soil. Herbivores ate plants; carnivores ate herbivores.

The alpha version of the game was just the framework, a natural world with no intelligent life. Wind could snap trees, and lightning could spark fires. Rivers could be rerouted or made into lakes if something dammed them. What's more, all changes were just as permanent or as transient as in the real world. If animals weren't killed, they died of old age or sickness. A random drought could devastate plants, kill weaker root systems, and allow new species to dominate.

After the ecosystem was in place, Jeri's team introduced humanoids: men, dwarves, elves, and goblins. A handful of other beings were dropped in with the first expansion. Although they appeared to be typical computer-controlled non-player characters (NPCs), they weren't. All of them were endowed by their creators with the best artificial intelligence the developers could dream up. Just as the creatures imitated the behavior of living animals, the races simulated human beings, with their own needs and motivations. Each programmer tried to outdo the others, and it was interesting to see characters acting on what they saw fit. None of the programmers was exactly sure what would happen once their creations were released into the virtual world, but they had great hopes.

At first things went well. The races lived in caves, hunting and gathering to survive, but the developers wanted more. The code was designed so that the characters would learn from observation and would experiment by combining random existing ideas to create new concepts. This aspect was less successful. Since multiple possibilities were attempted, some truly bizarre developments occurred. For instance, there were mass deaths as characters tumbled off cliffs or drowned while attempting to swim across an ocean. The team remedied this fatal disregard for common sense by adding restrictions to the Free Choice Code. Nevertheless, by the time the beta was opened to a limited public, none of the NPC population had advanced past the Stone Age. The virtual characters had tried thousands of random actions, but none had resulted in building a structure or discovering how to utilize fire.

Everything changed once *Realms of Rah* opened its doors to live players. Exposed to real people who knew enough to make tools, dig minerals, and start fires, the NPCs learned by observation and imitation. Their world evolved quickly after that. Language and technology advanced at a blistering pace, with one notable exception. Writing didn't exist. DysanSoft, still anchored to traditional game concepts, desperately wanted a written language to facilitate quests and stories. Much to the programmers' frustration, the computer-generated inhabitants of Rah never developed this skill. Six months before version 1.0 was set to release, the development team was forced to hardcode the written language into the game and fudge everything related to it. NPCs still couldn't read, and their vocabulary was limited to a set number of prerecorded scripts.

Out of random chance, similarities to the real world cropped up— as when the inhabitants of a large, powerful kingdom decided to build a tower to find God. This completely random event made headlines around the world, sparking arguments between philosophers, scientists, and religious groups. There were calls for *Realms of Rah* to be shut down. Ironically, the uproar actually boosted subscriptions by putting the game on the world's radar. More and more NPCs joined the effort to find God, until players were unable to locate the necessary vendors and resources they needed and began to file complaint tickets. Fearing the game was spinning out of control like a poorly balanced washing machine, corporate ordered the developers to intervene.

This time, instead of allowing them to fix the problem by inserting a Common Sense Code tweak, corporate forced the developers to lobotomize their creations, drastically reducing NPC freedom. This huge step backward launched a civil war inside DysanSoft. Rah programmers, who felt the integrity of the project was being destroyed by "suits," quit en masse. Only three of the original developers stayed: Samuel Mendelburg, Ajit Banerjee, and Jeri Blainey.

With the game closed to all players, those two mindless characters were the only ones in the tavern besides Troth. He was in corner near the fireplace, looking like he normally would with four notable exceptions: his helmet was on the floor, the rawhide at his tunic's collar had been untied and pulled loose, his weapon wasn't in his hands, and he sat in a chair rather than standing at attention.

Troth was a goblin, huge and green—a member of the Ozak tribe formerly of the Ankor Mountains. Mountain goblins were bigger than forest, swamp, or plain goblins, and Troth was one of the largest. He had to be. Troth was a guard to King Zog, the ruler of the Ankor Goblin horde, and designed to be intimidating. Dark-green skin, which was almost black, covered exaggerated muscles. He had a neck as wide as his bald head, a lantern-jaw formed into a natural-state frown, and small eyes that had watched her intently since the door opened. Troth's battle-ax leaned against the wall to the right of the hearth—in easy reach.

Jeri wasn't worried. She was running a default first-level character without gear but in god-mode, immune from harm.

"Hail, Troth," her character said when she targeted him and pressed the H key.

"Hello." His voice was a preprogrammed gravelly growl, but there was a hint of apprehension. His little eyes narrowed as well. "Who are you? How do you know my name?"

Both of Jeri's eyebrows rose. "Whoa—they weren't kidding about you, were they?" she said to her computer screen.

Lacking a decent microphone, she typed, "My name is Havalar. A friend told me about you. Said you were here." Her in-game voice spoke the words.

"Who is this friend?"

"Ozerath." Zach had played the same human wizard since starting at DysanSoft, so there was no doubt about the name.

Troth looked less suspicious but more inquisitive. He leaned forward, placing his massive arms on the table. "What did he tell you about me?"

"He said you were a very interesting fellow, and I should talk with you."

"About what?"

Jeri decided to stay in character, for a while at least. "Ozerath wasn't specific, but that's the way with wizards, isn't it?"

"Yes, it is. Have a seat." He kicked out the chair opposite him. It skidded back with the sound effect Jeri had picked out three years earlier when the sound pack was upgraded. "You came a long way. You must be tired."

This surprised her. "How do you know how far I came?"

"You're elven. The elven lands are a long way off."

His reasoning skills were impressive, but she didn't have all day. "What are you doing here, Troth?" she asked, taking the seat.

"Sitting." He glanced over at Dashion and Edgar and added, "I would have ordered a drink and something to eat, but those two never stop playing that game. I've watched them for hours. The thing is, they make the same moves over and over. I've tried talking to them, but the one insists I go chop wood because he has a bad back, and the other doesn't say anything except uninspired insults."

Uninspired insults? Jeri had programmed Troth herself and his vocabulary did not include the word *uninspired*. Troth had learned that himself.

"This is a tavern," he continued, "but I haven't seen anyone working here. Odd, don't you think?" He gestured at the hearth. "Look at this fire. It's been burning nonstop since I arrived. No one has added wood, but the flames haven't diminished. Don't you find that strange?"

"No. But that's not important. I'm curious. Why did you leave Eridia and come here?"

Troth raised an eyebrow. "Who are you really?"

Jeri took her hands off the keyboard for a moment. She had an eerie sense that Troth was looking through the screen at her—at the real her. "I told you; I'm Havalar."

"Let me rephrase," Troth said. "*What* are you?"

"An elf—you were right about that. I'm an elven enchantress."

Troth nodded. "And have you come to make me forget what I've discovered?"

What he's discovered?

She considered asking what that was, but instead decided on, "What makes you think that?"

"A while ago, there were a bunch of people here, everyone asking questions, everyone curious, and then they vanished all at once. That can be quite disconcerting. Don't you think? Since then, the only one around has been Ozerath—and now he's gone and here you are. I think I did something wrong, something unexpected. I'm supposed to be like them." He pointed at the checker players. "Like I used to be. Day after day, season after season, I guarded a door, and then I left."

"Why did you leave?"

"Well, it was pretty boring for one thing. But mostly, it stopped making sense. A lot of things didn't add up, like the fire and the checkers players. Some things adhere to rules, others don't, but even the rules aren't logical. Everything seems so arbitrary. Why should the sun come up every day? Why do I have to eat? Why do things fall when I let go?" He paused to look out the window at the snow. "Why is there anything at all?"

She could see why Ajit was impressed. Troth had managed to utilize his Random Combination Code on questions and was mimicking real life inquiries to a spooky degree. But it was just like the tower the NPCs tried to build, which was just like the lemming cliff-jumping—just random accidents that gave the illusion of independent thought. That's what the game was supposed to do. What she saw was an NPC that had evolved into what the original design team had always hoped for—a real-life mimic. Somehow his character had been overlooked during the great purge of intelligence, when DysanSoft made a corporate decision to get out of the innovation business. They wanted robotic quest givers, not inhabitants that appeared to be able to think.

"Nice talking with you, Troth."

In her hotel room, she stood in preparation to logging out.

"Are you going back to your world now?"

"What?" She paused.

"You enter this world from somewhere else, don't you? This"—he pointed at her avatar—"isn't you at all, is it? You're probably not even an elf. Maybe not even female. This is just a game for you, isn't it?"

Jeri stared at the screen, stunned. She didn't reply. Instead, she reached for the coffee and knocked it over, spilling the beige liquid across the desk. She pulled tissues from a box to sop it up.

Troth stood, moved toward her, and waved a hand in front of her face. "Are you still there?"

"Yes," she replied. She misspelled the three letters and had to back-space. Her hands, she discovered, were shaking a bit.

This is real. It has to be. Either that or I'm still sleeping.

"What's it like where you are?" he asked, sounding not at all like the muscle-bound mountain goblin he was modeled to be. "Are you still in your reality? Or this one?"

"What makes you think there's more than one reality?" she asked.

"Lots of things. Like I can't remember being born. I know what happened yesterday, and the day before that. I can keep going back, but I don't remember being born or how I got here. And what about death? Everyone dies. But why are we born, if we're just going to die? It makes no sense."

Jeri felt chills. She'd asked herself similar questions, most recently during her father's funeral, who'd past a year before. She hadn't considered the "being born" thing, but now that she thought of it, why couldn't anyone remember that? Everyone just accepted the fact, but why? Brain not developed enough? Was that it, or—

"And where did everything come from? Why is there something rather than nothing? And why *this* something?"

"You're a very philosophical goblin."

"Am I even a goblin? I don't know." Troth looked down at himself and his left hand slid along the skin of his right forearm. "Is this all I am? Or is there a part of me that is more than this?"

The Valkyries began riding again, and Jeri nearly fell out of her chair. She crawled across the bed and saw Meriwether's name and grinning photo on her phone. She answered it knowing what he would ask, but having no idea what she would answer.

"Let's have it," Meriwether said before she even said hello.

"Well, it's—it's definitely not a bug."

"Then what is it?"

"I, ah . . . ah . . ."

"Spit it out, Jeri. What the hell is happening?"

"I . . . I actually think it might be real."

"Real? What do you mean "real"? *What's* real?"

"I think Troth might be alive."

"Alive? Are you high?"

Clearly this wasn't the answer he wanted from her.

"Jeri, Troth is computer code. You wrote him. You made him. He's ones and zeros; he's pixels on a screen."

Pixies, she thought. *What if the blond was right after all?* It seemed more reasonable to think Troth was made of mischievous fairies than dots.

"This has gone on too long. My *no comment* stance isn't cutting it, and now the Chief of Staff is calling from the White House. I'm getting paranoid about a Black Hawk helicopter landing on my front yard and guys in dark suits and glasses taking me away. James Hartwell and a majority of the board—who am I kidding—the *entire* board wants this issue to disappear. Great advertising, but there is such a thing as *too* much. Pull the plug, Jeri. You're the Project Lead. Tell your team to delete Troth from the game, or reset it, or whatever it is you need to do to make this stop, but I want the game up and running normally by seven. Do you understand me?"

"Yeah. I understand."

She ended the call and set the phone down and looked at her computer screen. The small window reserved for in-game dialog was littered with messages from Troth.

While she watched, another appeared. "You're not here," he said. "I can tell. I've seen others stare like that."

More appeared in rapid succession. "Where are you, Havalar? Can you hear me? Havalar? Havalar? Havalar? Don't go. Don't leave. Havalar, I'm scared."

That last comment made her sit back down in front of the keyboard.

"I'm here." Her character repeated her typed words.

Relief washed over his face. "Thank you. I thought . . ."

"What did you think?"

He hesitated. "You're a god, aren't you? Or maybe you're *the* God."

"Why do you say that?"

He shrugged. "The way you're dressed. I've seen those same clothes on very weak people. You're what people refer to as Level One or Newbie. Most of those can be killed by piddling spiders or small rats, but I don't think a spider would kill you. I don't think *I* could kill you. I don't think you fear anyone, not even Azogath himself, because he's not a real god but *you* are."

He lowered his head and traced the table's wood grain with a finger. "I also think you're trying to decide whether to kill me, because I'm not supposed to ask these questions or think these thoughts."

"Listen," she typed, "I have to go."

"No!" he shouted, bumping the table as he moved closer. "No, please. I need to know. If I'm going to die, I want to know if there is a God and if there is any meaning to my existence."

Jeri pressed a hand to her lips, shocked at the rush of sympathy and self-hatred inside her. The clock read 5:58. It would take a while to reformat the drives and reload the code, and then they would need to test. Time was short, but she felt a responsibility to Troth. He was asking the same questions everyone did, but she could give him some answers. She owed him that much.

"I created you," she typed.

Troth's eyes went wide. She thought he might fall to his knees, but he didn't. Instead, he asked, "Are you going to kill me?"

She couldn't bring herself to say the words, so she typed "/nod" to make her avatar answer through body language.

He shook his head and stared at his feet. "Why did you bother making me then?"

Jeri thought about that for a moment. There was only one answer, but it killed her to type it. "For entertainment. For fun."

He stared at her. She expected more shock, perhaps outrage, but he didn't even seem surprised.

"So, it really is just a game, isn't it? All this is fake. Invented."

"How did you know?"

"Like I said, too many things don't make sense. An existence that starts nowhere and goes nowhere is pointless. Appearing out of nothing and vanishing back into it—that's not sensible. And the world is flawed."

"What do you mean by 'flawed'?"

356

"There's all sorts of problems. Kobolds, for example. They're constantly attacking travelers. And the wars between the goblins and the men cause such loss, and rats infest every city. No matter how hard we try, no matter how many rats are killed, there are always more."

"That's . . ." She thought a moment, her fingers hovering over the keys. "By design."

"You wanted an evil world?"

"It's not evil. It's a challenge. What fun would it be to have a world with nothing to do? Nothing to fix? Nothing to save? Your world is for enjoyment, regardless of what a person's idea of pleasure is. If you want to get rich, kill kobolds and sell their hides. You can do that. If you want to help defenseless people, well, there are the kobolds, aren't there? There's something for everyone."

He paused, his eyes darting in thought, his brows furrowing. "What about—why do children—why do some people die before they even get a chance to play?"

Jeri thought a moment, then it hit her. "You're just seeing people log into the game and then back out. Not everyone likes this game. They probably find another one they like better."

"Do people come back? I've met people that seem familiar but aren't. Sometimes they are of a completely different race, or a different gender. Still, I'd swear I knew them before."

"A player can be more than one person, but not at the same time."

Troth looked at her. He stared into her eyes. "I'm not going to come back, am I?"

She emoted for her head to shake.

Troth's big lower lip began to tremble and his eyes grew glassy. "A shame. I recently discovered how to read. The symbols represent sounds, don't they? The sign outside this place says 'The Chimera Tavern,' doesn't it?"

Jeri picked up her phone and used the "recent list" to call Meriwether. Asking Siri to do something she could do herself suddenly felt wrong. "We can't shut it down," she told him. "It's murder."

"Jeri, it's just a game."

"It's not a game—not anymore. And Troth—Troth is a freaking

genius. Seriously, he could be smarter than Stephen Hawking. He's Einstein and Socrates rolled into one. He taught himself to read!"

"Troth isn't *anything*. We're shutting it down."

"No, we're not," Jeri said. "I'll quit, Brandon. I'm not kidding."

"That threat didn't work the last time, kiddo, and it's not going to this time either."

"I'm telling you, I won't do it." Her hand clutching the phone was sweating.

"You don't have to. I am."

"You . . ."

We're shutting it down.

"Where are you, Brandon?"

Her phone vibrated and a text message appeared. *Ajit: Meriwether brought security. Pulling the plug!*

"God damn it, Brandon, don't you do it!"

"You've gone away again, haven't you?" Troth asked. "Please don't leave. I don't want to be alone. I'm scared. I know that sounds strange. I look like a big, strong goblin, but . . . well, you made me, so you should know."

That's when she lost it. Lack of sleep, maybe. Years of frustration, possibly. Most likely it was that big green face looking back at her. Troth was scared to death but blinking back tears and trying to act brave.

"Brandon, you bastard!" she screamed into the phone. "DO—NOT—TURN—OFF—THE—SYSTEM!"

The call ended.

"No!" she cried and slapped the desk, splattering coffee on her computer screen.

"Can you still hear me?" Troth asked.

"Yes! Oh shit, Troth," she furiously typed. "I'm so sorr—"

Troth and the Chimera Tavern vanished, and Jeri found herself staring at a "connection lost" screen.

The tears came. She sobbed harder than she had at her father's funeral. She fell onto the bed and bawled into the foam pillows as the dawn's light began to fill the room.

An existence that starts nowhere and goes nowhere is pointless. Appearing out of nothing and vanishing back into it—that's not sensible.

Jeri looked out at the rising sun. *Isn't that what I thought when Dad died?* She wiped her eyes.

I know what happened yesterday, and the day before that. I can keep going back, but I don't remember being born or how I got here. And what about death? Everyone dies. But why are we born, if we're just going to die?

Jeri stood up, walked to the window, and looked out. Beyond the parking lot, traffic backed up on the freeway as hundreds of people set off to work—just like they did day after day.

I've watched them for hours. The thing is, they make the same moves over and over.

Jeri placed her hands on the glass of the window.

"Is this a game?" she asked.

A knock at the door made her jump.

"Sorry," she said in a raised voice. "I forgot to put out the DO NOT DISTURB. Can you come back later to make up the room? I shouldn't be long."

"I'm not from housekeeping, Jeri," an unfamiliar voice said.

"Who are you? How do you know my name?"

SAM SYKES

I don't think Harry Potter is realistic.

I know that sounds stupid, what with him being a wizard who fights three-headed dogs and stuff, but I never thought that a kid with all that power would have his life nearly so put together. I remember what it was like being that young—craving approval from adults, being terrified of girls, cursed with an endless inner monologue as my thoughts shifted toward existential angst and further away from my previous record of emotional depth: boy, I sure do like Ninja Turtles.

I don't think magic would make that less complicated, and I wrote this story to explore that.

Dreadaeleon and Cesta are kids. Kids with a lot of power but no idea how to use it. Kids who realize that adults don't know everything. Kids who learn that the truth sucks, teachers lie, and the opposite sex is never impressed by what you do. You know, a classic tale of growing up.

Except with fireballs.

THE ETHICAL HERESY

Sam Sykes

Even over the smoke, he could smell her.

A breeze picked up and wended its way across the clearing, as though deciding to tidy up a bit, lest someone take offense to the scent of brimstone. It carried the acrid tinge of flame past his nostrils.

And with it, her.

Not that she smelled particularly unusual—she wore no perfume and her clothing carried the same pungent aroma of ink and paper that his did. Maybe it was just today and these circumstances that made him notice her scent. After all, something clean and pleasant would be impossible not to notice among the reek of cooked flesh.

Absently, he felt his neck slowly turn to his left to steal a glimpse of her standing beside him.

Focus, old man.

With that thought, Dreadaeleon turned his attentions back to the center of the clearing.

Listen, don't speak. Observe, don't stare. Learn, don't dream. Remember what Lector Vemire said. He sniffed, tried to ignore the stink. *After all, it's not every day you get to see a man die.*

Though what currently stood at the center of the clearing could only barely be called a "man" after what Lector Vemire had done to him. Rather, the heretic resembled more an overdone roast, his bony legs like a pair of spits.

Hair, cloth, and flesh had been treated to smoke and flame. All that remained of him was four limbs, a torso, and round head encased in a sloughing, steaming mass of red and black.

The heretic opened his mouth, as if to speak. But only a wisp of black of smoke escaped.

The heretic took a step forward, as if to challenge. But his legs trembled and snapped beneath him.

The heretic fell to his knees, stared out of steaming, empty eye sockets, and collapsed to the earth and lay still.

And as the man he had burned to death lay smoldering before him, Lector Vemire straightened up, brushed a stray piece of ash from his coat, and spoke a single word.

"Next."

He offered a pointed glance to Dreadaeleon, who nodded shakily. He glanced to his left.

And she glanced back.

An apprentice one year his senior, Cesta stood clad in the same boots, breaches, and shirt beneath a well-worn brown coat that he did. And though they had both begun their duties with their clothes hanging off their bodies, her body had begun to fill hers out in ways that made him all too aware of how big his still fit around him.

It certainly didn't help that she stood an infuriating half-a-head taller than him.

Still, his inadequacies didn't seem to catch her notice. Beneath black hair cropped close around her ears, her face was bright. A small mouth curled into a smile and her narrow eyes twinkled.

He felt his own smile creep shakily onto his face in return: a nervous, ungainly grin, ill-fit for a lady like her.

Girl, he reminded himself. *Not lady. She's an apprentice, just like you.*

From twenty paces away, Lector Vemire cleared his throat.

And apprentices have duties.

Cesta took the lead; he followed. Together, they bent at the knees, backs erect as they extended their hands out. Together, they spoke the words they had spent so many nights rehearsing, locked in the library. Together, they felt their eyes go bright with red light as the Venarie flowed into them, through them, out of them.

The air rippled around their hands, snaked across the clearing to seize the charred corpse in an invisible grip. They raised their arms slowly and, unsteadily, the corpse rose off the ground and into the air. They swung their arms, the corpse following like a particularly awkward dog on a particularly unsteady leash, as they magically guided it to a nearby burlap tarp and set it down.

And there it lay neatly between two other tarps: one holding a similarly charred carcass and one still empty for the moment.

They released the corpse, the gesture, and the power all at once. Only after the magic rushed out of him and the light dissipated from his eyes did Dreadaeleon realize he was breathing hard. A drop of sweat slithered down into his eye and he pulled a greasy curl of black hair from his forehead.

That was barely twenty feet, he chastised himself. *Disappointing, old man.*

However disappointing that was, it wasn't *half* so depressing as the sight that awaited him when he looked up.

Cesta, of course, was scarcely breathing hard. Only the barest hint of sweat caressed her brow, and not a single strand of her neatly trimmed hair was out of line. She was a year older than him, but her studies weren't *that* far ahead of his. And yet, levitation and projection, effortless to her, made him weak in the knees.

Then again, that might also just be her scent.

It was hard to tell these days.

"Proceed."

Lector Vemire spoke again, drawing the attentions of everyone in the clearing: Dreadaeleon, Cesta, and the next man to die.

He came shambling up to stand upon the patch of blackened grass where both of his fellows had died. Once, he had been rigid with pride, as all heretics were. Now, he stood bent and gaunt; the weight that had fallen from his body seemed to have been laid upon his shoulders. His eyes were sunken, his gray hair was long and stringy, and his clothes hung in tatters around his body. He had the muscle of a young man draped in the skin and hair of an elder.

To look at him, Dreadaeleon thought, he hardly seemed worth killing. Surely, disease and exhaustion would do it with far less effort, if not less time.

But heresy was heresy.

And duty was duty.

The heretic met Lector Vemire's gaze, eyes quivering in sunken sockets. Slowly, he glanced behind his shoulder. Two Venarium agents stood at his back, fifty paces away, hands folded behind their backs and eyes locked onto him, should he try to escape. At them, he merely sneered, before he glanced to his left.

His eyes settled on Dreadaeleon for a moment, considerate and desperate all at once; a caged animal searching the bars of his prison for any weakness. Dreadaeleon squirmed under the man's gaze, suddenly all too aware of his inadequacies, all too aware of the billowing way his clothes hung off him and the sweat dripping from his brow.

And yet he resisted the urge to look away.

However weak he might feel, it wouldn't do to show it to this man. *Heretic*, he corrected himself. *He's nothing but a heretic now.*

Once, he had been a man.

Once, he had had a rank.

Once, he had had a name.

"Former Senior Concomitant Amouran Athalas."

Lector Vemire's voice, nasal and authoritative, commanded the man's attention. His gaze swept back to the rigid man with the neat hair and pristine brown coat addressing him.

"You stand accused and guilty of nothing less than absolute heresy," Lector Vemire said in slow, clear words. "A summary of charges against you includes disregard of Venarium protocol, violation of Venarium protocol, use of Venarie in assault upon Venarium agents, use of Venarie in assault upon non-sovereign entities, use of Venarie in the name of a non-sovereign cause—"

"My family."

Amouran's voice was shaky and trembling. His glare was dark as he turned it upon the Lector.

"I used my magic in defense of my family," he hissed. "They were being attacked by soldiers intent on collecting tax they weren't entitled to, what else was I supposed—"

"*Abandoning Venarium post without leave*," Vemire spoke over the man's rasping defense, continuing with the litany of charges, "fabricating evidence in report to a Venarium superior, and fraudulent acquisition and unauthorized expenditure of Venarium resources."

Vemire narrowed his eyes, letting the list stand for a cold moment, as if to allow Amouran to challenge them. But the man remained silent, scowling resentfully at the Lector.

"Against these charges, you have been found guilty by the presiding Lector of the region absent a Tower Jury."

"A one-man conviction," Amouran said, sneering. "Efficient."

"The standing sentence, pending appeal, is termination and Harvesting." Vemire stared down the man for a moment. "However, acting within the rights granted by regional tower, Tower Defiant, the presiding Lector is approved to offer leniency in the event that the convicted offered testimonial and physical cooperation."

The breeze stopped, mercilessly. The smell of cooked meat shifted to the roiling reek of generic dead flesh and began to fill Dreadaeleon's nostrils. He absently reached to cover his nose with his sleeve before looking sidelong at Cesta and seeing her standing perfectly still, perfectly attentive, perfectly silent.

As everyone else was.

As he willed himself to.

The silence lingered in the clearing. And when it broke, it was with a seething word.

"Well?"

From Vemire.

The Lector's icy expression thawed, as a frown seared across his face. His eyes betrayed their usual impassive stare, narrowing in what one might call contempt, if one could believe a Lector capable of such emotion.

Comparatively, Amouran's perpetual sneer looked downright serene.

"I want to hear you say it," the heretic said.

"Don't be a fool, Amouran," Vemire replied. "I read your history. You were a promising concomitant, well on your way to earning a spot as a Librarian. You can't possibly throw it all away for—"

"For freedom?" Amouran asked, chuckling blackly.

"For *heresy*," Vemire snapped. "For a simpering fool who will eagerly spew rhetoric about freedom and liberty and just as eagerly leave you alone to face the consequences, as he's done now." He took a tentative step forward. "Tell me what you know of the heretic Lathrim, and I'll see to it your sentence is commuted to penitent study."

A smile cracked Amouran's face. A dark and ugly scar across a tired and ghastly face.

"How kind of you, Rondash," he said. "Instead of killing me outright, you'd see me mercifully locked away into a study to file paperwork for the rest of my life until wizards could cut me open and Harvest my corpse." He lay a skinny hand across a sunken chest. "Why, I was a fool to forsake my duty to the Venarium for the chance to see my family again and save their lives. To think, all this time, I could have been experiencing the endless *thrills* of having my soul crushed out of me year by—"

"Enough." A single word, and the chill returned to Vemire's voice, cast his face into a mess of hard lines. "You have my ultimatum. I will have your answer."

Amouran said nothing. He slowly craned his head around, taking in the clearing around him. He glanced at the two Venarium agents at his back before his eyes settled, once again, upon Dreadaeleon. The boy shuddered beneath his gaze and instantly cursed himself for doing so.

Stop it, stop it, stop *it,* he chided himself. *Don't show him you're weak. Not in front of Cesta. You're an apprentice, soon to be a concomitant. He's a heretic. Show him you're brave. Meet his eyes, old man, meet his eyes.*

Dreadaeleon did so.

He met Amouran's eyes, stared past the rims of the sockets and into the hollows beneath. Like any apprentice of the Venarium, his life of study and training had been fed with ample cautionary tales of the dangers of heresy. He had heard the stories of the reckless fiends who disregarded Venarium law and violated Venarium truths in the name of selfish pursuits of power. And in his dream, he always imagined their eyes would be wide, wild and red with power.

Not like Amouran's eyes. While the heretic's eyes were red from sleepless, tortured nights, there was nothing even the slightest bit insane about them. They looked at him with a soft, yielding gaze accompanied by a long sigh.

As though *he* were the pitiable one.

"Trial by ordeal."

Amouran turned to Vemire, all the despair fled from his face and replaced with grim resolve. Vemire closed his eyes and sighed, as though he had anticipated this.

"Are you sure?" the Lector asked.

"I can prove that I still have worth to the Venarium by combat," Amouran said. He slid into a stance that Dreadaeleon recognized easily: wide legs, feet firmly planted, all the better to channel the force of lightning. "If I win—"

"You will not, Amouran."

Vemire slid into a stance that mirrored the heretic's. He drew in a deep breath. When he opened his eyes again, they were alight with the crimson glow of magic. He words resonated through the clearing, lent a power that stilled breeze and silenced smoke.

"You may act when ready."

And Amouran did.

He did not bother breathing. His eyes erupted with the power almost immediately, Venarie flowing into his stare as swiftly as electricity flowed into his fingers.

Cobalt sparks raced down his arm, danced across his fingertips as he thrust one hand out, two fingers aimed straight for Vemire's heart. Breathless, blazing, bellowing, Amouran screamed.

And the sky screamed with him.

The bolt that shot from his fingertips was massive, an arcing serpent of electricity that flew from his fingers, screaming toward Vemire in a jagged scar across the sky. It swallowed everything the heretic had left in him—his rage, his fear, his sorrows—and grew fatter for it, splitting the sky as it shrieked.

But Dreadaeleon could see it in his stance, in the way he shuddered with every breath. He was powerful, and his passions lent him strength, but he was also exhausted, weak, hungry.

And Vemire was not.

Two steps to the right. The Lector measured each step to take him no farther than he needed to go. And the lightning bolt, fat and gorged as it was, went hungry, flying past him and disappearing with a faint crackle of electricity.

Two fingers thrust out. The Lector took aim. One breath. The Lector narrowed his eyes. One word. The Lector responded in kind, firing off a bolt that was no wider than a spear's shaft and existed for no longer than two breaths.

And Amouran fell dead.

The heretic collapsed. A single black hole punched through his chest loosed a long, slow sigh of steam. His body convulsed once, twice, and then lay still.

"A waste," Vemire muttered. He glanced over the carcass to the two Venarium agents standing nearby. "Amend the list of charges against the heretic Lathrim. He's responsible for these deaths. He'll answer for them." The two agents nodded and he stalked past the dead heretic. "Take care of these bodies while I consult my apprentices. We begin the search immediately after."

Dreadaeleon was still staring dumbly at Amouran's steaming corpse when Vemire came striding up. He noticed Cesta, snapping to attention with her hands folded behind her back, long before he noticed the looming shadow of his Lector standing over him. He mimicked her stance a moment too late to escape a disapproving glare and subsequent resigned sigh from Vemire.

"Tell me what happened," he said.

It did not go without notice or without bitterness from Dreadaeleon that he directed this question to Cesta.

"It was his stance, Lector," she replied. "His legs buckled slightly. He wasn't firmly planted, and so the recoil of the lightning's expulsion swayed him and knocked his aim off. Otherwise, the force behind it would have killed you."

Vemire nodded. He cast a glance toward Dreadaeleon. "And?"

Dreadaeleon blinked. "And . . . uh . . ."

"And his arm was held too taut," Cesta mercifully interjected. "The blowback almost certainly sprained it, preventing him from casting another spell. Not that it mattered. You obviously would have killed him, regardless."

"And yet, these are all apparent after the fact," Vemire said. "I still opted to let him strike the first blow without that knowledge. Why?"

Cesta opened her mouth to answer, but found no words. She cleared her throat, pointedly looked away.

"Because he's a heretic."

Dreadaeleon, to his credit, did *not* squeak when Vemire turned a scrutinizing gaze upon him. Rather, he chose a spot just beside the Lector's eyes to stare at while he continued.

"That is, uh, the heretics are known for reckless ideals," Dreadaeleon said. "They expend magic—uh, sorry, Venarie—without care for the cost or discipline needed to control it. Thus, ah, you could probably almost kind of guess that he wouldn't be able to control his spell."

He glanced at Vemire's eyes long enough to assure himself that, yes, Vemire *was* still staring at him and, yes, the Lector's stare *did* still scare the piss out of him. He shot a sideways look to Cesta for support.

"Right?"

She shot him a helpless wince in reply. Whether it was this that caused Vemire to sigh deeply or not, he didn't know.

"Close," the Lector said. "But 'close' is not good enough for what we do." He laid a hand on each of their shoulders. "Understand that heretics are not merely 'reckless' or 'undisciplined.'"

He gestured with his chin to the three carcasses nearby, where the Venarium agents were already hastily wrapping the corpses of the heretics in herb-soaked bandages that would preserve them long enough to get to the nearest tower capable of Harvesting.

"We don't carry out such heavy sentences for character flaws," he said. "The Venarium stands for discipline, control, and safety. It is by those laws that wizards do not destroy themselves and only by *all* of us adhering to those laws do we keep our Venarie from destroying each other. It is by those laws that you entered my tutelage."

Technically, it was by twenty pieces of gold paid to Dreadaeleon's father by means of a so-termed "bereavement fee" by Venarium accounting that earned Dreadaeleon his spot in Vemire's study.

He had been too young to recall much about his father beyond his drunken aggressions, let alone be upset about the prospect of being removed from him. And it was simply a policy to which all nations adhered that children who showed displays of magical ability be turned over to the Venarium's care.

Absently, he found himself glancing sidelong to Cesta. Did she have a similar story, he wondered?

You should ask her, old man. He opened his mouth. *Wait! Not right now.* He closed it. *Take it easy. Wait until you're alone. It's a tender subject, after all, isn't it? Well, it wasn't for you, but she gets so emotional . . . doesn't she? Women tend to. That's what the stories say. So you bring it up, easy-like, and when she bursts into tears, you—*

"Apprentice."

He nearly broke his neck with how quickly he snapped back to attention, staring up into Vemire's gaze.

"Trust me when I say I'm loathe to enlist you in this task at all, let alone without more study on what heretics are capable of." He glanced over his shoulder at the two Venarium agents. "But our protocol is clear. Regions that suffer a diminished Venarium presence are under different obligations."

Dreadaeleon's eyes suddenly widened.

You know this, old man! Quick, show her! I mean him! Both of them! Go!

"In the—"

"In the event of an incident warranting enhanced Venarium attention," Cesta suddenly spoke over him, "and at the Lector's discretion, all ranks concomitant and below may be mobilized for purposes of neutralizing said threat."

"Excellent, Cesta." Vemire nodded. "So long as you understand what we do and why we do it, I believe you'll be all right." He glanced at Dreadaeleon. "Mostly all right."

Dreadaeleon winced. *You probably deserved that, old man. Quicker, next time.*

He whirled about, made a few forceful gestures out in the general direction of the surrounding forest.

"What information we gleaned suggests Lathrim cannot have escaped more than ten miles," he said. "His comrades stayed behind to cover his retreat. He will be cold, wounded, and spent, likely in the northern direction. I will be taking that route. The attending concomitants will take northeast and northwest. The apprentices shall stay together and cover the east.

"Farther west lies the city of Redgate. The heretic will avoid civilized places for fear of being spotted by additional Venarium presence. In the event you should find him, be certain of your own safety before summoning the others. All orders shall cede to my judgment."

A pointed glance over his shoulder.

"Dreadaeleon, you shall cede to Cesta's."

With that, the Lector turned about and began stalking north. The agents fanned out in their commanded directions.

Dreadaeleon watched their poise as they left: heads held high, arms straight and slightly raised, all fingers spread out. A very typical detection stance, all senses open for the slight, almost imperceptible fluctuations in temperature and pressure that would denote magic use.

Vemire would be able to detect recent expulsions of magical energy for up to thirteen miles, so long as he concentrated. And he was concentrating.

Which meant, of course, that he didn't notice the rude gesture Dreadaeleon hurled with impotent vigor at his back.

But if he *had* . . .

Dreadaeleon kept it up until he became aware of Cesta glancing curiously at him. He felt a sudden rise of heat to his cheeks as he lowered his hands, letting the too-big sleeves of his coat fall over them.

She merely smiled at him, patted his head, and began stalking off to the east.

As though he were a particularly naughty child.

He resisted the urge to hurl the same gesture at her and instead hurried to catch up.

"SO, THE PROBLEM, as I see it, is that he doesn't *really* think I'm a wizard. Like, he looks at me and he sees the coat and the boots and the fire that I can shoot out—when it works; I was having an off-day that one time when it didn't, it wasn't my fault—but he doesn't see a wizard.

"But that's *his* fault. They shouldn't even let him be a Lector if he can't see the possibilities. I learned everything I needed to, I can recite the oaths backward and forward, and I know every stance, but I can't *work* when he's always *yelling* at me and if he could just *see* that, we'd have no problem."

Dreadaeleon took in a long, slow breath. Dreadaeleon let out a long, slow sigh.

"I just . . . he must be wrong about me. He *must*."

He opened his eyes and looked up the slope of the hill.

"Right?"

From atop the hill, Cesta looked back blankly.

"I, uh, just asked if you got that thing you stepped in off your boot."

"Oh!" He stomped his feet on the grass. "Yeah, it fell off a little ways back. Thanks."

"Okay." She nodded. "Good."

"Right, good." He scratched an itch that wasn't there at the corner of his eye. "That other stuff was just on my mind a little lately and, you know, the timing . . ."

"Yeah, no, I got that."

"Okay, just so you . . ." He cleared his throat, made a lengthy show of looking at his feet. When the earth, unmercifully, refused to open up beneath him and end this particular moment, he spoke once more. "So, uh, do you see—I mean, *detect*—anything?"

Cesta closed her eyes. She drew in a breath. She raised her hands up above her shoulders, and the sleeves of her coat fell back to reveal the tone of her arms. When she opened her eyes again, a faint red light glowed behind her pupils. Slowly, like some particularly purposeful top, she rotated in place.

Dreadaeleon knew what she was seeking: the fluctuation in temperature that would reveal the use of fire or ice, the atmospheric tingle that followed an expulsion of lightning, the subtle increase of pressure that followed levitation and use of force. And because he knew what she was seeking, he knew she couldn't find it, even before the light faded from her eyes and a frown creased her face.

"Nothing," she muttered. A short, haggard breath. Then the light flared back to her eyes. She stomped her foot and a wave of invisible force roiled out, bending the grass and nearly knocking Dreadaeleon to his rear. "*DAMN IT.*"

"It's not your fault!" He hurried on unsteady feet to join her at the top of the ridge. "It's . . . interference or . . . or . . ." He looked out over their surroundings, his frown matching hers. "Or something."

Between the city of Redgate to the west and the encroaching Silesrian forest to the east, the area in which Venarium Tower Fifteen—alias "Defiant"—operated resembled less a landscape and more a particularly low-key battle between two decidedly unenthused forces of nature. Here, the rolling hills of the west met the ever-reaching forest of the east, clashing in the center in a haphazard series of dense copses broken occasionally by hills rising up with lazy defiance.

The earth was still damp from recent rains, and gray clouds still mumbled thunderous complaints overhead, suggesting they weren't quite done. The scent of sodden earth and plant cloyed his nostrils, made it hard to focus. That, combined with the many hills to hide behind and trees to hide within, meant that Dreadaeleon found it increasingly hard to fault Cesta's frustration.

"It's not your fault," he offered. He looked overhead. "It's the rain, I bet. All the lightning from the rains is interfering, somehow."

"Really?" She looked at him flatly. "Lightning from the sky, completely distinct from the latent electricity we generate and amplify through Venarie, is interfering. How on earth would that even work, Dread?"

"Well, see, that's the thing, it's not *on* earth, it's up in the sky and it's . . . it's somehow . . ."

Her stare might have been an ax lodged in his skull for how keenly he felt it. He looked away, rubbed absently at his arm. And she merely sighed.

Well done, old man, he chided himself. *What are you thinking? That she'll become so infatuated with your desire to explain away her failure that she'll pull your trousers off here and now?*

He coughed.

Well, he certainly wasn't thinking that *anymore.*

"Forget it," Cesta sighed. "I'm sorry, Dread. I'm just stressed." She took off down the hill at a decisive stalk, leaving him to hurry after her. "There's got to be a reason we can't find him. He's . . . he's *cheating,* somehow."

"Cheating?" Dreadaeleon asked.

"I don't know. Masking his magic. Using some kind of device. It's not unheard of, right?"

"I guess." He stumbled on a rock that she had strode over. "I mean, I've read about that in some . . ."

Don't say "children's books."

". . . some kind of . . . something . . . somewhere."

Nice.

"Maybe he's using some kind of meditation technique, then," Cesta muttered. "Hiding his power that way, containing his expulsions."

"Really? How would that even—"

"Well, then, what do you think it is?"

She whirled on him with a snarl. He cringed away, rubbed at the back of his head.

"I . . . I don't know, I guess. I hadn't really thought about it."

"Hadn't really thought about it," she repeated.

"Well, I mean, we're just apprentices. No one really expects us to find him." He dared a glance up at her. "Right?"

If her stare had been like an ax lodged in his skull, her scowl was more like a vise tightening about his neck. He averted his gaze as if he were looking upon a profane idol and not merely a pretty, angry girl. But it did him no good. He could feel her—the tension in her jaw, the tremble of her fists—as she leveled her ire at him.

"*That*," she hissed, "is why the Lector doesn't take you seriously, Dreadaeleon. You don't understand what it is you have."

Ah, look alive, old man. She's about to recognize your skill!

"You were given a gift, a power that elevates you above the rest of humanity. Flame comes to you with a thought, lightning with a flick of your fingers. You possess *tremendous* power."

He puffed up a little.

Here it comes.

"All of which is wasted because you also possess the mind of a child."

He paused.

Does . . . does she mean you're carefree or . . .

"Do you not grasp what we're doing here? Did you hear *nothing* Lector Vemire said?"

Ah, no, she just thinks you're stupid. Bad luck.

"You didn't. If you did, you would realize that there are no expectations. Your common barkneck farmer expects lightning to stay in the sky and rocks to stay on the ground, and *we're* the ones that shoot it out of our fingers and hurl boulders with a thought." She stomped the earth. "We're not children with chores, Dreadaeleon. We are *wizards*. We make the rules. It's up to us to enforce them."

Her eyes were not burning with the magical light. She didn't exude so much as a bit of Venarie. She didn't need to. Dreadaeleon's legs felt weak and his breath felt heavy, just as surely as they would if she were using her power to crush him into the earth.

Vemire's disapproval had always been something easier to contend with, if not outright ignore. The Lector's perpetual glowers, frequent sighs, and occasional chastisements were a constant in Dreadaeleon's life, a weight he had learned to shoulder. But Cesta—Cesta who never was at a loss for an answer, Cesta who never assumed the wrong stance for a spell, Cesta who was already taller than him and looked down on him—had words that made him feel like he was bleeding: a bright red warmth that washed over him, permeated him.

And it did not go away when she stopped looking at him.

"We'll do it the barkneck way, then." She pointed down the hill to a nearby copse of trees. "It was raining, so he's probably seeking shelter. We can look for likely sites within our designated search radius and go from there."

A moment. She cast a glance over her shoulder at him. Her eyes were no longer quite so hard, her voice no longer quite so sharp.

"All right?" she asked softly.

He nodded at her weakly. "Yeah. All right."

And together, they set off down the hill.

OVERHEAD, THE SKY had a one-sided conversation with them. Heedless of their ignoring it, the gray clouds muttered with distant thunder, loosed the occasional chuckle of rain, let the wind sigh. And though he was cold and wet, Dreadaeleon did not mind the noise.

Largely because he couldn't hear it over his own thoughts.

Well done, old man. She dressed you down like a six-copper prostitute, and you simply stood there and took it. What were you thinking, doing that? That she'd be impressed with your ability to look at your feet and whimper? This'll get back to Vemire, you know. She'll tell him you were too cowardly to even stand up for yourself. Should have said something to her then.

He looked up, glared at the back of her head. He felt his fists tighten, his jaw clench.

Should say something to her now.

And within him, something began to boil. Something deep and solid and red-hot. Not a fire—too thick, too real for that. Nor blood—too bright and wild for it to be blood. This flowed into him like smoke, filled every vein down to the tips of his fingers and clouded his mind.

You should show her, old man. Show her you're not afraid of her or of Vemire or of anyone else. Show her that you're made for greater things, that she's as blind as Vemire is. Show them all, every last stuffed coat in the Venarium, what you're made of and—

"Look."

He blinked.

He looked.

And he wasn't quite sure when they had arrived here.

The trees crowded closer together here, their eaves helpfully leaning out to block the worst of the rain, permitting only a few determined drizzles in to sodden the needle-and-leaf-strewn earth. Trees long-fallen leaned against hillsides, forming a number of natural shelters.

One of which had the remains of a campfire lingering under it.

"He was here!" Cesta's gait had a decidedly enthusiastic spring in it as she rushed to the fire. "The heretic! Lathrim!" She looked to Dreadaeleon, her eyes wide and smile wider. "He was *here*!"

"Well, maybe," Dreadaeleon replied, scratching his head. "It's not like he's the only traveler. Someone else could have been by." At her blank stare, he forced a weak smile onto his face. "But it's . . . *probably* him? Most likely?"

"No," she said, shaking her head. "Look here." She pointed to a tiny plume of smoke rising from the blackened remains of the fire. "The embers are still a little warm. Whoever was here couldn't have been here more than a day ago."

What, she's an outdoorsman now too? Outdoorswoman. Sorry.

"The other heretics were discovered last night," she said, grinning ear-to-ear. "He *had* to have been here, Dreadaeleon. It *had* to have been him."

"Okay, we can send for Vemire, then." He reached into his coat pocket, felt the corner of a sheet of paper prick his finger. "I've got the parchment he gave us to—"

"Before we do that," Cesta interjected, "let's make sure our situational knowledge is complete." She shook her head. "We can't summon the Lector out here and just point to a few embers, right?"

"Well, yes. I mean, no. That's why I said that it only *might* be—"

"Good!" She shot him an enthusiastic nod. "Fan out. Find evidence of his passing and we'll see if we can't figure out which way he went."

Whatever other objections he might have had—such as the fact that heretics were presumably more advanced in power than a pair of apprentices and, thus, assumably quite dangerous—went unspoken.

Cesta, who threw herself to the earth in a search for tracks with a rabbit-like enthusiasm, was clearly not listening.

Not that it matters, he thought as he turned around and began his own search. *When has she ever listened to you, old man? She's never once shown an interest in you, has she?* He paused, blinked. *But then, when was the last time you asked anything about her? Do you even know anything about her? She's got a birthmark right above her left asscheek, but you can't let her know you know that. No one must know you know that. What else? She's driven, determined, focused—*

Focus, old man. That's what you're here for, remember. You're an agent of the Venarium, hunting heretics for the order. It's important that you study everything, every log, every tree, every . . .

"Rock."

It was, indeed, a rock that loomed before him. A tall, malformed cylinder, nothing particularly spectacular about it.

Except for the scorch mark that blackened its gray face.

He reached out, felt soot come off on his fingers. He sniffed at it curiously. Warm, recent, and accompanied by a very familiar odor. Flame of a magical nature, born of a person's body heat, always had a very thick, heady aroma, not quite as clean as natural flames.

He glanced around, saw other traces: a sheen of frost upon the bark of a nearby tree, a branch hanging half-severed, the new wood beneath blackened at the edges by electricity.

Someone had been expelling magic here. Clearly, not enough to do any real damage beyond a few alterations to the landscape. But it was evidence enough, just as Cesta had been hoping for.

But why? He scratched his chin. *Heretics reject the law of the Venarium, but not the laws of magic. Using magic just to damage a few trees and rocks would serve no purpose but to expend energy and exhaust the wizard. There's literally no reason to do it.*

A sudden chill coursed through him. His skin prickled as the temperature dropped severely. He drew in a gasp and tasted cold on his tongue.

Unless, of course, as bait for a trap.

He saw the frost first as he whirled about, a cloud of white mist haloing the top of a fallen log. And burning through them, a pair of eyes alight with a red glow, piercing through the veil of cold and scowling.

But not at him.

"*Cesta!*" he screamed.

Across the clearing, she looked up at him, then followed his gaze to the top of the log. Her cry of alarm shifted clumsily into words of power, hands thrown up and sending the air before her shimmering with an invisible shield. Sloppy words, weak stance, hasty spell.

It was hardly a surprise that the spear-sized icicle that slammed into her sent her flying.

The tails of her coat fluttered like a bird's wounded wings as she went sailing, but the air was thankfully unstained by any crimson. The icicle, then, had merely shattered her shield and not pierced her flesh.

That's good, Dreadaeleon thought.

"Apprentices?" a deep voice asked.

And that is not.

A figure, tall and slim, leaped from the top of the log. His descent slowed unnaturally as he fell, so that his boots did not so much as crunch a single leaf when he landed. Adjusting the cuffs of a clean coat, he stepped forward and regarded Dreadaeleon coolly through clear, bright eyes.

Admittedly, Lathrim did not look like what Dreadaeleon was expecting.

His skin was pale and clean, his black hair unwashed but kept in a neat braid, and his trimmed beard betrayed only a few unruly strands. His angular face showed no gauntness or hunger. And while his eyes bore dark circles from sleeplessness beneath them, they were not the blood-shot, wild stare that he had seen on the heretics who had earlier burned.

"The Venarium cannot possibly be so shameless as to send children after me," he said, shaking his head. "I was hoping to lure Vemire out, not his pets."

Ah, so that's why he was expending such minute amounts of energy, Dreadaeleon thought. *Only a Lector would be able to detect such trace amounts. Go on, old man, tell him he can't be so clever if mere children figured out his scheme.*

That would have been a good thing to say, he knew.

Of course, it was not what he said.

"B-by order of the V-Venarium," he stammered, "of T-Tower Defiant, I command you . . . you to . . ."

"And they've already drilled that nonsense into you, have they? I suppose the first thing one trains a dog to do is bark." Lathrim shook his head and turned away from Dreadaeleon. "I've no interest in fighting the Venarium's thralls, boy."

"N-no," Dreadaeleon said, shaking his head. "I have to . . . to take you in. I swore an oath."

"You swore servitude." Lathrim waved a hand, dismissive, as he began to stalk off into the underbrush. "I pity you, boy, but not enough to humor you. Now go to tend to your fellow dog, she looks almost as sad as—"

The heretic's voice was cut off by the sudden bolt of cobalt electricity that arced over his head. It struck the branch of an overhanging tree, severing it neatly and sending it to the earth, smoking. He glanced at the fallen branch for a moment before looking behind him at the boy in the too-big coat, an overlarge sleeve billowing around a skinny arm that ended in a pair of smoking fingers.

"I'm not a child," Dreadaeleon said, his eyes bursting into light. "I am a *wizard*."

To his ears, that sounded pretty good. Strong, forceful; admittedly, he probably would have sounded *more* forceful if his spell had come even remotely close to striking its mark.

As it was, the toll from the magic spent had already torn itself out of his body. He felt his legs weaken, his breath become heavy, a sheen of sweat appear on his forehead. He wasn't ready for a spell of that magnitude; even a clumsy show of force had taken too much out of him.

But that feeling, that wispy power that boiled angrily inside him, came flowing back into him. It bid his legs to hold steady, his breath to keep going, his eyes to burn, and his mind to reject any thought of retreat.

"As you like."

Lathrim made a slow bow. Then shot up, a single palm outstretched. He spoke a single word. And, in a single moment, a gout of flame erupted from his hand and roiled toward Dreadaeleon in a cackling blaze.

To his credit, "hurling oneself to the side in a blind panic" did not *exactly* qualify as "retreating." But the tax on Dreadaeleon's body made it hard for him to scramble to his feet; he felt smaller and weaker than ever before. And when he clambered up, that sense of power that bolstered him began to dissipate like so much smoke.

The flames retreated back into Lathrim's palm with another word, leaving behind only a black char line where the flames had eaten away the leaves. No stray flames or sparks had remained.

Son of a bitch, Dreadaeleon thought. *He can control his fire. This is too much, old man. You have to get out of here. You have to find Vemire. You have to . . .*

He forced that thought silent. Cesta was still here, with this madman, this *heretic*. Whatever he *had* to do was irrelevant. Whatever he was going to do was all that mattered.

"Don't think I enjoy this."

Of course, at the moment, what he was going to do seemed to fall along the lines of "die horribly, possibly while crying."

"You deserved better than the life the Venarium promised you, boy. You deserved better than to be turned into their slave and sent to die on a mad errand." Lathrim advanced toward him, palm still outstretched and glowing with flame. His eyes burned brightly. "Take some solace, at least, that the ones who follow you will be safer for the example you'll make."

His body screamed at him to run; he ignored it. His heart screamed at him to panic; he ignored that too. A wizard's power was in his mind, his thought, that which elevated him above the common barkneck.

Think, old man, think.

But any spell he could have called to mind powerful enough to kill this heretic would be too big to control, and the toll would kill him besides. He looked at Lathrim, transfixed by the fire that sparked to life in the heretic's palm. It was only by chance that his eyes drifted to the earth, where the fallen tree branch lay.

And it was only by fear that he acted quickly.

A word, shouted. He reached out with an invisible force, sending the air rippling past Lathim. The heretic glanced at it, unimpressed. But he was not aiming for the heretic.

That unseen force seized the tree branch, surely as it had seized the carcass earlier. And with another word and a fierce gesture, Dreadaeleon pulled.

Sloppy. Hasty. An ugly, ugly spell.

But it didn't need to be pretty.

The branch came hurtling up behind Lathrim. Its jagged tip found the heretic's leg, pierced his thigh. His concentration broke in a wail of pain as Lathrim fell to one knee. *Now* his eyes bore all the wild agony of the heretics that had come before him and they were fixed on Dreadaeleon.

He spoke a word. He raised his palm. Fire burst from his hand . . .

. . . and was extinguished just as rapidly.

Another word, spoken louder, drowning out his own. The air rippled around him as another force crashed against him and sent him flying. With a shout, he flew across the sky, leaving only a few embers behind as he crashed against a nearby tree trunk and lay still.

Dreadaeleon looked up as Cesta came staggering toward him, breathing heavily, barely standing from the exertion. And yet, she had enough to look at Dreadaeleon and grin broadly.

"Good work, Dread," she gasped. "Good work."

And that little ego boost was *just* enough to keep him from collapsing over and pissing himself from exhaustion.

THERE YOU GO, old man. One fold after the other, left over center, just like they told you. How'd the rhyme go? "Once for the neck, twice for the wing?" No, that doesn't even rhyme. Just . . . oh, that doesn't look good at all, does it? Well, just fold that part like . . . yeah, and then do that *part like . . . ah! And there you go!*

He looked down at the tiny amalgamation of paper and blood sitting upon the palm of his hand. In this light, as the sun set behind the gray clouds overhead, it looked a *little* like a bird, he supposed. A bird that had been in a terrible accident, anyway.

But whatever deficiencies his paper-folding skills might have had, he at least got all the important parts down: the parchment had two wings, a head, and critically, the smeared stain of blood uncovered by his various clumsy folds.

He sighed. It would have to do.

He spoke a word to it—the only word it was designed to understand. The blood began to glow, revealing strange sigils painted onto the paper in the red life. With a sudden stir, the paper bird's wings began to twitch. Clumsily, it took flight, lifting off his hand and rising past the eaves of the trees overhead and into the sky.

Dreadaeleon watched its little red glow as it sailed high, until it finally went too far for him to track and winked out of existence. He was not worried, though. The little creation would head unerringly toward the source of its blood sigil—the Lector himself—and deliver itself and the message it carried.

Depending on how far Vemire had actually traveled, it could be anywhere from one to three hours.

Which made Dreadaeleon smile.

That gave him at least a *pretty* good chance of coming out of this situation without being burned alive.

"Did it work?"

He glanced over his shoulder. Cesta stared up at the sky, searching for the messenger bird.

"It should have," Dreadaeleon replied. "Lector Vemire prepared the spell himself before we left. I can't see any reason why it should *fail.*"

His voice cracked slightly on that last word. Whether that was a betrayal of the fear lurking at the back of his head or perhaps just overdue puberty, he wasn't keen to explore. And Cesta did not seem to care, one way or the other. When she looked at him, her grin was positively ecstatic.

"Can you believe it, Dread?" she asked. "We did it. We *did* it. Vemire expected us to only be of assistance, but we actually caught the heretic all by ourselves."

"Right. Yes. That's good." Dreadaeleon nodded along. "But, uh, let's still be careful. He's still a heretic and we should be—"

"We took all the necessary precautions," she countered. "He's bound and gagged. He can't cast. There's nothing to be worried about."

"Vemire said the heretics were dangerous, though."

"And they are. When they're not bound and gagged." She held up her hands. "Okay, yeah, I know. We'll still be cautious, but let's savor this a little, hm?"

He looked past her, toward the meager fire they had built up and the prisoner sitting beside it. His hands firmly tied before him, his ankles likewise secured, Lathrim stared dully over the gag tied about his mouth. His eyes were empty, but not with the resigned blankness that came in defeat. Rather, to Dreadaeleon, he looked almost . . . bored.

Perhaps Cesta saw that too.

Perhaps that was why she strode toward him with a swagger that would look haughty even on a man six cups deep.

"Did you hear that, heretic?" she said. "The Lector will be on his way shortly. I expect your judgment will be extremely swift. The Venarium protocol is quite clear on matters of heresy."

Lathrim did not so much as glance up at her. Not that she seemed to notice.

"But surely you already knew that. Surely you did not commit your crimes without knowledge of the price you'd eventually pay." She walked a long, dramatic circle around the fire. "We were briefed on your charges before we left, Lathrim. Two Venarium agents were killed trying to calm you down when you snapped. You snatched priceless components when you fled Tower Defiant and took three Venarium agents with you."

She paused, turned, fixed a glare down at Lathrim, who did not return it.

"They're dead now, you know." She thrust a finger at him. "Because of you. Because of the lies you told them. Because of the filth you spewed. You convinced them to betray the Venarium and they died for you."

"Cesta." Dreadaeleon took a step forward, reached out toward her. "Maybe you shouldn't—"

"And you don't even *care!*" Cesta shouted over Dreadaeleon, ignoring him as she stepped toward Lathrim. "Five people are dead because of you! Five people who had lives to lead, lost because of your wretched lies, and you don't even *blink* to hear it." She knelt down, reached out for his gag. "What do you have to say for yourself, you piece of—"

"*Cesta! No!*"

She glanced up at Dreadaeleon, cast a baleful scowl at him. "It's fine, Dread. Any spell he tries to cast will be futile without his hands." She sneered at Lathrim, tore his gag free. "Isn't that right, heretic?"

Dreadaeleon braced himself. Though his body was still weak from his earlier spells, he immediately reached inside himself and searched for more power, more of that hazy, boiling strength. He unconsciously began to slide into a stance, ready for any spell the heretic might speak.

But the heretic spoke no spell. For a long time, he did not speak at all. And when his lips finally did move, he merely smacked them once or twice, then looked up at Cesta, and spoke softly.

"May I have some water, please?"

A sigh of relief washed over Dreadaeleon. It didn't seem like an unreasonable request. And yet, to see Cesta's face screw up in anger the way it did, one might have thought that asking for water was on par with insinuating certain proclivities involving her mother and livestock.

"What did you say?" she snarled.

"Water," Lathim repeated. "If it's not too much trouble."

"If it's not too much . . ." She shook her head. "Did you not hear a *damn* thing I said? About the men you killed? About the laws you broke?"

"I did. I grew thirsty as I listened. The icicle I hurled at you earlier took moisture from me that I must replenish." He blinked. "Am I not entitled to that?"

"What? No!" Her fist clenched. Her eyes blazed. "You're a heretic! Traitor to the Venarium and all the laws we hold sacred. You're no more entitled to water than you are entitled to—"

"To what?" Only now did Lathrim's eyes snap out of their glazed-over look. Only did he now seem to be paying attention. "To justice? To a reasonable trial?"

"The Venarium will offer you trial by ordeal if you—" Dreadaeleon began, but he did not get far.

"The Venarium will pit me into a deathmatch with a wizard six times my skill and watch me die," Lathrim interrupted. "Is that the only justice I'm entitled to? Even in slave-holding nations they grant more rights to people than a wizard is granted in the Venarium."

"There are no *rights*, heretic." Cesta straightened up, folded her arms across her chest. "There are laws. Laws that must be obeyed so that magic does not destroy the world and its people."

"Its people?" Lathrim asked. "The same people you look down upon? The 'barknecks?'"

"We don't look down upon them," Dreadaeleon said. "We . . . we protect them. They aren't like us. They don't have what we do."

"So we protect them," Cesta added. "The laws protect us *and* them. The laws protect us all."

"And so the laws demand that you're torn from your families and serve the Venarium's will until you're dead and can be harvested like scrap." Lathrim sneered. "And so the laws demand that you forsake justice and trials so that order may be protected. And somehow, after you've abandoned everything that makes you human, you're entitled to protect others? What sense does that make?"

"A heretic wouldn't understand," Cesta snarled. "A heretic *never* understands. They can't be reasoned with."

"Heretics must be punished for the crime of heresy. Heretics cannot be reasoned with, thus negating the need to ever talk to them. Thus, a heretic cannot defend himself from punishment for the crime of heresy," Lathrim replied, voice soft and cool as a breeze. "Such paragons of knowledge, you Venarium. Such airtight logic you've created for yourselves."

"We didn't create this," Cesta said. "These are laws. They've been in place since time immemorial."

"You can't believe that," Lathrim said. "If they've been around forever, if they are truly so all-pervasive, how is it only the wizards know about them? Does the average 'barkneck' know about them?" He quirked a brow. "Did your mother, before you were taken from her?"

Dreadaeleon had known Cesta all his life. And in all that time, she had never once seemed to flinch. Those few spells she did not master immediately, she practiced day and night. Those *very* few spells that blew up in her face, she got right back up and started practicing again.

Where he looked at his feet, she looked into Lectors' eyes like she was their equal. Where he mumbled, she proclaimed. Where he staggered and fell, she took a breath and kept going. Somehow, he assumed that was the way it would always be.

Until now, at any rate.

The look she wore on her face was not one of pain, as though he had slapped her. Nor was it one of fury or even anger. Rather, all the color from her face seemed to drain, all the light from her eyes seemed to fade. What was left behind was a perfect circle of white, broken only by her mouth hanging open, silent.

"Trace amounts of Venarie begin manifesting around five years of age," Lathrim said, his words soft and deliberate. "The Venarium comes to collect shortly thereafter. They pay a collector's fee and take the child back to a Tower to be trained. But some . . ."

He looked down at his bound hands. He flexed his fingers.

"Some manifest sooner," he said. "And some parents will not part with their children for any price."

"Cesta?" Dreadaeleon stepped closer to her. "Cesta, are you all right?"

She did not answer. Cesta's empty eyes were locked on Lathrim.

"Speak to any apprentice, they will tell you what they know of their parents." The heretic glanced at Dreadaeleon. Sadness was in his eyes. "I suspect you might remember a little, hm? A face? A voice? A phrase they used to say? But within every Tower, you will find a few apprentices who recall nothing, know nothing of a life outside the Venarium. Not even a ghost of a memory."

He looked at Cesta. His eyes were free from malice. The smugness in his voice had fled. What was left was something as dark and bleak as hers were white and empty.

"Do you remember your mother, girl?" he asked.

"Shut up," Cesta whispered.

"Your father? An aunt? An uncle? A childhood pet? Anything?"

"Shut up!"

"What do you suppose they told her to tear you from her breast? What price did they offer you?"

"Heretic, I'm warning you."

"Heretic." He laughed. "I never even entertained the word until I learned how *I* had been taken. Do you suppose you were made the same way? Did they take you from her? Did she fight them? Did they raise their hands and speak their words and—"

She did not tell him again.

Her response was no word. It was a sound. It was loud and booming, exploding with life. No form. No style. Just noise.

And power.

The invisible force rippled across the sky, struck Lathrim against the side of his head and sent him flying. He struck a tree, collapsed.

"Cesta!" Dreadaeleon cried, rushing toward the fallen heretic. But no sooner had he drawn close than Lathim went flying once again.

The invisible force shot up from beneath him, sending him flying up into the air. He hovered there for a moment, dirty clothes flapping in the breeze, before he came tumbling down.

Quick, old man, Dreadaeleon thought. *A spell! Reach out for him! Get him! Stance strong, arms out, deep breath, and—*

He didn't finish that thought. It was impossible to hear himself think over the heavy crunching sound of Lathrim's body hitting the ground. Dreadaeleon's mouth fell open as he looked from the unmoving heretic to Cesta.

But Cesta was not looking at him.

Her eyes were ablaze with red light. Her arms were moving in rigid, furious motions, as though she were conducting a symphony and Lathrim's body was the sole instrument.

And it played a shrill, screeching note for her.

Lathrim sounded not nearly so eloquent in flight. His screams were lilting things, fading in and out as he was hurled from the earth to the sky, from the sky to a tree, from a tree to a stone, from a stone to the earth. Over and over, the symphony played a discordant harmony:

390

Cesta's screams driving the crunching bone of Lathrim's body, Lathrim's agonized howls fighting to be heard over the wind moaning in sympathy.

Against such a cacophony, Dreadaeleon's own cries for sanity—for Cesta to stop, for Lathrim to recant, for someone to do *something*— were but one chiming note, easily ignored and completely lost.

Until, at last, the song came to an end.

Cesta's voice was a hoarse, wheezing breath. Her arms hung limp at her sides. She slumped to her knees, drenched in sweat and muscles trembling. The magic had devoured her, eaten away everything inside her to perform that feat of violence, leaving her only enough to keep her eyes—dark and lightless—open to admire her work.

Lathrim was painted all over the clearing. He was smeared upon the bark of the trees and the grass of the hills and the stones jutting from the earth. And at the center of the many stains, his body lay almost comically twisted in its anatomy.

Still.

Breathless.

Dead.

"Gods, Cesta," Dreadaeleon whispered as he approached the dead heretic.

"There are no gods, Dreadaeleon," Cesta said, breathless. "What happened to him, he brought upon himself."

"You killed him." He looked at her, mouth agape. "You *killed* him."

"He was a heretic. He was going to die anyway. He *deserved* to die for what he said about me, about . . . about . . ."

Whatever words she had left were lost. Her mouth hung open, a hoarse, choked sound emerging. Her eyes trembled, yet she had no tears to spend. Her voice, her tears, her sorrow—the Venarie had taken all of it, poured it into what she had done to Lathrim.

And left her with nothing but silence.

You can't let this go, old man.

And in that silence, he could hear himself. In cold, clear thought, he spoke.

The laws are there for a reason. It's not her place to pass sentence on a heretic, let alone carry it out. You can't let her go with this. You have to report it to Lector Vemire. You have to—

"Dread . . ."

He turned. Cesta made a move to try to stand, but her quaking limbs could not support her. She fell once more to the sodden earth. She stared at Dreadaeleon with a face that tried to hold what little life she had not used up to kill Lathrim. And her voice, what was left, tried to croak out a response.

"I'm sorry . . . I didn't mean . . . I didn't . . ."

It doesn't matter that she didn't, old man. You have to do what's right by the Venarium. These are the laws.

He opened his mouth to tell her this. Yet what came out what something else.

"It's fine," he said. "It's okay."

No, it's not okay! Don't do this.

"He was going to die anyway, like you said. Right?" He shook his head. "We'll tell Vemire . . . we'll tell him that he tried to attack you. We somehow overpowered him."

Not like this. Not because of this.

"We'll make it work, Cesta." He walked to her side. He leaned down and laid a hand upon her shoulder. The smile he offered her was warm. "It's going to be fine."

And as she looked up at him, the ghost of a smile at the corners of her lips, he could almost believe his own lie. He *would* have believed it, even. If not for the cold voice in the back of his head that hissed out a single word.

Coward.

The hours passed slowly.

Dreadaeleon had been thankful for this, at first. It had given him time to position Lathrim's body in such a manner as to suggest a struggle. It had given him time to give Cesta water, help her closer to the fire, let her fall asleep. Vemire's return was slow, and he was grateful for that.

392

At first.

But as the hours passed in silence, he found himself at a loss for what else to do but wait for Vemire. And so he sat at the edge of their little camp and stared out over the distant hills, left alone with nothing but his thoughts. And while they were certainly conversational, he found their company less than ideal.

Well done, old man, well done. This is how you'll prove your worth, eh? Covering up a crime, lying to your superior . . . and let's not forget you simply stood by and watched Cesta kill him, hm? Based on just a few harsh words he said.

I mean . . . they were really *harsh words, but still. Wizards aren't supposed to let emotions rule them like that, or else . . . well, that* happens, *doesn't it? It's not too late. Vemire hasn't arrived yet—what the fuck is taking him so long—you could still tell him the truth when he comes. You could still come clean and prove your worth . . .*

And watch Cesta suffer for it. She'd be sanctioned. Disciplined. Maybe even stripped of her rank. Or would she? Vemire likes her, maybe he'd go easy on her. But Lathrim had knowledge we could have used. He won't like that we killed him. No, that she *killed him, old man. You're not a murderer, just the accomplice. Let's not be sloppy here. Anyway, that's settled. You can't do that to her. You can't let her suffer.*

He closed his eyes. He drew a breath. He stilled his thoughts.

So long as she's safe, this is all worth it. Believe that, if nothing else.

The hours did not so much pass as crawl. They crawled up onto his back and settled down upon his shoulders, bearing his head low. The stress that had propelled him to action now seeped out of him like water from a sieve. He felt his eyes begin to droop, his head begin to bow, his vision begin to go dark.

His ears were the last to go. And an instant before they did, he heard the sound of rustling behind him.

He looked up and over his shoulder. There, he saw Cesta, busying herself with their satchels. She was busily attaching the last waterskin to it, taking the few bits of food he carried and loading them into hers. She attached the pack to her belt and rose up on shaky feet.

And then she noticed him watching her.

"I thought you were asleep," she said, voice still weak.

"I wasn't," he said, slowly rising to face her.

She looked away from his eyes and her stare fell upon his empty satchel. "There's food back at the tower," she said. "You'll be all right. Vemire will be here soon."

"And you won't be."

He hadn't intended to say that. He had meant to ask it, instead. He had meant to give her a moment to deny it, to reassure him. But he didn't. And she didn't. And they merely let his words hang between them for a very long, cold time.

"I can't remember her, Dread." When Cesta finally broke the silence, it was with words that sounded soft and painful. "My mother. I can't remember her name, what she looked like. But I had to have had one." She looked up at him. Fear shone bright in her eyes. "Right?"

"Yes. Of course." He took a step toward her. She took a step back. He frowned. "But . . . what does that have to do with anything?"

"Lathrim said he . . . said he learned how he had been taken," she said. "They took him, he said. They took him when he was an infant, killed his parents to do so."

"Heretics lie," Dreadaeleon said. "Heretics *always* lie. That's what makes them heretics."

"Heretics must be punished for the crime of heresy," Cesta said. The death of a chuckle escaped her lips. "Just like he said. We kill them for thinking the wrong things, saying the wrong words."

"The wrong words, from us, can *kill*," Dreadaeleon said. "We're not children, like you said. We're wizards." He shook his head. "If you're worried about this, ask Vemire. He'll be here and he'll—"

"Why would he tell me the truth, Dread?" She clenched her teeth. "If I *was* taken . . . if I was *made*, like a tool or a horseshoe, why would he tell me? Why wouldn't he just lie?" She turned. "I have to go, Dread. I have to find out for myself."

"What? Find out *what?*"

"I . . . don't know. Lathrim said he found out. There has to be a way."

"How are you going to find it? The Venarium will be after you. You'll be a *heretic*, Cesta. Listen to reason."

"Reason is a matter of debate, discussion," she said. "The Venarium does not allow that. There is only law."

"Law that protects us. Law that keeps us together." His voice cracked. He didn't care. "Cesta, we're supposed to stay together! We're supposed to . . . to . . ."

"I know."

She took another step.

"I'm sorry."

And another. She shed hesitation, began a full stride away from him, disappearing into the night.

"What do I tell the Venarium, then?" he called after her. "What do I tell Vemire?"

If she answered, he was too far away to hear her. If she looked back, it was too dark to see him. If either of them had anything they could have said to stop this, to bring her back, to bring him with her, it went unspoken.

And he was left, once again, with silence.

"Don't blame yourself."

He looked up. When Vemire had arrived, he couldn't say. When his eyes had begun to sting with tears, he didn't know. But as he looked up through bleary vision, Vemire did not look back at him. His eyes were out over the darkness into which she had disappeared.

"Perhaps it's my fault," the Lector sighed. "I didn't teach you the lessons you should have learned. You came away from my tutelage with the knowledge of the law, that discipline and power are intertwined. But what I never told you . . ."

He looked down at Dreadaeleon and frowned.

"Is that everything is a test to see if we are prepared for the burden of that."

"A test?" he asked. "This was a test?"

"I arrived hours ago. I have been observing you since then. You conducted yourself as well as you could have been expected to, appre—" He caught himself, considered. "Dreadaeleon."

Dreadaeleon looked out over the darkness. "What's going to happen to Cesta?"

Vemire did not say anything for a time. "To us, knowledge is everything, Dreadaeleon. Everything. And I can give you that knowledge, if you'd like." He closed his eyes, folded his hands behind his back. "But if you'd rather not hear me say it . . . I would not blame you."

And, alone in a thoughtless silence, Dreadaeleon did not speak another word.

He simply stood there and stared into a darkness where there had been a girl he had once known.

JOE ABERCROMBIE

It will come as small surprise that I'm a big fan of Fritz Leiber's Fafhrd and the Gray Mouser, the quintessential sword and sorcery double act. I'd written a few short stories closely tied to my novels, but since I was being asked to contribute to quite a few anthologies and often with a sword and sorcery tone, I felt I needed some characters who didn't tie too tightly into my other work and about whom I could easily base further stories—some characters with a long career of misadventures, you might say. My mind turned naturally to a barbarian and a thief with a strong, humorous, but occasionally tempestuous relationship, a taste for love and fast living, and with a knack for landing themselves in endless trouble. I'd written a lot about men in my First Law books, though, and sword and sorcery does rather tend to be dominated by male heroes, so I thought a female sword and sorcery odd couple might be an interesting twist. Thus were born Javre, Lioness of Hoskopp, and Shevedieh, the best damn thief in Styria. And every good duo needs an origin story, of course . . .

SMALL KINDNESSES

Joe Abercrombie

When Shev arrived to open up that morning, there were a pair of big, dirty bare feet sticking out of the doorway of her Smoke House.

That would once have caused her quite the shock, but over the last couple of years Shev had come to consider herself past shocking.

"Oy!" she shouted, striding up with her fists clenched.

Whoever it was on their face in the doorway either chose not to move or was unable. She saw the long legs the feet were attached to, clad in trousers ripped and stained, then the ragged mess of a torn and filthy coat. Finally, wedged into the grubby corner against Shev's door, a tangle of long red hair, matted with twigs and dirt.

A big man, without a doubt. The one hand Shev could see was as long as her foot, netted with veins, filthy and scabbed across the knuckles. There was a strange shape to it, though. Slender.

"Oy!" She jabbed the toe of her boot into the coat around where she judged the man's arse to be. Still nothing.

She heard footsteps behind her. "Morning, boss." Severard turning up for the day. Never late, that boy. Not the most careful in his work but for punctuality you couldn't knock him. "What's this you've caught?"

"A strange fish, all right, to wash up in my doorway." Shev scraped some of the red hair back, wrinkled her nose as she realised it was clotted with blood.

"Is he drunk?"

"She." It was a woman's face under there. Strong-jawed and strong-boned, pale skin crowded with black scab, red graze, and purple bruise to make Shev wince, even if she rarely saw anyone who wasn't carrying a wound or two.

Severard gave a soft whistle. "That's a lot of she."

"And someone's given her a lot of a beating too." Shev leaned close to put her cheek near the woman's battered mouth, heard the faintest whistling of breath. "Alive, though." And she rocked away and squatted there, wrists on her knees and her hands dangling, wondering what to do. She seemed to spend half her time wondering what to do these days. Time was she just dived into whatever messes she pleased without a backward glance, but somehow the consequences always seemed nearer to hand than they used to. She puffed her cheeks out and gave the weariest of sighs.

"Well, it happens," said Severard.

"Sadly, yes."

"Not our problem, is it?"

"Happily, no."

"Want me to drag her into the street?"

"Yes, I want that quite a lot." And Shev rolled her eyes skyward and gave another sigh, maybe even wearier than the last. "But we'd best drag her inside, I reckon."

"You sure, boss? You remember the last time we helped someone out—"

"Sure? No." Shev wasn't sure why, after all the shit that had been done to her, she still felt the need to do small kindnesses. Maybe *because* of all the shit that had been done to her. Maybe there was some stubborn stone in her, like the stone in a date, that refused to let all the shit that had been done to her make her into shit. She turned the key and elbowed the door wobbling open. "You get her feet."

When you run a Smoke House you'd better get good at shifting limp bodies, but the latest recipient of Shev's half-arsed charity proved quite the challenge.

"Bloody hell," grunted Severard, eyes popping as they manhandled the woman down the stale-smelling corridor, her backside scuffing the boards. "What's she made of, anvils?"

"Anvils are lighter," groaned Shev through her gritted teeth, waddling from side to side under the dead weight of her, bouncing off the peeling walls. She gasped as she kicked open the door to her office—or the broom-cupboard she called an office. She strained with every burning muscle as she hauled the woman up, knocked her limp head on the doorframe as she wrestled her through, then tripped on a mop, and with a despairing squawk toppled back onto the cot with the woman on top of her.

In bed under a redhead was nothing to object to, but Shev preferred them at least partly conscious. Preferred them sweeter-smelling too, at least when they got *into* bed. This one stank like sour sweat and rot and the very end of things.

"That's where kindness gets you," said Severard, chuckling away to himself. "Wedged under a mighty weight of trouble."

"You going to giggle or help me out, you bastard?" snarled Shev, slack springs groaning as she struggled from underneath, then hauled the woman's legs onto the bed, feet dangling well off the end. It wasn't a big bed, but it looked like a child's with her on it. Her ragged coat had fallen open and the stained leather vest she wore had got dragged right up.

When Shev spent a year tumbling with that travelling show there'd been a strongman called himself the Amazing Zaraquon, though his real name had been Runkin. Used to strip to the waist and oil himself up and lift all kinds of heavy things for the crowd, though once he was off-stage and towelled down you couldn't get the lazy oaf to lift a thimble for you. His stomach had been all jutting knots of muscle as if beneath his tight-stretched skin he was made of wood rather than meat.

This woman's pale midriff reminded Shev of the Amazing Zaraquon's, but narrower, longer, and even leaner. You could see all the little sinews in between her ribs shifting with each shallow breath. But

SMALL KINDNESSES

instead of oil her stomach was covered in black and blue and purple bruises, plus a great red welt looked like it had been left by a most unfriendly axe-handle.

Severard gave a gentle whistle. "They really did give her a beating didn't they?"

"Aye, they did." Shev knew well enough what that felt like, and she winced as she twitched the woman's vest down, then dragged the blanket up and laid it over her. Tucked it in a little around her neck, though she felt a fool doing it, and the woman mumbled something and twisted onto her side, matted hair fluttering over her mouth as she started to snore.

"Sweet dreams," Shev muttered, not that she ever got any herself. Wasn't as if she really needed a bed here, but when you've spent a few years with nowhere safe to sleep, you tend to make a bed in every halfway safe place you can find. She shook the memories off and herded Severard back into the corridor. "Best get the doors open. We aren't pulling in so much business we can let it slip by."

"Folk really after husk at this time in the morning?" asked Severard, trying to wipe a smear of the woman's blood off his hand.

"If you want to forget your troubles, why live with them till the afternoon?"

By daylight the smoking room was far from the alluring little cave of wonders Shev had dreamed of making when she bought the place. She planted her hands on her hips as she looked around, and gave that weary sigh again. Fact was it bore more than a passing resemblance to an utter shit-hole. The boards were split and stained and riddled with splinters and the cushions greasy as a Baolish kitchen and one of the cheap hangings had come away to show the mould-blooming plaster behind. The prayer bells on the shelf were the only things that lent the faintest touch of class, and Shev gave the big one an affectionate stroke, then went up on tip-toe to pin the corner of that hanging back where it belonged, so at least the mould was hidden from her eyes, even if her nose was still well aware of it, the smell of rotten onions all-pervasive.

Even a liar as practised as Shev couldn't have convinced a fool as gullible as Shev that it wasn't a shit-hole. But it was her shit-hole. It was

402

a start. And she had plans to improve it. She always had plans.

"You clean the pipes?" she asked as Severard stomped back from opening the doors, brushing the curtain away.

"The folk who come here don't care about clean pipes, boss."

Shev frowned. "I care. We may not have the biggest place, or the most comfortable, or the best husk," she raised her brows at Severard's spotty face, "or the prettiest folk to light it for you, so what's our advantage over our competitors?"

"We're cheap?"

"No, no, no." She thought about that. "Well, yes. But what else?"

Severard sighed. "Customer service?"

"Ding," said Shev, flicking the biggest prayer bell and making it give off that heavenly song. "So clean the pipes you lazy shit, and get some coals lit."

Severard puffed out his cheeks, patched with the kind of downy beard that's meant to make a boy look manly but actually makes him look all the more boyish. "Yes, boss."

As he went out the back Shev heard footsteps coming in the front, and she propped her hands on the counter—or the hacked-up piece of butcher's block she'd salvaged off a rubbish heap and polished up—and put on her professional manner. She'd copied it off Gusman the carpet-seller, who was the best damn merchant she knew. He had a way of looking like a carpet might just be the answer to all your problems.

The professional manner slid off straight away when Shev saw who came strutting into her place.

"Carcolf," she breathed.

God, Carcolf was trouble. Tall, blond, beautiful trouble. Sweet-smelling, sweet-smiling, quick-thinking, quick-fingered trouble as subtle as the rain and as trustworthy as the wind. Shev looked her up and down. Her eyes didn't give her much choice in the matter. "Well my day's looking better," she muttered.

"Mine too," said Carcolf, brushing past the curtain so the daylight shone through her hair from behind. "It's been too long, Shevedieh."

The room seemed vastly improved with Carcolf in it. You wouldn't find a better ornament than her in any bazaar in Westport. Her clothes weren't tight but they stuck in all the right places, and she had this way of cocking her hips. God, those hips. They went all over the place, like they weren't attached to a spine like everyone else's. Shev heard she'd been a dancer. The day she quit had been a loss to dancing and a gain to fraud, without a doubt.

"Come for a smoke?" asked Shev.

Carcolf smiled. "I like to keep a clear head. How can you enjoy life otherwise?"

"Guess it depends whether your life's enjoyable or not."

"Mine is," she said, prancing around the place like it was hers and Shev was a valued guest. "What do you think of Talins?"

"Never liked it," muttered Shev.

"I've got a job there."

"Always loved the place."

"I need a partner." The prayer bells weren't all that low down. Even so, Carcolf bent over to get a good look at them. Entirely innocently, it would appear. But Shev doubted Carcolf ever did an innocent thing in her life. Especially bend over. "I need someone I can trust. Someone to watch my arse."

Shev's voice came hoarse. "If that's what you want you've come to the right girl, but . . ." And she tore her eyes away as her mind came knocking like an unwelcome visitor. "That's not all you're after, is it? I daresay it wouldn't hurt if this partner of yours could pick a lock or a pocket either."

Carcolf grinned as if the idea had only just come to her. "It wouldn't *hurt*. Be good if she could keep her mouth shut too." And she drifted over to Shev, looking down at her, since she was a good few inches taller. Most people were. "Except when I wanted her mouth open, of course . . ."

"I'm not an idiot."

"You'd be no use to me if you were."

"I go with you I'll likely end up abandoned in some alley with nothing but the clothes I'm standing in."

Carcolf leaned even closer to whisper, Shev's head full of the scent of her, which was a far stretch more appealing than rotten onions or sweaty redhead. "I'm thinking of you lying down. And without your clothes."

Shev made a squeak like a rusty hinge. But she forced herself not to grab hold of Carcolf like a drowning girl to a beautiful, beautiful log. She'd been thinking between her legs too long. Time to think between her ears.

"I don't do that kind of work anymore. I've got this place to worry about. And Severard to look after, I guess . . ."

"Still trying to set the world to rights, eh?"

"Not all of it. Just the bit at my elbow."

"You can't make every stray your problem, Shevedieh."

"Not every stray. Just this one." She thought of the great big woman in her bed. "Just a couple of 'em . . ."

"You know he's in love with you."

"All I did was help him out."

"That's why he's in love with you. No one else has." Carcolf reached out and gently brushed a stray strand of hair out of Shev's face with a fingertip, and gave a sigh. "Is that boy knocking at the wrong gate, poor thing."

Shev caught her wrist and guided it away. Being small didn't mean you could let folk just walk all over you. "He's not the only one." She held Carcolf's eye, made her voice calm and level. "I enjoy the act. God knows I enjoy it, but I'd rather you stopped. If you want me just for me, my door's always open and my legs shortly after. If you want me so you can squeeze me out like a lemon and toss my empty skin aside in Talins, well, no offence but I'd rather not."

Carcolf winced down at the floor. Not so pretty as the smile, but a lot more honest. "Not sure you'd like me without the act."

"Why don't we try it and see?"

"Too much to lose," muttered Carcolf, and she twisted her hand free, and when she looked up the act was on again. "Well. If you change your mind . . . it'll be too late." And with a smile over her shoulder deadly as a knife blade, Carcolf walked out. God, that walk she had. Flowing like syrup on a warm day. How did she get it? Did she practice in front of a mirror? Hours every day, more than likely.

The door shut, and the spell was broken, and Shev let go that weary sigh again.

"Was that Carcolf?" asked Severard.

"It was," murmured Shev, all wistful, a trace of that heavenly scent still battling the mould in her nostrils.

"I don't trust that bitch."

Shev snorted. "Fuck no."

"How do you know her?"

"From around." From all around Shev's bed and never quite in it.

"The two o' you seem close," said Severard.

"Not half as close as I'd like to be," she muttered. "You clean the pipes?"

"Aye."

Shev heard the door again, turned with a smile stuck half way between carpet seller and needy lover. Maybe it was Carcolf come back, decided she wanted Shev just for Shev—

"Oh, God," she muttered, face falling. Usually took her at least a little longer than that to regret a decision.

"Morning, Shevedieh," said Crandall. He was trouble of an altogether less pleasant variety. A rat-faced little nothing, thin at the shoulders and slender in the wits, pink at the eyes and runny at the nose, but he was Horald the Finger's son, and that made him a whole lot of something in this town. A rat-faced little nothing with power he hadn't had to earn, which made him tetchy brutal, and prickly spiteful, and jealous of anything anyone had that he didn't. And everyone had something he didn't, even if it was just talent, or looks, or a shred of self-respect.

Shev hitched that professional smile back up, though it was hard to think of anyone she wanted less in her place. "Morning, Crandall. Morning, Mason."

Mason ducked in just behind his boss. Or his boss's son, anyway. He was one of Horald's boys from way back, broad face criss-crossed with scars, ears all cauliflowered up, and a nose so often broken it was shapeless as a turnip. He was as hard a bastard as you'd find anywhere in Westport, where hard bastards were in plentiful supply. He looked over at Shev, still stooping on account of his towering frame and the low ceiling, and gave an apologetic twitch of the mouth. As if to say, *Sorry, but none of this is up to me. It's up to this fool.*

The fool in question was peering at Shev's prayer bells, and without bending down, mouth all twisted with contempt. "What's these? Bells?"

"Prayer bells," said Shev. "From Thond." She tried to keep her voice calm as three more men crowded past Mason into her place, trying to look dangerous but finding the room too tight for anything but uncomfortable. One had a face all pocked from old boils and eyes bulging right out, one had a leather coat far too big for him, got tangled with a curtain and near tore it down thrashing it away, the last had his hands shoved deep in his pockets and a look that said he had knives in there. No doubt he did.

Shev doubted she'd ever had so many folk in her place at once. Sadly, they weren't paying. She glanced at Severard, saw him shifting nervously, licking his lips, held out her palm to say, *calm, calm*, though she had to admit she wasn't feeling too calm herself.

"Didn't think you'd be much for prayer," said Crandall, wrinkling his nose at the bells.

"I'm not," said Shev. "I just like the bells. They lend the place a spiritual quality. You want a smoke?"

"No, and if I did I wouldn't come to a shit-hole like this."

There was a silence, then the pock-faced one leaned towards her. "He said it's a shit-hole!"

"I heard him," said Shev. "Sound carries in a room small as this one. And I'm well aware it's a shit-hole. I've got plans to improve it."

Crandall smiled. "You've always got plans, Shev. They never come to nothing."

True enough, and mostly on account of bastards like this. "Maybe my luck'll change," said Shev. "What do you want?"

"I want something stolen. Why else would I come to a thief?"

"I'm not a thief anymore."

"Course you are. You're just a thief playing at running a shit-hole Smoke House. And you owe me."

"What do I owe you for?"

Crandall's face twisted in a vicious grin. "For every day you don't have a pair o' broken legs." Shev swallowed. Seemed he'd somehow managed to become more of a bastard than ever.

Mason's deep voice rumbled out, soft and calming. "It's just a waste is what it is. Westport has lost a hell of a thief and gained a very average husk-seller. How old are you? Nineteen?"

"Twenty-one." Though she sometimes felt a hundred. "I'm blessed with a youthful glow."

"Still far too young to retire."

"I'm about the right age," said Shev. "Still alive."

"That could change," said Crandall, stepping close. As close to Shev as Carcolf had been and a very great deal less welcome.

"Give the lady some room," said Severard, with his lip stuck out defiantly.

Crandall snorted. "Lady? Are you fucking serious, boy?"

Shev saw Severard had that stick of hers behind his back. Nice length of wood it was, just the right weight for knocking someone on the head. But the very last thing she needed was him swinging that stick at Crandall. He'd be carrying it up his arse by the time Mason was through with him.

"Why don't you go out back and sweep the yard?" said Shev.

Severard looked at her, jaw all set for action, the fool. God, maybe he was in love with her. "I don't want—"

"Go out back. I'll be fine."

He swallowed, gave the heavies one more glance, then slid out. Shev gave a sharp whistle, brought all the hard eyes back to her. She knew well enough what having no choice looked like. "This thing you want. If I steal it, is that the last of it?"

Crandall shrugged. "Maybe it is. Maybe it isn't. Depends whether I want something stolen again, don't it."

"Whether your daddy does, you mean."

Crandall's eye twitched. He didn't like being reminded he was just a little prick in his daddy's big shadow. Shev had always had a problem with saying the wrong thing. Or the right thing at the wrong time. Or the right thing at the right time to the wrong person, maybe.

"You'll do as you're told you little gash-licking bitch," he spat in her face, "or I'll get my boys to burn your shit-hole down with you in it. And your fucking prayer bells too!"

Mason gave a wince, and a disgusted sigh, scarred cheeks puffed out. As if to say, *He's a rat-faced little nothing, but what can I do?*

Shev stared at Crandall. Damn, but she wanted to butt him in the face. Wanted to with all her being. She'd had bastards like this kicking her around all her life, it'd almost be worth it to kick back just once. But she knew all she could do was smile. If she hurt Crandall, Mason would hurt her ten times as bad. He wouldn't like it, but he'd do it. He made a living doing things he didn't like. Didn't they all?

Shev swallowed. Tried to make her fury look like fear. The deck was always stacked against folk like her.

"Guess I haven't got a choice."

Crandall blasted her with shitty breath as he smiled. "Who does?"

NEVER CONSIDER THE ground, that's the trick to it.

Shev straddled the slimy angle of the roof, broken tiles jabbing her in the groin as she inched along, thinking about how much she'd rather be straddling Carcolf. Down in the busy street to her right some drunk idiots were haw-hawing way too loud over a joke, someone else blabbering in Suljuk, of which Shev didn't understand more than one word in thirty. Down in the empty alleyway on her left it seemed quiet though.

She inched to the chimney, keeping low, just a shadow in the darkness, slipped the loop of her rope over it. Looked solid enough but she gave a good heave to check. Varini used to tell her she weighed two-thirds of nothing but even so she'd almost dragged a chimney clean off once and would've taken a tumble into the street with half a ton of masonry on her head if it hadn't been for a luckily placed windowsill.

Careful, careful, that's the trick, but a healthy streak of good luck doesn't hurt either.

Her heart was pounding now and she took a long breath and tried to settle it. Out of practice was all. She was the best thief in Westport, that was well known. That was why they wouldn't let her stop. Why *she* wouldn't let her stop. That was her blessing and her curse.

"Best thief in Westport," she muttered to herself, and slid down the rope to the edge of the roof, peering over. She could see the two guards flanking the doorway, lamplight gleaming on their helmets.

About the right time, and she heard the whores' voices, shrill and angry. Saw the guards' heads turn. More shrieking, and she caught the briefest glimpse of the women struggling before they went down in the gutter. The guards were drifting down the alleyway to watch, and Shev smiled to herself. Those girls put on a hell of a show for a couple of silvers.

Seize your moment, that's the trick to it.

In a twinkling she was over the roof, down the rope, and in through the window. It had only taken a few coppers to get the maid to leave the shutters off the latch. She pulled them shut as she dropped onto the other side. Someone was on their way down the stairs, a light tread, unhurried, but Shev was taking no chances. She nipped to the candle and pinched it out with her gloved fingers, sank the corridor into comfortable darkness.

The rope would still be dangling but there wasn't much to do about that. Couldn't afford a partner to hoist it back up. Had to hope she was long gone by the time they noticed.

In and out quick, that's the trick to it.

She could still hear the whores screeching in the street, no doubt having attracted quite the crowd by now, folk betting on the outcome and everything. There's something about women fighting that men can never seem to take their eyes away from. 'Specially if the women in question aren't wearing much. Shev hooked a finger in her collar and dragged a bit of air in, squashing a stray instinct to go and take a peek herself, and padded softly down the corridor to the third door, already slipping out her picks.

It was a damn good lock. Most thieves wouldn't have even bothered with it. Would've moved along to something easier. But Shev wasn't most thieves. She shut her eyes, and touched the tip of her tongue to her top lip, and slid her picks inside, and started to work the lock. It only took her a few moments to tease out the innards of it, to tickle the tumblers her way. It gave a little metal gasp as it opened up for her, and Shev slipped her tongue and her picks away, eased the knob around—though she was a lot less interested in knobs than locks, being honest—worked

410

the door open a crack, and slipped through, just as she heard the boots on the stairs, and felt herself grinning in the darkness.

She hadn't wanted to admit it, least of all to herself, but God she'd missed this. The fear. The excitement. The stakes. The thrill of taking what wasn't hers. The thrill of knowing just how damn good she was at it.

"Best fucking thief in Westport," she mouthed, and eased over to the table. The satchel was just where Crandall had said it'd be, and she slipped the strap over her shoulder in blissful, velvet silence. Everything just the way she'd planned.

Shev turned back towards the door and a board creaked under her heel.

A woman sat bolt upright in the bed. A woman in a pale nightdress, staring straight at her.

There wasn't supposed to be anyone in here.

Shev raised her gloved hand. "This is nothing like it looks—"

The woman let go the most piercing scream Shev ever heard in her life.

Luck's a treacherous bitch and won't always play along. Then cleverness and caution and plans will only get a thief so far. Boldness will have to take you the rest of the way. Shev raced to the window, raised her black boot and gave the shutters an almighty kick, splintered the latch, and sent them shuddering open as the woman heaved in a whooping breath.

A square of night sky. The second storey of the buildings across the way. She caught a glimpse of a man with his head in his hands through the window directly opposite. She thought about how far down it was, and made herself stop. You can't think about the ground. The woman let blast another bladder-loosening scream. Shev heard the door wrenched wide, guards yelling. She jumped through.

Wind tugged, flapped at her clothes, that lurching in her stomach as she started to fall. Like doing the high drop when she was tumbling with that travelling show, hands straining to catch Varini's. The reassuring smack of her palms into his and the puff of chalk as he whisked her up to safety. Every time. Every time but that last time when he'd had a drink too many and the ground had caught her instead.

She let it happen. Once you're falling, you can't fight it. There's an urge to flail and struggle but the air won't help you. No one will. No one ever will, in her experience.

With a teeth-rattling thud she dropped straight into the wagon of fleeces she'd asked Jens to leave under the window. He looked suitably amazed to see her floundering out from his cargo, dragging the satchel after her and scurrying across the street, weaving between the people and into the darkness between the ale-shop and the ostler's, the shouting fading behind her.

She reeled against the wall, gripping at her side, growling with each breath and trying not to cry out. The rim of the cart had caught her in the ribs, and from the sick pain and the way her head was spinning, she reckoned at least one was broken, probably a few more.

"Fucking ouch," she whispered through gritted teeth. She glanced back towards the building as Jens shouted to his mule and the wagon rolled off, a guard leaning out of the open window, pointing wildly across the street towards her. She saw someone slip out of a side door and gently push it closed. Someone tall and slim, a strand of blond hair falling from a black hat, and a satchel over her shoulder. Someone with a hell of a walk, hips swaying as she drifted quietly into the shadows.

The guard roared something and Shev turned, stumbled on down the alley, squeezed through the little crack in the wall and away.

Now she remembered why she'd wanted to stop, and run a Smoke House.

Most thieves don't last long. Even the good ones.

"You're hurt," said Severard.

Shev really was hurt, but she'd learned to keep her hurts as hidden as she could. In her experience, people were like sharks, blood in the water only made them hungry. So she shook her head, tried to smile, tried to look not hurt with her face twisted up and sweaty and her hand clamped to her ribs. "It's nothing. We got customers?"

"Just Berrick."

He nodded towards the old husk-head sprawled out on the greasy cushions with his eyes closed and his mouth wide open and his spent pipe beside him.

"When did he smoke?"

"Couple of hours past."

Shev gripped her side tight as she knelt beside him, touched him gently on the cheek. "Berrick? Best wake up now."

His eyes fluttered open and he saw Shev, and his lined face suddenly crushed up. "She's dead," he whispered. "Keep remembering it fresh. She's dead." And he closed his eyes and squeezed tears down his pale cheeks.

"I know," said Shev. "I know and I'm sorry. I'd usually let you stay long as you need, and I hate to do this, but you got to get up, Berrick. Might be trouble. You can come back later. See him home, eh, Severard?"

"I should stay here, I can watch your back—"

More likely he'd do something stupid and get the pair of them killed. "I been watching my own back long as I can remember. Go feed your birds."

"Fed 'em already."

"Feed 'em again, then. Just promise me you'll stay out till Crandall's come and gone."

Severard worked his spotty jaw, sullen. Shit, the boy really was in love with her. "I promise." And he slipped an arm under Berrick's and helped him stagger out of the door. Two less little worries, but still the big one to negotiate. Shev stared about, wandering how she could be ready for Crandall's visit. Routes of escape, hidden weapons, backup plans in case something went wrong.

The coals they used to light the pipes were smouldering away in the tin bowl on their stand. Shev picked up the water jug, thinking to douse them, then reckoned maybe she could fling them in someone's face if she had to, and just moved the stand back against the wall so she could reach for it easily, coals sliding and popping as she set it down.

"Evening, Shev." She spun about, trying not to wince at the stab of pain in her side. For a big, big man, Mason sure had a light tread when he felt the need.

Crandall ducked into the Smoke House behind him, looking even more sour than usual. She watched two of his thugs crowd in behind him. Big-Coat with his big coat on and Hands-in-Pockets with his hands still stuffed in his pockets.

The door to the yard creaked open and Pock-Face sidled through and shouldered it shut. So much for the escape route. Shev swallowed. Just get them out fast, and say as little as possible, and do nothing to rile them. That was the trick to it.

"Black suits you," said Mason, looking her up and down.

"That's why I wear it," she said, trying to look relaxed but only getting as far as queasy. "That and the thieving."

"Got it?" snapped Crandall.

Shev slipped the satchel out from under the counter and tossed it to him, strap flapping.

"Good girl," he said as he caught it. "Did you open it?"

"None of my business."

Crandall pulled the satchel open. He poked around inside. He looked up at her, with far from the expression of delight she'd been hoping for. "This a fucking joke?"

"Why would it be?"

"It's not here."

"What's not?"

"What was supposed to be in here!" Crandall shook the satchel at her and the frowns his men wore grew a little bit harder.

Shev swallowed again, a sinking feeling in her gut like she was standing at a cliff edge and could feel the earth crumbling at her feet. "You didn't say there'd be anything in it. You didn't say there'd be some champion screamer in the room either. You said get the satchel, and I got it!"

Crandall flung the empty satchel on the floor. "Thought you'd fucking sell it to someone else, didn't you?"

"What? I don't even know what *it* is! And if I'd screwed you I wouldn't be standing here waiting with nothing but a smile, would I?"

"Take me for a fool, do you? Think I didn't see Carcolf coming out of here?"

"Carcolf? She just came . . . cause she had a job . . . in Talins . . ." Shev trailed off with that same feeling she'd felt when her hands slipped from Varini's and she'd seen the ground flying up to greet her. Crandall's men shifted, one of them pulling a jagged-edged knife out, and Mason gave a grimace even bigger than usual and slowly shook his head.

Oh, God. Carcolf had finally fucked her. But not in a good way. Not in a good way at all.

Shev held her hands up, calming, trying to give herself time to think of something. "Look! You said get the satchel and I got it, what else could I do?" She hated the whine in her voice. Knew there was no point begging but couldn't help herself. Looked to the doors, the thugs slowly closing on her, knew the only question left was how bad they'd hurt her. Crandall stepped towards her, face twisting.

"Look!" she screeched, and he punched her in the side. Far from the hardest punch she'd ever taken, but as bad luck had it his fist landed right where the wagon had, there was a flash of pain through her guts and straight away she doubled up and puked all down his trousers.

"Oh, that's *it* you fucking little bitch! Hold her."

The one with the pocked face caught her left arm, and the one with the stupid coat her right and stuck his forearm in her throat and pinned her against the wall, both of them grinning like they hadn't had so much fun in a while. Shev could've been enjoying herself more as one of them waved his knife in her face, her mouth acrid with sick and her side on fire and her eyes crossed as she stared at the bright point.

Crandall snapped his fingers at Mason. "Give me your axe."

Mason winced. "More'n likely it's that bitch Carcolf behind all this. Nothing Shevedieh could've done. We kill her she can't help us find what we're after, eh?"

"It's past business now," said Crandall, the little rat-faced nothing, "and onto teaching a lesson."

"What lesson will this teach? And to who?"

"Just give me your fucking axe!"

Mason didn't like it, but he made a living doing things he didn't like. Wasn't as if this crossed some line. His expression said *I'm real sorry*, but he pulled out his hatchet and slapped the polished handle into Crandall's palm anyway, turning away in disgust.

Shev twisted like a worm cut in half but she could hardly breathe for the pain in her ribs, and the two bastards had her fast. Crandall leaned closer, caught a fistful of her shirt and twisted it. "I would say it's been nice knowing you, but it fucking hasn't."

"Try not to spatter me this time, boss," said Pock-Face, closing the bulging eye nearest to her so he didn't get her brains in it.

Shev gave a stupid whimper, squeezing her eyes shut as Crandall raised the axe.

So that was it, then, was it? That was her life? A shit one, when you thought about it. A few good moments shared with halfway decent folk. A few small kindnesses done. A few little victories clawed from all those defeats. She'd always supposed the good stuff was coming. The good stuff she'd be given. The good stuff she'd give. Turned out this was all there was.

"It is a long time since I saw prayer bells."

Shev opened her eyes again. The red-haired woman she'd dragged into her bed that morning and forgotten all about was standing larger than life in Shev's smoke room in that ripped leather vest, peering at the bells on the shelf.

"This is a very fine one." And she brushed the bronze with her scabbed fingertips. "Second dynasty."

"Who's this fucking joker?" snarled Crandall, weighing the hatchet in his hand.

Her eyes shifted lazily over to him. Or the one eye Shev could see did, tangled red hair hanging across the other. That hard-boned face was spattered with bruises, the nose cut and swollen and crusted with blood, the lips split and bloated. But she had this look in that one bloodshot eye as it flickered across Crandall and his four thugs, lingered on Mason a moment, then away. An easy contempt. As though she'd taken their whole measure in that one glance and wasn't troubled by it one bit.

"I am Javre," said the woman. She had some strange kind of an accent. From up north somewhere, maybe. "Lioness of Hoskopp and, far from being a joker, I am in fact often told I have a poor sense of humour. Who put me to bed?"

Pinned against the wall by three men, the most Shev could do was raise one finger.

Javre nodded. "That was a kindness I will not forget. Do you have my sword?"

"Sword?" Shev managed to croak, the forearm across her throat easing off as its owner turned to sneer at the new arrival.

Javre hissed through her teeth. "It could be very dangerous if it fell into the wrong hands. It is forged from the metal of a fallen star."

"She's mad," said Crandall.

"Fucking loon," grunted Hands-in-Pockets.

"Lioness of Hoskopp," said Big-Coat, and gave a little giggle.

"I will have to steal it back," she was musing. "Do any of you know a decent thief?"

There was a pause, then Shev raised that one finger again.

"Ah!" Javre's blood-clotted brow went up. "It is said the Goddess places the right people in each other's paths." She frowned as though she was only just making sense of the situation. "Are these men inconveniencing you?"

"A little," Shev whispered, grimacing at the dull ache that had spread from her side right to the tips of her fingers.

"Best to check. You never can tell what people enjoy." Javre slowly worked her bare shoulders. They reminded Shev of the Amazing Zaraquon's too, woody hard and split into a hundred little fluttering shreds of muscle. "I will ask you once to put the dark-skinned girl down and leave."

Crandall snorted. "And if we don't?"

That one eye narrowed slightly. "Then long after we are gone to the Goddess, the grandchildren of the grandchildren of those who witness will whisper fearful stories of the way I broke you."

Hands-in-Pockets shoved his hands down further still. "You ain't even got a weapon," he snarled.

But Javre only smiled. "My friend, I am the weapon."

Crandall jerked his head towards her. "Put this bitch out o' my misery."

Pock-Face and Big-Coat let go of Shev, which was a blessing, but closed in towards Javre, which didn't seem to be. Big-Coat pulled a stick from his coat, which was a little disappointing since he had ample room for a greatsword in there. Pock-Face spun his jagged-edged dagger around in his fingers and stuck out his tongue, which was uglier than the blade if anything.

Javre just stood, hands on her hips. "Well? Do you await a written invitation?"

Pock-Face lunged at her but his knife caught nothing. She dodged with a speed even Shev could hardly follow, and her white hand flashed out and chopped him across the side of the neck with a sound like a cleaver chopping meat. He dropped as if he had no bones in him at all, knife bouncing from his hand, flopping and thrashing on the floor like a landed fish, spitting and gurgling and his eyes popping out farther than ever.

Big-Coat hit her in the side with his stick. If he'd hit a pillar, that was the sound of it. Javre hardly even flinched. Muscle bulged in her arm as she sank her fist into his gut and he bent right over with a breathy wheeze. Javre caught him by the hair with her big right fist and smashed his head into Shev's butcher-block counter, blood spattering the cheap hangings.

"Shit," breathed Crandall, the hand he was holding Shev with going limp.

Javre looked over at the one with his hands rammed in his pockets, whose mouth had just dropped open. "No need to feel embarrassed," she said. "If I had a cock I would play with it all the time too."

He jerked his hands out and flung a knife. Shev saw the metal flicker, heard the blade twitter.

Javre caught it. She made no big show of it, like the jugglers in that travelling show used to. She simply plucked it from the air as easily as you might catch a coin you'd tossed yourself.

"Thank you," she said. She tossed it back and it thudded into the man's thigh. He gave a great spitty screech as he staggered back

418

through the doorway and into the street.

Mason had just pulled his own knife out, a monster of a thing you could've called a sword without much fear of correction. Javre planted her hands on her hips again. "Are you sure this is the way you want it?"

"Can't say I want it," said Mason, drifting into a fighting crouch. "But there's no other way for it to be."

"I know." Javre shook her shoulders again and raised those big empty hands. "But it is always worth asking."

He sprang at her, knife a blur, and she whipped out of the way. He slashed at her and she dodged again, watching as he lumbered towards the door, tearing the curtain from its hooks. He lunged at her, feathers spewing up in a fountain as he hacked a cushion open, splinters flying as he smashed the counter over with his flailing boot, cloth ripping as he slashed one of the hangings in half.

Mason gave a bellow like a hurt bull and charged at her once more. Javre caught his wrist as the knife-blade flashed towards her, big vein popping from her arm as she held it, straining, the trembling point just a finger's width from her forehead.

"Got you now!" Mason sprayed spit through his clenched teeth as he caught Javre by her thick neck, forced her back a step—

She snatched the big prayer bell from the shelf and smashed him over the head with it, the almighty clang so loud it rattled the teeth in Shev's head. Javre hit him again, twisting free of his clutching hand, and he gave a groan and dropped to his knees, blood pouring down his face. Javre raised her arm high and smashed him onto his back, bell breaking from the handle and clattering away into the corner, the ringing echoes gradually fading.

Javre looked up at Crandall, her face all spotted with Mason's blood. "Did you hear that?" She raised her red brows. "Time for you to pray."

"Oh, hell," croaked Crandall. He let the hatchet clatter to the boards and held his open palms up high. "Now look here," he stammered out, "I'm Horald's son. Horald the Finger!"

Javre shrugged as she stepped over Mason's body. "I am new in town. One name strikes me no harder than another."

"My father runs things here! He gives the orders!"

Javre grinned as she stepped over Big-Coat's corpse. "He does not give me orders."

"He'll pay you! More money than you can count!"

Javre poked Pock-Face's fallen knife out of her way with the toe of her boot. "I do not want it. I have simple tastes."

Crandall's voice grew shriller as he shrank away from her. "If you hurt me, he'll catch up to you!"

Javre shrugged again as she took another step. "We can hope so. It would be his last mistake."

"Just . . . please!" Crandall cringed. "Please! I'm begging you!"

"It really is not me you have to beg," said Javre nodding over his shoulder.

Shev whistled, and Crandall turned around, surprised. He looked even more surprised when she buried the blade of Mason's hatchet in his forehead with a sharp crack.

"Bwurgh," he said, tongue hanging out, then he toppled backwards, his limp hand catching the stand and knocking it and the tin bowl flying, showering hot coals across the wall.

"Shit," said Shev, as flames shot up the flimsy hangings. She snatched up the water jug and flung it, but the meagre spray made scarcely any difference. Fire had already spread to the next curtain, shreds of burning ash fluttering down.

"Best vacate the premises," said Javre, and she took Shev under the arm with a grip that was not to be resisted and marched her smartly out the door, leaving four dead men scattered about the burning room.

The one who'd had his hands in his pockets was leaning against the wall in the street, clutching at his own knife stuck in his thigh.

"Wait—" he said, as Javre caught him by the collar, and with a flick of her wrist sent him reeling across the street to crash head first into a wall.

Severard was running up, staring at the building, flames already licking around the door frame. Javre caught him and guided him away. "Nothing to be done. Bad choice of décor for a place with naked flames." As if to underscore the point, the window shattered, fire gouting into the street, Severard ducking away with his hands over his head.

"What the hell happened?" he moaned.

"Went bad," whispered Shev, clutching at her side. "Went bad."

Javre scraped the dirty red hair out of her battered face and grinned at the ruin of Shev's hopes as though it looked a good enough day's work to her. "You call that bad? I say it could have been far worse!"

"How?" snapped Shev. "How could it be fucking worse?"

"We might both be dead." She gave a sharp little laugh. "Come out alive, it is a victory."

"This is what happens," said Severard, his eyes shining with reflected fire as the building burned brighter. "This is what happens when you do a kindness."

"Ah, stop crying, boy. Kindness brings kindness in the long run. The Goddess holds our just rewards in trust! I am Javre, by the way." And she clapped him on the shoulder and near knocked him over. "Do you have an older brother by any chance? Fighting always gets me in the mood."

"What?"

"Brothers, maybe?"

Shev clutched at her head. Felt like it was going to burst. "I killed Crandall," she whispered. "I bloody killed him. They'll come after me now! They'll never stop coming!"

"Pfffft." Javre put one great, muscled, bruised arm around Shev's shoulders. Strangely reassuring and smothering at once. "You should see the bastards coming after me. Now, about stealing back this sword of mine . . ."

MAZARKIS WILLIAMS

Being a child is not fun and innocence and happy memories. Not all the time, anyway. Being a child can be terrifying. Awful things happen, and children lack both the agency to protect themselves and the maturity to process their emotions.

When I was about five, one of my cousins went missing. There was a search, an uncertain space between when he was no longer part of our lives but we had not yet found his body. I remember that time very well, and yet I don't remember when I found out he was dead. I don't think anyone told me.

My experience is not special. Terrible things happen all the time, and parents try to protect their children from the details.

But children glean many things from adult conversations. Very often adults don't tell them anything; they talk over the little ones' heads. But children know. They know when something is wrong. Their imaginations can go into all the darkest places. They know there are people who can do harm, and for the most part they don't want to be one of them. I think that's what this story is about.

THE RAT

Mazarkis Williams

"I saw a rat nosing around outside. Put the cat to it, will you?" Nana May's clean hands wound her yarn into a ball. "I won't have it showing up and ruining everything. Not today."

Emil glanced around. "Greygirl!" He heard no answering yowl, so he got on his knees to look under the table and behind the spinning wheel. "Is Greatpapa very old, Nana?"

"Old, yes," she said with a sigh. "More than some tales."

Emil made a show of looking for Greygirl behind the ladder that led to his mat in the loft, but his mind was on the old stories. "Nana May, wasn't your papa in the Wizard War?"

"And don't you go asking about that, either." Nana May's eyes strayed to Emil's set of wooden soldiers, carefully carved by his own papa three years ago, crowded around a vase on the tiny side table. "He doesn't hold with great tales any more than he holds with rats. Just leave it be." She rose to put the yarn into her wool-box. All her wool was yet undyed, the same black and grey as her hair.

Emil moved to the doorway of the tiny cottage, his anticipation now tinged with a familiar unease. Nana May always said leave it be.

She didn't like to talk about his father, Alain; or the blight in the garden; or the way her witch-charm was ripped from the door and smashed under someone's heel. She had once said in a bitter moment that her papa would never come to the cottage because of *his* papa. Now Alain was dead, drowned in the river, and so Greatpapa came, bringing his own secrets with him.

From now on Nana May would sleep in the other side of the loft where Alain used to sleep, and Greatpapa would take her little bedroom in the back. Emil missed his father's warm voice in the darkness, but Nana May had her own kind way of speaking. It was only the things she wouldn't say that made him want to spite her. He folded his arms over his chest. "Papa said that *I* would be the man of the house now."

Nana May smiled at him the way a person did at a new lamb or spring flower. "Plenty of time remains for you to be the man. Never fear."

She didn't understand. But the bitter words gathering in his mind slipped away when he caught sight of two figures on the road. "Here comes a man with a lute, Nana, and he has a very old man with him."

"That won't be your greatpapa, then," said his nana, flashing her dark eyes at the doorway. "He don't hold with musicians either."

But the two men were heading straight for the door where Emil stood. "It's him, Nana!" said Emil, his voice rising in excitement. He cleared his throat. "It's your father," he said, a bit deeper.

Now THEY WERE upon him. Emil's greatpapa leaned on a walking stick but still managed to twist his head around, checking the path behind him and from side to side, as if he expected an animal to attack at any moment. The musician was young enough to hold his shoulders straight, but he carried snow in his hair. He squinted at Emil, creases forming to either side of his hazel-colored eyes.

"Welcome to our home, Greatpapa. Welcome, stranger," said Emil, bobbing his head like a bird.

"You Alain's boy?" asked his greatpapa, looking him up and down with eyes like the winter sky. His cheeks folded away from his nose like two pale fans. "Never did like that sneak, but you look all right." Some spittle flew out of his mouth and landed on Emil's chin. Emil tried his best to ignore it.

Greatpapa hadn't noticed. He waved his walking stick toward the other man. "This here is a fellow who showed me some kindness on the road. Being me, I didn't have no kindness to give back, so I brought him to your nana. May's always been good, in her way."

Unfazed by the odd introduction, the musician stepped over the threshold, looked Emil in the eye, and held out a hand. "I'm Horace. I am very pleased to meet you."

Horace looked like the kind of person who noticed things, who watched and asked questions. Emil knew right away he did not want to let him into the house, but he shook hands as Nana May had taught him. "Please, come inside."

Greatpapa shuffled in behind Horace, making it only halfway through the door before he stopped again. "You ain't got no rats, do you?"

"No, Greatpapa. We have a cat, and she's a good ratter." Too late he remembered he had not found Greygirl.

The old man nodded, and for the first time Emil saw a smile on his face. He still had three good teeth, and his tongue was pink and shiny. "That's my May," he said.

Emil blushed. He hadn't lied, not exactly.

Before long they sat around the small table, shoved between the spinning wheel and the fireplace, eating the stew Emil had been smelling all day as it bubbled in its pot. "This is delicious," said Horace, with a wink at Emil. Emil glared back at him.

"May always did cook a nice supper," said Greatpapa, smacking his lips together. "It's too bad I ain't been able to come before now."

"You could have come anytime, Father," said Nana May, as pleasant as could be, but at the same time allowing no contradiction.

"This is a lovely part of the country," Horace said into the silence that followed. "I have never been to these parts before."

"Well, you're in for a treat," said Nana May. "Soon you'll find the hills, and the lakes between them, blue as can be, made from the tears of giants."

"That's a story," said Greatpapa, "that some liar told to you."

"And what is the truth, Father?" Nana May asked.

He shrugged. "You don't care. If you did, you'd already know the truth."

Nana May appeared to accept this, and said nothing, though Horace regarded Greatpapa with some curiosity. The old man stared into the fire with a baleful look, then continued, "Nobody cares. The wizards tell some story and we all believe it. Giants' tears!" He snorted.

"You don't like wizards?" Horace asked, though Nana May shook her head at him.

Greatpapa turned from the fire, suspicion sharp in his eyes. "You do?"

"In truth, I don't think a person can like a wizard, or dislike one, either. They're not like other people." Horace shrugged and took another bite of stew. Emil thought suddenly of the rat and looked around the room, searching for Greygirl.

"I don't know from like or dislike, but it's easy enough to hate the wizards. 'Specially after what they did in the war." Greatpapa's spoon made a bang when he threw it into his bowl, and Emil jumped, his attention back at the table.

Horace was looking at Emil, his hazel eyes so direct that Emil found himself wriggling in his seat. "And you? What do you think?"

His greatpapa bent toward Emil before he could answer, and it took a force of will not to lean away as the old man spoke. "Never fight alongside a wizard, boy, and never trust one, and surely never *be* one. Sneaks all, they are."

Horace cleared his throat and put down his own spoon. "You were in the war? Sir, so few survived to tell of it, I feel obliged to ask—"

Greatpapa jerked his head backward to look at the door, though nobody was there. "Who would ask me about that? What kind of person?" His wintry eyes narrowed and he pointed a finger at Horace. "You know what? You remind me of my grandson," he said, more of an accusation than an observation.

428

Emil grabbed at the edge of the table, stuck between protest and revelation. His father had been nothing like Horace. Alain possessed great and secret talents, and if only the townsfolk had known the things his father did, they would have loved him instead of hated him. Horace seemed the opposite: the kind of man people always liked, but who didn't deserve it. And yet.

"Forgive me," said Horace, more to Nana May than to Greatpapa, "I was rude."

Nana May gave a sigh of relief, and everyone picked up their spoons.

AFTER DINNER, GREATPAPA seemed to have calmed enough to doze, his head tilted back as he drew in long, noisy breaths. Emil stretched out upon the rushes, pretending to sleep, but his body was tense, his mind racing. Nana May and Horace talked, their voices low in the darkness, believing themselves alone.

"I was sorry to hear about your son," said Horace.

Emil opened his eyes to slits and watched Nana May's boot twist against the floor. He had a sickening feeling. Once again the bard was sticking his nose in where it didn't belong. "Thank you," said Nana May. "I lost both my husbands and then my son. Now it's just me and Emil, but we do all right. It's just, our crops . . ."

Horace lowered his voice. "Is the boy . . . ?"

"Yes," murmured Nana May.

She had answered the bard's question, but not in a way Emil could decipher. He crushed a sage leaf between his fingers and let the scent wash away his anger. Always when his papa was alive there had been whispering, Nana May with concern and the townsfolk with darker looks. That Alain is bad luck, they muttered. Vermin. Then one day papa left to buy the seed and ended up floating in the river. But he hadn't died, not then. The water had filled his lungs and killed him slow.

Now they whispered about Emil.

His father had gasped for air at the end, and sometimes Emil felt he could not breathe either, caught between one secret and the next.

But Horace saw him watching and winked, then brought out his lute. Emil sat up, relaxing his guard. It wasn't often that he got to hear music now that his parents were gone. Sometimes at the harvest festival a bard would come and sing an epic tale, but there were so many folks there that he could never get close.

The music was sweet and measured, the perfect gift for Nana May. Emil watched seven kinds of delight cross her face before she settled into a pleased blush. It was the face she gave whenever he said her dress was pretty, or the bread particularly fine. In another life Emil would have warmed to the bard now, perhaps given him a smile. Instead he focused his gaze on his boots. After a time the music was finished and a respectful silence settled over the room.

Greatpapa rubbed at his ear. He must have woken up to listen. "Well, I come here to die," he said, "and this has been a fine welcome. I hope my goodbyes are just as nice."

"Goodbye? But aren't you going to live with us, Greatpapa?"

"Not for long."

Emil looked to Horace, but Horace was looking around the cottage, at the dingy chairs and the spinning wheel and the iron cooking-pot, as if taking inventory. Was he going to stay, then? Emil's hands closed into fists.

Nana May said, "Horace, you best sleep up in the loft with Emil tonight. I'll settle my papa in bed and wrap myself in a few blankets right here."

Before Emil could protest, Horace leapt from his seat. "Outrageous! I won't hear of you sleeping on the floor."

Nana May rubbed her eyes. "I want to be near my papa. And I'm too tired to climb that ladder anyhow."

Though Emil felt he should have protested more, Horace made a graceful bow. "As you wish, my lady." He spoke as if he were with a real lady with jewels and everything. The bard fished in his pocket. "And as a host-gift, I'd like to present this." He drew out a carved wooden sparrow. Its polish gleamed in the light of the dying fire. Emil took a step forward. He knew that the bird was meant for his nana, but nevertheless it held a message for him too.

"Your music was gift enough," said Nana May, her eyes sparkling as she gazed at the offering.

"I have never had stew so tasty, bread so soft, nor company more enchanting. I must insist."

Nana May held out one trembling hand and wrapped it around the bird. "My son carved too," she said in a voice barely more than a whisper.

"What?" said Greatpapa. "I never heard of him doing anything useful."

"He carved," repeated Nana May, pointing to the wooden soldiers.

"What . . ." sputtered Greatpapa, backing away, as if he were facing a bear and not a pile of toys. "Why would he carve those?"

"They're toys, Papa," said Nana May.

"Toys?" Greatpapa showed all his three teeth and waved his head from side to side. "No!"

Horace stepped closer to the soldiers, eyes lighting with interest, so Emil sprang up to stand in front of them. "Those are mine," he said.

"I would never take them from you," said Horace with a laugh. "Only, may I look?"

Their eyes met for two heartbeats. At last Emil stood aside, but he hovered next to Horace all the same. He could hear his greatpapa muttering behind him, too low to hear. Horace reached out and wrapped his long fingers around a wooden archer. He sighed and nodded in relief as if some hope had been confirmed, then smiled at Emil. Emil focused on the musician's hands. They were just as calloused and strong as his papa's had been. "Do you know which soldiers these are?" asked Horace.

Emil nodded. "This is the army of the great hero Nehrem on his last campaign into the Mountains of Hosnan." He opened a drawer. "And this is the Hosnian army. I don't keep them out, usually." His father had carved these of redwood. Their faces sneered with hatred.

The musician examined these soldiers too. "The detail is perfect. The uniforms, the hats, and the weapons are exact."

"Ain't nothing exact when it comes to a war," grumbled Greatpapa, "or the telling of it."

Horace ignored him and asked Emil a question instead. "Do you know all about the Hosnians and their powerful sorcerers?"

Emil nodded. Nehrem had saved the land from the terrible magic of the north. Everybody knew that.

"I'LL SHOW YOU something amusing." Horace cleared a space on the eating table and lined up the armies so that they faced one another. He brought over two candles. They made his eyes shine like beacons, but didn't light up the table very well. Something about the sure way he moved in the darkness felt familiar to Emil. Nana May took a few steps closer, the sparrow still in her hand.

When all the soldiers were in place Horace began to speak, his voice deep and sonorous. "It is well past midnight. The Army of Nehrem have been fighting for a day and half again, and have lost many men. They are trapped in the Valley of Dreams while the Hosnians have the high ground. The Hosnians have a thousand sorcerers while the Durenin wizards number only five. All seems lost." As he paused, something moved on the table. *The rat!* thought Emil, his heart skipping a beat, but he blinked, and saw it for what it was.

The wooden figures were beginning to move. Horace could make the soldiers move just as his papa had. Emil remembered sitting on Papa's lap at the table while he told the great tales. He leaned forward for more, his eyes watering with happiness as the Hosnian army raised their swords and lances and stepped forward.

"No . . ." said Greatpapa, but Emil was too pleased with the story to look up at him and ask why.

"In the moonlight Nehrem raises his arms and his voice and says, 'People of Durenin, for what do we fight? We do not fight for the Valley of Dreams, or the Mountain before us, or for the glory of one battle. We fight for our people and their Goddess Ruhala. This is the moment when we choose whether to scatter before the enemy and abandon the lands of our goddess to this cruel world, or to soak the ground with our own blood so that our children never need face fear.'"

As Horace spoke, the hairs tingled on Emil's arms as if he were listening to Nehrem himself.

The Hosnian army took backward steps, as if Nehrem's sacrifice put them in awe.

"No," said Greatpapa again, only louder, and this time Emil did look at him. The old man stood up from his chair, his face twisting but not with anger, not exactly. "Stop this right now! The battle didn't go that way. The men all died, that's true, and as they lay there, with nobody to bury 'em, the rats ate 'em—" He took three headlong steps and swept the wooden soldiers from the table, "—because the wizards and sorcerers joined together against us! *That's* the peace we bought with our blood, and you know it well!"

"I didn't," said Horace, his voice steady. "I don't. I've never met anyone who was there, except you."

"Lying sneak! *You knew.* You tricked me, but that's over. You will not speak to the boy again. You will not look at him." Greatpapa pounded his cane against the floor, shuddering the planks.

Emil watched Nana May and looked for some hint, some answer. *You knew.* She did not look his way. He got on his knees and reached for his soldiers, but Greatpapa pinned his hand between the cane and the floor. "Leave 'em," he commanded, "they're filthy, lying things, just like this here wizard." He turned to Horace and spoke in a voice so low and certain that Emil thought he must have been an intimidating person to fight against, back when he was a soldier. "Get. Out."

Emil kept still. The soldiers were all he had left of his father, and he was afraid for them.

"Emil, why don't you go outside," said Nana May in a shaky voice, "and show Horace where he can sleep in the hayloft?"

"Yes, Nana May." As the cane released Emil's hand, he slipped one of the wooden men, an archer from Nehrem's army, into his right boot. And then, because he saw it on the floor by Nana's foot, the sparrow. His deeds unnoticed, he scrambled outside and waited in the darkness by the open door.

"You'll have to go," he heard Nana May say to Horace, all polite. "I'm sorry about this. You are welcome to the barn, but you must be gone by morning." When she got upset, which wasn't very often, she trembled all over like a leaf in the wind. Emil could imagine her right now, standing by the table, her chin shaking something awful.

"Naturally." Horace's voice sounded stiff. Angry. Emil felt sorry for Nana May. He knew she liked Horace. "I thank you for the hospitality." A few heavy footsteps, and now the bard—no, wizard—stood beside Emil on the porch.

"Papa," said Nana May, her voice thin and quiet.

Horace laid a hand on Emil's arm, but Emil shook it off, listening.

"Nehrem was a coward who made a coward's bargain," said Greatpapa. "Now his sons will sit the throne for as long as the blood is in the soil and the wizards can make use of it." He drew in his breath. "*Our* blood . . . The sacrifice, they call it now!"

"Papa . . ."

"The Valley of Dreams, indeed."

". . . not all the wizards are bad." Nana May's voice was weak, finished, the last autumn breeze chased out by winter. She barely believed it herself, Emil realized, and with that, he felt a deep sadness.

Emil heard the scattering of more wooden soldiers. "It twists them all around, the magic. Your son would have betrayed us just the same."

Horace tried once again to pull him away, a tight grip over rough wool.

"Please, Papa . . ." Then Nana May made a little gasp of fear, and Emil tried to move forward. He needed to know what was happening. He needed to go in to her, to save her if necessary, but his legs wouldn't move, and in any case Horace held tight to his arm. Emil heard the wood-ax thunk against the floorboards. "I'm going to chop every last one of these worthless toys."

"Papa! You'll kill yourself."

"If you knew the things I did in the war, you wouldn't be coming at me when I got an ax in my hand. Now lay off, woman, and let me do my work." The ax hit again. *Crack.*

Emil stood and listened for what seemed a long time. *Crack. Crack.*

He felt conscious of the carvings in his boot, pressing against his leg, and the sound of Nana May crying, and the scent of Horace behind him, all pine needles and wax. What he did not feel was his papa. He truly was gone.

The ax, its job finished, fell with a bang upon the eating table.

Emil's face was wet with tears. He heard someone else weeping too. Greatpapa.

"If I die tonight, don't let the rats get me. Don't let them eat me."

Nana May sniffed, not the crying kind from before but more of a Nana May sort of sniff, the kind she used when Emil was slow to his tasks. "There are no rats in here, Papa."

"Rats are everywhere, May. Even in the mountains. Fed on my brothers. My friends. I tried to stop 'em. But there's a good girl, keep 'em off of me."

"Yes, Papa, I will."

EMIL FELT CUT in two. He wiped his tears and turned away. "Come," he said to Horace, "I'll show you where to sleep." As he walked through the darkness, he thought of his papa and the warm feeling that came in the room when he used to carve, how it buzzed and tasted of life, round and sweet. He remembered Nana May saying it ruined the vegetables and brought rot to the apple trees. No more carving, she had said. Emil could feel the garden now, limp and diseased in the night, gnawed and chewed by pests and vermin, even though his papa was long gone. It hadn't been the carving after all, and that made him angry.

"Why did you have to go and do that?" he asked the bard.

"Do what?"

"Come here, ask questions, make the soldiers move . . . you've ruined everything!"

"Have I?"

"Of course you have." Emil pulled open the barn door. "You can forget about staying here too! I saw you smiling at Nana May, and looking at all our things as if they were yours! Well, you can forget it."

Horace leaned down, put his face on a level with Emil's, and looked into his eyes, man to man. "I wasn't going to stay."

"Then what were you going to do? Take Nana May away with you?"

Horace laid a hand on his shoulder. "It wasn't your Nana May I came for," he said, his eyes so direct, always so direct and honest, that Emil knew it for truth.

And so he ran. He sprinted toward the river where his father had found his end, and from there into the woods, where crickets chirped and roots tangled around his feet. When he thought he had gone far enough that Horace would not find him, he sat with his back against a tree. Only then did he realize he had heard no shouts, no running footsteps. Horace had let him go.

Emil gathered his thoughts. It had to be him who made the garden sick. It had to be him who brought bad luck, just like his father. He sat so long the forest grew quiet all around. His neck ached; his throat was sore.

The night opened in his mind.

When he closed his eyes he could feel Greygirl hunting by the riverside, and the rats who ran from her, their hearts racing. Horace was at the river too, waiting for him in stillness, one hand on his lute. Nana May lay in her blankets, short little breaths showing her ready to wake at any moment, and quieter than all of them, Emil felt the dim light that was Greatpapa, flickering like a candle, but not ready to go out. Not yet. Emil breathed in the fierceness of that tiny flame. It was not anger that drove the old soldier; it was fear, fear so deep that it was part of him, bone and flesh and all. Emil remembered the toys turning in Papa's hands, the power going into their tiny wooden forms. It had seemed a small trick, but now he knew it for wizardry; and he knew just as well as his greatpapa did that bringing toys to life and laying waste to an entire army was the same thing, only a different size.

Papa. Now he understood.

In the morning, Emil woke with a stiff back and his chin against his chest. He reached down into his boot for the wooden soldier, but found the sparrow instead. He pulled it out and studied it, from its sharp beak to its carefully rendered feathers and delicate feet. He ran his fingers over its wings and felt a sympathetic trembling in the wood. Emil made a fist around the carving so that nobody, not even the real birds above, could see. The sparrow's wings tickled his palm as it stirred, waking to his will.

BRIAN MCCLELLAN

I'll admit, when Shawn Speakman first asked me to contribute to the *Unbound* anthology, I was pretty disappointed. Here was this awesome collection of short stories from a fantastic group of authors, including several of my friends and writing heroes, and there was absolutely no way I had time to write anything for it. I had a to-do list a mile long. So I politely declined, kicking myself the whole time.

A while later, Shawn asked me if I'd be interested in contributing to *Unfettered II* and, as I was so annoyed I'd had to turn down *Unbound*, I immediately said yes. I wrote "The Siege of Tilpur," a short story set in the Powder Mage universe, and sent it in. Later still, I noticed that Shawn was still announcing contributions to *Unbound*. I asked him if we could bump my story up by one anthology if I wrote a second for *Unfettered II*, and he agreed!

Long story short, I'm crazy excited to have "The Siege of Tilpur" in *Unbound*.

I hope you are too!

THE SIEGE OF TILPUR

Brian McClellan

Sergeant Tamas closed his eyes and listened to orders being called back and forth across the front lines, voices punctuated by the report of artillery blasting away from the next hill over. Captains shouted at their lieutenants, lieutenants shouted at their sergeants, sergeants at their infantry. It was only a matter of time before some poor infantryman snapped and started screaming at the drummer boys for the simple release of having someone of his own to bark orders at.

It was all nonsense, of course. "Hold steady, boys," or "keep your heads up," or "first man over the top gets a hundred krana." Everyone was in line, bayonets set, flintlocks primed, ladders to shoulders, tensed and just waiting for the signal. The only thing the shouting accomplished, as far as he was concerned, was to allow the officers to unleash their own damned uncertainty in as manly a fashion as possible.

Meanwhile the infantry baked in their uniforms, jackets and pants already soaked with sweat. If General Seske waited another half hour to give the order to charge, the desert sun might just reduce the entire Adran army to withered husks.

"This is bullshit," a voice said behind him.

"Quiet down, Farthing," Private Lillen responded in her lazy drawl. "I'm trying to get in a nap before this things starts."

"I'm not joking," Farthing said. "This is utter bullshit. We're charging the broad face of a bloody fort in full daylight with nothing but ladders and light artillery. It's not going to work, just like it didn't work last time or the time before that. We're all about to be buggered by grapeshot and sorcery. Might as well call us 'his royal majesty's Adran bullet-absorbers.'"

"You'd think you'd have gotten used to it by now," Lillen said.

"Used to it? Explain to me how one gets used to a fireball to the face? The same way you get used to napping on your feet? Because I can't figure that one out either."

"You want to desert?" Lillen's pleasant tone turned mocking. "Because you've been telling us you're going to desert for almost three years now and it hasn't happened yet. I'm beginning to think I'll be long dead by the time you finally do it, which is a shame because I want to be there when they haul you back into camp and put you in front of a firing squad."

"You bitch. I'll cut you for that."

"Shut up, Farthing," Tamas said. "And take your damned nap, Lillen. You've got about eighty seconds left. If anyone can do it, you can."

"Yes Sarge," both soldiers said, subdued. There were a handful of snickers from the other nine members of Tamas's squad but he didn't look back. Let them have their bitching and their petty squabbles. It was *their* only outlet right before a charge of this importance and Tamas's squad, unlike plenty others, weren't lacking in courage and loyalty. They'd be on his heels from here to the fort and straight to the pit.

Tamas kept his eyes on the fort. Over a mile away, thick puffs of smoke rose from Gurlish cannons as they returned fire at the Adran artillery. Gurlish cannons weren't as good as the Adrans'—they lacked the range and the punch needed to clear the distance, but occasionally one would get lucky and an eight-pound ball would ricochet off the ground and knock out an Adran field gun or plow through the ranks to a chorus of screams.

On the other hand, the sorcery protecting the Gurlish fort was as potent as any, and had shrugged off almost two years of shelling. The Adran artillery blasted against the walls to no visible effect. He wondered why either side even bothered.

The only conceivable way of taking the fort of Tilpur would be up and over those walls into the teeth of Gurlish bayonets and pikes.

The fort itself was no great marvel of military engineering. It had six thirty-five-foot walls and six onion-domed towers, with broad space on the parapets that would allow the Gurlish to bring no less than twelve cannons to bear on any approach. The garrison was supposedly two thousand men, but his own estimates put it at half that number. Not that it mattered. A fort like that could be effectively defended by a few hundred.

Tamas pried the paper end off one of his powder charges with a grimy thumbnail. He touched the loose black powder to his tongue, shivering at the sulfuric taste. His resolve tightened instantly, his senses sharpened. Sorcery lit his veins, giving him the strength of four men and speed that would let him run the distance to the fort in less than three minutes. Not for the first time he wondered how regular soldiers tolerated the stress of battle without a powder trance.

Strength and speed and sorcerous courage were wasted in the infantry line where battle was about mass rather than individual prowess, but his *betters* had decided to put him here regardless. All he could do was wait, hoping he survived long enough to make it over those walls. He emptied the rest of the powder charge into his mouth.

The euphoria of a powder trance took a hold of him, removing what little fear he had.

Behind the artillery, a man on horseback approached General Seske. Salutes were exchanged, the general nodded, and an order was given. "It's time," Tamas said over his shoulder.

Somewhere, a boy rattled out a single pair of beats on his side drum. Along the lines, men fell silent.

"Advance!" came the long-anticipated order.

The next five minutes were a maelstrom of blood and horror straight from the pit. At three-quarters of a mile the Gurlish Privileged opened up with their elemental sorcery. Fire and ice rained down on the Adran infantry from the fortress walls. Some of it was blocked by the Adran Privileged marching in the rear, but far too much of it pierced their protection to leave charred bodies in the wake of the army.

At five hundred yards the cadence of the drums doubled and Tamas broke into a run, musket gripped in both hands, teeth clenched against what would come next. Behind him his squad spat defiance and curses at the bombardment.

Whole platoons were leveled in a torrent of grapeshot. The Gurlish managed two salvos before the front lines, Tamas and his men included, were beneath their line of fire.

"Ladders!" Tamas yelled as he reached the rocky base of the fort. Ladder teams rushed forward and raised their long ladders against the walls as musket balls and stones hailed down from above.

Tamas took stock of the Adran infantry, assessing the situation in a heartbeat. Hundreds lay dead and wounded on the field behind them, but an equal number had managed to reach the relative safety found at the base of the walls, and more still advanced across the rocky, barren ground of the desert floor. He hoped it enough to scale the walls and take the fort.

Just get me over the top, he prayed to no god in particular, shouldering his musket and readying to throw himself on to the first steady ladder. The sorcery raining down from above intensified, blasting scorch marks into the earth. The rear lines began to waver. Tamas cursed them silently, urging them to steady.

Somewhere back by the Adran artillery a bugle let out a long, mournful note. "No, damn it," Tamas swore. "We can do this." He looked up at the top of the fort wall. "We have enough men, we can do this!"

All around him, men broke off the assault and fled toward the Adran lines, abandoning ladders, kit, and muskets.

"Sarge, that's the retreat," Lillen said, grabbing Tamas by the arm.

He shook her off. "I know, damn it! Why are we retreating? This is as close as we've ever gotten. Bloody fools!"

"Sarge!"

"I know, I'm coming." Tamas cast one more look toward the top of the walls. All he needed to do was get inside.

"WE COULD HAVE made it over those walls, sir." Tamas paced back and forth in the small space of his captain's tent. The dry desert air tasted of defeat, the whole camp brooding, sullen, and quiet this evening save for the cries of the wounded in the surgeons' tents.

Captain Pereg sat with his boots up on his cot, leaning back in his chair while he stared, perplexed, at the layout of playing cards sorted face up on his bedside table. The jacket of his dark-blue uniform lay on his bed. The buttons of his white undershirt were undone, the collar wilted and damp with sweat. He scratched at one brown muttonchop, picked a card up, paused, then returned it to its place.

"Captain!" Tamas said, jerking Pereg's attention away from him game. "We could have made it."

The captain let out a long sigh. "I don't know what you expect me to say, Sergeant. General Seske did not agree, and he had a much better view of the battlefield than you."

"I was *on* the battlefield, sir."

"And he could see the big picture. There's no need to second-guess the general. He's been an officer for well over a decade."

"That somehow precludes him from making terrible decisions?"

"Too many soldiers died before they could reach the walls. The attack could have lost us even more men."

"Or could have been a successful follow-through that ended the siege," Tamas retorted.

"Seske's a general. *Our* general."

"Through no merit of his own," Tamas grumbled.

Pereg lifted a card, stabbing it in Tamas's direction. "Now look here, Sergeant. I won't have you disparaging the king's officers, not even in private—especially my aunt's husband, even if we don't have the best of relationships. You're a damned good soldier, and I'll put up with you because you're worth any three sergeants, but do not forget your place. You're a commoner. Seske has noble blood."

"That's the problem, I think."

Pereg shrugged. "And one we can't do a thing about."

Easy for you to say, Tamas thought to himself. *You're the youngest son of a baron. You'll be a general in twenty years yourself while I'll be lucky to make captain in that time.*

"You only lost, what, one man from your squad today?" Pereg asked.

"Gerdin's wounded, but we don't think he'll make it through the night."

"See?" Pereg said, flicking a bit of sand out of his ear, "you should be ecstatic. You've lived to fight another day and brought most of your men through it with you. That's a victory in my book."

I like you, Pereg, but you're an idiot. "We were lucky. Nothing more. Captain, I *need* to get over that wall."

Pereg looked up from his cards sharply. "You're not still going on about a promotion, are you?"

"You said yourself, sir, I'm a commoner." Tamas leaned over Pereg's table. "The only way I can become a commissioned officer is through valor in combat."

"You're a powder mage," Pereg said. "A damned killing machine if I've ever seen one. In any other country you would have been hanged just for what you are. The Privileged," he lowered his voice, looking over his shoulder as if a sorcerer might be hiding in the corner of his tent, "the Privileged do not like your kind having any power. You should be grateful you've made it to sergeant. Get to master sergeant one day and you've got yourself a career to be proud of. By Kresimir, you're only nineteen and already a sergeant!"

Pereg was right, of course. Never mind his common blood—powder mages were universally despised by the nobility and their pet sorcerers. They claimed it was a base magic, used only by the very dregs of humanity. Tamas knew the truth—he knew they were scared of what he could do. He tried to figure out how to express to Pereg the urgency of his situation, of the weight on his chest every morning that he didn't make progress toward climbing the ranks. He couldn't afford to relax for even a single campaigning season, because everything about his career was stacked against him.

"I'll clear the damned fort by myself if I have to, sir. I just need to get inside the walls and the garrison will fall. I guarantee it."

"And I," Pereg said, scowling at his cards, "need to win this game or I'll break a fantastic streak."

Tamas wanted to kick the chair out from under Pereg and watch him fall on his ass. "The queen of rooks," he said.

Pereg's scowl deepened as he searched the cards, then his face brightened. "Ah, there we go. Thank you, Sergeant! Look, go give your men an extra ration of beer for work well done today." He looked up, tapping the queen of rooks thoughtfully. "And take my advice—ambition is not becoming of a commoner. It'll only get you killed."

"How's Gerdin?" Tamas asked when he returned to the small group of tents occupied by the twenty-second squad of His Royal Majesty's Ninth Infantry.

Private Farthing looked up from poking a long bit of sagebrush into the dung fire. He was of medium height, with a pockmarked face burnt from years in the Gurlish sun. When Tamas met him he'd been a round little cuss, gasping with every step, but the campaigns had turned him into a battered strip of shoe leather. "Died thirty minutes ago," he said.

Tamas sank into a stool beside Farthing and rubbed his temples. Another man gone. Three dead from the previous failed charge at Tilpur's walls, and two the time before that. He wondered if they'd bother to give him any new soldiers or if they just planned on waiting until *he* bit it so they could incorporate his squad under another sergeant.

"And Mordecia's arm?" Tamas asked.

"Just a scratch. She'll be good to go in a week as long as it doesn't fester. Sarge, can I ask you a question?"

"What is it?"

"Rumor has it that another sergeant heard me complaining on the line today. They, uh, they won't put me in front of a firing squad, will they? It was just a little moaning on my part. They know that, right?"

Tamas stared into the low, flickering glow of the dung fire. "I'm not going to let them shoot you over a little bellyaching in the face of death, Farthing," he said with a sigh. "Anyone asks tell 'em the sun was getting to you. Worst thing you'll get is a week digging latrines."

Farthing breathed a relieved sigh. "Thanks, Sarge. You're a decent fellow. Want to hear some good news?"

"Always."

"Remember my cousin? The maid in General Seske's retinue?"

"Yeah."

"Saw her tonight. Said that she overheard that we've orders to pull out. Today's attack was the last big push and the higher-ups don't think Seske has the ability to take the fort before the end of the campaigning season."

Tamas let his face go slack, forcing a neutral expression. Inside, he felt like he'd been kicked in the gut. The end of the campaigning season, and he had yet to make master sergeant. If they pulled out without another fight he wouldn't have a shot of promotion until next year. He couldn't—wouldn't—wait that long. "Good," he said "That's very good."

"Anyway," Farthing continued, throwing another chip of dung on the fire. "How'd your talk with the captain go?"

Tamas grunted a response. He already had a reputation as an upstart, but even *he* knew better than to bitch about superior officers to his men. Besides, he had more to worry about. Good news? This was horrible news. His career—his life—stalled for another season because Seske wasn't more creative than tossing men at the enemy cannons and hoping the Gurlish ran out of grapeshot.

They sat in silence for several minutes, listening to someone from a nearby squad sing a quiet drinking song, the tune slowed down to account for the mood of the camp.

"Sarge, can I ask you something else?" Farthing said.

Tamas nodded.

Farthing scooted his stool a few inches closer to Tamas and looked around, then lowered his head. "This is bullshit, isn't it? I mean, throwing us at that big damned fort thousands at a time when they know we won't make it over the wall anyways. That's bullshit. Right?"

"Not our place to say," Tamas said, feeling a knot in his belly. This *was* bullshit, all right. The orders to pull out likely hadn't had a last assault written into them, which meant that Gerdin, and hundreds of other poor souls, had died on Seske's wishes and optimism. It wasn't any way to conduct a war. Tamas was a sergeant, a powder mage of low birth, and even *he* could see that. "But," he added, "if you don't shut your trap you *will* end up with more than latrine-digging duty."

"Yes, Sarge," Farthing said, falling quiet.

Tamas got up to walk through the orderly rows of tents, looking up at the desert sky. There was a certain rugged beauty in this place, thousands of miles away from home, but it was the stars that did it for him, shining bright without the interference of the street lamps of Adopest. He found a hill where he could see the stars above Tilpur, three miles away.

From this distance the fort looked like an upturned footstool into the desert, with full command of the only freshwater spring for eighty miles in any direction. Rumors were that they had provisions enough for another two years, and being built directly on the spring meant they never had to worry for water.

Tilpur had never once fallen out of Gurlish hands. The Kez had besieged it. The Brudanians. The Adran army had besieged it twice and, if General Seske's maid was to be believed, this second attempt had fallen short. The finest minds of the Adran officer corps could not figure out how to crack it.

It was too bad, Tamas thought bitterly, *that the finest minds of the Adran officer corps were inbred dimwits from the least talented echelons of the nobility.*

Though, as much as he hated to admit it, he'd not been able to figure out a way through those sorcery-warded walls either. Were ineffective artillery and suicidal charges really the best options available to a modern army, the pride of the Adran nation?

He let his eyes wander over the distant silhouette of Tilpur and down to the mouth of the spring. It flowed from beneath the forts walls into a year-round river giving birth to an oasis below the southern wall. The oasis stretched for miles, a haven for wildlife and even the Adrans themselves, providing the only bit of respite in this inhospitable place. Tilpur was a prize that every army coveted and none could gain.

All he had to do was get inside their walls at the head of a few hundred infantry and he'd clear the fort in hours . . . the thought trailed off and he stared at the moonlit silhouette, pondering. What if he didn't even *need* a company of men at his back?

He sprinted back into the camp where Farthing, Lillen, and all the rest were gathered around the embers of the dung fire.

"Lillen," he said, after catching his breath, "do you still have that floor plan you drew of Tilpur?"

Lillen crawled into her tent and came back a moment later, handing the rolled-up parchment to Tamas. He spread it on the ground, poring over the detailed drawing before looking over at Farthing. "Do you think you could get me a dozen sets of crampons?"

GENERAL SESKE WAS normally a jovial man, never too far from his wine and always able to find some native girl or hanger-on to share his bed. But something—probably the order of withdrawal combined with his failure to take Tilpur—had him in a foul mood when Tamas was finally able to rouse him from his bed at nearly one in the morning.

Seske was in his late forties. His dark skin marked him as a foreigner, but his marriage to an Adran duchess guaranteed him his rank in the Adran army. He ran his hands through his sparse, graying hair before pulling a thin silk robe on over his undershirt. He squinted at Tamas, then at Captain Pereg, who looked not all that more enthusiastic about the hour than Seske himself.

"What is this, Pereg?" Seske asked.

Pereg fidgeted with his bicorn hat. "I'm very sorry to get you out of bed at this hour, Uncle, but there's been an, erm, development."

"Development? What kind of development? I was having the very best of dreams. So unless Tilpur just tumbled down or Kresimir himself has returned to the realms of mortals, I hope the next thing out of your lips is a damned good explanation."

Tamas cleared his throat and moved a few things aside to lay Lillen's drawing out on Seske's map table. "Sir," he said, "I'm very sorry to interrupt your . . . sleep, but I think I may be able to give you what you're looking for."

"What's that?"

"A Gurlish surrender."

"Pereg, who the bloody devil is this?"

"Sergeant Tamas, Uncle. One of the best infantrymen under our command."

"Tamas. Tamas. Why do I know that name?"

"He's the powder mage, sir."

Seske harrumphed loudly. "Bah. Powder mages. Nothing better than dogs, if you ask me. No offence, Sergeant Tommy. Purely a professional opinion. I'm sure you're a good chap. Can't help what you're born with and all that. Now tell me, Pereg, why the pit is he in my tent?"

Tamas cleared his throat again. Late hour it may be, but a general should have a better attention span than a petulant child. He kept his expression appropriately reserved. "Sir, I have a plan to break the siege."

"What's that you say?" Seske searched his robe until he found his spectacles and put them on, peering at Tamas. "What do you mean?"

"If you'll humor me a question, sir?"

Seske adjusted his robe, raising his chin to look down his nose suspiciously at Tamas. "Go on."

"Why have we not sent a raiding party over the walls into Tilpur during the night? Men to spike cannons, slit throats, foul their powder—that sort of thing."

"Not very gentlemanly."

"War is seldom gentlemanly," Tamas said.

Seske snorted. "Because a raid would be bloody suicide."

"Only slightly more suicidal than a frontal assault with our infantry," Tamas said, hurrying on before it could occur to Seske to be offended. "But that "slightly" is what matters. Order men on a genuine suicide mission and you'd have a mutiny on your hands. Am I correct, sir?"

"Yes?" Seske said, his eyes narrowing.

"Even a frontal assault or a Hope's End has a tiny chance of success. A small number of men over the walls at night, however, will only find themselves trapped and slaughtered like dogs once they descended into the fort itself to light the munitions. Once they were inside, the hope of escape would close to none. Except . . . if you'd be so kind and take a look at this."

Seske shuffled over to the map table and lifted Lillen's floor plan, examining it in the light of the oil lamp hanging over the tent. "Where'd you get this, Sergeant? Since when do we give quality drawings like this out to the rank and file?"

"One of my infantrymen apprenticed with an architect before signing up," Tamas said. "The floor plan is her own make, based on reports from our intelligence."

"Oh, right then. She's very good."

"Yes, sir, she is. Now, if you'll direct your attention to this point here," Tamas indicated the spot with his finger, "you can see where the fort's main well descends from the courtyard into the ground here, about fifty feet to reach an aquifer below the fortress."

"Yes."

"And, if you'll look here, you can see where a spring emerges from the rocks just below the fort."

"Of course."

"I think this could be the key, sir."

Seske scowled at the map for several moments, adjusting first his spectacles, then the light from the lamp over his head. "I'm not sure what you're getting at. We've already considered trying to poison them out, but as any fool knows the water flows out from the aquifer, making it impossible to foul their water source."

"That's not what I mean at all, sir. Remember, I'm talking about a raid. Take a look at the two spots I indicated. What do you see?"

Seske sighed. "Absolutely nothing. I've stared at a drawing just like this for hours a day all damned summer."

And telling me you found something where I did not would imply that I'm an fool, Seske's tone warned. Tamas stifled a frustrated groan. Seske *was* a fool, but Tamas was a mere sergeant, and showing up his commanding officer wasn't going to land him a promotion.

"It's not obvious, sir," Tamas dissembled, "but as you can see, there's only a few dozen yards between the fort well and where the spring comes out of the rocks. That's not very far for a man to hold his breath."

"Are you suggesting that we send men through the spring and up the well?"

"Against the current? No, sir. What I'm suggesting is that the well offers an easy escape route. If we sent, say, fifteen men over the walls with rope and crampons in the middle of the night, those men could spike the Gurlish cannons, set fire to their powder stores, maybe even kill a few guards, and then escape down through the well once the alarm is raised. It may not sound like much, but the advance we made earlier today was so very close. If we disabled even a portion of their cannon we could mount another charge and get men over the wall and into the fort."

"Not very gentlemanly," Seske muttered. "Underhanded tactics like this make us no better than the Gurlish."

"Perhaps," Tamas said, "But, sir, it could crack Tilpur. And the officer who cracks Tilpur would earn the favor of the king himself."

Seske looked at the map, then at Tamas, then at Pereg. "Tell me," he said to Pereg, "this is a joke?"

"It's not a joke, sir," Pereg said. "It's sound reasoning."

"That's because you're a strategic potato, Pereg." Seske slapped the map with the back of one hand. "Assuming a group of men can scale the walls, and spike enough cannons to make the effort worth it, it's still a suicide mission. Any fool can see that. They'd have to be either bloody arrogant or damned desperate to volunteer for the mission."

"I'd like to suggest someone who's both, sir," Tamas said.

"Eh? Who's that?"

Tamas smiled. "Me, sir."

"I TOLD YOU to get me crampons."

"Begging your pardon, Sarge," Farthing replied, "but this isn't the bloody Mountainwatch. We're in the middle of a desert."

Tamas turned his spare pair of boots over in his hands, examining Farthing's work. "This is just a chain looped around the toe and heel."

"It'll do in a pinch," Farthing said.

"Will it do to climb a wall? And this isn't a pickax, it's a bayonet with the tip bent at a right angle."

"With a strap to hold your wrist if you lose your grip," Farthing pointed out proudly. "It's not a bad job in just a few hours, if I do say so myself."

"And how many sets do you have of all this?"

"Five crampons and two sets of pickaxes, Sarge."

Five. Tamas needed twelve to fifteen men for this raid to be effective. Five soldiers would have to work quickly, with no hope of fighting their way out if they got cornered. But it would have to do. No, he thought, reconsidering. This might be better. Five men would move far more silently than fifteen. "I'll take one set," he said. "Draw lots for the rest."

"Begging your pardon, sir, but I wouldn't send you up there with my equipment without coming myself," Farthing said. "Draw lots on the other three. I'll go."

Tamas glanced down at the chain wrapped around the toe of his boot. "Glad to hear you'd stake your life on this stuff. All right. The moon is waning. We go tomorrow night. Pray for fog."

A CLEAR SKY, it turned out, wouldn't be a worry. Clouds raced over the desert the next morning and by evening thunder had forced the army to hunker down beneath their tents, every stitch of equipment lashed down, only the unfortunate infantrymen on guard duty showing their faces as night fell. Wind buffeted the camp, sporadic sheets of rain soaking the cracked soil and forcing men to move their tents to higher ground to avoid flooding.

Lots were drawn, and Tamas led his fraction of a squad across the no-man's land between the Adran artillery and Tilpur. He was accompanied by Farthing, Lillen, Krimin, and Olef, the latter two being the unit's cook and musician, respectively. They left just after dark and crept across the desert, hiding beneath scrub bush during the worst of the lightning.

By the time they reached the base of the fort the rain had become a torrent. Tamas's heart was in his throat as he looked up at the thirty-five-foot walls, slick and foreboding.

This was worse than suicide.

"Here," Farthing said, passing out strips of tanned hide. "Bite this between your teeth. If you fall, bite harder and hope the ground is soft. If you scream we're all dead men."

Tamas gestured for the squad to gather around, faces huddled near his. He pointed up at the walls, hoping that he wasn't dragging four soldiers along with him to their deaths. "You see those walls?" he asked, his voice swept away by the downpour. "Those are our worst enemies tonight. They determine whether we rest beneath the godforsaken Gurlish plains for eternity or go home as heroes and I, personally, would rather have the latter."

The soldiers chuckled, but he pushed on, his voice solemn. "This," he said, "is not idle arrogance. This is not men marching in a straight line toward grapeshot and sorcery. This is five shit-upon infantrymen looking to end this damned siege on their own terms, and not the terms of their so-called betters." He paused, shielding his eyes from the rain. "Because we could go home, a winter spent in Adopest only to come back here and march into the face of death once more. Or we can do what five thousand men cannot and take this damned fort. Are you with me?"

Four fists thumped against their chests in a silent salute.

"I'd rather have you four than all the Adran army," Tamas said, realizing as he did that he meant it. "Let's climb."

Farthing, by far the most experienced climber, went first. Tamas waited until the count of sixty before he sprinkled a black powder charge on his tongue and followed Farthing up.

He used the bent bayonets as pickaxes, questing with the tips for cracks in the masonry, securing each foothold meticulously, working his way up inch by agonizing inch. Within minutes his muscles burned, even strengthened as they were by the powder, and his arms and legs trembled at the unaccustomed exercise.

He bit down hard on his bit of leather, feeling the weight of the weapons and tools hanging from his belt. A shudder ran through him at each heavy gust of wind, making his body sway dangerously. He dared not look up into the pelting rain, nor down lest he succumb to a wave of dizziness.

Every moment he expected a loose bit of masonry to send him

tumbling to the ground or the shout of a guard above, followed by the raising of an alarm. The chains beneath his toes slipped as he climbed, his picks scratching too loudly against the stone.

He paused every so often, pushing outward with his sorcerous senses, looking for black powder. The towers to his left and right each contained concentrations of powder, clustered together like fireflies at dusk on a warm Adran spring. The guards, it seemed, were content to take shelter and assume the storm would stall a nighttime attack.

Tamas finally reached the lip of the wall where he paused to rest before taking a deep breath and lifting himself to look over the edge.

Farthing was already on a parapet, securing a rope to toss down behind them. Body trembling, Tamas pulled himself over and set about lowering his own rope. Together they secured a third, then Tamas leaned over to wave to the three almost imperceptible figures below.

He watched them begin their climb, then turned his attention to the towers. Reaching the top, as he'd told them before the climb, was not the end of their woes. It was only the beginning. His heart hammering in his chest, he drew his knife and approached the nearer of the two towers.

The guardhouse in the tower was quiet, dark, and cool. He could sense the black powder inside, enough charges for two men. Slowly he pushed open the door, wincing as it creaked, only to be greeted by the sound of snoring.

Tamas crouched beside the two Gurlish guards, watching the rise and fall of their chests. They were slumped together, their faces haggard but peaceful, deep in the sleep of the exhausted. Their uniforms were torn and dirty, patched in a dozen places with whatever material they could find during the siege. He found himself hesitating as he raised his knife. As much as he scoffed at the idea of a gentlemanly war, this was different than combat on the parapets or in the field. This was murder.

But what, he reasoned, was a pair of cold-blooded murders next to the lives of all the Adrans who would die trying to take this place?

He cut the throat of the first, and then stabbed the second twice, jerking the blade quickly in and out, once in the lung and once in the heart. He left them to die, resting against each other as they had in sleep, and wiped the blood off his knife.

He found the cannons in the dark, his trance-fueled preternatural senses allowing him to see better than most. He produced a barbed spike from his belt and positioned it above the touchhole of one cannon, raising his hammer, eyes on the sky through the window. Lightning flashed, and he brought the hammer down as the crash of thunder followed. He did the same five more times, three strikes to drive each spike, before heading back out to find Farthing and the others.

They had cleared the opposite tower, their knives dripping. Tamas gathered them around with a gesture, and pointed at the next tower. "Spike as many cannons as you can," he said quietly. "Once you hear an alarm, run for the ropes and get off the wall as quickly as possible."

"What do you mean?" Lillen asked, adjusting her sodden jacket. "I thought we were using the well for our exit?"

"A watery grave," Tamas said, shaking his head. "A story to get Seske to let us make the attempt."

"We won't torch their munitions?" Farthing asked with a scowl.

"I'll do it," Tamas said. "Alone."

"You'll get yourself killed."

"I can move faster than all of you together. I'll light their munitions and be back here before you're done. Time's wasting. Move."

He stifled the rest of the protests and exchanged his hammer, spikes, and boot knife with Farthing for a long fixed-blade knife and a loaded pistol. He checked to make sure the powder was dry before heading around the length of the wall, alone, and into the spiral staircase of the nearest tower.

He reached the bottom without incident and paused beside a thick wooden door, listening. Low voices reached him above the distant thunder. Opening the door a crack, he spied a small group of Gurlish soldiers squatting in a circle, playing dice by the light of a single oil lamp. He watched them for a moment, absently drawing a new powder charge to sprinkle on his tongue.

The grit of the powder between his teeth, Tamas drew Farthing's knife and took one long, deep breath.

He dashed into the guardhouse, clearing the space between the door and the gambling infantrymen in two long strides. His heart thumped, the power of the powder trance flowing through him, making the infantrymen's every movement seem slow and unwieldy.

He killed the quickest of them as he went for his musket. The second lost her life to a flick of Tamas's knife, while the third managed to draw his own and deflect Tamas's slash as he leaped for the door, a cry on his lips. Tamas jumped after him, reversing his grip on the blade midair and ramming it into the base of the man's spine, jerking it free and sinking it once more between his ribs.

Tamas turned as the fourth guard brought the stock of his musket to bear, slamming it across Tamas's jaw with enough force to drop a camel. Tamas staggered back, his head ringing from the blow, grateful for the powder trance that kept him coherent. He caught the next swing of the musket and jerked it out of the guard's hands, jamming the stock into the man's throat. The Gurlish collapsed, gasping and gurgling.

Tamas's hands shook from the speed of the fight, his chest heaving. His head pounded, and there was a slash across his thigh—a distant burn from within the powder trance. It was hard to think through the fog, and his preternatural sight seemed adversely affected by the blow to his head. More powder did nothing to help.

The temptation to retreat back up the tower and follow the squad back over the wall was strong. Surely they'd spiked enough of the cannons? Would destroying their munitions really make a difference?

Of course it would. Spiking the cannon would hobble the garrison. Destroying the munitions would destroy their spirit and perhaps even force a surrender without the need for any more Adran blood. Tamas couldn't stop here. He was too close. His men needed him.

He could sense a large concentration of powder down below the next tower. But he had to move fast.

He dashed to the next guardhouse without incident, looking up through the rain to check on the squad's progress. He could see dark figures hunched over the cannons, moving along the wall slowly. No alarm.

Yet.

He broke the chain to the grated door of the munitions dump with a few sturdy blows of the butt of his knife, then crept down the stairs in complete darkness where even the vision from his powder trance, impaired as it was, only gave him the slightest impression of stairs and walls.

The stairwell became cool and quiet, the sound of the rain gone, thunder muffled above him as he descended. The stairs led down into an open room where he could sense the barrels heavy with gunpowder. Using the knife, feeling his way, Tamas went about prying the lids off several before upending them, kicking them haphazardly across the room. He could taste the dust from the black powder on his lips.

He snatched up one powder keg and left a line of powder from the center of the room to the edge of the stairs, where drew a demolition cord from his pocket and unraveled it up the first few steps. He pressed pinch of black powder against the tip of the cord and then concentrated, focusing on the powder with his sorcery.

The cord flared to life, illuminating the munitions room, throwing shadows on the walls. Tamas watched it burn for several moments, finding himself enraptured by the flickering ember as it hissed toward the black powder.

Until something caught his ear.

The shout was distant, muffled, but it had him on his feet in a fraction of a second, sprinting up the stairs to the courtyard. He burst out of the munitions room and into the chaos of men shouting in Gurlish.

Half a dozen soldiers poured out into the rain from the barracks, their muskets raised at the four figures racing across the top of the walls. Tamas reached out with his senses, lighting their powder with his mind. The explosions blew apart the muskets, searing Gurlish faces. One unlucky man with a powder horn hanging around his waist was ripped clear in half by its detonation.

Three men emerged from the nearest guardhouse. Tamas threw himself forward, knife drawn, making short, bloody work of the soldiers before dashing inside. He drew his pistol as he mounted the stairs, listening to the shouts of the Gurlish as soldiers swarmed the courtyard. He reached out with his senses, detonating all the powder he could reach.

It wasn't enough. By the time he gained the top of the wall, the courtyard below was swarming with figures, muskets raised, shooting blindly up at the parapets. Tamas risked a glance out of the guardhouse and his heart fell.

He'd gotten turned around down in the courtyard and gone up the wrong staircase. The ropes were on the opposite side of the fort. His squad was gone, whether captured or already over the edge he did not know, but he was alone in a hornet's nest of Gurlish soldiers with no way to get off the walls. A thirty-five foot fall would at *least* break his legs, even with the powder trance.

He'd have to make a run for the ropes.

Only a sixth sense, a tingling at the base of his spine, made him throw himself backward into the guardhouse as fire swept across the parapet, nearly blinding him with its brilliance. His mouth turned went dry.

The Gurlish Privileged sorcerer had joined the hunt.

How many Privileged did the garrison have? One? Two? He couldn't remember. He did know he wouldn't last thirty seconds against a Privileged. Show his face, and he would be incinerated instantly. Stay here and he would be incinerated when they found him. A pair of broken legs was beginning to look like a good option.

He reached out with his powder-enhanced senses, searching for the Privileged. He could sense one nearby, down in the courtyard and a second one not much farther . . . reaching the top of the wall where Farthing's ropes marked their escape.

The Privileged was going after Tamas's fleeing quad. He would kill all four of them down on the desert floor with only the snap of his fingers. They'd be dead before they had a chance to scream.

Tamas lifted his pistol, praying to Kresimir that the first Privileged, down in the courtyard, was not looking his direction.

He leaned out of the gatehouse and found the second Privileged, pinpointing him in the gloom by his aura of sorcery and the white gloves raised above his head. It wasn't a long shot, perhaps fifty yards at most, but it would be near impossible with a pistol in these conditions.

For anyone but a powder mage.

Tamas let his breath out slowly, forcing his hand steady as he pulled the trigger. He willed the bullet forward, drawing power from a powder charge in his other hand, nudging the bullet's trajectory with his mind as he adjusted for rain and wind. It flew for what felt like an eternity—yet couldn't have been more than a fraction of a second—and blew the side of the Privileged's head clean off.

Tamas discarded the pistol and leaped back into the guardhouse as flames slammed into the wall just to his left. He waited, heart pounding, and thought about the drop.

He could hear the sound of boots on the on the stairs below him, and the whispering of orders. He reached out, touching off powder, and flinched away from the explosion. Sooner or later they'd figure out who he was—what he was—and the Privileged would fill the tower with flame from top to bottom.

He felt the bit of leather in his pocket, remembering Farthing's words; *bite this between your teeth. If you fall, bite harder and hope the ground is soft.* He put it between his teeth.

That's when he remembered something he'd seen in the courtyard, not more than a dozen feet from where he could sense the Privileged—the dark, stone pit of the fort well. He pictured Lillen's drawing in his head, considering the fifty foot drop into the cold water below. It might just be more survivable than the drop from the walls *and* they wouldn't be likely to chase him.

Tamas reached out with his senses, getting a good feel for where the Privileged was in relation to himself—twelve feet along the wall, eight feet from it, and about thirty feet down.

"I hope," Tamas said to himself as he climbed to his feet, "that he's a fat son of a bitch."

Tamas raced out of the guardhouse, a dozen paces down the parapet, and then leaped into the courtyard, pushing off with every bit of power the powder would give him. His arms cartwheeled as he soared through the air, his bowels turning to jelly as he fell, the dark ground, crawling with Gurlish infantry, coming up to meet him.

The last thing he saw before impact was white gloves reaching upward. Then he slammed into a body, the Privileged crumpling beneath him with a scream. Tamas rolled out of the fall and managed to come up on his feet, stumbling on a turned ankle. The bullet from a hastily fired musket tore through his shoulder. He grit his teeth against the pain and detonated all the powder within reach. The blast deafened him, and he hoped it sowed enough confusion as he limped toward the well.

Another bullet ripped through the arm of his jacket, and the whistle of another buzzed past his ear. Smoke from the detonated powder hung in the damp air, filling his nostrils, urging him on. He reached the lip of the well and threw himself over the edge, knowing that the fall itself would likely kill him.

It didn't matter, he just had to get away.

He crashed into something solid—a moment of confusion overwhelmed him before he realized why he wasn't falling. An iron grate covered the well, preventing his descent. He gasped, staring up into the rain, and felt his heart sink. Here he was, in the middle of the Gurlish fort, and now cornered like a rat in a cage.

He was going to die the same way he lived: arrogant, desperate, and still a goddamned sergeant.

A Gurlish infantryman loomed over him. Hands grabbed him by the ankle and arms, trying to pull him up. Tamas reached for Farthing's knife, only to find it gone from its sheath. Helplessly, he watched as the infantryman raised the butt of his rifle and brought it down on his head. Tamas raised one hand to ward off the blow, feeling the sharp pain as his wrist broke.

Something shifted beneath him. There was a grating of metal on metal as the grate collapsed. Tamas gasped, and then suddenly he was falling. The blackness of the well swallowing him, the vision of the Gurlish infantrymen zooming away. His legs hit the side of the well, sending him tumbling head over heels until he hit water far below.

The breath was knocked out of him and he sank, stunned, into the dark. He felt his limbs scrape along mossy stone, the pain of his wounds overwhelming him to the point of numbness. He tried to scrabble for purchase and air, but found neither.

He felt his limbs weakening, barely able to keep himself from gasping in a lungful of water.

There was a sudden rumble through the water, and then a glow from somewhere ahead lent him one last burst of strength. He pushed himself forward and suddenly his head broke the water as he was swept along in the current of the river below Tilpur.

Above him, flames licked the sky over the fort. He stared up, incredulous, able to think of nothing but the air in his lungs, before he realized that the munitions had gone up.

With a laugh that came out as a choked sob, Tamas struggled toward the shore.

TAMAS WALKED THROUGH the main gate of Tilpur fortress three days after his nighttime raid. His arm hung at his side uselessly in a sling, wrist set and bandaged with his uniform jacket hanging off his shoulder. Everything hurt—his head, his wrist, his ribs, his shoulder, his legs. A light powder trance held the pain at a low buzz in the back of his head. He felt naked without his musket hanging off his shoulder or a shako on his head, and seeing the courtyard in the daylight sent a shiver down his spine. He half expected a Gurlish soldier to lean out the window of the barracks and take a shot at him.

But the fort had been emptied of Gurlish forces two days ago. Less than six hundred men, a good portion of those wounded, had survived the detonation of the fort's munitions. The garrison commander had immediately called for a parlay and surrendered without condition. Their forces were now camped out on the plain, disarmed, while the Adran officers decided what to do with them.

It was, without a doubt, the biggest turnaround of the season, if not the entire campaign. And General Seske had yet to call for Tamas.

He paused inside the courtyard, watching as Adran soldiers made repairs. The munitions explosion had collapsed a large part of the courtyard and destroyed most of the barracks when the ground dropped a dozen feet beneath it. Bodies were still being hauled out of the rubble, while the sorcery-protected stones of the inner wall were being scrubbed clean of the soot and ash from the explosion.

Overseeing the whole operation was General Seske, standing up on the walls near where Tamas and his squad had gone over the top. He was surrounded by aids, a broad smile on his face as he handed out orders and cracked jokes with his officers, standing with thumbs hooked through his belt, bicorn cocked forward like he'd conquered Tilpur himself.

It did not, Tamas thought, bode well.

Seske's gaze swept past Tamas, pausing for just the slightest moment, his smile faltering, before moving on. Instead of a gesture or a grin or anything to acknowledge the man who'd just handed him an enemy fortress, he continued bantering with his officers.

Tamas made a circuit around the fort, examining the repairs, taking a look down into the well and examining the ancient, rusted grate that had almost gotten him killed. He counted fifteen paces from the well and scuffed at the black, stained stone with one toe, chuckling to himself. The Privileged he'd landed on, he'd found out later, had died almost instantly, spine snapping like a twig at the impact. The stain under Tamas's boot was likely his blood.

"Sergeant," a voice said.

Tamas looked up to find one of Seske's aids beside him. "Yes?"

"The general would like to see you."

Tamas followed the aid to the nearest gatehouse and up the steep, narrow stairs, the pain in his side deepening with each step. By the time he reached the top of the wall he was covered in sweat and quite dizzy. He searched his pockets for a powder charge, only to come up empty.

Seske was alone when he approached. The general gazed out over the camp of the Gurlish prisoners, a scowl on his face. He did not turn as Tamas approached.

Tamas saluted with his left hand. "Sir," he said.

"I suppose," Seske said, "that you think you're getting a promotion for this?"

Tamas let his salute fall, trying to fight the dizziness caused by the climb. His powder trance was almost gone. "I wouldn't presume, sir."

"No. No you wouldn't. I've spoken with Pereg. He was rather excited by the Gurlish surrender and let it slip that you're a man of ambition. You want to be commissioned. Is that true?"

Tamas's mouth went dry. He took a deep breath to steady himself. "I would like to serve my king as an officer, sir."

"So that's a yes?" Seske shook his head. "I won't have it. Not in this army."

Tamas bit back an angry retort. Surely there would be a good reason? "I'm not sure I understand, sir."

"The king will likely grant me lands for this victory. Pereg himself will be made a major, which will please his aunt to no end, and for both those things you have my thanks. But an officer should be of noble blood. Nothing will convince me otherwise. Don't be hard on yourself. I understand your birth is not your fault. But this is the way of the world and you need to get used to it."

I'll have his thanks? Tamas looked at Seske, then looked at the perilous drop off the edge of the wall. One quick shove and . . . and what? He'd be trundled off to a court-martial and then shot? All to silence a single braggart?

"You won't get a promotion for this," Seske said, "but you'll be rewarded with a stipend. Your whole squad will receive medals from the king the next time you're in Adopest. I've even recommended that your wounds be healed by a Privileged to shorten your convalescence. A man like you can be awfully useful, after all. Perhaps I'll send you over to consult at the siege of Herone." He paused. "Bah, don't look so glum. You'll make master sergeant within a few years. But as you said yourself . . . don't presume. You're dismissed, Sergeant."

Tamas stared at Seske for several moments, disbelieving. He didn't want a stipend, or Seske's thanks. He didn't give a damn about any bloody medal. He wanted a commission—a commission he earned killing two Gurlish Privileged and taking the fort almost single-handedly. From the self-satisfied expression on Seske's face, the general thought Tamas should be *thanking* him for not giving him a promotion. Tamas could practically hear what Seske was thinking: *this is for your own good, you common upstart.*

"I said you were dismissed, Sergeant."

"Thank you, sir," Tamas managed to grunt, throwing up a half-hearted salute. Seske didn't seem to notice.

He stumbled down the stairs, barely able to hold himself up, and stopped to rest in the main floor guardhouse of the tower. He leaned his head against the cool stone. Was this all that awaited him in his career? Did his superiors have any respect for the risk of an infantryman? Or was bravery just a word meant to spur him into the face of the grapeshot for the glory of others?

"Sergeant."

Tamas looked up to find Captain Pereg had joined him in the guard room. He felt a spike of anger go through him even as he struggled to raise his arm in a salute.

"No, don't," Pereg said, his forehead creased. "I came here to apologize. Seske told me he wasn't going to give a promotion for this, and I can see from your face you've just had that discussion." He grimaced. "I know it's a disappointment and, though it's not much of a consolation, I've written a letter of commendation to go in your file in Adopest. I'll be sure a copy gets to someone other than General Seske."

"Thank you, sir," Tamas said.

"No, thank you. I wanted you to know that I'll be turning down my promotion under the objection that you didn't get one."

"That's unnecessary, sir," Tamas said.

"It's the least I could do. At least one officer in the Adran army should show appreciation for what you've done."

Tamas thanked Pereg once more and walked back into the heat of the desert sun. He paused, catching his breath, and looked down at his ragged hands. A cane may be a good idea, at least until Seske granted him access to a Privileged healer. He scowled, then looked up, aware of a sudden silence.

Every soldier working on the repairs to the fort had stopped. They stood, looking toward him, squinting in the sunlight. One of them raised their hand in a salute. Slowly, the others joined him, until over a hundred infantrymen were saluting him in silence.

Tamas wiped a tear out of his eye and stood up straight and returned the salute. He'd done this for a promotion, yes, he reminded himself. But he'd also done it for something more important—to save lives that would otherwise have been thrown away. And these infantry, these good men and women saluting him, knew.

And they'd remember.

Kristen Britain

"Mr. Island" has been awaiting its day in the sun for over twenty years and is the result of my love for coastal Maine and my exposure to nineteenth-century history via my career as a National Park Service Ranger. One day in the early 1990s, as I sat at my computer, the voice of Mrs. Grindle simply started pouring out of me and "Mr. Island" was born.

When I finished, I had this hard-to-categorize story. Was it science fiction? Fantasy? Romance? Historical? When I workshopped it, the instructor encouraged me to seek publication, which was nice, but where might I find a market willing to publish such a cross-genre piece? I was stumped.

Years passed and "Mr. Island" remained filed away. I pulled it out a few times to tinker with it but was still stymied by where I might submit it. I hoped that one day the right market would come along, for I was very fond of this story and had faith in its quality.

And lo, an invitation *did* come for an anthology of science fiction and fantasy that, as the title *Unbound* implied, did not hold to a restrictive theme. Hooray! It may have taken twenty years, but at last "Mr. Island" found its home.

MR. ISLAND

Kristen Britain

The beacon on Schooner Head swept beams of light through the crisp autumn night as I strolled along the Shore Road with my husband, Mr. Grindle. Flecks of gold glinted across the black bay, and the bell buoy by Heddybemps Rock clanged in the roll of ocean swells. It is said that during a squall, the spirits of mariners lost on Heddybemps can be heard keening in the wind.

Over the years, that jagged rock has exacted a price from those who depend on the ocean for their livelihood. Hardworking fishermen and brave shipmasters can win a fortune by plying the waves, but there is always the sacrifice.

I shivered and clasped my cloak tightly about my shoulders. Such thoughts of men lost are mournful, and tonight's gathering was a happy one, a gathering for a survivor of Heddybemps Rock. Indeed, we were finally to meet this mysterious gentleman for the first time though he had crashed upon our shores a month ago. A foreigner he was, Dr. Hutchinson had said.

"Who tends the lighthouse, I wonder," my husband mused, "if Isaiah Fernald is at Dr. Hutchinson's?" Mr. Grindle's investments in many ships caused him earnest concern for the operations of all lighthouses.

"Tilda, I expect, or one of the girls."

Mr. Grindle frowned. "It's not right," he said, "leaving such an important task to the girls."

I pressed my lips together, and we strode on in silence, leaves scratching across the road in a breeze. Mr. Grindle believes the woman's sphere centers solely around the home, hearth, and family, and more than once he has railed against those women in Boston and New York who seek the elective franchise.

Others joined us along the rutted road, either in pairs or singly. Light spilled out of the doctor's house in bronze puddles. I took one more breath of the chill salt air before stepping into the confines of the Hutchinson home and handing my cloak over to their hired woman.

The house was bright and had a festive feel to it. Many of the good citizens of Schooner Harbor occupied the formal parlor where a blaze crackled in the fireplace. A giddiness pervaded the conversation, my friends and neighbors filled with expectancy.

"Mrs. Grindle, I am glad you're here!"

Lydia Pendleton had recovered recently from an accident in a Lowell textile mill. A surge in the flow of water that powered the turbines sped the carding machine she tended out of control and ruined her hand forever. She swathed it in linen and a mitten so none could see it.

Though her parents were simple fisher folk, she had earned enough in the mills to purchase fine city clothes, and she'd become worldly and educated there, though, since the war, the mills now attracted immigrants rather than Yankee country girls to operate the machines.

"You look well, Lydia."

"I'm excited." Her large brown eyes were bright and comely. She'd earned a dowry, but none would have her for her crippled hand. "We're finally going to meet Isaiah Fernald's strange sailor."

Isaiah Fernald stood by the fireplace in his Sunday best: a coarse wool coat and trousers. His long gray side-whiskers swayed as he regaled the men with a story he'd told hundreds of times before, his shadow large against the wall.

"That night I couldn't see my hand before my face in that fog . . ."

470

"When do you suppose we'll meet Mr. Island?" Lydia asked me, too eager to listen to Isaiah's story again.

"Soon, dear."

"I hear he'll travel the lyceum circuit and speak of his journeys."

I had heard this too and feared that Mr. Island's sensational story would distract the populace from those who spoke on behalf of women's rights and the freedmen.

"I seen his ship all aglow, close on Heddybemps . . ." Isaiah paused his narrative to light his pipe. Smoke drifted in a cloud over the assembled.

Lydia touched my sleeve. "Why, look, there's Tilda and the girls. Who's tending the light?"

The girls, ten and eight, peeked into the parlor, then darted away, giggling. Mrs. Fernald hovered near the doorway, smoothing her faded skirts. She watched the festivities with a shy smile but declined to join in.

Mr. Grindle noticed as well and fairly echoed Lydia. "Isaiah, who watches the light?"

Isaiah sucked on his pipe, eyes twinkling above his ruddy cheeks. "Why, the light watches itself," he said mysteriously. "Thanks be to Mr. Island."

Murmuring broke out in the parlor among the men, but before discussion could grow too loud, Dr. Hutchinson burst upon the gathering, his expression jovial. "Gentlemen, gentlemen. And ladies. Do not question our poor keeper. Isaiah is true to his word. The light keeps itself thanks to a clever mechanism devised by Mr. Island. But come, ladies and gentlemen, please be seated."

Skirts swished as ladies found plush parlor chairs to sit on. Isaiah took up his confident pose by the fireplace again and cleared his throat.

"When I seen the vessel near the Rock, I told Tilda, you mind the light now. And I sent the girls to fetch the doctor. I pushed the dory down the ways. The sea was like to grab and pull it under. It filled with rain and ocean, but I rowed. I thought, this is the night I pass the Gates of Heaven, this is the night of Judgment. But I guess *He* wouldn't have me." Isaiah laughed.

"Then I seen the light shine off the hull of the vessel. I rowed alongside it and tapped it with my oar. It rang hollow. Wasn't wood, nor steel, but I'd no time to think it peculiar. I just thought of the poor bastards trapped inside."

Gasps passed through the room at his coarse language, and Miss Agatha Richardson, a spinster of seventy years, fanned herself with a handkerchief.

"Isaiah," the doctor said. "Remember, you are in fair company tonight."

The mantel clock ticked loudly while Isaiah regarded the doctor with annoyance. He puffed on his pipe and turned back to his audience. "Just when I was wondering how to help, a hatch opened and Mr. Island stuck his head out. As luck would have it, he was the only soul aboard. I hauled him into the dory, and just in time, for the ship sank straight away. I took him to my house. The doctor awaited us there. When we got Mr. Island inside, we knew he was from away."

"Thank you, Isaiah," the doctor said before the lighthouse keeper could go on. "I shall resume the story now."

Isaiah allowed the doctor a baleful glance before surrendering his coveted position at the polished oak mantel. The doctor assumed his place and hooked his thumbs in his waistcoat pockets.

"Mr. Island is an interesting specimen as you will see. He grasps little English, but is learning as fast as I can instruct him. He is a mariner from far away, an island of some sort, we gather, which we have never heard of before. We endowed him with his unusual name." Here the doctor smiled. "Upon sighting Sheep Island from the light tower and learning the word 'island,' he grew excitable and could not stop saying the word. Thus, his surname. 'Joseph' is after my own grandfather, for he, too, was a mariner.

"Mr. Island and I will travel the lyceum circuit starting next month. I am sure the country will want to meet him. May I present, without further ado, Joseph Island."

A hunched figure shuffled into the parlor. He wore a black suit, a gold watch and fob glistening in the firelight. At first his features were shadowed but became visible in the lamplight. Several ladies cried out and hid their eyes, and even the gentlemen were taken aback.

All averted their gaze, all except Lydia, who paid rapt attention to his every movement.

Joseph Island looked manlike enough, but his skin was flaccid and wrinkled like a dead porpoise that has washed ashore. His blunt nose fell beneath wide eyes, black liquid pools that reflected the lamplight. There were small openings along his jawline that may have been ears, but they resembled nothing with which I was acquainted. His hands, when I examined them more closely, had only three stubby fingers each.

Though most had shrunk back upon viewing his deformities, we remained politely restrained. The doctor sensed our duress and did the only sensible thing he could do: he served tea. Some might have desired stronger spirits, but the doctor was, after all, a temperance man.

Mr. Island gazed at the floor, blinking slowly, as though deliberately. His stubby fingers played with the watch fob. Once I saw him take the watch out and listen to its steady ticking rhythm as a babe might listen to his mother's heart. It seemed to comfort him. I detected a reticence on his part, or perhaps more accurately, a sadness. That is until the hired woman, Margarite, carried the tea service in on a silver tray.

"Tea!" Mr. Island grinned. "Two sugarz, pleeze."

My neighbors and I looked on in amazement at his outburst. Margarite smiled tolerantly as she dropped two teaspoons of sugar into a teacup, evidently familiar with this peculiar guest.

Isaiah guffawed and patted him on the shoulder. "Never saw such a bugger for tea."

After that, the tension in the parlor eased and gay chatter filled the room. Mr. Island watched and listened from his chair.

Through it all, Lydia scrutinized him. When he gazed in her direction, balancing the saucer on the tips of his three fingers, he smiled again. I saw a dimple form on the edge of Lydia's mouth. But then Mr. Island's grip on his teacup slipped and hot tea soaked his front. He gazed mournfully at his knees. The parlor stilled as he moaned. It was the loneliest sound I have ever heard, and my heart ached for him.

Lydia wasted no time in coming to his aid. She took a handkerchief from one of the gentlemen and blotted his coat. She held her mittened hand before him. "See," she said, "I have trouble holding my teacup, too. I have to do it all with one hand. I can understand your difficulty."

Lydia kept speaking in reassuring tones as she blotted. Mr. Island looked from her hand to his, and back again. "Difficultee," he said. "Yez. Difficultee, teacup."

"Yes," Lydia replied. "Difficulty. Teacup." Then a wondrous thing happened and the two laughed together as if bonded by an understanding that made the rest of us outsiders.

The occasion came for Mr. Island to tell us his story. He shuffled to the mantel and the room hushed.

"From across ocean I come. Great ocean." The gilt-framed mirror over the mantel reflected the back of his head. Thin sandy hair wisped around his crown. "My land. Iz called Evanonway."

From the corner of my eye, I saw Miss Richardson mouth the name of his land as if to etch it into her mind.

"Long I travel. I explore, see new placez. I see Izaiah's light but I come too close." Now he looked out the window. "My land, I need to go back. Harvest. Time for harvest. To help famlee."

"What is your land like?" asked Reverend Foster. "Your Evanonway. I've not heard of it before."

"Treez. Much smaller, not so big as here." Mr. Island's eyes drifted upward as if the room were surrounded by the tall spruces and pines indigenous to much of Maine. "I live by the sea too."

"'Course you do," Isaiah said. "You live on an island."

Mr. Island smiled at his friend. "Yez. Island. It is not so different."

"What continent is your island near?" Reverend Foster asked.

Mr. Island glanced first at Isaiah, then at Dr. Hutchinson, in puzzlement. "Cont-continent?"

"Yes. Like Africa, for instance, or Europe."

The folds above his forehead deepened. "This I do not know."

Dr. Hutchinson placed a hand on Mr. Island's shoulder. "He has much of our language yet to grasp, Reverend."

When it appeared little else was forthcoming, whether due to the insurmountable language barriers or bashfulness on Mr. Island's behalf, the ladies removed to the sitting room across the hall. Many of the women pulled out needlework and conversed about childcare and matters of domestic economy.

Lydia suffered the evening silently, for her crippled hand prevented her from even the simplest of needlework. I caught her often peering across the hall, where the French doors enclosed the men in the formal parlor but did not hinder their thunderous laughter. No doubt she wondered about our mysterious Mr. Island and the faraway port he had sailed from. Evanonway. Though he was ugly beyond words, she had formed a bond with him, and I wondered if it would blossom into something more. Tilda Fernald noticed Lydia's glances too and smiled.

For my part, I closed out the inane chatter of the women. Mr. Grindle and I had not been given children, and my mind cried out to discuss something other than croup and pox. I, too, looked at the closed French doors. But to actually cross the hall and open the doors and join the men would have been considered promiscuous at the very least.

OCTOBER CAN BE beneficent with the sun warming the day and frost coating the ground by night. Or, the weather can be surly with heavy leaden clouds hanging low over the ocean. No matter what the climate, I observed Mr. Island strolling, or rather his shuffling equivalent, along the shoreline on a daily basis. Ensconced on Schooner Head at the base of the lighthouse, he would look out to sea. For hours.

On one such excursion, Lydia joined him. The wind swirled leaves around them as they walked, and from their intense expressions, I knew they attempted to communicate with one another. They did not watch the ocean for long that day, for Lydia grew chill. Mr. Island put his topcoat around her shoulders and escorted her to her parents' home.

Later in the week, I chanced to meet Lydia along the Shore Road as I walked to the village on errands. "Lydia, dear," I said, "what is it that Mr. Island watches for when he stands beneath the lighthouse?"

Lines creased Lydia's brow. "I believe he wants to go home and he thinks about that. He is trying to think of a way to retrieve his ship."

"Why, it must be shattered to pieces by now!"

"I don't know," Lydia said. "He believes his ship to be whole."

"Well, it's too treacherous to go anywhere near Heddybemps. He must resign himself to that and perhaps find passage on some other ship."

"For some reason, he doesn't find other ships to be good enough."

Over the days that followed, I espied Lydia accompanying Mr. Island to Schooner Head. It appeared they were beginning to understand one another much better now, their conversation and gestures animated. Lydia's laughter, a sound unheard since she returned from the mill, carried on the wind to my dooryard.

Isaiah Fernald often sat carving on a stick outside the lighthouse and barely grumbled when Mr. Island and Lydia passed by. His sunny nature had grown irritable at best now that the light kept itself. The egg-sized lamp Mr. Island had installed in the light tower didn't smoke the Fresnel lens or brass housings as kerosene once had, and so there wasn't even polishing to occupy the lighthouse keeper.

We fear that Isaiah's idleness may lead to his consumption of demon rum as it is the way with men of the sea. I pity Tilda, whose shy smiles have turned to anxious frowns.

Mr. Island surprised my husband and me by stopping at the house one afternoon. I led him to the piazza where Mr. Grindle sat reading in the warmth of Indian summer. As I turned to step back into the house to leave them, Mr. Island stopped me.

"Pleeze. Stay, Meezus Grindle. Stay."

I hesitated on the step and my husband raised a brow. "Wouldn't you like some tea?" I asked, uncertain as to why I was being detained. After all, it sounded like he wanted man-talk. To talk business with my husband.

"No, pleeze. I just talk. Talk ships."

"Well, surely you don't need me."

"Stay. Where I come from, mates are . . ." He paused, searching for the appropriate word. "Partnerz."

My husband was incredulous but did not protest for fear of offending our guest. I settled onto the rocker, frankly relieved to be off my feet. All the mad preserving of fruits and vegetables, the beating of carpets and cleaning in preparation for winter, had sapped the energy from me, even with the help of our housekeeper.

"What is it I can do for you?" Mr. Grindle asked. "Are you interested in investing in the new ship I'm building in Searsport?"

"Ah, no. I need *my* ship." Mr. Island jabbed a finger at his chest. "I need your help, George Grindle. I need my ship."

Mr. Grindle smoothed his mustache. "Joseph, I'd help if I could, but your ship is broken on the bottom of the bay. It's foolish to even think about salvaging it."

Mr. Island's wrinkled brow furrowed deeper. "Not foolish. Not broken. I know this. I know how to . . . salvage, but, uh, I have no monee."

"Money? You want me to finance the salvaging of your ship? I wish to help, Joseph, you know that, but not only is it a dangerous endeavor, it's an expensive one. Can't we find you passage on some other ship?"

"No, no, no. No good. Only *my* ship take me home."

I could tell my husband wanted to help, but he is, after all, a businessman, and Mr. Island's request was not a good investment.

"Obviously Mr. Island is in desperate need," I said, before I knew I was saying it. "It seems we must help him in some way. Remember Paul: *And now abideth faith, hope, charity, these three; but the greatest of these is charity.*"

My husband glared at me, but Mr. Island beamed. "Yez, I provide George with macheenze that make his ships better. Faster than wind. Faster than steam. He gives me monee."

That gave my husband pause. Speed in shipping was everything, and he harbored a not-so-secret desire to relive the days of the swift clippers of the '50s; he often cited the record of the *Flying Dragon*, which sailed from Maine to San Francisco in only ninety-seven days. Our hardy down-easters proved competitive but lacked the glamour of the days of the Gold Rush, when speed and grace, not necessarily cargo, were the mariner's dream.

"You have machines that will improve my ships?" he asked.

Mr. Island nodded. "You give me monee. I make macheenze."

Once Mr. Grindle realized he would receive some compensation for his assistance, his benevolence toward Mr. Island could not be mistaken.

When the interview concluded, I showed Mr. Island to the front door. He paused on the threshold, only to turn around and look up at me with those queer black eyes of his.

"I am most grateful," he said. "You convinzed George."

"I did no such thing. You offered him a form of recompense that he found impossible to ignore. These engines you proposed will make his ships difficult to surpass. Sailing around Cape Horn as speedily as possible is more important than you may know."

"Perhapz." He rubbed a wrinkled cheek with his three fingers. "But you helped all the same. It is important that I return home. Your ships, they will not cross the ocean I must cross. The ocean I must cross to my island."

He bore his sadness well but now and then it resurfaced. I have never been far from home, certainly not across the wide ocean, and now I was sure, after witnessing Mr. Island's melancholy, that I never wanted to travel afar. I will remain content with the curios and stories brought back from foreign lands by my brother and the various ship-masters in my husband's employ.

"I do have one request," I told Mr. Island after a moment of thought. "A favor you may return if you like."

His sadness vanished at once in his eagerness to please.

"When you travel the lyceum circuit at the end of the month, I ask that you remember to mention women's rights and universal suffrage!"

Mr. Island laughed. "I will, I will!"

"One more thing," I said. "You must promise not to hurt Lydia. She's quite taken with you and if you were to leave . . ."

His laughter died abruptly, and the sadness returned to his eyes. "I am . . . taken by her too."

THE REST OF the month brought frenzied activity to Schooner Harbor. Mr. Island spent much of his time at the shipyard drafting plans for my husband's ships and working with machinists as they built engines to his specifications. The rest of his time he spent at the sail loft, where he manufactured special filaments that were woven into sailcloth. My understanding was that the sails would collect the energy of the sun, in turn rendering power to the engines.

Even when the sun hid behind the clouds, Mr. Island assured us enough energy would be stored to keep the engines running, and if not, the sails would catch the wind as always and continue to impel the ship forward. Mr. Grindle was well pleased. His ships would not be likely to falter in a dead calm, and he'd outpace any competitor to port.

One day he brought home a sample of the new sailcloth and the filaments made it gleam with pearlescent beauty. I could only imagine how splendid a fully rigged ship would look with sails bent and the sun full upon it.

Meanwhile, Mr. Island left the lightkeeper's house to reside with Dr. Hutchinson. Isaiah Fernald had grown surly, and we suspected the rum. Mrs. Fernald and the girls hurried through town on their errands, their expressions wan and bereft of joy. There was talk of the government relieving Isaiah of duty. After all, the light kept itself. In fact, rumor had it that all lightkeepers would be replaced by a replica of the device that kept Schooner Head Light aglow.

Mr. Island spent long hours poring over plans and drawings in anticipation of removing his ship from the ocean floor. I chanced to see him one evening through an undraped window, bent over his desk, examining the pages of a logbook in the glow of a candle. No one was privy to these plans but Lydia.

November blustered in, cold and rainy. Lydia waved a handkerchief in farewell as Dr. Hutchinson drove off with Mr. Island to the train station to begin their lyceum tour. Beneath the hood of Lydia's cloak I saw tears. It could have been rain but I think not.

Lydia spent evenings with me, huddled by the warmth of the stove in the kitchen, writing letters to Mr. Island. That is, I wrote the letters for she was not capable with her maimed hand. The content consisted of, as one may guess, sentiments of youth, the sentiments of love. I recall a few I wrote Mr. Grindle during our courtship.

She narrated, blushing girlishly as she did so, and I inked the papers wondering throughout it all how such an odd looking fellow, with all his deformities, could capture the heart of this sweet young woman.

"Lydia," I said, "what will you do if he is able to leave for his own land?"

"I don't believe he'll be able to do it," she said with complete assurance. "All of the men say it's impossible for him to recover his own ship. Even your Mr. Grindle."

I laid my pen down on the table and looked her squarely in the eyes. "It appears that Mr. Island is capable of a good many things. If he should succeed in retrieving his ship, what then?"

"I will go with him."

I shook my head at her confidence, then remembered love can drive one to do a great many things. "My dear, he comes from a very foreign place. It will not be easy."

"I shall manage quite well," she said and would speak no more of it.

Mr. Island wrote Lydia in return, and she shared portions of his letters with me, whether out of her own excitement and desire to share them, or out of a feeling of obligation toward me for writing him letters on her behalf, I do not know, though I suspect the former.

She showed me his fine renderings of Faneuil Hall and Boston's waterfront. He could not write in English, but his drawing skill was excellent. The letters, crafted by Dr. Hutchinson's ornate hand, spoke of the wonders of Boston and New York, and of the society there.

In a side note to me, he said he spoke on behalf of women's rights just as he'd promised. He called on Mrs. Elizabeth Cady Stanton in New Jersey, the most radical leader of the struggle, but she was not home. How thrilled I was that he tried.

The Boston paper my husband subscribed to, however, told a different story of Mr. Island's exploits, stories of which I did not have the heart to relate to Lydia. One evening, as the bitter November wind lashed rain against our windows, Mr. Grindle and I sat in the parlor, he with his paper, me with wool and needles. I was knitting a pair of mittens for my little niece.

The house groaned with the wind, and the fire spat and hissed like an angry cat as rain seeped down the chimney. Over the cacophony, I heard my husband grumble at the paper.

"What is it?" I asked him.

He snapped the paper in his hands. "Our Mr. Island has made friends with every industrialist in Boston."

"This is good."

"Humph. Just so long as he doesn't sell any secrets of my ship engines." Mr. Grindle stroked his mustache. "It says here that though Joseph was well received by society people, he faced much heckling and ridicule while speaking. Apparently it is generally believed he is suffering from delusions borne of reading Jules Verne, that he is malformed not only physically but he is quite mad as well." He looked up at me. "Was he reading Jules Verne?"

"I do not think he could read our language, or French, for that matter." I found the account very dispiriting, for I knew Mr. Island only for the kind fellow he was. Unusual, yes, but certainly not mad.

"Hmm. Well, in any case, he has created quite a sensation." Mr. Grindle read on and *tsked*.

I dropped my knitting into my lap. "Go on, George Grindle, what else does the paper tell you?"

"His audiences could not endure his foreignness, apparently. They hurled rotten vegetables at him." He paused again, brows raised. "What in Heaven's name would possess Joseph to endorse woman's suffrage?"

I wondered if Mr. Island's poor reception was the result of his foreignness, as my husband put it, or because he endorsed suffrage. Miss Susan Anthony received similar treatment for the cause.

"It says here," Mr. Grindle said, "that Lucy Stone does not wish to associate the cause with Joseph Island."

I was not surprised. She did little to associate with Mrs. Stanton and those of a more radical mind either. A gust of wind rattled the windows and I sighed. It would be a long winter. More so for Lydia Pendleton.

MR. ISLAND RETURNED from his tour months early. Snow frosted the blocky granite shore the day he and Dr. Hutchinson drove in on a sleigh in early January. It was a bright blue day but frigid. Frigid down to the marrow.

Lydia ran to welcome them home and Mr. Grindle and I followed.

Her enthusiastic greeting was cut short by a gasp of shock. Mr. Island disembarked from the sleigh painstakingly and stiffly. He stood more bent than ever and, though it was difficult to tell beneath the buffalo robe he wrapped about himself, he appeared fragile.

He greeted Lydia with a feeble smile, and Dr. Hutchinson hastened to support him. Lydia grabbed his other side. He took mincing footsteps to the doctor's house. My husband and I glanced at one another and followed behind.

In a flurry of a ragged and patched coat, Isaiah Fernald rounded the doctor's house. He'd been turned out of the keeper's house in late November by the Lighthouse Service. Where he lived no one knew exactly, though some spoke of a hermit taking refuge in an old fish shack on Barred Cove. Tilda and the girls removed to Castine, where Tilda still had family. No one spoke of it though it was known.

"YOU!" Isaiah shouted at Mr. Island, a plume of steam issuing from his mouth. He slipped on some ice to his knees. He gripped an empty bottle.

"Izaiah," Mr. Island said, barely above a whisper.

"Your fault."

We could tell by Isaiah's drawl and inability to stand erect that he'd been at the rum.

"Your fault," Isaiah repeated. "Your fault I've lost it all. My lighthouse. My . . . my little girls." He sobbed into his hands, oblivious to the snow soaking through his trousers. We watched the spectacle, entranced.

Mr. Island reached out with a gloved hand. I had knitted the gloves at Lydia's request, the only time, I daresay, that I'll ever knit gloves with only three fingers.

"Izaiah," he whispered. He reached. His hand trembled.

"Your fault!" Isaiah staggered to his feet and lobbed his bottle at Mr. Island.

Lydia would've shielded Mr. Island if she could have reacted quickly enough. None of us could. The bottle shattered on his shoulder. Splinters of glass glinted on his turned cheek.

"Scoundrel," my husband muttered. "I will take care of Isaiah. You get Joseph into the house." Isaiah lay in a crumpled heap in the snow, and my husband grabbed him by the collar.

We bustled our ill friend into the back bedroom he had occupied before beginning his travels. I caught his eyes once. They had lost the luster I remembered. They brimmed with creamy tears. At least, I took them for tears. So many things about Mr. Island were strange that it was difficult to know.

And after that episode, I knew Lydia's tears. She desperately wished to help him if she could.

He gazed at her in a dispirited way and in a quavering voice said, "Leave, pleeze. Leave."

Weeks passed before he would see anyone. Eventually he did summon Mr. Grindle and me. We arrived in the Hutchinson parlor to find him draped in a shawl and sipping tea by the fire. He looked better than on that first day of his return but still fragile and weary. A greenish discoloration encircled his eyes and mouth.

Margarite served us tea, and after Mr. Island assured himself of our well-being, he said, "I need my ship. I need my island, or elze I do not get well."

Mr. Grindle squirmed in his chair. "I am sorry," he said. "As you know, winter is a treacherous time to work. The cost of labor is inordinate at this time of year."

"I am rich," Mr. Island said. "Very rich. I show them, them in New York, Boston, and Philadelphia, how to make macheenze. Macheenze that work better. Monee is not a factor."

"The weather is."

Mr. Island nodded. "Neverthelezz, we begin."

I took turns with Lydia and Mrs. Hutchinson watching over Mr. Island in his weakened state. At first he made a go of it, fighting the illness, but soon he was bedridden. He wrote frequently in his logbook and consulted with my husband on the salvaging of his ship. When my husband wasn't available, he pressed me.

"Meezus Grindle, what progress do they make?" He lay covered by quilts and blankets, but still, chills racked his body.

I pushed the velvet drapes aside from the window that overlooked

the harbor. Snow swirled outside. A chickadee hopped from one swaying branch to another. "It appears they've rigged a platform, but the
seas are too rough to erect it this day." I turned away from the drafty
window and adjusted my shawl.

"I fear I will not make it through the winter." Indeed, the sickly
green discoloration mottled his cheeks. A cure for his illness proved
beyond Dr. Hutchinson's powers. "I fear I will not see my home again.
My ship, it will not be salvaged."

Lydia entered to take the night watch. She stirred the embers of
the fireplace and sparks shot up the chimney. "Of course it will be," she
said. "And you will take me to Evanonway."

Her words, though brave, belied desperation as if all her optimistic
energy might imbue him with the strength to go on.

"Dear, dear Lydia," he said. "I wish it, but Evanonway is too far for
you. Too far."

Lydia knelt beside his bed. She placed her mittened hand over his
and used the other to brush his wispy hair away from his face. "You will
improve, Joseph, and then we shall discuss it. But now you need rest. I
will watch you throughout the night."

They gazed at one another for a time without saying a word. I
feared to move lest I break the spell. Finally, Lydia stood and bent over
him. She pressed her lips to his brow in a chaste kiss. He caressed her
cheek with his deformed hand. Before they remembered my presence, I
slipped through the door. But even as I did so, their voices carried to me.

"Rest now, Joseph. You've all my love. Rest now."

"In Evanonway," he replied, "we say, *arem, mi doran*. You make
me alive."

MAY BRINGS ALL seasons to Maine, the warmth of summer sun and
the frosty breath of latent winter in the wind. With May comes the
thawing of the earth.

I inhaled the mixed scents of freshly turned soil and sea air. Gulls
wheeled overhead, and the sails of fishing sloops dotted the cobalt bay.

Mr. Island's derricks, mounted on the platform by Heddybemps Rock, stood unmanned, lifeless.

I wound my hands in my shawl and stood leeward of Mr. Grindle. The cemetery rises on a high spot above our village and few trees protect it from the scouring of the wind.

Reverend Foster stood with his head bowed over Mr. Island's grave. The wind snatched words of prayer from his lips and whipped them past my ears.

Mr. Grindle purchased the headstone and had it engraved upon it simply, "Here rests Joseph Island, far from home, a mariner, died March 20, 1870, of illness." A saber and flag were carved in relief above the words on a headstone left unused after the war. When I protested, my frugal husband chastised me. "Joseph was a traveler, an explorer. Do you think his courage any less than that of our Union soldiers?"

Dr. Hutchinson had donated the plot, very near where his ancestor, Joseph Hutchinson, reposed in eternal sleep.

Lydia looked out to the ocean, and what she saw, I could not say. Her face, thin and white from the exertion of nursing Mr. Island through the long, dark winter, was without expression. No tears traced her cheeks. Her grief had been silent all along.

The good citizens of Schooner Harbor had donned black and gathered as once they did one October evening. This time it was not to greet the stranger from far away but to bid him farewell. My husband knelt to the ground and took up some loose soil. He sprinkled it on the pine coffin. Others followed his lead.

Earlier I had plucked starflowers, so tiny and white and sturdy in the uncertainty of May, and I planned to leave them by his stone.

I stopped by the edge of the grave, reflecting on Mr. Island's time with us. It had been less than a year, but his influence went well beyond Schooner Harbor, with his clever knowledge of machines. I suspected our world would never be the same again.

But for me? I had simply lost a friend. I had been able to see beyond his misshapen appearance, beyond his foreignness, and see the kind soul within. I believe it was so for most in our small village.

I looked for Lydia in the crowd, grateful so many had assembled to say their good-byes, but she was walking away. The flowers fell from my fingers and I slipped between my husband and the reverend. Miss Richardson, weeping openly, grasped my arm and squeezed it.

"Time, my dear, will heal all wounds."

I loosed myself from the spinster. By this time, Lydia was at the bottom of the cemetery path, had passed through the wrought iron gate, and was striding in the direction of the lighthouse. I hoisted my skirts up and struck out after her.

"What is wrong?" my husband called after me. "Are you overcome?"

For perhaps the first time since we had met, I ignored my husband. Mr. Grindle means well, but he seldom understands the workings of a woman's heart. It was not mine I was thinking of, rather Lydia's. It was too soon to contemplate another burial.

Lydia flew along the road without impediment while I mired in the mud. Chin up and back held straight, she hurried ever faster, ever out of reach. Mud sucked at my ankles. I despaired of catching up with her before it was too late.

She entered the lighthouse grounds. She passed the keeper's house with its boarded windows, passed the light tower in need of a whitewash. I, too, entered the grounds, and only then did the gap between us close.

I found her standing on the very edge of Schooner Head's cliff face. I trembled and panted, but she stood calm as she overlooked the frothing sea far below, calm as though she had floated there to fulfill her dreadful purpose.

"Lydia, dear," I said.

"Do you know, he once pointed to the moon and called it an island? He said there were more islands than we knew over greater expanses than we could fathom."

"Lydia—"

She turned wide brown eyes on me. "I want to be with him."

Her dark cloak slipped to the ground, and she teetered on the edge. In desperation, I must have leaped the yards that separated us. I clamped my hands around her arm. She struggled and my insides roiled. I feared she'd topple the both of us over the edge.

"Lydia," I said, "do not do this. This is not what he would wish.

Lydia, do you hear me? Joseph wished for you to go on. Who will remember him and his fate? Who will tell his people should they search for him?"

Something awakened in her, and she looked at me again. This time she saw me. "Yes. Someone must tell his people." She fell to her knees weeping. My own, weak from preventing this near lover's leap, sank into the earth. I folded Lydia in my arms.

"We shall not speak of this to anyone, Lydia," I said. "We must go on as best we can. Cherish his memory, yes, but live on." I stroked her hair, which spilled out from beneath her bonnet, and whispered any comforting platitudes I could think of till she calmed. In time, we separated.

WE STROLLED IN silence along the Shore Road toward the village. As we drew abreast of the Hutchinson home, the doctor stepped outside, still garbed in his mourning clothes.

"Lydia, one moment please." He carried a book.

"Yes, Dr. Hutchinson?" she asked.

"My dear girl, I know how fond you and Joseph were of one another. In fact, he spoke of you often."

A ghost of a smile played on Lydia's lips.

"I've a token for you. Joseph's logbook. He was my friend, poor fellow, but I think this would mean more to you."

Lydia received the logbook gently as if it might crumble in her hands. "Thank you, Doctor. It means so very much to me, really."

The doctor smiled, but his eyes remained sad. "It's as it should be. Joseph was a fine draftsman, but the written parts are in his own tongue." He tipped his hat and reentered his home.

Lydia opened the book to pages full of, what looked to me, gibberish. Knotted characters looped across the page. She leafed through the book, and there appeared drawings of plans for machines of some sort. Again, they proved nonsensical to me. Could these be the plans I saw Mr. Island poring over through the window months ago? The plans for retrieving his ship? Or plans of the ship itself?

One drawing was of an oblong object that reminded me more of a bird than an oceangoing vessel. Very foreign. Then I recalled Isaiah Fernald's story of rescuing Mr. Island, of his oar ringing against the hull of a strange ship.

"Oh, look," Lydia said. She pointed to drawings of gnarled trees and flower blossoms, nothing like I have ever seen. A fanciful creature with legs and a long curving tail cavorted in the ocean. Perhaps it was a drawing from his imagination. "I believe this is Evanonway," Lydia said. "Joseph's home."

She flipped a page and unmistakably, there she was, her own portrait drawn amidst the gnarled trees, one of the strange blossoms clasped in her hand. An unfamiliar mountain range loomed in the background, above which Mr. Island had drawn two moons. Lydia held the book to her breast. I placed a hand on her shoulder to steady her.

"I shall be all right," she said.

And indeed she was, at least on the outside. She turned distant as if her thoughts were thousands of miles away, and every day, despite poor weather, she ventured up to the cemetery to gaze at Mr. Island's grave, just as he had once watched the sea. So long she had waited for love, and when it found her, it was taken away.

Work commenced on the platform above Heddybemps Rock. Mr. Grindle had grown interested in Mr. Island's ship and did not wish to halt progress. Lydia now looked seaward from the cemetery to view the work.

THE FIRST TIME I saw Mr. Island's ship hauled up on shore, the hairs on the back of my neck stood on end. Isaiah Fernald had been right. It was a strange vessel, and not one bit of it made from wood or steel. It was smooth and white like a giant egg, unmarred as if it hadn't sat submerged on the ocean floor all winter. It possessed wings, giving it the avian appearance I had seen in the logbook. Only the minutest hairline seams could be found where we supposed the hatch was, but none could gain entrance.

Word of Mr. Island's vessel reached the cities, and summer folk flocked to Schooner Harbor instead of Camden or Mount Desert. Rusticators by the score took lodging in the homes and barns of our neighbors, ate of their food, and purchased goods from Bayard Bascomb's store. They spent their afternoons on picnics and buckboard frolics. It was agreed by all that our small village had never experienced such a season of prosperity.

Lydia found no peace at the cemetery. Like pilgrims, the rusticators trampled the path to the gravesite. What revelations they expected, I do not know. There was a brief scare that someone might excavate the grave and make off with Mr. Island's remains. The local men set up a vigil to deter such an attempt.

Lydia's story was learned and soon she was beleaguered by those wishing to record it. She sought refuge in my home. None too few followed her and gazed wistfully into my dooryard, but when she failed to reappear, they tired of waiting and went off to puzzle over the ship.

I drew Lydia into the kitchen and sat her by the cold stove. She put her face into her hands. "Oh, Mrs. Grindle, won't they ever leave?"

"When the days grow crisp," I said, "they will return to the city. Poor dear, this is hard on you."

Lydia then looked up, her eyes searching. "You have been a good friend to me. No, more than that. More a good aunt, or even a mother."

I warmed at her words, glad she thought so well of me. I was very fond of her too.

"I believe," Lydia said, "that for all Joseph protested my going to his land, it was what he truly wanted. His book has shown me that, if not in words, then in pictures. I intend to make a go of it."

That evening, I stacked the Willoware on the sideboard and reflected on her words, realizing that making "a go of it" had been her objective since the moment she decided not to leap to her death from Schooner Head.

I gazed out the window. In the fading light, a figure hurried by, skirts flaring behind her. Lydia!

I took my shawl from its hook and hastened out the door to the shore, where Mr. Island's ship sat luminous and sleek in the moonshine. Lydia leaned into it as if embracing a lover.

She pressed her hand down on its smooth surface, traced the seam of the hatch with her fingertips. "Open, please open." She spared me a brief a brief glance, then turned her attention back to the ship. "*Avar*," she said.

The hatch slid open and white light bathed Lydia, bleaching her dress. "He taught me some of his words," she explained. She gazed inward and a startled expression crossed her face. I approached slowly as if my feet were anchored to the ground.

Lydia stepped into the vessel. She stood framed in the hatch, the intensity of the light knifing past her and into my eyes, obscuring what lay beyond. Lydia turned round and round, enraptured by her surroundings.

"Lydia," I said, feet still dragging.

"I am sorry, Mrs. Grindle. This time you cannot stop me."

"I know, dear. I know." I knew also, at that instant, how it is to be bereft of a daughter.

The light embracing her, she smiled and stepped inward. "It is amazing in here," she said. "Farewell, Mrs. Grindle. Thank you. Thank you for everything." And she was lost in the light.

The hatch *shooshed* closed.

I lifted my skirts and strode back down the Shore Road. The land vibrated and a hum filled the air like thousands of bees. I walked on and did not look back. I did not look back till the vessel hovered above the ground, lights blinking on the tips of the wings. A beam of gold from the lighthouse stroked the vessel. And then, in the beating of a heart, the ship was gone.

It is not my way to visit the cemetery after dark, but this night I did. I stood by Mr. Island's headstone and gazed at the sky, where bright points of light dazzled the eyes. I wondered if one of them might be Lydia. I wondered how she would fare in Evanonway, if the folk there were polite and would receive her with warmth. If they were at all like Mr. Island, I did not fear for her. How brave she was to leave behind all she knew!

I watched the stars for some time, feeling the push and tug of the breezes, first the cold from the ocean, then the warm from the land.

Did Mr. Island's homeland have the tang of salt in the sea air? Would Lydia grow homesick for all she had known? Would she return?

At our very first gathering at Dr. Hutchinson's home, Mr. Island had said of Evanonway, "Yez. Island. It is not so different."

JIM BUTCHER

My goal with Harry Dresden was never to write the mysterious wizard. I wanted to write the nerd next door, a nerd who just happened to be working forces that relatively few other people knew about. An intrinsic part of writing that character was giving him problems that regular people have, and exploring what happens when the supernatural collides face-first with the mundane. Harry has bills to pay. He has rent to make. He has to get his mail, do his laundry, walk his dog, pay his taxes, fix his car . . .

And it seemed completely natural to me that he would also have to do jury duty.

What I found out while writing this story was that Harry's personality really came more into conflict with this cornerstone of American civic duty than did his supernatural profession. And of course, since it was Harry, I couldn't just throw him into a case where he would sit around and make a calm and reasoned judgment. I mean, what fun would that be?

So I threw him into the judicial system as it functions in a world with supernaturally connected robber barons, politically active succubi, and Chicago politicians all vying for power.

Enjoy!

JURY DUTY

Jim Butcher

"I don't believe it. They found me," I muttered grimly. I looked left and right, checking around me for lurking threats. "I don't know how, but they did it. I've been back in the world for less than a month, and they found me."

Will Borden, engineer and werewolf, set down a heavy box of books on the kitchen table and looked at me with concern. Then he came over and looked down at the letter in my hands before snorting. "Such a drama queen."

"I'm serious!" I said and shook the letter. "I'm being hunted! By my own government!"

"It's a summons to jury duty, Harry," Will said. He opened the fridge and helped himself to a bottle of Mac's ale. He had to navigate around a few boxes to do it. I didn't think I'd had much out on the island, but it's amazing how many boxes it takes to hold not much. It had taken most of a day to ferry it all from the island into Molly's apartment in town. She rarely used the place these days and had given it to me to live in until I found my own digs.

"I don't like it," I said.

"Too bad," Will said. "You got it. Look, you probably won't be selected anyway."

"Summons," I said, glowering. "It's a freaking command. They want to see what a real summoning is, I could show them."

Will laughed at me. He was younger than me, shorter than average, and built like a linebacker. "How dare they intrude upon the solitude of the mighty wizard Dresden."

"Nngh," I said, and tossed the paper onto the top of a box of unopened envelopes—my mail, which had accumulated for more than a year, most of it junk. Some of it had been at the post office. More had been set aside by the new owner of my old address, formerly Mrs. Spunkelcrief's boarding house, and now the Better Future Society. I hadn't been able to stomach asking the new owner for my mail, but Butters had gotten it for me.

"Maybe I won't show up," I said. I paused. "What happens if I don't show up?"

"You can be held in contempt of court or fined or jailed or something," Will said. He scratched his chin thoughtfully. "Now that I think about it, they actually leave it kind of vague, what's going to happen."

"Good threats are like that. More scary when you can use your imagination."

"They aren't the mob, Harry."

"Aren't they?" I asked. "Pay them money every year to protect you, and God help you if you don't."

Will rolled his eyes and got another bottle from the fridge. He opened it for me and passed it over. "Mac would kill you for drinking this cold, et cetera and so on."

"It's hot out," I said, and took a long pull. "Especially for this early in the year. And he would just give me that disappointed grunting sound. Damned government. Not like I don't have things to do."

"Is justice worth having?" Will asked.

I eyed him.

"Is it?"

"Mostly," I said. Warily.

"Well, that's why there's a legal system."

"What does justice have to do with the legal system?"

"Do you really want to tear it all apart and start over from 1776?" Will asked.

"Not particularly. I have books to read."

He spread his hands. "The courts aren't perfect," Will said, "but they can do okay a lot of the time." He reached into the box and picked up the summons. "And if you really think the courts aren't working, maybe you should do something about it. If only there was some way you could directly participate . . ."

I snatched the letter back from him with a scowl. "Think you're smart, huh."

"You're kind of a solitary hunter by nature, Harry," Will said. "I'm more of a pack creature. We're smart about different things, that's all."

I read a little more. "There's a dress code too?" I demanded.

Will covered up his mouth with his hand and coughed, but I could see that he was laughing at me.

"Well," I said firmly, "I am *not* wearing a tie."

Will lowered his hand, his expression carefully locked into sober agreement. "Viva la revolution."

So I WENT to court.

It meant a trek downtown to the Richard J. Daley Center Courthouse, whose name did little to inspire confidence in me that justice might indeed be done. Ah well. I wasn't here to create disorder. I was here to preserve disorder.

I went up to the seventeenth floor, turned in my card along with about a gazillion other people, none of whom seemed at all enthusiastic about being there. I got a cup of bad coffee and grimaced at it while waiting around for a while. Then a guy in a black muumuu showed up and recounted the plot of *My Cousin Vinny*.

Okay, it was a robe, and the guy was a judge, and he gave us a brief outline of the format of the trial system, but it's not nearly as entertaining to say it that way.

Then they started calling names. They said they only needed about half of us, and when they had been going for a while, I thought I was about to get lucky and get sent home, but then some clerk called my name, and I had to shuffle forward to join a file of other jurors.

There were lines and questions and a lot of waiting around. Long story short: I wound up sitting in the box seats in a Cook County courtroom as the wheels of justice started to grind for a guy named Hamilton Luther.

The case was being handled by one of the new ADAs. I used to keep track of those people pretty closely, but then I was mostly dead for a while, and then living in exile and my priorities shifted. When you live in a city with a reputation for political corruption as pervasive as Chicago's, and work in a business that sometimes treads close to the limit of the law (or twenty miles past it), it's wise to keep an eye on the public servants. Most of them were decent enough, I guess, by which I mean they're your basic politician—they had just enough integrity to keep up appearances and appease political sponsors and at the end of the day they had an agenda to pursue.

Once in a while, though, you got one who was thoroughly in someone's pocket. The outfit owned some of those types. The unions owned some others. The corporations had the rest.

The new kid was in his late twenties, clean-cut, thoroughly shaven, and looked a little distracted as he assembled notes and folders around him with the help of an attractive female assistant. His gray suit was tailored to him, maybe a little too well tailored for someone just out of law school, and his maroon tie was made of expensive silk that matched the kerchief tucked into his breast pocket. He had big ears and a large Adam's apple, and his expression was painfully earnest.

On the other side of the aisle, at the defendant's table, sat a study in contrast. He was a man in his fifties, and if he'd ever been in college it had been on a wrestling scholarship. He had shoulders like a bull moose, hunched with muscle, and his arms ended in fists the size of sledgehammer heads. The dark skin on his knuckles was white and lumpy with old scars, the kind you get in back-alley fistfights, not in a boxing ring. He had shaven his head. There was stubble around the edges but the top was shiny. He had a heavy brow, a nose that had been broken on a biannual basis, and his suit was cheap and ill-fitting. He had a couple of folders on the table with him, along with a pair of thick books. The man looked bleakly uneasy and kept flicking nervous glances across the aisle.

If that guy was a lawyer, I was an Ewok. But he sat alone.

So where was his public defender?

"All rise!" a large man in a uniform said in a voice pitched to carry. "Court is now in session, the Honorable Mavis Jefferson presiding."

Everyone stood up. After a second, so did I.

I guess you could say I'm not really a joiner.

The judge came in and settled down at her bench, and the rest of us sat too. She was a blocky woman in her early sixties, with skin the color of coffee grounds and bags under her eyes that made me think of Spike the bulldog in those old cartoons. If you didn't look closely, you'd think she was bored out of her mind. She sat without moving much, her eyes half closed, scanning over a document on her own desk through a pair of reading glasses. There was something serpentine about her eyes, a suggestion of formidable, remorseless rationality. This was a woman who had seen a great deal, had been amused by very little of it, and who would not be easily made a fool. She finished scanning the document and glanced up at the defendant.

"Mister Luther?" she said.

The bruiser in the bad suit rose. "Yes, ma'am."

"I see that you have taken it upon yourself to serve as your own defender," she said. Her tone was bored, entirely neutral. "While this is your right under the law, I strongly advise you to reconsider. Given the severity of the charges against you, I would think that a professional attorney would offer you a much more comprehensive and capable legal defense."

"Yes, ma'am," Luther said. "I thought that too. But all the public defender wanted to do was plea bargain, ma'am. And I want to have my say."

"That too is your right," the Judge said. For a second, I thought I saw a flicker of something like regret on her face, but it vanished into neutrality again almost instantly. Her tone took on the measured cadence of a cop reading formal Miranda rights. "If you go through with this, you will not be able to move for a mistrial based on the fact that you do not have adequate representation. This trial will proceed and its outcome will be binding. Do you understand this warning as I have stated it to you?"

"Yes ma'am," Luther said. "Ain't no take-backsies. I want to represent myself, ma'am."

The Judge nodded. "Then you may be seated." Luther sat. The Judge turned toward the prosecutor and nodded to him. "Counselor." There was a pause about a second and a half long, and then she repeated, in a mildly annoyed tone, "Counselor?" Another impatient pause. "Counselor Tremont, am I interrupting you?"

The young ADA in the fine suit blinked, looked up from his notes, and hastily rose. "No, your Honor, please excuse me. I'm ready to begin."

"Thank goodness," the Judge said in a dry tone. "My granddaughter graduates from high school in three weeks. You may proceed."

Tremont flushed. "Um, yes. Thank you, your Honor." The young man cleared his throat, adjusted his suit jacket, and walked over to face the jury box. He held up a glossy professional headshot of a handsome man in his thirties and showed it to us.

"Meet Curtis Black," Tremont said. "He was a stock broker. He liked to go rock climbing on the weekends. He volunteered in a soup kitchen three weekends a month, and he once won an all-expenses-paid vacation to Florida by making a half-court shot during halftime at a Bull's game. He was well liked by his professional associates and had an extensive family and was owned by an Abyssinian cat named Purrple.

"You have doubtless noted my use of the past tense. Was. Liked. Volunteered. But I have to use the past tense, because one year ago, Curtis Black was brutally murdered in an alley in Wrigleyville near the corner of Southport and Grace. Mr. Black was bludgeoned to death with a bowling pin. His skull was smashed flat in the back, and the autopsy showed that it had been shattered into a dozen pieces, like plate glass."

Tremont took a moment to let the graphic description sink in. The room was very still.

"The state intends to prove," he said, "that the defendant, Hamilton Luther, murdered Mr. Black in cold blood. That he followed him into the alley, seized the bowling pin from a refuse bin, and struck him from behind, causing him to fall to the ground. That he then proceeded to continue beating Mr. Black's skull with twelve to fifteen heavy blows while Mr. Black lay stunned and helpless beneath him.

"This is a serious crime," Tremont continued. "But Mr. Luther has a long history of violent offenses. Forensic evidence will prove that Mr. Luther was at the crime scene, that he left his fingerprints on the weapon, and that the forensic profile of the attack matches his height and build closely. Eyewitnesses and security cameras witnessed him fleeing the alley shortly after Mr. Black entered it, the victim's blood literally upon his hands. The evidence will prove Mr. Luther's guilt beyond any reasonable doubt and, in the end, you must find him guilty of this horrible crime. Thank you."

"Thank you, counselor," the Judge said, as Tremont returned to his seat. "Mr. Luther, you may present your opening statement."

Luther rose slowly. He glanced around the jury box, licked his lip nervously and approached the jury.

"Ladies and . . . and gentlemen," he said, stammering a little. "I know I got a past. I did a dime in Stateville for putting a guy in the hospital. But that was my past. I ain't that man no more." He swallowed and gestured vaguely over his shoulder, toward Tremont. "This guy is going to tell you about all this CSI stuff that says I did it. But all those reports and pictures don't tell the whole story. They leave a lot of stuff out. I ain't a lawyer. But I'm gonna tell you the whole story. And then . . . then I'll see what you think about it, I guess." He hovered for a moment longer, awkwardly, then nodded and said, "Okay. I'm done."

"Thank you, Mr. Luther," the Judge said. "You may return to your seat."

"Yes ma'am," Luther said, and did so.

"Mr. Luther, you are charged with first degree murder," the Judge said, still in her rote-memory voice, "how do you plead?"

"I . . ." Luther looked down at some notes in front of him and then up again. "Not guilty, ma'am."

Hell's bells.

The full legal might of the state of Illinois was being thrown at Luther. The man seemed sincere enough. But apparently the only defense he had to offer was a story. A story from an ex-con, no less.

I wanted to hear him out. I knew all about being judged for things that were out of my control. But I was pretty sure Luther was going back to jail.

"Mr. Tremont," the Judge said. "Is the prosecution ready to begin?"

"Yes, your Honor," Tremont said.

"Very well," she said. "You may call your first witness."

TREMONT SPENT THE afternoon driving nails into Luther's coffin, thoroughly, methodically, and one at a time.

He did exactly what he said he would do. He brought out each case of physical evidence, point by point, and linked Luther undeniably to the scene of the crime. Luther had been photographed by a grainy black-and-white security camera coming out of the alley's far side, spattered in blood. His fingerprints were on the murder weapon, in the blood of the victim. The officer who arrested him had taken blood samples from his skin and clothing matching those of the victim. He additionally gave testimony of Luther's past criminal record, which had landed him in jail as young man.

When given a chance to cross-examine, Luther shook his head, until he got to the testimony of the arresting officer, a black man in his late forties named Dwayne. He rose and asked the officer, "When you brung me in, was I injured?"

Officer Dwayne nodded. "You were banged up pretty good. Especially your head."

"Where at?" Luther asked.

Dwayne grunted. "Back of your head."

"Any other injuries on me?"

"You were one big bruise," Dwayne said.

"How big was the victim," Luther asked.

"About five-four, maybe one-fifty."

"Weightlifter or something?"

"Not so you'd notice," Dwayne said.

Luther nodded. "You known me a while. How come?"

"I was the one who arrested you the first damn time."

"Officer," the Judge said.

"Beg pardon, your Honor," Dwayne said hurriedly.

"I remember that too," Luther said. "In your experience, a businessman like that handle a guy like me?"

"Unless he's armed, or got a lot of training, no."

"One more question," Luther said. He squinted at the officer and said, "You in my neighborhood ever since I got out. You ever think I'd be trouble again?"

"Objection," Tremont said. "He's asking for pure conjecture."

Luther frowned and said, "Beat cops deal with ex-cons on a regular basis professionally, ma'am. Figure that qualifies him as an expert opinion on potential, uh . . ." He consulted his notes and spoke in a careful, clear tone. "Recidivism."

The judge eyed Luther and said, toward Tremont, "Overruled. You may answer the question, Officer."

"No," Dwayne said. "I've seen you with your kids. I wouldn't have called you for it."

"In the arrest report," Luther said, "does it say what I kept asking the officers?"

Dwayne cleared his throat and looked down at a notepad in front of him. "Yeah. The suspect kept asking 'Where is she?' and 'Is she all right?'"

"Who was I talking about?"

Officer Dwayne turned a page and cleared his throat. "The suspect claimed that he only began the confrontation with the deceased after witnessing the man drag a female child, Latino, around the age of ten, into the alley," he read. "Subsequent investigation could not confirm the presence of any such person."

"How hard did they look?" Luther asked.

"I'm sorry?"

"You heard me," Luther said. "In your opinion, how hard did the investigating detectives look for a little girl who might clear an ex-con from being guilty of a murder of a big-shot businessman?"

"Objection."

"Overruled."

"I'm not a detective," Officer Dwayne said. "I can't speak to that. But I'm sure they followed departmental guidelines."

My finely honed crapometer, garnered during my days as a legitimate, licensed private investigator went off. Cops were as thorough as they could be, but that wasn't always supremely thorough—that was why private investigators could stay in business in the first place. It was understandable: a city the size of Chicago has an enormous caseload, detectives are always buried in work, and the investigations get triaged pretty severely. The preponderance of evidence, absence of witnesses, and Luther's status as an ex-con would have made this case a slam dunk, a low priority—and most of the time, the cops would have been right. Once the evidence was all taken and dissected and duly reported upon, as far as the police were concerned, they had their man. And there was already a mountain of fresh justice waiting to be pursued on behalf of new victims. Even the most dedicated and sincere police detective could understandably have dropped the ball here.

"Sure," Luther said. He sat back down again and said, "I'm done."

The judge looked at the clock and asked, "Mister Tremont, do you have any further witnesses?"

Tremont listened to something his assistant whispered and rose. "Your Honor, the prosecution rests."

"Then so will we," she said. "Mister Luther, the defense can begin its case in the morning. I remind the jury that the details of this case are confidential and not to be discussed or disclosed. We will reconvene here at 9 a.m."

"All rise," the bailiff said, and we did as the judge left the room.

I frowned as Luther was escorted out.

Something did not add up here.

If Luther had been a professional tough, a little guy like Curtis Black wouldn't have a prayer against him. I had been around enough tough guys to size Luther up. I wouldn't want to take him on in muscle-powered combat if I could avoid it, not even now with all the extra physical stuff the Winter Knight's mantle had given me. Doesn't matter how much you bench press, some people are damned dangerous in a fight, and you're a fool to take unnecessary chances against them. Luther struck me as one of those men.

Also, Tremont was way too young a kid to be pulling a high-profile murder case like this one. This was the kind of flashy prosecution DAs loved to showboat. Killers brought to justice, the system working, that kind of thing. They certainly didn't hand the case off to some kid straight out of law school. Which meant that the old hands in Chicago thought that something about this case stunk to high heaven as well.

I didn't know the law really well, but I have a doctorate in the parts of Chicago that never showed up on the evening news. If Luther was telling the truth, then Curtis Black couldn't have been human.

Problem was, most humans didn't know that. Even if Luther was telling the truth about Black, he wasn't going to get a fair shake from Chicago's justice system. Hell's bells, the cop acquainted with him wasn't even giving him much. Nobody was going to go to bat for him.

Unless I did it.

He was a father. For his kids' sake, I wanted answers.

I glanced at the clock as I filed out with the rest of the jury. Nine tomorrow morning. That gave me just under sixteen hours to do what wizards do best.

I left, and began meddling.

"WELL?" I ASKED the rather large wolf after he had been casting around the alley for a while.

He gave me an irritated look. He sat, and after a few seconds, shimmered and resumed the form of Will Borden, crouched naked on the dirty concrete. "Harry, you are not helping."

"Did you find anything or not?" I asked.

"This isn't as easy as it looks," he said. "Look, man, when I'm wolf, I've got a wolf's sense of smell—but I don't have a wolf's freaking brain. I've been learning how to sort out signals from the noise, but it's freaking hard. I've been doing this since my freshman year, and I could follow a hot trail, but you're asking me to sift background. I don't even know if a real wolf could do it."

I looked around the alley where Luther had beaten Black to death with a bowling pin. It had been nearly a year to the day since the murder. There was nothing dramatic to suggest a man had died here, and the bloodstains had long since faded into unrecognizability with the rest of the grunge. We were far enough down the alley to be out of sight of the street except for a slim column of space that cars crossed in under a second. "Yeah, that was a long shot anyway."

"You going to wizard up some information?"

"After this long, there's nothing left," I said. "Too many rains, too many sunrises. Not even Molly could get much."

"Then what are we going to do?"

"Get furry again. We might be here a while."

He frowned. "Why?"

"I think the girl might come by in the next few hours."

"Why?"

I shrugged a shoulder. "Let's assume Luther's telling the truth."

"Sure."

"This little guy grabs a little girl and drags her into the alley. Luther jumps him from behind and gets thrown into a wall. Fights him, hard, and beats him to death with a bowling pin. What can we deduce?"

"That Black was stronger than normal and tougher than normal," Will said. "Some kind of supernatural."

I nodded. "A predator. Maybe a ghoul or something."

"Yeah. So?"

"So a predator, operating in the middle of a town? They don't tend to openly grab little girls off the street, because someone might see it happen."

"Like Luther."

"Like Luther. But this guy did. He didn't go after a transient sleeping in an abandoned building, or someone wandering down a dark alley to buy some drugs, a prostitute, any of the usual targets. He went with something dicier. He's going to do that, he's going to cut down on every random factor he can."

"You think he stalked her."

I nodded. "Stalked her, learned her pattern, and was waiting for her."

Will squinted up and down the alley. "Why do you think that?"

"It's how something from Winter would do it," I said. "How I would take someone in a busy part of town, if I had to."

"Well. That's not creepy or anything, Harry."

I showed my teeth. "Not much difference between wolves and sheepdogs, Will. You should know."

He nodded. "So we wait here and see if she's still going by?"

"Figure if she still goes by here, she'll do it fast and she'll be worried. Should make her stand out."

"You know what else stands out on a busy Chicago street? A timber wolf."

"Thought of that," I said, and produced a roll of fabric from my duster's large pockets.

"You're kidding," Will said.

I smiled.

"And what's in the guitar case?"

I smiled wider.

A FEW MINUTES later, I was sitting on the sidewalk with my back against a building, with an old secondhand guitar in my lap, the case open beside me with a handful of a change and an old wadded dollar bill in it. Will settled down beside me, wearing a service dog's jacket, resting his chin on his front paws. He made a little groaning sound.

"It'll be fine, boy."

Will narrowed his eyes.

"Just keep your nose open," I said, and started playing.

I started with the Johnny Cash version of "Hurt," which was pretty simple. I sang along with it. I'm not good, but I can hit the notes and keep the rhythm going, so it more or less worked out. I followed it up with "Behind Blue Eyes," which gets a little harder, and then "Only Happy When It Rains." Then I followed it up with "House of the Rising Sun," and completely mangled "Stairway to Heaven."

There wasn't a ton of foot traffic on a weekday evening on this street, not in a fairly brisk late March, but nobody really looked at me twice. I made about two and a half bucks in change the first hour. The life of a musician is not easy. A patrol car went by, and a cop gave me the stink-eye, but he didn't stop and roust me. Maybe he had things to do.

The light started fading from the sky, and I was repeating my limited set for the fifth or sixth time when I started to think about giving up. The girl, if she was still following the same pattern, definitely wouldn't be running around town alone after it became fully dark.

I was singing about how you'd get the message by the time I'm through when Will suddenly lifted his head, his eyes focused.

I followed the direction of his gaze and spotted a girl of about the right age getting off of a bus. She started walking right away, down the street, though she stayed on the other side, directly toward the El station a block away.

"There we go," I said. "Kid walking a regular route alone gets jumped in Chicago, kid's probably using public transit, running on a schedule. Makes her real predictable. Perfect mark for a predator."

Will made a low growling sound.

"I think I'm kinda smart, yeah," I said to him. "Get her scent?"

Will nudged me with his shoulder and growled again.

I frowned and looked around until I spotted a rather large and rough looking man descending from the bus at the last second before it left for the next stop. He started down the sidewalk, in pursuit of the girl. He wasn't maniacally focused on her or anything, but he wasn't moving like someone coming home tired after a day of work, either. I recognized his pace, his stance, his tension, just as Will had. He was a predator in covert pursuit of his prey.

Worse, he had a smart phone. His thumbs were rapping over it as he walked after the girl.

"Damn," I said. "Whoever Black was, he was connected. I'm on the creep. You stick with the girl."

Will gave me one brief, incredulous look.

"I'm six-nine and scarred, you're furry and cute. She's eleven, she's going to like you."

Will gave me a flat look, his gold eyes utterly unamused. On a wolf, that's unsettling.

"I don't know," I said. "Wag your tail and paw your nose or something. Go!"

I'll give Will this much, he knows when actions matter more than questions. He took off at once, vanishing into the oncoming evening.

Meanwhile, I put my guitar in the case, set it back into the alley, rose, and focused my will and my attention on the thug. Wizards and modern technology don't get on well, and nothing dies as fast as cell phones when a wizard means to shut them down. I gathered up enough power to get the job done without taking out the lights on the whole block, flicked a finger at the man pacing the girl, and murmured, "Hexus."

A wave of disruptive energy washed out across the street and over the man and his smart phone. There was a little flash of light and a shower of sparks from the phone, and the man flinched and dropped the device. Most people would have stared at it or looked wildly around. This guy did neither. He sank into a defensive crouch and started scanning his surroundings with wide eyes.

He knew he was being threatened, which meant he had some kind of idea that a wizard might be about. That meant he was no mere thug. He was clued in enough to the supernatural world to know the players and how they might operate. That meant he was elite muscle, and there were only so many players who he might be working for.

I checked the street, hurried through an opening in traffic, and went straight for him. He spotted me in under a second and ran without hesitation, both of which impressed me with his judgment—but he took off after the girl, which meant that he wasn't giving up, either. I swerved to pursue him, leaped and pulled my knees up to my chin in the air, hitting the hood of a blue Buick with my hands as I flew over it, and came down still running.

We rounded a corner, and I understood what was happening.

The thug I was pursuing wasn't the grabber. He was just riding drag, making sure the girl didn't bolt back the way she came. I saw the girl ahead, being hurried into a doorway by three more men, and my guy poured it on when he saw them.

I slowed down a little, taking stock. The goons ahead had seen me coming behind their buddy, and hands were going into coats. I flung myself into the doorway of an office supply store, now closed for the evening, and the thugs all hustled through their own door, without producing guns on the street.

Suited me. I had been hoping to get them somewhere out of the way anyhow.

I waited until they were inside, gave them a five count, and then paced down the street. The door they'd gone through belonged to a small nightclub. A sign, hanging up on the door, read "Closed for Remodeling."

The door was locked.

It was also made of glass.

I smiled.

I HUFFED AND I puffed and I blew the door in with a pretty standard blast of telekinetic force. I tugged my sleeve up to reveal the shield bracelet I'd thrown together out of a strip of craft copper and carefully covered with the appropriate defensive runes and sigils. I channeled some of my will down into the bracelet, and the runes hissed to life, spilling out green-gold energy and the occasional random spark.

"All right, people!" I called into the club as I stepped through the door. "You know who I am. I'm here for the girl. Let her go, or so help me God I will bring this building down around your ears." I wouldn't, not while the girl was still in here, but they didn't know that.

There was silence for a long moment. And then music started

playing from deeper inside the club. "Bad Romance" by Lady Gaga.

"Okay," I muttered. "Have it your way."

I advanced into the darkened club, my shield bracelet throwing out a faint haze of light from the runes—just enough to keep me from bumping into walls. I went through the entry hall, past a collection window where I supposed cover fees would be paid, to double doors that opened onto the bar and dance floor.

I raised my left arm as if wielding an actual shield, the bracelet glowing, and stepped forward into the club.

The little girl was sitting in a booth against the far wall. The four thugs were fanned out on either side of her, guns in hand but pointing at the floor. Sitting with the little girl in the booth was the ADA's pretty assistant. When I came through the door, she lifted a hand, clicked a remote, and Lady Gaga's voice cut off in the midst of wanting my bad romance.

"Far enough," the woman said. "It would be a shame if someone panicked and this situation devolved. Innocents could be hurt."

I stopped. "Who are you?" I asked.

"Tania Raith," she replied, and gave me a rather dizzying smile.

House Raith was the foremost house of the White Court of Vampires. They were seducers, energy drainers, and occasionally a giant pain in the ass. The White Court was headed up by Lara Raith, the uncrowned queen of vampires, and one of the more dangerous persons I'd ever met. She wielded enormous influence in Chicago, maybe as much as the head of the Chicago outfit, Gentleman Johnnie Marcone, gangster lord of the mean streets.

I made damned sure to keep track of the thugs and precisely what they were doing with their hands as I spoke. "You know who I am. You know what I can do. Let her go."

She rolled her eyes, and spun a finger through fine, straight black hair. "Why should I?"

"Because you know what happened the last time some vampires abducted a little girl and I decided to take her back."

Her smile faltered slightly. As it should have. When bloodsucking Red Court had taken my daughter, I took her back—and murdered every single one of them in the process. The entire species.

I'm not a halfway kind of person.

"Lara likes you," Tania said. "So I'm going to give you a chance to walk out of here peacefully. This is a White Court matter."

I grunted. "Black was one of yours?"

"Gregor Malvora," she confirmed. "He was Malvora scum, but he was our scum. Lara can't allow the mortal buck who did it to go unpunished. Appearances. You understand."

"I understand that Gregor abducted a child. He did everything he could to frighten her, and then fed on her fear. If Luther hadn't killed him, what would he have done to the little girl?"

"Oh, I shudder to think," Tania replied. "But that is, after all, what they do."

"Not in my town," I said.

She lifted her eyebrows. "I believe Baron Marcone has a recognized claim on this city. Or am I mistaken?"

"I've got enough of a claim to make me tickled to dump you and your brute squad into the deepest part of Lake Michigan if you don't give me back the girl."

"I think I'll keep her for a day or two. Just until the trial is over. That will be best for everyone involved."

"You'll give her to me. Now."

"So that she can testify and exonerate Mister Luther?" Tania asked. "I think not. I have no desire to harm this child, Dresden. But if you try to take her from me, I will reluctantly be forced to kill her."

The girl's lower lip trembled, and tears started rolling down her face. She didn't sob. She did it all in silence, as if desperate to draw no attention to herself.

Yeah, okay.

I wasn't going to stand here and leave a little kid to a vampire's tender mercies.

"Chicago is a mortal town," I said. "And mortal justice is going to be served."

"Oh my God," Tania said, rolling her eyes. "Did you really just say that out loud? You sound like a comic book."

"Comic book," I said. "Let's see. Do I go for 'Hulk smash,' or 'It's clobberin' time . . .'"

Tania tensed, though she tried to hide it, and her voice came out in a rush. "Bit of a coincidence, don't you think, that Chicago's only professional wizard wound up on that jury?"

I tilted my head and frowned. She was right. In fact, the more I thought about it, the more this felt like a turf war. "Oh. Oh, I get it. Luther was one of Marcone's soldiers."

"So loyal he went to prison for ten years rather than inform on Marcone," Tania confirmed. "Or maybe just smart enough to know what would happen to him if he did. He went straight after he got out, but . . ."

"When he got in trouble, Marcone stood up for one of his own," I said. "He pulled strings to get me on the jury."

"Luther was getting nailed to a wall," Tania said. "Marcone controls crime, but Lara has a lot of say over the law, these days. I suppose he thought someone like you might be the only chance Luther had. Gutsy of him, to try to make a catspaw of Harry Dresden. I hear you don't like that."

Dammit. Marcone had put me where there'd been a guy getting fast-tracked to an unjust sentence and known damned well how I would react. He could have asked me for help, but I'd have told him to take a flying . . . leap. And he'd have known that. So he set it up without me knowing.

Or hell. He and Mab had been in cahoots lately. Maybe he'd asked her to arrange it. This had her fingerprints all over it.

"Tania," I said. "It's hard for me to tell with vampires, but I'm guessing you're pretty new to this work."

She winked at me. "Let's just say that I'm old enough to know better and young enough not to care." She picked up a drink from the table. "This one is over, Dresden. You can't do anything here. You can't produce evidence in the trial—not as a juror. You can't get to Luther to tell him you found the little girl—and even if you could, you aren't taking her away from us. Not until it's too late. The girl is the only evidence that Black wasn't a poor victim, and I have her. This one is done. Marcone lost the round. I win." She winked at me. "What does Marcone mean to you? You don't owe him anything. Why not sit down, have a drink, help me celebrate?"

I stared at Tania for a minute. "No," I said quietly. "You just don't get it. This isn't about Lara and Marcone anymore. It's not even really about Luther." Then I looked at the little girl. "Honey," I asked, making sure my voice was a lot gentler. "Do you want to go home?"

She looked at me. She was cute enough, for a kid her age, with caramel skin and big green eyes. She nodded, very hesitantly, flinching as if she thought Tania might hit her.

"Okay," I said.

Tania was staring at me as though she couldn't quite grasp what was happening. But her voice was harder when she said, "Gentlemen? The wizard doesn't like the carrots. It's time for the stick."

To my right, from behind the bar, another four men rose. They were holding short-barreled shotguns. To my left, from the bathrooms, another four thugs appeared, clutching various long guns.

"I'll count to three," Tania said. "Boys, when I get to three, kill him."

Crap. They were flanking me. My shield was excellent, but it was not omni-directional. No matter which way I turned it, one or more groups of thugs would have a shot at my unprotected back.

"One," Tania said, smiling. "Two."

"Comic book, huh?" I said. "Have it your way."

"Three," she chirped.

Guns swiveled to me. A dozen men took aim.

"Hexus!" I snarled, unleashing a wave of disruptive energy.

And every light in the place blew out in a shower of sparks, plunging the club into darkness.

Guns started going off, but only from the most confident or stupid gunmen, so I wasn't cut to ribbons. I was already moving. Hitting a moving target isn't easy, not even when it's fairly close. Hitting one in the dark is even harder. Hitting one moving in sporadic flashes of light is harder yet.

I got lucky, or none of them did, however you want to think of it, and I got to the thugs to one side of Tania in one piece.

One of them got off a shot at the sound, but I caught the round on my shield, and the resulting shower of sparks showed the men on my flanks that I was among their compatriots, and no one shot at my back. I knew Lara hired almost exclusively from former military, mostly Marines. Men like that don't shoot their buddies.

I dropped the shield and threw a punch at the guy in front of me. Ever since I'd started working for the Queen of Air and Darkness, I'd been stronger than the average wizard. Or the average champion weightlifter, for that matter—and I knew how to throw a punch. I connected with the man's jaw, hard, and shouted, "BAM!" as I did.

The thug reeled back, his legs going wobbly and useless as he ragdolled to the floor. I threw a stomping kick toward the belly of the guy next to him, shouting, "POW!" I hit him in the dark, somewhere more or less near his belly. His gun went off randomly as he was lifted off the floor and thrown ten feet back into a wall. He was trying to scream, breathlessly. I winced. I hadn't meant to hit him *there*, but those are the breaks.

I raised my shield again and dropped, just as the bad guys with shotguns realized that I didn't have any of their buddies standing near me. I trusted the shield and turned my face away from the blinding shower of green-gold sparks it sent flying up as buckshot hammered into it. The copper band got hot on my wrist, even as I flung my right hand out toward the group of goons by the bathroom and shouted, *"Forzare!"*

Raw telekinetic force hit three of them—one was the guy from the street, who again impressed me with his smarts by diving to one side, out of the wave of energy. As shotguns pounded my shield, he slid to a stop with an automatic braced in both hands, took a breath, and aimed carefully, only moving his finger to the trigger after he had his sights lined up on me.

Crap. To steal from Brust, no matter how turbo-charged the wizard, someone with brains, guts, and a .45 can seriously cramp his style.

Fortunately, I wasn't in this fight alone.

I'd been counting on Will to join in at the right moment, and he didn't let me down. Two hundred pounds of gray-brown timber wolf (wearing a service dog cape) hit the Smart Gunman at a full sprint, bowling him over. A flash of white fangs sent the gun flying.

Total elapsed time since I'd killed the lights? Maybe three and a half seconds.

Will threw himself into the guys I'd knocked around by the bathrooms, and I turned to discover that I'd been right about Tania. She was new to this kind of game. She'd been sitting there with a stunned look on her face at the abruptness of the violence.

I flung myself into the booth with her, getting as close as I could, wrapping my left arm around her neck hard enough to pull her head in against my body and still have my shield ready to stop more gunfire—but the Smart Gunman screamed, "Check fire, check fire!" the second I did.

The shooting stopped. There was an abrupt silence in the club, which was filled with the sharp scent of gunpowder.

For a second, I felt a cool, sweet sensation flooding into me. I realized that Tania had slipped a hand beneath my shirt and was running her fingertips over my stomach.

If anyone ever tells you that being fed on by a vampire of the White Court is not a big deal, they're lying. It's ecstasy and heroin and sex and chocolate all rolled into one, and that's just the foreplay.

So I stopped her by tightening my grip on her until it threatened to break her neck. Tania let out a little yelp and whipped her hand away from my skin.

I met the wide eyes of the little girl and said, "Hold on, honey. I'm going to take you home in just a second."

"You can't!" Tania said.

I scowled and flicked her skull with the forefinger of my free hand in annoyance. "Wow, you're new at this," I said, panting. Five seconds of combat is enough cardio to last a while. "How old are you, kid?"

"I'm twenty," she said, her teeth clenched with discomfort, "and I am *not* a child."

"Twenty," I said. "No wonder Lara sent a babysitter along with you."

Just then, the room flooded with green chemical light. I eyed the Smart Gunman, who had just fired up a chemical glowstick from a pocket. I nodded my head at him, holding it a moment, and said, "I'm Dresden."

He pushed himself up from the floor with his left arm, holding his right in close to his side. It bore long lacerations, and the blood looked black in the green light. He nodded back to me and said, warily, "Riley."

I twisted my upper body just enough to drag Tania around a little. She let out a squeaking sound. "Can you see the score here, Riley?"

He studied the room, wincing, and said, "Yeah. How you want to play it?"

"Guns down," I said. "Me, the wolf, the girl, and Miss Raith here will walk out. No one comes after us. Once we're on the street, I'll let her go."

He stared at me, and I could see the wheels turning. I didn't like that. The guy had been too capable to give him time to work something out.

"You boys just gave me a twenty-one gun salute, and the front door to the club was broken open, Riley," I said. "Police response time around here is about four minutes. How long do you think it will take someone to call it in?"

Riley grimaced. "Give me your word."

"You have it," I said.

"Okay," he said. He looked around the room and said, "Stand down. We're going to let them leave."

"Damn you, Riley!" Tania snarled.

I pressed the still uncomfortably hot copper bracelet against her ear, and she yipped. "Come on, Miss Raith," I said. I stood up, keeping her head locked in my arm. She could have made a fight of it. White Court vampires can be unbelievably strong, if only in bursts. She didn't seem up for a physical fight, but I wasn't taking chances. I moved carefully and kept my balance, ready to move instantly if she tried anything.

"Come on honey," I said to the little girl. I extended my free hand to her. "I'm going to take you home."

She stood up and reluctantly took my hand.

Will padded out of the shadows to walk on the other side of the girl, his teeth bared. On a wolf, that is an absolutely terrifying expression.

As I went by Riley, I asked, "Lara giving Tania here a lesson?"

"Something like that," he said. "You hurt her, things will have to get ugly."

"I get it," I said. "You'd have had me if I hadn't cheated."

"You aren't cheating, you aren't trying hard enough," he replied. "Another time, maybe."

"I hope not," I told him, sincerely.

And I walked out with a vampire in a headlock and a little girl overlapped in the protective shadows of a wizard and a werewolf, while Lara Raith's soldiers looked on.

"YOUR HONOR," THE foreman of the jury said to the judge. She paused to turn to me and give me a deadly glare, "After two days of deliberation, the jury has been unable to reach a unanimous verdict in the case."

Luther, lonely at his table, blinked and sat up straighter, his eyes opening wider.

The assistant DA made an almost identical expression. Beside him, Tania sat staring stonily forward, with her hair combed over her singed ear.

The judge eyed the jury box with weary resignation, and her gaze settled on me.

"What?" I said, and folded my arms. "I believed him."

She rubbed at her eyes with one hand and said something beneath her breath. I listened closely, which is much closer than most people can, and thought I heard her mutter, ". . . goddamned supernatural assholes . . ."

She lifted her eyes again and spoke in that rote-repetition voice. "That being the case, I have no choice but to find a mistrial. Mister Tremont, the prosecution's office will need to notify me about whether or not the people mean to continue pursuing this case against the defendant."

I eyed Tania, smiling.

If the White Court tried to push this trial again, I could produce the girl, Maria, as a witness. Maria was currently being watched by a number of werewolves and wasn't going to go anywhere. If they continued pushing Luther, I could drag their ugliness out into the light—

and if there was anything the White Court hated, it was looking ugly.

Tania gave me a sulking glance. Then she muttered something to Tremont, who blinked at her. They had a brief, heated discussion conducted entirely in whispers. Then Tremont looked back up at them. "Ah, your Honor. The state would like to drop all charges."

"It would?" the judge asked. Then she rolled her eyes and said, "Of course it would. All right people, justice is served, court is adjourned." She banged her gavel down half-heartedly and rose. We all stood up as she left the courtroom, and then we began filing out.

Luther sat there dazed as the bailiff approached and removed his handcuffs. Then he was buried by a pair of quietly squealing children who piled onto him, and were shortly joined by a woman with tears in her eyes. I heard him start laughing as he hugged them.

I left, because there was something in my eyes.

Outside, in the parking lot, someone approached me and I felt a tug at my sleeve. It took me a second to recognize the judge in her civilian clothes—a plain pair of slacks and a white shirt.

"Let me guess," she said. "Someone found the girl."

"The girl from what's-his-name's testimony?" I asked, guilelessly.

"And if the girl had gotten up in front of everyone and answered questions, it would have made things awkward for whoever was behind Black. Am I right?"

I scratched at my nose with one finger and said, "Maybe."

She snorted and turned to walk away. "Worst jurist ever."

"Thanks," I said.

She stopped and looked at me over her shoulder with a faint smile. "You're welcome."

I hung around long enough to see Luther leaving the building with his family, a free man.

Maybe Will had been right.

Justice served.

SHAWN SPEAKMAN

I write short stories for many different reasons.

In the case of "The Dead's Revenant," it's because I needed help with my next two novels.

Tathal Ennis is a terribly complex wizard. He has been alive a very long time and is seeking answers to questions that no human has ever truly actively sought. I knew he would make a cameo in my next novel, *The Everwinter Wraith*, with a much larger role in its sequel, *The Splintered King*, but when I came to his cameo, I didn't know him well enough. Actually, I didn't know him at all beyond his function for the overall story.

I decided I had to take a break from writing *The Everwinter Wraith* to better explore the ruthless wizard of the Fallen Court.

I learned more than I bargained for.

Here is his first short story, "The Dead's Revenant."

And let the heavens fall . . .

THE DEAD'S REVENANT

Shawn Speakman

Viewing the village of South Cadbury, Tathal Ennis intuited its death.

It was a familiar knowing. Death had drawn him like iron to a lodestone for the entirety of his long life, and the future had always been his to see. Now he peered down on the village and knew its death better than even those who inhabited it—its bloody past, its dying present, and its ill-fated future. Old Ellis sitting at his shadowy corner table in Camelot Pub as he did nightly, eyes bloodshot, consuming death in every pint. Widow Cora and twin spinster Eleanor rocking beside their hearth, the former's husband long in his box but both women readying to join him with every creak of their chairs. Young Tim Becket tossing in sleep, his nightmares darker than the purpling new bruises that mingled with old yellow and old green, all delivered by a grandfather who abhorred weakness.

Even Ruindolon Arl, the long-lived Elf who had managed to avoid discovery, lived the death of heartbreak. Every minute. Passing. Failing. Exiled from his home, he experienced a slower death than his human neighbors, but death all the same.

Death existed in the very bones of South Cadbury.

And Tathal Ennis would possess that death at life's expense.

South Cadbury was one of the oldest villages in Britain, and its soil had known more blood than even the legends recounted. He knelt, touched the gritty ground, and closed his eyes, sending spell-heightened senses into the land—searching for one death so dark it stained Britain deeper than all others. It was here he would call that death forth.

And he sensed it was nearby.

With a sickle moon slicing the sky, Tathal stood and strode toward the village, unsure exactly where the grave existed but satisfied nonetheless. He breathed in the air's hint of lavender. He had smelled it before, on this very path, centuries earlier. That visit had brought him in search of the Archstone, the rarest of keys, needed to expose the secrets of Stonehenge. While he had not found the relic within South Cadbury, he always recalled sensing the darkness buried nearby—a suspicion of its source seeded and taken root. Now he hoped that past would bear fruit in the present.

He had now come for a lesser talisman, a soul, and a victim. They would not be all three found in one.

As stunted trees bore witness to his passage, the magic of his birthright tingled, warning of danger. It did not take long to locate it. Three pairs of lantern eyes peered from the gloom, watching with feral interest. Tathal understood their nature. He too felt more comfortable hunting at night. The lead dog growled low. Tathal slowed and glared at the brazen affront. With a last look, the dogs vanished like smoke on a breeze. Like most night creatures astute to his passage, they wanted no part of Tathal Ennis. They knew death better than most beings— the night filled with it—and they would not risk their lives against a creature they sensed would deliver it all too easily.

He continued unimpeded and took in the breadth of the land beyond South Cadbury. The beauty of southwest Britain had become song over the ages. He did not need to enact the magic of his halfbreed blood to see every aspect of verdant hills rolling into the distance. The world turned. The night passed. And, not knowing who entered it, the village slept as it had for centuries.

Most of it, anyway.

The warm glow of lights within Camelot Pub beckoned him onward. It was not yet midnight, and several patrons would still be awake with the last of their pints.

Tathal would start his search now.

When he entered the pub, curious eyes quickly ignored him. He did not blame them. He knew the story of those in his presence, and at their core they could sense some truth about him. Drinkers mostly. Six of them. There were four American tourists as well, arrogant with imagined superiority.

A barmaid, whose most attractive days were behind her, served them all and, sitting at the small bar, the owner who had slept with her once but remembered only how lackluster it had been.

And then there was the drunk.

Old Ellis sat in the corner, where Tathal had divined he would be. He walked to the old man's table, standing over him.

And waited.

"Bugger off," the old man slurred, gray-grizzled cheeks drooping.

Tathal willed a gold coin into his hand. He set its discernible weight on the table.

"I am looking for information."

Old Ellis glanced at the coin with bleary eyes. He then took in the visitor, seeing him for the first time. Any light at newfound wealth died in his eyes then. He grunted and looked into the bottom of his pint.

Like the dogs, Old Ellis knew when not to challenge.

"Sit then," he snorted. "The Queen cares not."

Tathal pulled a chair over. "I have been led to believe that you are an expert of these parts, and South Cadbury in particular," he said. Pride, even the pride of a drunk, had its uses. "There have been many battles in this part of Britain. Hard won. Lives lost." He paused but the other did not speak. "Those lives lose a great deal they can't take with them when they pass beyond. The armor they wore. And the weapons they carried."

"What are you looking for?" Old Ellis asked.

"I seek a sword. Ancient. Millennia old."

"Do I look like the owner of an antique shop, *friend*?" Old Ellis grunted.

"My path has brought me to you," Tathal said. "If you do not know what I need, then you know who does know."

"South Cadbury is tiny. Everyone knows everyone. Secrets aren't secret here."

"So who do *you* know that can aid my search?"

Old Ellis fingered his new coin for the first time. And remained silent. Tathal waited. Drunks were more often than not obstinate folk, their wits vanishing with drink.

But greed's thirst had no slaking and even the most inebriated soul had a price.

Tathal pulled another coin free.

"Yes?"

"I know of the blade," Old Ellis admitted, eyeing the coin but taking a drink instead. "Everyone does."

"Go on."

"That bitch," the old man mumbled. He lifted the glass again to cracked lips. "Cora. And her sister, Eleanor. The bitches of Cadbury, I calls them. They have a sword. Hangs over their fireplace. A terrible-looking thing. Long broadsword. Old. Cannot say if they still have it. Been many years since I entered that damn house, I tells you." Old Ellis gave Tathal a watery look. "It's like a damn family member, that sword. They love and polish it. I don't see them parting with it, if that is what you are thinking."

"I have a way of being persuasive."

Old Ellis fingered his second coin. "Aye, you do."

"How do you know of it?"

"The sword?" Old Ellis croaked a snort. "Let's just say Eleanor and me had a thing going. Until that bitch dog Cora helped end it. Said I drank too much. Convinced her sister I was no good. Screw them both, I says."

Tathal nodded. "Well, I believe you have been very helpful."

"Piss off then," Old Ellis growled, emptying his pint, ready for another one with his newfound fortune. "And tell that old bitch Cora I'll see her in Hell."

Tathal stood and walked away. He would not follow Old Ellis's request. Honey caught more flies than vinegar.

And old women loved to be flies.

He made his way back to the bar. And waited.

"What can I get you?"

Tathal turned. Robin Lindholm stood behind him, bar apron tied tightly over round hips and a scarf trying its best to hide her ample bosom. It failed. With his eyes, he traced the curve of the woman's lips and smiled. She had eyes that did not flinch from the death in his. Women were like that sometimes. They courted death for the excitement. She was no great beauty but that did not matter. When his future called, Tathal answered.

And she possessed knowledge he needed.

"Good evening. Miss?"

She showed her wedding band. "Married. But you knew that already."

"It is always wise to check before falling too hard."

"A charmer, huh? Just my luck. And here I thought tonight would be boring," she said with a short laugh that took a decade off her face. "You are not from South Cadbury. A tourist here to see the Camelot and all of its glory?"

"No, although if my instincts are correct I will be walking there this night to see what might be left."

"It is a pleasant evening for that."

"It is a pleasant evening for *many* things," he said, winking.

She blushed but barely. She was too far from maidenhood to turn crimson. "What can I get you?" she repeated.

"The world. For now though, you will suffice."

She chuckled. "A charmer indeed. I'll see what I can do. In the meantime, I'll bring you a water and a list of what we still have available tonight."

Her hips swaying with an exaggeration he had not observed earlier in the night and undoubtedly her husband had not seen in many years, she left him then. Tathal watched her go and grinned, amused.

Ever since he had been a boy, the universe had put possibilities before him. It took boldness to seize those moments and use them to whatever end he desired.

And he had gotten good at squeezing the life from them.

Robin Lindholm was one. She too would die, of course.

And like the rest in the village of South Cadbury, all too soon.

HE WAS WAITING for Tim Becket when the boy stepped free of his home.

After delaying in order to be the last patron at the Camelot Pub and seducing the barmaid on the very table where he had sat with Old Ellis, Tathal had spent the rest of the night wandering South Cadbury. It had been many years since he had done so, and much had changed. Newer buildings had been built among the old. The population had grown, if barely. The people were as proud as ever—in their care of the small village and one another. And when the morning began to chase the last of night's darkness west, Tathal sensed the universe had chosen that the village should die before it saw another dawn.

Leaning against the dilapidated home, he watched Tim Becket creep out the door, the snoring sounds of his grandfather, Old Ellis, rumbling from within.

The boy startled like a fawn and froze when he saw Tathal.

"There is no need to worry," Tathal said. "I am a friend."

Tim Becket looked at him like the dogs had. Not surprising, he thought. Fresh bruises darkened the other's right cheek. The boy knew physical abuse at the hands of family, the slowest kind of death.

"I understand you know South Cadbury better than anyone," Tathal said. "And I am in need of a guide."

"I should go," the boy said, already reaching back toward the door.

"Where to?" he said, folding his arms over his chest. "Back to a beating?"

Steel and a flash of anger entered the boy's eyes. They vanished quickly and the meek child returned. Tim Becket stood between two worlds, uncertain, but he did not flee. Tathal admired that.

"I have been hit. Many times," Tathal continued. "Often as a boy even. I had a mean father. He hated me. Still don't know why."

The boy remained quiet, eyes still wary.

"What is your name?"

"Tim," the boy answered. "Tim Becket."

"That is a strong name. And a prouder surname in these parts," Tathal said, looking up into the morning sky. "Becket is the name of one of the most powerful archbishops in the history of the Catholic Church. He was Thomas. A defiant man. Murdered by knights of the King of England. For believing he was above the law of the throne, his law being that of the Church." Tathal paused and smiled. "Ironic that the God he put before all others did not come to his aid when the swords bled him of life."

"I am related to him in some way," Tim Becket said, frowning. "Not sure how."

"Are you ready to be strong? Like your forebearer?"

Tim nodded, though his eyes still held mistrust. "What do you want?"

"As I said earlier, I have been told that you know South Cadbury better than anyone," Tathal said. "I am here to see an older woman named Cora. She has a twin sister named Eleanor, I believe."

"The widow Cora?" the boy asked. "She lives not far from here."

"Can you show me?"

"What's in it for me?"

Tathal had to suppress a grin. The boy was quick. World smart. The kind of intelligence that came from a lifetime of pain and misery. In another century in another village, Tathal might have even spared the boy's life. After all, he had taken on a number of apprentices over the years, often young boys and girls who could be molded into whatever instrument Tathal needed to fulfill his long quest. But that time had long since vanished and the needs of his immediate future did not require a henchboy.

Instead, he reached into the folds of his long jacket, pulled forth a vial, and showed it to the boy.

"Do you know what belladonna is?"

Tim Becket shook his head.

"Do you wish to be free of his fists? Free of the pain? The tears?" Tathal didn't have to say whose fists, whose pain, whose tears.

The boy gazed at the vial and its contents, the dark liquid within negating the sunlight that had just risen high enough to be felt.

"What will it do?"

"You know what it will do, Tim Becket," Tathal insisted. "Do not be coy with me. You are too smart a lad to do that."

The boy stepped near. He took the vial. It was a dark stain of menace in his pale hand. In many ways, Tathal thought, the vial's color matched the death that marked Tim Becket's swollen cheek.

Sometimes even death had a sense of irony.

"I leave it in your capable hands to choose," Tathal said. "Now. Show me where Cora lives. The morning passes and the day will not wait."

Tim Becket hid the vial in his pants pocket and turned. "This way," he said.

Tathal strolled after the departing boy, easily keeping up with him. He marveled at the resiliency of those in pain. The human soul was capable of surviving suffering of the greatest sort. But few possessed the courage to throw off pain's shackles. That too was a part of the human condition.

Tathal had given Tim Becket the key to undo those shackles. But the boy still had to place the key in the lock and turn it.

Tathal thought he would.

Old Ellis would likely not live out the night.

And unlike the rest of the people in South Cadbury, his death would not be at Tathal's behest.

WIDOW CORA LIVED in the middle of South Cadbury, in a home as old as the village's origins.

After Tim Becket had shown him to the proper door and left with his vial of poison, Tathal knocked. And waited. He heard stirring on the other side but it was soft, like old bones moving beneath a heavy quilt. When the door opened, Tathal found he was staring into the blue eyes of a woman who appeared to be as old as sin. She did not have much time to live. Long months. Or short years. White hair sat bundled in a ratty bun upon her head, and wrinkles had eroded her thin face toward hollowness, her lips pursed in a permanent state of distaste and disappointment.

Hunched against her own mortality, she glared at Tathal as if the seconds he had already stolen from her were her precious last.

"Yes?" the old woman asked impatiently.

"Are you the Lady Cora?"

"I don't know about the lady part. But I'm Cora."

Tathal brought the charm to his smile. "We don't know one another, bu—"

"Of course we don't know one another," she snapped. "I would remember you. Yes, yes?"

"Direct. My kind of woman," Tathal purred, hating her but hiding it. "To the point then. I am here in search of a very rare sword. I have long known about its existence but not its location. That search has brought me here, to your very door."

"There is no sword here," Cora said bitingly. She moved to close the door. "Now good day to you."

Tathal stopped the door with a swift arm. "I saw a flicker of knowing in your eyes, Lady Cora. You know the sword of which I speak."

Fury filled the crone's face, an anger that shook her wrinkles.

"How *dare you* try to intimi—"

"Stop being an old bitch, Cora," a tired woman's voice said from inside the house. "You are being rude by not inviting him. So do that. Hear him. Then kick him out."

Cora's thin lips pulled back from yellowed teeth in a kind of snarl.

"Now, Cora," her sister insisted.

Clutching her blanket closer, Cora opened the door wide enough for entry. Tathal followed her into dim light. It was small and quaint like most old homes in this part of England—a lifetime of photos, paintings, and ancient-looking embroidered tapestries hung on the walls. A number of crosses also pointed at Tathal, while a large painting of Jesus Christ upon his killing cross hung over the fireplace. No sword was in sight. It was plain to see that these sisters were the devout. The pious. The righteous religious.

Several doorways led to other parts of the home. He doubted they were used much. Looking about the main living room, Tathal could tell the Catholic ornamentation was newer than the home's other memories. These two had come to their faith later in life. And they almost solely occupied this room.

Strange how becoming dust concerned no one's soul until life's eventual end.

Cora went to an empty rocking chair in one corner near the fireplace. Opposite her in her own rocking chair sat the mirror image of her twin.

"Good day to you, Lady Eleanor?" Tathal presumed.

"You have yet to give us your name?" Eleanor noted. While the first twin possessed downright crabbiness, the second gazed upon Tathal with an airy lightness that reminded him of the fey.

"Tathal Ennis. I'm pleased to make your acquaintance."

Cora scoffed. Amused by her sister's cantankerous mood, Eleanor returned her attention back to their visitor.

"Tell me of the sword you seek?" she asked.

Tathal did so. He had nothing to hide. He knew its general size and make. He knew who had carried it during the Battle of Camlann and who would carry it before the next dawn. The power Tathal possessed had confirmed the existence of the sword and that existence in South Cadbury. To say he knew more about the sword than anyone alive would have been a severe understatement.

When he had finished, Eleanor chewed her lower lip, thinking.

"We know of the sword," she said finally.

"The past is the past," Cora hissed with a fiery tone, age having not worn her down fully. "It should remain there, Sister."

"Sometimes, Lady Cora, the past is the key to the future," Tathal encouraged.

The old woman stared at him with flashing blue eyes. "The past is pain. Nothing more." Cora rose from her seat. "My sister will see you to the door."

Cora left, vanishing into another room. Tathal watched her go. He would hate to have to interrogate her; it was too early to begin the bloodshed. It may take him several hours yet to find the sword.

It would not do to draw too much attention to himself too soon.

"She has always been strong-willed," Eleanor said apologetically. "Not to her husband though. That bastard did as he pleased."

"Your sister is right. The past *is* pain," Tathal said, ignoring his own dark memories. "I do not care about marriages or husbands though. As I have said, the sword is important to me. To the world."

"How? It is a relic from a dead age. Useless, really."

"Oh, it is *quite* useful, I assure you."

Eleanor frowned, closely observing him. Tathal suddenly felt exposed, as if this woman was capable of peeling back his multifaceted layers to view the driven man the centuries had made.

Witches sometimes had that power.

"I see the look in your eye," Eleanor said, her demeanor suddenly matching her twin's. "I have seen that look before. In those consumed by a desire far beyond their reach. My sister's husband was one such man. Pain followed in its wake." She paused, considering. "If passion once put you on the path for this sword you seek, that passion has become fervor. Tathal Ennis, it is not my place to aid that kind of evil. Good day. The door is where you left it. I hope you consider my words, words from an old woman who has seen how intemperance can destroy lives."

"You are making a grave mistake, Lady Eleanor," Tathal growled, darkening. "I *will* possess the sword. And I *will* act by any and all means to learn its whereabouts . . . no matter the consequences to those I meet along the way."

Eleanor stopped rocking in her chair. Up until now their conversation had been light of bearing, filled with the banter of strangers. Tathal had changed that. She sensed the threat in his words; she weighed the danger against its validity.

Fear had its uses, after all.

"It was an heirloom," Eleanor answered, face pinched, the amusement once so alive in her eyes now gone cold before the man who would kill her if it meant gaining his prize. "And my sister sold it."

"To whom did she sell it?" Tathal pressed.

"The sword had belonged to his family. Her bastard of a husband. He was a nasty, ill-tempered man. While my sister hated him, she loved

533

him too. He prized the sword as an account of his family history and it sat over that fireplace. I always felt he adored it in a way that he never did my sister. Or God, for that matter. I hated that sword."

"Then you have no ties to it."

"No. Why is it so special to you?" Eleanor asked.

"It too is a part of my past. And more importantly, my future."

Eleanor nodded and took a sip of her tea. The fight was gone from her. "Then who am I to get in your way? Especially when you have . . . argued . . . your case so well. Cora sold the sword you described to pay for her husband's funeral."

Tathal kept his disappointment in check. The sword was not here. "Do they still have it?"

Eleanor shrugged. "Only they would know. And God, of course."

"I am not speaking to God. But soon. Soon."

Before she could utter anything, Tathal left the home. He sensed the twins no longer mattered; he had gained from them what the universe required. Sunshine became his companion even as he strode toward the church. He would not tarry. The universe had a way of intervening upon and undoing even the simplest and most sure plans. Now that he knew where the sword had gone, he would not be denied. Every life event led to the next. But others could see the possibilities of those events just as well as he and mold them like he could. And those powerful people were out there.

Wariness slowed him. Arrogance could kill. Irony had ever been an enemy, and his path led him to the heart of it. It was not chance that put him in direct confrontation with the disciples of his enemy.

With Saint Thomas a Becket Church.

TATHAL WAITED UNTIL the moon and stars held firm the heavens.

He walked through South Cadbury, the early night as pleasant as the previous had been. Having not grown up in Britain, Tathal could appreciate the land's beauty. It possessed magic—had since long before the days of Uther and Arthur—and that magic had created a proud people who protected its history and secrets with bravery born of cultural identity. It existed in the very foundation of its faith—a faith he now went to confront. A direct affront undoubtedly considered blasphemy by those who followed the Word and its hypocrisy.

The priests of Saint Thomas a Becket Church would do their best to maintain their secret. It would not matter. They did not understand they were blind.

And he was not.

Tathal continued his way southwest, uphill and beyond the tiny village. The Church of Saint Thomas a Becket sat against the night in the shadow of an ancient hillside fort, the remains reportedly the famous Camelot. As he grew closer to the church, he noticed flowers, bushes, and vines through the sparse trees, life that tried to beautify the harsh reality of the dead's province where timeworn tombstones broke the graveyard like shattered teeth. It was an interesting dichotomy, life and death so intertwined.

He paid the irony no mind. Instead, he focused on the present. He could not dismiss the Word entirely. There were other forces in the world—like the demon wizard Myrddin Emrys—capable of countering his. But he would not go into tonight risking failure by being a tourist. He would tread with absolute care.

The lights of the church drew him onward, a moth to the flame. He would not be burned though. He sent his magical halfbreed senses into the night.

There were people inside the church.

Two by his estimation.

Moving over the well-maintained grounds like a wraith, Tathal stepped up to the church's entrance and tried the door. It was not locked. He entered the small parish house of worship like he had so many other places during his long life—without sound.

He could just make out faint voices, those in earnest discussion.

The church was not large. Opposite from where Tathal stood, two men were talking in the chancel where a finely carved crucifixion formed a reredos below stained glass windows gone dark with the coming night. The older of the men had graying hair cut short and the fine clothing of a rector; the young man wore a simple suit lacking ornamentation that barely contained his strong broad shoulders.

Tathal strode past rows of pews toward the two men with confidence born of the knowledge that this was the exact place he was meant to be.

"Good evening," Tathal greeted.

Both men turned, the rector a bit startled and his companion solid as a rock.

"And to you, sir," the older man said. "What brings you to the Church of Saint Thomas a Becket this night?"

"I have come for answers," Tathal said simply.

"I pray I have the answers then," the rector said. It was clear Tathal's sudden appearance still unnerved him. "I am Reverend John de Brug, rector of this parish. And this young man is Churchwarden Peter Fursdon." He looked up toward the shadows. "We were just discussing some work that had been done to our ceiling. A church this old needs love more often with each passing century." He returned his gaze back to Tathal. "Well, what brings you to us this night, son? God is filled with possibilities and it is clear you require something of Him."

"I know possibilities and probabilities better than most," Tathal said, looking about the church as he walked toward the two men. The sword was not prominently featured on any of the walls. That would be too easy. "There is a high probability that a phone in this very church will begin ringing soon, faint but with authority on the other end. There is a probability, lesser than the first, that sirens will approach from the village proper, growing louder even as the phone remains faint." He returned his gaze back to the rector and stopped a dozen feet from him. "Still, an almost zero probability that you both survive this meeting. Although if you aid me, I promise at least one of you will."

Silence permeated the church. The reverend wrung his hands before him, a nervous tick of which he was likely unaware. "Who are you and what do you want?" he asked, all warmth gone from his voice.

"I am looking for something. I have been told that it is here."

The other man frowned. "I'm not sure I understand."

"Remember what I said when I walked in?" Tathal questioned. "Answers. The first answer I seek is in the form of a sword."

Reverend John de Brug and his churchwarden looked at one another, betraying their knowledge.

"Son, I do not understand what you mean," the rector lied.

"And it is best you leave now," Peter Fursdon said, stepping in front of the rector, his size taking up most of the aisle.

"Do not come between me and what I desire, boy," Tathal growled, a spell already forming within his mind. "I have walked centuries for this moment, and I will not be denied by the likes of either of you."

"Blasphemy," Reverend John de Brug hissed, fists clenched.

"Free will is the will of the Word, right?" Tathal asked pointedly. He had already tired of the game. "And I *will* have the sword. Where is it?"

Before a reply could be given, the churchwarden lunged at Tathal, the man's size belying his aggressive speed. Tathal almost did not weave the spell in time. A number of words paired with three gestures and the magic of his blood burst from within into the church to paralyze the man in the middle of his haphazard attempt. Still conscious, he went down in a mess of arms and legs, unable to use either. It took only a moment, but Tathal had neutralized the major threat.

Besides, as Tathal had felt in the universe, he still needed Church-warden Peter Fursdon—and more importantly, his brawn.

"Now, where were we?" Tathal asked as if nothing had happened.

The rector had not moved. "The weapon you seek will not bring you peace, no matter what you want to use it for."

"No, it won't. Life is like a chess match, Priest," Tathal said, unable to hide his contempt for the reverend and all he stood for. "There are pieces upon the board. A player can react to a move. Or a play can be the reason for reaction. The sword is one play in a much larger game. It is a reaction piece, leading to a greater gambit. And I will have the most important answers this universe has to offer."

"You defy God!"

"No," Tathal said. "I defy His tyranny."

The reverend darkened. "Son, that game will lead to your damnation."

"I hated the last man who called me 'son,' you know," Tathal mused. "Hate can be a most powerful magic if wielded by someone tempered by it."

"Whosoever hateth his brother is a murderer: and ye know that no murderer hath eternal life abiding in him," John de Burg quoted.

"Ahh yes," Tathal said, remembering the Bible passage. "John 3:15, right? You are correct about one thing. I *am* a murderer. But I have been alive for far too many centuries to not wonder about eternity and my place in it." He put his foot on the neck of the churchwarden. "I will counter with this: 'Believe those who are seeking the Truth; doubt those who find it.'"

"I do not know what you plan," the reverend said. "The sword is filled with a miracle, a weapon that does not show its true age. I am not a dumb man. It has been imbued in some way. And if it has been given certain properties that are outside the realm of science, it must be the Word's doing. Since God exists, then evil exists." John de Brug paused. "You are a part of that evil, on some quest that has rotted your heart, a search for answers that leads to your death and those you meet. I beg you. Forgo that quest."

"A brave speech," Tathal said, smiling. "Where is the sword?"

"Would you destroy the world to have your answers?"

Tathal looked to the Christ, pinned to his cross even as his cross was pinned to the stone wall of church.

Christ had to have wondered, while dying, what his Father was thinking.

Tathal had similar questions.

Just then a phone began to ring, from a distant small office within the church.

"To be born with such an unerring sense of right is a hardship most will never know," Tathal said, looking back to the priest. "You believe you know what duty is. But like many of your brethren, you have been misled. I intend to discover that which has been hidden from the world."

"This is Lucifer's work!"

Tathal laughed. "Lucifer? Hardly. A pawn, nothing more. Lying in his pit and waiting, no doubt. No, I seek a greater prize."

He pulled a knife from concealment and, kneeling, put it against Peter Fursdon's neck, never once taking his eyes off of the rector.

"For the last time, Reverend. Where is the sword?"

Reverend John de Brug did not move.

"His blood will be on your soul."

Indecision. It crashed over the reverend like a wave. The silence of death hung within the church. The old priest moved toward the chancel. Tathal watched closely. There were no ways of exit there. After fumbling out of sight behind the stone relief of Christ on his cross, the rector withdrew and returned with a long wooden box, waxed and glowing in the dim light of the church's interior.

"This is what you seek," Reverend John de Brug said.

Returning his knife to its shadows, Tathal gazed upon the box. A small leather belt kept it closed.

"Set it down on the pew. And back away," he said.

The rector did so.

While reaching to undo the belt and peer at his prize, Tathal hoped his trip to South Cadbury had not been in vain.

That's when the rector, like a cornered viper, struck.

Reverend John de Brug leaped at Tathal, roaring, trying to bowl the other over through physical force. It worked. Both men went tumbling into the pews. Fire erupted along Tathal's side even as he lashed out with all the rage a wounded and surprised wizard could muster—the words for the first spell he had learned blazing in his mind and gathering on his lips. He then saw the bloodied knife about to plunge into him again. He gripped the other's wrists, bracing them and their blade from falling, even as he shouted a language not heard commonly for hundreds of years.

Just as the rector gained leverage, Tathal finished the final word.

And fire sprung to life on the rector's chest.

John de Brug screeched in panic, his attack halted. It was enough. Left cold by the magic that had stolen his body heat to create flame, Tathal drove his fist into the rector's neck. The reverend tumbled backward onto the church floor, squirming, choking, unable to breath.

Tathal regained his feet. He peered down at the beaten man.

"Brave of you," the wizard said, breathing hard from the fight. "No one has dealt me a blow in almost a century. Still, that was a pitiful attempt at being a hero," he added, straightening his clothing. "There are no such things, you know. Heroes. Only men with the will to see *their* will done."

"A hero will be called to answer for your evil," Reverend John de Brug croaked.

"I look forward to killing this man."

"He is no man," the rector gasped, rubbing at his throat even as his clothing still smoked.

Tathal did not care. Undoing the belt, he pulled the sword free of its case. The weapon was heavy but he did not look at it.

He didn't need to.

"You will need me," Reverend John de Brug croaked.

Tathal looked down at the churchwarden before meeting the eyes of the rector, the coming death rising inside.

"I no longer need you."

With a rage he had befriended in his youth, Tathal brought the sword down. Repeatedly. Again and again. The old priest screamed in agony as steel punctured his abdomen in numerous spurting wounds. Blood began to pool about him.

It was a baptism the centuries-old church had likely never witnessed.

Tathal took a step back as the other man mewled and whimpered like a feverish child, bloody hands clutching at his shredded middle. He would let the reverend suffer for his affront, death too great a gift to give. The wizard looked to his own wound. Fire lanced his side. Breathing hurt. His own crimson bled out. The cut was not deep. The knife had scraped along his ribs. He had been lucky. But barely.

"You are mine," Tathal said to the churchwarden, whose rage and fear could not be quelled by even the paralyzing spell the wizard had used. "Rise. And become an extension of my will."

As if a puppet on strings, Peter Fursdon regained control over his body and pushed himself up off the floor. Of course, he was not *in* control. Tathal maintained that. Getting a better look, he was pleased to see the strength in the younger man—a brutish strength but lithe enough to be quite quick. The churchman would be perfect for what was needed.

"You have killed him," Peter Fursdon whispered, suddenly realizing he could use his voice.

"Yes. In time. A short time, methinks."

"You could have killed us easily, gotten the information you wanted easily," the churchwarden growled, his fury returned. "Why toy with us?"

"When one plans on speaking to the Word," Tathal said, hefting the sword and finally examining it. "It is important to practice."

"There are forces of good in this world. In South Cadbury even."

"I know," Tathal agreed. "And I look forward to killing them."

Looking away, he called upon his magic. It stirred immediately. And snaked its way up the blade—into the very metal—alive and revealing the secrets the weapon held. Many men and women had died upon the sword. He could sense that. But Tathal focused on one particular bloodletting—one set down and recorded as part of an epic battle in this part of the world. The magic then took a small part of what it had found and entered the world, reaching, delving, seeking for the one Tathal hunted.

It did not take long.

Frowning, he went to a window and gazed northwest with eyes keener than any night bird.

To a hill, far in the distance, where a black stain with straight lines jutted from England—a tower, with darkness carved from the faint light of moon and star.

A tower created to imprison.

Tathal let his magic die, replacing it with burning conviction. He could see his quest's endgame.

And it was nigh.

Carefully wrapping the sword in cloth and tugging on the magical strings of his new puppet, he left the dying Reverend Peter de Brug and his holy place. He exited the church and returned to the cool caress of the night. The scent of sweet lavender became his companion once more. For a moment, he looked backward, discerning if he had made a mistake in letting the rector live even moments longer, moments that might lead to downfall.

But he sensed nothing. The path he took was his to win.

With the churchwarden following against his will, Tathal embraced the journey before him.

An hour after leaving South Cadbury, the six bells of the Church of Saint Thomas a Becket pealed with a manic undertone that echoed over the countryside, music not meant to sound the time.

Tathal listened to them fade with every step.

It was a nice night for a walk.

No one witnessed his arrival to Glastonbury Tor.

It had taken the rest of the night and most of the following day to make his way across the south of Britain. Tathal had embraced the journey as he had done all of the events in his life—with patient conviction. Now he stood at the base of one of the oldest places in England, its settlement dating back to the Iron Age. And at its apex, a tower lorded, its construction older than he but not by much. He had been here before but never could have guessed part of his future lay buried in the tor's past. Death, it seemed, could hide from even one such as he. But he now possessed one of the most marvelous blades in history and it had drawn him here like a lodestone, leaving no doubt. Buried in the hillside's depths, darkness slept.

And in that darkness, he would find a powerful tool that would protect him from Heliwr Richard McAllister and his foulmouthed fairy guide.

With the churchwarden behind him, Tathal paused, sending magic into the surroundings for what felt like the hundredth time since they had left South Cadbury. He was not worried about the tourists who frequented Glastonbury Tor; they had vanished with the coming of night. No human was present on the tor, as far as Tathal could gauge. No night predators of significance were about either.

Yet Tathal and his charge were far from alone.

The bells of Saint Thomas a Becket church had summoned aid. Tathal had no idea who—or what—tracked them. Spirit. Demon. Fey. Angel. Any number of other entities not human. He could feel his tracker's otherworldliness. It was a subtle suggestion on the air that grew stronger as the distance between them lessened.

As fog began to infiltrate the lowlands, Tathal made his way above it, up the steep path toward the hill's top. The tower of Saint Michael's Church had stood on Glastonbury Tor for centuries. Once part of a much larger complex, the tower was all that remained, the memory of an age long since past. The Dissolution of Monasteries had been hard on all of the important buildings of ancient England. The tower was all that remained of a much greater church, its square spire three-stories tall and featuring corner buttresses, perpendicular bell openings, and a sculptured tablet bearing the image of an eagle below the parapet. The tower stood with resilience against the ages, sealed with concrete where weather and use had pitted it.

Tathal now recognized that the tower had survived not by chance but by design. Men of secrets and power had preserved it at a time when they dismantled other churches.

Those men understood what he now discerned.

The tower held a dark secret.

Tathal walked the grounds, taking it all in. He did not hurry. Reverend John de Brug did actually teach him something: never take a moment for granted. When one was as old as he, life depended on being cautious. In his arrogance, he had almost lost his life. He would not be careless again.

That's when four arrows shot with lightning speed punctured the night.

When he had sensed their pursuer, Tathal had readied for the attack. The arrows bounced off a thin skein of magic he had maintained throughout the journey.

They were no ordinary arrows.

At least he knew who pursued him.

"You might as well show yourself, Elf," Tathal said, trying to keep the edge out of his spell-thick voice. "Few can follow me. Fewer still can harm me."

Movement showed in the darkness, quickly vanishing below the hill's horizon.

"Are you by chance a warden of this place?"

No answer.

"Or merely someone seeking revenge for last night?"

"Wizard, I protect more than an evil like you can fathom," the darkness said.

In the voice, Tathal heard many things. Pain. Intelligence. Loneliness. Caution. Rage. Heart.

And the last fracturing more with every passing sunrise.

"I know you, better than I know many in your village of exile," Tathal said, still peering into the gloom in an attempt to discover the other's whereabouts. He felt like the universe was testing him with one last trial. "I felt your presence when I first entered South Cadbury. Are you the final piece to the puzzle of this night?"

"I am not," the Elf snarled, now on Tathal's left. The wizard kept his magic up.

"I know your story, Ruindolon Arl. The exile. The anguish. Shall I tell you the tale I know?" When the Elf said nothing, Tathal continued. "In a name, your exile is Rylynn Etton. Also known as Rylynn of Beauty. Her name says it all, yes?" No answer. "She was your love," he continued. "And you, her love. Young love. The kind that many legends recount. But we know how those stories end, don't we, Ruindolon Arl? The King of the Elves wooed Rylynn for his own. Royalty has ever done such things. It failed. The love you shared held true. Until the King used threat against you to win her hand. And in your jealousy and anger and righteousness—emotions only the deepest depths of one's heart know—you attempted to assassinate your liege. And failed.

"I do not begrudge the attempt, you understand," Tathal said. "It is undoubtedly what I would have done. It was just poorly executed. Like your attempt on *my* life."

"I have much to pay for," Ruindolon Arl agreed, now somewhere behind him.

Tathal followed the voice. "You will serve my needs this day, Elf. And be released from pain."

"You know me," the Elf said flatly. "But I know you as well. Why you are here. There are graves in the Misty Isles that hold great power.

You seek one of those deaths here, beneath us. Not a forever death but a revenant of death chained beneath the weight of his bastardized past. The death you seek, it will undo you." He paused, voice already in a different place near the tower. "I know you will not relent. But the priest is an innocent in this. Let him free."

Tathal grinned, magic tingling in his chest and at his fingertips. "Innocent like Rylynn's flower beneath the sweaty body of the man you failed to kill?"

No answer.

"Innocent like Rylynn's loins as they mount *her* king?"

Nothing.

"Innocent like the children Rylynn *will* bear him."

Rage in the deathly silence.

With the churchwarden bidden to protect his back, Tathal swept the tor and the interior of its tower, eyes scanning the darkness. Nothing. Elves were capable of hiding in ways that human eyes could barely detect. But Tathal knew his barbs had buried deep; the Elf would not hide for long.

Even with that knowledge, he barely had time to throw up his magical ward as a shadow darker than the sky fell from the heights of the tower.

Ruindolon Arl hit him like a boulder, snarling, both men crashing to the ground. Short sword slashing, the Elf was relentless. His shielding spell barely holding, Tathal fought the fey creature physically, unable to break free of the other's grip. Only magic kept the sword from killing him. Panic he had not felt in a very long time crystalized the moment—the crumbling of his protective spell as his own strength waned, the green eyes of his assailant flashing hatred, the dewy smell of the grass they fought upon, the sounds each of them growled even as they labored for breath, and the human attire the attacker wore to blend in with his neighbors.

The killing would have been moments away if not for Peter Fursdon.

Tathal directed the churchwarden with a thought. Unable to ignore the command, the big man responded immediately.

Before the Elf could avoid it, a fist like a cinder block connected with his cheek.

And Ruindolon Arl crumbled.

Almost as quickly, unseen thick lines of magic chained the dazed Elf. Tathal regained his feet, wiping the indignity of grass and dirt off his clothing.

"Besides, there is no innocence *left* in this world."

"You are wrong," the Elf growled.

"Wait until you see what I have in store for you."

Ruindolon Arl struggled against his invisible shackles. It would do the fey creature no good. If they could contain the elemental fury of a Praguian golem during World War II, the Elf would be no problem.

Tathal turned back to the tower and entered its hallowed walls. The floor lay exposed to the night air; it had once been dirt but had more recently been covered in stone. Stars twinkled cold fire through the tower's absent roof. He could see with his wizard eyes the wards that ran through the walls, pulsing with a faint blue-white veil of magic created to imprison the death he sought. Tathal began his work. The spells came easily. Like a handful of other wizards in the world, Tathal had lived long enough to acquire an unimaginable amount of knowledge. He used it now. Spoken words of enchantment. Accompanied hand movements. Focused intent. Tathal calmed his mind from the heat of battle and tore strand after strand of another magician's work away.

It took barely ten minutes to undo the magical jail. Glancing to ensure the Elf remained frozen, Tathal ordered the churchwarden to stand at the center of the tower.

And began the last part of his work.

Tathal unwrapped the sword. It had once been plunged into the chest of a father by an enraged bastard son. The wizard handed it to the churchwarden.

Peter Fursdon took the broadsword, resistance and hate in his eyes.

"Soon those eyes will look at me with more fury than you can imagine, Priest," Tathal said, grinning. "But it will not be your soul within them."

The churchwarden tried his voice. Tathal liked the silence.

"To my work," he said.

Prison undone, Tathal beckoned the dead. Rather, he called for one fatal revenant. Ghosts inhabited the land everywhere, and summoning the wrong one would complicate the night. It did not take long to find the right death though. The wail started first, a hoarse scream that became a banshee from hell, its rage consuming the hilltop. Tathal focused on it, the sword the key. The weapon became a lightning rod, drawing the spirit from his hidden grave beneath the tower to the sword with which it had once dealt death. Ethereal emanations seeped from the floor and gathered about the young churchwarden, settling around him—entering him. Peter Fursdon screamed.

Tathal paid his pain no mind. The culmination of his plan settled into its new body even as the wizard witnessed a ghostly illumination of golden armor beginning to form about the once-churchman, invisible to all but those who knew magic.

As the armor coalesced, Tathal saw the rent in the breastplate where the killing stroke had fallen more than fifteen centuries earlier, the final result of the spirit's attempt at overthrowing his king—his father—and taking his place upon the throne.

The anguished screams of the revenant and its new host died on the night.

"Speak," Tathal said.

The man before him took a deep breath. He stood taller, prouder, replaced with stern steel not original in his making, chin lifted, regal and powerful. The soul that stared at Tathal was not that of the churchwarden.

It was a spirit far darker.

"What is the name your mother gave you at birth?" Tathal asked.

The flicker of annoyance crossed the other's face. "I am Mordred, bastard of King Arthur Pendragon of Caer Llion."

"And who am I?"

"You are Tathal Ennis, wizard of the Fallen Court," Mordred growled. "And I will kill you, cur."

"That remains to be seen," Tathal said, admiring the revenant's bloodlust. It would come in handy soon. "You are no longer Mordred.

You are now *the* Mordred. My knight. My protector. An extension of my will. I have given you freedom from eternal torment. And whether you like it or not, you are mine to command. Yet I would not do so without giving you a gift as well—what you most yearn for."

"And what is it you think I desire, wizard of the Fallen Court?"

"Revenge against your slayer."

The Mordred frowned darkly, staring off into the night, thinking. When his gaze returned to the wizard, he had sensed what Tathal knew to be true.

"There can be no witnesses," Tathal asserted.

"I understand."

Tathal nodded. "A first test then."

Sword gripped and invisible armor encasing his new mortal body, he charged Ruindolon Arl from the tower even as Tathal undid the Elf's magical shackles. The fey creature was on his feet as quick as a cat, steady and strong in the way of the Seelie Court, his own short sword brought up in protection. The Elf would be more than a match for any human. It was time to see if the Mordred lived up to the history and legends of his previous life.

The two combatants met, steel meeting and ringing. No sound escaped the Mordred. Every step, every feint, every parry, and every attack was carried out with precise and systematic ease. The Elf had more speed—if barely—but his much shorter weapon lacked the reach that his foe possessed.

After several minutes of combat, though outmatched in almost every way, the Mordred swept the Elf's feet from out under him.

And drove his sword into the chest of Ruindolon Arl.

Eyes big with surprise and fear, the Elf lay pinned to Glastonbury Tor, his blood a darkness upon the hill's grass.

He took his memories of Rylynn the Beauty with him.

"Well done, my Mordred," Tathal breathed.

The dead knight gave the wizard a dark look. Before Tathal could say something more, the Mordred pulled free his weapon and in moments vanished down the tor, an ancient ghost in a new, powerful body. It would take him several hours to reach South Cadbury, but

when he did, the sword that Tathal had fought so hard to acquire would
lay waste to all it touched.

Death would enter the town. And leave none alive.

"Now we will see, Myrddin Emrys," Tathal hissed to the stars and
moon. "You have your unfettered knight. But now I have mine."

The night responded with the silence of the dead.

Feeling confident in his future once more, Tathal Ennis descended
Glastonbury Tor, leaving the body of Ruindolon Arl behind. He cared
not who found the Elf and what that would mean for the world. Instead,
he entered the night that cloaked his passage. The Mordred would join
him when he had finished his task.

When that happened, the wizard had two more places to visit, two
more items to acquire. Then he would have his answers.

He breathed deep of the night and couldn't help but grin.

The prelude of the world's end began now.